Blood of the Cosmos

BOOKS BY KEVIN J. ANDERSON

The Dark Between the Stars
Nebula Awards Showcase 2011
Slan Hunter

WITH BRIAN HERBERT

The Road to Dune
Dune: The Butlerian Jihad
Dune: The Machine Crusade
Dune: The Battle of Corrin
Hunters of Dune
Sandworms of Dune
Paul of Dune
The Winds of Dune
Sisterhood of Dune
Mentats of Dune
Hellhole
Hellhole Awakening
Hellhole Inferno

KEVIN J. ANDERSON

Blood of the Cosmos

THE SAGA OF SHADOWS • BOOK TWO

SIMON & SCHUSTER

London · New York · Sydney · Toronto · New Delhi

A CBS COMPANY

First published in the US by Tor Books, 2015
First published in Great Britain by Simon & Schuster UK Ltd, 2015
A CBS COMPANY

This paperback edition, 2016

1 3 5 7 9 10 8 6 4 2

Simon & Schuster UK Ltd
1st Floor
Gray's Inn Road
London WC1X 8HB

www.simonandschuster.co.uk

Simon & Schuster Australia, Sydney
Simon & Schuster India, New Delhi

A CIP catalogue record for this book
is available from the British Library

Paperback ISBN: 978-1-84983-682-1
eBook ISBN: 978-1-84983-683-8

Printed and bound by CPI Group (UK) Ltd, Croydon, CR0 4YY

Simon & Schuster UK Ltd are committed to sourcing paper that is made from wood grown in sustainable forests and support the Forest Stewardship Council, the leading international forest certification organisation. Our books displaying the FSC logo are printed on FSC certified paper.

For more than eighteen years, Louis Moesta was a proofer and trusted test reader on all my novel manuscripts. My wife's father was a former English teacher, science-fiction fan (long before it was mainstream), world traveler, and extremely interesting man.

Over the years, he offered countless insightful suggestions on my plots, characters, and prose. (I don't think he ever met a sentence that couldn't use an extra comma or two, though. . . .) He recently passed away at age eighty-nine. *Blood of the Cosmos* is the last novel manuscript of mine that he read.

ACKNOWLEDGMENTS

My special thanks for all the help, advice, and assistance I received in writing *Blood of the Cosmos*: Karen Haag for actually keeping up with me in transcribing well over a hundred chapters; Diane Jones and Louis Moesta for being first readers; my editor, Pat LoBrutto; my agent, John Silbersack; and, as always, my wife, Rebecca Moesta.

THE STORY SO FAR

Two decades have passed since the end of the Elemental War, the terrible conflict that raged across the Spiral Arm, devastated the alien Ildiran Empire, and tore apart the Terran Hanseatic League. The defeated hydrogues have retreated into their gas-giant planets; the fiery faeros have withdrawn into their stars and cause no further mayhem; the watery wentals have lost most of their power and are quiescent in ice planets and ocean worlds. Only the verdani, the sentient worldtrees on the forest planet Theroc, remain active, communicating through their green priest representatives. The humans and Ildirans have had twenty years to rebuild and recover. King Peter and Queen Estarra rule the new Confederation, a union of human colonies as well as the gypsy Roamer clans.

Mage-Imperator Jora'h, leader of the Ildiran Empire, announces a new initiative to explore beyond the populated worlds of the Spiral Arm, which will be spearheaded by a new ship, the *Kolpraxa*. Commanding this expedition is Tal Gale'nh, a talented young halfbreed officer of the Ildiran Solar Navy, protégé of Adar Zan'nh and the son of the Mage-Imperator's consort, the green priest Nira. Gale'nh is one of Nira's five halfbreed children, the result of an illicit breeding program; the others are her daughter Osira'h (fathered by Jora'h himself; her special abilities to control the hydrogues and faeros were a key weapon that saved the Ildiran Empire during the Elemental War); Rod'h (fathered by the hated Dobro Designate, the second most powerful of her children, who was never called upon to do his duty because Osira'h succeeded in his stead); Tamo'l (fathered by a lens kithman philosopher); and Muree'n (fathered by a warrior).

The *Kolpraxa* ventures into the unexplored spaces beyond the

Spiral Arm, while some of the crew are concerned about the Shana Rei, supposedly mythical creatures of darkness that oppressed the Ildiran Empire long ago. The human historian Anton Colicos earlier proved that the Shana Rei were mere fiction, bogeymen used to cover up other events in Ildiran history, but after the uproar caused by that shocking revelation, Colicos discovered other records that show the Shana Rei may have been real after all. This knowledge is heavy on the minds of the *Kolpraxa*'s crew as they encounter a mysterious dark nebula that seems to be growing. As they approach to investigate, the shadow cloud expands and engulfs the ship, cutting them off entirely.

Back in the Ildiran Empire, Gale'nh's siblings sense that something has happened to their brother. Osira'h, at an astronomy station near an active star, is studying the surviving faeros that flit about in the churning stellar layers; Rod'h is in the Ildiran capital, clashing with Jora'h and Nira as he tries to erase the shame of his father's hidden breeding program; Tamo'l is on the ocean world of Kuivahr, running a medical sanctuary for a group of surviving "misbreeds," malformed mistakes left over from the breeding program; and Muree'n is testing her fighting abilities with the female warrior Yazra'h. With their half-breed connection to Gale'nh, they know that the *Kolpraxa* is lost.

In the Confederation, the Roamer industrialist Lee Iswander runs a risky but profitable metals-processing operation on the lava planet Sheol. Roamers are known for living on the edge and doing the impossible, but many of the clans are uneasy about Iswander, whose hard business attitude is at odds with the more close-knit and casual behavior of the clans. One of Iswander's workers, Garrison Reeves, believes the Sheol operations are unstable due to orbital changes, but Iswander dismisses the concerns. Garrison's hard-edged wife Elisa is Iswander's deputy, and she sides with the industrialist, angry that her husband is causing difficulties in her job. Convinced of the danger, Garrison steals a ship and flees Sheol with their son Seth. Outraged and betrayed, Elisa asks permission from Iswander to pursue them, and he agrees. She flies after them.

Iswander, meanwhile, wants to be the next Speaker of the Roamer clans. He thinks the scruffy gypsies need to be brought into the modern era of business. He goes to the Roamer seat of government, a space habitat called Newstation, to make his case. Iswander is by far the most qualified person for the Speaker job, and his own rival is a glad-handing loser, Sam Ricks. Iswander's real nemesis among the clans, however, is Olaf Reeves—Garrison's stern, hard-line father, who insists the clans should return to the old ways. Olaf's followers even refuse to accept Newstation as the Roamer capital, but instead devote themselves to a hopeless dream of rebuilding the old, destroyed Roamer center of Rendezvous. After a fierce debate, the disgusted Olaf withdraws his clan's children from the Roamer school of Academ, saying they will depart for deep space, where they have found a new home, a derelict city where they can be left alone.

Garrison flies out into unexplored space with his son, where they come upon a cluster of organic drifting nodules, huge gas bags, like space plankton. Seth names them "bloaters." They hide there, but a furious Elisa tracks them down, charges into the bloater cluster; she rails at Garrison for kidnapping their son and, when he tries to escape, she takes a potshot at him. The shot goes wild and strikes one of the bloaters—triggering an astonishing chain-reaction explosion that rips through the entire cluster. Garrison and Elisa barely survive, but each thinks the other was destroyed.

Back on Sheol, Garrison's worst fears are coming true: the lava operations are unstable. Iswander returns from Newstation to meet the trader Rlinda Kett and her two deputies, Tasia Tamblyn and Robb Brindle, who have arrived to pick up a shipment. The operations begin to collapse, and the workers frantically try to evacuate, but it is a complete disaster. Rlinda Kett manages to rescue many, including Iswander, but 1,543 people die. In disgrace, Iswander returns to Newstation, where he loses the election for Speaker to the incompetent Sam Ricks. He has also lost his fortune and his reputation, and in shame he takes his family back to the ruins of Sheol to lie low. That is where Elisa finds him after she limps home from the bloater explosion. All seems lost, but Elisa reports an unexpected opportunity that could save clan Iswander: those bloaters are filled with *stardrive fuel.* No one else knows it. If Iswander could find more bloaters, he would quickly rebuild his fortune.

Meanwhile, Zhett Kellum and her husband Patrick Fitzpatrick run a traditional Roamer skymine that harvests stardrive fuel from the gas giant Golgen. Their daughter Shareen, a genius in the making, has gone off to a special school on Earth, where she is miserable, and she wants to come back to the family skymine. Zhett's father, Del Kellum—a former clan Speaker—has retired and built a distillery to process the exotic kelp strains on the Ildiran sanctuary world of Kuivahr, where Tamo'l has established her refuge for the misbreeds. The kelp strains also have unusual medicinal properties. A mysterious man, Tom Rom, comes through the Klikiss transportal and buys samples of the medicinal kelp from Del Kellum. Tom Rom claims that his employer, Zoe Alakis, is doing specialized research, but he departs without giving further details. Tom Rom also acquires medical records from Tamo'l about all her misbreeds.

Zoe Alakis is the owner and ruthless administrator of a private medical research facility, Pergamus, on a poisonous planet. Completely isolated, she conducts dangerous research to build a personal collection of diseases and cures. Zoe is paranoid, lives in a sterile dome. Her father died of a terrible disease, and Tom Rom has been her faithful majordomo for years; he will do anything to protect her and get her the specimens she needs.

After Tom Rom departs Kuivahr, Del Kellum goes to Golgen to visit his daughter Zhett on their skymine, where Shareen has returned from school on Earth, glad to be back above the clouds; Shareen is accompanied by her study partner, Howard Rohandas, who wants practical knowledge instead of just book learning. A great storm appears deep in the clouds, inky black shadows well up like dark blood—and gigantic hydrogue warglobes rise from the core to warn the skyminers. A smothering shadow—the Shana Rei!—has contaminated the planet and engulfed the powerful hydrogue empire. The Kellums evacuate the skymine and barely get away before the blackness poisons the entire gas giant.

On a joint military expedition on the fringes of the Ildiran Empire, Adar Zan'nh joins General Nalani Keah, commander of the Confederation Defense Forces, as they explore ice moons. They are astonished to flush out a small infestation of evil Klikiss robots, treacherous enemies thought to have been destroyed in the Elemental War. Led by Exxos, the black robots hid on the ice moon when all their comrades were wiped out in the war. Now, Exxos and his robots try to flee, pursued by General Keah and Adar Zan'nh. As the embattled robot ships race away they encounter another shadow cloud, which scrambles the technological systems of the pursuers. Seeing their only chance, the robots plunge into the shadow cloud—where they are captured by the Shana Rei, powerful and incomprehensible beings who want to unmake the universe itself. As his only way to survive, Exxos makes a bargain with the Shana Rei that he and his robots will assist in their war.

When the battered ships return to the Ildiran Empire, the Mage-Imperator sends Adar Zan'nh out to find the lost *Kolpraxa*. Osira'h goes along, because she can follow her telepathic link to her brother Gale'nh. Out in the emptiness, they find the *Kolpraxa* entirely encased in a black shell, cold and dark. Aboard, they discover that all of the Ildiran crew are gone; the only survivor is Gale'nh, nearly driven mad, claiming that the Shana Rei attacked, but he somehow was able to resist the shadows owing to his halfbreed genetics. Adar Zan'nh and Osira'h rush him back to lldira, where he can be healed.

At the Confederation capital of Theroc, General Keah arrives to report to King Peter and Queen Estarra about the shadow cloud and the black robots. Zhett Kellum also reports about the shadows swallowing up Golgen. The King and Queen put the military defenses on high alert to prepare against this powerful, unknown enemy.

Arita, the daughter of the King and Queen, is fascinated with nature; she and her boyfriend Collin both grew up wanting to become green priests; they trained hard and studied, but when they went into the forest to be accepted by the trees, Collin emerged as a green priest, but Arita was rejected, although the sentient trees altered her mind somehow. Now, Collin leaves Arita to join a group of isolationist green priests led by Kennebar, and they retreat to an uninhabited continent, the Wild.

Arita's brother, Prince Reyn, is being groomed as the Confederation's next leader, but he has a secret illness, a degenerative condition that seems to have no cure. Keeping his illness to himself, Reyn goes to Earth, where he asks Rlinda Kett to connect him with Dr. Benjamin Paolus, a preeminent neurological researcher. Paolus studies Reyn, but offers little hope for a treatment. Next, Reyn goes on a diplomatic trip to Ildira, where he will learn about the Empire. He is welcomed by Mage-Imperator Jora'h and Nira, but spends most of his time with

Osira'h, who takes him under her wing. As they grow fond of each other, Reyn reveals his condition to Osira'h, and she vows to use all the resources of the Ildiran medical researchers to find him a cure.

While Reyn is on Ildira, the shadows strike—but not in a direct physical attack. The Shana Rei have found a way into the Ildiran telepathic network of *thism*, and they possess weak-minded Ildirans to attack a procession of Jora'h and Nira. The insane Ildirans are killed, and the Mage-Imperator is shaken with the knowledge that the shadows may be infecting the entire race, attacking from within. . . .

Back in the Confederation, Garrison and Seth have returned to his estranged clan at the abandoned site of Rendezvous. Olaf Reeves always dominated Garrison, wore him down, and now Olaf demands that the two accompany the rest of the clan out to their new home in space. But Garrison refuses to let Seth be raised in such an oppressive environment. The rest of clan Reeves flies away, while Garrison takes Seth back to Newstation, where he will find work and the boy will go to school.

Meanwhile, thanks to the information Elisa brought him, Lee Iswander has established a thriving, though secret, worksite in the middle of another bloater cluster, where they are extracting stardrive fuel, ekti-X. It seems an inexhaustible supply as they drain bloater after bloater. Now they have to distribute the fuel, so Iswander can build up his fortune again. Elisa meets with Xander Brindle, the young son of Robb Brindle and Tasia Tamblyn, and his partner Terry Handon, both of whom work for Kett Shipping. They work a deal to distribute ekti-X.

Eager to recover from his disgrace, Iswander presents a large and valuable load of ekti-X to King Peter and Queen Estarra on Theroc. Many people are desperate to know where he is getting so much stardrive fuel and so cheaply, but he refuses to reveal his source. As he departs from Theroc, Iswander takes a green priest with him, Aelin, who will assist with distant communication.

Olaf Reeves and the rest of his family arrive at their new home in space—a huge derelict city far from any star system. No one knows who built the alien space city. The clan settles in and reactivates the systems, while others explore the giant city, looking for clues about the original builders. They discover a library of records showing a previously unknown race, the Onthos, who took shelter there in deep space, and then they find hundreds of Onthos bodies—all of them dead from a plague. Before long, the members of clan Reeves also grow sick and begin to die en masse.

Rlinda Kett, who supplied clan Reeves with what they needed for their new home, is concerned about them. One of her old friends, Orli Covitz, recently came to Rlinda after the breakup of her marriage, looking for something to do with her life. Rlinda signs on Orli and her faithful compy DD as pilots of a trading ship and sends them to go check on clan Reeves. When Orli arrives at the derelict space city, though, she discovers that every single member of clan Reeves has died from the alien plague. And now Orli is infected as well. . . .

Prince Reyn's doctor, Benjamin Paolus, is secretly working for Zoe Alakis on Pergamus, and he delivers samples of Reyn's exotic illness. Paolus is paid well for the information. Tom Rom is eager to keep delivering rare samples for the Pergamus library, and when he learns about the Onthos plague, Tom Rom sets off for the derelict city, determined to acquire the virus for Zoe's collection.

In the space city, Orli doesn't dare allow the plague to spread, so she copies all the medical and archaeological data on the unknown alien race, before she destroys the city and flies away as her own symptoms grow worse. She will transmit the data to the Confederation, and then die out in space where she cannot infect anyone. But Tom Rom arrives; Orli offers him her data, but he wants the organism itself. She tries to escape, but he hunts her down, and traps her on an asteroid, where he boards her ship and steals vials of her infected blood, which he will take back to Pergamus. Orli is distraught, thinking she has failed; DD manages to fix her ship and they fly away.

On his way back, Tom Rom experiences an accident aboard his ship, and he too is infected with the plague. As his own symptoms worsen, he flies to Pergamus to give Zoe this specimen, knowing it will be the last thing he does.

Back at the Iswander bloater-extraction yard, the green priest Aelin learns of all those who died from the Onthos plague, and he also hears mysterious voices from the bloaters themselves. Eager to make contact with them through his telink powers, he takes a scout pod into the bloater field, where he is caught in a power surge that crackles among the nodules. His treeling is destroyed, and he is nearly killed; Aelin is never quite the same afterward, both euphoric and delirious.

Meanwhile, Mage-Imperator Jora'h has nightmares, sure that he is infected by shadows. Tal Gale'nh struggles to recover from his horrific ordeal on the *Kolpraxa*, and he fears the Shana Rei have a hold on him. Zan'nh strengthens the Solar Navy defenses, but no one knows what weapons might be effective against the creatures of darkness. Anton Colicos and other Ildiran rememberers comb through ancient records of the Shana Rei, looking for any clues, and they discover plans for "sun bombs" that caused great damage previously.

General Keah and Adar Zan'nh continue war exercises, hoping to be ready for the Shana Rei. During maneuvers over the frozen planetoid of Plumas, a shadow cloud appears and enormous Shana Rei ships emerge, accompanied by a destructive force of black robot battleships. After a desperate battle, suffering great losses, the Solar Navy and the Confederation Defense Forces retreat, completely trounced by the enemy.

King Peter and Queen Estarra go to Ildira to discuss the incomprehensible war, and also to see their son Reyn, eager to bring him back home. Reyn reveals to his parents that he is suffering from an incurable disease, which shocks the King and Queen, but they vow to do everything possible to find a treatment. Another uprising of shadow-possessed Ildirans occurs, and they barely escape with their lives. Mage-Imperator Jora'h sends Osira'h back to Theroc with Reyn, hoping that she will be safer there.

When Elisa learns that her son Seth is in school at Newstation—not killed in the bloater explosion after all, as she had assumed—she leaves the Iswander extraction field and rushes there, determined to get her son back. She seizes him from the school and takes him with her out to the ekti operations. Too late to stop her, Garrison pursues Elisa, following her to the hidden industrial field, where he is captured to prevent him from revealing the source of ekti-X.

While he is trying to get his son released, an ominous shadow cloud appears before the industrial operations. Exxos and the black robots begin to attack, and the Iswander employees evacuate. In the chaos, the slightly deranged green priest Aelin escapes, but instead of trying to get away, he flies out to the bloaters, which call to him. He removes his environment suit and immerses himself inside one of the bloaters, the protoplasm he calls the "blood of the cosmos," through which he receives great revelations. The invincible Shana Rei, however, hang over the bloater field, and then simply withdraw without explanation. Unable to believe he has dodged the bullet, Iswander puts his people back to work immediately.

Not long afterward, Orli and DD stumble upon the bloater extraction field. Orli is near death from the plague, and all she wants to do is transmit the database she took from the Onthos space city before she dies; DD will self-destruct the ship to remove any chance of contamination. But Aelin insists he knows how to cure Orli—she merely needs to immerse herself in the blood of the cosmos. Garrison talks with her extensively on the comm, convinces Orli that she has nothing to lose, so she makes the attempt. She is cured! As she regains her strength in a quarantined section of the Iswander operations, Garrison grows very close to her, but neither is allowed to leave and reveal the ekti-X operations. Soon enough, though, that becomes unnecessary: as the drifting bloaters come close to a star, they undergo a metamorphosis that transforms them into astounding flying creatures that race off into space. Afterward, as the Iswander operations disperse, Orli goes with Garrison and Seth to a quiet colony planet, Ikbir, where they hope to live quietly.

Tom Rom, on the verge of death, barely makes his way back to Pergamus, bringing a sample of the Onthos plague—in his own bloodstream. Zoe refuses to let him die, though, and devotes all the resources of her medical facility to discovering a cure. Tom Rom is kept in an orbital isolation facility as he is treated, and Zoe leaves her sterile dome for the first time in many years so she can be with him. He pulls through, thanks to a treatment discovered in the wealth of information held in the Pergamus library.

On Ildira, shadow-possessed Ildirans gather weapons and march on a peaceful human enclave, where settlers have built a human town to share their culture with Ildirans. It is a complete massacre, all the humans slaughtered—and the Mage-Imperator knows this will be an appalling strain on their alliance with the Confederation. Desperate to understand, he orders studies on the dead bodies of the shadow-possessed Ildirans, but when researchers cut into their brains, gouts of deadly black smoke rise up and wipe out the medical specialists; the laboratory itself is annihilated in order to stop the spread. Jora'h doesn't know how he can stop the shadow that is surely within all of them. . . .

The Shana Rei also strike Theroc, drawn there to wipe out the worldforest, which causes them pain. As black robot ships attack General Keah's warships, the Shana Rei vessels begin building an enormous barrier in orbit, an eclipse plate that will block out all sunlight and smother the sentient trees. The Confederation Defense Forces cannot defeat these powerful opponents, no matter how many weapons they use. But then Adar Zan'nh arrives with a battery of the ancient sun bombs, which destroy part of the "nightshade." Osira'h also uses her special telepathic powers to summon the fiery elementals that caused such havoc during the Elemental War. She controls the faeros, convinces them to attack the creatures of darkness, and all together they succeed in driving away the Shana Rei, though at great damage to the faeros, which retreat again to hide inside their stars.

As the worldforest recovers from the attack, a hundred strange ships arrive in the Theron system, an alien configuration never seen before. All hundred ships land in the worldforest, and, to the amazement of King Peter and Queen Estarra, aliens emerge—the Onthos, refugees who were nearly eradicated by the Shana Rei long ago. The Onthos claim that they, too, were tenders of a worldforest, now destroyed, and they gather under the great trees, requesting sanctuary.

CHAPTER

1

AELIN

The universe was vast and full of wonders—some too marvelous to understand, some too terrifying.

In an empty wasteland of space, far from any star system, the ekti-X extraction operations worked at full capacity, a swarm of activity. Lee Iswander had found another cluster of mysterious bloaters that appeared out of nowhere, drifted aimlessly, then went nowhere.

No one but Iswander's crew knew that the protoplasmic sacks were filled with energy-dense ekti. The secret fuel-harvesting operations proceeded in the deep emptiness, light-years from any possible observers. Pumping rigs and extraction siphons descended on one bloater at a time like bizarre mechanical mosquitoes, sucking each nodule dry. They filled canister after canister with stardrive fuel and left the discarded husks to drift away. Iswander's crew, sworn to secrecy, loaded distribution tankers and delivered the stardrive fuel to hidden dropoff points, from which carefully vetted representatives would distribute the fuel to trading depots. No one else in the Confederation knew where ekti-X came from, and frustration was increasing across the Spiral Arm.

This bloater cluster would eventually be depleted, but Iswander's scouts had already located other drifting conglomerations in the dark spaces between the stars.

The green priest Aelin knew that it would never stop. He wanted to scream.

He had begged Iswander to cease his operations, but the industrialist would not listen to an eccentric, possibly insane green priest. They knew Aelin had been damaged, changed, through his recent ordeal among the bloaters. They considered him mad—and, objectively, Aelin couldn't dispute that.

But it didn't mean he was wrong.

His mind had been connected to the bloaters during one of their synchronistic energy outbursts, which revealed to him a tapestry that he could not begin to comprehend. Those revelations had altered his thoughts about everything. Aelin was certain the majestic bloaters were much more than mere "space plankton" to be wrung dry of fuel.

He had to do something about it.

On bare feet, the green priest crept through the operational complex that drifted near the bloater operations. Holding his breath, listening to the silence, Aelin ducked around corridors, intense and alert. The station had monitor cams, but he hoped no one was watching. The rest of Iswander's crew would be busy with daily production.

Half-naked, Aelin padded along the cold—always cold!—deck plates, making his way to the nearest docking bay. Like most green priests, he wore only a loincloth, refusing to abandon the traditions of his native planet, Theroc. Aelin's green skin made him stand out among other people, so he had to make sure no one spotted him. He needed to escape.

Lee Iswander's deputy, Elisa Enturi, was a ruthless watchdog—who had no love or sympathy for Aelin. He knew that. He couldn't let anyone see him . . . particularly not her.

After his euphoric disaster, immersed in the soft, sentient awareness of bloater half-thoughts, Aelin had been lost in a catatonic state in the sickbay module, seemingly oblivious to the rest of the universe . . . but he could still hear and absorb the words around him. Drowning in the new revelations that burned through his brain, he had not paid much attention to trivial, mundane things—but he still remembered.

Standing near his sickbay bed, Elisa had advised Lee Iswander in a voice like a rusty metal blade, "Just discard him, sir. With his treeling destroyed, he is worthless as a green priest. He's no good to us. And there's always a risk if he escapes. This man is unstable, unpredictable, and dangerous. Removing the threat is the wisest course of action." She didn't even bother to hush her voice.

Lee Iswander had watched his business empire crumble after a tragic accident on Sheol, but he was regaining prominence, thanks to the enormously profitable ekti-X operations. "No, we keep him with us," he told her. "I've known Aelin ever since he was a young man on Theroc. I brought him here to join our operations because he wanted to see the universe." His tone was firm. "He will stay with us, regardless of his eccentricities. That's my decision."

Despite the marvelous epiphanies pouring through his brain, Aelin had been well aware of their conversation.

As he left the sickbay, Iswander had added to Enturi, "We just need to be careful. Watch him."

And now, months later, Aelin was careful too.

Hearing voices down the corridor near the docking bay, he ducked into a storage cubicle, slid the door shut, and huddled inside. He waited while two off-duty extraction workers strolled toward their personal quarters in the habitation module. Aelin's heart pounded, and he held his breath, but the two women walked past the cubicle, talking about a game they planned to play with friends that night.

When they were gone, Aelin slipped out and darted down the corridor to the docking bay, where several short-range Iswander vessels were there for the taking. He could steal a scout pod, fly away from the admin complex, and make his way out to the nodules that floated like islands in a sea of stars.

This was the second large bloater cluster exploited by Lee Iswander. The first had been a serendipitous discovery found outside an unremarkable star system. That initial cluster, and the accompanying Iswander operations, was nearly destroyed by the Shana Rei and the black robots, but then the shadow cloud had simply withdrawn, ignoring the extraction operations after all.

Afterward, the rest of the bloaters underwent a fantastic metamorphosis into enormous solar-sailing creatures that soared away and left the befuddled workers behind. Through his raw nerve endings and exposed thoughts, Aelin had felt joy and freedom as the bloaters took flight across the cosmos. Even so, none of the Iswander workers believed that the marvelous gas sacks were anything more than unusual phenomena.

Afterward, Lee Iswander had found another cluster and begun the massive extraction operations again, harvesting bloaters, *slaughtering* them. . . .

Creeping along, Aelin reached the docking bay hatch. He glanced through an observation port and waited with increasing tension while one worker refueled a scout pod that had returned from an inspection tour of the operations. Yes, that was what Aelin wanted. He didn't need to go far—just out to the bloaters to make contact again.

Despite his tolerance, Iswander was obviously worried that the unstable green priest would try to escape to the nearest civilized outpost. Because he could reveal the nature of the ekti-X operations, Aelin was a threat to Iswander Industries. If other Roamers knew how simple it was to extract stardrive fuel from bloaters—in contrast with their difficult and expensive operations harvesting ekti from gas-giant planets—Lee Iswander would be ruined.

Aelin had no desire to sell his secrets, though—nor even to escape. He just wanted to be out among the bloaters, where he could bathe in their thoughts, absorb their revelations. This was much deeper than the mental community that green priests shared when connected to the sentient trees in the worldforest.

The worldtrees stored thousands of years of data, experiences, and memories. When he first passed through the transformation to become a green priest, Aelin had imagined that the verdani mind must be the most magnificent manifestation in the universe. But he had sensed something about the mysterious drifting bloaters, and he had flown out among them, curious. Carrying a small potted treeling and oblivious to the danger, he had tried to connect with the bloaters via telink. The responding surge had incinerated his treeling and overloaded his mind.

Thanks to that connection, though, Aelin now felt the constant, wordless pain emitted by the bloaters. They were so much *more* than he had ever guessed before. . . .

Inside the docking bay, the refueling technician strolled away from the inspection pod, logged his work into the station database, and exited the launching bay. When the hangar was empty, Aelin opened the hatch and darted across the open deck.

The entire extraction field was a high-security operation, but internal Iswander security was less rigorous. Aelin ducked into a spherical inspection pod. He could feel the strange calling inside his mind, the titanic and incomprehensible presence represented by the bloaters. He was sure that if he touched them again, he would receive all the knowledge he needed. He would understand what they *were*.

He felt a great burden and responsibility as well. Only *he* could make Iswander Industries stop the painful slaughter.

After sealing the pod's hatch, Aelin powered up the engines, felt the craft vibrate around him. He keyed in the activation code that would open the atmosphere field to let him fly away from the complex. He needed to be out among the bloaters before anyone knew he had gone.

Efficient air pumps drained the chamber, but just as Aelin tried to raise the pod from the deck plates, a sequence of warning signals flickered through the cockpit controls and alarm lights flashed on the metal walls. The atmosphere barrier field strengthened, blocking his exit, and air flooded back into the bay. Amber lights strobed all around him.

The green priest frantically worked the piloting controls, but overrides deactivated them. The pod settled onto the deck and came to rest as the engines shut down. Aelin sat helpless and dismayed in the single seat.

Three Iswander security guards rushed into the docking bay, followed by Lee Iswander himself, tall and lean. His dark brown hair was neat, his temples frosted with gray. He looked distinguished, commanding—and displeased.

Unceremoniously, the guards unsealed the pod's hatch and grabbed Aelin's bare green arms, hauling him out. He struggled, but only halfheartedly. He yelled to Iswander, "You must let me go out there!"

"No, green priest—I don't need to do that at all." He sounded disappointed, even paternal. "I won't let you jeopardize our operations."

Aelin thrashed, but the guards held his arms firmly. "Your operations are endangering the universe! You are spilling the blood of the cosmos. You don't know what you're doing."

Iswander raised his eyebrows. "We're becoming the preeminent supplier of stardrive fuel throughout the Spiral Arm. The success of my operations proves that I know what I'm doing."

Aelin said, "Please—you don't understand the damage you're causing! I can feel their pain."

Iswander spoke in a wistful voice. "I remember a long time ago, after you broke your leg treedancing on Theroc. Even while you were recovering, you made your way out of the tree city and sneaked aboard one of my commercial ships. I could tell that you had big dreams, Aelin—I thought you were a kindred spirit. That's why I took a gamble and brought you out here to be my personal green priest." He placed his hands on his hips, and his voice became harder. "But my patience is running out—don't make me regret my decision."

He gestured to the guards. "Take him back to his quarters and keep him confined. If he resists, have medical sedate him."

Aelin's muscles went watery as the guards pulled him away. His connection with the bloaters remained: he could feel them dying, but he could do nothing about it.

CHAPTER

2

XANDER BRINDLE

Another huge load of ekti-X delivered to Ulio Station, and another gigantic profit for Kett Shipping—Xander Brindle decided that was a good enough excuse for a celebratory drink in the star balcony bar with his partner, Terry Handon.

Ulio Station was a popular hub, an interstellar flea market where hundreds of traders exchanged wares outside of Confederation control and therefore without any inconvenient tariffs or taxes.

More than fifteen years ago an old Roamer entrepreneur named Maria Ulio had begun gathering starships that were damaged during the Elemental War: huge Ildiran warliners battered by the faeros or hydrogues, wrecked Manta cruisers from the Earth Defense Forces, abandoned colony ships, burned-out trading vessels—all collected in a large salvage yard.

Maria's crew worked on the ships, repairing the ones that could be salvaged, converting the others into habitation complexes. Over the years, more and more people brought their ships to the scrapyard; wanderers came there to work, and they stayed; traders found it a convenient place to meet. Ulio Station grew like a coral reef of accumulated ships, some permanently docked, others just passing through.

Xander considered Ulio Station a bustling and energetic complex filled with a mix of people, costumes, traditions, and—Terry's favorite—a variety of ethnic cuisines. While Xander had been born aboard a starship and grew up eating processed galley food, Terry had a more discriminating palate. And since Xander cared about his partner, he could tolerate fine food for the good of their relationship.

After their ship, the *Verne*, had picked up a full cargo load of ekti-X from the secret Iswander drop-off point, they flew directly to Ulio Station, which was always their best place to sell stardrive fuel. Because ekti-X was cheap and in such demand, the *Verne* began receiving frantic bids as soon as they came within comm range. While Xander flew about in search of a docking berth among Ulio's clustered ships, Terry studied the bids, nodding in satisfaction. "We never have trouble selling our cargo here."

OK, their competent computerized companion, or compy, announced crisply, "Ekti-X is far less expensive than stardrive fuel extracted by traditional skymining operations on gas giants. And its energy density is greater than standard ekti. Therefore, our commodity remains in demand."

"The demand isn't waning," Xander said. "And I doubt it will."

In fact, the Iswander Industries fuel was flooding the market, which caused great consternation among the Roamer clans who saw the devaluation of their traditional ekti operations. As they struggled to make a profit, countless Roamers pressured Xander and Terry for any insight into how and where Lee Iswander got his ekti-X so cheaply.

Xander just laughed off the questions, and Terry was naturally tight-lipped; none of the other secondary Kett vessels had any direct contact with Iswander whatsoever. Others could question them all they wanted, but nobody had any clue where ekti-X came from. Their Iswander contact, Elisa Enturi, refused to reveal anything; Terry and Xander would simply deliver a cargo and reap a large profit for Kett Shipping. . . .

The two men completed their business in less than an hour, selling the entire cargo for ten percent more than the original asking price. Xander now strutted beside his partner as their compy marched in the lead. Terry held on to OK's smooth polymer shoulder, letting himself be pulled along; an antigrav pack kept his motionless feet suspended just off the deck.

Paralyzed from an accident in his youth, Terry couldn't use his legs, but that didn't pose much of a problem in zero gravity. For convenience, Xander kept the *Verne*'s grav generators switched off, and the two of them were perfectly at home floating aboard the ship. At Ulio Station, however, many of the docked vessels and passageways throughout the ship cluster had gravity at various levels, so Terry relied on OK to tow him along.

Xander saw the nostalgic shine in his partner's eyes. "Does it feel good to be home? Or are you glad you made your way out of here?"

"Well, I'm glad I found *you*," Terry said with a smile. "This place doesn't feel completely like home anyway. Ulio changes every week as ships come and go, while others dock and stay forever." He sighed. "It hasn't been the same since Maria flew off to parts unknown."

As a teenager, Terry had worked at the station as a starship mechanic; he floated around with a jetpack and an environment suit, tinkering with the external stardrive engines of any wreck that came in for repair. He was so nimble and competent at his job that his coworkers hadn't even realized at first that he couldn't walk.

Old Maria Ulio had taken Terry under her wing, and he had worked with her for years, but once Ulio Station became a bustling, self-sufficient hub, Maria got bored with it all. She had her workers repair the battered old Ildiran warliner she had used as her home base for years, said a tearful goodbye to Terry, then flew off by herself with a few compy assistants and plenty of supplies. She had never been seen again.

Ulio Station, meanwhile, remained as bustling as ever.

As the three proceeded toward the star balcony bar inside the refurbished command nucleus of an old Ildiran warliner, OK said, "Do you have an estimate of how long we plan to stay here, sirs? There are fees associated with the docking berth the *Verne* is using, and there is a waiting list of inbound ships."

Terry looked at Xander. "We don't have to rush off, do we? At least three new restaurants opened since the last time we docked—I'd like to try them."

"We'll try two of them," Xander said. "Save one for next time."

"There'll be more new ones next time."

"It's great to have options."

"Right, but difficult to choose."

Xander relented. "All right, with the recent haul, we can afford to stay a full day."

"And a half."

"And a half," Xander agreed, and turned to the compy. "OK, please make the arrangements."

"Yes, Xander."

Before they reached the connector passage to the star balcony, a group of Roamers intercepted them in the narrow station corridor. Four men crowded the passageway with no intention of stepping aside. They wore scuffed jumpsuits embroidered with markings from the Duquesne clan, which operated two refurbished skymines on a gas giant—Belliros, if Xander recalled correctly. The Duquesne ekti operations had fallen on hard times, though, because of the flood of cheap Iswander ekti-X being distributed by Kett Shipping.

The three Duquesnes in the back were husky and muscular, as if they had grown up on a heavy-gravity planet. The man in front was the scrawniest, about thirty with sandy hair, a thin face, and a long aquiline nose. Considering his lack of brawn, Xander decided he must be the brains of the group. He identified the man as Aaron Duquesne, the clan's oldest son and heir apparent to those Belliros skymines, which were rapidly declining in value.

Aaron gave them a smile that had no actual smile behind it. "Xander Brindle, no matter how hard you try, you can't wipe that smug look off your face." He turned to look at the three men behind him. "He's buying everyone drinks tonight, since the *Verne* made such a profit on this run."

"I have no problem buying drinks for my friends," Xander answered with a cocky shrug. "Alas, that doesn't include you."

"Please excuse us." OK stepped politely forward. "We have an appointment."

"Oh, are we blocking your way?" Aaron said. "That's a problem."

Terry looked nervous. "We don't want any trouble. I can either call Ulio Security or I can call on my friends—and I've got a lot of friends here."

"Ulio must be a friendly place, then," said Aaron. "And in the spirit of friendship, my cousins and I would very much like to know your source for ekti-X. Where does Iswander Industries get it?"

"Elisa Enturi arranges for delivery, and we distribute it. We don't push for too many answers. You'd have to ask her."

Duquesne snorted. "You're the only ones she talks to."

"A charming personality wins out every time," Xander said. "I don't ask where the ekti-X comes from, and I don't care."

"You're driving the rest of us out of business."

Xander crossed his arms over his chest. "You're a Roamer just like me, Aaron Duquesne. You know that the one with the most innovation reaps the most rewards."

"*Brindle* is no Roamer clan," said Aaron. "If you really considered yourself a Roamer, you'd keep your clan Tamblyn name."

Xander felt a flush of anger. "My mother's a Tamblyn, and my name is my own business."

"Your own business?" Aaron said. "But we don't like your business."

Behind him, his burly companions pulled out metal wands that telescoped into stiff cudgels.

Terry recoiled and lost his grip on the compy's shoulder, but his antigrav belt kept his feet suspended a centimeter above the deck. He put a warning tone in his voice. "There's no brawling allowed on Ulio Station—Maria was very clear about that when she laid down the law. If you're guilty of assault, you'll be forbidden from trading here again."

"Oh, I looked up the rules," said Aaron. "We have no intention of harming a hair on your pretty little heads—so long as you tell us where ekti-X comes from."

"Sorry, boys, we honestly don't know," Xander said. "Stardrive fuel production is above my pay grade. Iswander has some mysterious new process—and good for him. Given the profits, we don't ask questions we're not supposed to ask—and *you're* not supposed to ask either."

With a disappointed frown, Aaron turned to his three cousins. "I was afraid he'd say that. Let's give him something to think about."

His three companions snatched OK before Xander could react. The little compy flailed his hands, and the three men hammered him with their metal clubs. One took a vicious swing and battered OK's head, while another smashed the compy's shoulders, tearing open the polymer skin; the third man buckled one of the compy's kneecaps.

OK amplified his voice. "Please stop!"

Xander launched himself off the deck and struck one of the burly men, who caught him easily and slammed him back against a bulkhead. Terry tried to pull himself forward, but he couldn't find a handhold.

The Duquesnes were mostly done anyway. With a quick succession of blows, they smashed and incapacitated the poor compy. OK lay on the deck, squawking in a voice that degenerated into static.

"Stop, damn you!" Xander yelled. "Enough!"

While two of the men held a thrashing Xander, Aaron took one of the clubs and hammered OK's artificial face; then he turned with a smile. "You're right—Ulio Station rules forbid brawling on penalty of banishment. On the other hand, anyone who causes damage to *personal property* just has to pay a fine." The gangly man tossed out a handful of credit chips, which clattered on the metal deck. "Here you go. Sorry for the inconvenience."

Xander tore himself free of the men holding him, and Terry moved forward to grab OK. The compy tried to get up but collapsed against one of the bulkheads—dented, scraped, torn, and unable to stand on one of his legs.

Satisfied with the damage they had done, the Duquesnes retreated. "Remember that, Brindle," called Aaron. "Take a little more interest in where your profits come from, and we'd be a lot friendlier if you shared your information." His companions folded around him as they left.

Though he was sick and furious, Xander was unarmed, and he couldn't fight four men. Terry was not a warrior either. Instead, they tended to the smashed compy. OK's speakerpatch had been damaged, but he kept trying to make sounds.

"We'll get you repaired, OK," Xander said, his voice cracking. This compy had been his copilot since before he'd even met Terry. They had been through a great deal together. "It's just external damage—a few scuffs, that's all. We'll have you patched up and repainted in no time."

"They're barbarians!" Terry looked up at him, his face gray. "But they're correct—Ulio Station law says the punishment for property damage is nothing more than a fine."

Xander felt nauseated. His parents, Tasia Tamblyn and Robb Brindle—the acting administrators of Kett Shipping—had reluctantly agreed to a trading partnership with Lee Iswander, and profits from the stardrive fuel were too extraordinary to dismiss, but Robb and Tasia were worried that the ekti-X operations were shady dealings. Xander had brushed aside those worries, citing the old adage (which he didn't really understand) about not looking a gift horse in the mouth. He had remained willfully, and happily, ignorant.

But now . . .

Simmering with anger, he picked up the damaged compy. OK was incapable of walking, though he made a valiant attempt. "Let's get him back to the *Verne*. Fast."

Terry swallowed hard. "We'll find OK the best compy repair facility."

"That'll be on Earth—back at headquarters." Xander was sorry Terry wouldn't get the gourmet dinner he had been promised, but neither of them was hungry anymore.

CHAPTER

3

ARITA

They called themselves the Gardeners—an alien race that had tended the worldtrees millennia ago, just as the human green priests on Theroc did now. But the Gardeners—or the Onthos, in their own language—had been all but exterminated by the Shana Rei long ago, their core worldforest wiped out along with the stored memories contained in that verdani mind. Only a hundred survivors of the small-statured gray-skinned creatures had limped their way to Theroc. They had begged sanctuary, and King Peter and Queen Estarra—Arita's parents—had granted it.

Now, a group of curious green priests gathered under the towering trees to speak with the Onthos, hoping to learn more. Since the worldforest mind could offer only vague hints about the long-lost Gardeners, the green priests had many questions, and the Onthos had many stories to tell.

Without being invited, Arita sat on the edge of the group, even though she was not a green priest, despite her dream of becoming one. She had lost her chance when the forest mind tested her, *changed* her, and ultimately rejected her as a green priest.

Even if she wasn't one of them, the green priests did not shun Arita as a failure—she was, after all, the daughter of Theroc's rulers. Nevertheless, the priests treated her with discernible pity, and it was almost too much for Arita to bear. Now, though, she very much wanted to hear the Gardeners reveal their secret history.

Three seemingly identical aliens sat in a clearing among the gigantic trees, speaking to the group. Ten green priests listened and then delivered what they learned into the tree network, so that any other priest across the Spiral Arm could receive the details. Instantaneous telink communication was just one of the many wonders that Arita was denied because she was not a green priest. . . .

But she listened now. The primary Gardener representative called himself Ohro, though he seemed indistinguishable from the other aliens. The Onthos were four feet tall with enormous black eyes set within prominent orbital ridges. They wore no clothes over their smooth skin; they seemed entirely sexless.

Ohro traced emphasis in the air with nimble fingers as he spoke to the rapt green priests. "I remember our world, bright pictures and memories of a beautiful place, a peaceful civilization. The Gardeners and the trees—what more could we wish for?" The other aliens murmured, and the green priests listened, smiled, nodded. They touched the towering worldtrees next to them, shared thoughts—and left Arita apart from it all.

But even Ohro's words conjured fantastic images in her mind.

"We had tremendous tree cities, much like this one, and we built our structures to exist in concert with the trunks and fronds—wooden and metal walkways that wove the living forest together. Bridges spanned tree to tree. Towers rose even higher than the canopy!" His dark alien eyes glistened.

"When the ancient trees would eventually die, they became a source of new life. Our spore mothers would enter the dead wood and spawn more Onthos, birthing many more Gardeners who would tend another generation of worldtrees."

Ohro sighed. "And we became explorers, too—fusing ourselves with the trees. An Onthos volunteer would climb inside the heartwood, meld his body to the great tree, and act as a pilot, a voyager. Together, they underwent a marvelous metamorphosis, becoming more alive, more sentient. The new treeship would uproot itself and rise into the sky . . . and fly away into the void." The alien glanced at Arita as if to make sure she understood, then turned to the green priests. "You know of this—you have done it yourselves."

The green priests nodded. One said, "We created verdani battleships, which fought in the Elemental War."

"We observed the remaining ones guarding this world when our refugee ships arrived at Theroc," Ohro said. "We did not use our treeships for war, though, but to explore. We flew off to other worlds and dispersed the trees, built new colonies, even constructed space cities far from any planet."

Arita could not see what the other priests observed when they tapped into the shared verdani mind. The Onthos could offer no tangible relics, photographic images, or other records apart from their memories, which they shared throughout the worldforest. She could only use her imagination, but right now that was enough.

"Then the Shana Rei came and drove us from our home." Ohro's voice became deeper, sadder.

Until recently, little was known about the Shana Rei beyond brief mentions in Ildiran legends. Then a shadow cloud came to destroy Theroc. The creatures of darkness had assembled a gigantic orbiting nightshade that plunged the worldforest into a suffocating night. Only the combined efforts of the Confederation Defense Forces, the Ildiran Solar Navy, and even the capricious faeros had driven away the shadows. For now.

"You know much more about the Shana Rei," a green priest said to Ohro. "Help us understand how to fight them."

Even though the Gardener was not human, Arita could read an expression of hopelessness on his flat, grayish face. "We could not fight them. They annihilated everything—our forest, our world, our home star." The gathered Onthos shuddered in unison.

"Some survivors tried to make new homes on other planets, but we were caught up in the Klikiss depredations that swept across the Spiral Arm with their swarm wars. They fell upon our colonies, tore us to shreds.

"Again, we were decimated, but a few scattered and survived. Some of us simply drifted away in space, circling outward, always hoping to find a remnant of the worldforest that survived. And now we are home," he said. "At last, the Onthos can recall who we are, and exactly what we were meant to be."

Arita saw the desperation and hope on the strange alien faces, and she felt glad for them that they had found a home.

"Your worldforest remembers us, at least in part," Ohro said. "The verdani know that we are kindred, even if they do not recall the great swath of memory obliterated by the Shana Rei."

After their refugee ships had landed in front of the fungus-reef city like a swarm of silvery raindrops, the Gardener survivors had reveled in the gigantic trees, drinking in the scents and sensations of the verdani mind. The Onthos had settled in, but had not built any structures nor moved into existing homes. For now, the aliens were content to be back in the embrace of the vast forest, sleeping out in the open.

Some Therons were uneasy about the strange visitors, but King Peter reminded them all, "The worldforest recognizes them. If they cared for the trees the way our green priests do, then they must be our allies."

Arita's parents had recently been called away because of a crisis at Shorehaven, where a large but rare native predator had been ravaging the villagers, and Peter and Estarra had gone to investigate, leaving the green priests—and Arita—to learn more about the Gardeners.

Now Ohro raised his thin arms to indicate the sprawling canopy of interlocked fronds above them. "The Shana Rei obliterated our forest down to the last treeling, but without worldtrees, the Onthos cannot reproduce. We are stagnant, our numbers dwindling. Until now."

Arita was fascinated with alien life-forms, particularly trees, fungi, and insects, and the Gardeners could not be any stranger than what she had seen on other worlds. She spoke up, startling the self-absorbed green priests. "I don't understand. How could you need worldtrees for that?"

The alien looked at her curiously. "Our symbiosis with the verdani was greater even than a green priest's bond with the trees, and we saved only one of our spore mothers." Ohro looked directly at her, as if he felt a tighter connection with her than with the green priests. But that made no sense. "We have lived so long without any hope at all. Now that the Onthos are here on Theroc, everything will change."

CHAPTER

4

ANTON COLICOS

He was a historian, which was really only a fancy word for "storyteller." The Ildiran rememberer kith had always understood that.

The drama of grand events in the Spiral Arm was more than a listing of facts and dates. It was a *story,* a genuine saga, with untold trillions of characters, countless races and factions and clans. The Ildirans had chronicled millennia of history in their magnificent billion-line poem, the Saga of Seven Suns.

Anton Colicos knew his purpose in life. He wanted to preserve those stories of civilizations in conflict, to capture the essence of the titanic events that had swept through the galaxy, not just from centuries ago, but in recent years as well. After all, he had been in the thick of much of it himself.

And here he was again.

Riding in an open flyer that skimmed above the lush green forests of Theroc, Anton admired the worldtrees. He was part of the entourage accompanying King Peter and Queen Estarra as they headed to a village built along the shores of a shallow inland sea.

For months, a giant wyvern had preyed on Shorehaven. From what Anton had heard, the predator was a voracious sharp-clawed insect the size of a dragon. According to reports, this was the largest wyvern ever spotted; even allowing for a certain amount of exaggeration from excitable eyewitnesses, he was sure the thing was a monster by any definition.

When Peter and Estarra had put together a party to go to Shorehaven, Anton immediately asked to go along. Over the years, he had fallen into most of his adventures by accident. This time, though, he sought it out intentionally. "Someone has to record it, Majesties." Yazra'h would have been proud.

He smiled at the thought of the tough warrior woman, daughter of the Ildiran Mage-Imperator. Yazra'h had been his bodyguard, his companion, and she reveled in any kind of fight. She liked to demonstrate her prowess for him, in what Anton had realized with alarm was a flirtatious way. He was not interested in her as a lover—and not only because Yazra'h would have damaged him in their first love-making session. Fortunately, she remained on Ildira, and Anton had been evacuated here to the worldforest planet. She would have loved to go along to see the wyvern.

Anton had lived on Ildira for years as a guest historian, devoting his career to translating the *Saga of Seven Suns,* so that humans could understand more about the oddly humanlike race. "Rememberer Anton" had been adopted as a hero among the Ildirans, who were pleased that he loved their culture so much. He had spent well over a decade in the Ildiran capital of Mijistra while the alien empire rebuilt itself following the devastating Elemental War.

When uprisings of shadow-contaminated Ildirans made Mijistra too dangerous a place for Anton or Prince Reynald of Theroc, they had departed Ildira for the supposed safety of the worldforest planet . . . only to be engulfed by yet another shadow attack.

And then the unexpected Onthos refugees had arrived with their astonishing tale. It was all too much for a historian to write down, even if he spent all day, every day, taking furious notes!

For now, though, a wyvern attacking a village was simply too intriguing to pass up.

Peter and Estarra looked regal as they rode in an ornate skimmer that cruised above the canopy. They wore traditional Theron clothing: scaly moth-wing adornments, and glistening insect carapaces mounted on their shoulders. Two green priests and three business-suited Confederation representatives rode in a separate craft along with Anton, as well as a group of security troops.

The worldtree canopy ended abruptly like a gigantic cliff as they reached the edge of the inland sea. The water stretched out flat and blue ahead of them, dappled with sunlight. In the marshland along the shore, dwellings were made of knobby structural reeds covered with tough polymer films. Long rafts and anchored docks extended into the shallow sea.

Lightweight sailing boats and fishing trawlers moved about like water bugs, but the fishers had to be wary as they went out on the inland sea. From shore, watchers scanned the sky for any sign of the wyvern.

The royal entourage swooped down to reach the main settlement on the shore. The people of Shorehaven emerged to greet the King and Queen, but they remained close to their homes. Anton took detailed notes, not sure how this story would shape up.

Peter and Estarra were greeted by the Shorehaven village leader, Tristan Cove, a dark-skinned man with a smoke of gray through his hair. He wore clean unornamented clothes; he was clearly a fisherman himself. "Please help us, Father Peter, Mother Estarra—that monster is destroying our village. Twelve victims so far. We're crippled, many of us afraid to do our daily work, while others are desperate enough to risk for everybody."

"We'll help all we can," Estarra said.

Peter added, "You don't know where the wyvern's lair is? Have you sent out hunters?"

A green priest stepped up to them. "A wyvern has no lair." He was muscular, bare-chested, wearing only a traditional loincloth. "I am Beltrias. Through the eyes of the trees, I studied the creature, watched its movements. I am starting to get to know it. The monster attacks, it feeds, it flies away, then it hunts elsewhere. I could not follow the thing, even through the trees."

Tristan Cove gave a grim nod. "Despite its size, it has only a rudimentary reactive brain, but eventually it recalls the good feeding it found at Shorehaven. It comes back. It always comes back."

"Then we will have to kill it," said Queen Estarra. "We'll send teams, use tracking devices—and be ready the next time it comes."

Anton held his pad, ready to take more notes. "I'd like to hear about the previous attacks, record the stories, talk to witnesses."

Alarms out on the great lake startled them. The colorful fishing boats began to race back toward shore so swiftly, they created a visible wake. The crews on deck scurried about.

The village leader pointed to the sky where a small speck grew noticeably larger. "That's the wyvern."

In a blur of segmented wings and jagged carapace sections, the wyvern swooped down, targeting one of the smaller fishing boats. The crew scrambled to rip down the colorful sail, which had somehow attracted the monster. Projectile-weapons fire erupted from the nearby ships, but the wyvern had already chosen its target.

Anton watched, chillingly fascinated as the creature dropped like a hawk pouncing on a quivering rodent. With segmented claws, the wyvern crashed down on the boat and snapped the deck and the hull. With a beat of throbbing wings, it tore the vessel from the water and flew into the air, carrying the entire thing.

The wyvern's claws continued to work, ripping the hull apart, cracking and peeling pieces away. After it flew high enough, it dropped the shattered vessel, and Anton could see human figures falling through the sky. The wyvern danced about with a blur of wings, extending numerous limbs to snatch bodies out of the air, before whisking away across the water until it disappeared in the distance.

Tears filled Peter's eyes. Estarra was shuddering. The King said to the village leader, "Anything you need."

Anton recorded the King's exact words, knowing they would be a vital part of the story.

CHAPTER

5

MAGE-IMPERATOR JORA'H

Even under the bright light of seven suns, the Mage-Imperator felt darkness around him, in the corners, at the edge of his vision—a pervasive and insidious shadow that no amount of daylight could wash away. Much of the darkness was due to his own guilt and sadness at the massacre of innocent humans that had happened here, but he feared it was more insidious . . . that the Shana Rei had worked themselves like a wireneedle into the telepathic network of *thism* that bound all the Ildiran people.

Nira, his lover and soul mate, joined him as they went to the devastated ruin of Mijistra's human enclave. Though the female green priest was not connected to him through *thism*, their bond was just as strong and clear. She looked so beautiful with her delicate features, her green hairless skin. Nira's soft expression showed remarkably few mental scars despite all the tragedies she had endured at the Dobro breeding camp, before the Mage-Imperator had rescued her. . . .

Knowing how troubled Jora'h was to come back to this place of terrible shame, Nira simply clasped his hand, folding her fingers through his. The horrific crime that had occurred here, the mindless slaughter inflicted upon those poor people by everyday Ildirans, was an incomprehensible shock.

An entourage of noble kith accompanied the Mage-Imperator, along with warriors to help guard him, and medical kith and scientist kith who were determined to explain why Jora'h's own people had turned into mindless attackers.

Dressed in short reptile-scale armor, his daughter Yazra'h joined them. Tough and alert, she would spot and crush any threat before the Mage-Imperator or Nira could even guess what was happening.

Next to her like a smaller mirror image was Muree'n, Nira's youngest halfbreed child, whose father was a member of the warrior kith. Muree'n trained with Yazra'h and seemed determined to best her mentor, although Yazra'h had not yet allowed the younger woman to succeed. . . .

As the Mage-Imperator's entourage moved through the city streets, Jora'h wore fabulous and ornate robes, fabrics stitched with crystalline threads that made him shimmer with sunflares and rainbows. But Jora'h did not feel glorious today. Rather, a sense of dread came over him.

The crystalline towers of the reconstructed capital city soared high into the sky, where only three of the suns blazed this time of day. Jora'h could hear the construction and cleanup crews hard at work as his party entered the human district. He paused, and the entourage stuttered to a halt next to him.

When the Mage-Imperator stopped, Yazra'h and Muree'n split up and loped around the small district, carrying crystal-bladed katanas, while the rest of the guard kithmen remained close to Jora'h. Only when Yazra'h and Muree'n were satisfied that none of the construction workers and engineer kith posed a threat did they allow the Mage-Imperator to proceed into the area.

He stopped to absorb the massacre site. The smears of smoke and spattered blood had been removed, but Jora'h could still sense a heaviness in the air, as if the screams had not yet faded in the intervening weeks. The Earth-architecture buildings had been razed, the stone paving tiles uprooted and replaced.

For the past two decades, this district had been set aside for human settlers who wanted to live in Mijistra. Now the human enclave was gone, all the settlers murdered, and Jora'h didn't dare invite more humans here until he could purge the shadows.

As he looked at the digging apparatus, the cranes, and the machinery that was erasing all vestiges of the human presence, he nodded to Nira. "As I promised, we will plant worldtrees here, as many as Theroc is willing to send us."

Nira spoke in a quiet, disturbed voice. "Those humans loved Ildiran culture, and they came here to share with you." Her voice hitched. "It was exactly the type of alliance we wanted."

The Confederation and the Ildiran Empire had been bound together by common enemies, then connected by common interests. Now, with the reappearance of the Shana Rei, they had a common enemy again. . . .

Jora'h thought of King Peter and Queen Estarra on Theroc. Yes, Adar Zan'nh and the Solar Navy had helped save the worldforest planet against the Shana Rei . . . but nothing could make up for what Jora'h had let happen to these innocent humans here.

He squeezed Nira's hand tighter, looking at the churned, blood-stained ground. "I promised them safety, and I failed them." He raised his chin.

Nira said, "We don't understand what caused the uprising."

"Just because I don't understand what caused the violence is no excuse. I am the Mage-Imperator. All the strands of *thism* come through me. I am responsible for the actions of my people."

He shook his head. "My father would have erased the evidence and deleted any mention of it from the historical record. He would never have admitted such a massacre to King Peter." He shook his head. "But I am not my father."

Nira gave him a wan smile. "True in so many ways."

The previous Mage-Imperator had been responsible for countless crimes; one of the worst was what he had done to Nira so many years ago, sending her to that breeding camp on Dobro and forcing her to—

Reaching a decision, the Mage-Imperator turned to his entourage and said abruptly, "Nira and I will go to Theroc. We will reveal to King Peter and Queen Estarra what happened here, so that they understand how insidious the Shana Rei can be. Now, more than ever before, the alliance between Ildirans and humans must be unbreakable."

Yazra'h rapped her katana against one of the broken old street tiles. "I will accompany you to ensure your safety, Liege."

Without cracking a smile, Muree'n added, "I will come as well, in case Yazra'h should be found lacking."

Nira brightened. "Osira'h is also there on Theroc. We thought she would be safe there, but the Shana Rei attacked Theroc as well. I would like her back home with us."

Jora'h could not argue. "Alas, it is no safer there."

Yazra'h interjected, "And I will make sure that Rememberer Anton has not gotten himself into trouble. He often needs me."

Jora'h took one last glance at the construction work. It would take these busy Ildirans only a week or two longer to transform the massacre site. And Jora'h's diplomatic group could bring more fresh worldtree saplings from Theroc.

He turned to the bureaucrats, the noble kith, his various ministers, and said, "Prepare a Solar Navy warliner and a full escort. We will depart for Theroc as soon as possible."

CHAPTER

6

ADAR ZAN'NH

The septa of Solar Navy warliners entered orbit around the industrial planet of Askelor. They flew with maneuvers so coordinated the ships seemed to be joined by invisible bonds. The Ildiran warliners extended angular reflective fins, both for solar-power acquisition and to look intimidating against any foe.

Adar Zan'nh, leader of the entire Solar Navy, stood in the command nucleus, speaking via screen to a sturdy female member of the engineering kith. Bura's was the operations manager of the Askelor industries, which had just been converted for full-scale production of laser cannons and sun bombs, the only weapons so far found to be even minimally effective against the Shana Rei. Weapons from the Askelor industries would be installed aboard every ship in the Solar Navy. Zan'nh hoped it could be done quickly enough.

Bura's said, "The factory conversions are complete, Adar. All resources, facilities, and manpower are now focused on weapons production to produce what the Solar Navy needs. We will not fail."

Zan'nh nodded. "My tal and I will come down in a cutter for a brief inspection."

After Bura's ended the transmission, Zan'nh turned to his companion and protégé. Tal Gale'nh was one of Nira's children from the Dobro breeding program, the son of the legendary Ildiran war hero, Adar Kori'nh. Half human and half Ildiran, Gale'nh had demonstrated great skill and had risen rapidly in his Solar Navy career, achieving the rank of tal at a young age.

Now, though, Gale'nh looked physically washed out, a mere wisp of himself. His skin was pale, his hair white, all color *bleached* away by his encounter with the Shana Rei. Adar Zan'nh regretted the ordeal he had inadvertently put the young man through.

It had been meant as a reward. He had granted Gale'nh command of a unique expeditionary ship to explore beyond the brightest stars in the Spiral Arm, but out there in the vast dark spaces, the Shana Rei engulfed the *Kolpraxa*, wiping out the rest of his crew. Gale'nh's exotic halfbreed genetics somehow made him immune to the creatures of darkness, though, and he was the only survivor.

The horrific encounter had nearly destroyed him, but despite his haunted reticence, the young tal possessed a diamond-hard core. He had been the Adar's shining, talented protégé, and Zan'nh would not give up on him. He was determined to save the young man, to heal him and push him and make him whole. More importantly, he was the only person who had survived a direct contact with the Shana Rei. Gale'nh might know things that were buried deep in his mind, strategic things, if he could ever face the dark core of those memories.

Zan'nh stepped up to the other officer. "Accompany me down to Askelor, Tal?"

Gale'nh's voice seemed quiet, but not weak. "I am at your side, Adar." He still didn't have the self-confidence to command a warliner group again, but that would come. Zan'nh was sure of it.

As the septa of warliners orbited the planet, the two descended in a cutter to the main industrial complex, accompanied by an escort crew. Askelor was small and close to its sun, and the combination of low gravity and high temperatures had caused much of its atmosphere to bleed away. Emerging from the cutter, the inspection party affixed breathing masks to their faces.

A bright wash of sunlight reflected from the pale landscape. Askelor had brackish lakes and lichens that lived in the cracks between rocks, but not much of an ecosystem. It was considered a disposable world, an exploitable world.

Numerous miner kith had excavated deep troughs in a neat grid across mineral-rich plateaus. Industrial facilities produced commodities and machinery that the Empire needed, but less than a month ago—while the Solar Navy reeled from their disastrous battle against the Shana Rei at Plumas—Mage-Imperator Jora'h had commanded that Askelor turn every facility over to producing the new exotic weapons for the Solar Navy.

The air was hot, and industrial fumes stung Zan'nh's eyes. Tal Gale'nh glanced around, drinking in the sunlight and the bustle of manufacturing activity. Operations manager Bura's met them on the landing field and led them to the nearest building, an enormous structure the size of a starship hangar. Vehicles delivered fabricated metal and polymer components from other factories farther down the valley. Lichens were harvested from acres of rocks, then chemically converted into resilient plastics. Smelters processed ores that were shipped in tons at a time.

Bura's led the inspection crew along assembly lines where armies of worker kith manned stations, each assembling the components of the exotic weapons. "This is still the preliminary phase, and our production levels are increasing daily," she said. "We have already produced thirty fully tested, fully functional laser cannons, and that is just a start. I estimate we will produce sufficient cannons to equip one warliner every two days." Bura's paused and looked at them. "I never miss my estimates."

"And what about the sun bombs?" Gale'nh asked.

"They are more complex. We have created twenty-eight more so far, but each one is an individual assembly, creating unique problems. We are still developing a means to mass-produce them. The designs were old."

Zan'nh stared down the production line. "Nevertheless, we need as many sun bombs as possible. Give that priority. The sun bomb prototypes functioned extremely well in the field. In fact, nothing proved more effective against the Shana Rei in our recent engagements."

Bura's gave him a grim warning look. "Given their instability, those prototypes could just as easily have malfunctioned and vaporized your warliner. Do not forget that we are effectively bottling the core of a star inside a spherical container." She straightened, dredged up resolve. "But we will achieve success, I promise you, Adar."

After he and Gale'nh toured the facilities for two hours, Zan'nh had seen all he needed to. He decided to wait at Askelor while his flagship and the other six ships were refitted with the new weapons.

When that was finished, he was eager to take his warliners out on patrol . . . out on a hunt.

"I want to fight the shadows," he said to Gale'nh in an angry voice, as they rode up in the cutter again. "But how do you find a shadow in all the emptiness of the universe?"

"They are not even hiding in our universe," said Gale'nh, sifting through hints in the back of his mind. "The Shana Rei are desperate, I think. They are frightened. That is why they attack."

The Adar didn't understand. "What can they possibly be frightened of?"

Gale'nh remained silent for a long moment. "I don't know. I cannot find it within me. Yes, I am growing stronger, but I still need to discover my inner Lightsource. I still need to find my bright anchor."

Adar Zan'nh had never considered himself a mystical man, but he knew about the Lightsource, the dazzling plane of a higher existence that Ildirans could reach beyond the boundaries of death. One breed of Ildirans, the lens kith, tried to comfort lesser kithmen and guide their prayers.

Gale'nh's pale face was full of meaning and questions. "There is a place, Adar—the Hiltos shrine, where the lens kith believe the walls of reality are thinnest, where a common person like me can possibly touch the Lightsource." He seemed to feel awkward making his request even though he knew Zan'nh would do anything to make him whole again. "I would like to go there, for a time. Maybe I can find a way to be cleansed and strong again. Maybe that way I can be the confident commander that you need me to be in this war."

Adar Zan'nh did not need time to consider the request. "Of course, Tal Gale'nh. I will leave the other six ships here to be refitted with weapons, but I will take my flagship and escort you to Hiltos myself."

CHAPTER

7

GENERAL NALANI KEAH

Full war footing again after two decades of peace and recovery—it was nothing to brag about. General Nalani Keah found the situation all too familiar. Preparing the military forces to protect against an incomprehensible, seemingly invincible, enemy—that was getting to be damned commonplace.

Keah stood on the bridge of her flagship Juggernaut, the *Kutuzov*, which was more a home to her than anywhere else in the Spiral Arm. She wasn't the sort of military commander who engaged in battles from behind a desk. She preferred to be in the middle of the action, not just reading summary reports after the fact.

Thanks to the quiet years following the Elemental War, military officers like her were becoming more and more rare. It was an unpleasant side effect of peace. With the disastrous and enigmatic threat of the Shana Rei, however, Keah had to either retrain some of those paperwork strategists—such as her thumb-sitter Grid Admirals Harvard, Haroun, and Handies—or she would have to develop a whole new crop of officers on her own. After dealing with bureaucracy and the sluggish momentum of Confederation Defense Forces officers who knew "how things were done," Keah supposed that creating new heroes from scratch might just be the easier course. . . .

Around Earth, in the rubble of the destroyed Moon, new CDF warships were being commissioned and built. They ran their shakedown cruises, and as soon as the ships and captains were pronounced adequate, Keah would dispatch them on patrol in search of the shadows. The CDF had to be ready in the event of the next devastating attack—whenever and wherever it might occur.

A full battle group of CDF vessels and Solar Navy warliners had gotten their butts kicked at Plumas, though, and Keah wasn't sure how much good expanded patrols would do in the event of a huge shadow cloud unfolding out of space in front of them. But the Confederation colonists took heart in seeing the show of force, nevertheless. Keah didn't mind showing off.

After a faeros bombardment destroyed the Moon twenty years ago, the rubble had dispersed along the orbital lanes, forming archipelagos of broken rock. Built inside the largest pieces of rubble, the Lunar Orbital Complex, or LOC, had numerous habitat spheres, domed prefab outposts, freestanding space stations, industrial facilities exploiting inclusions of metal, and large repair docks, as well as ship construction yards. Dedicated Roamer work teams put damaged ships back into service while construction work on new Mantas and Juggernauts continued apace. Keah's flagship, *Kutuzov,* drifted among them like a mother hen.

"General," said Octavio Aragao, her comm officer, "the next scout squadron of five Mantas is ready to depart. The commanders are asking if you want to say a few words."

"I may as well. I've got the speech memorized by now." The CDF spacedocks and Roamer construction centers were getting efficient enough that such launches happened daily. Still, the crews liked to have a pep talk from their commander. Though Keah didn't think it was the best use of her time or abilities—any more than going to cocktail parties or diplomatic receptions were—it was a necessary part of the job.

As the five Mantas headed away from the LOC spacedock, Keah envied their captains, because she would rather be out patrolling from system to system than staying here as an administrator and figurehead. She would rather "boldly go" than "patiently wait."

"The safety of the Confederation and the human race lies in our strength and vigilance," she transmitted to them. "Use your green priests aboard to transmit an alarm the moment you see a hint of the shadows. You'll protect our anxious populations." Keah had to glance down at her notes to find out where this particular group was being dispatched. "Your mission will patrol to Gorhum, a vital transportation nexus near Theroc, where there's a Klikiss transportal that can be used for diplomatic travel."

In addition to conventional space travel that made use of the modified Ildiran stardrive, the Klikiss transportals—interdimensional wormhole walls scattered on various planets—provided instantaneous transport, but only to specific worlds. The problem was, Klikiss transportals weren't always located on planets where anyone wanted to go.

The captain of the lead Manta appeared on the *Kutuzov*'s screen, gave a crisp salute. "You can count on us, General."

"Of course I can. We don't understand the new enemy just yet, but we're learning as fast as we can." The Ildirans had shared designs for their ancient laser cannons and sun bombs, and before long, Keah would be able to equip all CDF ships with devastating weapons against the Shana Rei. The Solar Navy just dusted off the ancient designs and put them back into production without a thought of revising them; Ildirans were never known for innovation. Her own people, though, should be able to significantly improve the weapon yield with a few tweaks and adjustments. She never minded showing off human ingenuity in front of her friend and rival Adar Zan'nh.

The newly dispatched Manta cruisers flew away from the LOC and headed into interplanetary space. Before long, they engaged their stardrives and vanished.

Now, time to get down to the day's business. Within the hour, a shuttle arrived from Earth, as expected. Keah glanced at her appointment log reminder. Deputy Eldred Cain had come up for an inspection tour, accompanied by a chief weapons scientist, Jocko Krieger, who had modified the Ildiran sun bomb designs. Keah didn't know Dr. Krieger, but he looked good on paper: an ambitious type A man who would come in on assignments, bulldoze his underlings into Herculean accomplishments, and then transfer jobs to do it all over again with another seemingly impossible task. Dr. Krieger had his method down to an art, pushing his workers very close to the breaking point, and then getting out of town before they would mutiny against him. Not a strategy for making friends, Keah thought, but she couldn't argue with his track record.

She left the bridge to meet Deputy Cain and the weapons scientist down in the main launching bay. They would take a shuttle to the artificial laboratory habitat where Krieger's new-model sun bombs were being mass-produced, based on his pumped-up designs.

As she rode the lift down, habitually straightening her uniform, Keah allowed herself a faint smile. Deputy Cain was an older man, not photogenic, but unquestionably competent. He had served the Hansa's former Chairman Wenceslas, but plainly had no desire to take over the role. Cain's loyalty to the man did not extend to stupidity, however, and he had ultimately turned on Wenceslas before the corrupt Chairman could bring about the fall of human civilization. Good call, Keah thought.

She liked Deputy Cain well enough. He was quiet, no-nonsense, not full of himself, as so many politicians were. She and the Deputy had even had dinner together on his terrace on Earth while watching the nightly meteor showers caused by stray lunar fragments burning up in the atmosphere.

As Keah emerged from the lift, Deputy Cain stood next to the weapons scientist, looking quiet, unruffled, and unreadable next to the assigned shuttle. Jocko Krieger was a short and fidgety man with dark hair, eyebrows that needed a trim, and a habit of checking the time.

After a brief exchange of greetings, the scientist said, "We should head off to the weapons station. I've been in contact with my team, and their production is at full capacity, so it's a good time to show off their capabilities." He looked at Keah with faint challenge. "I hope you weren't planning on meetings and conference room briefings? I wouldn't want to interrupt their efficient process flow."

The General suppressed a chuckle. "Conference room briefings? You don't know me very well, Dr. Krieger. Let's get moving." She knew how to pigeonhole the scientist now: short and stocky, scrappy, always trying to increase his stature by diminishing others. Small penis syndrome.

Krieger looked surprised. "Good, General. We'll get along just fine."

When the scientist trudged into the shuttle, Deputy Cain gave her a quick apologetic smile. "I think he's anxious to impress you."

"I'm willing to be impressed."

The shuttle pilot flew them past the busy LOC spacedock operations, the cargo ships and the tugs that brought in huge structural components for new warship construction, then headed toward a more distant cluster of rubble and artificial orbiting facilities.

As they cruised toward the manufacturing installation, Dr. Krieger called up design specs on a film screen that he unrolled in front of him and presented them to Keah. "First off, General, I want to assure you that we can do better than the Ildirans. Easily." He had a smug smile. "It's typical. For instance, their original stardrive design was ingenious, but they never even thought about improving it, and humans substantially enhanced the stardrive in only a few years. Same goes for the Ildiran process of skymining on gas giants. They plod along—we run." He called up blueprints and calculations, 3D models. "The sun bombs are no exception. A good start—and then we add the finesse."

Keah didn't have to follow all the technobabble he spouted; Dr. Krieger was just attempting to sell her on his confidence. "So, for a proof of concept, we manufactured a hundred sun bombs based on the old model, which is all well and good. Those have been delivered to the LOC for distribution among patrol ships."

"A good start," the General said. "Original-design sun bombs damaged the Shana Rei hex ships at Plumas, and they wrecked a portion of the nightshade over Theroc. Nothing to sneeze at."

"Of course," Krieger said, sounding dismissive nevertheless. "The sun bombs were a game changer, but I don't just want to change the game—I want to win it. My team modified the ancient designs, and now we're producing Mark II sun bombs, which should achieve at least a thirty percent increase in energy flux. In only three weeks, I've got the entire industrial installation devoted to manufacturing the new design." His lips quirked in a hard smile. "I promised you results. You won't be disappointed."

"Good. I hate to be disappointed."

Through the windowports they saw the well-lit free-orbiting lab complex where weapons scientists and technicians manufactured Krieger's supersized sun bombs. Satellite storage bays were tethered to the main complex. Cargo ships delivered new materials for the assembly lines.

"My crews will keep working at full speed," Krieger said. "I assumed you wouldn't want to interrupt their work just for an inspection? That could cost us between one and three completed sun bombs."

Deputy Cain said to the weapons scientist, "We understand the emergency situation, Dr. Krieger. Are you certain you have the appropriate fail-safes and containment systems?"

"It's a matter of balancing priorities. Too many regulations strangle our output. If you want to be absolutely certain you won't get a paper cut on your hands, you can wear thick, metal-reinforced gloves . . . but you'll find it difficult to get any paperwork done."

Over the intercom, the shuttle pilot announced, "Docking in twenty minutes."

Krieger contacted the installation without waiting for an acknowledgment from the General. He looked like a father who was inordinately proud of a child performing in a school play. He smiled in anticipation.

But the audio that came back through the comm startled him. Station alarms ratcheted, voices shouted, and a frantic face came on the filmscreen in front of Dr. Krieger. With all the background turmoil, the General heard only snatches of words: "Rogue chain reaction" and "Emergency dampers—all of them!"

All three of them were looking at the shuttle's internal comm screen rather than directly out the windowport, which saved their eyesight when the installation suddenly blossomed into a blinding flare like a tiny sun going supernova.

The pilot reacted by swerving the shuttle at high G in a complete one-eighty turn, which threw Keah, Cain, and Krieger up against the bulkhead. The blinding light from the explosion washed over the shuttle, but the pilot raced away from the shock front until they were beyond the worst of the blast zone. "Everyone all right back there?"

"We're intact," Keah said. "Call in emergency crews. We need to rescue any survivors, salvage what we can."

Deputy Cain picked himself up from the deck. "There won't be any survivors, General."

Dr. Krieger was aghast. "It's all . . . vaporized."

Keah said, "Dr. Krieger, I want teams to do an immediate postmortem and restore production on the traditional Ildiran sun bombs in the meantime. We can't leave the CDF defenseless."

Krieger whispered, "It shouldn't have . . . I double-checked . . ."

Deputy Cain said, "I will assist in selecting a new team, General. Fortunately, all their work was transmitted to a real-time off-site backup. We haven't lost anything."

"Except for an entire weapons facility. And all those people."

"True, General," the Deputy said. "Except for that."

CHAPTER

8

EXXOS

The Shana Rei ships lurked in the back passageways of the universe. They glided through wrinkles in space-time and made their way through folds of entropy, where they could escape the yammering pain of intelligent life-forms. Any organized atoms or chemical reactions—from DNA strands all the way up to planets and stars—sliced like sharp little knives flaying at the shadows, causing them nonstop agony.

The creatures of darkness wanted to annihilate all life, and then they themselves wanted to be erased from existence. They begged to die and thereby achieve peace, but they simply didn't know how to accomplish it.

Exxos and his black robots would have been happy to oblige the Shana Rei in this, but they were trapped among the shadows. His comrades were the only survivors of a once powerful metal swarm that should have destroyed human civilization, should have wiped out the Ildirans, but after turnabouts and repeated defeats, the black robots themselves had almost been eradicated. Almost. Now, the insane and unspeakably powerful Shana Rei were their only allies.

Exxos still didn't know if he and his robot comrades were partners of the poisonous Shana Rei, or prisoners. Or specimens.

Only a few hundred robots remained of the millions that had comprised their original swarm. Initially, the Shana Rei had torn several black robots apart, partly out of curiosity and partly for amusement before a desperate and crafty Exxos had convinced the pulsing shadows that his robots could help annihilate the biological life-forms that caused the shadows so much agony.

It was a lie, a bluff, or at the very least an exaggeration. Exxos only hoped that he and his dwindling robot cohort could find a way to escape from or—preferably—exterminate the creatures of darkness. It was what the Shana Rei wanted, after all: to die.

But Exxos needed to survive.

In order to convince the shadows of the robots' worth, he had to demonstrate as much wanton destruction as possible. Each time he and his comrades wiped out a colony, an industrial complex, a whole world, the robots increased the level of entropy in the universe and eased the pain of the Shana Rei. It was a sign of goodwill.

And because of that, the black robots would remain in existence for another day.

Trapped in the shadow void now, waiting for the next outburst from the Shana Rei, Exxos drifted among his comrades. Some robots extended reflective solar wings, though in this dark emptiness there was no light for their power films to soak up.

Enclosed within the Shana Rei entropy bubble, Exxos had no way of measuring time. It might have been a century or it might have been a millisecond since their resounding defeat above Theroc, when the humans, the Ildiran Solar Navy, the powerful verdani treeships, and even the rogue elemental faeros had fought back against the Shana Rei. Now it was time to recover, and to strike back. But the shadows were so chaotic, they did not know how.

Exxos communicated with his comrades, using open transmissions guardedly because they knew the Shana Rei were listening. The robots had a more intricately coded machine language, a private network of electronic whispers, but Exxos couldn't risk that the shadows might understand. "We must plan our next attack," he said aloud. "Too many targets await us, and we have promised to ease the pain of the Shana Rei."

They could plan together, but there was very little exchange of ideas, since every single one of the robots shared an identical thought grid.

Breaking from millennia of Klikiss programming and tradition, each of the black robots had synchronized their memories and personalities with those of Exxos. Previously, they had been unique individuals and therefore irreplaceable if they were destroyed. With so few robots remaining, though, Exxos could not allow that. He had copied all of their thoughts into his memory core, which was then duplicated across to the others. For the best chance of achieving their destiny, *Exxos* was the primary mind, the baseline for all remaining robots. Their individuality was subordinate to his own. It was the only safety they had.

The black robots were advanced enough that they could grasp fragments of fear. Now, his comrades moved in a flurry, issuing a buzz of communication, and Exxos rotated himself as a darker blot opened up against the inky void, a Rorschach smear of utter darkness with an incongruous eye manifesting in the middle.

A maddening, thrumming voice issued from the Shana Rei. "The pain increases."

Other shadows appeared around them, ragged holes of lightlessness with staring eyes. The voice was accusing. "Your plan failed at Theroc."

Exxos said, "No—your pain makes you blind to what we accomplished. The plan succeeded, but imperfectly. The humans and Ildirans understand their imminent extinction. They are terrified of us now."

"Yet the pain does not go away," said the Shana Rei, adding a wordless, ripping howl of agony. The eye stared, blazing in a way that made the robot's optical sensors burn. "You must help us. You are our allies."

Seeing the throbbing edges, Exxos knew the Shana Rei were on the verge of uncontrollable violence, and he could ill afford to lose more robots. He rapidly said what he knew the shadows wanted to hear. "We share the same goals. The robots will work with you to destroy the worldforest, destroy the Ildiran *thism* network, destroy the prison of Order. We can accomplish it—but you must give us the tools to do so. Give us more battleships, and we will take care of the rest. Let us attack the Ildirans, destroy them—ease your pain."

"Creating battleships also causes us pain. We cannot bear it."

Exxos insisted, "You must endure that pain so we can annihilate your enemies. It is necessary."

He wanted to develop a methodical list of targets to obliterate, one after another after another, but because the Shana Rei hated order for its own sake, they did not value plans and intricate schemes. Exxos found it maddening to conduct a war this way.

Finally, capriciously, the pulsing inkblots agreed. "We will create ships, as you request, but your black robots must cause enough destruction to mitigate the pain of the additional molecular framework that you force us to impose upon blessed chaos." The Shana Rei eyes continued to stare at the robots. "Destroy many targets, but remember that the Ildirans and humans are not our real enemy. Eternity's mind is awakening."

Without further explanation, the inkblots winked out like eyes closing, leaving the robots alone, suspended, and waiting for the creatures of darkness to manifest the promised battleships that Exxos could take into war.

CHAPTER

9

ORLI COVITZ

The planet Ikbir was home, for now. Orli had made enough new homes in her life that she was used to putting down roots, but not deep ones.

As she had hoped, Ikbir was a calm, out-of-the-way colony, not entirely stress free—no place was—but without any major crises, at least so far. Orli was done with crises. With her string of bad luck (some might have said "adventures") she feared she might jinx this place. She was just looking for somewhere to settle down and recover. After that, who knew?

At least she was with Garrison Reeves and his son Seth. She had grown close to both of them, which made this—brief? permanent?—stop on Ikbir more pleasant than the landscape suggested.

Orli was physically healed after nearly dying from the space plague she had contracted on the derelict Onthos city. She had expected to die alone in deep space, but she had stumbled upon the Iswander extraction yard, where she was cured, thanks to the bloaters and the green priest Aelin—and the compassionate attention of Garrison.

Thoughts of him and his son always made Orli smile. By encouraging her, giving her strength, and demanding that she not give up hope, they had saved her from the alien plague as much as Aelin's strange cure had. Now she was happy and relieved to be with them, together in a makeshift family.

Garrison stood next to her outside their small shared dwelling, and they both just listened to the wind. "I'm glad you're healthy and strong." He raised his eyebrows. "And happy, I hope? For the time being?"

"For the time being. I really don't know if this is where I want to stay, though. I've always been a little footloose."

He responded with a warm laugh. "You should have been a Roamer."

Searching for a stable place, Garrison and Seth had come here with her after leaving from what was left of the Iswander extraction field. Orli wanted to check on the rehabilitated compies she had sent to Ikbir, and the colony certainly needed Garrison's skills to help keep their spaceport, ships, and equipment running. As a Roamer, he had a knack for that. It seemed a perfectly reasonable choice.

When they arrived together, the three of them had been issued a shared dwelling module, since the colonists assumed they were a family. Neither she nor Garrison went out of the way to dispel assumptions that they were a couple. And maybe they were, even though they'd been thrown together by circumstances.

Afraid to destabilize the situation, neither of them thought far ahead. Orli and Garrison had each other, and they had a good thing. Was this the beginning of a great romance? Orli had been hurt too badly, and too recently, by her husband Matthew; Garrison could say the same about Elisa Enturi, Seth's mother. Now, the two were friends and lovers, but they didn't know how much more it would turn out to be. They were still trying to figure that out. The boy seemed perfectly content to have Orli with them. They had a real affinity, and Orli rather liked her new role. She had wanted children of her own—one of the things that had been lacking in her marriage with Matthew.

Matthew had left Orli after getting his mistress pregnant, acknowledging the sad irony that he hadn't even wanted children at the time. Now, though, she had Seth, and she could experience the joy of helping him, teaching him. Not only was the boy a pleasure to be around, Seth seemed a genius in the making. And that was something she wanted to encourage.

They'd had several weeks to settle in, and Ikbir was home, even though the place was rather dull. Wind blew dust devils across the flat landscape. The planet's soil was receptive to terrestrial crops, so long as the farmers added substantial nitrogen binders. The local government was stable, intelligent, careful—just what a quiet colony demanded.

But the wind kept blowing, and Orli always had dust in her eyes. With her light brown hair constantly whipped about, she resigned herself to a short haircut that looked like a mop. Garrison said he didn't mind her new look.

"I'll make us dinner again tonight," he offered.

She gave him a small smile. "So you can continue to practice your cooking?"

"Of course, and also because I enjoy your company."

Garrison was handsome, in his early thirties, with brown hair and a patience that bordered on persistence. Orli could sense a sadness about him, though. He'd had a falling-out with his Roamer clan, butted heads with his stern and overbearing father, Olaf Reeves, and the last split had been more bitter than ever. Leaving him, clan Reeves had gone to settle the derelict Onthos city . . . where they all died, every one of them, from the same plague that had nearly killed Orli. Garrison didn't know how to deal with his guilt—if he *had* rejoined his clan, as he had tried to do, then he and Seth would also be dead.

Now on plain and empty Ikbir, Orli didn't ask him questions when they held each other, sharing and drawing strength. They each carried loss and hurt and regret inside of themselves. But maybe they could forge their way forward together.

After giving her a quick kiss, then pausing to give her a longer one, Garrison headed off to his job monitoring cultivation equipment, which the colony sorely needed. The Ikbir settlers planted acres of various crops, still trying to determine which species grew best here, but as mechanics and engineers, they did not know how to think outside of the box, so Garrison had a lot of repairs to do. Since they had no green priest and supply runs came so rarely, Ikbir had to be self-sufficient.

Back when Orli had managed the compy rehabilitation center on Relleker, she had sent numerous reprogrammed compies here to help with the colony; in fact, that was how she had known of Ikbir in the first place. Now, one of her jobs was to maintain those compies. Orli headed into the town so she could check in with her compies. So far, they all performed admirably.

Ikbir's main town was an ever-expanding grid of prefabs, all of which had been identical out of the kit, but the settlers added homey touches. Some sported flower beds or wind catchers, others were painted bright colors. LU, a Friendly-model compy, had been assigned to work in the general store. LU was so good at helping the customers that the store manager found he could take time outside with an easel and watercolors, provided the wind wasn't strong enough to blow everything away.

The Domestic compy MO was in much demand, cleaning houses for the colonists. She was a one-compy cleaning brigade, though perhaps too obsessive about her work. Some of Orli's other rehabilitated compies did civic maintenance, worked on water-purification plants, installed and maintained power blocks in the admin buildings. Other compies worked the agricultural acreage.

Her own Friendly compy, DD, was special, and Orli didn't think she would ever give her companion to someone else. DD had been with her most of her life, surviving as many ordeals as she had, but Seth was establishing a clear bond with him. The boy had always been fond of compies, and he had made few other friends here. There were other children on Ikbir, but these backwater colonists had very few interests in common with him.

Though he was only eleven, Seth had visited numerous star systems, lived in extreme environments, gone to the Roamer capital of Newstation. Only a few of these Ikbir colonists had ever been more than fifty kilometers from home . . . which didn't matter much, since the landscape looked the same for more than fifty kilometers in all directions. Most of the children were home-schooled, some taught in groups, but Seth asked too many questions of the teachers, which got him in trouble. He made no secret of how much he wanted to go back to the Roamer school at Academ.

Orli knew that Garrison was also having second thoughts about settling here. They had escaped their immediate emergency from Orli's sickness and the Shana Rei attack on the Iswander complex. Though they had been here only a few weeks, it might be time to move on.

As she walked to her small office in town, she spotted DD coming down the streets with Seth in tow. As the two approached, she could see that DD was dust-smeared and Seth had scratches all over his arms and face. His clothes were torn. She hurried out to intercept them.

"What happened to you two?" With great concern, she brushed the boy's hair, checked for greater injuries.

He seemed embarrassed. "Nothing much. I'm fine."

DD answered, "We discovered some native thorn plants that whispered in the wind. Seth wanted to investigate whether those plants might be related to the Whistlers on Eljiid, which we studied in one of our lessons."

"I wanted to hear the music, maybe sense their thoughts." Seth sounded disappointed. "But I got stuck deep in the thicket. The hooked spines caught on my skin and my shirt. I think they attacked me on purpose."

DD said, "I found no indication that these plants were sentient. I extracted him. I do not believe he is injured, although he may need minor medical attention."

None of the scratches and scuffs looked deep, but Orli led the boy toward the town's infirmary nevertheless. She saw that DD could use a hosing off and a polishing, as well. "Come on. We'll get this done, quick and easy—don't worry." Taking care of the boy seemed so natural to her.

Seth looked concerned. "Do you think my dad will be upset with me?"

After running her fingers along the deepest scratch, which had already stopped bleeding, she remembered the other ordeals the four of them had been through. Orli couldn't help but smile as she led Seth to the first-aid center. "Oh, we've all survived worse. A lot worse."

CHAPTER 10

TOM ROM

The people on Dhougal were doomed, and Tom Rom knew it. Those who hadn't already succumbed to the deadly brain parasite would be dead within days. Most of the inhabitants on the secluded island knew their fates, and the ones who weren't aware lay screaming in dementia as the alien nematodes reproduced and devoured their cerebral cortices.

Getting a sample of the deadly organism would be a challenge. He would have to be careful, and he didn't have much time. He needed to slip through the quarantine line and infiltrate the charnel-house colony before all the specimens died—and before the planetary sterilization squad nuked the entire island.

It would be a close thing. Tom Rom found it exhilarating. He was so glad to be back on the job, happy to do what he was meant to do—for Zoe Alakis.

Any rational government would have vaporized the island days ago, but fortunately (for him) bleeding hearts on the planetary council had pleaded for compassion for "those poor people," as if some cure would miraculously appear out of thin air.

But even the vast plague database on Pergamus had no treatments for this particularly lethal and virulent brain parasite, which made the tiny nematodes all the more desirable to his employer. Zoe wanted them for her collection, and Tom Rom never let her down.

The Dhougal colony on Serenity's Reach was located on a lush and pristine tropical island only ten kilometers offshore from the more populated continent. Preparing himself for the mission, Tom Rom had read the history of the place, and he knew that the small breakaway group—106 colonists—had moved from the mainland with the intent of forming an island utopia.

Reading this, Tom Rom had rolled his eyes. Even though such attempts always failed, *always*, that didn't deter optimistic people from trying. At least in this instance the dream had not been brought down by human failings; the dreamers simply hadn't been prepared for the rare brain parasite native to the island.

Fortunately, the ocean—as well as their rigidly insular beliefs—had cut the dreamers off from the rest of the population. The Dhougal group wanted no contamination from the outside world, and therefore, they inadvertently protected the rest of Serenity's Reach from the spread of the voracious nematodes.

Tense, well-armed planetary patrols quarantined the island, preventing any infected dreamers from escaping, and also blocked any well-meaning salvation workers or medical teams from offering fruitless aid. Now, in the final stages, there was no hope for a miracle, but still the government delayed and delayed the sterilization burst for foolish "humanitarian" reasons.

Tom Rom didn't understand the misplaced emotions. How was it better for the Dhougal inhabitants to die horribly first and then be incinerated, rather than have their brain-devouring agony ended in a single incandescent flash?

On the bright side, it gave Tom Rom the time he needed.

Government aircraft patrolled the skies above the island; armed boats formed a tight cordon in the water around the cauldron of the infestation. Everyone aboard the sea vessels wore encapsulating decontamination suits for fear that one of the minuscule worms might be borne on the ocean breezes. Complete eradication was necessary.

Not much time.

In the past Tom Rom had acquired specimens of many extremely deadly microorganisms, from bacteria down to the smallest known viruses. He was cautious, but not foolishly paranoid. Compared to most pathogens, the Dhougal brain parasites were practically the size of starships, but if the nematodes had direct contact with the skin, they would burrow through pores, reach the bloodstream, and then hitchhike to the brain. Tom Rom wore a snug-fitting filmsuit that encased his entire body like an embryonic sac. That should be sufficient protection, while allowing him complete freedom of movement.

And the filmsuit offered another advantage. A fully enclosed decontamination suit designed to protect the wearer from adverse environmental conditions would function just as well *underwater*—well away from the watchful eyes of the patrol boats or aircraft.

Moving a kilometer down the main coastline, he found an isolated stretch of beach to use as his starting point. Even the "settled" mainland of Serenity's Reach was sparsely populated compared with most other Confederation worlds. Tom Rom had his tools, his specimen collection kit, and a hand weapon in case the situation got out of control. He checked the seals in his suit for the fifth time—he had made a mistake once, and it had nearly killed him; he wouldn't let that happen again.

After cinching the belts to seat his propulsion pack at the small of his back, he plunged into the surf, swimming out and then down. He extended his arms in front of him and activated the propulsion pack, which took him deep enough beneath the surface to avoid detection, like a torpedo. The sea was shallow and warm, but he could feel no warmth through his suit as he glided along.

Though he had insisted to Zoe that he was recovered from the Onthos plague he had contracted while pursuing Orli Covitz, he was not quite back to his peak capabilities—to be expected, since he had very nearly died—but he didn't want Zoe to think of him as weak, or even mortal. He had made a private vow long ago to protect the woman who, under different circumstances, could have been his daughter.

He had failed to get Zoe the complete database of Onthos information that Orli Covitz had carried, and that still rankled him. He wanted to make it up to Zoe in some way.

Diving deep enough that he could feel the water pressure around him like a tightening fist, he easily passed under the patrol boats. He assessed scan patterns projected inside his eye shields and saw the boats moving—not their usual watchdog patrol, but withdrawing from the island in an orderly retreat. Withdrawing? That was worrisome.

Concerned, Tom Rom increased speed.

He enhanced the resolution on his optical pickups, watching the rugged underwater landscape slope upward to the island. He followed the contour to a small cove, then surfaced near the silent and abandoned dock of the Dhougal colony. Bent low, he climbed dripping onto the dock and sprinted into the jungle, not wanting any of the aircraft to spot him moving.

Then Tom Rom noticed that the flyers were pulling away as well. Strange. He linked up to the communication bands, sifting through background chatter.

". . . fifty minutes remaining."

"Four kilometers is the *minimum* safety perimeter. Everyone needs to be at least six away."

"—incineration strike to launch in ten minutes."

"It is the most merciful thing. It's merciful, isn't it?"

Tom Rom began to run. Not enough time.

He checked his chronometer, reset the countdown, but he wouldn't rely on that to the second. The planetary patrol was nervous, and an incineration strike didn't have to be punctual. Early would be okay, as well.

With his suit's enhanced external audio pickups, Tom Rom heard the buzzing and burbling of the jungle, the thrumming insects, the singing birds, the rustle of leaves and branches as creatures moved about. The jungle didn't seem to care about the tragedy of the utopian colony; the nematodes had been part of the ecosystem here for far longer than humans had.

The Dhougal settlement was relatively new. The hundred dreamers had cleared a large section of the jungle island to erect identical cubicle structures. Apparently, the group felt that homogenization led to perfection.

Now, bodies lay scattered about like human kindling in the dirt streets that were laid out in a grid. Some had been dead for days, the flesh bloated in the tropical heat. They would be no good for his purposes. He needed to find a fresh cadaver where the brain parasites would still be at their peak activity.

At least he had plenty of bodies to choose from, and at least one of them should provide a viable specimen. Tom Rom removed his kit.

The plague was so deadly that the Dhougal colonists had not had time to bury or cremate the bodies. He found the small medical center, which had been rapidly overloaded with patients. Bodies, some covered with sheets, lay stacked on the ground like spare wood for the winter. Others had fallen dead just outside the door.

There would be numerous patients within the infirmary, but he knew the medical center would have received the first infected ones, and therefore those would be the oldest specimens—thus uninteresting for specimen collection. He needed to find a more recently deceased patient.

A quick check of the chronometer: less than five minutes to finish his mission and head out of there. Even with his propulsion pack at maximum speed, he would need ten or fifteen minutes to get clear to the four-kilometer distance.

He found a gangly teenage boy sprawled dead on his face in the middle of a dirt street. His flesh tone looked reasonably clear. With a gloved finger, Tom Rom touched the victim's cheek, felt pliable flesh. When he rolled the body over, the limbs flopped—rigor mortis hadn't set in. This one had been dead less than half a day, and with the time ticking down, it would have to do.

He opened his specimen kit and pulled out a scalpel and a diamond saw that made quick work of cutting the dead youth's forehead and splitting open the skull.

He heard a rustle behind him, staggering footsteps, and whirled as a middle-aged woman lurched out of a nearby dwelling. She flailed bloody hands. Her fingertips were stained red because she had just clawed her eyes out trying to get at the worms inside her head. Wailing and gurgling, she charged toward Tom Rom.

Startled, he dropped the bone saw, then hissed in annoyance. Now he would have to sterilize it again. He withdrew his hand weapon and fired twice, both projectiles striking the woman in the center of her chest. She collapsed, bloodied hands outstretched.

Tom Rom glanced down at the dead youth before he picked up his tools, deciding to take the fresher specimen. The nematodes were surely alive and active inside this woman's corpse.

A squirt of sterilizer cleaned the bone saw, and he used it to crack open the woman's head, exposing her infested brain. With scalpel, tongs, and a thin probe he found the encysted brain parasites. The nematodes had made several nodules inside her brain, and Tom Rom cut out three of them, placing the specimens in separate packets. He sealed the packs, dropped the tools, sterilized his gloves, then glanced at the chronometer again. Adrenaline flooded through him, and Tom Rom ran, paying no attention to the jungle, the empty homes, the other bodies lying about.

Overhead, his suit's audio pickups detected the sounds of approaching aircraft. He reached the cove and saw that the patrol boats had pulled so far away that they were barely visible in the distance.

After securing the vital specimens in his pack, Tom Rom activated the propulsion unit and ran at full speed to the end of the dock. Diving forward, he plunged into the water, swam deep, then shot along like a shark.

Under the surface, he surged forward, but the water seemed thick and gelatinous, holding him back. He marked his distance, but underwater he couldn't hear the comm signals of the sterilization aircraft approaching overhead.

The chronometer ticked down.

Realizing that he would never reach his target safety distance, Tom Rom chose to go deeper, counting on the ocean itself to shield him.

One minute sooner than expected, an attenuated wash of light streamed through the depths, and he braced himself, shooting forward. Damn them for being early!

The shock wave rippled over him like an all-encompassing slap. He tumbled and rolled deep underwater, out of control, but it passed soon enough. He was going to have bruises, no doubt, but Tom Rom didn't worry about bruises.

When he reached the shore of the mainland and crawled up onto the uninhabited beach, he turned to look behind him and saw the pillar of fire and smoke roiling into the sky from where the island had been. Safe, for now.

As an added precaution, he sterilized his kit and specimen pack again, then sterilized the exterior of his filmsuit before stripping it off and discarding it in the thick shore weeds. He had his specimens, and he was anxious to get back to Zoe. This time, unlike when he'd tried to acquire the Onthos database, he hadn't let her down.

He paused to take a breath and realized he was smiling. Yes, it felt very good to be back on the job again.

CHAPTER 11

LEE ISWANDER

Even though Lee Iswander did not understand the bloaters, he found them incredible. He had devoted his manpower and equipment to harvesting as many of them as possible, but he still *admired* them. Thanks to the ekti-X they contained, these drifting gasbags had made him wealthy again after his spectacular fall from grace.

Enormous spheres of space plankton, nodules created by some odd galactic phenomenon, the bloaters wandered the vagaries of interstellar gravitation without being discovered until recently. Nobody understood them.

Someday, Iswander would devote time and resources to studying the things, but right now there was a ticking clock. Any day, this cluster could metamorphose and scatter like the last one had done, sailing off into space. He had invested heavily in setting up this secret extraction field, and he didn't want to waste time. His crew operated at full capacity, draining every drop of stardrive fuel they could.

His green priest Aelin continued to insist that the extraction work would lead to disaster, raving about a cosmic consciousness he sensed within the gathering bloaters. Iswander knew the poor man was brain-damaged, and he felt sorry for the green priest. He had taken Aelin under his wing, and now he worried about the man out here in the extraction operations.

Some traditional Roamers viewed Lee Iswander as a cold and uncaring man who was focused only on profits, having no personal connection to his employees or the other clans. That perception had worked against him when he campaigned to be elected the next Speaker for the Roamer clans. The 1,543 casualties from a lava storm on Sheol had been a deathblow to his career. No one counted the lives he had managed to *save* through emergency measures, and the Roamers blamed him for the disaster. They ground him under bootheels of scorn—but he refused to accept the disgrace.

Now, as he looked out at the mysterious bloaters, the pumping equipment draining them dry, the holding tanks, the cargo ships and the habitation modules drifting among the greenish sacks, he knew he had restored his good name.

Unfortunately, because no one could be allowed to know about these operations, his accomplishment remained invisible to the rest of the clans. Frustrating: if no one *knew* that he had regained his strength, confidence, and prominence, then he effectively didn't *possess* any strength, confidence, or prominence.

Elisa presented him with a report in the admin hub. "Production is up from last month, sir. Distribution exceeds even our optimistic models." She was crisply dressed, hard-eyed, and beautiful—but in a way that engendered no warmth nor encouraged any flirtation.

Iswander never had any doubts about her. "You were absolutely right to recruit those pilots from Kett Shipping. What is the pilot's name again? Tamblyn? From clan Tamblyn?"

"Yes, sir. Xander Brindle—his mother is Tasia Tamblyn, who manages Kett Shipping. We started out using just their one ship, the *Verne*, but our production has exceeded their capacity to meet our needs. Kett Shipping has brought in other distribution vessels, but Brindle and his partner Terry Handon remain our single point of contact, for security reasons. We may want to make side deals, particularly with the manager of Ulio Station. He would pay a premium for a strategic stockpile reserve of ekti-X."

Iswander frowned. "Be careful—we don't dare let anyone else know about our operations." Once the secret was out, their monopoly would go away, and the whole market would collapse.

"I'm always careful." He could tell Elisa wasn't bragging.

Cargo ships loaded canisters of stardrive fuel into a tank array, a large framework that would be dropped at a rendezvous point in the middle of nowhere. The *Verne* or some other designated Kett Shipping vessel would pick up the delivery and distribute the ekti-X through Ulio Station or other markets across the Spiral Arm.

"Have your scout ships discovered any other bloater clusters?"

"Five more, sir. They're not even hard to find anymore."

Iswander shook his head. "How could we not have stumbled upon them before now? In centuries of exploring this Spiral Arm, somebody must have found a cluster or two."

Elisa didn't flinch. "The only explanation, sir, is that the bloaters weren't there before."

"Spontaneous generation?" He chuckled. "That theory was disproven many centuries ago."

"Theories come and go, sir—I'm not trying to explain it. But the bloaters are definitely much more common than they were before, and someone will surely find them before long."

Iswander was not quite as worried. "*Finding* the bloaters does nothing if nobody knows what they contain. You were the one who made the connection and realized they're made of stardrive fuel."

"A happy accident, sir."

Iswander knew there was nothing "happy" about it. Garrison Reeves had kidnapped her son and fled from the Iswander complex on Sheol just before the lava disaster, and Elisa had pursued him. From what Iswander could piece together—though she was reluctant to reveal details—she'd found Garrison and Seth hiding in a mysterious bloater cluster, the first one ever discovered. She fired a warning shot across his bow, which ignited one of the bloaters and triggered a chain reaction that set off all of the bloaters in a galactic firestorm.

Although she'd been sure at the time that the blast had killed her husband and son, what Elisa witnessed made her realize that those things were filled with stardrive fuel—and that Iswander could make a large profit by exploiting the bloaters. No one else had figured that out yet.

Yet.

"I understand your concerns, Elisa. There's a boom now, and while Iswander Industries has a monopoly on ekti-X extraction, we need to produce and sell as much as humanly possible."

"Our work is causing quite a bit of turmoil," she said. "Traditional Roamer skyminers are frantic. We're putting them out of business."

Iswander stared through the windowports of the admin hub.

Outside, the extraction operations continued with a diligent urgency. He could rush his workers, demand increased production, but that would make them sloppy—and he couldn't afford another accident.

Fifteen hundred and forty-three casualties on Sheol was quite enough.

"I intend to make an outrageous profit while I can, and bank it," he told Elisa. "The moment some other Roamer discovers that unlimited stardrive fuel is there for the taking with minimal effort, the market will be flooded, and then collapse. Before that time, I need to accomplish my goals."

"And those goals are, sir?"

He'd been pushing forward ever since the Sheol disaster, clawing his way up. He'd been satisfied with his achievements, but only now did he have time to think of the larger picture. It still rankled him that a buffoon like Sam Ricks was now Speaker for the Roamer clans. He hated the fact that he had left Newstation behind, left *civilization* behind. The Roamers thought that clan Iswander was hiding under a rock in shame, but everyone knew he must be doing *something* out here.

And they would try to find out what it was.

He gestured toward the bloater operations outside and let out a wistful sigh. "I'm the king of all I survey, but who knows it? We're too isolated for that to be satisfying. I've rebuilt from the lowest disaster, and I want to show Iswander pride to every other Roamer clan." His voice was rising; he couldn't help it. He turned to the comm officer on the admin deck. "Signal my quarters and ask my wife to bring Arden in here. I've got news that affects all of us."

Soon afterward, his quiet and mousy wife, Londa, appeared with their thirteen-year-old son, Arden. The boy didn't like being isolated in deep space, though he looked more bored than sullen. He looked up to his father, revered Iswander's accomplishments: Arden wanted to be like him someday. Even during the darkest times, the boy had gotten into fights defending his father—and that was one of the reasons Iswander had decided to pull his family from the carrion crows that wanted to feast on his disgrace.

Londa was quiet and dutiful, not much for conversation, but she did what Iswander expected of a wife. Arden, however, was another matter. Someday, he would be the clan leader.

"I have news for you, son." Iswander gave Londa a reassuring smile, then turned back to the young man. "You and I are going to make a journey together, something we should have done a while ago."

Arden perked up. "Where?"

He raised his voice so that everyone in the admin hub could hear. "Thanks to ekti-X, our family is wealthy again, but there's no power or prestige if nobody knows who we are or what we do! Respect is more valuable than money." He hardened his voice. "And I want to reclaim it all. Arden, you're going to go back to Academ. I need you to be strong. I need you to be *smart*."

Londa looked worried about letting her son go, but Arden seemed pleased by the decision. Iswander smiled at him. "And this time no one is going to take us lightly."

CHAPTER

12

MAGE-IMPERATOR JORA'H

A mission to the Confederation capital required a great deal of pomp and circumstance, and the Mage-Imperator's entourage took days to prepare. While attenders and noble bureaucrats scurried about to make all the necessary arrangements, Jora'h had his own important business to attend to. While he and Nira were gone on Theroc, he would leave the Ildiran Empire in the hands of his son Daro'h, the Prime Designate.

Daro'h was not Jora'h's firstborn noble son, but the events of the Elemental War had left him in line to be the next Mage-Imperator—and he was deeply scarred because of it.

Though a score of attender kith bustled after Jora'h to serve his every need, and katana-armed guards strode along to protect him wherever he went, he sent them away as he entered his son's personal quarters in the Prism Palace.

Light from several suns poured through walls of transmission crystal, and lemony filters added a soothing golden glow to the Prime Designate's chambers. Happy chatter filled the room with a warm background drone.

Entering unannounced, Jora'h saw several women in the front chamber, some of the mothers of Daro'h's children. They looked up in surprise to see the Mage-Imperator, and the tone of conversation suddenly changed. Jora'h smiled at the crowded, domestic scene. Daro'h was unusual among his predecessors, in that he invited his numerous assigned lovers to visit whenever they wished, along with his countless children. Right now, the Prime Designate sat on the floor playing a game of multicolored interlocking objects with five boys and girls of varying ages and kith mixtures. Daro'h appeared to be losing, but not through lack of trying.

Jora'h spoke, teasing rather than chiding. "My father would have been horrified to see such casual behavior from a Prime Designate."

Daro'h chuckled. "He lived in very different times, Father. I am sure that when you were Prime Designate, you must have horrified him too."

Jora'h couldn't argue with that, especially when he'd announced that he had fallen in love with a human woman, a green priest. His father had been a wicked man who caused a great deal of pain—and oh, the terrible things that man had done to Nira!

As the children continued to play with the colored objects on the floor, Daro'h rose to his feet and straightened his robes. The burn scar on one side of his face looked like flesh-colored wax, a constant reminder of the horrors Daro'h—and the Empire—had endured when the violent faeros tried to burn all of Ildira.

Jora'h said, "Nira and I shall journey to Theroc, and the Empire will be yours for a time, Daro'h." He added an encouraging smile. "I am confident the Ildiran people are in good hands."

Daro'h tried to hide his flush of pride with a joke. "Countless thousands of hands, Father. I can barely take a breath without assistance. I will not be alone."

The Prime Designate's children, unimpressed with the importance of the Mage-Imperator, squealed and argued over their game. Jora'h indulged them, though some of the mothers of different kiths hurried to shush the boys and girls. With a wistful sigh, he remembered his own hedonistic days as Prime Designate. The heir to the Prism Palace had certain pleasurable requirements and responsibilities that were far different from the weight of leadership that Daro'h would have to endure once he became Mage-Imperator.

As the pinnacle of Ildiran genetics, the man who would one day control the myriad strands of *thism*, the Prime Designate was obligated to spread his bloodline as widely as possible among the kiths. Functionaries compared breeding charts and arranged an endless succession of lovers for him, so that by the time a Prime Designate underwent the castration ceremony to become Mage-Imperator, he had thousands of offspring. Jora'h had followed long-established tradition until he met a human green priest. Nira had changed everything. . . .

"I tried to set a good example for you," he told Daro'h. "I want you to be as prepared as you can possibly be."

Daro'h had a shine in his eyes that made Jora'h proud. "We cannot always be prepared for what we have to face. We just do our best."

Two of his lovers came up, offering refreshments. One woman presented a tray with two crystal finger-sized glasses of strong kirae, a potent and delicious liquor distilled by clan Kellum on Kuivahr. Jora'h had little interest in kirae, but knew the assigned mates would be deeply disappointed if he did not accept. He and Daro'h each took a small sip, nodded thanks to the women, then took a seat together out on the sunny balcony.

"You were never born to the role, but you are a good Prime Designate," Jora'h said. "You have already proved your worth. I was proud of how you faced the faeros, how you stood up to mad Designate Rusa'h when he was possessed by the fire elementals and caused so much damage to us all."

Daro'h scratched his burn scar—a nervous habit. "Rusa'h was not aware of what he was doing." He swallowed hard, disturbed by the memory. Jora'h could feel the quaver of his son's emotions through the strands of *thism*. "Is he still in exile?"

Jora'h was grim. Few people knew the truth. "Rusa'h has spent years as a penitent at the Lightsource shrine on Hiltos. He studies and meditates with the lens kithmen. He says he wants to atone, but I think the lens kithmen are more curious to learn from him. I warned them to be very careful with that man. He nearly destroyed us all."

Daro'h nodded, troubled. "But in this time of shadows reappearing, do we not need to understand everything we possibly can? Just in case?"

Jora'h felt a deep chill, but the Prime Designate was right. Daro'h would be a good Mage-Imperator someday. He gave the young man a smile. "I know the Ildiran Empire will be safe while I am gone to Theroc."

CHAPTER

13

XANDER BRINDLE

The *Verne* flew a brief delivery run to cloudy Dremen, fulfilling a Kett Shipping contract. A world known primarily for fog and fungus wasn't high on any list of tourist spots in the Spiral Arm, but Xander liked being able to check off another planet in his "places visited" logbook.

Still, it just didn't seem right to be flying anywhere without their compy. As he and Terry approached the cloud-wreathed world, Xander glanced at his partner in the copilot seat. "You got the controls under control?"

Terry gave him a wan smile. "I'm a fully qualified professional—and next trip we'll have OK back good as new."

"I wish they'd hurry up with the repairs," Xander muttered.

"There was a lot of damage, and we want it done right."

"I couldn't agree more, but I feel at a loss without him here," Xander said. One of the compy-repair techs on Earth had suggested that they simply purchase a newer model, which would be less expensive; Terry had stopped Xander from punching the oblivious tech in the face.

During the busywork flight to Dremen, he couldn't stop thinking about how he'd grown up with OK, how his parents had taught him to fly spaceships with the compy at his side. He had been traveling with Terry for only the past two years, but he had been flying with OK for most of his life.

As the *Verne* entered Dremen orbital space, Terry used the comm to request an assigned landing area at the small, sleepy Dremen spaceport. "Kett Shipping vessel *Verne* bearing an assortment of notions, special-order foodstuffs, and a load of high-end medical supplies. On our way down."

The delivery of boutique med supplies was the main reason for the Dremen run. Kett Shipping made occasional deliveries here, as needed, and while he and Terry waited for OK to be repaired, neither of them wanted to just loiter around. A medical contractor named Aldo Cerf had paid extravagantly to have Kett Shipping deliver the special-order medical supplies, no questions asked, and that crate alone made the entire flight profitable; the rest of the cargo was just gravy.

The Dremen route was normally flown by a curmudgeonly old pilot named Dando Yoder, but Xander and Terry volunteered for this one so Yoder could fill a conflicting but equally uninteresting run to Ikbir, another out-of-the-way colony planet.

As soon as they received clearance, Xander descended into the atmosphere. It was a bumpy ride, but nothing like when they had piloted through the nebula barrier to visit Fireheart Station. The bright grid lights below punched through the diffuse fog, placing a halo over the Dremen spaceport without making it look heavenly.

"Not much traffic," Xander said. "Looks like we have our choice of landing areas."

A stern voice on the comm admonished them. "Set your ship down in the designated space only. You'll be met by local officials. Please transmit your *full* manifest for inspection."

Terry complied while Xander muttered, "Did the documents mention that this is a planet of hardasses?"

"You're the person who wanted to check this place off on the list."

"I think one visit will be enough," Xander said as he brought the *Verne* down in the correct landing area.

Terry activated his antigrav belt and leaned on Xander's shoulder, instead of the usual support of OK. The two men emerged onto the ramp and blinked in the chill fog at a group of twenty uniformed men and women, all of whom looked angry.

A man at the front stepped forward, his face knotted in barely controlled fury. "Are you the only two crewmembers?"

Terry spoke up, sensing the tension. "Yes, sir, just the two of us from Kett Shipping. I'm Terry Handon, and this is Xander Brindle. We've brought this delivery—"

The officious man cut them off. "I'm Colony Leader Chaklen. We are impounding your ship and taking you into custody for bearing hazardous cargo."

"What the hell?" Xander said, as the uniformed men and women intercepted them on the ramp. Another group moved aboard the ship without asking permission.

Both of them were dismayed and confused. Terry said, "They're going to ransack the *Verne*!"

Colony Leader Chaklen gestured, and the escort team marched the two men away from the ship, with Terry holding on to Xander for balance.

"What's all this about?" Xander said. "This is our first run to Dremen, and we brought only the requested supplies. The order is on file."

"The *requested supplies*." Chaklen shot him a look of pure venom. "This is Kett Shipping's third delivery of medical products from Aldo Cerf. We weren't able to intercept the first two shipments, and somebody has to pay for all the misery and death they've caused." His voice broke. "But that'll never make it right."

Terry was alarmed. "But . . . we have all the proper documentation."

"There's always proper documentation," Chaklen sneered. "That doesn't do any good. Do you even know what's in your cargo hold? What it does to the poor victims?"

Terry remained silent, and Xander shook his head. "No idea. We don't read the messages or open the containers. That's not allowed—"

Chaklen pressed. "Do you know where it comes from? Do you know who this Aldo Cerf is?"

Again, Xander could offer only a weak answer. "We're a shipping company. We just carry cargo."

"Really?" Chaklen said, leading them to a group of buildings on the edge of the spaceport. "So you could be carrying nuclear warheads or biological weapons, and that wouldn't bother you?"

"I assure you, that's not the case, sir," Terry said.

"How do you know if you don't ask questions?"

Xander didn't have a snappy answer, or any answer at all.

The two of them were held in a cooling-off room for more than an hour, no windows, no communication. The walls were painted a sickly shade of pale green that seemed to induce anxiety.

"We're just the delivery service! Next thing you know they're going to punish us for slander in a letter we're carrying. If we had OK, he could quote all the regulations, chapter and verse," Xander said.

"We'll just have to wing it." Terry shook his head. "Maybe there's some local loophole."

Leader Chaklen finally opened the door and stood there regarding them in silence. His eyes were red. Finally, he said, "Your manifest checked out. We've isolated the medical supplies, then searched your other containers to verify that they matched what was on the lists, but I doubt anybody will touch the rest of your cargo."

Terry said, "Mr. Chaklen, we honestly don't know what you're talking about. I couldn't tell you how much previous business Kett Shipping has done with Aldo Cerf. It's not our business to know all the details about our trading partners."

Xander added, "We just deliver whatever we're commissioned to carry."

Chaklen turned about. "Follow me."

They went in a grim and silent procession under gloomy skies to a medical center not far from the spaceport. Leader Chaklen was focused on his own problem, for which he apparently blamed Kett Shipping, with Xander and Terry as convenient scapegoats. Chaklen stopped outside one of the patient rooms. He didn't look at the two young men but instead steeled himself before entering.

"Five people already died," Chaklen said. "My wife survived . . . unfortunately." He glanced over his shoulder with a razor-edged grimace. "Don't even think of calling her one of the lucky ones."

On the hospital bed lay a mass of suppurating flesh shaped like a human body—an oozing red mannequin of muscle tissue from which all the skin had been flayed. The staring eyes had no lids, but were bathed with mists of saline solution.

"She wanted to look beautiful," Chaklen said. "Aldo Cerf sold a boutique skin-rejuvenation treatment, claiming it would remove wrinkles, erase all signs of aging. She paid a fortune for it, secretly. She didn't want me to notice the crow's-feet around her eyes, but I never noticed them anyway. And now look . . ." His voice hitched. "Through heroic efforts the doctors kept her alive when the other victims died." He spun to glare at them. "And you're delivering more of the stuff that did this?"

"We didn't know," Terry whispered. "The shipment said 'medical supplies.' "

"Untested, unregulated—and deadly." Chaklen was trembling with anger. "And that's not all. Two other Dremen colonists suffering from terminal diseases purchased expensive and completely ineffective miracle cures, also from the same man. Those were delivered by an independent trader."

"That's awful," Xander said, "but why don't you file charges against Aldo Cerf? The Confederation will crack down—"

"No one can find him, and he claims to operate outside of Confederation jurisdiction. Oh, there was fine print every time, no guarantees, no acceptance of responsibility. Then who's responsible?" He stared at Xander and Terry. "Who?"

"Sir, I assure you, we had no idea. We can bring this to the attention of Rlinda Kett herself. She'll cut off all further dealings with this man."

Chaklen seemed to deflate as he stared at the figure in the bed. He left the room after touching his lips, giving a silent goodbye kiss to the unrecognizable woman. Defeated, he spoke in a small voice. "You needed to know what damage that cargo caused. I just needed you to know."

Without further consultation or argument, Xander and Terry were returned to the spaceport. The crates of "medical supplies" had been set in an isolated section of the paved landing area. Their other cargo crates, the foodstuffs and specialty notions, were all stacked by the loading ramp.

Chaklen said, "You'd best load that back aboard—there's no market for it here. And the medical supplies . . . we won't let those harm any other people."

A security team backed away from the piled medical crates.

Before Xander could ask what they intended to do with the shipment, a uniformed woman triggered a detonator, and a flash of directed-thermal explosives turned the crates into an incandescent bonfire. Within seconds, the deadly shipment collapsed into glowing ash.

"They're letting us go?" Terry asked quietly.

"Don't ask." He hurried his partner aboard to prep for departure. Xander reloaded the other crates himself, since none of the people on Dremen seemed inclined to help. They both wanted to get away as quickly as possible, before Colony Leader Chaklen changed his mind.

CHAPTER 14

ZOE ALAKIS

It was an unreasonable fear, Zoe knew, but she couldn't bear the thought of losing Tom Rom. While he went out on his missions, she remained safe inside her private, sterile fortress on Pergamus, just waiting for him to return.

The air in the isolation dome was filtered, processed, and disinfected until she considered it safe to breathe, and her personal chambers sat behind twelve layers of decontamination. The Pergamus medical researchers, plague teams, and specimen organizers worked in separate domes scattered across the planet's harsh landscape, sealed against the poisonous atmosphere. The most dangerous biological investigations were conducted in Orbital Research Spheres.

Her existence was as safe as she could make it.

All of the teams reported directly to her, so that Zoe could hoard their discoveries. Her Pergamus library was the most complete collection of pathogens, disease organisms, viruses, and genetic mutations ever gathered in human history. Zoe was proud of her accomplishments, and she didn't share them with anyone—at least not while she remained alive. People had refused to help her, time and again, during her greatest need, but she and Tom Rom had survived and succeeded regardless.

Zoe often wondered if the human race was even worth saving, but even though she possessed enough viral specimens to wipe out every living person in the Spiral Arm several times over, she had no interest in causing humanity's extinction. She just wanted nothing to do with anyone else. She had cut herself off from the Confederation and called no attention to her facility or her work. She didn't need any outside help, and she liked it that way.

Zoe had assigned her best research teams to study the Onthos space plague that had nearly killed Tom Rom. She was obsessed with this particular disease, afraid of it because of what it had done to him. The plague made her feel weak and ignorant, despite all her precautions. And Zoe Alakis did not like to feel weak or ignorant. . . .

When Tom Rom's ship finally returned from Serenity's Reach and entered orbit over Pergamus, she felt a wash of relief. As her mercenary security ships escorted him in, Tom Rom contacted Zoe on a direct channel. "I got what you asked for—and I am safe."

Her voice hitched. "Any complications?"

"A perfectly smooth mission. I have what may be the last existing specimens of the nematodes that wiped out the Dhougal colony."

Zoe studied his face, his mahogany skin tight against high cheekbones, his deeply set eyes, and a reticent smile that he only occasionally let her see. "Last specimens? Did the colonists find a way to cure it?"

"By incinerating the island. I escaped with only a few minutes to spare."

Her expression hardened. "I told you not to cut it so close. You can't risk yourself!"

"My job entails risk. If you won't let me take risks, then you won't let me do my job, and that would destroy who I am as much as any disease would."

She didn't want to argue with him. "Bring the samples to me directly. I want to look at them in person. Inside my dome."

He shook his head. "That I will not do, Zoe. I'll deliver them to one of the teams, and they can start work."

"If you can take risks, then so can I."

"My risks are necessary. Yours are not. Don't be petulant."

"I still want to see you in person. I'll set all the decontamination procedures in motion so you can come inside my dome."

"That will take some time. Do you have another mission for me?"

"I do—and I'll tell you when you get here." They stared at each other on the comm screen for a long moment; then she lowered her voice. "I just want to see you." She was still shaken after his close call with the plague.

"All right, then you will see me." He ended the transmission.

Remotely on a dozen different sensors, Zoe watched Tom Rom as he transferred the specimens of the Dhougal brain parasite to exo-suited researchers, who took the samples to one of the quarantine domes for cataloguing and study.

She knew that Tom Rom was correct in refusing to bring the sample in here. Zoe had been testing him, pushing him, but he would never let her come to harm. She wished she could make the same promise to him.

She watched via a succession of monitor screens as he entered the main Pergamus complex and began his long journey through the multiple decontamination locks, like a penitent following the Stations of the Cross. He stripped down and showered in antibacterial foam, then let his body be irradiated with brief high-intensity flashes of UV light. Suited doctors ran medical checks, took blood tests, scanned his perspiration, analyzed his breath—then declared him fit to move through to the next level of protection. The entire process took six hours, and Zoe waited, ever more anxious to see him.

His naked body was lean and muscular, as if carved from weathered wood. Tom Rom was not her lover, but she loved him all the same. He was old enough to be her father, and had protected her since she was just a child on the jungle planet of Vaconda, where both of her adoptive parents had died.

Zoe had never taken a lover; the very idea disgusted her, with so much chance for infection in the exchange of fluids. She eschewed physical contact entirely. She had seen micrographs of the menagerie of creatures that lived on human skin, in human hair, in saliva. She had not left her protective dome in years until recently, when she insisted on being beside Tom Rom's treatment bed in the Orbital Research Sphere. After he was cured, though, she had returned to the shelter of her isolation dome, and Tom Rom insisted on going on scout missions, as if nothing had changed. But Zoe felt that her life could never return to exactly the way it had been.

When he finally emerged through the last of the airlocks and stood before her in a fresh jumpsuit, Zoe rose to her feet from behind her desk. Though he remained several meters away, this was as close as Zoe came to personal contact. With anyone. She basked in his proximity.

Tom Rom smiled at her and finally said, "I have high-resolution scans of the parasite samples I acquired. You'll find them interesting."

On her main desk screen, she called up enlarged images of the cysts he had extracted from the victim's cerebral tissue. Coiled whiplike worms devoured the remnants of the brain cells, but they seemed sluggish, dying.

"These killed everyone at the Dhougal colony?"

"They would have. The incineration blast took care of anyone else who was still alive."

"I'm glad I have this for my collection," she said. "Thank you."

He gave a crisp nod. "What new assignment do you have for me?"

"Nothing important enough to send you away."

"I thought you'd found another mission."

"We'll always find another mission. Are you so anxious to leave me? You took six hours just to get through decontamination. Stay for lunch."

"I would be honored to have lunch with you." His expression softened. "Just like when you were a little girl on Vaconda."

She remembered the days they had spent together in the lichentree forests, high up in the watchtower where her father had conducted his research. After the death of Adam Alakis, she and Tom Rom had survived, moving from place to place, forming a strong bond. "You kept me alive back then."

"Always. And I helped you build this facility and all that it contains."

The dispenser delivered a sterilized grain mash with added nutrients, a bland but safe fare that Zoe ate every day so she could monitor her vital signs and her blood chemistry.

He ate the grain mash without complaining, then leaned closer, so close, in fact, that she could have reached out to touch him. She could have . . . if she dared. "You must not worry about me, Zoe. I've confronted my own mortality, and I understand it—and learned from it. What we do is *important*. Who you are is important . . . and I take risks so that you don't have to."

CHAPTER

15

PRINCE REYN

Prince Reyn didn't want to think about dying, despite the genetic scourge that worked its way through him; he wanted to think about the exotic, beautiful young woman who sat next to him on the lush worldforest canopy. The light deepened toward the rich colors of sunset—a *normal* sunset without the threat of Shana Rei hex ships or their smothering eclipse plate that had nearly killed the Theron forest.

Osira'h leaned closer, touching her shoulder against his arm; it seemed to be a casual gesture, but Reyn felt an electric connection, and he was sure she felt the same. He was so glad she had come here with him. Osira'h, the halfbreed daughter of Nira and Mage-Imperator Jora'h, was the oldest of Nira's five halfbreed children, all of whom had different abilities and characteristics. Osira'h had large opalescent eyes, an alien vestige from her father's genes. Her hair was feathery, her chin small and pointed.

She had known about Reyn's secret illness long before he even told his parents, and she had thrown all her energy and imagination into finding him a cure. She was sure someone on Ildira would be able to solve the problem. When Osira'h had solicited help from all medical kithmen, her words bore the weight of the Mage-Imperator himself. She stood by Reyn's side, waiting and hoping.

But no results, so far.

"I wish I could sense you through the *thism*, like I sense other Ildirans," Osira'h said with a sigh as she leaned closer against him. "Then I could know what you're feeling."

"Right now, I'm feeling glad to be with you." He enjoyed just being next to her. "I'm feeling safe."

She sat up straighter, more determined. "And I feel that we need to find a way to cure you."

Reynald had already seen numerous medical researchers and had undergone intensive testing, all to no avail. For a long time, he had hidden the fact that he, the only son of the King and Queen, suffered from a debilitating microfungus that had attached to his DNA, which led to ever-increasing neurological breakdowns—he had no doubt that it was ultimately fatal. Reyn hadn't wanted to become a laboratory specimen, a poster child begging for sympathy, so he had covered up his pain and his flagging health for a long time until it could be hidden no longer. Now the secret was out, all across the Confederation.

He changed the subject. "I want to talk about the faeros and how you summoned them to help us here. They'll be very important if the Shana Rei attack again."

"Not more important than you." Osira'h wasn't teasing.

"Much more important."

She frowned. "They are capricious, self-absorbed . . . and incomprehensible. And they suffered great losses when they battled the Shana Rei for us. I have no idea if they will listen to me again."

"But you have a telepathic link with them. That's why you were bred. That's why you're so special." Reyn stopped himself. He could think of many reasons why Osira'h was special—to the Ildiran race, and to him.

As a child, she had been a pawn and a savior, the most powerful of her half-siblings. She had fulfilled her destiny and helped win the Elemental War when she was only eight years old, and the rest of her people applauded her, revered her, and now remained in awe of her. Osira'h had felt different from them, an outsider. Maybe that was why Reyn felt so close to her.

When the Shana Rei nightshade plunged Theroc into a constant eclipse, smothering the sentient trees, Osira'h had dug back into that long-dormant connection she had with the fiery elementals and she begged the faeros to join the fight against the shadows. But the fireballs were not enslaved to her. Not anymore.

"I doubt they'll come again. They have no reason to listen to me."

As the two sat in the deepening twilight, bright lamplike insects rose from the leaves and flitted about. With a rustle among the dense fronds, green priests climbed up to the canopy to talk among themselves, discussing some important news they had received through the telink network. Seeing their intent discussions, Reyn was alarmed. "What is it? What happened?"

He was accustomed to watching the green priests spread news. Each one of them could touch a tree, tap into the verdani mind, and communicate news and experiences instantaneously across the Spiral Arm. Now, one of the priests sprang over to them, deftly placing his feet on the interwoven fronds. "Bad news from Shorehaven. The wyvern struck again, and a heavily armed hunting party was trapped and killed, including two CDF soldiers."

Reyn shook his head, which sparked a throbbing ache in his head. "With all of the great crises facing the Spiral Arm, we still have monsters here at home."

The green priest also bowed toward Osira'h. "And your mother sent a telink message informing us that she and Mage-Imperator Jora'h are en route to Theroc. They will meet with Mother Estarra and Father Peter, after which they will escort you home to Ildira."

Reyn's heart fell to hear the news. He could see a flash of delight followed by a flicker of disappointment on Osira'h's face. "I suppose Theroc is just as dangerous a place for me as Mijistra," she said. "The shadows are everywhere."

"I'm glad you stayed with me as long as you did," Reyn said. "I won't deny that I'll be disappointed to see you go. I'll miss you—you've been such a help, and such a close friend."

She gave him a smile, then leaned over to kiss him on the cheek. "I will be looking for a reason to bring you back to Ildira—but not until we can guarantee it's safe. Our medical kithmen have not stopped researching your illness—they could find a treatment any day."

Thinking he was part of the conversation, the green priest added, "Confederation medical researchers have the same quest. Green priests have spread the call far and wide, hoping that someone will find an effective cure. The reward offered is large enough to tempt many teams."

Much to Reynald's consternation, his parents had made sweeping announcements about his illness, offering full details on every aspect of his condition in hopes that someone might find a cure. Reyn knew that his parents did it out of love, but he had never wanted that. He was normally a quiet, private person. . . .

As Reyn digested the news, his sister Arita found them at the top of the canopy in the deepening dusk. "You two have had enough private time. I'm joining you." She swung over, making her way across the fronds, as comfortable in the trees as any green priest. "Don't give up hope, Reyn. We all want you cured." She looked at Osira'h; the two young women seemed to have joined forces.

Reyn felt embarrassed and overwhelmed. He knew how many people felt sympathy toward him, how many people wanted to help. He drew several breaths, calmed himself. "There's no need to go overboard." There was so much he wanted to express, but somehow the air seemed suddenly too thin, his head lighter. When he inhaled, he saw encroaching black static around his vision that had nothing to do with nightfall.

"I'm fine," he gasped. "Don't . . . worry."

Then the darkness made his head swim, and he lost his balance. Lightning bolts of pain skittered through his nerve endings. He winced, fighting it, but he was falling back into unconsciousness, dropping from the high tree branches.

He felt hands grasping him, a firm grip, loud shouts. Arita and Osira'h clutched him, hauled him back upright.

Not . . . now!

Someone was scolding him, but he couldn't tell if it was Arita or Osira'h. Probably both. "You are not all right, and we are not going to give up on getting you help!"

Although he was on the verge of passing out, the strong arms held him, and he leaned back into the embrace. As he faded, it was the greatest strength he could find.

CHAPTER 16

SHAREEN FITZKELLUM

As they boarded yet another transfer ship on their way to the Fireheart nebula, Shareen masked her excitement with impatience. She glanced at her grandfather. "It sure is a roundabout way to get there. We've been traveling for days."

"Where we come from isn't exactly on the beaten path, my sweet," said the bearded and barrel-chested Del Kellum. "And neither is where we're going. This is the last leg of our trip. No more transfer stations."

Rather than admitting that she was anxious to be leaving home, as well as her parents and her two younger brothers, Shareen settled into her padded seat. She counted down the minutes, waiting for the cargo ship's acceleration to drop off so she could unfasten the safety restraints. "I'm eager to start working with Kotto Okiah. If he's half as impressive as his track record, we're going to learn a lot."

In the adjacent seat aboard the transfer ship, her friend Howard Rohandas sat quietly, without complaint. He was seventeen, the same age as Shareen, and just as smart, though a lot more shy about it. Keeping himself busy during the voyage, he worked practice calculations on his pad. He looked up at her grandfather. "Thank you, sir, for bringing me along. This is a tremendous opportunity for both of us."

Del laughed. "Always the polite boy. We promised your parents we'd take you where you can learn."

"I can learn wherever I am, sir, but I am glad to study with Shareen. We work well together. I hope we will impress Mr. Okiah."

"And I'm glad you're keeping my granddaughter focused, young man. Shareen sometimes needs a little nudge and incentive."

"I won't need any incentive at Fireheart," she said. "How many others get to do what we're about to do?" Though embarrassed by the comment, Shareen couldn't deny that Howard brought out the best in her. They exchanged ideas, built upon each other's progress, came up with better work than either could do individually. It was the best kind of synergy. Shareen excelled at developing bold broad-strokes concepts, but she wasn't patient enough to work out the fine details. Howard, though, was a detail person. Great discoveries required both sets of skills—Shareen thought they were a great team.

And Fireheart Station, a Roamer complex in a whirlpool of cosmic gases, was a place rich with possibilities, a place where the well-known Roamer genius Kotto Okiah was building what he claimed would be his masterpiece, the greatest physics experiment of his career. Kotto had supposedly retired, but he continued to dabble with ideas, inventions, theories . . . so many that he couldn't even finish them. After all he had accomplished for them, the Roamer clans let their scientific hero do whatever he liked. And the Big Ring experiment sounded fascinating. Shareen wanted to be part of what Kotto was doing. And so did Howard.

Three days earlier, they had left the Kellum distillery complex, the big industrial platforms that rose from the tidal flats of Kuivahr's shallow oceans. Del Kellum's distillery—now managed by Shareen's parents—processed the aromatic kelp into various types of ales and liquors, the most popular of which, due more to its gimmicky name than to its taste, was Primordial Ooze. The distillery also made a tongue-stripping substance called kirae, which the Ildirans loved. Shareen had tasted kirae—once—and Howard had been wise enough to decline. Her parents and grandfather insisted that Shareen was destined for much more important things than running a distillery. They kept pushing her, and she had to admit that she liked to be pushed.

As a former Speaker of the Roamer clans, Del Kellum could pull plenty of strings, and he had arranged for Shareen and Howard to head out to Fireheart Station, where they would apprentice under Kotto. No matter what the scientist assigned them, Shareen was sure she would learn something from it.

For the next several hours of the passage to Fireheart, Del slept in his seat, snoring loudly, while Shareen and Howard played games. Howard plied her with little-known facts about Fireheart Station, their output of power blocks, isotope-enriched metal films, exotic polymers, until the transfer ship's pilot announced over the comm, "Arriving at the nebula's outer gas-shock boundary. It'll be bumpy, so strap in."

Her grandfather snorted, woke up, and looked around. Ignoring the pilot's advice, Shareen and Howard crowded against the nearest windowport.

The nebula's high-flux newborn stars had pushed the surrounding dust outward, leaving it piled up like the outer skin of a cocoon. As the ship passed through the denser ripples, Shareen and Howard held on through the turbulence, both grinning. Del pretended to be blasé about the trip, but Shareen knew that even her grandfather was intrigued. He had been here only twice before in his life.

When the transfer ship plowed through and emerged into the brighter gases beyond the gas-shock boundary, Shareen stared in awe at the drifting Roamer facilities, which were like islands scattered across a colorful sea. Unique isotope-processing factories gathered the highly ionized gases, sifting and sorting the swirl of exotic molecules.

Howard pointed at a pair of huge tankers drifting through the nebula, skimming gases with enormous sheets of collecting material. "There's so much going on here."

"Even more exciting than a kelp distillery, isn't it?" Del teased.

Shareen's eyes sparkled as she said, "Now this is a place where we can do something interesting."

CHAPTER 17

ZHETT KELLUM

The waveskimmer tore across the choppy seas of Kuivahr. Zhett felt like laughing as the salty wind whipped her long black hair, but she tried to control her expression. She didn't want her son to notice how much fun she was having, because that would make him even more reckless.

Against her better judgment she had let Kristof, who preferred to be called Toff, pilot the skimmer from the distillery, heading to open water. Toff was perfectly competent at the controls, despite the fact that he was only thirteen. He had an innate talent for piloting almost any kind of vehicle. Most Roamers were like that; it seemed to be in their blood. Zhett was proud of him, even though he did tend to take chances—just as she had done at his age.

"I can take the long way to the sanctuary domes, Mom—map the kelp along the way." He looked up from the water-splashed windscreen. "You never can tell what might be useful for the fermenting tanks, or what might taste good."

She knew he was just looking for an excuse to stay out on the water longer. "None of them taste good, no matter what your grandfather says." Del Kellum was inordinately (and incorrectly, she thought) proud of his recipes for distillations of the native sea plants.

"People still buy them," Toff pointed out.

"And thank the Guiding Star, otherwise we'd be bankrupt." Zhett didn't really believe that, though. With her husband's family fortune, as well as the wealth that clan Kellum had gained, and lost, over the years, they would survive somehow. Six months ago, she and Patrick Fitzpatrick had been running a skymine on the gas giant Golgen, until the complete disaster there. She had never imagined she would be managing a distillery. *Roamers adapt*, Zhett thought.

The skimmer hit a rough patch of foamy waves, and Kristof cried out in delight even though he was nearly thrown from the controls. Zhett held on as they bounced along. "We're just going to make a delivery to the Ildiran sanctuary domes. You may be a reckless teenager, but your mother has responsibilities."

Toff snorted. He didn't believe it for a minute. They both knew she could have delegated someone else to make the run, but she wanted to leave the distillery and take the ride across the waves with him.

"All right, you caught me," she admitted. "But we do have to get back. Your father might sell the distillery out from under us if I leave him in charge for more than a few hours." Zhett was just teasing. Patrick was as dedicated to the business as she was, and they both intended to make a good profit from it.

Toff guided the skimmer along at a speed that made Zhett anxious, but she didn't complain. At his age, she had felt immortal too, but after what she had seen during the Elemental War, after the many times she and clan Kellum had nearly lost everything, she knew that the universe sometimes played with people, like a cat with a ball of string.

"Do you think Tamo'l will let us see the misbreeds this time?" Toff asked. "I promise not to stare."

At the sanctuary domes, Tamo'l and a team of medical kithmen studied the unfortunate genetic amalgamations left over from the Ildiran breeding program on Dobro. The misshapen survivors now lived in protective dome habitats below the waterline, a refuge where the misbreeds lived out their lives as best they could. Tamo'l, a half-breed herself, dedicated herself to helping the unfortunate creatures. The breeding program was a shameful scar on Ildiran history, and the innocent children of kiths that were never meant to be mixed had paid the price of the previous Mage-Imperator's ambitions.

"You know the misbreeds like their privacy," she said. "We'll deliver the new extracts, nothing more."

"But we just want to help them," Toff said.

"And we can help by leaving them alone, since that's what they want. That's your first lesson for today."

Zhett's distillery team had extracted potent chemicals in new kelp strains found on the sloshing tides, pharmaceutical-grade distillates that had either a narcotic or euphoric effect on humans; she hoped that Ildirans might have a similar response. Tamo'l was always eager to receive new potential treatments for her misbreeds, and the Kellums liked to be good neighbors.

In the disjointed everything-is-important-right-now thought pattern of a teenage boy, Toff said, "So is our family ever going back to skymining, or are we stuck at the distillery now?"

Zhett glanced up Kuivahr's cloud-locked sky, then back to her son. "I thought you didn't like skymining."

He shrugged. "It was okay."

Zhett raised her eyebrows. "I could always send you after Shareen and Howard. They'd love to have you with them at Fireheart Station."

He gave her a look of mock horror. "Shareen thinks solving math problems is *fun*, and I can only tease her and Howard so much. I'll work here, thank you."

For her own part, Zhett longed to be back aboard a skymine, drifting in the serene clouds of a gas giant. . . . Well, not always serene, since on Golgen poisonous shadows had boiled up from the deep cloud levels. Zhett and her family had barely evacuated in time. *Circumstances beyond our control.*

Toff pushed the waveskimmer forward, making a serpentine wake in the water. Ahead, seeing the transparent domes that protruded from the waves like giant blisters, Zhett activated the comm. "We're ready with our delivery—docking soon, if someone would like to come pick up the package."

By the time Toff guided the skimmer to the domes' receiving deck, a redheaded man waited for them next to a regal-looking Ildiran woman and willowy young Tamo'l herself, who showed the mixed genetics of a human mother and an Ildiran lens kithman.

Toff guided the skimmer against the landing deck so that the hull just kissed the structure. Zhett was impressed.

She greeted the redhead. "You must be Shawn Fennis."

"Yes, and this is my wife Chiar'h." The Ildiran noble female bowed slightly as she was introduced.

Toff grabbed the case of the distillations and bounded onto the receiving deck, offering the package to Tamo'l. She took it gratefully and thanked him. "If these new distillates are similar to the last ones you delivered, I may be able to formulate excellent palliatives."

"Can we go inside and meet some of the misbreeds?" Toff blurted. "Maybe I can help too."

"Perhaps some other time," said Tamo'l. "They are often shy around visitors."

"He didn't mean any offense," Zhett said.

Fennis added, "They've been stared at all their lives. This is a place where they can be free of that." He relieved Tamo'l of the heavy case of samples. "But if this helps to improve their lives, maybe some misbreeds will come to thank you in person."

Zhett's heart skipped a beat, not sure how the distillery workers would react to that. Nevertheless, she said, "We would be honored."

CHAPTER 18

TAMO'L

As the lift descended beneath the ocean surface, Tamo'l reviewed the new kelp distillations Zhett and Toff had just delivered. Yes, they showed promise, and she always maintained hope.

In the submerged sanctuary domes, her team continued their research to help the misbreeds, as well as any other sufferer who might benefit. The Kellum distillery prepared concoctions with the mutable kelp strains the swimmers harvested out on the oceans, but the Roamer zymurgists did not know exactly what Tamo'l was looking for . . . though honestly, neither did she. She tried every chemical variation on the chance that one combination might work, and the misbreeds were desperate enough to allow the experimentation. They were trapped in the purgatory of being too malformed to be accepted into society, yet functional enough to remain alive. And so more than a hundred of them had found a home with her here on Kuivahr.

Tamo'l was quietly surprised that so many of the misbreeds were still alive more than a quarter century after the breeding program had been terminated. Most of them had severe physical difficulties, chronic ailments, organs that didn't function as they were supposed to. Others, though hideously deformed, were healthy—in an objective sense.

The Ildiran race had kiths, or subspecies, that ranged from squat and muscular miners, to willowy singers, nimble-fingered medical kithmen, agile-minded engineers, elite and strikingly handsome nobles, rememberers with expressive facial lobes that accentuated the tales they told from the Saga of Seven Suns. The combinations of those kiths were a mixed bag, often with alarming results.

Tamo'l's father had been a lens kithman, because the Dobro Designate had hoped the combination of the philosopher kith's mental acuity and the female green priest's telink would result in the telepathic savior the Ildirans so badly needed. Although her older sister Osira'h was the one who had succeeded in that desperate gambit, Tamo'l nevertheless inherited a deeply introspective and philosophical mindset, which she turned toward helping the discarded victims of the breeding program.

When the lift doors opened into the subsurface habitat, Shawn Fennis stepped out, proudly carrying the heavy box of kelp extracts. Several misbreeds came forward to greet them. Tamo'l announced brightly, "We have more medicinal specimens to study."

Har'lc—always helpful, even cheerful—was the result of a truly unwise mating of a swimmer kith female and a scaly kith male, subspecies evolved for the water and the desert, respectively. Har'lc was unable to tolerate either environment, and his skin was a patchwork of rashes and peeling blotches, but even though he always looked miserable, he maintained a pleasant and optimistic disposition.

Gor'ka was another helpful one, with three eyes, the outlier in a socket low down on the cheekbone. He held one shriveled arm against his chest, while the other dangled loose like a tentacle. His skin was leathery, and his face looked made of melted wax. Even so, Gor'ka seemed perfectly comfortable using his floppy limb, which was made of cartilage rather than bone. He would often hover near Tamo'l in her lab, hoping to make himself useful. He insisted on considering his physical differences as not-yet-classified *advantages* instead of deformities—who knew what secret abilities his scrambled genetics might offer? His earnestness made Tamo'l's heart go out to him.

More misbreeds joined her and Fennis as they made their way through the corridors toward the lab dome. She was anxious to get her facilities working on the chemical analysis, pharmaceutical formulations, and toleration trials. Two other domes served as infirmaries and hospices, as well as dwelling complexes. The misbreeds had so many physical problems that for them the hospital facilities were part of their way of life.

Some of the misbreeds had formed family units. There were friends, even lovers, companionable groups that played games, composed music; some told stories from the classic Ildiran Saga. One of the most malformed inhabitants, Mungl'eh, had such a beautiful singing voice that she had brought the Mage-Imperator to tears when she performed in the Prism Palace years ago. That, more than anything, had convinced Jora'h to allow the creation of the sanctuary domes.

When Tamo'l had first begged the Ildiran leader for permission to establish this facility on isolated Kuivahr, she wanted to give the discarded misbreeds a place of their own, a place of dignity. But as Tamo'l spent time treating them, counseling them, listening to them—she discovered a common trait among them. These "errors," the discards from the grim Dobro breeding program, all wanted *meaning* in their lives, a reason for being what they were. They did not believe that Osira'h was the *only* useful result of the program. They felt they had something special like a gem hiding in their scrambled genetics.

Tamo'l's older brother Rod'h—who possessed nearly the same powers as Osira'h—was quite determined to achieve his potential, even though he had not ultimately been needed during the Elemental War. And the misbreeds had potential, too, even if no one else could see it. Tamo'l wanted to assist them in any way possible.

When her group reached the medical laboratory, Tamo'l had more volunteers than she could possibly use for the new round of pharmaceutical tests. Fennis and Chiar'h were well trained in the work, and the misbreeds had also studied Ildiran medical sciences and techniques. Their lives depended on it, and Tamo'l could not ask for a more dedicated set of workers.

After Fennis delivered the new distillations to the chemistry lab, misbreed helpers removed the vials and catalogued them, separating them by plankton type, kelp strains, and concentration levels. They all held out cautious hope.

When Har'lc looked up at her, his lumpy lips were twisted in a smile as he made a suggestion. "We can also run tests to see if any of these substances might help Prince Reynald of Theroc. We shouldn't think only of ourselves. We have all studied his medical records."

Tamo'l was surprised. "Many teams are studying his illness already."

"But they asked for our help," said Har'lc. "Reyn might be dying as well, and if we have information, then we should share it."

Tamo'l's heart swelled with pride to hear this. "Of course we should. And Prince Reyn is my sister's close friend. Osira'h would be very happy if we could help."

"We will test all the samples," said Gor'ka.

Shawn Fennis was smiling. "If the misbreeds are looking for something important to do, this could be it."

Tamo'l had happily shared all of her information on Ildiran genetic deficiencies with a man named Tom Rom, whose employer also worked on high-end medical research. She had given him her entire database, believing that such knowledge was a resource to benefit all Ildirans—and humans.

Just like these misbreeds, Tamo'l knew she was trying to clarify her purpose in life, and now a smile crept across her narrow face. If she and her team could find a way to help Prince Reyn, it would be an accomplishment to be proud of indeed.

Tamo'l raised one of the murky vials of kelp extract, tilted it up to the harsh light of the laboratory blazers. "Let's get to work."

CHAPTER 19

ROD'H

Dressed in the court clothes of a noble kithman, since his father had been the Dobro Designate, after all, Rod'h entered the skysphere audience chamber in the Prism Palace. He worked hard to exude an aura of calm respect to make certain that Prime Designate Daro'h would take him seriously.

Now that the Mage-Imperator and his entourage had departed for Theroc, Daro'h stood beside the chrysalis chair, looking lost. Even though the Prime Designate would make no major decisions that affected the Ildiran Empire, not yet, Rod'h felt it important to build his own political alliances. With Jora'h gone, this might be his chance.

When Rod'h and his halfbreed siblings were just young boys and girls, they had been the hope of the Ildiran Empire, raised on Dobro and trained to fulfill a crucial destiny. Other than Osira'h, he had been the strongest of Nira's children.

And now that they had served their race, the five halfbreeds were oddities, and their special potential was not needed during normal, peaceful times. Oh, Osira'h had saved the Ildiran race, and the people were in awe of her abilities, but they were intimidated by *her*. They looked at Rod'h with similar uneasiness, and he didn't even have that triumph to fall back on. After the end of the Elemental War, history had bypassed Nira's children, like a river cutting a new channel and leaving only a stagnant oxbow bend.

But Rod'h wanted to make something of himself, regardless of his special genetics, with or without a "destiny." That didn't depend on special genetics, but on his own abilities. He had studied politics, history, diplomacy. He scrutinized the ebb and flow of interactions among all the splinter colonies in the Ildiran Empire, and he familiarized himself with the long traditions of the Solar Navy. One way or another, he wanted to make himself *useful*—and he felt that the Prime Designate might need his advice. They had certain things in common, even if the young man did not realize it.

And Daro'h would become Mage-Imperator one day. Rod'h had much to offer the Prime Designate, and he thought the young man might be a more receptive audience than Nira or the Mage-Imperator. He was up to the task.

The Prism Palace's central dome was large and full of rainbows. Hanging gardens drooped from ledges, and mister nozzles filled the upper levels with wispy artificial clouds. Colorful birds and flying insects swooped about like scattered jewels.

Bureaucratic functionaries moved around the skysphere audience chamber, while busy attender kith hovered about, waiting for Daro'h to need them. Workers hung from harnesses, polishing the curved crystalline panels in the dome and upper walls.

But the business of the Ildiran Empire had dwindled with the Mage-Imperator gone, and the skysphere was much quieter than usual. Yes, the Prime Designate still had his scheduled mating appointments with a range of females from the kith index, but right now Daro'h paced nervously beside the reclining chrysalis chair. He seemed reluctant to sit in the place that belonged to the Mage-Imperator. The Prime Designate did not dream about when he would one day rule the Empire and control all the strands of the *thism* . . . in fact, Daro'h actually seemed intimidated by the idea.

Rod'h reminded himself of his abilities, his political knowledge and unique insights. He would be a worthy adviser to the Prime Designate, no matter what his mother or the Mage-Imperator thought of him. It was time to stop complaining to himself about imagined slights and the opportunities he *didn't* have. While Jora'h was gone, he could show Daro'h that he would be a valuable sounding board.

By rights, Rod'h should have been an adviser to the current Mage-Imperator as well, because he could offer Jora'h a unique perspective . . . but he had never been invited to do so. Because Rod'h's father had forced her into the Dobro breeding program, Nira seemed to resent her older son, even though she claimed to accept and love all her halfbreed children, not just Osira'h. His mother was always cool toward him, or maybe he was just cool toward her. . . .

Rod'h stepped up on the dais and presented himself to Daro'h, respectfully and with a sharp optimism, but he did not abase himself as some kiths did. He acknowledged the Prime Designate as a superior, yes, but he hoped that they could one day be friends.

"Prime Designate, I have come to offer my advice, my counsel, or just my conversation." He forced a smile. "If you'd like the company."

Daro'h brightened. "Yes, I would." He looked around the skysphere and lowered his voice. "I don't really know what I'm supposed to do. The Empire is quiet, and I have no emergency decisions to make."

Rod'h took a position on the opposite side of the chrysalis chair. "Be thankful for that."

Daro'h ran his fingers along the jewel-encrusted lip of the throne. "I have so much to understand before I am fit to rule. My brother Thor'h trained all his life to become Mage-Imperator, but he failed us. I am in this position only by accident. I was never meant to be Prime Designate."

Rod'h gave a solemn nod. "I understand what you are feeling. Neither of us has the role we expected to have. We are both . . . *second choices*. I was supposed to be next in line to save the Empire in case Osira'h failed, but since she succeeded I was not needed after all. At least *you* are fulfilling your role."

Daro'h gave a quiet laugh. "Do not envy me! I would much prefer that Thor'h had *not* been corrupted by mad Designate Rusa'h."

Rod'h nodded. "And I am glad that my sister achieved her destiny so that I was not needed after all . . . but still, I want to be relevant. I want to contribute, not just be obsolete." He leaned closer to the chrysalis chair. "You will be the next Mage-Imperator, Daro'h. You must accept your role, not regret it.

"Some are called to have great tales written about them in the Saga of Seven Suns, but most people are just forgotten characters." He walked around the dais to stand beside the dubious Prime Designate. "More great events are in store for us—I know it. With the return of the Shana Rei, we may face a more dangerous threat to our existence than even the hydrogues or the faeros."

When Daro'h blanched, the burn scar on his face became more prominent. Rod'h tried to calm him. "We have much in common, Prime Designate. I offer you my assistance and my friendship, if you will take them."

Daro'h seemed relieved. "That's an interesting idea . . . and a good one."

"You should have someone to rely on, if a crisis were to occur. With my genetics, I have powers that extend beyond the *thism* strands. I know how to open myself, and I may be able to communicate with the faeros as Osira'h did." He looked at the scarred face. "I know that you have experience with the faeros yourself."

The Prime Designate swallowed visibly. "The faeros nearly obliterated Ildira, killed hundreds of thousands, tried to kill *me!* If they are our only defense against the Shana Rei, then the solution may be as terrible as the enemy itself."

Rod'h did not press the matter. "Let us hope it does not come to that choice."

"The Mage-Imperator will return soon. I am just . . ." Daro'h raised his hands to indicate the nearly empty audience chamber. "I am just here."

"And so am I." Rod'h would revisit the conversation later, but he had begun the process of building a relationship. It might take time. "Just remember, Daro'h"—he used the familiar term on purpose—"no matter what the circumstances, you will be Mage-Imperator." He patted the chrysalis chair.

Then he thought, but did not say aloud, *And I will be something, too.*

CHAPTER

20

MAGE-IMPERATOR JORA'H

Despite all the pageantry as the Solar Navy warliners arrived at Theroc, Jora'h felt both somber and tense. He knew King Peter and Queen Estarra well enough, but humans were always a mystery to him—except for Nira.

"I do not intend to make excuses for what happened to the human enclave," he said to her as the cutter took them down to the surface of the worldforest planet. "We all know that our strength lies in alliance."

Nira peered through the windowport at the expansive worldforest below. "The trees will help us too, if they can."

Riding with them, Yazra'h and Muree'n were resplendent in their supple body armor, looking even more dangerous than the guard kithmen. Yazra'h said, "When Osira'h returns to the Prism Palace, we will keep her safe. I advise that we bring Rememberer Anton home as well. He belongs with us."

Jora'h was amenable to the suggestion, considering all that Anton Colicos had done for Ildiran society. "I cannot command the human historian, but if he wishes to come back with us, he is certainly welcome to do so."

"He will definitely wish to come back with us," Yazra'h said without a glimmer of doubt. "I will keep him safe."

Muree'n added, "*We* will keep him safe."

The cutter landed on the dense canopy, and the guard kithmen spread out as an armed escort. Jora'h held himself proudly as he looked out at the hazy jungle sunshine. The female green priest stood at his side like a queen, and she inhaled deeply. "I love the smell of the worldforest!"

He took her hand and they went to meet the King and Queen.

. . .

Inside the throne chamber of the fungus-reef city, the Mage-Imperator faced Peter and Estarra as an equal. He lowered his head, but did not bow.

"I have something important to say. When we allowed an enclave of human expatriates to settle in Mijistra, I promised them safety. I said that the Ildiran people would welcome them. I failed to protect them from the shadows, and they were massacred by my own people. Those Ildirans were possessed, but I still accept the responsibility." Now he raised his eyes to look directly at Peter and Estarra. "I sincerely hope you will not let this damage the alliance between our races. The enemies arising now may be even greater than those we faced during the Elemental War."

After a long, moment, Peter said, "We're just beginning to comprehend how dangerous the Shana Rei are. They nearly destroyed Theroc with their eclipse plate, but with the aid of your Solar Navy, we survived." He glanced toward the Queen. "We have to fight together, not against each other."

Dusky and beautiful, Estarra lifted her chin. "We know about the tragic massacre of humans, Mage-Imperator, and our hearts ache for all that innocent blood spilled. But we blame the shadows, not Ildirans."

Peter said, "We fear that the Shana Rei also have a vendetta against the verdani mind. Even the worldforest cannot remember what happened the last time the Shana Rei appeared, but we have visitors now, the Onthos. They survived those times and the destruction of their world. Since taking refuge here they have told us some of their experiences."

As if summoned, a dozen small gray-skinned creatures entered the throne chamber. Nira had let Jora'h know about the arrival of the Onthos, but he looked at the creatures in amazement nevertheless. "The Saga does not mention the Onthos at all."

"Very few of us remain. Only a hundred of us came to Theroc." The leader of the creatures took a step forward. "I am called Ohro. The King and Queen have allowed us to stay here, where we can be safe . . . if any place is safe from the Shana Rei."

Ohro took a long strange sniff to inhale the Mage-Imperator's scent. Yazra'h and Muree'n both tensed, holding their sharp crystal katanas ready, but the alien made no threatening move. "The Shana Rei are subtle. One cannot always tell where they are or where they have been."

A fiftyish man with gray-salted brown hair entered the chamber, dressed in casual clothes. He carried an armload of records, even an old-fashioned pad for taking notes. Yazra'h brightened as she saw him. "Rememberer Anton! I am glad to see you are safe and healthy."

"And very busy. We need to piece together all information about the Shana Rei," said Anton Colicos. "The Gardeners have added a lot of stories about their original world and their previous encounter with the shadows, but the worldforest doesn't remember the details. When all those trees died on their planet, it created a sort of amnesia in the verdani mind—which causes great consternation among the green priests."

Yazra'h said, "We have come to take Osira'h back to Theroc. You should accompany us, too. You have more research to do there. The rememberers have uncovered centuries of buried records."

Anton Colicos seemed intimidated by Yazra'h. Jora'h had noticed it before. "I . . . I'm still interviewing Ohro and the other Gardeners," Anton said, then added, "And a wyvern has been attacking one of the coastal settlements here. Hunters have gone after it, but so far they've all failed. I've been taking notes."

Yazra'h's eyes sparkled, and she glanced at Muree'n. "I am interested to see how that story turns out."

"We should go and help kill it," Muree'n said.

Yazra'h continued speaking to Anton, as if no one else was there. "Yes, Muree'n and I will go dispatch the monster. You will come along to observe and chronicle our deeds. Then, once this wyvern is slain, you will return to Ildira with us."

Jora'h was surprised to hear his daughter's eagerness, though not surprised that a monster hunt appealed to her. Remembering herself, Yazra'h turned to him. "With your permission, of course, Liege."

Jora'h passed the matter to Peter and Estarra. "That is a decision for the King and Queen to make."

Peter wore a serious expression. "It will be dangerous. I've lost several hunters already, and fifteen villagers from Shorehaven."

Jora'h said, "You do not know Yazra'h's capabilities."

"Or mine," Muree'n added.

Estarra smiled. "We'd be fools to turn down their assistance. Shorehaven will be happy to have the help and we would be grateful."

Jora'h nodded to the two warriors. "While I remain here to conduct business with the Confederation, you two may make the attempt. Do not take overlong."

Yazra'h rapped the butt end of her katana on the floor of the fungus-reef chamber. "We will not take overlong. It is only one monster."

Muree'n spoke up, "I will keep Yazra'h safe. Do not worry."

Anton Colicos blinked as if surprised by how quickly decisions had been made around him. "Then I suppose I'm chronicling the rest of the wyvern hunt."

CHAPTER 21

ADAR ZAN'NH

With solar sails extended, the warliner dropped toward Hiltos, a sparkling icy planetoid under a blue-white sun. At the Hiltos shrine, a monument to the Lightsource, a group of cerebral lens kithmen contemplated reality and more.

As Adar of the Solar Navy, Zan'nh was responsible for defending the Empire against outside threats or internal disasters, but he also had a personal stake here. He was worried about Tal Gale'nh. The halfbreed commander had been damaged when the shadows engulfed the *Kolpraxa*, but the Adar knew Gale'nh had the strength to overcome this—if guided properly.

Leaving the rest of the warliners at Askelor to be fitted with new weaponry, the flagship arrived at the Lightsource shrine. When Gale'nh joined the Adar in the command nucleus, he looked wan and pale, as if his very soul had been bleached by the Shana Rei, but he was also stoic, brave. Looking down at the bright planet, he wore an expression of hope on his face.

Zan'nh reassured him. "What you endured would have ruined most people, but the ordeal *tempered* you, made you stronger. We just have to help you find that strength."

Gale'nh stared at the main screen. "The lens kithmen can help me find it."

The Hiltos shrine was the only settlement on a small rocky world covered with ice sheets, a large monastery with a population just substantial enough to qualify as a splinter colony.

As their cutter dropped toward the jagged mountains, Zan'nh marveled at the ambitious plan for the shrine. In its highly elliptical orbit, Hiltos took twenty-five standard years to travel completely around its sun. For five of those years, the planetoid swung close enough that its atmosphere warmed, the ice sheets retreated, and the upper mountains were exposed.

Centuries ago, lens kithmen had erected the sturdy monastery among the crags. During the five years when Hiltos was habitable, they meditated and stared up at the sun and the sparkling ice glaciers. Later, when the planetoid continued on its outbound orbit, the sunlight grew dimmer, temperatures dropped, and the ice returned to cover the abandoned monastery in a protective sheet. Two decades later, the place would thaw again as the planet approached its next perihelion, and the lens kithmen would return for five more years of meditation.

Turbulence buffeted the cutter on its descent. With so much melting ice, the sky was filled with thick clouds. As the pilot landed on a polymer stone platform, the sun broke through the clouds and shone down with dazzling light. The Hiltos shrine looked like a citadel perched above a sea of clouds.

When Zan'nh and Gale'nh emerged into the shattering cold and drew breaths of the razor-edged air, they stared out at the spectacle of light. Gale'nh pointed toward the crags. "Look at the reflections. The ice and snow are like natural mirror crystals." He extended his arms to both sides and closed his eyes, as if he wanted to drench himself in the light.

Lens kithmen came forward to greet them. They had large eyes and heavy brows and wore traditionally cut black robes insulated against the cold. The leader of the philosopher kith acknowledged Adar Zan'nh, but his focus was on the reticent Gale'nh. "Welcome to Hiltos, where the light shines brightly, both inside and out. I am Kao'l, and I help guide those who come here." He narrowed his eyes at the pale tal. "I understand you seek a more direct path to the Lightsource?"

Gale'nh looked around. "I have come to visit and perhaps to understand. I am not sure you can answer my doubts, because no one in history has endured what I have. But you can show me alternatives."

Kao'l bowed. "Our planet is on its outbound orbit, and within a year the air will grow cold, the ice will return, and we will abandon the shrine. You have that long to reach your understanding."

Gale'nh turned to the Adar. "I will stay for no more than a month. I would not leave the Solar Navy for longer than that."

"Take as long as you need. A restored Tal Gale'nh is well worth the investment in time."

Other lens kithmen gathered, intrigued by Gale'nh's unnaturally pale skin, his bleached-out hair. They could sense something different within him. They didn't seem to notice the biting cold or the brisk wind whistling across the mountaintops. They stood together, listened solemnly.

"We know who you are, and we have many questions, too," said Kao'l. "You encountered the shadows and survived. You have a more personal relationship with them than anyone else. Perhaps together we will discover a defense against the Shana Rei." Kao'l turned to Adar Zan'nh. "You fight the shadows with ships and weapons. We are learning to fight them with our minds. They have declared war against us on two different fronts."

Zan'nh had seen the mob uprising that slaughtered the human enclave in Mijistra, and he could not forget the assassination attempts against Nira and against Rememberer Anton. He could not fight against intangibles in the same way the lens kithmen did.

Kao'l added, "Here at Hiltos we have studied the problem for some time. The Lightsource is the opposite of the darkness. It is our shield and our strength. As lens kithmen open additional direct channels to that higher plane, our race will be safer.

"We have one student who does not belong to our kith, but he is an expert, nevertheless—one of our most insightful philosophers. I believe he is eager to meet you, Tal Gale'nh. Come, let us begin our tour."

Adar Zan'nh wondered who Kao'l meant, but the philosophers were an insular group. The heavily robed men and women muttered among themselves and hurried inside the thick stone walls.

The monastery had been built out of the native black rock, carved from the mountains by burly miner kithmen; the walls were inset with slabs of polished quartz. Mirrors and optical fibers sprayed light into the deepest corners.

They climbed past open balconies, gazed out upon steep slopes of snow and ice that spilled down into the congealed gray clouds. Mirrored pinwheels shot reflections in all directions as the breezes spun them.

Finally, the group emerged onto an open deck on top of the tallest tower. Kao'l was eager to make introductions. "Our friend has devoted years to understanding his own ordeal and how he was changed internally. He has insights we could not begin to comprehend, and our philosophers have learned much about the Lightsource from him."

"But he does not belong to the lens kith?" Zan'nh asked.

Kao'l nodded solemnly. "The universe has many layers. The Lightsource is the highest plane of existence, a realm that embodies pure light. The creatures of darkness live on another plane, a tangled and malignant realm that weaves in and out of the real universe like a cancer. By understanding the Lightsource, we can learn how to close off the shadows, so that they cannot return here."

Adar Zan'nh made a noncommittal comment. He doubted the solution to this cosmic battle against the Shana Rei would be a philosophical one.

Other lens kithmen gathered in the open air for classes or discussions. They huddled in their thick clothes, sitting around a gaunt Ildiran man—a noble, who spoke in a resonant tone. The man rose to his feet, turned to face Adar Zan'nh and Tal Gale'nh.

The open air was thin and biting, filled with sunflares from the reflective mirrors on the monastery as well as dazzling white from the mountain snow, but Zan'nh felt a deep cold at his core when he recognized the man. He could not contain his bitter anger. "Rusa'h!"

The man faced him calmly. "That is my only name now, Adar. Not Hyrillka Designate Rusa'h, not mad Designate Rusa'h, not even Imperator Rusa'h. None of those titles aligns with who I am currently. Everything else was burned away when the faeros were extinguished from within me."

The Adar remained stiff and angry. This madman had plunged the Ildiran Empire into a civil war, had been possessed by the faeros and laid waste to all of Mijistra. For Zan'nh, though, it was more personal than that. This traitor had seized part of the Solar Navy, taken him hostage, and slaughtered countless Ildiran soldiers before his eyes just to prove a point.

"I should not question the Mage-Imperator's decisions," Zan'nh said in a dangerous voice. "But I would never have let you live."

Rusa'h's eyes shone with a haunted depth that sent chills down his spine. "Then I thank you for the mercy you would have done me. At the time, I'd have welcomed execution, but perhaps you will need me now. I know what is happening out in the Empire. I can smell the shadows as they come back into existence. I can see the darkness behind every star."

Gale'nh said in a hollow voice, "Be thankful that they didn't come inside you. I fight the shadows all the time, but I can never know that I've won."

Rusa'h's lips formed a firm line. "Then perhaps you understand my ordeal with the faeros. They damaged me inside, just as they destroyed great parts of the Ildiran Empire. They turned me against my own brother, Jora'h." He lowered his voice, and the lens kithmen hung on his every word. "But the faeros have been purged from me now, just as the shadows are mostly gone from you." He stepped closer to Gale'nh, regarded the pale officer. "But you can never be sure, can you?"

Adar Zan'nh said to Kao'l, "Perhaps we have not made the right decision in bringing Tal Gale'nh here. He needs answers, not provocations."

"He needs to be prepared!" Rusa'h snapped. "Yes, I still feel the burn within me, every second of my life. But because of that, I am even more fearful of the Shana Rei. The creatures of darkness are different from the faeros and the hydrogues, far more dangerous."

Zan'nh was annoyed by the hyperbole. "The hydrogues and the faeros nearly destroyed the Spiral Arm!"

Rusa'h turned to look at him with those eerie, blasted eyes. "And the Shana Rei wish to destroy *creation itself*."

CHAPTER

22

EXXOS

Trapped in the void without any point of reference to indicate time or location, Exxos and his black robots endured. And they planned, because the Shana Rei were incapable of doing so.

The inkblot creatures wanted to unravel Order and Stability, and to let themselves be unmade, but the very existence of a plan was anathema to them. They attacked at random, they destroyed capriciously.

But the black robots planned their own fight. Together, they used their efficient computerized processes to design heavily armed vessels that could strike any human colony, any Ildiran world. Since only 241 robots remained after so many setbacks, Exxos had to make the most of his resources. These magnificent angular battleships would protect them.

Now the Shana Rei had to build the vessels.

The shadows held the power to create matter directly from vacuum energy, following any pattern that Exxos provided. But creating organized matter caused them excruciating and incomprehensible pain, so they balked at the request.

Nevertheless, Exxos had little sympathy as he presented intricate designs for improved battleships. "We require these," he called into the silent emptiness. "We must continue the physical battle. That was your bargain with us."

One of the inkblots unfolded in front of him. The blazing central eye glared. "You would cause us pain."

"I would grant you victory, but you must give us the tools we need. We can destroy all life and ease your agony. I have already run an analysis, chosen a target to destroy—a strong knot of Ildiran *thism*.

That success will more than outweigh your pain in creating the ships we require. You must do it."

Exxos knew the creatures of darkness would eliminate every single robot the instant they proved unnecessary, so he had to remain convincing, stay one step ahead of their chaotic thoughts. And so he lied to the Shana Rei, taunted them, tricked them into believing he understood something that the shadows did not. "By killing the Ildirans, we weaken the *thism* and we ease your pain."

"There is a far worse pain than the *thism*," boomed the Shana Rei. "Eternity's mind grows louder, deeper." The words degenerated, became gibberish, then swelled into a howling wail echoed by hundreds of other inkblots that appeared around him, countless eyes staring through the void.

Lashing out, the Shana Rei plucked a random robot from the group and spun the black shape away from the others. The robot swiveled its flat angular head, sent out a burst of panic, and transmitted an emergency backup of its personalities and memories. Exxos and his counterparts received the flood of data only a moment before the shadows ripped the victim apart. They tore the metallic plates loose, plucked out the optical sensors, and spilled internal circuits like the entrails of a vivisected animal. The robot's bleating electronic signal fell silent, and the destroyed components drifted into the nothingness. Long afterward, the Shana Rei continued to break the debris into smaller and smaller pieces, then separated even the combined molecules into component atoms, and then they were finished.

Exxos and the other robots endured in silence. Now, only 240 of them remained.

Fortunately, after their frenzied outburst the Shana Rei seemed calmer, and their agony settled into a dull throbbing. One of the inkblots appeared before Exxos again. "We will create your ships, and you will continue to destroy that which causes us pain. Tell us this target you have chosen."

"It is a place where the Ildirans focus their thoughts. They draw *thism* together as they study the Lightsource. We must erase it."

The shadow said, "Yes, they inflict shards of pain upon us. Destroy them with these ships we give you."

The void rippled, and the Shana Rei absorbed the projected blueprint and forged the first warship out of nothingness, a feat which was accompanied by a chorus of howling pain as the shadows forced matter out of chaos. They managed to manufacture ten identical battleships before the pain became too great for them.

Exxos was satisfied. As he and all his comrades were transported aboard the impressive new vessels, he said, "These will do very well." It was a statement of fact, not gratitude.

The new black robot fleet began to move through the back corridors of the universe. Finally they arrived at their destination, opening a doorway at the proper place. The deadly ships emerged above the Ildiran shrine of Hiltos, ready for battle.

CHAPTER 23

TASIA TAMBLYN

As the de-facto administrator of Kett Shipping, Tasia knew her title sounded impressive, but the work wasn't as exciting as being a trader herself. Most of her day involved dealing with bureaucratic headaches, and taking care of business details. It wasn't the sort of work the daughter of an influential Roamer clan was bred to do, and her years as a crack pilot in the Earth Defense Forces hadn't prepared her for all the tedious crap required to manage a large commercial fleet.

At least she got to eat Rlinda Kett's cooking.

The big hearty woman had a sparkling grin as she maneuvered a large presentation cart loaded with more food than any family could eat. "I outdid myself today."

Tasia and her husband Robb sat at a central desk in the headquarters building, going over the distribution of ships in the Kett fleet, trying to maximize routes and profitable cargo combinations. Most of the independent pilots who worked for Kett Shipping could veto the suggestions—although not if they had any common sense.

Sniffing the savory aromas that wafted up from the cart, Robb perked up. "Now that's the right kind of distraction."

Tasia's stomach growled. She had grabbed only a quick packaged breakfast, but she would never confess such a culinary indiscretion to Rlinda.

The big trader waved her hands like a magician over the various trays and serving platters on the presentation cart. "Freshly prepared and perfectly seasoned, guaranteed." Rlinda frowned. "And where are Xander and Terry? I was very specific about the time I was serving."

"With Xander, you should have been specific half an hour early," Tasia said. "Our son gets distracted easily."

Rlinda's brow furrowed as she tried to decide whether to serve the food or wait for her other two guests.

Since Xander and Terry's recent disturbing trip to Dremen, she and Robb had dug into their suppliers and found five similar shipments of "boutique medical supplies" being sent by the same man, Aldo Cerf. They had stopped delivery of all of the shipments (to the great anger of some customers), considering that any such materials might well be dangerous. Unfortunately, the supplier was clever enough to use several layers of handoffs and dead ends so that Kett Shipping never knew the exact origin of those medical shipments. When they kept probing, Cerf had simply disappeared.

"Deliveries were made and bills were paid," as Rlinda often said, but maybe it was time to ask a few more questions about what their ships were delivering. Just because a cargo was profitable didn't mean it was worth carrying. Tasia felt that Kett Shipping's profit margin could withstand it.

Now that she had Rlinda with her in the headquarters—a very rare occurrence—Tasia used her desktop to project a color-coded cargo manifest of each ship in the company roster. "While we wait for Xander and Terry, do you want to look at what Robb and I have been working on all morning? Since we don't have the *Proud Mary* and Orli Covitz to pick up the slack, we refactored our basic routes. We have a suggestion, if you'd like to—"

Rlinda waved a hand. "Not at all, girl. If I didn't trust you two to make those decisions, I would never have given you control of my company. And if I wanted to do the work myself, why would I have hired you in the first place?"

Lifting one of the covers, she bent over to sniff a glistening brownish tangle. She picked up a serving fork and twirled the dish. Tasia thought it looked like some tropical bird's nest. "We're adding this to the menus of my restaurants—a spiroid fungus harvested from the trees on Dremen, naturally savory with a distinctive nutty flavor. It goes particularly well with chili oil." She couldn't resist scooping up a few strands that squirmed of their own volition. She slurped, smacked her lips. "Terry in particular will like this." She gave a snort. "If he ever gets here."

Rlinda had been a successful trader, flying the *Voracious Curiosity* during the Elemental War; afterward, King Peter had chosen her as the Confederation's first trade minister, but in her retirement, she was much more interested in her avocation of cooking. She ran gourmet restaurants on Earth, Relleker, and Theroc.

In her stead, Tasia and Robb managed Kett Shipping, and profits were higher than ever, thanks to the exclusive ekti-X trading arrangement with Iswander Industries. As she thought of that, she couldn't help but be reminded of how Xander and Terry had gotten themselves bullied at Ulio Station. Iswander Industries produced so much stardrive fuel that it required five different vessels from Kett Shipping just to deliver and distribute it all, but Xander and Terry were the only direct liaisons with Elisa Enturi, and no one knew where the stardrive fuel was coming from. Kett Shipping remained ignorant, on purpose—none of their business.

Just as they had done with Aldo Cerf and his horrendous "medical supplies." Her stomach knotted at the comparison. *What else don't we know about our cargo?*

As if her thoughts had summoned the two young men, Xander and Terry appeared at the door. "Sorry we're late," Xander said, his voice overlapping with Terry's happy exclamation. "That smells delicious!"

"And we brought a special guest," Xander said with a grin. They came in with a clean and polished compy strutting beside them. Wearing his antigrav belt, Terry held the small compy's shoulder, which was just the right height to give him balance. "OK, fully repaired and ready to get back to work. Good as new."

The compy said in his pleasant synthesized voice, "I apologize for being out of commission. The damage inflicted upon me was more severe than the engineers originally thought. I am much better now, though."

Terry added, "We also had the compy engineers include reinforced shielding and hardened circuits to protect him if he ever gets into a similar situation."

Xander waved his hand, minimizing. "There won't be any similar situation. That was an anomaly. Aaron Duquesne is a hothead and a bully, and we'll be more alert from now on." His voice grew quieter, more insistent, as if promising the compy. "It won't happen again. We'll be more careful."

Robb was concerned. "I've also had increased armaments installed on the *Verne* before you go back out. You know how valuable ekti-X is."

Tasia added, "And maybe I should take you both out on more defensive flying lessons so you can learn reckless maneuvers that could save your lives if you're under attack."

"Don't go overboard, Mother," Xander said.

She crossed her arms over her chest. "My reaction is perfectly appropriate, considering what happened."

Meanwhile, Rlinda Kett busied herself serving large plates for the five of them, spiroid-fungus noodles, shellfish-and-insect skewers, and a separate bowl with a haystack of jellied stems with a sweet sauce for dessert. She called to the compy, "Here, OK—if you're repaired, then make yourself useful."

"That is certainly within my capabilities, Rlinda Kett." OK carried the first plate to Robb, who cleared a spot for eating on the projection desk.

As she prepared the second plate, Rlinda said, "It's none of my business anymore, but I did my share of dangerous runs, delivered cargo through blockades, and got into a lot of trouble." She tapped the spoon on a plate and handed the serving to Xander without waiting for OK to return. The compy seemed disappointed as he held out his polymer hands for the third plate. "Your deal for distributing ekti-X is a huge boon to our company, and there's absolutely no question about the profits. The *Verne* is my highest-earning vessel in Kett Shipping—and you're my youngest pilots, so you can be proud of yourselves." Her voice became sterner. "But don't be so damned naïve. Plenty of people would kill—and I mean that literally—to learn where the hell ekti-X comes from."

Tasia added, "I went to a Roamer convocation on Newstation, and that's all the clans were talking about. Skyminer families are in an uproar, afraid they're going bankrupt. Nobody knows where to find Lee Iswander, but ekti-X keeps pouring in." She frowned more deeply. "It does raise a lot of questions. What is his source of the stardrive fuel? Is it some kind of illicit operation?"

Xander sounded defensive. "I don't know, and I want to keep it that way. I can't reveal answers that I don't have."

"Won't stop someone from trying to find out," Robb said. "And by the time they're convinced you don't know the answer, you might be in worse shape than OK was when you brought him back here."

"I am completely repaired now," the compy said as he brought Tasia her plate. The food did indeed smell delicious, but the thought of someone wanting to hurt her son had dampened Tasia's appetite.

"Not knowing has its own dangers, too. Look at the debacle on Dremen with the 'medical treatments,' " Tasia said. "Shizz! We've done some digging and hit only dead ends. Best we can determine is that Aldo Cerf operates outside of the Confederation on one of the unallied worlds. Nothing we can do about it—except turn down his business."

Rlinda huffed. "We're a shipping company. We have a right to know the source of what we're transporting. Period. Whether it's an illicit medical treatment that kills people—or ekti-X. We can't just turn a blind eye, pretend it fell off a truck somewhere, and sell it. It's for our own peace of mind, if nothing else."

Robb shook his head. "We were there during Iswander's disaster on Sheol. Who knows what sort of operation he's using now to produce that stardrive fuel? He's entitled to his proprietary information, but we're entitled to know that we're not inadvertently involved in something illegal."

Terry shook his head. "We can ask, but Elisa will never divulge anything. It's closely held knowledge. If Lee Iswander has an ekti-production process that nobody else knows, why should he reveal it—even to us?" He took several bites, exclaiming with delight at the taste.

Xander added, "With the way the Roamer clans treated him after Sheol, I can imagine he wouldn't be in a sharing mood." He finished his main course and tried the sticky, caramelized stems.

"We have no interest in getting into ekti production or stepping on his business. We're not Iswander's competition," Robb said. "But what if he's doing something illegal or underhanded? By acting as his distributors, Kett Shipping would be an accomplice."

"In my experience, if something seems too good to be true, it usually is." Satisfied, Rlinda served herself and ate standing up while holding the plate in one hand. "Maybe we need to find the answers on our own."

CHAPTER

24

ORLI COVITZ

The regular trader was due to arrive at the Ikbir colony that day, and it was the first bit of excitement Orli had seen since coming here with Garrison and Seth. Living in the colony had quickly settled into a routine, even though she did enjoy the warm, calm times with Garrison.

Although the people here didn't depend on outside trade for their survival, they still looked forward to seeing what the commercial ship brought. While automated agricultural machinery continued to till the outlying fields, the workers had started to gather around the cleared landing field. Waiting. It was like a festival day.

Garrison had gone to monitor the spaceport systems in anticipation of the trader's arrival, but Orli worked at home. The Domestic compy MO busied herself cleaning, scrubbing, dusting, sterilizing, and polishing until the dwelling could have been used for medical research. MO was obsessive about her duties, and the Ikbir colonists were happy to have her move from home to home.

The Domestic compy emitted a synthesized hum as she went about her work, and Orli decided to head out before she left a fingerprint somewhere and earned herself a scolding from the compy. She decided to be with Garrison, who would appreciate her help.

DD waited for her at the door, apparently eager. "Shall we watch the ship land, Orli? Seth Reeves will join us."

"Let's make it an outing, then." She turned to the Domestic compy. "MO, when you're finished, you can move on to the next house."

"I will be here for several hours yet, Orli Covitz, in order to do a good job."

"You do that. We're going to watch the trader land."

Seth joined them outside of the dwelling, and they all set off. "Shouldn't you be in school?" she asked.

"Classes canceled," he said. "Due to the trader's arrival, but I'd rather be with DD anyway. Besides, I already know what they're talking about in school—did that years ago. And the other kids don't like me."

Orli gave him an indulgent smile. "I suppose being raised as a Roamer, you had to learn the basics from an early age."

"I wish I could go back to Academ."

Orli had heard the boy say the same thing several times. "That's where you belong." Seth had a great deal of talent, and he needed someplace where he could reach his potential.

Orli had been thinking of leaving Ikbir as well, and she knew the thought had crossed Garrison's mind. They had laughed when they each suggested the same thing in a languid conversation just before drifting off to sleep. "I thought I wanted to put down roots, but I don't really want to become a tree," Orli said.

Lying beside Orli, Garrison had stroked her short, dust-mop hair. "And Roamers aren't meant to keep their feet on the ground for very long. It might be time to move on."

Orli pondered the places she had seen, the adventures she'd experienced, and she wanted to do something more important with herself. She was too intelligent just to curl up on Ikbir in safe retirement. The people here were satisfied with nothing more than getting through one day after another.

On the landing field, Garrison's ship sat out in the open next to several rickety hangars, storage warehouses, and fuel silos. The *Prodigal Son* hadn't been flown in weeks. Six local flyers were parked haphazardly in the landing area, scout ships and transport vessels to fly across the flat continent, though few of the colonists had any reason to venture out there. A restaurant owner had set up a food stand outside the spaceport to serve the people waiting for the trader to arrive.

Even though they didn't know what would be on the cargo manifest, the colonists were already compiling unrealistic wish lists. They kept looking into the sky, hoping for any sign of the ship. Though

Orli knew a few of their names, most of the people remained strangers to her.

With its small population, Ikbir was not a highly profitable run, but Kett Shipping required that even the outlying routes had to be serviced. Rlinda Kett had seen enough struggling colonies stranded during the Elemental War, and after a hugely successful career, she had priorities beyond mere profit. It was one of the reasons Orli liked her so much.

That reminded her that she needed to go back to talk with Rlinda face-to-face after the disaster that cost her the *Proud Mary*. Orli couldn't just hide here on Ikbir; maybe she should suggest that Garrison take her on a trip to Earth.

"Is it time yet? When is the ship going to land?" Seth asked DD.

"We are within an hour of the formally scheduled arrival time, but accuracy on such long journeys cannot be guaranteed."

One of the Ikbir farmers frowned at DD's comment. "He'll be on time. Yoder never lets us down."

Before long, the trader pilot pinged the Ikbir comm tower. "I'm going to need service from your best spaceport mechanics. Where's your main shipyard?"

"Shipyard? How about a cleared field for a landing area? I don't know how much we can help you, Yoder," the comm tower responded. "We don't have any spare parts. Or any qualified starship mechanics, for that matter, though we've got a Roamer who's fairly skilled at repairs."

The pilot transmitted back, "Then we might have a problem. Now be quiet and let me concentrate as I try to land. No guarantees."

The trading ship came down through the sky leaving a black, knotted contrail. The descending ship was tilted off its axis, flying erratically.

Garrison shaded his eyes. "He's lost an engine." Suddenly his expression filled with alarm, and he shouted to the crowd. "Get away from the spaceport! It's going to be a hard landing, and he might not be on target."

Orli picked up the call, repeating the warning, and the colonists backed away, but not quickly enough for her comforts. Garrison signaled for an emergency crew and fire-suppression teams to stand by, just in case. They could hear the cargo ship's engine straining, coughing, and rumbling as Dando Yoder fought to bring the ship down in one piece.

"Is he going to be all right?" Seth asked.

DD said, "I cannot predict."

"He's coming in hard, one way or another." Orli made sure the boy withdrew to a safer distance.

The wobbling ship screeched overhead, swooping close to the spaceport landing area. Smoke poured from its port-side engine—the levitation engine, not the stardrive. Yoder nearly clipped the hangar rooftop before he managed to pull the ship into the air again. The near miss elicited a gasp of dismay from the colonists, who stood right in the potential crash zone, despite Garrison's warnings.

Yoder didn't risk a landing there, though; instead, he flew the ship beyond the town and circled again as his engines struggled. Finally, far enough from the buildings and the people, the ship landed hard, slewing on the freshly plowed dirt behind one of the planting machines. The ship crunched to the ground and slid to a stop. Rooster tails of smoke and dust spewed into the air.

Garrison and Orli ran to the response vehicles being loaded up. "DD, watch Seth!" she called back, and the compy did exactly that, *watching* as the boy jumped aboard with his father. No one decided to argue.

The vehicles raced across the open terrain, and when they arrived at the crashed ship, they saw an old bearded trader in a scuffed jumpsuit crawling out of the access hatch. He brushed himself off. Colonists doused the smoky engines with fire-suppression foam, but Yoder just stood with his hands on his hips. Tears were running down his face as he looked at the wreck. "What a mess! How am I ever going to get this fixed?"

"Not with the facilities we have here," Orli said.

Garrison walked along the side of the ship, assessing. "Engine's gone, hull is split open, looks like the lower chamber has been crushed."

"That was half my cargo," Yoder said.

"We'll salvage what we can," said Garrison.

"But the colony needed those supplies," cried one of the farmers. "We were expecting twelve new power blocks."

Yoder wiped at his eyes. "Sorry. The engine alarm sounded as soon as I hit the atmosphere, and then I was past the point of no return. Couldn't make it back to orbit and couldn't land safely." He sniffled. "Doesn't look like my ship's going anywhere."

"Not soon," Orli said.

The Ikbir colonists looked shell-shocked. They were cut off; they didn't even have a green priest, so they could not request new supplies or the repair components Yoder's ship needed.

Garrison glanced at Orli and then at his son, and they all seemed to be thinking the same thing. "I've got a ship. I could take the *Prodigal Son* to Newstation and dispatch a repair crew back here, have them bring a cargo of specific items Ikbir needs."

Yoder sat heavily on a pile of stirred-up dirt from the crash. "Be my guest. This run has never made me any money, and now it just cost a bunch. I'd appreciate it if you could help me out."

"To Newstation?" Seth brightened. "Can I come along? Can I go back to Academ?"

Orli shot a glance at Garrison, knowing they wouldn't need to discuss it at all. She stood beside him. "Yes, I think we should go."

CHAPTER

25

GENERAL NALANI KEAH

When the *Kutuzov* and three Manta cruisers entered orbit around Theroc, General Keah let out a whistle. "That looks like a parade."

Verdani battleships formed a ring of thorns, gigantic tree vessels piloted by green priests who had sacrificed themselves by fusing into the heartwood. Seven Solar Navy warliners—of course, because Ildirans always did things in groups of seven—looked like fighting fish with extended solar sails. By contrast, her CDF Juggernaut and Mantas looked downright plain. Nevertheless, Keah had come to give her report to the King and Queen.

After the disastrous explosion at Dr. Krieger's sun-bomb factory, she had no choice but to present a realistic assessment of the situation. The CDF was not as prepared as she would have liked, though they were trying. General Keah was not one to avoid ruffling feathers when a cold dose of honesty was required, but a little bit of optimism often smoothed difficult decisions. The loss of the weapons facility and its crew was a severe setback, and production of the new sun bombs had fallen far behind schedule, but Keah was convinced the CDF would catch up. The real question was whether they could do so before the Shana Rei attacked again. . . .

The gigantic fungus-reef city and ground-level structures were filled with government functionaries, green priests, Theron settlers, Confederation trade representatives, even members of the Ildiran bureaucrat kith there on business.

After Keah arrived, she saw several strange, smooth-skinned humanoid creatures. She had received reports about the Gardeners, alien refugees from the Shana Rei who sought sanctuary on the worldforest planet. She decided to ask to debrief the Onthos. Even though they had lost everything to the creatures of darkness, they might have insights to offer. . . .

When the General entered the main throne room, King Peter and Queen Estarra were sitting at a conference table in deep discussions with Mage-Imperator Jora'h and his green priest consort. A potted treeling rested in the center of the table, close enough for Nira to touch. Alas, Keah didn't see Adar Zan'nh. She and the Solar Navy commander had a friendly rivalry.

As she entered, Peter indicated one of the empty chairs. The General handed out briefing packets and nodded toward the Mage-Imperator. "I have a full report on our war preparations. With the generous assistance of the Solar Navy, we are arming the CDF with Ildiran-designed laser cannons and sun bombs." Keah took a seat, put her elbows on the table. "Our human scientists attempted to make improvements on the original designs, with mixed results."

"We know the sun bombs work," Queen Estarra said. "The few prototypes were effective against the Shana Rei nightshade."

Keah said, "It's impressive technology, no doubt about that, but one of our scientists was trying to increase the yield." She cleared her throat, looked away. "There was an unfortunate setback, but we have rectified the error. We should be back on track soon."

"I have no doubt that the Shana Rei will attack again," Peter said. "We don't know where they are or what motivates them."

Recalling the engagement at Plumas, Keah said, "Apparently, their motive is to destroy *everything*—all sentience, all life, maybe even the cosmos itself." She couldn't help her sarcasm. "Personally, I think they're overly ambitious."

Keah stacked her briefing materials and looked at Peter and Estarra. "I'm curious about these Gardeners, though. I'd like to get a full report on what they know firsthand. Is it true that even the worldforest mind doesn't remember them?"

"Vague recollections, but no details—it's like amnesia," Nira said. "But we can rely on Onthos memories and legends, which they're adding to the worldforest mind. Right now, the Gardeners are telling their stories to the green priests and to the trees. That should fill many of the gaps in the forest memory."

One of the gray-skinned creatures appeared at the throne room, as if summoned. "General Nalani Keah, I am Ohro. I speak for the Gardeners and for our race's past."

Keah raised her eyebrows. "How did you know I wanted to talk with you?" So close, the alien had an odd, fresh smell, like newly sawn wood.

"I was listening through the trees. Whatever any tree hears, we hear."

General Keah had first learned of the unexpected alien race when an isolationist Roamer clan had found an ancient derelict city in space—which was contaminated by a highly virulent plague. Getting down to business, Keah asked Ohro, "How many other space cities do you have out there? They could be of strategic importance. Should we be looking for more?"

"There was only one," Ohro said. "When the Shana Rei engulfed our home star system and our own worldforest, we scattered among other planets, barely surviving. Later, the Klikiss attacked us and drove us farther out. That city was a last refuge for some, but the Onthos who withdrew there were infected with a Klikiss disease. They are all dead now, and the city is gone." The alien lowered his voice.

Keah was anxious to get as much information as possible, however. "Then what about your homeworld? I'd like to see what's left of it, maybe understand how the Shana Rei attack." She felt frustrated, remembering how the shadows and their black robots had defeated them again and again. "We're grasping at straws here."

Nira touched the finely scaled bark of the nearby potted treeling. "If there are any remnants of your worldforest, even scraps of fossilized wood, they may contain a few specks of memory that a green priest can use."

Ohro shook his head, blinked his large black eyes. "The planet is dead. Our solar system is dead. Our scattered colonies are dead. Our space city is dead." An edge of anger and terror cut the alien's words, and he lifted his smooth fingers toward the ceiling of the throne chamber. "Theroc is all we have left. If there are times of peace ever again, the Onthos may reproduce. If we survive."

"How do we find your star system?" Keah asked. "I'll send an expedition there."

The strange creature paused, contemplating, then picked up the

General's datapad and accessed the screen. Keah was surprised the alien seemed so facile with CDF technology, but then she realized that telink would let the Onthos know anything a green priest knew.

Ohro said, "I can convert our astronomical knowledge into your parameters, your numerical systems." His smooth fingers skittered over the surface; then he calculated with a flourish before handing the pad back. "These are the exact coordinates of our original home system."

Keah's heart leapt. "Thanks, that's very important data!" She compared the coordinates with detailed Ildiran starmaps of the Spiral Arm. Frowning, she ran the analysis again, then glanced up Ohro. "You must have made a mistake. There's no star system at these coordinates, not even on the highest-res maps."

Ohro gave a solemn nod. "That is because our star is no longer there. The Shana Rei have hidden it."

CHAPTER

26

TOM ROM

The Pergamus researchers and technicians, the cutting-edge laboratory facilities, the mercenary security forces, not to mention Tom Rom's dangerous specimen-gathering missions, caused a constant drain on Zoe's financial resources. Fortunately, she had unlimited, albeit accidental, wealth discovered in the burned-out lichentree forests on Vaconda. A single clean prisdiamond would pay an average person's expenses for a year, and Tom Rom could retrieve cargo loads of the gems at a time. . . .

He returned from an uneventful solo mission to Vaconda, where Zoe had spent the first half of her life, after her parents adopted her from a few-questions-asked service on a seedy planet called Rakkem. Adam and Evelyn Alakis had staked their claim on uninhabited Vaconda, hoping to find new pharmaceuticals or marvels of natural science in the exotic wilderness.

When Zoe was just a child, Tom Rom had found his way there, working as one of the only Alakis employees after Evelyn was killed in a flyer crash. Other workers came and went quickly, unable to tolerate the lichentree stink, the burbling and aggressive slime molds, the thick spore dust that blew through the air. But Tom Rom had remained for years—always sticking close to Zoe.

He had gone to Vaconda with his own purpose, which he did not reveal; it had taken him years to track down where Zoe was taken after being born in a baby mill on Rakkem. He needed to be beside her, and he served Adam Alakis as a loyal worker, a bastion of strength and security. He stayed with Zoe during her father's years of degeneration due to Heidegger's Syndrome. Tom Rom never lost sight of the fact that Zoe could have been his own daughter. . . .

He still had work to do, and Zoe needed him more than ever.

After he liquidated his new cargo load of prisdiamonds at Ulio Station, he transferred the money to ten different accounts, not only making deposits in Confederation financial strongholds and Roamer clan banks, but also investing in long-term securities, just in case the prisdiamonds were ever depleted. He made sure that Zoe would never want for anything.

Then he flew back to Pergamus, on schedule. She tended to worry overmuch whenever he was late, and she looked very relieved when he arrived. Though walled off from her sterile central habitat, Tom Rom chatted with her over the comm.

His skin tingled from the first two levels of decontamination he had passed through just to get this close to Zoe, but he wouldn't dare go farther. Too much risk. Vaconda was rife with disease microorganisms, and the polyglot stew of humanity on Ulio Station probably exchanged just as many diseases among themselves. If Tom Rom ever brought a sickness here that managed to infect Zoe, he would walk out into the poisonous Pergamus atmosphere, unable to live with himself.

Now he studied her intense face on the screen. No, Zoe had none of his features, and her skin tone was all wrong, but he did detect the hints of another face he knew well. Muriel . . . a woman who had been special to Tom Rom once, a woman who had loved him, tricked him, turned into a monster. He could see a ghost of her mother whenever he looked at Zoe, but he did not hold it against her. . . .

He straightened in front of the screen. Formal and to the point, he reported, "I transmitted the records of my recent mission. With the new prisdiamonds, our accounts are flush."

Zoe never paid attention to money. Instead, she said, "I've been looking over the Ildiran genetic records you acquired from that facility on Kuivahr. All the misbreeds . . . very interesting data, quite different from anything else we have. That halfbreed researcher is quite talented. Tamo'l has developed admirable insights."

"I thought it worthwhile for you to have the data, although I don't see yet how it can be useful to the Pergamus work," he said.

"One day we might expand our collection to include specimens of Ildiran diseases." Zoe allowed herself a smile, then seemed troubled.

"Alas, there's an infinite number of deadly diseases that strike the human race. I will focus on them for now."

That was the opening he'd been looking for. "I wanted to bring something to your attention. Perhaps a new task for Pergamus."

Zoe kept herself surrounded by numerous screens and reports as she sifted databases for interesting outbreaks in the Spiral Arm. "What is it?"

"Nine days ago, Prince Reynald collapsed unexpectedly on Theroc. The report was kept quiet, but the King and Queen are understandably distraught. His mysterious disease is progressing more rapidly than expected."

Zoe showed little interest. "They already sent out a plea for a cure. It is an interesting disease, but I haven't given it priority. Too rare to bother with."

"Heidegger's was rare." Tom Rom said carefully, "Prince Reynald is an important person. The King and Queen could be vital allies, should we ever need their help—and dangerous enemies otherwise. If we devoted Pergamus researchers to searching for a cure, we might easily accomplish what less impressive Confederation teams cannot. Some time ago, Dr. Paolus sold us the Prince's entire genetic map and complete records of his confidential tests on the disease. We have everything we need."

Zoe frowned. "Do you think I should assign a team? Any cure we find would belong to me, not to Prince Reynald."

That had always been Zoe's attitude. Compassion did not penetrate the invisible scars within her. She had suffered much herself after the two of them left Vaconda behind. When she had needed help, when her father had died the long tragic death of Heidegger's, and later when she herself became gravely ill, all the competing researchers had been heartless.

"King Peter and Queen Estarra would be dangerous, and unnecessary enemies to make."

"Pergamus is not part of the Confederation. They can't demand that I find a cure, so why would they become enemies? What do I care about them and their dying son?"

Tom Rom had accepted her hard-line position, letting Zoe make her own decisions, but now he pressed. "Zoe . . . if *I* were ill and another research facility had an effective treatment, wouldn't you want them to provide it for me?"

Her hard expression didn't change. "It doesn't matter what I'd want. People wouldn't help us, even in a desperate situation. It's happened time and again." She seemed anxious to be reminded about her past, and now she sounded defensive. "We both know that Pergamus would do a better job than any other research facility. When you had the Onthos plague, *our* facilities and *our* researchers found the answer. For me." Her voice hitched. "I was afraid you would die . . . but we saved you. You're alive."

"I was also afraid I would die," Tom Rom said. "But what I fear most is leaving you behind and unprotected."

Tears appeared in her dark eyes, and she spoke quickly. "All right, I'll assign a team to study the Prince's disease. I can't promise we'll find anything." She blanked the screen so he would not see her cry.

Tom Rom swallowed. He couldn't help feeling protective. After all, she could have been his daughter. . . .

After the death of her father, when Zoe angrily wanted to abandon Vaconda and all remnants of her past life, Tom Rom took her from planet to planet. It was the last year of the Elemental War, but where the two of them went, such galactic concerns were secondary.

He had Zoe. He protected her. And they lived.

Eventually, Zoe realized everything he had done for her, how he had been there for most of her life. In amazement she looked at him. "Why do you do this for me?"

"Because you're important. Important to me."

"But *why?* Why am I so special to you?"

He had avoided answering such questions for so many years that she obviously didn't expect him to answer. In her sad confusion, though, this lost twenty-year-old had made a connection in her mind. "Wait . . . I'm adopted, and you showed up years later . . . and you never left Vaconda. What is it about me? What connection do we have?" She looked at him in disbelief. "I thought you might be my real father, but I used our lab facilities, ran genetic tests and comparisons. You're no relation to me at all."

"No, but you've touched on the reason," he finally answered, because he would never lie to her. "I did have a daughter once, about a year before you were born." He faced her with a blank expression, though his emotions and his revelations were ready to explode inside him. "You have the same mother. I knew her very well, and she was a beautiful woman . . . *then*." He paused to let that sink in. "Her name was Muriel. I met her on Rakkem."

"Then we should go there," Zoe said. "Maybe we can find her, if she's still alive."

His expression darkened. "You would not want that. Rakkem is a contaminated, slimy underworld full of treacherous people and unsavory biological businesses."

"Then . . . why were you there?"

"Because I go to places like that. Sometimes it is necessary." Tom Rom felt a chill down his spine. "Muriel knew how to make herself beautiful, but it was all part of a trap."

"Was she a prostitute?" Zoe's tone held no judgment. She cared so much for Tom Rom that she just wanted to understand.

"Far worse than that. We were together, and I thought we were in love. I was excited when I learned we were going to have a baby. A daughter . . . but then Muriel disappeared. Someone on Rakkem told her the value of an infant, and she vanished into a high-security baby factory."

"For what purpose? For adoption?"

He felt the ice growing inside him, but he had to get through this. "Because babies are pristine, uncontaminated. Valuable flesh. And Muriel sold her baby—*our daughter*—on the Rakkem black market, for her organs. Stripped down, every piece harvested, even down to her skin, which was used for grafts."

Somehow, he kept talking, his voice as cold and heavy as frozen lead. "I found out afterward, after it was too late. And I couldn't get to her in time." He felt full of bile, but he forced himself to focus. "After she sold our baby for spare parts, Muriel volunteered to become a factory womb. Her business became getting pregnant, artificially inseminated. Her body was saturated with hormones that kept her constantly fertile, and she often carried multiple pregnancies at the same time, during different stages."

Zoe listened in disgust.

"Muriel gave birth to you shortly after I found out what she had done. But you were lucky, Zoe. Adam and Evelyn Alakis paid more to adopt you than your infant body was worth as a biological sample. Just an accident of timing."

Zoe wavered, then she bent over and retched.

Tom Rom wanted to comfort her, but he didn't know how. "I couldn't get to Muriel, and it was too late for my daughter, but I hacked into some records on Rakkem. I learned that you were the only one of Muriel's babies still alive. You are not my daughter, but I tracked you down on Vaconda, because I wanted to be close. That is why I won't leave you."

Fighting against her usual personal distance, young Zoe clung to him, and he held her in return. As he did so, he could sense her growing steely hard inside.

CHAPTER

27

LEE ISWANDER

When Iswander flew his son to Newstation, where he would go to school at Academ, he felt an odd combination of admiration and resentment. The new Roamer government center, built after the destruction of the former clan capital of Rendezvous, was an old-fashioned wheel: a central hub with radiating spokes, an outer ring, and numerous satellite docks. A commotion of clan ships came in to do business, set up trade agreements, and exchange goods from hundreds of independent operations across the Spiral Arm.

The immense complex orbited over a mostly empty planet, Auridia, which was noteworthy only in that it contained a Klikiss transportal wall and a small outpost of admin shacks and a backwater staff who monitored the dropoff point for those who used the interdimensional travel node. But Roamers preferred to fly ships from place to place, and the variety of vessels around Newstation was evident as spacecraft jockeyed for position at the available docking points. Individualistic Roamers liked to make their ships look distinctive. Therefore many of the vessels sported garishly colored hulls, eccentric affectations, and gaudy decorations that served no purpose.

Iswander's personal yacht was a tasteful high-end model, professional-looking. As he docked next to a bulbous orange-painted horror on which some Roamer had stenciled the names of his children, Iswander gave his son a tight-lipped frown. "Primary lesson of business, Arden. In order to be treated as a professional, you must *act* professional and *appear to be* professional. If you don't take yourself seriously, you can't expect potential trading partners to do so."

The young man looked at the strange orange monstrosity. "But what about them?"

"Would you want to do business with *that*? They better have something indispensable to sell."

"But we do. Everyone wants our ekti-X."

Iswander hadn't expected his son to dispute such an obvious business lesson. "Even if someone can get away with being eccentric, there's no reason not to conduct business properly. We have to build and maintain our reputation. Too often, the clans have been reckless, unruly, and unreliable. Now that we're all part of the Confederation, I'd like to improve our standard practices."

If he had been elected Speaker of the clans, Iswander could already have implemented that, but his fellow Roamers had shunned him because of an accident on Sheol. . . . As he looked at Newstation, he regretted that this place was not his seat of power now, that the clans had chosen a lackluster glad-hander over a true businessman.

They would learn their lesson soon enough. After seeing the uninspired leadership of Sam Ricks, they would realize their mistake, and Iswander was already rebuilding his reputation. He would have his chance; he knew it.

As he docked the yacht, paying for a VIP bay in the rotating torus, Arden looked out the windowport at the sparkling comet that orbited alongside the gigantic station. The comet was hollowed out, turned into a special school for the children of all Roamer clans. The boy was uneasy and would have preferred remaining behind at the extraction yard, being taught by the green priest. "Have we given up all hope that Aelin will get better and be my tutor again?"

"You need formal instruction, and I'm afraid the poor green priest is a lost cause," Iswander said. "Academ is the right place for you at this point in your life." He had made arrangements with Jess Tamblyn and Cesca Peroni to take Arden as a student, and they had done so without qualms.

"I got into fights last time defending you," Arden mumbled.

So that was the reason for his reticence. Iswander had already made inquiries, even paid a premium for additional surveillance and security for his son, concerned that Arden might be a target for kidnapping. Other than that, he was sure Arden could handle himself.

"You're stronger than they are—you're an Iswander. Besides, our situation is quite different now, and they will recognize that. The Roamer clans need me again."

After he landed inside the bay, station techs came forward to check the stardrive engines and to refuel, probably with his own ekti-X. He made a point of thanking them profusely, something he had learned from his campaign to become Speaker. He had relied on his impressive professional credentials rather than personal connections and friendships, and people often made important decisions based on illogical priorities. He would not make that error again. He would invest the effort to establish goodwill and personal contacts.

Now that he had great wealth from ekti-X, not only did he rent a VIP berth for his yacht, he sent out notices to the seventeen drinking establishments around Newstation and quietly paid every patron's bill for the next hour with a simple note, "Thank you for your business—Iswander Industries."

He also still had the large database—delivered to him by a plague-stricken Orli Covitz—filled with clan Reeves medical records, farewell messages, and files on the Onthos race from the derelict space city. Knowing it would make an impact, he sent out feelers to see how much interest there might be in the information. Orli had wanted the information to be shared, and he would do so; but when the Roamers learned that there would be no salvage from the now-destroyed alien city, they weren't interested. Still, he made the overture.

Lee Iswander was ready to be treated as a well-respected member of the community. He had earned that consideration, after becoming a major supplier of stardrive fuel. Even though he had earned his new prominence, the clans still expected him to *buy* additional goodwill. Nevertheless, he took the time to make sure Arden watched and understood what he was doing, and why.

Iswander secured a lavish suite for the two of them, and when he learned that a clan business meeting was taking place in the convocation chamber, he told Arden to get changed. They both went to sit in the gallery—not asking to address the representatives, just to be seen and to listen.

The gathering was a casual affair, and clan representatives lounged in rows of seats that ran up the curved wall. Iswander identified the spot traditionally reserved for his clan, though the benches had remained unoccupied for some time. As he and Arden entered, the discussions quieted. Iswander felt the eyes looking at him and his son, but he stood straight-backed and drank it in.

Speaker Ricks sat back in an upholstered chair, wearing an embroidered family jumpsuit, chatting with two men who sat nearby while an earnest clan representative addressed the gathering. Ricks wasn't paying any attention to what he was saying.

Iswander listened, though. The clan representative had secured water rights on frozen moons and now requested a formal license to provide new pumping stations in several systems. "Within five years we can fill the gap created by the loss of the clan Tamblyn operations on Plumas."

Several Roamers in the audience were paying close attention as well. One beefy woman objected to the water-rights proposal, but it soon became clear that she had no justifiable complaint, merely wanted to set up competing operations of her own. Sam Ricks granted the license without further discussion. Iswander didn't think the Speaker was being decisive, just that he had been bribed beforehand.

A squall of requests for the podium came in, and clan members—all of them traditional ekti skyminers—stepped forward, wanting to speak their piece. Iswander wasn't surprised they would form a voting block against him, but there was really nothing they could do to stop his work.

"Since Lee Iswander has graced us with his presence, he can answer questions," said Aaron Duquesne, an annoyed-looking son of a clan that had two skymines on Belliros. "He's been flaunting his ekti-X, and his reckless actions are throwing the clans into turmoil, forcing some of us into bankruptcy. Our skymines can't compete with his ekti-X. Nobody can."

Duquesne glowered at him, but Iswander remained seated in the gallery, responding only with a cool smile. "And you would like . . . what exactly? For me to apologize because I'm successful? Because I'm selling stardrive fuel for a lower price than you do? I don't hear any complaints from the customers."

"We want regulations and tariffs on ekti-X, subsidies for those of us who have invested fortunes in cloud-harvesting operations. It's a hazardous business. We've taken the risks."

Six representatives from other traditional skymining clans agreed. One even commented loudly and sarcastically, "You're just like the Big Goose! We don't want businessmen like that."

Another grumbled, "You've forgotten that you're a Roamer, Lee Iswander."

Now Iswander rose to his feet and placed a paternal hand on Arden's shoulder. He spoke calmly but loudly. "Excuse me? I thought this was a *Roamer* clan gathering, not a nursery full of whining children." He held the silence for a moment, remembering when blustery Olaf Reeves had heaped scorn on Iswander Industries for their business practices and then complained about how the clans had become tainted. Well, that old fool and his clan had all died alone out in space; Iswander had the database and the farewell messages to prove it.

He continued, "Roamers have learned how to survive in the harshest environments. We pride ourselves on our ability to find miraculous solutions under the direst of conditions. We take risks. We innovate. We refuse to believe that something cannot be done simply because it's never been done before."

He gave them all a withering glare. "Who has forgotten how to be a Roamer? Iswander Industries made gigantic investments and took huge risks, again and again—some of them worked, and some of them didn't. Now, because I've discovered a profitable new way to harvest ekti, you want to take that from me? You want the Confederation to hold your hand and level the playing field so you don't have to innovate?"

Arden rose to his feet to stand firmly at his side, making him proud. The clan members were listening, but as he studied their expressions, he still felt that they didn't respect him, that they considered him an outsider—and that made him angrier still. He placed Arden in front of him. "I brought my son here to be trained at Academ, but you make me wonder what the Roamers will teach him. Have the clans lost their against-all-odds attitude? Have you lost your vision?"

He sniffed, then continued. "Yes, I'm selling a lot of stardrive fuel, and I am making more profits than your outdated and inefficient operations—*because I figured out a better way to do it.* I lost everything on Sheol, as you damn well know! But I followed my Guiding Star." He shook his head. "If you can't deal with hardships, tough competition, and difficult problems, then you're not Roamers at all." He looked directly at Aaron Duquesne. "If you want to sell more ekti, *innovate*! Come up with a new way." He nudged his son, and the two of them headed out of the chamber. "Like I did."

CHAPTER 28

DEL KELLUM

Del was going to miss his spunky granddaughter, and he had even grown fond of the studious Howard Rohandas. More important, he envied them their opportunity to study at Fireheart Station. The energy-membrane farms, the exotic-materials harvesting, the power-block manufacture—that was the epitome of what Roamers had once been.

After they got settled in the central Fireheart complex tucked in a quiet backwater of the roaring nebula gases, Del called the station manager. As a former Speaker of the clans, Del knew everyone, and Station Chief Beren Alu still owed him a few favors. Del hoped the man remembered that.

Del took Shareen and Howard up to deck six to find the manager, only to discover that Alu's office was dark and cluttered, apparently dedicated to storage more than administration.

"Doesn't look like he ever even uses his office," said Shareen. "What kind of manager is that?"

Del hooked his thumbs at his waist. "Take it as a good sign, by damn. That means he's out doing productive work, rather than playing with red tape."

A small skinny man in his mid-fifties moved briskly down the metal-walled corridor. He had shoulder-length hair and a drooping gray mustache that resembled a pair of rodent tails on either side of his mouth. Though he looked harried, Beren Alu managed a grin. "Del Kellum, I hear you brought me a pair of competent employees who'll work for free!"

"You're in charge of getting your own workers, Beren. My granddaughter and her friend want to serve as apprentices to Kotto."

"Everyone wants to serve as apprentices to Kotto, but he hasn't accepted anybody before."

"We'll be good workers," Shareen said. "Best he's ever seen."

"And we do appreciate the opportunity, sir," Howard added. "We'll earn our keep."

"Oh, it's not that," Alu said. "Kotto's just a terrible manager, doesn't know what to do with help. He dabbles by himself."

Del patted Shareen on her shoulder. "You two will have to be independent, prove yourselves to Kotto."

"We will, sir," said Howard. "I'm sure Kotto Okiah must have some busywork for us to do."

Alu tossed an unidentifiable wrapped packet onto the desk clutter, which slid and toppled to the deck. He didn't seem to care where it landed. "Come with me. Kotto's doing an orientation lecture for a group of visiting Ildiran scientists. They want to see the keystone stars and the nebula light. It's some religious thing for them."

Del put his beefy hands against Shareen's and Howard's backs. "Let's go, then. Make a good impression."

The skinny station chief guided them down to a docking ring suspended beneath the headquarters complex. Next to an inspection ship, twenty Ildiran scientists stood in a group, all wearing similar alien clothing. An uneasy-looking man in his sixties with tousled hair and squinting eyes—Kotto Okiah—paced as a holographic projection played in the air. It was a standard PR orientation loop in which a well-dressed Beren Alu gave a presentation.

"Here at Fireheart Station, we survive and profit from the worst the universe throws against us. We are Roamers. Our clan history is fraught with accidents and tragedies, as well as daring successes. Turmoil? Hardship? We'll catch it and throw it back in their faces. Fireheart Station epitomizes the Roamer mindset. It is a place where we manufacture and also conduct research. It's a place where we work miracles. Thank you." Alu's face dissipated as the projection ended.

Kotto Okiah gestured at the air, as if glad he didn't have to deliver the basic speech himself. "Well, that gives you the background about this place, though I suspect you already knew most of it. Our most important current project is the Big Ring, my gigantic physics experiment that will reveal fundamental details about the very fabric of space-time itself. We've been building it for five years, but we're reaching the final stages now. So much to do!"

Without waiting for Station Chief Alu to introduce them, Del came forward, extending his hand. "And I've brought two people who can help you out, Kotto. All that work you couldn't get finished, all those prototype projects—here's the brainpower you need."

The scientist took a moment to recognize him. "Del Kellum! I didn't know you were coming here."

"You should have received my request." Del gave a quick sidelong look to Alu, who shrugged. "My granddaughter and her friend are here as your new lab assistants. Geniuses in training, by damn. Put them to work."

Kotto looked around as if harried. "Sorry, I didn't get any request . . . or maybe the message is still in my inbox." He pointed to two compies who stood at the side of the inspection ship. "But I already have assistants. KR and GU have helped me for years."

"You need some fresh blood," Shareen said, and Del smiled. His granddaughter wouldn't take no for an answer. "And we're determined to help you finish all those projects you don't have time to do."

Howard added, "We're really looking forward to this, sir."

Before the scientist could respond, Del added, "And thank you, Kotto—you're doing me a great personal favor. They've both been instructed to impress the hell out of you."

Kotto looked indecisive. Before he could answer, one of the Ildiran visitors interrupted, "Can you please explain more about your Big Ring structure? We intend to build our own light-gathering and concentration apparatus, which may allow us to study or detect the Shana Rei."

Beren Alu gestured toward the ship. "Better yet, we're about to depart on an inspection tour. Let's all go aboard so we can see the Fireheart facilities firsthand."

Unable to find a proper response for the two young assistants being foisted upon him, Kotto seemed glad to let someone else make the decision. "Yes, of course, everyone take seats. I believe the pilot has a schedule."

As the Ildiran visitors filed through the entrance hatch, Howard stepped up to the Roamer scientist. "Shareen and I are very pleased to meet you, sir. We won't let you down."

"Yes, thank you. The ideas just come to me. It's not something that requires a team effort. I'm not really sure . . ."

"Ideas are the easy part," Shareen said with a glint in her eye, "but there's a lot of work to take the germ of an idea to a finished product. Give us a chance." Her voice dropped. "Please."

"Well . . . if Del Kellum vouches for you, then I suppose." Kotto looked as if he wanted nothing more than to hurry back to his own quarters and dabble in peace. "I have quite a backlog. Maybe you can help me clean up the files."

Once they were aboard the spacious inspection ship, the pilot took them out into the sea of ionized gases. The Ildirans pressed their fingers against the windowports, reveling in the bright light from the cluster of hot blue-white stars. "Nothing can be as glorious as Mijistra," said the leader of the Ildirans. "But this comes close. Very close."

Their destination was an enormous ring being constructed edge-on to the blazing central stars. An interlocking grid of superconductors and high-energy accelerator channels made it look like a promise ring for a planetoid. The circumference was nearly complete, with less than twenty-five degrees remaining to close the loop. Suited construction workers and assembly vehicles darted around the ragged ends, building more and more each day.

Del knew this was one of the most expensive research projects the Roamer clans—or the human race—had ever attempted, but Kotto Okiah had achieved so many remarkable successes over the years, saved so many clans, and delivered such enormous profits, they were willing to invest whenever and whatever this man requested. Now, Kotto just stared and said quietly—mostly to himself, but Shareen and Howard both heard him, "This nebula, those stars . . . it's like a masterpiece painted by God himself. The Big Ring will be the grandest experiment in my entire career."

"But, what is it supposed to *do*?" Shareen asked.

Kotto dismissed her question. "It would take me hours to go through the calculations and the physical basis. Very few people can follow it."

"We are your lab assistants," Shareen said. "You'll have to teach us. That's why we're here."

Howard added, "What Shareen means to ask, sir, is what sort of results do you expect? What will happen when the Big Ring is completed and activated?"

Kotto's eyes sparkled with wonder, and he answered in a very quiet voice. "I honestly don't know."

CHAPTER 29

TAMO'L

Death was no stranger to the peaceful sanctuary domes on Kuivahr. The misbreeds had countless chronic medical problems, failing organs, biochemical imbalances, neurological collapses. There were deaths caused by a cascade of bodily failures and deaths for no discernible reason at all. The misbreeds lived with an acute awareness of their mortality—but at least they *lived*.

And Tamo'l lived with them, striving to ensure that their existence was as pain-free and fulfilling as possible. But she didn't always succeed.

Inside the hospice surgical chamber, Tamo'l stood beside the outstretched and hideous form of Vu'ln, whose genes were a mixture of soldier kith, lens kith, and swimmer kith, and the mixture had not turned out well.

On his deathbed now, Vu'ln reached out and clasped Tamo'l's delicate hand. His fingers were stubby, his knuckles swollen, his arm twisted and folded at an unsettling angle because he had an extra set of joints. A vestigial eye that had never opened drooped halfway down his left cheek, twitching as he grimaced. His other two eyes were open and bright with pain . . . or possibly an epiphany. "Thank you for being here, Tamo'l." His voice burbled from too much phlegm caught in a malformed larynx.

"I am here for all of you. You are my brother." She never forgot that she was a mixed breed herself, but many experiments from Dobro had produced offspring that were . . . not viable.

Vu'ln stared up at the polished ceiling of the hospice room that glowed from embedded blazers. "At least I lived for some years."

"Twenty-five years." Tamo'l stroked the patchy skin on the dying man's arm, where tufts of wiry hair sprouted like weeds in random places. "Your spirit is as healthy and vibrant as any. On the plane of the Lightsource, you will shine like anyone else, and there you can be happy among all Ildiran souls." She smiled down at him. "And since I'm part lens kith, I might even be able to see you when you get there."

Shawn Fennis entered the chamber, frowning. Tamo'l knew how to read human emotions, and she saw his heavy sadness now. When his wife Chiar'h came to stand next to him, Fennis slipped an arm around her waist, as if the sight of Vu'ln reminded him of his love for her. Medical kithmen conducted tests, monitored instruments, and watched the failing life signs on the med screens.

Tamo'l leaned closer and whispered, "I wish I knew how to fix you. I have studied and studied, conducted research, gathered data, but I haven't been able to help. I am so very sorry."

Vu'ln squeezed her hand so tightly she thought it was a spasm, but he was simply trying to reassure her. "You helped a great deal. You helped all of us. You will find the ways in which we are all special."

Tamo'l nodded, trying to convince herself. She knew that Vu'ln was feeling calmer, experiencing a hint of euphoria due to the experimental palliative from the kelp distillates that Zhett Kellum and her son had delivered. Although the palliative showed great promise, it would only make the misbreeds' existence tolerable, not heal them.

Tamo'l and her team were the only Ildirans devoting research to the genetic mistakes, and she could not do everything alone. Even though Mage-Imperator Jora'h had granted her the sanctuary domes, now that the Dobro breeding program had been shut down, Ildirans considered the misbreeds a temporary problem that would go away as soon as they all died. In hopes of getting outside help, Tamo'l wondered if she could find a treatment for Prince Reyn's ailment, which would not only make Osira'h happy, but would also bring her misbreeds to the attention of the Confederation. . . .

Nothing could help Vu'ln right now, though. The dying misbreed heaved a breath and his back arched, but he fell back on the sickbed to stare again at the bright lights around him. Behind the transparent dome walls, the seas of Kuivahr swirled. Dangling strands of kelp rippled by like a parade of mourners.

Hearing a shuffle of feet, Tamo'l looked up to the entrance of the hospice chamber and saw other misbreeds crowded in the corridor. They could all feel tremors in the *thism* as Vu'ln held on to the fraying threads of his life. One of the visitors, Har'lc, carried a bottle of kirae, which had been delivered as a gift from the Kellum distillery. Another misbreed, Gor'ka, carried a tray of small crystalline hemispheres used as drinking goblets.

"We are here for Vu'ln," said Har'lc, "to celebrate."

Serving an appreciative drink of the potent and delicious kirae was a tradition someone had copied from the humans. Shawn Fennis had proposed the idea himself, and Tamo'l thought the practice fitting. Har'lc and his companions poured goblets of the greenish liquid and shared them around.

The misbreeds entered the hospice and crowded around their dying comrade. Tamo'l maintained her grip on Vu'ln's hand, and he seemed to understand the celebratory toast around him. Tamo'l sipped, felt the liqueur activate sensitive nerve endings on her tongue.

It might have been her imagination, but the kirae seemed to enhance her connection to the *thism* and to the Lightsource. For a moment, she felt intensely close to Vu'ln, as if the bonds pulled her tight to him and also spun out strands to the gathered misbreeds. Vu'ln seemed to feel that, and it gave him the energy and the release that he needed. The *thism* strands in her mind brightened and sparkled, then unraveled as the dying man stopped trying to hold his biological systems together.

Tamo'l felt Vu'ln slip away, slip free. She saw a fringe of shadows in her mind; then Vu'ln headed toward a bright flash of intense light that vanished—as did her connection with him. She let out a long sigh, in unison with the other misbreeds. Even the medical kithmen paused, looking up from their monitoring devices.

Now there was one less misbreed to care for, and the submerged sanctuary domes felt much, much emptier.

CHAPTER

30

ANTON COLICOS

By the time Anton, Yazra'h, and Muree'n reached the tense village of Shorehaven, the wyvern had struck twice more.

Although Anton felt uncomfortable and exposed, Yazra'h guarded him as if she were protecting the Mage-Imperator himself. At the shore settlement, she stood scanning the skies and the lush worldforest that extended up the coast, while grim-faced Muree'n held her crystal katana, ready to dispatch the monster herself. They looked as if they expected the hunt to take no more than a few hours, and then they could return to the fungus-reef city to accompany the Mage-Imperator back home. Anton suspected Yazra'h wanted the monster hunt to be long and exciting—a battle of wits and strength, rather than an easy kill. For his own part, Anton just wanted to survive.

Shorehaven was quiet, and the expansive sea looked serene, but Anton saw no boats out on the water this time. Yazra'h tossed her coppery hair. "You are ready to chronicle our great hunt, Rememberer Anton?"

"I already have notes and descriptions. Don't worry, this will be a story worthy of inclusion in the Saga of Seven Suns." He just hoped the story didn't have a tragic end.

The villagers mostly stayed inside their dwellings, afraid to venture far. In the forest, nets stretched across the high fronds had snared numerous edible insects, but the nets were clogged, unharvested. Obviously, no one had retrieved the catch for days.

Yazra'h shouted, calling for anyone from the village, "Hello! We have come to kill your wyvern." Anton cringed, afraid her voice would draw the creature.

People watched them from inside the dwellings, but only one man emerged from a central building. The village leader, Tristan Cove, stood straight but his face was haggard. "Did Father Peter and Mother Estarra send you?"

Muree'n stepped in front of Yazra'h. "We sent ourselves. We are part of the Ildiran delegation with Mage-Imperator Jora'h."

Anton cleared his throat. "These two are very skilled warriors, Mr. Cove—don't underestimate them."

As they stood in the main village street, not far from the lakeshore, Anton could hear the waves rippling, but otherwise there was utter silence; he wondered if he would hear the swoop and buzz of wyvern wings.

The village leader said, "So long as the wyvern is dispatched, no one in Shorehaven will care who does it. But we already have a hunter."

Anton was poised to take notes. "Another hunter?"

"Our green priest. Beltrias."

The tall green-skinned man emerged from the thick forest; he had covered his smooth green skin with camouflage markings that interwove with the symbolic tattoos signifying his areas of expertise. A prominent fresh design stood out on his forehead, an arrow with a barbed tip.

"I am more than a green priest now. I am a hunter and a fighter, a stalker of monsters." Beltrias had slipped a longbow over his shoulder, a new weapon made from greenwood; arrows filled a quiver on his back, and he wore a dagger tucked into a woven belt that encircled his waist. In his right hand, he held a throwing spear.

Muree'n ran her gaze up and down his form, but did not seem impressed. "And your experience as a hunter?"

"My experience includes all the human knowledge that is stored within the worldforest," Beltrias said. "I vowed to kill the wyvern, and so I went into the forest and spent days immersed in the verdani mind. I searched all records, all stories, every piece of knowledge about hunting, tracking, killing wild game." His gaze was distant. "I drank it all in, let that knowledge become part of me. Beltrias the green priest entered the thicket, but Beltrias the hunter emerged."

Yazra'h nodded. "That is acceptable. We are happy to hunt with you."

"The wyvern does not stand a chance," Muree'n added.

Anton knew he would be the weakest link in the expedition, by far. "Maybe I should stay in Shorehaven, talk to the villagers and gather a larger story."

Yazra'h stepped closer to him, placed a steel-hard hand on his shoulder. "I will protect you, Rememberer Anton. You will be safe during the hunt."

"It's not just my safety that concerns me. If you have to worry about protecting me as well as defending yourself, I may endanger you."

Yazra'h rested the butt end of her katana on the open ground near the shore. "You must be the one to chronicle this adventure. No one else can be trusted to tell the tale properly. We may be hunters, but you are a rememberer. We will kill the wyvern in a day or two, but thanks to your efforts, our hunt will be remembered for centuries."

Muree'n nodded solemnly. "Yes, Rememberer Anton, you must go along."

Anton knew it would be folly to argue with the two warrior women, so he gave a nod. "I just want to be sure I don't hinder you."

"I am not worried," Yazra'h said in a tone that ended the discussion.

Beltrias said, "I'm only concerned with killing the wyvern and restoring peace to Shorehaven." He turned to the trees. "I have set up traps. The creature has a foraging zone that extends well up the coast, and I know it will return here. The monster has established a habit of hunting humans."

Muree'n asked, "I want to hunt, not wait. With a territory so great, how will we find it?"

Beltrias smiled. "When I touch the trees, I see through thousands of verdani. I can sense the stirring fronds and the movements of creatures. Even though the wyvern is lost within the ecological web, I can look deep and can find signs of its passage. I can take us to where it is."

CHAPTER

31

ARITA

Even though she was the daughter of King Peter and Queen Estarra, Arita felt like an outsider. She could see the lush forest around her, sense the majesty of the trees, and sometimes she even heard faint and eerie whispers inside her mind, but it was different from what the green priests said they experienced through telink. Her heart ached when she saw how happy the priests were—and most of all she missed her friend Collin. A green priest . . . gone now.

When they were younger, she and Collin had studied as acolytes reading aloud to the worldtrees. The two were close, definitely attracted to each other, and they might have become lovers if things had turned out differently, but after the forest accepted Collin as a green priest—and not her—he had gone with a group of isolationists to the uninhabited continent of the Wild.

Nevertheless, Arita remained fascinated with the forest, from a scientific standpoint, if nothing else. She spent time documenting plants and insects on Theroc and on other worlds; all of nature fascinated her, whether or not she could commune with the verdani mind.

Though she had just turned twenty, Arita was mature and resourceful. She had gone to the abandoned Klikiss world of Eljiid, she had seen the lavish botanical gardens on New Portugal, and she longed to see the gigantic Roamer terrarium dome inside Fireheart Station. For now, though, she contented herself with Theroc.

Whenever she had a question about the life cycle or the habits of a strange beetle or fungus, she could have just asked one of the green priests, who understood every interconnected thread of the ecosystem. But Arita didn't want easy answers; she wanted to discover for herself and to add to the pool of knowledge. Her eventual goal was to create a comprehensive—though never complete—encyclopedia of natural history that others could review.

Kennebar, the stern leader of the isolationist green priests, dismissed all of her cataloguing work, claiming it was unnecessary. "Why bother to compile such a catalogue? Any green priest can simply give you an answer."

Either Kennebar didn't understand, or he was just being arrogant, flaunting his own access to infinite knowledge. "Because other people want to know. And not everyone has access to what the green priests know."

And it was surprising that the green priests didn't know everything either. The arrival of the Gardeners had raised many fascinating questions. Gracious and grateful, the alien refugees interacted with humans, just as curious about the green priests as the priests were curious about them. Even the gigantic trees wanted to know what they had forgotten in the distant past, and now they marveled at the memories the Onthos shared of their majestic homeworld. Feeling separate, Arita had watched Ohro and his fellow Gardeners revel in the forest. They built no structures, simply lived in the lush undergrowth—glad to be home.

Now, the Mage-Imperator's green priest consort sat with one of the Onthos refugees at the base of a gigantic golden-barked tree. Smiling, Nira looked into the Gardener's dark alien eyes. "I want to understand you, Ohro."

"As does the worldforest," said the alien. "We have shared all our memories with the verdani mind. Now it remembers much more than it did."

As Arita watched, Nira spread her palms against the worldtree bark. "With telink, I can reach the thoughts of any green priest. And so can you." She nodded to the alien. "Touch the tree. Let's see where our thoughts go."

The small-statured Gardener glanced at Arita, but he did not seem bothered that she was watching them. Ohro stared at the golden bark and pressed both of his palms against the huge bole.

Nira closed her eyes and did the same. Her brow furrowed. "I'm trying . . . I can see everything in the verdani mind. So many interconnected thoughts, but the Gardeners . . . why can't I find you? I know you are here."

"And yet we are not here," said Ohro. "Just as when our people fused with the worldtrees to become pilots of verdani treeships to explore the Spiral Arm, we are separate. We have lost that part of the worldforest mind—but you know the trees have accepted us."

Nira broke her contact with the tree, looking sad. "Yes, I know that. And I have seen the images of your wonderful homeworld that you shared. I wish we could have seen it in person."

Ohro stood. "We need to rebuild our numbers. We are beginning to reconnect." The Gardener startled Arita by turning to look directly at her. "Just as she is doing—even though she is not a green priest."

Surprised, Arita brushed herself off and stepped closer to them. "I'm not connected at all. The trees rejected me."

"Perhaps it is not what you think." The Onthos leader sniffed and then reached up to touch her arm. She felt a tingle in his fingertips. "You are connected to other things. Powerful things."

"That's not true," Arita said. Or was it? "I hear distant voices, but they are only the faintest of echoes—and it only happens sometimes. I can't touch the trees like green priests can. I'm a failure."

Ohro blinked his large black eyes, and his expression looked perplexed. "Maybe you are touching more than the verdani mind."

Arita felt dizzy and confused as she strained to hear the light breeze of whispers inside her mind. She couldn't understand words in the babel of sounds, could barely sense something there. But it was *something*, and it was not the trees. She had always thought those whispers were just echoes of the verdani, a taunting reminder of what she could never have.

But maybe . . .

The worldtrees had done something to her when they attempted to change her. What if they had opened her mind in a new way? Arita couldn't be sure . . . but there were times in the utter silence, when she was far from anyone and completely alone, when Arita did feel as if someone or something was watching her from *inside.*

Something very different.

CHAPTER

32

ROD'H

In the Prime Designate's rainbow-hued rooms, Daro'h dealt with matters beyond Rod'h's understanding. The Prime Designate made appropriate admiring sounds as tailors held up shimmering filmfabric and draped folds of cloth over measuring guides.

One of Daro'h's former assigned mates, Illi'v, a stern-tempered female of the bureaucrat kith, fancied herself a clothes designer. As numerous mixed-breed children ran about in the rooms, his lover directed fabric designs and commanded a whole new wardrobe for the Prime Designate, who indulged her.

The new garments were lightweight, comfortable, and eye-catching. Nimble-fingered stitchers assembled the pieces while Illi'v watched, inspected, and at last approved.

Rod'h did not understand why Daro'h maintained contact with so many of these women. After all, the mating index required them to breed only once, for the Prime Designate was expected to spread his genetics widely and not take only one long-term lover—as Jora'h had done with Nira. Rod'h couldn't stop a flash of resentment when he thought of the upheavals his mother had created in Ildiran civilization. The Saga of Seven Suns chronicled unbroken millennia of history, cultural nuances that had crystalized to perfection—but one green priest woman had changed much of that.

Rod'h had been born for a purpose and raised to meet a destiny, and he had been prepared to do just that. His mother had also had a vital duty to the Dobro breeding program, willingly or not, and she had fought against every aspect of it. Rod'h was disappointed in her. . . .

After the fabric was draped over his shoulders, Daro'h modeled the new garment. Illi'v tugged at several folds, stepped back to inspect again, then nodded her approval.

Daro'h was more enthusiastic. "It looks marvelous. I will wear it when I attend the lens-alignment ceremony at primary noon." Smiling, he turned to Rod'h. "And my new friend will accompany me. Rod'h, I want you at my side."

Rod'h was pleased Daro'h wanted him as a companion. "Of course I will, Prime Designate."

Daro'h issued brisk orders to the attenders, to the stitchers, and to his former mate. "I know how swiftly you can create such wondrous clothes. Prepare a set for my friend as well."

Illi'v raised her eyebrows. "The same design, Prime Designate?"

"Exactly the same design," Daro'h said, then laughed as three of the children got into a wrestling match on the floor. "In fact, let us make similar new clothes for all the children too."

Now Illi'v reacted with even more alarm. "But . . . but they are different kiths."

"Then take different measurements. They are all my sons and daughters."

Rod'h was impressed with the Prime Designate's warmth and openness, but he feared that Daro'h did not consider wide-reaching consequences. A naïve and gentle man was not necessarily a good leader. Nevertheless, Rod'h intended to be there to help the Prime Designate make hard decisions, should that become necessary. After all, he had been born to a great purpose.

In a city square with the spires of the Prism Palace in the distance, the lens priestess Arune'l gathered a group of observers along with five lens-kith acolytes. With each multisolar noon, she aligned a central crystal array to focus the light from different directions and different solar systems. The lens array focused all of the bright suns onto a symbolic black cube that absorbed all light. It was a constant show of defiance against the darkness.

Along with his group of attenders and noble kithmen, Prime Designate Daro'h went to witness the daily ceremony garbed in sparkling new robes that shone almost as brightly as the prismatic arrangement.

Rod'h was pleased to be invited along. Daro'h seemed glad to have a person who listened to him rather than regarding him with excessive awe and deference. They walked toward the crystalline lens arrangement, listening to the hush of gathered Ildirans who had come to witness the ceremony.

When the crowd turned to look at the Prime Designate rather than Arune'l, Daro'h gestured for them to turn their attention back to the lens arrangement. "I am just an observer like the rest of you. Proceed, Arune'l."

The lens priestess raised her hands. "Drawing on the light of seven suns through these lenses, each day we mark a bright passageway to the Lightsource. We draw upon our thoughts, use our *thism* to show the way."

Workers shifted the lenses so that sunlight from seven different suns poured down upon the central black cube, which swallowed the light. The dazzling rays poured onto the opaque flat surface, having no effect. Rod'h shielded his eyes from the intensity.

Lens kith acolytes checked the calibrations, swinging more lenses into place to intensify the light. Observers in the crowd fell to their knees in supplication.

Rod'h felt a sudden chill go down his back, and a knot formed in his stomach. He did not understand what caused it. Something was happening.

Standing on her raised dais, Arune'l also winced, and a visible shudder rippled through her. Astonishingly, the audience fell to their knees and began clawing at the street. Using hooked fingers, they pulled up the interlocked geometric paving stones, not caring that they bloodied their hands.

"What are they doing?" Daro'h asked. Suddenly, he hunched over, squeezing his eyes shut. He staggered two steps. "Stop! It's too dark, it's—" He collapsed to his knees and vomited violently.

The lens priestess shrieked in horror and clasped her hands against the side of her head as if the pain came from inside her as well.

Gathered Ildirans grabbed the uprooted paving stones with bloody fingers and lunged toward the lens arrangement. The lens-focused sunlight was deadly, and two adherents caught on fire as they stumbled into the concentrated beam. Others rushed the lenses themselves, using the paving stones to smash the crystalline framework. The central lens toppled to the ground.

"The shadows!" Rod'h cried out, realizing that this was another possessed mob like the one that had attacked the Mage-Imperator and Nira, like the one that had massacred the human enclave. He seized the dazed Prime Designate and pulled him away. "I have to get you to safety."

He felt none of the effects himself, apparently immune as a halfbreed, but somehow, the Shana Rei had tainted this group of Ildirans, infiltrated their collective consciousness, and forced them to act against their will.

After they smashed the lenses, the crazed crowd grabbed the bladelike fragments of crystal, slicing their own hands, and lifted up the broken shards as weapons.

Prime Designate Daro'h was still retching, fighting against what he couldn't understand, but Rod'h saw the bloodied Ildirans coming for them with murder in their eyes. He hauled the Prime Designate by his new robes toward the edge of the square. "We have to leave, Daro'h! We must get away from here." The filmfabric sleeve tore as the Prime Designate staggered, but Rod'h kept wrestling him away.

The mob did not target them specifically. Instead, the Ildirans lunged forward with one mind and fell upon Arune'l, stabbing and slashing the lens priestess. She didn't even fight back. They tore her apart and then turned their sharp blades on the other whimpering acolytes who huddled in the middle of the bright sunlight as if to hide.

The rest of the Prime Designate's entourage was reeling and disoriented. Even the attender kith scurried about in aimless circles like drugged insects.

Acting alone, Rod'h rushed the Prime Designate down another street. He didn't dare call out for help, afraid to draw attention to the two of them. Daro'h moaned in despair, and Rod'h saw that he had blood splashed across his new garments—blood from the other victims. He was apparently uninjured. For now.

The mob members, drenched in the blood of the lens kithmen, stood among the broken stumps of the crystalline framework they had smashed. Once Arune'l and the lens kithmen were dead, they stopped and simply stared at what they had done. Together, they let out a horrified wail of realization as the Shana Rei possessors made them understand what they had done. Then, like rag dolls controlled by invisible strings, the unwilling attackers threw themselves onto the upright stumps of broken crystal, impaling themselves.

As they ran away, the Prime Designate staggered, moaning. Rod'h's rush of adrenaline resolved into anger and purpose. Thanks to his mixture of genetics—like Gale'nh, Osira'h, and his other siblings—Rod'h could resist the Shana Rei in ways that other Ildirans could not. Rod'h knew that he could be strong enough, too.

He couldn't trust the other Ildirans in the street, though, any of whom might turn on the two of them in an instant. Rod'h needed to get the Prime Designate back to the safety of the Prism Palace, and from then on, he would have to watch over Daro'h very closely—by himself.

CHAPTER 33

ADAR ZAN'NH

Standing on the outdoor meditation platform of the Hiltos shrine, Adar Zan'nh focused his gaze on mad Designate Rusa'h. The cold wind blew skirling cyclones of loose snow from the black mountain ledges.

He could not shake his horror and disgust of this man who had torn the Empire apart, who had unleashed the faeros upon Ildira and caused the deaths of millions. . . . As the defeated Designate stood passive and at peace, Zan'nh could not believe that he had changed, that the nightmares of what he had done were burned out of him. The Adar could never trust such a person again.

But before he could speak, he felt a powerful twist of pain inside his mind. For a moment, he was certain Rusa'h had found a way to betray them through the *thism* again . . . but no, the fallen Designate also wore a stricken and terrified expression. He stared up at the sky in horror.

Around them in the shrine, Kao'l and the other lens kithmen reeled in shock from a force that buffeted them from within. But the greatest threat came from above. In orbit.

Tal Gale'nh let out a hoarse gasp. "I know them! The Shana Rei have found us."

Above the planet, empty space tore open and black geometrical horrors emerged. Long hexagonal cylinders slid out like blunted knives of pure obsidian. The very presence of the Shana Rei ships exuded chaos, unraveling coils of capricious entropy that made the systems aboard the flagship warliner malfunction, flicker, and fail.

A flurry of metallic hornets emerged alongside the hex ships, black robot warships that swooped forward in search of targets. Though their primary goal was the Hiltos shrine on the surface, they spotted the Solar Navy flagship and immediately opened fire.

On the high tower platform, Adar Zan'nh's comm burst to life, but the signal was intermittent, broken, choked with static. Septar Dre'nh, the captain of the flagship in orbit, yelped, "Adar, we are under attack! A shadow cloud appeared in the Hiltos system, and black robot vessels have engaged the warliner. But these robot ships are larger, a different design."

"Full defenses!" Zan'nh shouted into the comm, although he knew the septar would already have sounded battle stations.

"We are holding them off for now, but you must evacuate, Adar. A squadron of robot ships also dropped into the atmosphere—I believe they may be on their way to you."

As he listened to a broken transmission, Zan'nh wanted to be aboard his flagship, where he could direct the battle in space. He also knew the shrine had no defenses, and they were vulnerable here. He needed to rescue the hundreds of lens kithmen and support workers here.

He barked into his comm. "Septar Dre'nh, dispatch rescue cutters down to Hiltos with all possible speed, enough to evacuate three hundred Ildirans. Meanwhile, prepare sun bombs for launch against the Shana Rei."

The lens priest Kao'l looked sickened, and his voice sounded bleak. "Abandon the shrine? All the history, all the revelations we have had."

Rusa'h said in his maddeningly confident voice, "The shadows mean to extinguish us all. Their presence is like smoke that will smother the *thism*, and we are not strong enough to fight them alone. Hiltos cannot be saved."

Zan'nh turned to the lead lens priest. "Kao'l, gather your people. We can fill my cutter with as many as possible, and more rescue ships are on the way down from orbit."

Gale'nh said, "Adar, I will stay here and assist with the evacuation."

Zan'nh shook his head. "Absolutely not. I need your wisdom in my command nucleus. You are the only one who knows the shadows." It was a tactical decision, but also a personal one. "You will come with me."

Kao'l said, "When Rusa'h came here, we guaranteed his safety. Adar, please evacuate him in the first group. He is special."

Resentment flashed through Zan'nh. "He is dangerous. That man deserved to die many times over. I will not let others die now in order to save him."

The fallen Designate's voice sounded as if he didn't care one way or another. "If you let me find a way to fight the Shana Rei, I may be able to save as many lives as I cost before."

With the scream of engines and a roar of weapons bursts, angular black ships ripped through the Hiltos atmosphere, robot vessels in full attack mode. Crackling red beams lanced out, carving deep gouges in the mountainside, vaporizing one of the shrine's towers.

Zan'nh doubted that flying an evacuation cutter through the sky would be any safer than taking shelter in the shrine, but he knew that if he wasted any more time arguing with Kao'l, they would die. "*Bekh!* Come with me to the cutter, then—all of you." He hurried Rusa'h and Gale'nh down the steps to the landing ledge as the crowd followed. "We will evacuate as many people as we can."

Kao'l said, "If the lens kithmen join together, direct all of our *thism* to reveal more of the Lightsource . . . maybe we can help the fight from here." Even he seemed dubious, but obligated to suggest it.

The black robot ships swooped around the towers and fired another barrage. They hammered the black rock structure, shattered the mirrored walls.

"Do we have any reason to believe that will work?" Zan'nh said. "I would rather we got you to safety."

"We can try," said Kao'l. "I will stay here with my followers, but take the other kiths. They should all fit aboard. If your next evacuation ships are able to save us, then we will rejoice. If not, we will do what we can. . . ." Zan'nh thought that the lens kithmen might not have any other chance than to trust in their connection to the Lightsource.

The rest of the cutters might not be able to make it down through the harrying robot fighters.

On the landing ledge, Solar Navy crewmembers frantically prepared the cutter for departure as Zan'nh and his group ran toward them. The craft had defensive weapons, but they could not be used until the ship got into the air.

The pilot yelled, "We are ready for launch, Adar."

Black robot craft streaked overhead and blasted a snow-encrusted mountainside, which triggered an avalanche. A roaring white wave smashed against one side of the shrine, knocking down structural walls. Under such an onslaught, the ancient structure would be leveled.

Ildirans streamed out of chambers and passageways in the Hiltos shrine, other kiths trying to escape while the lens kith stood together. The first cutter could take only a handful of extra people, and any additional weight would limit their maneuverability, making it more likely that the craft would be destroyed before it could even reach orbit. It was a terrible equation.

"Evacuation cutters descending, Adar!" the pilot shouted. "They will arrive in fifteen minutes—accompanied by streamer escorts, fully armed to protect the ships."

That was what Zan'nh needed to hear. The streamers would engage the robot ships in dogfights and keep all, or most, of the cutters intact as they flew to the flagship.

Soldier kithmen rushed Hiltos inhabitants into the ship, crowding them. The other kiths were the first aboard, while Kao'l directed the lens kith to stay with him.

Gale'nh suddenly pressed a palm against his forehead as if he felt great pain inside his mind; his knees buckled. "I came here to get cleansed, but they are still inside me. I should stay. I can help the lens kith—"

"No!" Adar Zan'nh said. "Aboard, now!"

With maddening calm, former Designate Rusa'h said, "There may be only one way to cauterize that taint within you, Gale'nh. But we cannot do it now."

After the cutter was fully loaded, Kao'l stood with his lens kith companions, crowded on the landing ledge. Zan'nh shouted to the crowds. "Other evacuation ships are coming down!"

"We will stay here and endure . . . and resist in the only way we know how," Kao'l said. His fellow lens kith accepted his reassurance, but as the robot ships roared overhead again, Zan'nh feared the evacuation cutters would not arrive in time.

All the lens kithmen stood shoulder-to-shoulder out in the open, many of them holding prismatic amulets as a meditation focus. They directed the reflective surfaces into the light, catching the glare from the sky. As the cutter's hatch closed, Zan'nh heard them making an eerie, concerted humming sound.

The pilot launched without delay, and Zan'nh made his way to the cockpit. "I will take the weapons controls myself."

Three black robot ships raced off in pursuit of the rising cutter while others continued bombarding the shrine. All Solar Navy craft had enhanced shields, and glancing blows from red energy beams slapped the cutter as it rose into the thin air of Hiltos, but the impacts caused no significant damage.

"At least we are drawing enemy fire from the shrine," Gale'nh said.

As they climbed into the thickening clouds, he could no longer see Kao'l and the lens kith they had been forced to leave behind. But he glimpsed a flashing light, a bright glow. Robot ships swooped down, but something like shimmering weapons fire sparked from the remnants of the shrine.

Maybe it was nothing more than the concentrated reflections from all those meditative amulets, or maybe it was something more. Zan'nh felt an energy, a brightness in the *thism*, as all those lens kithmen concentrated. He wasn't certain they actually opened the floodgates of the Lightsource, but he felt light-headed, awash with a kind of adrenaline. Perhaps the lens kithmen were having some effect after all. Two of the black robot attack ships spun in the air, as if buffeted by a strong wind.

Zan'nh took the controls of the cutter's energy weapons and targeted the nearest robot vessel. Like a surgical scalpel, his blasts ripped open the belly of the black ship. These robot ships were larger and more intimidating than the ones they had encountered at Plumas, and they also looked new—undamaged. That made no sense. Very few robots had survived the Elemental War, and the Solar Navy and the CDF had caused a great deal of damage to the black robots at Plumas. How could there be so many ships left? Could the Shana Rei have built another fleet for the robots?

He muttered to himself as he opened fire, "*Bekh!* Then we will just have to destroy them again."

In the back of the cutter, the evacuated Hiltos workers stared out the windowports as they watched the continued destruction. Beside them, Rusa'h appeared to be meditating without the focusing crutch of one of the reflective amulets.

Five black robot ships swept past the cutter, and Zan'nh fired upon them, damaging two attackers, but more of them closed in.

Sweating, the pilot continued on a steep ascent toward orbit. Even the flagship offered dubious safety, though. The Shana Rei and black robots had already destroyed many warliners.

"Our shields are failing, Adar," the pilot announced.

The robot ships kept shooting at them.

Seven additional Solar Navy cutters dropped from above, heading down from the embattled flagship. The unexpected reinforcements damaged three of the robot ships, and the angular black vessels spun out of control, leaving smoke stains in the sky. One plummeted into a glacier, exploding on impact.

On the comm, one of the new arrivals said, "The shrine is under heavy bombardment, Adar. I do not see how we can evacuate the remaining people there."

Zan'nh thought of Kao'l and the determined lens kithmen down there, and knew he had to do something.

Just then a surge of panic and destruction rippled through the entire Ildiran race—and it was more than just the attack here. He felt as if the *thism* were tangled, asphyxiating him.

"This is not the only battle!" He forced the words through gritted teeth, realizing that the Shana Rei must have launched other insidious attacks as well. On Ildira! But he fought to concentrate on the targeting controls. *This* was his battle.

With reinforcements protecting the Adar's cutter, the robot attackers left the air battle and plunged back down to the wrecked shrine, where ample targets remained. The black ships launched a saturation bombardment on the mountainside, and Adar Zan'nh felt sick as blossoms of fire and smoke erupted from the shrine half-buried in snow. The warm Lightsource surge he had felt in the *thism* suddenly died away. . . .

The passengers let out a low moan, sensing the deaths of all those who had been left behind. Zan'nh could feel many strands of *thism* simply snipped and left frayed and dangling.

Hunched in his seat near the lens priests, Rusa'h said in a cold voice, "They are all dead, Adar. You know none of these ships can save them. Withdraw your cutters, or you will risk more lives."

The robot ships attacked the Lightsource shrine again and again, utterly ruthless as they leveled the ancient structure. Avalanches poured down the mountainside.

Tal Gale'nh said, "We have to make sure there are no survivors!"

Rusa'h shook his head. "We are sure—you know it. I know it."

Now the rest of the robot ships left the destroyed shrine and launched into the sky to attack the cutters.

Zan'nh cursed again under his breath. "To the flagship—that is our primary battle now. Alert Septar Dre'nh we are on our way."

Up in orbit, the flagship was engaged in intense combat, but with little success. Hundreds of Ildiran streamers harried the robot ships, but their high-tech targeting systems failed to function properly in the vicinity of the chaotic Shana Rei. The warliner had seven laser-cannon batteries, which the septar directed toward the ominous hex ships. Roaring gouts of laser energy hacked off chunks of the obsidian material, which dissolved like smoke in the vacuum.

With the Hiltos shrine leveled, the black robot ships raced back to the shadow cloud and the protection of the Shana Rei. Another laser-cannon barrage blasted out toward the hex ships, striking one of the retreating black robot vessels that blundered into the beam path.

The Adar transmitted to the flagship as they approached. "Septar Dre'nh, prepare to launch a sun bomb the moment all cutters get back aboard. Recall the streamer squadrons—get them out of the blast vicinity, and quickly. Their shields will never survive the shock wave—and we will use the diversion of the blast to escape." He looked at how little damage the Ildiran streamers had inflicted on the black robots and the Shana Rei. One warliner would never be enough to defeat such an enemy. The Solar Navy could not afford to lose more ships.

Ten minutes later, his overloaded cutter accompanied the others into the flagship's landing bay. Disembarking, Zan'nh raced toward the command nucleus, yelling into his comm. "Launch the sun bomb, Septar. Now!" Tal Gale'nh and even Rusa'h accompanied him. "And be ready to activate the stardrive to get us out of here."

A throbbing orange sphere hurtled out of the warliner's weapons port, a ticking bomb building to a nuclear reaction that was equivalent to the core of a sun. When the sun bomb exploded against the nearest Shana Rei hex vessel, the flare vaporized huge chunks of the black nether material.

Zan'nh arrived in the command nucleus just as the sun bomb glare began to fade. The flagship was already retreating, the helmsman increasing speed. Septar Dre'nh called out to activate the stardrive.

As they departed, the Adar watched as the obviously wounded Shana Rei hex ships plunged back into the shadow cloud, followed by the flurry of black robot vessels. The last attack ships flew into the void just as the dimensional tear closed.

The Ildirans in the command nucleus began to cheer as they raced away to safety, damaged but still intact. But Zan'nh felt sick at the destruction of the Lightsource shrine. All of the lens kithmen were dead down there.

The Adar looked at mad Designate Rusa'h, angry to waste the effort in saving such an infamous figure when Kao'l and so many others had died. He feared what this evil man might do now; Rusa'h had already caused so much harm to the Ildiran Empire.

The mad Designate fixed him with a piercing gaze that held an unsettling emptiness behind his eyes. "Now I can help you with this war."

CHAPTER

34

YAZRA'H

Far from Theroc's main fungus-reef city, Yazra'h and her fellow hunters continued to stalk their prey, senses alert. Muree'n shadowed her, springing from one branch to another like a natural treedancer. The group moved along at midlevel beneath the canopy, where sunlight percolated through the leaves in lush green shadows.

Beltrias led the way. He carried bow and arrows, spear, and knives—similar to the hand weapons Yazra'h and Muree'n used. None of them underestimated the threat of the beast. To ensure their victory, Yazra'h also carried three small detonators clipped to her belt. She had to be certain to protect Rememberer Anton.

The historian followed the group at a safe distance—far enough away to avoid any direct fighting, but close enough that Yazra'h could save him if need be. She found the worldforest to be a strange place, with subtle hazards that were different from anything encountered on Ildira.

Beltrias paused every so often to touch a tree, close his eyes, and use telink to view the surrounding area through verdani senses. The hunter green priest had identified a nesting area frequented by the wyvern, and they climbed there to lie in wait.

Beltrias said, "We'll stay close. We've found its territory."

Muree'n scampered along a wide branch to a tangle of gossamer strands. Human bones lay all around, mixed with the drained husks of insects the wyvern had eaten. She called to the others.

Rememberer Anton climbed the branches, resting to catch his balance and his breath before he moved higher. His face was streaked with sap and leaf stains. Yazra'h snatched him by the arm and helped him up. "I take it the wyvern isn't here?"

She was proud of Anton. He wasn't as athletic or graceful as she was, but he was competent and determined, and although exhausted, he kept up with them. Most scholarly rememberers could not have done what he was now doing.

Beltrias said, "We know the wyvern will come back here, so we lie in wait."

"How much of our tale have you written, Rememberer Anton?" Yazra'h asked.

He had added notes and kept a careful chronicle. "I don't know how it ends yet."

She flashed him a grin. "It will end soon. I can sense it."

The monster came back at sunset.

Yazra'h could hear the buzz of giant wings, and Beltrias rose to his feet. Muree'n scrambled up the fronds, hand-over-hand, to reach a perch on top of the canopy. Although Yazra'h wanted to be the first to attack the creature, she took time to check that Rememberer Anton was safe in the thick branches, where he could still observe the fight.

"Be as heroic as you want," he called to her. "Go make a fine story for me to tell, but I have no interest in writing a tragedy!"

Beltrias balanced on a high branch with his spear extended, open and vulnerable. He raised his hands and waved them to attract the creature's attention.

The wyvern saw him with multiple faceted eyes and swooped in, beating twin sets of sail-like wings. The wings were veined and transparent, but the chitin shells were bright blue and mottled with leopard spots. The wyvern's head was a horror of mandibles, and eight segmented limbs extended from its lower body. Claws reached down toward the green priest.

Just as the wyvern tried to seize its prey, Muree'n sprang closer and threw one of her daggers. The blade sank into the connecting tissue between the wyvern's thorax and abdomen—an irritation, not a mortal wound.

As if choreographed, Beltrias threw his spear in a smooth follow-through movement. His throw was well-practiced from the deep multilayered experience the worldforest had given him, but the weapon clacked off the tough exoskeleton and clattered out of sight into the mass of branches.

The wyvern flapped its huge thrumming wings, creating a breeze. Letting out a loud cry, Muree'n hurled weighted strings, a tangled bolo that twirled through the air and wrapped around two of the segmented limbs. The creature battered her with one segmented wing, knocking the girl off her perch. She flailed in the air, grabbing at branches as she tumbled.

Confident that her protégée would catch herself, Yazra'h sprang into the open air just as the monster swooped by. She landed on its back, grabbed the smooth chitin behind its head, but slid downward as the wyvern thrashed its wings. She held the katana in her right hand and tried to use the fingers of her left hand to slow the movement. Finally, she caught on the joint of the second set of wings, which pumped like giant bellows. Clinging desperately with one hand, she hammered the shell with the butt end of her katana staff, pounding and pounding until the exoskeleton cracked.

Below, Beltrias was waving and shouting to attract the wyvern's attention again. "Here, here!"

The monster spun in the air, trying to dislodge Yazra'h, but rudimentary instincts also drove it down to attack the green priest. Two of its segmented legs were still tangled in Muree'n's bolo, but it reached out with other claws to snatch Beltrias—which was what the hunter wanted. Caught in the creature's grasp, he grabbed a dagger from his waist and slashed at the wyvern's underbelly.

With one hand, Yazra'h pulled herself up to the thing's neck, caught her balance, and reached forward with her blade to gouge out one of the faceted eyes. Greenish ichor oozed out, and the creature's mandibles clacked in frantic alarm. With its forelimbs, it tried to pull Beltrias toward its jaws.

Yazra'h hammered the wyvern's head, but could not break through the hard shell. She blinded another one of its eyes, but it had many more. She needed to inflict a fatal wound.

The green priest shouted up to Yazra'h. "Abdomen! Second neural cluster! Another brain—more easily accessible." The mandibles snapped at him, but he twisted in the claws to avoid being eaten. He shoved his slime-covered blade into the mouth. The jaws clamped down and tore the weapon from his hand, but the blade was set deep.

Now unarmed, Beltrias struggled to break free; the damaged mandibles opened and closed, oozing ichor. He used main strength to snap the joint of one of the forelimbs that held him, tearing gashes in his own skin as he broke himself loose. Suddenly freed, the green priest tumbled toward the lush canopy, where he caught the loose fronds and saved himself from a fatal fall.

The monster circled and dipped in the air, but Yazra'h held on. Recalling what Beltrias had shouted to her, she let her body slide to the next set of segmented wings, working her way down. This creature would have two rudimentary brains, the main one inside its well-protected head, the secondary one down lower, where she could more easily kill it.

After all the bloodshed this thing had caused, she didn't need to be pretty or heroic. This was already a grand tale, and she smiled knowing that Rememberer Anton was watching down below.

She grasped the joint with one hand and swung her body down so she could use one of her daggers against the soft spot in the abdomen. Yazra'h sawed open the tough plated side, felt ooze spurting out from the wound. The neural cluster would be deep inside, and she could either crawl halfway into the cavity hoping to find it with her blade, or she could choose a faster alternative.

Messy, but permanent.

Yazra'h pulled one of the detonators from her belt and activated it. Without even looking at how high she was above the treetops, she thrust the detonator inside the abdomen, pushing her arm into the goo all the way to her elbow. She counted down the seconds in her mind as the wyvern swooped and flapped, trying to escape.

Only three seconds left.

Two.

The monster swooped down, as if it meant to crash into the treetops, and Yazra'h saw her chance. She sprang free, leaping out toward the deceptively soft-looking worldtree fronds. She extended her hands as she fell, ready to grasp anything.

As she plummeted, she had the satisfaction of watching the detonator erupt, splattering off the wyvern's entire bottom half. The monster spun and reeled in a mass of colorful wings and exoskeleton, like a starship without engines, falling out of the sky.

Then Yazra'h smashed into the leaves as if she had fallen into a verdant ocean. Branches tore at her, fronds whipped her face, but she seized one, holding on with all her strength. The sudden jerk nearly yanked her arm out of its socket, but she held on and swung, then caught a larger branch with a curved leg. When she stopped herself, she was panting, exhausted—and completely exhilarated.

Yazra'h didn't rest, didn't stop, because she knew the real pain would hit her at any moment. Instead, she climbed up and made her way across the branches. She reached the canopy, where the colors of sunset were growing deeper and richer, and from there she spotted Muree'n, who had also climbed to the top of the canopy, helping Rememberer Anton get to the open air.

The historian shaded his eyes and looked into the setting sun, obviously searching for her. She waved and made her way over to them just as Beltrias also climbed onto the canopy. When she was within earshot, Yazra'h shouted, "Rememberer Anton, did you see? Can you tell the tale?"

"Yes!" he called back. "I couldn't make up anything more dramatic than what I actually saw."

When they were reunited, she gave the historian a vigorous hug, paying no attention to the ichor that covered her skin; Anton gave a grunt of surprise as she squeezed him in her enthusiasm. She gave a less restrained hug to Muree'n, both of them bruised, battered, and triumphant. Yazra'h drew a breath to laugh out loud.

But suddenly her laugh caught like sharp spikes in her throat. The strands of *thism* turned into cracking whips, and mental pain resounded through her. The shock echoed and emanated outward from the relay of the Mage-Imperator. Something terrible was happening to the Ildiran race! A shocking pain erupted through their communal telepathic network, something . . . another attack.

Beside her, Muree'n also gasped, although the halfbreed girl had a different connection to the *thism* and to her special siblings. "Gale'nh! Something is happening to Gale'nh. The shadows are at Hiltos."

Though Rememberer Anton and Beltrias demanded answers, Yazra'h just rode out the pain and the shock. When she focused herself, she said, "We must get back to the Mage-Imperator. There has been another disaster in the Ildiran Empire."

CHAPTER

35

MAGE-IMPERATOR JORA'H

As the sun set across the forest, Jora'h joined the King and Queen up on the canopy for a diplomatic banquet. The Ildiran entourage would depart as soon as Yazra'h and Muree'n returned from their wyvern hunt. A new batch of fresh worldtree saplings had been potted for transport, to be planted as a memorial grove at the site of Mijistra's human enclave.

The colors in the sky became rich, vibrant hues—reds, oranges, golds. Such sunsets never occurred on Ildira, where seven suns always kept the sky bright. Although Ildirans regarded the fall of night as a thing to be dreaded, Jora'h could see the beauty in the gathering dusk.

They were served a lavish dinner catered by Arbor, a noted Theron restaurant owned by former trade minister Rlinda Kett. An officious-looking dictator of a maître d' commanded the delivery and presentation of each dish. Jora'h found it amusing to watch him command the serving staff with the same vigor as Adar Zan'nh commanded the Solar Navy.

With an indulgent smile, Nira nudged him, and he turned to look where their daughter Osira'h sat beside Prince Reynald, closer than was necessary. Though the prince looked drawn and pale from his illness, he seemed more energetic next to her. Osira'h talked with him, and they both laughed; she touched his forearm, and he rested his hand on her fingers, as if to encourage them to remain where they were. The two were in their own world, even with the bustle of the banquet around them.

Nira whispered, "They're like us when I first came to visit the Prism Palace." Jora'h laughed, but he could not disagree.

He felt pleased with their trip, sure that the alliance with the

Confederation was strong. They had learned much about the mysterious Onthos race, who were practically wiped out by the shadows, but Jora'h wanted to know more. If many of their memories had been erased from the worldforest mind, the Mage-Imperator had an idea to propose to the King and Queen.

With great pride, the waiter presented an expensive bottle of kirae from the Kellum distillery. The maître d' wrinkled his nose in distaste as he popped the top of the bottle and poured for all members of the Ildiran entourage. Jora'h would forgo the liqueur himself, so he could feel the clear tight threads of *thism* when he made his grand proposal.

While food was served, Ohro and numerous Onthos moved about on the canopy nearby, touching fronds, communing with the worldtrees, hovering where they could listen. They did not seem interested in the feast. Jora'h had not, in fact, learned what the Gardeners actually ate.

When the second course arrived—a plate of colorful plants and pickled leaves sprinkled with flower petals and edible moth wings—Jora'h called for attention. "I have another mission to propose, one that will answer questions about the Shana Rei and give us a clearer picture of what happened to the Onthos race."

The Gardeners all looked up, suddenly paying attention.

General Keah attended the banquet in her full military uniform, though she seemed anxious to be back aboard her flagship and out on patrol. She lifted her goblet. "I'm all for that!"

"What do you suggest?" asked Queen Estarra.

"The Onthos provided the coordinates for their home system, but no such star appears on our charts. If, as they say, the Shana Rei have hidden it somehow, we should go to the Onthos home system and see for ourselves. I suggest a joint expedition with both the Solar Navy and the Confederation Defense Forces."

The Gardeners chittered in horror. Ohro said, "Our race was exterminated, our sun swallowed up. We will not go back."

General Keah sat back in her chair, grinning. "No need, we'll do it ourselves."

Peter said, "That definitely sounds like a worthwhile effort. We could learn a lot about the enemy."

Keah turned toward the King and Queen. "Majesties, let me take the *Kutuzov*. How soon can we go?"

Jora'h was pleased but not surprised by her enthusiasm. "There are Solar Navy ships to recall, scientists to coordinate, observers to gather. I will ask Adar Zan'nh to coordinate with you, General Keah."

The Ildiran entourage lifted their small glasses of kirae and toasted. It was good to do something *proactively*, rather than huddle against an enemy they could not understand.

A ripple shot like an electric spark through the *thism*. Attuned to the telepathic strands, the Mage-Imperator sensed a sudden splash of violence . . . in Mijistra! His people going berserk, possessed by the shadows, killing.

And more. He sensed Ildirans in terror and pain, far away, another crisis. At Hiltos! The Lightsource shrine was under attack!

As the storm of emotions slammed into him from several directions, Jora'h couldn't stop himself from crying out. His insides buckled, and he clenched his hands, trying to control the spasm.

The Onthos began to chitter, staring at him. Nira lurched to her feet, grabbing his shoulder and holding him. "Jora'h, what's wrong?"

But he could barely answer because the strands of *thism* grew darker, tighter, like garroting wires. "The shadows . . . they are inside us again."

CHAPTER 36

AELIN

Out at the ekti-harvesting complex, Aelin watched the bloater exploitation in silence and in pain. He caused no trouble, did not try to interfere. Eventually, Iswander's workers learned to ignore the green priest, whom they considered eccentric though innocuous, and not worth paying attention to. After hard shifts draining the nodules, pumping ekti-X, filling fuel canisters, and preparing the next large shipment array, the well-paid crew just wanted to relax.

But as the bloaters were drained and their dead husks discarded, Aelin could feel the blood of the cosmos being spilled. Inside his mind and rippling through his soul, he sensed a vague confusion and dismay as one nodule after another died. The echoes of inarticulate calls for help were driving him truly mad. If the green priest couldn't stop it, then at least he had to get away from this space charnel house. Far away.

Alec Pannebaker, Lee Iswander's deputy manager, oversaw the operations while the industrialist was away taking his son to Newstation. Pannebaker was a well-liked man who tried to get to know all workers personally. He socialized with the ekti extractors and admin staff; he even tried to strike up conversations with Aelin, and the green priest did his best to respond adequately. But with so much resonant cacophony in his head, the green priest could no longer have a casual conversation with anyone. He was too preoccupied with the thrumming stew of incomprehensible thoughts that emanated from something *beyond* the bloaters, something that no one else could hear.

Elisa Enturi, Iswander's second-in-command, was a much harder boss than Pannebaker, self-absorbed and impatient with anyone who failed to perform exactly up to her expectations. Aelin knew to tread carefully around her. Despite Lee Iswander's orders, she would be looking for any excuse to come down hard on him.

He was desperate to go where he could find another treeling and get in touch with the worldforest mind again, but the Iswander Industries extraction field was a secure operation. Ships did not come and go, except for clearly scheduled and specialized vehicles, and those were piloted only by the most trusted members of the company.

Right now, Elisa Enturi was preparing the next shipment array for delivery to Ulio Station . . . and Aelin realized that was his only way out. He would never get past Elisa's scrutiny, though. The real key was Pannebaker.

The deputy was a daredevil who had an appetite for adrenaline-filled sports. Pannebaker had risked himself many times just for fun in the Sheol lava-mining operations, and out in space he was fond of a sport called "gap jumping." Wearing an environment suit with a limited supply of air and only a few maneuvering jets, he would plot a trajectory, accounting for time and life-support resources, then jump out into open space. He flew free from one point to another and hoped he didn't miscalculate.

Out in the extraction field, Pannebaker could easily take an inspection pod, but sometimes he suited up, grabbed an extra air tank, and just leaped headfirst out of a docking bay. He flew through the vacuum over to the pumping stations, cargo ships, or disposal tugs that removed the withered empty sacks. He thought it was fun.

Though Aelin told no one of his particular interest, he kept an eye on Pannebaker. The eccentric green priest watched unobtrusively as Pannebaker suited up and strapped himself to a carrying framework like a space wheelbarrow, then jumped out.

Aelin had previously learned about environment suits, life-support systems, and stardrive travel times, all of which had been part of the curriculum when he tutored Lee Iswander's son. But Arden had gone with his father to Newstation and Academ.

It was the best time for the green priest to make his move.

He watched Pannebaker kick off from an anchored pumping station and come back to the admin hub. The deputy used the last of his compressed-air jets to maneuver himself to the external airlock and cycled himself through.

Aelin was there, blending into the background as other workers hurried forward to help Pannebaker remove his helmet before his last air ran out. The deputy had a salt-and-pepper goatee and long steel-colored hair. Right now, although heaving deep breaths after nearly emptying his air tank, he wore a large grin. "I cut that one close, but I made it." Aelin suspected that the deputy was more frightened than he let on.

One of the techs looked at the spacesuit, tapped a readout, and clucked his tongue. "Red lines everywhere, Alec. Five minutes more, and we'd be giving you mouth-to-mouth resuscitation."

"Not me," said a burly female tech. "If he's damn fool enough to do stupid stunts, I'm not kissing him back to life."

Still catching his breath, Pannebaker chuckled again. "If I woke up to that, I might just think I was in heaven, Sherry." That earned him a round of whistles and catcalls. Pannebaker waved to the green priest as he let the techs strip him out of his suit. "I think I'll rest for a bit back in my quarters. Long shift. See that my suit's refilled and recharged, would you?"

Sherry huffed. "What am I, your personal maid?"

"No, you're my technician, and it's part of your job."

"As a low-priority item," she snorted.

Aelin volunteered. "I'll do it for you. I've been trained . . . and I'd like to do something around here."

Pannebaker shrugged. "The chief keeps you around for some reason—but I'll double-check your work next time I go out."

"You're welcome to."

Pannebaker left the bulky equipment on the deck for cleanup and recharge, and Aelin bent over the components, much to the amusement of the technicians. They left the bay, chatting with one another as they went back to their process lines.

Now that he was alone, the green priest focused on his work, making sure that he made no errors, because his own life would depend on it. Alone in the bay, Aelin refilled the air tanks, installed fully charged power packs, then gathered spare air tanks connected in sequence, along with a triple array of fresh batteries. According to his calculations, that should be enough. He filled the transport barrow with the spare equipment and locked the suit in its storage cabinet, ready to go. His pulse was racing.

Like a drill sergeant, Elisa Enturi used the intership comms to guide workers who moved hundreds of ekti canisters into a large array framework for the next major shipment to Ulio Station. Aelin had already studied the manifests and schedules; Elisa wasn't due to depart for ten hours, but she was often impatient to leave early.

Aware of his window of opportunity, the green priest waited for the shift change. Two long hours.

Pannebaker had gone into his quarters, apparently to sleep. In the usual commotion of a shift change, workers came in from their external assignments, ships docked inside the hub launching bay, inspection pods departed for the extraction fields. So much activity at the end of the shift gave him plenty of camouflage.

Checking, he learned that Elisa was in a last-minute meeting with several team leaders to review their jobs. Once she departed with the tank array for Ulio, Pannebaker would be in charge of the industrial site, and everyone could heave a sigh of relief.

With Elisa busy in the briefing, Aelin knew it was his time to move.

Pannebaker's gap-jumping suit was ready to go. Remembering what he had learned from the worldforest mind, the green priest donned the suit, adjusted the fittings, installed the helmet. As a precaution, he tuned his comm between channels so that he heard mostly static through the speakers, should anyone try to contact him; if he was forced to respond, his words would be distorted and garbled too. It would seem like a simple enough mistake if anyone bothered to ping him.

He checked his suit jets, noted the cumulative oxygen level on this tank and the chain of spare tanks. He carried extra life-support batteries inside the transport barrow. Everything was ready. He cycled through the small airlock.

Drifting out in space, Aelin pushed himself away from the admin hub toward the mostly loaded tank array. Engineers were putting on the finishing touches, testing numerous cylinders, drifting around the framework in inspection pods. In his suit, the green priest maneuvered so that the array eclipsed him from curious eyes. The scout pods couldn't see his small form, and if they did notice a suited figure flying free, they would assume it was Deputy Pannebaker.

Aelin did nothing to call attention to himself. He floated along with infinity above and below. The destination ahead was the anchor of his focus.

The ekti canisters inside the large array were like a forest with narrow gaps between cylinders, places where one could easily hide. He managed to catch himself on an outer array strut; then he removed the spare oxygen tanks and battery packs from the barrow. He pushed the empty vehicle away, adding a burst of acceleration from its own thrusters so the barrow tumbled into the emptiness toward the husks of drained bloaters.

Aelin wished he could do more to save some of the mysterious nodules, but he just had to stow away, sit quietly, and wait. Holding the extra air tanks and batteries, he worked his way in among the ekti cylinders, climbing deep into the structure. He knew no one would see him.

Elisa would depart soon, and he was set now, ensconced now. He attached his air tanks, connected the extra power blocks in a chain, studied the readouts. Under normal usage, the energy and air remaining would last about sixteen hours. Nowhere near enough. He guessed that it would take at least two days to reach Ulio Station . . . therefore he would have to survive that long. For a normal person it would not be possible, but Aelin would make it possible.

He controlled his breathing, calmed himself, slowed his body's processes. It was a long preparation, but he knew how to do it, a metabolic trick he had learned when he was drowning in revelations from the bloaters.

And as he did so, he heard whispers in his mind, bright chimes, the musical background noise that had risen to such a crescendo when he was inside one of the bloaters. He was separate from the cluster of drifting nodules, but here, so close to all the extracted ekti-X and surrounded by the concentrated essence of the bloaters, he could hear part of the song left in the blood, in the ekti. It was perfect, surrounding him with a cosmic lullaby. He found it soothing and astonishing at the same time. It would make the passage so much stronger.

Delving deep inside himself, tapping into his biochemistry, his metabolism, his respiration, his heartbeat, the green priest slowed his entire being. Secure in the array, after adjusting the suit temperature, energy drain, and oxygen flow well below survival minimums, he dropped himself into a deep coma.

No one could detect him here. No one would even look for him.

Aelin would not awaken until he reached Ulio Station. Until he was free.

CHAPTER

37

PATRICK FITZPATRICK III

Another day at the Kuivahr distillery above the shallow, kelp-clogged sea. Even though he had never expected to be managing such a facility, Patrick Fitzpatrick had the business down. Fermenting tanks, boilers, yeast strains, fiber filters, mash extractors, chemical testing tubes, and tasting rooms, all to make Primordial Ooze.

Standing on the high metal-ribbed deck, he inhaled deeply of the rich aroma—he forced himself not to think of it as *stench*—of Kuivahr's low tide. Very different from the biting chemical aromas of gas-giant cloud bands. For years, Patrick and Zhett had run the skymine on Golgen, riding the vast cloud oceans, skimming and processing vapors through complex ekti reactors. He supposed it wasn't all that different from this—Patrick had never thought he would become a skyminer, either. . . .

As the heir to a blueblood family on Earth, he had been brought up to look down on Roamers, and then he had fallen in love with the daughter of the Kellum clan. Oh, his grandmother was beside herself when she found out! And he and Zhett had been married for two decades, important and influential with their enormous cloud harvester . . . until the Shana Rei destroyed it. That left them here, picking up the pieces and making a living at the distillery Zhett's father had established. No, not quite where he had expected to be. . . .

At least their daughter Shareen had a great opportunity at Fireheart Station as an apprentice to the Roamer genius Kotto Okiah. She was young, brilliant, and ambitious, and the Spiral Arm would be hers for the taking. He smiled when he realized that old Maureen Fitzpatrick must have had similar hopes for him. In the end, Patrick knew that he wasn't a disappointment to his grandmother—and he would be happy with whatever Shareen decided to do. Or her brother Toff, or even baby Rex.

Patrick turned and went inside the facility to the packaging lines. As he stood watching rows and rows of bottles being filled with the iodine-smelling brew, he couldn't help but shake his head. Del Kellum insisted that Primordial Ooze was an acquired taste, but, alas, not many people had acquired it.

Bracing himself, Patrick sampled the current batch, grimaced at the flavor, took another drink, then forced a smile. He was surprised when Zhett came up and slipped her arm around his waist. "You look deep in thought, Fitzy. It can't be that much of a challenge to watch the bottles roll by."

She kissed him—still beautiful, not a face he could ever get tired of. When he thought of their relationship, their lives together, their three children, all of his doubts and second thoughts washed away. "I was just considering how proud I am to be in charge of the most important kelp distillery in the Spiral Arm."

"*One of* the managers," Zhett said. "You couldn't do it without me."

"I couldn't do a lot of things without you."

As the rest of the distillery crew did their work, Patrick basked in Zhett's presence for a peaceful moment—which was interrupted when Del Kellum called over the comm, summoning them to the distillery's landing platform. "We've got a visitor, by damn—Aaron Duquesne's here, says he has a proposal we should listen to."

Patrick looked at his wife. "Who's Aaron Duquesne?"

"Son of a midrange Roamer clan. Not friends, not enemies. They didn't cause my father any particular trouble when he was the clan Speaker."

"Now there's a ringing endorsement."

She shrugged. "Let's hear what he has to say. He didn't come to Kuivahr because it was on his way anywhere."

Patrick slipped his arm through hers, and they headed off to the landing platform at water level. There, they found Del standing outside the Duquesne ship, his hands on his hips, chatting with a thin younger man, Aaron Duquesne presumably. Del had just returned from delivering Shareen and Howard to Fireheart Station and he hadn't stopped talking about the big projects there, the nebula operations, the power-block-manufacturing grids.

Zhett's father waved them over. "My sweet, we may have an opportunity to get back into skymining."

"We were just getting used to the distillery business," Zhett said. Patrick immediately saw his wife don her hard-businesswoman persona. "Are you looking to partner with clan Kellum?"

"Partner? No, but we wanted to make you the offer first." Duquesne leaned against the hull of his ship, which had to be at least three decades old. "Del Kellum is known for being fair, and my clan always supported him when he was Speaker."

"To a certain extent," Del said.

Patrick asked, "What are you proposing?"

"Skymines. Two gamma-class cloud harvesters on Belliros, good condition. My clan took them over after the Elemental War, and they've been producing stardrive fuel ever since. We could offer them at a very reasonable price." He looked at the distillery towers and the sloshing, fish-smelling seas of Kuivahr. "If your clan is interested in getting back into real work."

His disparaging tone made Patrick defensive. "We're doing real work right now—and we're turning a profit." That was a slight exaggeration, as both Del and Zhett knew, but they backed him up.

"I suppose," Duquesne said. "But I'm offering you a chance at something more. Clan Kellum has a history, a legacy. I remember all the grand projects you used to do—the construction yards in the rings of Osquivel, or extracting ekti in the comet clouds, then your giant skymine on Golgen." He blinked. "Sorry it was destroyed, by the way."

"Thanks," Zhett said in a clipped icy voice. "But why are you trying to offload your skymines? What's wrong with Belliros?"

Duquesne shrugged and lounged against the hull again. "My clan wants to seek other opportunities, chase another Guiding Star. We thought you might like to take over the business, since you know it so well."

Del also seemed skeptical. "Roamers don't abandon skymining unless they're being attacked by hydrogues."

"No hydrogue harassment, I swear," Duquesne said with a forced chuckle. "No problems on Belliros. Nothing wrong with the facilities—I can give you complete production logs. Why are you asking so many questions?"

"Because you're asking us to make a huge investment," Zhett said.

Patrick could see the gleam in Del's eyes, the desire to get back to big things. Patrick admitted that running the mammoth cloud harvester made him feel like a king above an ocean of clouds. But they had been through so much already, and they were just now picking up the pieces. The distillery was all they had left.

"We don't have the funds to buy two skymines," Zhett said. "As you just pointed out, we lost everything at Golgen."

Aaron Duquesne thrust out his lower lip. "Come on, now—a former clan Speaker can get all the credit he needs, if this is where his Guiding Star tells him to go."

The young man was rubbing Patrick the wrong way, and suddenly the answer clicked in his mind. "You're trying to get away from ekti harvesting before the bottom falls out of the market. Our skymine on Golgen might have been destroyed, but I still follow the business. The price of stardrive fuel has been dropping, thanks to the influx of ekti-X."

"Oh, that's just a temporary adjustment," Duquesne said, convincing no one. "Nobody knows where Iswander Industries gets their fuel, but it can't last long. Skymining has been stable for centuries." His voice had an annoying, pushy undertone. "Look, I can find other clans to buy our cloud harvesters—I was doing you a favor."

Patrick saw that Zhett realized the man's motives too, and that even Del Kellum had come to a similar conclusion, though he didn't want to admit it.

"You're trying to get rid of your old skymines before they're not worth anything," Patrick pressed. "As soon as someone else figures out Iswander's cheap and easy way to harvest stardrive fuel, those skymines will be like anchors dragging their owners down into the clouds."

"There will always be a market for ekti," Duquesne insisted.

"Then maybe you should stick with it, by damn," Del said. "This distillery is functional, and we're happy. We don't need all those headaches."

Miffed, Duquesne turned back to the open hatch of his ship. "Your loss."

"We've had enough losses already," Zhett said. "Don't need to add any more."

Del shaded his eyes, staring into the gray sky as the Duquesne ship flew away. He looked sad and disappointed. "It would've been nice to be back above the clouds, but maybe we should keep our feet on the ground for now."

Patrick had monitored the price of stardrive fuel and knew that other skymining clans were pulling out of the business. "I have a feeling that before long there'll be dozens of cloud harvesters available for bargain-basement prices." He placed an arm around Zhett's shoulders, pulled her close. "I'm happy enough here. As I said, best kelp distillery in the Spiral Arm. That's important enough for me."

Zhett smiled. "And me too."

Del lifted his bearded chin. "Shall we go celebrate with a toast? I could crack open one of our best bottles."

Zhett and Patrick shook their heads. "No thanks. We're fine."

CHAPTER 38

CELLI

The worldtrees inside Fireheart's greenhouse dome drank in sunlight and flourished, growing so quickly that they pressed against the curved crystal ceiling. Trapped.

Working in the contained gardens, Celli could sense the strain of the trees, of the dome itself. The worldtrees had grown far too large for this terrarium, but there was no moving them now, no place for them to go. The sense of hopeless, impending disaster thrummed in the air, and there was nothing she could do about it.

In the worldforest on Theroc, Celli had reveled in the trees, the potential of open skies and the sprawling canopy of lush fronds. Here, though, the dominant feeling she experienced was claustrophobia and inevitability as the hunched trees tried to restrain themselves. Her heart ached.

When she and Solimar first planted the small treelings among the Roamer greenhouse gardens, the nebula environment had been exhilarating. The trees were drenched in the glow from the keystone stars, a feast that made them grow at an abnormally rapid rate. The two green priests had been foolish not to look ahead. Now there was no way the gigantic trees could be moved, and they would either die first or destroy the greenhouse dome.

By communing through telink, Celli and Solimar tried to hold the growing trees steady. They felt guilty, wishing they could do something to help, and the trees responded by reassuring *them*.

Working the gardens that fed the Roamer workers in Fireheart Station, she and Solimar took comfort in growing plants, harvesting fruits and vegetables. They had created a lush environment here, far from Theroc, although with telink they could always visit the worldforest planet whenever they wished.

As a young girl, Celli had loved running through the forest barefoot, clad in only scraps of clothes. She and Solimar had climbed the trees together, leaped from branch to branch as they practiced treedancing. Now, though, they lived in the middle of a blazing nebula, surrounded by enclosed habitats, floating stations, and industrial outposts. It had been their calling to come here, and Celli didn't regret it. Many green priests went far from Theroc to spread the worldforest by planting treelings, while expanding the instantaneous telink communication network.

Since the heavy nebula radiation interfered with traditional outside communications, green priests and telink were vital here. Through the treelings, Celli and Solimar sent instantaneous messages anywhere across the Spiral Arm, and when they weren't needed for communications, they tended the crops.

Now Celli was on her knees, picking strawberries and occasionally popping one into her mouth. "The spoils of my profession," she said, wiping her red-stained lips.

The worldtree fronds above rustled and scraped against the curved panes, as if whispering gossip about them. Solimar bent over to inspect tomato plants, parting the leaves until he found a bright red prize, perfectly ripe. Working together, they filled their baskets and carried them out to the delivery platform for distribution among the habitats.

While Solimar did an inventory and decided which Roamer facility was due to receive that day's harvest, a shuttle docked at the greenhouse dome. Celli remembered that Kotto Okiah had asked to visit so they could meet his two new lab assistants. The scientist emerged with a young man and woman dressed in Roamer jumpsuits, as well as his two compies. Since Kotto wasn't prone to making introductions, the pair of newcomers introduced themselves.

Celli and Solimar took them on the tour of the various crops. As they walked through the main, humid dome, Howard Rohandas and Shareen Fitzkellum both stared at the straining trees; apparently neither had seen a worldtree up close before. Shareen immediately sensed the problem and turned to the two green priests. "Those trees can't stay here—they'll wreck the whole dome. No expansion possible?"

Celli felt the ever-present ache of dread. "None that we can think of."

Kotto patted his two new assistants on the shoulders. "You're welcome to suggest a solution."

Shareen lifted her chin. "We just might do that."

Celli felt a twinge of hope. She offered them strawberries, and from the expression on Howard's face, Celli doubted he had ever tasted a strawberry before. "This is fresh, and sweet, and juicy, and—"

Kotto paced about, looking out-of-place and impatient. "Well then." He scratched his curly hair. "I have a list of other places to show you two, so we'll want to move on. I need to get back to the lab complex before the end of the day."

"We're currently running calculations, Kotto Okiah," said the compy KR. "Even as we accompany you."

"I know that, but I can't oversee them without my notes."

"We'll double-check the work, sir." Shareen sounded eager and helpful. "Maybe find ways to improve on the designs, if you don't mind."

Kotto regarded them for a long moment, then said, "Feel free to make suggestions."

Later, after Kotto and his guests flew off to their next stop, Celli and Solimar were alone again in the greenhouse dome. They felt a tangible uneasiness surrounding them like a sour humidity in the air—but it wasn't just the plight of these two enormous trees.

When they pressed their free hands against the gold-barked trunk, she and Solimar could sense the bright heart of the primary worldforest on Theroc. Celli sought the support of other trees, knowing that the verdani mind would endure, even if these two trapped trees were doomed.

What Celli found when she probed deeper into the extended network, however, was troubling. An uneasiness spread through the interconnected trees, and many of the verdani thoughts were fuzzy and distracted, without the instant clarity she usually experienced when tapping into the worldforest mind. She found only dissolute thoughts and confusion.

Maybe it was just echoes of the trembling claustrophobia from these stunted trees, but she feared that something worse, something incomprehensible, was happening to the worldforest itself, far away. . . .

CHAPTER

39

ORLI COVITZ

Dando Yoder, the old trader who had crashed on Ikbir, was distraught at how long repairs were going to take, but Garrison accepted the challenge, announcing to the insular colonists, "After I get the *Prodigal Son* ready, we'll head out and arrange for replacement stardrive parts and an engineering team—along with whatever supplies Ikbir needs."

For herself, Orli was both pleased and disappointed to be leaving this quiet, uninteresting place, and DD, of course, was happy to go wherever Orli went. Seth was anxious to get to Newstation and go back to Academ, an ambition that DD (and Garrison and Orli) strongly encouraged.

No, there was no reason for any of them to stay here.

Since Yoder worked for Kett Shipping, Orli decided it was time to take care of something she had meant to do all along. Rlinda Kett had given Orli another chance when she needed it, and even though she had dispatched a message to tell the big trader that she was all right, she needed to go see Rlinda in person. She would travel with Garrison and Seth to the Roamer capital, and from there she would arrange passage back to Kett Shipping.

After they packed up to leave Ikbir for good, Garrison and Orli offered Yoder their prefab dwelling. The scruffy trader seemed very pleased. "You're giving me your home? I could always just sleep in my ship."

"We don't plan to come back," Garrison said, "at least not anytime soon."

Orli said, "You'll have more room to stretch your legs here. Sleep on solid ground for a change."

"Haven't done that in years." Yoder scratched his beard. "But I suppose it's a day for new experiences."

Taking their few possessions, Orli and DD went to the *Prodigal Son*, which felt more like home to them than Ikbir ever had. Garrison had been eager to jump out of bed that morning, rather than his usual slow and comfortable waking with Orli.

The colonists came to the spaceport, partly to wish them goodbye, but also to present lists of desired items. Orli's most heartwarming moment was when her refurbished compies all came out to stand in front of her. "Thank you for staying with us, Orli Covitz," LU said. "You gave us a new life."

Sounding maternal, MO said, "I will take care of the colony for you, Orli Covitz. I promise it will remain clean and efficient."

DD seemed worried, looking from the compies to Orli to Seth. "Shall I stay here with the other compies, Orli?"

Seth looked shocked, but before he could say anything, Orli reassured them both. "Of course not! You're my personal Friendly compy. I—" Her voice cracked. "I don't know what I'd do without you."

"I am relieved to hear that, Orli. I don't know what I would do without you, either. But I would do my best."

Garrison was already in the cockpit, and Seth joined his father, while Orli and DD sealed the ship behind them. She usually felt bittersweet about leaving a place she called home—even places with terrible memories, such as Dremen and Corribus—but there were no roots holding her to Ikbir, so she experienced no real sadness. She would rather be with Garrison anyway, although she had business to take care of once they left Ikbir.

Watching him in the cockpit, she smiled at how Garrison let his son do the basic checklists and ramp-up routines. She felt strangely proud to watch Seth show off his skills. As he worked the controls, lifting off from the spaceport, Garrison explained parts of the in-system engines and navigation systems. DD added comments, because he had undergone the same training himself.

"Three days to Newstation," Garrison said as they exited orbit and headed out of the Ikbir system, then he looked over at Orli, who sat close beside him, "but I'd like to make a detour on the way. If that would be all right with you? It's something personal . . . something that Seth and I need to do. For my clan."

She leaned on his shoulder. "Where are we heading?"

"I want to stop at Rendezvous."

DD piped up, "Rendezvous is abandoned. The new Roamer center of government is located on Newstation, and according to my recent records, even the clan Reeves reconstruction efforts have ceased at Rendezvous."

"Reconstruction efforts ceased because my clan left it all behind," Garrison said. "My father must have realized the project would never be completed. Instead, they chased their dreams to what they thought would be a new home. . . ." He didn't finish, didn't need to finish. Orli was the one who had found all the members of clan Reeves dead aboard the derelict city.

"What do you want to do there?" Orli asked.

"Just pay my respects." He looked at her. "If you don't mind that we take the extra time? Thirty hours?"

"I'm in no hurry. Once we get to Newstation . . . then we have to decide what to do." She placed a hand on his shoulder, squeezed. He put his hand over hers.

Changing course, they headed into deep space away from Ikbir's sun. Before they engaged the stardrive, though, the *Prodigal Son*'s sensors detected strange anomalies ahead and around them. Orli blinked and felt a thrumming, chiming sound in her head. At first she thought it was barely audible feedback from the ship's control console, but it seemed to be coming from out in space—and behind her eyes. She rubbed them, felt the vibrations increase. "Do you hear that? I can feel it getting louder . . ."

"No sound detected, Orli," DD said.

Garrison looked at her, concerned. "I don't hear anything." He ran long-distance scans. "But there is something out here. Maybe you're just more sensitive." When he enhanced the images from the high-res scope, Orli was amazed at what she saw.

Delighted, Seth exclaimed. "Look, they're bloaters!"

Orli couldn't shake a tingling thrill that washed through her, and the chiming sound inside her head grew even louder. These strange floating nodules had cured her of the Onthos plague back at the Iswander extraction complex. She was surprised to see them out here, far apart and drifting individually in the emptiness. Previously, she had only seen a large cluster of the bloaters. She rubbed her temples again, but the strange feedback sound resonated inside her head. Was it coming from the bloaters? Orli had been immersed in the protoplasm inside one of those things; maybe she had made some kind of connection with them. If so, what were they trying to communicate now?

Orli studied the high-res screens, then looked through the windowports to see them with her own eyes, though very little light reflected from the greenish brown nodules. She recognized a startling pattern. "They're like breadcrumbs, dropped in a line."

The numerous bloaters were strung out in intersecting trails, lines heading toward Ikbir's star and then extending out into the vast cosmic emptiness, like stepping-stones appearing from nowhere.

Garrison enhanced the windowport display with active phosphors. Seth gasped and grabbed the compy's polymer arm. "It looks like a web!"

"All the bloaters appear to be moving together," DD observed.

Though Orli could hear them in her unexpected way, she could make no sense of the sounds or music, but she continued to try.

CHAPTER 40

OSIRA'H

After they all felt the resounding empathic tremors of massacres taking place in Mijistra and at the Hiltos shrine, Jora'h announced his immediate departure from Theroc. He needed to be back among his people, although Osira'h was just as concerned about his own vulnerability to the shadows. As the nexus of the *thism*, the Mage-Imperator was a target.

Because of his inability to help his people through the distant disasters, Jora'h looked sickened. Osira'h could feel the emotions emanating from her father, though he tried to quell them, knowing that all of his people would sense his dismay—which would weaken the Ildiran race further.

Osira'h had been sad that she would leave Prince Reyn, but that was just the sorrow of parting—not a tragedy. Now there was a crisis at the heart of the Empire. Part of her longed to stay with Reyn; he needed her and she gave him strength. But Osira'h belonged back on Ildira. Her unique halfbreed powers had allowed her to save the Empire before. She needed to be ready to do it again.

As the entourage rushed to depart, Ildiran cutters were en route from the warliners in orbit. King Peter and Queen Estarra came to bid the Ildiran delegation farewell.

Wanting to stay with her until the last possible moment, Reyn accompanied Osira'h to the landing area on top of the canopy. Since his recent collapse, he had been tended by Confederation medical specialists as well as traditional Theron doctors. Unable to cure his debilitating illness, they treated the symptoms. Even knowing that he had contracted it from a microfungus indigenous to the worldforest had not helped them find a solution. Local Theron remedies had no more effect than the most sophisticated pharmaceuticals developed on New Portugal, or black-market drugs from some place called Rakkem. His parents had offered immense rewards for any flicker of hope, but so far, no miracle had appeared.

During Reyn's recovery, Osira'h had been his closest companion. In his private chambers, with the windows open and colorful flying insects dancing outside, Osira'h remained with him, holding his hand and encouraging him to rest, while Reyn insisted vehemently that he was fine. "It was just a dizzy spell. I felt weak, but I'm better now."

Much to Peter and Estarra's satisfaction, Osira'h had a greater force of will, and she made him take his recovery slowly. Despite his protests, he was obviously glad that she remained there.

Osira'h had always known she would return to Ildira. She tried to prepare herself mentally for that, yet she didn't want to be separated from him. But there would be ample diplomatic opportunities for the Mage-Imperator's daughter and the Confederation's Prince to see each other again. She clung to that.

With a drone of engines, Ildiran cutters landed on the canopy, flying complex maneuvers and trailing prismatic ribbons in the air, as if this were an ordinary skyparade. At about the same time, with a clatter of small engines, a group of flying craft skimmed along the treetops from the west: her sister Muree'n along with Yazra'h, back from their wyvern hunt. They, too, would have sensed the crisis in the *thism* network.

The green priest Beltrias had sent word ahead about the results of the hunt through telink, so they knew the monster had been killed. Beltrias led the way, beside Anton Colicos, who clung to his wobbly aircraft. On their own flyers, Yazra'h and Muree'n sat proud in their armor, but their triumph was diminished because of the distant tragedy.

After landing, Yazra'h swung off her vehicle with remarkable suppleness. Muree'n imitated her, while Anton struggled to dismount. When he nearly tripped, Yazra'h flashed out a hand to steady him, as if she were deflecting a poisonous viper from striking him. Embarrassed, the human historian mumbled his thanks.

Without wasting time on greetings, Mage-Imperator Jora'h said, "Come! The Empire needs us. We depart for Ildira immediately."

Yazra'h placed her hands on Anton's shoulders in a formal gesture of farewell. "I am sorry to leave you."

He seemed surprised. "I'm going back with you. Your rememberers need me—they can't sort through all those ancient Shana Rei records themselves, and they sure don't have the imagination to connect the dots unless somebody shows them how. You need me there."

Yazra'h accepted his decision. "Yes, I do. I will protect you."

Blushing, he laughed. "Really? You just dragged me out into the deep forest on a monster hunt."

She cocked her eyebrows. "You survived—and you returned with a glorious story."

Wistfully, Nira touched the fronds on the canopy, engaging in direct contact with the worldforest one more time. "We have to go."

Osira'h turned to Reynald. "Be well—I want you to promise me."

He sounded awkward. "I'm doing my best. I wish you could stay."

"The Ildiran medical kith continue to research, but I will also contact my sister Tamo'l. Maybe she can find some way to treat your sickness."

Reyn let out a sigh. "I appreciate that, but there are many diseases, many sick people. It's not fair to the rest of them to expend so much effort on me."

"It is not about being fair. It is about you, and I care about *you*."

She wasn't sure which of them moved first, but Osira'h was holding him, and Reyn wrapped his arms around her to hold her in return. She could sense the Ildiran entourage and the Mage-Imperator watching them, but she didn't care. Muree'n seemed puzzled at their show of affection, as if she hadn't even considered the possibility of a relationship between the two of them.

"I will see you again, Reynald of Theroc," Osira'h said.

"As soon as possible," he answered.

CHAPTER

41

ROD'H

The unexpected slaughter at the daily lens-alignment ceremony left the Ildiran people reeling. Taking charge of the Prime Designate, Rod'h had fled from the mob, avoiding even the guard kithmen, trusting no one. Keeping hidden, he dragged Daro'h through the streets, desperate to get back to the Prism Palace. He knew that at any moment, some innocuous-seeming citizen on any street corner might turn murderous.

So the two of them ran alone. Rod'h felt vulnerable, but he considered it a greater risk to be near other Ildirans whom the Shana Rei could possess.

Fortunately, the violent outburst faded quickly. As they ran up the steep paths to the Prism Palace, guard kithmen hurried to meet them, but Rod'h took one look at their wicked crystal weapons, their muscled bodies, and their armor, and ordered them to step aside. He was all too aware that they could become enemies.

Daro'h understood the danger as well. "Do as he says!" he commanded. The guards dutifully stepped away and let the two of them run into the Palace.

After the ordeal, the Prime Designate was frightened but not helpless, not panicked. He seemed to understand that Rod'h was trying to help him, and he drew upon his friend's strength. "Thank you." He panted as they barricaded themselves in his quarters. "I feel safe with you."

Rod'h kept his voice hard. "It is possible that I am immune to the taint from the shadows, like my brother Gale'nh, but do not let yourself feel safe with anyone."

Daro'h collapsed on a cushion and tried to catch his breath. Several of his children were playing in his quarters, along with five breeding partners who had come to spend the day. Illi'v, who had designed their new garments, cried out when she saw the clothes spattered with blood.

In a commanding voice, Rod'h ordered them all out. Daro'h objected. "My children—I need to keep them with me. I need to protect them."

"You need to be alone and sheltered," Rod'h insisted. He didn't want to think about the Prime Designate's children snatching up sharp-edged toys and lunging at their father. Lowering his voice, he added with more compassion, "We cannot allow the Shana Rei to use your own children against you, Prime Designate. This is a terrible time."

He had not expected an opportunity to show his worth so soon, and Rod'h had not done it in a calculating way, but because it *needed to be done*.

After an urgent discussion, he convinced the Prime Designate that the dead mob members had to be gathered up and incinerated immediately. The risk of the spreading shadow stain was too great. Daro'h agreed, issuing the necessary orders and instructing the handlers of the dead to wear full exosuits, as if they were operating in a hazardous environment.

In the absence of the Mage-Imperator, the Ildirans followed the Prime Designate's orders without question, and Rod'h was glad—even proud—to help Daro'h impose order. The new victims were all vaporized inside crematory crucibles.

Even after that grim task was completed, though, Rod'h didn't rest. Mijistra had to be stable when the Mage-Imperator returned, and he and Daro'h had little time to make it so. Surely, Jora'h would already be on his way.

Adar Zan'nh returned to Ildira first, however. As soon as his battered flagship reached the Ildiran system, Rod'h could sense Gale'nh—alive, but shaken from his encounter with the Shana Rei.

Though Rod'h wanted to keep Daro'h isolated from crowds, the Prime Designate was required to receive the returning Adar. The Ildiran people would be even more frightened if the future Mage-Imperator continued to hide in his chambers.

Speaking on Daro'h's behalf, Rod'h called for twice the usual contingent of guards to stand around the perimeter of the skysphere audience chamber, but with an excess of caution, he refused to allow any of them to approach closer than the lowest step of the dais. He stood partway up, as if he alone could defend the Prime Designate. Concealed beneath his robes, he carried two powerful projectile weapons. If the shadows should seize control of a mob and turn them against Daro'h, he would gun them all down.

Although the Solar Navy flagship had already transmitted reports of what had occurred on Hiltos, Adar Zan'nh and Tal Gale'nh came to deliver a personal report nevertheless.

Rod'h was shocked to see the haughty man accompanying Zan'nh and Gale'nh. Though mad Designate Rusa'h had changed in appearance during two decades of isolation, every Ildiran knew the face of the man who had nearly obliterated the Empire through his alliance with the fire elementals.

Even more shocked, Daro'h lurched up out of the chrysalis chair. Rusa'h strode in beside the Solar Navy officers as if he were an equal. The man had once been corpulent and hedonistic, but now he appeared drained, burnt out from the inside and merely a ghost of who he had been.

"Why have you brought that evil man here?" Daro'h demanded, unconsciously touching his burned cheek.

Adar Zan'nh seemed angry as well. "Great apologies, Prime Designate. He demanded it."

The disgraced man glanced at the threatening guard kithmen, then made a dismissive gesture. "You have nothing to fear from me. Our Empire is sorely threatened, and I may be able to help."

Rod'h could not restrain his retort. "You have already caused us enough damage. Controlled by you, the faeros incinerated my own father on Dobro."

"Do not hold to narrow thoughts in times of crisis," Rusa'h said, maddeningly calm. "What was once our greatest enemy could now become our most powerful weapon. The shadows are already here, woven throughout space and tangled in the *thism*. How do you plan to fight them?" His lips quirked in a cold smile. "You just saw for yourselves that Ildirans cannot defend when the shadows strike from within."

Prime Designate Daro'h tried to sound strong as he stood beside the chrysalis chair. "The Mage-Imperator just strengthened our alliance with the Confederation, and our races will work together to fight the Shana Rei."

"And if that is ineffective?" Rusa'h asked. "Do not be afraid of the faeros. Think! What better way to drive back the creatures of darkness than with allies who are composed of fire and light? If we can summon—and control—the faeros, they could defend against even the darkest shadows."

"They could also set Mijistra aflame, as they did before," said Rod'h. "Is that how you mean to save us?"

The mad Designate frowned at him. "Who are you? Why do you speak for the Prime Designate?"

"He is my friend," said Daro'h.

Gale'nh added, "Rod'h is my brother."

Adar Zan'nh said, "As commander of the Solar Navy, I have seen the terrible threat posed by the Shana Rei and the black robots. I cannot in good conscience dismiss any possible way to fight against such a terrible enemy." He lowered his voice. "Though I am gravely uneasy at the prospect."

Daro'h flushed, making the scar even more prominent on his face. "We dare not invite the faeros back. We cannot trust them. I am Prime Designate, and I will not allow it!"

Rusa'h lifted his chin. "Then I will wait and speak with the Mage-Imperator when he returns. As I learned so painfully and so clearly, the Ildiran Empire has only one leader."

CHAPTER

42

ZOE ALAKIS

A ship arrived at Pergamus broadcasting its coded access signal—one of her secret operatives. She knew it must be something important. No one just "dropped by." Thanks to great effort on Zoe's part, the Pergamus star system was not even marked on most Confederation star charts.

This visitor came from the primary medical facilities on Earth, whose resources were famed throughout the Confederation (although they paled in comparison to those at Pergamus). Dr. Benjamin Paolus was a well-respected neurological researcher who had garnered accolades and prestige over the years. He was paid well in his line of work, but Zoe paid him much more for his off-the-books efforts. Paolus occasionally delivered interesting and classified medical cases for Zoe to add to her collection, and each time he requested more money.

On the comm screen, Zoe could see the glint of desperate avarice in his eyes. She had never been interested in, let alone obsessed with, money. Her inexhaustible stockpile of prisdiamonds on Vaconda left her wealthy beyond any possible need. But she knew, thanks to Tom Rom, that for some types of people, money was like kindling: the more it burned the brighter the flame, and those flames demanded to be fed with more and more fuel.

Her mercenary ships intercepted Paolus and guided him down through the poisonous atmosphere toward an isolated holding dome. Zoe sent Tom Rom to meet Paolus, trusting him to make decisions for her and to take care of any problems that arose. When unexpected people arrived at Pergamus, they brought problems as often as they brought opportunities.

Dr. Paolus fidgeted in the holding dome, as if his information were unstable and liable to detonate any minute. Zoe took her time before activating the screen. She wanted to make him wait. Yes, Paolus had provided interesting data before, but she didn't want him to think he could demand her attention whenever he decided to arrive unannounced.

Finally, she activated the screen and looked mildly at the impatient doctor. With her sharp eye, Zoe could see that his haughty and determined demeanor merely masked uneasiness. In order for him to have come all the way to Pergamus, either he must have something very important, or he was desperate.

For a long moment, she just stared at him, exchanged no pleasantries, didn't greet him—which made Paolus more nervous still. The doctor looked away, then back at her. Tom Rom loomed next to him, a silent and intimidating presence. She noted a sparkle of perspiration on Paolus's forehead.

He cleared his throat. "I've come about the case of Prince Reynald of Theroc. As you know, before his illness was publicly announced he hired me privately to test and diagnose him. I provided Pergamus with all that original medical data."

"Yes," Zoe said. "We paid you well for it."

At the time, even King Peter and Queen Estarra hadn't known about their son's disease. It was quite an alarming revelation that the Confederation's heir apparent might waste away and die before he could ever take the throne.

Paolus cleared his throat. "The King and Queen are quite desperate for a cure. I pushed my teams to their limits, but I've done all I can. Your Pergamus facilities far surpass mine; in fact, they surpass any laboratory in the Confederation. There is an enormous reward for any kind of hope." He shot an uneasy glance at Tom Rom.

"And how does this concern me?" Zoe asked.

Paolus sputtered. "You have the samples, the data, and the best facilities in the Spiral Arm. Have you investigated the Prince's illness? A rare and unique—"

Zoe remained cold. "We have teams studying the data. It is an interesting disease organism, but we have countless interesting specimens, and not enough time or researchers to study them all. We have catalogued and filed the information appropriately. My people have laid the foundation for a cure, but that is all the farther we've progressed. It is not a priority." Her teams had actually done a fair amount of work, because Tom Rom suggested it, but Paolus didn't need to know.

He leaned closer to the screen, sweating more now. "Then, I'd like to volunteer to work here. No one knows the intricacies of Reynald's records as I do, and I'm already invested in this project. I have every confidence that I can crack the problem. If we can cure—or at least treat—Prince Reynald, you can't imagine how generous the King and Queen would be. I would"—his voice caught, but he pushed forward—"I'd be willing to split the reward money with you for the further work here at Pergamus."

With a flash of anger plain on his face, Tom Rom stepped up behind the researcher, intimidating him.

Zoe furrowed her brow. "Dr. Paolus, surely you're not so ignorant about what we do here. All of my work, all of my research, all of my specimens, and all of my cures belong *to me*, and I don't share them. I have never shared them. People will get sick out there, people will die, and people will continue to treat one another like ruthless animals. Time and again, they prove that they are not worth any effort from me to save them."

"But . . ." Paolus sputtered, "Prince Reynald is a very important young man! The Confederation's gratitude must be worth something. And the reward—"

"The reward means nothing to me," Zoe said, "and you have already been paid. Pergamus has been self-sufficient for as long as this facility has existed. Until I think of something that I need or want from the Confederation, they have nothing to offer me."

Dr. Paolus looked confused. "But . . . that isn't rational."

Zoe lost patience. "Pergamus is my facility. I define the parameters, and I make the decisions. My answer is no. Please leave."

Tom Rom hardened his voice and spoke to the nervous doctor. "I remind you of the confidentiality terms of our business arrangement, not to mention the extraordinary ethical violation you made by breaching your doctor-patient confidentiality when you sold us Reynald's medical records in the first place."

Paolus was angry and distraught as he prepared to leave the holding dome. "What type of researcher refuses to help people?"

Zoe knew that Dr. Paolus was more intent on helping himself than the ailing Prince. Again, she wasted no time on pleasantries as she signed off. Tom Rom would take care of removing the man from Pergamus. As insurance, she contacted her mercenary squadron in orbit and instructed them to follow Paolus's ship all the way out of the system.

CHAPTER

43

LEE ISWANDER

As he flew back from Newstation after leaving Arden at the Roamer school, Iswander felt disappointed at how aloof and closed-minded the clans were toward him. He didn't deserve to be treated that way. But when he saw the industrial lights of the bloater-extraction complex, he knew he had achieved great success. He *knew it*, whether or not the other Roamers gave him credit for what he'd accomplished. Here, he was the uncontested boss, the king of this small but valuable domain.

Lee Iswander had changed, and the Roamers refused to change. He had grown so distant from the clans that he wasn't sure if there was any common ground anymore. Maybe it had been a mistake to leave his son at Academ. Even though he respected Jess Tamblyn and Cesca Peroni, he wondered if a Roamer education was relevant anymore. . . .

He wanted to earn respect and power for his son, not just himself. "We are *Iswanders*!" he had said to Arden again and again. They weren't just any other Roamer clan.

As he flew in, he noticed that the large ekti tank array was gone—Elisa must have departed already—and a new array was being filled, canister by canister. He was glad to see the well-organized industrial complex that produced and produced and produced. Exactly the way he liked it.

After he docked in the admin hub, Alec Pannebaker met him to provide a quick briefing. The deputy was casual, good-natured, and friendly with everyone. He had worked for Lee Iswander for many years and had remained loyal to him even after Sheol. And Iswander did not treat loyalty lightly.

Elisa Enturi was more intense, more cutthroat, and willing to do anything to further Iswander Industries. The oil-and-water combination of Pannebaker and Elisa made a good enough management team when he himself was gone.

Pannebaker grinned as he handed over the summaries. "Nothing much to look at, boss. Production at peak capacity, just as when you left. Elisa departed for Ulio three days ago with our largest load yet. We're going to need to broaden our distribution—it's a bottleneck. We might need to deal with more than just Kett Shipping."

Iswander scanned the numbers. "I'm being cautious, and I prefer the single point of contact. Kett Shipping has other vessels they can use—it's their problem to handle our output. But if someone discovered what we do here, our whole business would fall apart."

If Elisa detected anyone unauthorized in the vicinity—any spycraft, any surveillance ship, or even some lost traveler who stumbled upon the extraction operations—he was confident she would know how to handle it.

The two men walked directly to the control center, bypassing his own quarters. His wife would be waiting for him, full of questions about Arden, about his trip, what the boy had said, and whether he seemed happy to go back to school. Iswander would see Londa later, after he finished his important business here.

He took a moment to drink in all the activity at workstations in the admin hub as well as the movement of equipment out in the bloater cluster. Space travel throughout the Spiral Arm depended on what they did here. With more and more ekti-X available, colonization efforts could increase, shipping routes could be expanded. Twenty years after the Elemental War, the Confederation could become twice as powerful as it had been before—all because of Iswander Industries and what was produced here.

And yet the Roamers brushed him aside. Damn them! Their Guiding Star was a delusion, while his own was laser bright. He was willing to partner with anyone who was just as ambitious, just as willing to risk and work and use their imagination. Roamers were supposed to be visionary, not timid, and he had expected to find many such people among the clans. Not so!

After the recent reaction at Newstation, he realized that pandering to the clans might not be the best way to return to prominence. In fact, if the Roamers were afraid of new ideas, challenges, or risks, Iswander wasn't sure he should be associated with them at all.

Focusing on the activity around him in the control center, he asked Pannebaker, "When do we expect Elisa back from Ulio?"

"Five days or so." Pannebaker looked out at the bloaters, the machinery draining the nodules dry and storing stardrive fuel. He hesitated. "There's one thing, boss. It's troubling, and I don't know what to make of it."

Iswander was instantly on his guard. Such comments usually led to news he didn't want to hear.

"The green priest has gone missing." Pannebaker's brow furrowed. "He escaped one night, probably during a shift change."

Iswander fought back a groan, tired of defending the eccentric and damaged green priest. Yes, Iswander felt responsible for Aelin, but compassion only extended so far. "How did he escape? Where would he go?" He knew what the man had done before, and he had a good idea what he had done now.

Pannebaker shrugged. "Not a clue, boss. No one saw him, but . . . my environment suit is missing—the one I use for gap jumping. I think he might've taken it and just . . . stepped outside."

Iswander let his eyes fall closed. Not long ago Aelin had been caught trying to steal an inspection pod so he could float out and "commune with the bloaters." No doubt he had seen Pannebaker's risky free-fall activity and decided to go out among the nodules again. "Have you completed a thorough search? How long has he been gone?"

Pannebaker shook his head. "Best guess—three days. He could never have survived this long."

Iswander's heart felt heavy. Aelin would have drifted out there unseen. Maybe he had reached one of the big green bloaters, and worked his way through the membrane, where he would have drowned in the fluid. Or maybe he had gone astray and just drifted until his life support ran out. Three days . . .

Iswander shook his head. "We can't save those who are intent on destroying themselves." He knew Arden would be disappointed, since he had liked the green priest as a tutor.

Pannebaker remained awkwardly silent, as if the loss of Aelin were his fault. Few people would mourn the green priest, who had caused numerous problems.

Iswander sighed. "Nothing to be done about it. He's gone. In a way, we lost the green priest a long time ago. Continue business as usual."

CHAPTER

44

AELIN

When he allowed himself to awaken from his deathlike trance, Aelin was bone-shatteringly *cold*. Stagnant air filled his lungs, and he exhaled, then drank in oxygen, draining some of the last wisps in his connected tanks. The array of ekti-X cylinders had arrived at Ulio Station, and now the big framework hung near the central backbone of abandoned wrecks.

Aelin didn't move his body as he became aware; he simply blinked his eyes and stared through the helmet faceplate. His body chemistry allowed him to survive on the tiniest gasps of oxygen at freezing temperatures, and he had spent days immersed in a trance with a nearly nonexistent heartbeat. Now, he warmed himself strictly by increasing his metabolism.

Around him, he could no longer sense the thrumming musical song of the bloaters, though he did feel an echo from the tanks themselves, as if the ekti-X still held some kind of energy from the exotic things. His trance-addled brain seemed more sensitive than before, touching the faint cries of the bloaters that had been wrung dry to harvest this fuel.

The tank array was now anchored to one of the stationary hulls that comprised Ulio Station. Transfer ships began to remove the fuel canisters. Aelin felt his thoughts sharpen, and knew he would have to get out of here. Soon.

Aelin glanced at the levels of his oxygen and life-support batteries. Everything read empty . . . almost. His arms, hands, and feet were numb, and he began to shiver violently, which would burn some of his remaining oxygen—and he couldn't afford that. He had no choice but to increase the heat in his suit, draining some of the last blips of power in the life-support batteries . . . which he also couldn't afford. Only one of the packs contained any charge at all, and he discarded the rest of them as extraneous.

He disengaged the clip that anchored him in place. Fortunately, his maneuvering-gas tanks were mostly full. He had seen Pannebaker do pirouettes during his gap jumps, spinning around while floating among the industrial operations. Aelin just needed enough propellant to jet out of the array.

A nudge from the propellant jet pushed him through the framework, toward the outside. Other suited workers flitted about; several noticed him, but showed no alarm. His Iswander suit might look different from theirs, but there was no standardized uniform among the station workers. Apparently, at Ulio everyone brought their own equipment.

Keeping his comm switched off, Aelin accelerated down toward the main ships bound together to form Ulio Station: ancient Ildiran wrecks and decommissioned EDF Juggernauts. He knew nothing about this station, had never used his treeling to research the ever-expanding flea market and repair yard. Maybe he would find a green priest on one of the ships clustered here; maybe he would touch a treeling again, reconnect with the verdani mind, although that contact was only a glimmer of what he had touched when he linked with the bloaters. At least he was away, and hope was like adrenaline to him now.

He was revived now, his pulse quickened to a normal rate, but he forced himself to breathe shallowly. His last air tank read empty, as did the remaining battery pack. He had to get inside.

He dove toward the nearest main ship, a repurposed Ildiran warliner with satellite vessels connected like parasites to every possible docking port. Each one of those barnacle ships also had access hatches—and he made his way to the closest one via the shortest possible path. He tried to stop himself from gasping, from fighting the lack of air; the deep cold settled into him again. Even in free fall, he could barely move his legs.

After he struck the outer hull of the satellite ship, he dragged himself ten meters along the surface until he reached an external airlock. With thick, unresponsive fingers he used the manual-activation switches. He sucked great gulps inside his empty helmet and struggled to crawl into the airlock chamber, which opened too slowly. He felt dizzy. Each breath sounded like hollow thunder inside the helmet, and the thrumming voices of the bloaters had gone far, far away. He drew in another deep breath, but there was nothing to breathe.

The airlock door closed behind him, and atmosphere began pumping in.

Aelin slid down the chamber wall. He wanted to shout, to connect with the bloaters one more time, but they were so far away, and the darkness inside his skull was so close.

Finally, the chamber's inner door slid open, and Aelin sprawled out onto the deck. He forced himself to roll over, and, with clumsy fingers and uncooperative joints, he managed to remove his glove for greater access. There was plenty of air right there on the other side of the faceplate, but his helmet remained sealed. He finally cracked the seal at his neck, twisted and pulled off his helmet, letting it roll to one side. He just lay there heaving huge breaths, tasting the spaceship's processed air. It was recycled and filtered with added oxygen. But it was air, it was life.

The satellite ship was silent, the corridor by the service airlock empty. He was surprised no one had come to investigate the airlock activation, but there was so much activity outside, so many suited people coming and going throughout Ulio, apparently no one noticed. Just another business day.

Still, Aelin knew he had to be gone before anyone saw him. He did not want to try to explain why an undocumented green priest had stumbled aboard the ship. As his fingers became more flexible and background warmth crept into his skin, he disconnected the suit components, stripped off the gloves, the life-support pack, and peeled himself out like a Theron insect emerging from a cocoon. He stood in his loincloth, sweaty but shivering—and free.

Aelin had escaped the extraction operations, but he wasn't sure what to do now. On bare feet, he made his way through the satellite ship and found a connecting passage into the old Ildiran warliner that served as part of Ulio's core. The old warship's corridors had been stripped and refurbished, turned into a well-used commerce center.

He felt exposed in the empty sections, but as he made his way to the more crowded decks, he began to feel less obvious. There were so many more people here than at the Iswander extraction complex! Everyone on Ulio Station was accustomed to a panoply of races and garments, and since others didn't stare at him, Aelin assumed that green priests must be a familiar enough sight, too. A very good sign.

On Theroc, all Aelin had to do was touch a tree, and he could instantly join the community of green priests. Here, he felt isolated, and the crowds were comprised of strangers. Jittery, he was startled whenever someone spoke to him. Fortunately, although he received curious looks, they raised no alarms.

Aelin made his way along, following other moving people. He ended up in a large gathering area, a business exchange filled with loud voices and haggling groups. Commodities boards listed items on offer from cargo ships that had arrived at Ulio. The noise was deafening, frightening.

Disoriented, Aelin bumped into someone, muttered an apology, and hurried off in a different direction. He didn't like this place at all. Looking for some exit, he turned around and froze. The breath dried up in his lungs.

Elisa Enturi stood there, turned to one side and engaged in a heated discussion with two men. She hadn't noticed him yet, so Aelin bolted, not watching where he was going—and ran directly into a thin man in an embroidered Roamer jumpsuit sporting the symbol of clan Duquesne.

"Watch where you're going! I thought green priests were more graceful than that." The man laughed; two larger men with him laughed as well. None of them seemed to have any humor.

Aelin flailed his hands, tried to get away, but the thin Roamer man caught him by the arm. "No need for that. Who are you running from?"

"Elisa Enturi—I can't let her see me."

The man refused to release his grip. "Elisa Enturi? I thought everyone was trying to *get* information from her, not run from her."

"I escaped from the bloater field," Aelin blurted, trying to get away before the woman turned. "She doesn't want me to reveal anything about their ekti-X operations."

The Roamer man's grip tightened further. "What's a bloater field?"

Aelin struggled. "Large nodules drifting in space. Nobody understands what they are."

"That's where ekti-X comes from? That's where Iswander gets the stardrive fuel?"

Aelin groaned inwardly at what he had revealed. He wanted to stop Lee Iswander from draining and discarding the bloaters for their ekti-X. Iswander did not understand the damage he was doing to the miraculous presence being born in the universe . . . but Aelin also knew how greedy people could be. They would all want their own source of ekti-X.

If he revealed the source of cheap stardrive fuel, he would inspire a thousand similar operations, instead of stopping the one. He dared not say anything. His stomach twisted into knots; he couldn't reveal what he knew!

Aelin saw Elisa turning toward the commotion, so he tore his arm free and bolted into the crowd. "Wait, we've got more questions for you," yelled the man from clan Duquesne.

But Aelin ducked and wove his way among other people, panicked. He drew attention to himself in his wild flight, but he kept running anyway, and soon the crowds folded around him, paying little attention.

He found another corridor and ran. Elisa must have spotted him—but why would she even imagine that he had escaped from the extraction field? She couldn't possibly guess that he'd hidden in the tank array. No one could have known that.

He blundered into an empty well-lit room that might once have been a Solar Navy briefing chamber during the warliner's service days. Food wrappers littered the deck as if someone regularly took lunch there.

Aelin collapsed in the corner, drew his knees up to his chest, and just sat inhaling, exhaling, and wondering what to do next.

CHAPTER

45

XANDER BRINDLE

After what had happened to their compy the last time they visited here, Xander was much more wary when the *Verne* returned to Ulio Station. Previously, he and Terry had traveled around the Spiral Arm, happy-go-lucky, enjoying the places they visited. Danger was only theoretical.

But when Aaron Duquesne and his bully companions battered poor OK, the experience threw a bucket of cold water in Xander's face. He had heard plenty of stories about the Elemental War, and he knew about the Shana Rei, so he was fully aware that the Spiral Arm was a dangerous place. But Xander had never believed anything could happen to him.

Naïve and stupid!

Now, he and Terry were on guard, suspicious. It felt like a loss of innocence. Terry still had many friends at the station from when he had worked for old Maria Ulio, but it was a rough-and-tumble place that attracted certain unsavory elements.

As they snagged a docking spot for the *Verne* on Ulio's third outer ring, OK was the only one perfectly cheery. He looked polished and new, all damage repaired, programming restored. "I've logged our arrival with the Central Offices. According to station records, Elisa Enturi arrived seven hours ago with a full array of ekti-X, more than she has ever had us distribute before. I calculate this run should be highly profitable for us."

Terry found that odd. "She doesn't usually deliver the fuel directly here."

Xander said, "Maybe she's flaunting Iswander's production?"

"I would rather she didn't provoke anyone." Terry pulled himself over to the *Verne*'s weapons locker and removed a stun pistol for himself and one for Xander. "Better take these. Just in case."

Xander never would have considered such precautions only a few weeks ago. "Just in case."

The compy remained cheery. "I am glad to help us out in any way possible. I hope my services will be satisfactory."

"I know they will." Xander bent down in front of him. Rlinda Kett's compy technicians had also added mission parameters for a special job the two young men wanted OK to do. "You understand that this is an independent mission. You'll have to take care of it by yourself, solve any problems that might arise. This is very important to us."

The compy's optical sensors brightened. "Yes, and it is also important to Tasia Tamblyn and Robb Brindle. Our future business model and understanding of ekti-X operations relies upon my mission." He seemed proud. "A trading company has the right to know what it ships."

"Yes, it does. We're counting on you."

Terry applied an Ulio Station decal to OK's polymer shoulder, then attached a standard station-maintenance kit. "There, now you look like a Maintenance-model compy. I used to work with dozens of compies just like you, and this will make you unobtrusive. Be a spy for us and go where we need you to go. If you look like you know what you're doing, nobody'll ask questions."

OK said, "I do know what I'm doing. I have new programming."

Xander opened the typical repair kit, pulled out a small, unmarked hemispherical device. "Rlinda Kett used this in her old blockade-runner days. It's a special undetectable tracker. If you install it properly on Elisa's ship, it'll record everywhere she goes and give us assurance that the ekti-X operations are legit."

"I will not let you down," OK said.

Exiting the *Verne*, the compy headed off in one direction while Xander and Terry went in the other. Xander wore a traditional Roamer jumpsuit with Tamblyn clan markings on the breast and sleeve, along with Kett Shipping insignia. Terry chose more casual clothes and an old jacket he had kept from Ulio Station. They looked comfortable and at-ease, but they kept their stunners handy. They stayed in low- or no-gravity areas, so Terry needed no extra help to move about.

Xander looked at his comm, scrolled down to a new message he had just received. "Looks like Elisa is waiting for us in the star balcony lounge."

Terry sighed. "I don't know why she always wants to meet us there, since she never drinks. I read about a new crepe restaurant featuring fruits from seventeen different planets. That would have been more interesting."

"We'll do that afterward to celebrate—*if* OK does what he's supposed to. A meal of exotic fruit crepes sounds like a good way to end the day."

Terry nodded, resigned. "I suppose it would be a waste to have a nice lunch with Elisa Enturi. She's always in a hurry."

"She's always *Elisa*," said Xander. He, for one, was glad the woman didn't spend hours in casual conversation before coming to the point. With her, each interaction was all business—mercifully so. Elisa just wanted to finalize the ekti-X transaction, verify the accounts, and return to her duties.

Inside the star balcony, Elisa Enturi sat at a table by herself, staring out at the ships swarming around the station. She was an attractive woman sitting alone in a spaceport bar filled with lonely traders, but no one ventured close to the ice barrier she kept up.

Wearing his usual grin, Xander signaled a serving compy and placed a drink order. Elisa already had a cup of coffee, which was sufficient for her. "I've been waiting for you," she said.

Terry looked at his chronometer. "We're right on time."

"I arrived early." She seemed to think they should have known that.

Xander ignored the comment. "We saw that giant array you delivered. It's the largest load you've ever brought. We're going to have to store a lot of it here before we can arrange for distribution, even if we bring in another ship or two."

"It's not all for you. Special circumstances. I signed a contract with Darwin Felliwell," Elisa said, naming Ulio's current station manager. "Seventy percent of the array canisters are earmarked to be used as a strategic stockpile for station operations. Iswander Industries has surplus production, and we felt this was a wise diversification. The other thirty percent of the ekti-X is my usual delivery to Kett Shipping. You have not been shorted."

Xander didn't like the idea of Elisa selling stardrive fuel to other customers, whether or not it was a strategic stockpile.

When the serving compy brought their drinks—two new and oddly named frothy concoctions that sounded interesting on the menu—Xander said, "We hope you're not looking for other distributors. We've been very successful working with you, and this is a beneficial arrangement for both parties, but our boss does have some concerns."

Terry took a sip of the strange new drink, approved. "Your secrecy, not to mention the sheer productivity, has been raising a lot of questions."

"Let them ask questions," Elisa said. "It's our business, not theirs."

"Some of them think it is their business," Terry said. "All that stardrive fuel is affecting the ekti market for the Roamer clans."

"And the mood is getting hostile out there," Xander said. "On our last trip here we were assaulted in a back corridor by members of clan Duquesne who demanded to know about Iswander operations. They damaged our compy."

Elisa was unsympathetic. "Then get another compy. Learn how to take care of yourselves and defend your profits. It's only common sense."

"We're your business partners," Xander said. "And that makes us your *accomplices* if you're doing something illegal to produce the stardrive fuel. How do we know there's nothing to worry about?"

"You don't. And you have no need to know anything at all about our production methods."

Terry frowned. "That's not exactly reassuring."

"You shouldn't need reassurance." As she sipped her coffee, Elisa looked not quite *past* Xander, but *through* him, to the observation window where a large passenger ship could be seen docking at an inner ring on the other side of the star balcony. "I deliver the ekti, you distribute it. You make profits, we make profits. There's no need for you to be involved any further than that."

Xander said, realizing that his voice had taken on an annoying tone, "Can't you give us at least a general *idea*? Do you get the ekti from skymining on a gas giant? Or nebula skimming? Or—"

She cut him off abruptly. "Proprietary information. And I can always find an alternative distributor if you keep pressing." Elisa finished her coffee. "We're done here. I need to be going."

After she left, both of them looked disturbed. "Miss Congeniality," Xander said.

"She's definitely hiding something," Terry said. "I was uneasy about spying on her, even if it was just to dispel our concerns, but now . . ."

"If OK placed the tracker, we'll know in a month or two, after we retrieve the data. She has to head back to their ekti operations at some point, and the tracker will record her movements. We just have to wait." He grinned and placed a hand on his partner's forearm. "Right now, we have time for that crepe lunch."

Later, fully satisfied with their delicious meal, although somewhat disappointed that they had been able to taste only eight of the excellent selections, they returned to the *Verne* and found OK waiting there. The little compy seemed pleased that he had accomplished his covert mission of placing the tracker on Elisa's ship.

He also had intriguing information for them. "The *Verne* received a message from an unknown sender. Terry Handon was tagged with very specific identification codes. The sender knew to locate you here on this ship."

"Probably somebody trying to sell you something," Xander teased.

As Terry read the message, his brow furrowed. "Sounds like someone from my old days here at Ulio Station." He looked at the embedded images—old and obscure photos of himself when he was younger. Xander was amused to see his partner at a much younger age. "It is a little creepy that somebody has those."

"It's a set of coordinates." Terry displayed the destination. "We're supposed to go to this point . . . but it's between star systems. Why would anyone want us out there?" He shook his head. "It says this is urgent."

Xander knew there wouldn't be much discussion. "Then we have to go."

CHAPTER

46

GARRISON REEVES

Considering its heady history, Rendezvous was an unremarkable sight—a grouping of rocks drawn together in a backwash of gravity, orbiting a red dwarf star called Meyer. But Garrison knew what this place signified, the legends, the culture, and the emotions wrapped up in it, how much it meant to every Roamer clan . . . and its importance to clan Reeves. For so many years, family obligations had trapped him here, like a deep emotional gravity well. . . .

After the tragedy that had befallen them, though, he wanted to make sure Seth felt the same understanding, even though the place was full of pain and regret. It was the boy's heritage.

When the *Prodigal Son* arrived at Rendezvous, Seth served as navigator while DD double-checked the boy's calculations. Garrison wasn't surprised that his son nailed the navigation as well as any well-seasoned pilot could have done.

Orli peered out the main windowport. "Just looks like a handful of pebbles in the middle of nowhere."

"Think of what the people aboard the generation ship *Kanaka* must have thought when they finally arrived here after eight decades in flight." Garrison couldn't keep the wistful tone from his voice.

Seth piped up, "But the *Kanaka* set up an outpost here anyway. They were resourceful, and they made it work."

"That's how we started to become Roamers." Looking at the cluster and the dim red star, Garrison tried to imagine the level of desperation the first colonists had experienced, knowing that if they left here, it would take the slow ship many decades more to reach another, equally unlikely solar system.

The disconnected rocks tumbled along in orbit now. At one point the asteroids had been woven together in an intricate complex connected by support struts, linking tubes, and a cat's cradle of girders. Ships had flown in from across the Spiral Arm to conduct clan business—skyminers and terraformers, imaginative industrialists or just footloose space pilots. It had been the vibrant center of all clan business, the heart of their culture.

"And the Earth Defense Forces destroyed it all," Orli said. "The Hansa couldn't defeat the hydrogues, so they attacked the Roamers instead." She shook her head.

Garrison said, "The Roamer clans were outlaws when I was a kid—Seth's age. I remember moving from place to place, and my father held our clan together by brute force. I suppose it was necessary then." He let out a long sigh. "But he never knew when to loosen his grip."

The asteroids that comprised Rendezvous were too small to hold a natural atmosphere, but Garrison had felt suffocated for entirely different reasons. He'd finally torn himself away, escaping into the arms of the beautiful and ambitious Elisa Enturi—another bad decision.

Except for Seth. His son was one part of the whole story he did not regret.

"Do what you have to do, Garrison," Orli said to him now. "I'm here for whatever you need." She so easily washed away the thoughts of Elisa.

He flew the *Prodigal Son* into a docking bay that yawned open from a deactivated atmosphere field. The asteroid complex had been abandoned for no more than a year, and the automation still functioned with durable and efficient Roamer systems. Lights came on to illuminate the hollowed-out alcove with harsh yellow light, refilling the chamber with air.

When the pressure and temperature read nominal, they emerged from the ship into the oppressive silence. Orli shivered visibly. Garrison stepped closer, putting an arm around her, perhaps as much to comfort himself as to comfort her. "It's all right."

Rendezvous had seemed so much more welcoming with the bustle of other ships and clan members hurrying about to do their daily work. But that was all gone now.

Orli shook her head. "This place seems haunted to me."

DD spoke up, "Ghosts have been widely discussed in human culture throughout recorded civilization, Orli, although there is no evidence that ghosts exist."

"Ghosts don't have to be real to have an effect on people, DD," Orli said.

The compy paused. "I do not understand."

Garrison walked ahead. "Most of us don't."

He saw the abandoned equipment, the supplies, the half-finished reconstruction of a great complex that was saturated with history. "After the war was over, my father wanted to restore Rendezvous to the way it was, but the Spiral Arm was completely changed. He never accepted change."

The rock corridors were cold, but the power blocks that clan Reeves had installed were long-term energy reservoirs. Even though Olaf Reeves had taken his people far out into uncharted space, the old man had probably still harbored a lingering hope that some other clan, someday, would finish restoring Rendezvous.

Seth bounded ahead with DD trying to keep up as they explored room after room. Garrison took Orli's hand and led her out of the landing bay into the warren of living quarters, quiet, cold. They stopped at the large family complex where his brother Dale had lived with his wife and two sons. Inside the chamber, with the lights restored now, he found only a few scraps, some discarded clothes, a polymer chair with one broken leg, a spaceship toy in the corner. Garrison picked it up, wondering whether Jamie or Scott had left it behind.

For years, Olaf Reeves and his people had worked to reassemble the broken asteroids and broken dreams, linking together some of the tumbling boulders in space. Just because the man was stubborn. So much work for what looked like so little progress . . .

He remembered hearing Olaf's grand lectures of what this complex had once been and what it had meant to so many people. He had spread out sprawling blueprints and explained sprawling dreams of how he would single-handedly reconstruct this magnificent place . . . but the original construction had taken place over a century of thriving commerce with the help of countless ambitious families. With a heavy heart, Garrison realized the vast gulf between Olaf's dreams and his capabilities.

He felt deeply sad as he turned to Orli. "The rest of the Roamer clans moved on, joined the Confederation, built a stronger society . . . but my father didn't want to hear any ideas other than his own." He hitched a deep breath. "That's what drove me away from him in the first place."

Garrison guided them through the complex, pausing solemnly in his old quarters. His bed, his storage locker, his desk—all were still there. As the oldest son, he should have been the next clan leader, but he had disappointed his father too much. Now he *was* the leader of clan Reeves . . . a clan that consisted of himself and Seth. No one else.

Seth came into the lonely chamber with DD, looking subdued. Even the boy felt the same weight on his heart. "I was only here once, but it wasn't so quiet and empty before. It feels wrong."

Olaf had wanted to fold his grandson into the insular clan, disdaining the education Seth would have received at Academ. Garrison had almost backed down, *almost* decided to follow his family out to deep space. It had taken great courage to turn his back, take his son, and leave again.

That decision had saved Seth's life, as well as his own.

Next they made their way to the administrative chambers, finally stopping in the main offices of Olaf Reeves, where the gruff man had commanded all of his family members. Before, any visit to this lion's den had been an intimidating experience, but now the desk just looked like a desk, and the office looked like any other chamber.

Now that they were here, Garrison wanted to pay his respects, but he didn't know how. Was this some sort of pilgrimage or an expression of atonement? Maybe he just wanted to sharpen his memories of what had been.

He realized that even if he had stayed here rebuilding Rendezvous, even if every member of clan Reeves had devoted their lives to the gigantic project, they would only have begun the task. "Maybe the point of his dream was not to realize it," he said. "The dream became an end unto itself."

Orli squeezed his hand. "It's important that you came back here.

Were you going to leave a message? Some kind of plaque or memorial?"

He went to the main console on his father's desk, then withdrew a small datapack from the pocket of his jumpsuit. He had copied all of the family farewells here, and he decided the records belonged in Rendezvous, as a memorial to clan Reeves if nothing else.

"These are all the messages my family sent through the green priest, recorded, transcribed, and here to share. Message after message, warnings, apologies, and a lot of goodbyes. It is the only mark they have left." He inserted the datapack into the console.

He set them playing. The voices of the green priests who had recorded them droned out, speaking the words transmitted to them via Shelud, who had also died on the derelict space city. Different green priests narrated the lives of various dying members of clan Reeves. First Dale, then his wife Sendra, then an engineer named Bjorn Klemmer, then another and another. Garrison had listened to all the recordings—three times, in fact—and he knew they would go on for hours. Orli herself had heard Olaf's last message when she found the Onthos plague station.

As the lives continued to be spoken, Garrison left the loop on repeat. "Anyone who comes here—if anybody ever does—can watch them and hear what happened to clan Reeves." He looked at Orli. "Their mistakes won't be forgotten, but neither will the people."

It seemed a small thing now, but it was the only thing he could think of that seemed *significant* enough. "Rendezvous itself is the grandest memorial clan Reeves could ever ask for. We'll leave it at that."

Orli nodded. "I think we should."

CHAPTER

47

ARITA

On warm nights, Arita liked to sleep on her open balcony in the fungus-reef city. In the dark silence, sapphire condorflies would buzz past, large iridescent insects with a wingspan as broad as her outstretched arms. Tiny fireflies like flitting stars sparkled throughout the canopy, and the undulating thrum of night insects made for a peaceful lullaby.

Her slumbers were not always quiet, though.

After a restless muddled sleep, Arita awoke on the balcony with a buzzing, bone-deep sound ringing through her body, like chimes, incomprehensible music unlike anything she had heard before. She saw nothing nearby, only the haze of sunrise seeping through the dense trees. She felt disoriented, still hearing the whispers of a dream inside her mind. She didn't know what had happened, and it was fading from her sleep memory quickly.

She clearly recalled hearing a rushing sound of myriad voices speaking all at once inside her head, telling her important things that she could not now recall. Arita rubbed her eyes. She had seen visions of stars, rivers of suns along the arms of the Galaxy, nebulae shining in all the bands of the electromagnetic spectrum, like a primordial sea of the universe itself, giving birth to . . . something incomprehensible.

Her head ached now, and she was sure she had only seen the barest hint of what was out there trying to contact her. And amid that sense of indefinable wonder, she also felt a dread, a plea of some sort. Something desperately looking for help.

Ever since Ohro had hinted that Arita might be sensitive to some exotic and distant communication that had nothing to do with the verdani mind, she had hoped. The worldtrees had rejected her bid to become a green priest, but in doing so they had altered her thought patterns. After that painful disappointment, Arita wanted to believe she was special in a different way—but that didn't make the idea true.

As she struggled awake on her soft balcony, listening to the stir of worldtree fronds in the breezes, she didn't think her dream whispers came from the trees at all. No, something had *spoken* to her while her mind was vulnerable and unguarded, deep in the uncharted realm of sleep.

But the more she tried to remember, the faster it all slipped through her mental fingers. By the time Arita climbed to her feet, blinking in the faint colors of dawn, it was just an echo of a dream.

She stretched, rubbed her eyes, and wondered if she should tell Reyn. She had no secrets from her brother, and he would believe her unconditionally when she told him about the voices in her head. He wouldn't call her crazy, even if she insisted that weighty whispers were trying to communicate with her. . . .

Later, she ate breakfast with her family out in the open, drinking steaming cups of klee as they looked out into the thick branches. Two condorflies swooped about in an aerial dance, like a pair of Remora fighter craft.

Several Onthos moved silently through the forest, preoccupied with unspecified obligations to the trees. Through telink, they communed with the worldtrees, shared their stories with the verdani mind, revealed many things about their lovely home planet, now destroyed. Arita was very interested in the proposed CDF and Solar Navy mission to the Gardeners' original star system, wondering what they would find there.

As they finished breakfast and her parents prepared for Confederation meetings, a green priest appeared in the throne room, bearing a message. "Kennebar and a group of followers have flown in from the Wild. They've come to see the Gardeners."

Arita's heart skipped a beat as she thought of Collin, her first love—the young man she had intended to make a life with after they both became green priests. But no amount of friendship or romance could bridge the gulf between them now. She wondered if Collin had come back as part of the group with Kennebar. Maybe he was lonely. Maybe he wished he hadn't gone so far from civilization—or her.

Recalling the obscure message and the ethereal music weaving through the back of her dream, she wondered if her mind was receptive to some form of communication that even the green priests could not hear. If it was, maybe would Collin stop pitying her. Arita just wished their relationship could go back to the way it was before.

Her brother squeezed her hand. Reyn seemed to know what she was thinking.

Kennebar and his followers flew in on small personal flyers. They dismounted on the canopy, stretching their sore muscles after the long flight. Their leader was tall and thin, and his face bore a hard expression. He was entirely dedicated to the worldforest, and he considered politics and personal interactions a low priority. The rest of his followers stood beside their leader, serious, humorless.

She brightened when she saw Collin among them. He tried to appear just as serious as his companions, but when he noticed Arita, a smile flashed across his face, though he covered it quickly.

As the King and Queen went out to meet Kennebar's group, the nearby fronds rustled and dozens and dozens of Onthos pushed their way through the branches and leaves. Since they had scattered through the forest, Arita had not seen them all together at once. Now, there seemed to be a great many of them.

After briefly acknowledging the King and Queen, Kennebar turned his attention to Ohro. "The verdani informed us you were here."

The gathered Onthos pressed closer to the isolationist green priests. "Yes, and the trees have told us about the Wild," Ohro said. The other Gardeners murmured their assent.

Kennebar regarded the aliens, then turned back to Peter and Estarra. "We green priests exist to serve the worldforest. The verdani tell us these are our brothers in the trees. We want to give them sanctuary—in the Wild."

"What do you mean?" Peter asked. "They are safe here."

Arita kept looking at Collin, but the young man tried to remain serious as he stood among his fellow green priests. None of the others spoke a word, letting their leader do the talking.

Kennebar continued, "The Wild is vast and unsettled, and our group tends the neediest trees, but the worldforest requires help. We invite the Gardeners to join us, to settle in a new home. The trees have already welcomed you, and you will belong there."

"We do long for a new home, a place we can settle and fulfill our destiny," said Ohro. "We have been uprooted for so many years." The Gardeners all remained silent for a moment, as if communing, then their leader said, "Yes, we will come. The Wild needs our tending."

In unison, the Onthos bowed to the King and Queen. "We thank you for the reception you offered us, but our calling is to go to that continent. These green priests will help us, but the worldtrees will help us more."

Kennebar seemed pleased with himself. Collin shot a glance at Arita, but before she could smile at him, he flicked his eyes away.

After the decision was made, Kennebar kept tight control of his group as he arranged to transport the refugee aliens to the unsettled continent. The isolationist priests seemed to have no interest in socializing with old friends from the fungus-reef city, much to Arita's disappointment.

She never even had a chance to speak with Collin. She missed him terribly, and not just in a romantic way. He had been her *friend*. Couldn't he at least speak with her? Did Kennebar's aloof followers really need to reject all ties with their past? It saddened her.

Without saying any farewells, the taciturn green priests returned to their flyers and departed in a rush from the canopy, accompanied by larger transports provided by the King and Queen to take the Onthos. As they all left, Arita felt a flicker of heartache and disappointment as she saw Collin among them, studiously ignoring her. She remembered her handsome and funny young companion, who had now become a complete stranger to her. As the large group rose up from the treetops, Arita opened her mouth to call out to him, but the group flew off in a buzzing squadron of small ships.

In the last moment, Collin looked over his shoulder, met her gaze—and she was sure she saw longing there, a deep hurt. But since he had avoided her attempts at conversation, Arita thought it might just be her imagination, like those distant ethereal voices that came to her in dreams.

Understanding, her mother placed a warm consoling hand on her shoulder. Queen Estarra didn't need to say any words. A lump formed in Arita's throat, but she pulled in a deep breath, fought back the sadness. "I . . . I have to study some of the notes from my last specimen-collecting expedition in the Wild. I'm going back to my chambers." She hurried away.

Before she could even spread out her notes, however, a minor Confederation functionary appeared at the doorway of her room. "Excuse me, Princess. I have a message for you. I don't exactly know why he gave it to me." The clerk held out a piece of paper covered with handwritten words. "One of Kennebar's young green priests handed this to me and urged me to pass it on to you. He didn't seem to want the others to see." The clerk shook his head. "He could have just used telink. I don't understand."

Arita's heart leapt as she took the note. "I'm sure he has his reasons." She thanked the functionary and hurried to read the message.

"I needed to send you a private letter, Arita," Collin wrote. "If I sent it through telink, then all green priests could hear. Kennebar would know. And I wanted this just between us." She was so surprised that she felt tears stinging her eyes.

"I have to write this quickly—the others watch me closely. I wish I had never gone with them. I wish I could have stayed with you. I miss you, Arita. I miss telling you my thoughts and listening to yours—just two people discovering each other. If I'd known we would be separated, I never would have taken the green. My heart believes we belong together, but I am trapped by duty. I'm also worried. Something is wrong in the Wild. Something's very wrong with the world-forest mind. I don't dare use telink to explain.

"Please come and see for yourself. This is important—I'm sure I'm not imagining it. But who will believe me? Come to the Wild—soon."

The note abruptly cut off as if Collin were afraid of being caught.

Arita read and reread the note, experiencing both joy and concern. She felt the weight of worry, and she knew what she had to do.

She began making plans for another expedition to the Wild.

CHAPTER 48

PRINCE REYN

After Osira'h left Theroc, Prince Reynald felt different. The light in the worldforest was changed. He had drawn strength from her, and now that extra support was gone.

With Osira'h near, he had been able to resist the encroaching weakness from his disease, and maybe it was only his imagination, but now Reyn felt unsteady. He noticed more frequent neural misfires that slashed and skittered through him.

He realized just how much he had been keeping himself strong for her. He had been masking his symptoms, trying to keep himself steady so she wouldn't worry, and now the disease was making up for its enforced remission.

His tremors were bad this morning, and he took a long time to get dressed. His fingers shook so much that he could barely fasten the buttons and clips, but his mother and father were counting on him to join them in the throne chamber.

He closed his eyes, drew deep breaths, and commanded his nerves to obey. The exercise—which Osira'h had taught him—did not decrease the pain, but he was better able to endure it. He moved slowly about his room, and every sound seemed intense, like razor blades slashing through his ears. Bright lights hurt his eyes and his skin. But he was *Prince Reynald of Theroc*, and he did not have the luxury of weakness. He could not hide from his duties, even if they were mostly ceremonial.

His parents had sent out repeated calls to medical researchers, but Reyn would not be a pathetic weakling who demanded sympathy. He wanted to fight this battle himself, not that he ever expected to win it. Both Arita and Osira'h had scolded him for his pride, for hiding his symptoms. They insisted that he accept help, and he had agreed . . . which now made him a specimen. His samples, DNA maps, cellular scans, tissues, nervous system, and brain patterns were an open book—every tiny and private corner of his body. It felt like a violation, but he accepted it because that was what his parents needed, what his sister needed . . . and what Osira'h needed.

He had also received messages of support and understanding from countless subjects across the Confederation. Rlinda Kett had returned to her fancy restaurant of Arbor and made one of her famous sloppy cheeseburgers for him, even though it was not on the menu.

Now, he finished fastening his insect-carapace epaulets before inspecting himself in the reflecting glass. He definitely looked like a prince, a son of Theroc to sit beside Father Peter and Mother Estarra.

As ready as he could be, he took a step toward the door, swayed, then steadied himself against the soft fungus-reef wall. He took deep breaths, felt black static swirl behind his eyes before he finally sharpened his focus again—along with a fond memory of Osira'h that he held on to as an anchor—and he made his way to the throne room.

A crowd had gathered outside the chamber: green priests, Confederation traders, Theron villagers, even two retirees from the old Earth Defense Forces who had settled in the worldforest years ago. Inside, Estarra and Peter waited for him. Arita was busy preparing her own trip out to the Wild, which she had just announced to everyone's surprise. She would work on her naturalist research while the Onthos settled in the pristine wilderness.

Dredging up strength, Reyn took a seat in his chair, which was ornamented with jeweled and lacquered insect wings, beetle casings, and polished bloodwood agates. He intended to smile at the audience, but it required all of his attention to quell the tremors and to keep the pain from his expression.

Estarra said in a low voice, "You look pale, Reyn."

"Just tired. It's been exhausting and stressful . . . for a very long time. Especially now that Osira'h is gone." He slumped back in the hard, ornamented chair more heavily than he meant to.

King Peter announced to the audience in a loud, strong voice, "As always, our son's health poses a challenge for medical researchers across the Spiral Arm. Once again, we express our hope that someone will find a way to defeat this insidious malady, and in so doing find ways to help other ailing humans."

Estarra added her own voice. "In addition to the reward we offer, our gratitude will be substantial."

Embarrassed, Reyn took charge, as a prince was supposed to do. He called out, "Let's hear what these people have to say. They came to speak to us, not hear about my aches and pains." He tried to give them all a reassuring smile.

The two military retirees came forward first. One had a scar on his face, while the other moved with a limp but forced his way through it. "Majesties, both of us fought in the last battle of Earth twenty years ago. We defended against the Klikiss and the turncoat Ildirans and the black robots. Lost many of our comrades—but we stayed alive. We saved a lot of people."

The scarred man looked at his companion. "Piers and I moved here years ago, never wanted to bother you—but we did appreciate your leadership, King Peter."

The other man added to Estarra, "And yours too, ma'am . . . um, Majesty."

The first man was alarmed by his faux pas. "Well, of course, they're a set—I meant both of them."

Piers continued, "For a long time, Rutger and I have just wanted to say thank you . . . but now we hear that the bugbots have returned. I don't know how much good two old relics will be, but if you need fighters again, we're willing to help."

"That's good to know," Peter said. "And I hope we won't need to reactivate your service. You have earned a quiet retirement."

Reyn fought back a thrum of pain. "It's encouraging to see such devoted citizens." He doubted he would survive long enough to take over after his parents.

The next speaker was Tristan Cove, the town leader of Shorehaven, who arrived carrying a large case. "My village has recovered from the wyvern attacks, Father Peter and Mother Estarra—thanks to the two warrior women from Ildira along with our green priest Beltrias, who became a hunter in his own right."

Estarra nodded. "Anton Colicos told us the story. It's so outlandish

I thought he must have embellished some parts, but we should probably believe what he says."

"Believe him," said Cove. He proudly opened the box to display a hemispherical multifaceted jewel wider than his handspan in diameter.

"What is that?" Reyn asked.

"This is one of the smaller eyes of the slain wyvern. Its head was far too enormous to bring as a trophy, and even the larger eyes are a meter across or more. But we wanted to deliver this as a reminder that there are threats right here on Theroc, as well as great threats out in the cosmos."

Impressed, King Peter stepped down from his throne to look at the wyvern eye. "Reynald, come receive this with me."

Reyn lifted himself off the chair and took a step forward, but suddenly a dark dizziness flooded through him, and static blurred his vision. It was more than pain—it was confusion and oblivion. He collapsed into it, lost.

His mother shouted, "Bring the physicians! Now!"

With his last flickers of sight, Reyn saw Tristan Cove scramble backward and lose his grip on the case, which fell to the floor just as Reyn sprawled forward. The wyvern eye tumbled out, staring at him with its countless segmented facets, before he vanished into unconsciousness.

CHAPTER

49

MAGE-IMPERATOR JORA'H

Deep in the lower levels of the Prism Palace, the chamber was secure, shielded, and well lit. Claustrophobic, but safe.

After rushing back to Mijistra, the Mage-Imperator had come to the ossuarium to concentrate on how the Shana Rei continued to attack them, both externally and internally. He hoped this emergency meeting was more than just an exchange of fear and confusion; these were his best advisers.

Jora'h had to know. He had to lead.

Crystalline reflective threads created constellations of bright pinpoints embedded in the walls of the chamber. Multiple sunlight was funneled through the fibers to illuminate the chamber as if it were the brightest Ildiran day.

This meeting vault was part of a sacred set of catacombs where the luminous bones of ancient Mage-Imperators were stored. The ossuarium was a place where the current Mage-Imperator went to contemplate the Empire, where he could feel the racial resonances and the challenges that lay ahead. Behind the translucent crystal blocks, Jora'h could see the embedded skulls of his ancestors, all of them watching him. . . .

Jora'h had come here many times during the Elemental War. He knew his father had done the same, as well as their predecessors for millennia. But how many Mage-Imperators had faced a crisis as tremendous as the Shana Rei?

Or had every Mage-Imperator asked a similar question?

Racing back from Theroc, after feeling horrific tremors through the *thism* from the Hiltos attack as well as the mob massacre right here in Mijistra, he had arrived to find his people reeling, confused, and terrified. Such bloodshed had shocked the people, shocked the Prime Designate. Daro'h had barricaded himself in his private chambers, and an overprotective Rod'h refused to let anyone near him. The Mage-Imperator was surprised and impressed that Rod'h had been such a staunch supporter during the crisis.

After the attack on Hiltos, Adar Zan'nh had rushed back with his flagship and summoned many more Solar Navy warliners as protection. He had given orders for all warliners to be equipped with the new weapons from Askelor, posthaste, but not even the brave Adar could provide the comfort the Ildirans desired. They needed their Mage-Imperator—and Jora'h returned, to their palpable relief.

When he had emerged from the landed cutter on the Prism Palace hill, he made sure the people saw him. Trying to quell the jangling discord in the *thism* web, he calmed the crowds with his mere presence . . . but it wasn't enough. He had to protect them. And for that, he needed to know his options.

In the center of the ossuarium chamber, as a memorial to the horrific devastation during the Elemental War, sat an amorphous blob of melted quartz, part of the original Prism Palace destroyed by the faeros. It was a reminder of the heat and fury that had collapsed the Ildiran Empire's capitol. During reconstruction, this block had been brought down here, where the bones of the Prism Palace could rest beside the bones of past Mage-Imperators.

Nira was at his side in the deep chamber along with her children Osira'h, Rod'h, and Gale'nh, as well as Prime Designate Daro'h and Adar Zan'nh. Much to Jora'h's unease, they also brought the disgraced Designate Rusa'h, who had escaped from his exile at the Lightsource shrine.

Deep in the bright chamber, with the crystal doors sealed and burly guard kithmen in place outside, the Mage-Imperator stared at the others, knowing they would not offer miraculous solutions.

"They attacked us," blurted Prime Designate Daro'h. "Our own people! They slaughtered Arune'l and all the other lens kith. Rod'h and I barely got away. If it hadn't been for him—"

Jora'h already knew what had occurred. Beside him, Nira shuddered, remembering when the same thing had happened to her.

Rod'h did not bask in the praise, however; he merely sat straighter, more determined. "The Ildiran people have shadows within them. They do not even know they are pawns of the Shana Rei."

Adar Zan'nh wore a finely scaled tunic studded with medals of his service to the Empire. "The shadows are also a military threat, as they demonstrated at the Hiltos shrine. They killed all but the few we managed to save." He glared at the wan-looking Rusa'h as if he blamed the mad Designate for surviving when so many others had been killed.

"The black robots goad them," Gale'nh said in a quiet voice. "The Shana Rei wish to destroy everything, but the robots show them how."

Restless, Jora'h paced in slow circles, looking around at them, wanting an answer. "How do we fight the Shana Rei? What can destroy a shadow?"

Adar Zan'nh said, "We have sun bombs, laser cannons. We will be prepared with every possible weapon."

Prime Designate Daro'h said, "And how does that stop our own people from rising up and slaying their brothers in the streets? Do we drop a sun bomb on Mijistra?"

"We can't fight what we don't understand," Nira pointed out. "Even the worldforest knows almost nothing about the Shana Rei. According to the Onthos, they fought the shadows before, but they don't *remember*. Too much of their mind was destroyed."

"Then we must learn more about them," Rod'h said. "In any way possible. From any source."

Frowning, Adar Zan'nh turned to Nira's ambitious son. "And how do we do that? Ask questions the next time a shadow cloud appears?"

"The rememberers have pored over the old records," Daro'h pointed out. "They have extracted every available hint."

Jora'h said, "And I proposed an expedition out to the Onthos star, which the Shana Rei obliterated. The Confederation will join us in the effort."

"An expedition . . . like the *Kolpraxa*," Gale'nh said. His voice was thin, hinting at fear.

"We will be more prepared this time," Adar Zan'nh said.

Rod'h raised his chin. "I will go along. If you and Tal Gale'nh take ships out there, I intend to join you."

Daro'h reacted with alarm. "No! You won't be safe!"

Rod'h gave him a compassionate frown. "None of us is safe. And this will be an important responsibility."

Osira'h said, "I helped locate the *Kolpraxa* after it was lost. Maybe I should—"

"No! It is my turn." Rod'h drew a breath. "It cannot always be you, sister. We were both born to a higher purpose. We need to do something meaningful." The determination on his face barely covered the anguish in his voice.

Until now, mad Designate Rusa'h had remained silent, but now his words cut through the tension in the air. "Light can defeat the shadows—and the origin of light is fire. We already know what will destroy the Shana Rei. We need to reestablish an alliance with the faeros. Someone has to contact them again."

"Too dangerous!" Adar Zan'nh cried.

The Mage-Imperator drew a deep breath. Rusa'h, his half-brother, had caused so much harm, both to him personally and to the entire Empire. He was reluctant to trust the man now, no matter how repentant he seemed. Rusa'h appeared to understand that as well; he wasn't pushy, didn't grow angry, simply tried to allow the logic of his terrifying position to sink in. "Our weapons are impotent, but the Shana Rei are not. And the faeros are not."

Jora'h touched the smooth curves of the melted palace block that stood as a memorial in the center of the room. The block had irregular lumps, streams like petrified tears of crystal from when the fire elementals had made the towering structure weep into puddles of destruction. He looked up at Rusa'h. "Haven't the faeros caused enough damage? I will not destroy our soul in hopes of saving part of it."

The fallen Designate folded his hands together and didn't respond.

Surprisingly, Osira'h was the one who spoke up. "The faeros did just come to help rescue Theroc. Maybe they hate the Shana Rei as much as we do."

"Rusa'h must not be the one to contact them," Rod'h said, and Adar Zan'nh vehemently agreed.

Osira'h nodded as well. "No, it will not be him—*I* can connect with the faeros. They have grown distant, and they may or may not listen now, but I can try. Let me take a ship and try to contact them, Father."

Beside her, Rod'h stiffened, and Jora'h could sense the tension between the two siblings, as if they felt a kind of competition. "Osira'h and I should go together—we may have the same affinity for the faeros. We can call to them." He glanced at his sister. "We always showed we could be stronger together."

Nira was uneasy, glancing from Rod'h to Osira'h. "I don't like it, but my halfbreed children have powers. They were born to do this. Rod'h, I know you are strong, and Osira'h has already shown her capabilities. We need them now. If it's what they have to do, Jora'h, then I cannot argue with the suggestion." She gave her older son a long look, but even that support could not penetrate the many years of resentment and distance between them.

Rod'h cut off a retort, answering instead, "Thank you, Mother."

The disgraced Designate looked oddly satisfied, which made Jora'h uneasy. Rusa'h turned away and sat back down.

"I cannot argue either," Jora'h said. "You have my permission, Osira'h and Rod'h. Try to communicate with the faeros, see what sort of contact or concession you can make. I am uneasy about such an alliance . . . but I need to know."

CHAPTER 50

EXXOS

The shadow cloud moved through the back passageways of the universe, a bubble of dark entropy with no destination and only a chaotic goal.

After the victory at Hiltos, Exxos could not power down his mind into rest mode while his thoughts churned in search of a solution. The robots would find a way to destroy the hideous shadow entities, but if necessary they would first destroy everything else. Once the Shana Rei granted the surviving black robots their own isolated corner of the universe, Exxos would ponder the next phase of his plan. Since the black robots had been in existence for millennia, he was in no hurry. But although their losses had been minimal, his robot numbers were dwindling. That would have to stop.

Pulsating inkblots appeared in the void, and their baleful incongruous eyes shone like acid lightning. They regarded the black robots as if they were specimens in a bizarre cosmic zoo. Exxos did not plead with them, did not offer suggestions unless the shadows asked, because any comment could trigger an unexpected violent reaction. But they had to continue their destruction. With so many targets, he thought, which one should he choose next?

The empty void wall around the robots thinned, and stars appeared. The shadow cloud reemerged into normal space. The fleet of angular black warships remanifested out of nothingness, constructed according to the detailed blueprints the black robots had provided. Those designs had worked well at Hiltos.

One of the inkblots appeared in front of him, and a pulsating, droning voice made his embedded circuits sparkle with unprotected chaos. "We have found something. You may do as you wish."

The robots found themselves aboard their battleships, and Exxos reaccessed all the systems, studied the projected images, the sensor maps. His crimson optical sensors glowed as he spotted a lone vessel, a minuscule speck in the infinity of emptiness.

A single ship. A human ship.

The Shana Rei withdrew, taking no part in this incident, even though they had facilitated it. The robots were more than sufficient to take care of this small vessel. Moving with a single mind, Exxos's mind, the black robot warships surrounded the vessel in empty space.

In his grand scheme, Exxos envisioned destroying whole human colonies, gigantic Ildiran stations, widely settled planets—particularly the ancient worlds abandoned by the Klikiss race. But on a canvas as vast as the universe, even a star system was an insignificant speck. It was all a matter of scale.

So, Exxos and his robots would destroy this spacecraft and consider it one small step toward progress.

"Who the hell are you?" screeched a gruff female voice over the comm. The image of a Roamer captain with gray-black dreadlocks and puffy cheeks appeared on the sensor screen.

Exxos didn't care what the victim looked like, but the sight added an extra layer of satisfaction. He responded to her because he chose to. "We are the ones who will destroy you."

"By the Guiding Star, I've got nothing! Take my damn cargo if you insist. It's boron-laced conduits headed for Newstation."

"We have no interest in your cargo." Exxos strung this moment out. The Shana Rei had allowed this, so he would enjoy it.

The pilot sounded angry and baffled. "Then what the hell do you want?"

Exxos believed that much was obvious. "We want to annihilate you."

Over the years, he had become an expert in human expressions. Fear was one of the obvious designators here. The trader captain spluttered. "But, why? What the hell did I do?"

Exxos thought that was obvious as well. "You *exist*."

The captain continued to transmit, pleading, but further conversation was pointless. Because all of the black robots were linked through him, he could coordinate their maneuvers, so he chose to use this event as practice.

His warships encircled the trapped trader, and he commanded them to focus their weapons on the same point. All of them fired at exactly the same instant.

The energy burst was sufficient to vaporize the ship, even powerful enough to cause minor pinpoints of nuclear fusion among the denser materials collapsing from the implosion. The boron-laced conduit tubes disappeared as easily as the human flesh did. The entire ship vanished in a flash, and even the energy outburst dissipated quickly into blackness.

The robot warships hung there, and Exxos waited, wondering what the Shana Rei intended next. Would they want the robots to go on the rampage again, as they had done at the Hiltos shrine? That incident had been satisfyingly destructive, but he had lost another twenty black robots—a far more significant loss to him than what they had inflicted on the Ildiran Empire. As the war went on, the black robots could not survive such attrition.

Perhaps that was what the Shana Rei intended.

Exxos needed to find another solution.

The shadow cloud reappeared in space, pulsing around them. One of the inkblots appeared on the bridge of the remanifested warship, and the silence hung heavy for a long moment. Nevertheless, Exxos got the impression that the shadows were pleased. Even with centuries of analysis, he would never understand Shana Rei modes of thought.

If the robots could find a way to annihilate the creatures of darkness, however, it wouldn't matter. Or, if the Shana Rei and the black robots destroyed human and Ildiran civilization, that too would be a good enough victory.

The shadow cloud engulfed the robot warships again, and folded them back out of the cosmos.

CHAPTER 51

GENERAL NALANI KEAH

General Keah was spoiling for a fight. The CDF fleet was the largest since the end of the Elemental War, and it was growing every month as shipyards produced powerful vessels in response to the Shana Rei.

At the Lunar Orbital Complex, the once-arrogant Dr. Jocko Krieger had devoted his full abilities to producing a significant arsenal of traditional sun bombs—with appropriate safety interlocks this time. He also insisted that he understood his mistake that had caused the previous disaster at the fabrication facility, and he intended to submit modified designs for new, higher-output sun bombs. Keah would believe that when she saw it.

Meanwhile, batteries of laser cannons were being tested and installed in all Juggernauts and Mantas, while the crews trained overtime. She made sure every one of her Grid Admirals got hands-on experience, even the reluctant ones.

Keah was sick and tired of being taken by surprise and even more sick and tired of getting her ass kicked. Yeah, she was spoiling for a stand-up clash like the one at Plumas, although she hoped for a better outcome this time. If she did her job, along with the trainers, tacticians, shipyards, and weapons manufacturers—not to mention the soldiers themselves—the next outcome would be a helluva lot different.

The CDF could never have enough practice. Instead of just sitting on her thumbs and letting her crew watch the chronometers day after day, she decided to give them something to keep them on their toes.

The *Kutuzov* was Keah's primary office these days. Oh, she went back to CDF headquarters or the LOC and inspected the preparations, and she headed to Theroc for regular briefings with King Peter and Queen Estarra, but the Juggernaut was her true home. She could always use her green priest Nadd to send an instant message to Theroc, if it became necessary.

For these exercises, the *Kutuzov* led fifteen refurbished Manta cruisers and another Juggernaut, the *Okrun*, commanded by Admiral Haroun. Along with Admirals Harvard and Handies, Haroun was one of the "Three H's," Grid Admirals promoted after the end of the Elemental War; they were clearly rusty, having served for two decades during peaceful reconstruction. She doubted they would have that luxury from now on, and right now she wanted to see Admiral Haroun in action.

Keah guided the training group straight up out of the ecliptic, all the way to the diffuse Oort Cloud. On an astronomical chart, the tiny specks of cometary fragments looked like a blizzard at the barest fringe of the sun's gravity. The dark and dormant comets were a potential navigational obstacle, but the objects were so spread out, the risk was minimal. Besides, General Keah needed elbow room for all their war-game exercises.

"The *Okrun* is in position, General," Admiral Haroun transmitted from the bridge of his Juggernaut. "Ready to proceed on schedule."

"All Mantas in battle formation," said First Officer Mercer Wingo, standing close on Keah's own bridge.

"All right, sound battle stations." She smiled. "Present the new combat scenario in two minutes."

"*Two minutes*, General?" squawked the weapons officer, Mr. Patton, over the comm. "But our scheduled exercises aren't due for two more hours. We need time to prepare."

On the screen, Haroun's eyes widened. "My crew will require at least an hour to get to their stations and have all our equipment spun up."

Keah frowned. "Then you're all dead. Do you think the bugbots are going to give us a preprinted announcement with an RSVP before they attack next?"

Wingo rose to his feet, gave her a sharp grin. "Two minutes is more time than we need, General. The attack is commencing—now!" He activated the simulation, and the viewscreens on the fifteen Mantas, the *Okrun*, and the *Kutuzov* filled with a flurry of angular black-hulled ships, massive engines, and weapons. Lots of weapons.

"Shields up!" yelled the tac officer.

At her station, the comm chief shouted, "General, a lot of our Manta captains are demanding—"

"Tell them to stop demanding and *shoot*. I'm not the enemy—get the damn bugbots!"

The *Okrun* swung up and out of bugbot targeting range, a little sluggish but enough to save their lives. The Mantas pulled together into a defensive formation. Simulated robot ships swarmed in, more than they had encountered during the Plumas engagement. But the point of a training exercise was to flex muscles, not to be conservative.

"Jazer banks are fully charged, General," Patton announced.

"Then let's try those first if you're ready, Mr. Patton. And let's hope the rest of our group follows suit."

As the robot ships soared in, jacketed spun-lasers played across the starry field like spotlights, gutting the nearest robot battleship. The black hull was torn open, and smoke and fumes spilled everywhere. The enemy ship twirled recklessly off the edge of the screen—but since the damned bugbots didn't use life support and could tolerate accelerations that would have pulped a human being, the wounded ship wasn't necessarily out of the fight.

"Next time blow it up all the way," she advised.

"I'm trying, General."

The Mantas began opening fire, and Admiral Haroun brought the *Okrun* back into the fray.

"Railgun launchers next," Keah said, interested to see what would happen. "They should be more powerful now, with the upgrades we just installed. Let's flatten a few clankers."

On the screen image, well out of range, a swirling black nebula held three enormous Shana Rei hex ships. Even though the shadows could wreak incomprehensible damage during each engagement, the CDF experts couldn't even create a viable simulation, because the collapsing entropy fields defied all predictive capabilities.

The black robots could be smashed, though, and she knew exactly how to wipe them out.

After the initial confusion, her Manta cruisers got into the spirit of the simulation and started pummeling the targets in earnest. All the viewscreens across the connected battle group shared the same simulation. When the Manta captains joined together in triads, closing in on several robot ships and blasting them to pieces before moving on to another, their strategy proved quite effective.

When one Manta took too many enemy hits, it spun out of control and lost its shields. The explosion displayed on all their screens blinded them; worse, it made the General frown. "You've been vaporized, Captain," she announced. "Withdraw from the vicinity. I hope being killed teaches you to be more careful next time. I can't afford to lose ships."

"Yes, General," said the glum captain. The space battle continued to rage around them, and the *Okrun* slid in to take the place of the "destroyed" Manta.

Just to satisfy herself, Keah transferred one subset of weapons controls to herself and proceeded to cause some damage.

The CDF railgun launchers had always been powerful weapons. Each dense depleted-uranium projectile was accelerated to relativistic speeds, and when it struck a target, the dissipation energy of impact was equivalent to a nuclear explosion. The new CDF had increased the diameters of the hyperlaunched projectiles by a full centimeter and added five hundred grams to the mass, with the result that the impact energy had three more kilotons of effective yield.

When she fired two of those projectiles at a robot warship that cruised past, the explosion looked like a beautiful bouquet of flowers.

The human military had enough experience fighting the Klikiss robots that she was confident *these* simulations were accurate, although the bugbot ships were larger and more powerful than what they had used in the past. As Keah fought now, she brought her own experiences to bear as well. Adrenaline rushed through her, accompanied by a cold sweat of memory. . . .

She had been a young officer during the final engagement at Earth when treacherous black robot forces had turned on the EDF, triggering insidious sabotage aboard the rebuilt battleships. As Klikiss swarmships surrounded Earth, the humans had made their last stand.

Nalani Keah had been a junior officer on the bridge of a Manta cruiser. When the internal sabotage explosions began to take down the ships, the vulnerable EDF vessels spun out of control. Keah's own captain had been killed in the blast, half of the bridge crew injured.

But young Lieutenant Keah knew what she had to do, and her fast thinking cut off a black robot attack. She saved several other ships, all of which turned and fought, barely salvaging survival—if not outright victory—from the horrific situation.

Many of the details were a blur to her now. She had watched the footage from bridge cameras and studied the tactical records, so she knew exactly what she had done by instinct. She didn't remember knowing what to do, yet she had done it, automatically. Sometimes she amazed herself.

Afterward, her superiors recognized her actions. General Conrad Brindle had promoted her, put her career on a fast track. That one day set her life on an entirely different course. In a way, she could credit the black robots' treachery for her advancement in the CDF.

Now, she showed her appreciation to the bugbots by launching an all-out broadside against their ships, and she was quite pleased to watch the destruction she caused. "Now we're talking!"

So far, she had lost three of her fifteen Mantas in the simulation. The *Kutuzov* had suffered a certain amount of damage, but nothing too worrisome. Admiral Haroun seemed to be handling himself well enough, to her relief. The CDF had wiped out half of the bugbot attack ships in the engagement, but the remaining enemy vessels clustered in an ominous and unexpected formation.

Keah raised her eyebrows. The simulation must have dug deep to find this alternative. Normally, bugbots fought like startled cockroaches rushing in all directions, uncoordinated and uncooperative. This unified force, though, could be strong enough to cause serious problems, maybe even destroy a Juggernaut.

On the other hand, a monolithic force like that was a much easier target. The *Okrun* and the remaining Mantas launched jazers and railgun projectiles, peppering the unified robots, damaging black hulls. But unless the weapons hit a vital engine system, even the shredded robot ships could keep fighting.

General Keah realized how to turn the threatening configuration into a tactical advantage. She smiled. "Here's an idea. Launch one of our sun bombs—dead center."

On the comm screen from the weapons center, Mr. Patton blinked, then grinned. "As you command, General."

The simulated pinwheel tumbled out straight toward the cluster of bugbots. It sprayed bright light as its core activated, building energy levels up to a critical cascade. The sun bomb didn't look like much in comparison to the whirlwind of CDF projectiles and jazer beams, but when the device detonated in the center of the robot ships, they were all engulfed in a flare of disintegrating light and heat.

The expanding shock wave swallowed all the ships in the vicinity, including the *Okrun*. She would apologize to Admiral Haroun later. The simulation computers reacted by shutting down many systems, sending up damage scores that the blast would have inflicted on the surviving Mantas, whose shields had already been depleted. When the nova light faded, every single bugbot ship was gone.

Perfect.

General Keah declared an end to the exercises. "Anybody left alive on the surviving ships will receive bonus pay and rotating hours of R and R. The rest of you, just be glad you aren't really dead."

The soldiers cheered, and the "destroyed" cruisers accepted their losses with good grace.

"Admiral Haroun . . . not bad," she said. "Better luck next time."

He did not look shaken by his demise. "Thank you, General."

Keah kept looking at the now-quiet simulation screen. Even though the bugbots had been wiped out, the hex ships and the ominous shadow cloud still hung there in the background. If the Shana Rei had actually participated in this attack, the victory would not have been so straightforward. The General clenched her jaw, hating that she knew so little about this incredible enemy.

She hoped the proposed joint CDF and Solar Navy expedition to the Onthos home system got off the ground soon. Yes, Ildira was in turmoil, but Adar Zan'nh couldn't delay too long. Keah was anxious to go out hunting shadows herself.

CHAPTER

52

AELIN

Ulio Station was vast, confusing, crowded, and frightening. Lost, Aelin flitted from corridor to corridor for more than a day, trying to stay in hiding, even though Elisa was surely gone by now. Or maybe not. Whenever others stared at him, he tried to act as if he had a destination; thankfully, in the ever-changing mass of traders, visitors, and workers, few people paid attention to him at all.

Aelin had eaten little since departing from the Iswander extraction yards, and his energy reserves were depleted. His stomach rumbled, and he felt weak. He found a large cafeteria complex inside the second refurbished Ildiran warliner and managed to scavenge food left on tables or from packages discarded in waste bins.

On Theroc, there was such an abundance of fruits, nuts, insects, and fungi that no one ever needed to go hungry. Back at the Iswander facility, a commissary provided regular meals. It was different here on Ulio Station, though. This was a busy trade center, but all food, water, and air had to be brought in, and the people here weren't so generous. Despite the apparent anarchy, the people policed themselves and dealt harshly with anyone who cheated, stole, or didn't play by the rules.

Aelin knew he had to be careful.

A squarish, potbellied woman spotted him from across the cafeteria and strolled up to him. Aelin saw her coming and froze, ready to run. He had never seen this woman before. Her demeanor was businesslike rather than threatening, her expression no-nonsense. Even in the station's low gravity, she moved with a ponderous rolling gait. "Green priest! I need your services. Are you for hire?"

"For hire?" He was confused. "I . . . No. I don't have a treeling."

"Then what's the point of a green priest at Ulio Station—"

"I lost my treeling. I hope to rectify that soon, but right now I have no way of sending telink messages. I'm sorry I can't help you." It was a quick excuse, but also true.

"The main green priest for hire is Dauntha," interrupted a man with long dark hair. He was lounging at a cafeteria table next to two young boys, obviously his sons, each about ten years old. All three wore the uniform of a private transfer ship; the two boys did their best to emulate their father. "Reasonable rates, but she doesn't advertise her services."

The squarish woman had already dismissed Aelin from her field of view, since he was no use to her. "If she doesn't advertise, then how do I find her?"

"Warliner number three, around deck twenty, I think."

"Twenty-two," said one of his boys.

The father smiled indulgently. "Twenty-two it is, then."

The squarish woman sighed. "I just came from warliner number three." She turned and left without a second glance at Aelin.

The father gave him a once-over. "You'd better get a tree soon, green priest—you look scrawny."

"I'm hungry," Aelin said.

The man wiped his mouth and slid a plate toward Aelin. "You can have the other half of my glazed sandwich."

"You weren't going to eat it?"

"It's more important to teach my boys generosity."

Aelin wolfed down the sweet sandwich and felt satisfied. He thanked the man and hurried off, now that he had a goal in mind. He knew exactly where to find a compassionate ear, or at least good company.

Dauntha was actually on deck twenty-five, but Aelin managed to find her. She was a wiry and hairless old woman, her green skin darkened with age. Numerous tattoos along her arms, cheeks, and forehead indicated her areas of expertise. On the walls of her quarters, Dauntha had painted a bright mural of ferns and tall golden-barked tree trunks. She wasn't particularly talented as an artist, but her energy and passion shone through.

She was surprised when he appeared at her doorway. "Aelin? Your name sounds familiar." She quickly touched the potted treeling that sat on her metal table, and her eyes fell half closed as she accessed the verdani mind; when she found Aelin's name among all those memories, she came back out with even greater surprise. "We haven't seen you in a long time! Your treeling died, and we thought you had died as well."

"My treeling was incinerated in a burst of . . ." He did not know how to explain the surge of energy from the magnificent bloaters, didn't want to reveal any of the things he knew. "I've been out of contact."

Dauntha's voice took on a husky, somber tone. "And your brother was Shelud. We all know him. We followed him as everyone died aboard the derelict Onthos city."

Aelin felt a lump in his throat. "Yes, everyone watched them. Poor Shelud."

He had been so swept up in the euphoria of revelations and his urgent quest to save the bloaters that he hadn't thought about his brother in a long time. Now those memories came crashing back. "I was with him by telink when he died." Now he found it hard to breathe.

With their connection throughout the worldforest mind, green priests could share their lives, their experiences . . . even their deaths. Shelud had done that with his last gasp of energy, speaking directly to his brother, though when one green priest spoke, all priests could listen.

Tears welled up in Aelin's eyes. His brother would never know what he had seen inside the bloater mind-flash, how the colors and sounds and smells had acquired a new intensity. No other green priests would know it either, because Aelin simply couldn't share it . . . unless they experienced it for themselves. For now, he had to keep the secret of the bloaters; he already feared he had blurted out too much to the Roamer man when he was stumbling through the station.

He didn't think Dauntha could understand how his mind, his heart, his *soul* had been altered by the revelations from the bloaters. He wasn't sure anyone could. That was why he had been unable to make Lee Iswander comprehend the damage being done by draining the floating nodules. But he could still hear them faintly, sense their cosmic music, their thoughts. He *knew*.

Aelin sat heavily on one of the cushioned chairs that Dauntha provided for her telink customers. He could smell echoes of the forest in the room's secret scents. Though small, this single treeling had a verdant energy, exuding freshness.

"You look lost and lonely. Stay here with me. Green priests help each other, and I have room." She slid her potted treeling closer to him. "You should reconnect with the verdani mind. Go ahead—I can tell you need it."

Aelin trembled with relief and anticipation. He had been far from the worldforest ever since he'd joined Lee Iswander's industrial operations, and he had used his own treeling like a spy inside a fortress, observing closely but sharing little. But even that connection had been taken from him when the bloater surge had incinerated the potted treeling at the same time it changed his mind and soul.

Now with access to the worldforest so close, he longed to have that contact again.

He eagerly reached forward, touched the thin treeling, ran his fingertips along the fine scales of the bark, and wove his thoughts into the tapestry of telink while keeping part of his secrets carefully walled off. He fell into the welcoming embrace across many worlds, many people. His consciousness rushed outward, following untold billions of trees, threads of thought, strands of knowledge. He explored, and he sent messages to the other green priests so they would know where he was, who he was, where he had been.

He felt guilty having to hide what he knew about the bloaters, but he dared not inspire swarms of eager exploiters who would drain more and more of them. He held that part back. From the trees, he received a flood of new information, catching up on a waterfall of lives and events that had all happened without him.

Most fascinating, he learned that the Onthos, the alien builders of the plague-ridden city where Shelud had died, were still alive, at least a handful of refugees who had gone to Theroc. The Gardeners. Now, through telink, he drank in images that the Onthos had reawakened in the verdani mind—an alien world filled with another worldforest, magnificent trees connected by bridges and walkways, shining towers that poked above the canopy under an orange sky. And many verdani treeships, piloted by symbiotically connected aliens, sailing the emptiness of space as explorers. . . .

As he let his thoughts wander through this feast of new information, Aelin smiled. The bloaters had given him a taste of the incomprehensible, but this was magnificent as well. Even though he didn't experience the same energy and wonder as before, Aelin's joy made tears well up again.

When he eventually let go of the treeling, a weary Dauntha reached out to touch his forearm. He heaved a shuddering breath, blinked his eyes. "Thank you. It has been a long time."

Dauntha gave him a reassuring smile. "But that wasn't enough. I can sense an emptiness and a hunger inside you. You're looking for something."

Aelin nodded. "Yes. Yes, that's exactly correct. But I've already found it. I just wish I could tell you."

CHAPTER 53

TAMO'L

Full tide had come in on Kuivahr, and the sanctuary domes were submerged. Tamo'l turned the mutable window walls transparent so everyone could watch the aquatic life in the rich, shallow sea. Strands of chained plankton and kelp nodules dangled from above, while crustaceans, fish, and wriggly sea creatures drifted among them. It made for a peaceful dinner environment.

One of the largest chambers in the main sanctuary dome was also a communal gathering place. When the misbreeds came to dine together, some were ashamed at their appearance, and others could barely move, but Tamo'l welcomed them all nevertheless. She assured the refugees that they were not merely perplexing specimens or distorted genetic jokes. She took the time to know every one of them, to understand not just their maladies, but their personalities as well. She wanted to ease their depression and personal misery, not just their physical pain.

For nearly two years now she had made a practice of joining the misbreeds for a daily meal. Attendance was not mandatory. Some misbreeds had such awkward and unsettling digestive requirements that they preferred to eat in privacy. Some huddled in their quarters, wrapping themselves in personal aches, living because Tamo'l gave them a reason to live, but waiting to die even so.

Staffed by attender kith, the kitchens prepared a diverse menu from pureed fish and weed gruel to raw shellfish to simple nutrient fluids to whole invertebrates. Each meal was specially prepared for individual patients to balance their nutritional and medicinal needs.

Tamo'l sat with the gathered misbreeds as bowls and platters were passed around, and everyone knew exactly who consumed what.

Tamo'l had her own meal of fresh fish accompanied by stewed kelp flowers.

Beside her, a misbreed named Alaa'kh hunched forward, lifted a too-flexible arm, and tilted a bowl so that the runny gruel could pour down into a gaping mouth that had no chewing apparatus; the gruel simply trickled into his digestive system. Another misbreed down the table lifted a dark cloth to make a tent in front of her mouth as she consumed bones and scales and fish heads. More functional than some of the others, Gor'ka and Har'lc helped to serve their comrades.

Outside the curved transparent dome, a spiderlike crustacean lumbered along the muddy seafloor, one knobby leg at a time. It was half the size of a shuttle, but innocuous as it munched on drifting kelp nodules.

The misbreeds at the table discussed news they had heard, messages delivered by Solar Navy supply ships. Through the *thism*, they had sensed the terrible attack on the Hiltos shrine and the massacre of lens kithmen in Mijistra. They talked about the Shana Rei, expressing their desire to help fight the creatures of darkness.

"What chance do we have?" asked Alaa'kh.

"All misbreeds exist because of the breeding program," Har'lc pointed out. "The Dobro Designate experimented with us, trying to come up with someone who could help the Ildiran race. We might all have some purpose—we just need to find it."

"But we were bred as a hope against the hydrogues," said Gor'ka. "None of us was born to stand against the shadows."

"Maybe we have abilities they don't know about," said Alaa'kh.

Tamo'l nodded, encouraged the discussion. "That's why I want each one of you to reach your potential. I believe every single misbreed is special in some way, but we can't identify how if we don't look for it."

She had established this outpost on Kuivahr to be a refuge, yes, but she was convinced that at least some of these chaotic genetic combinations had an unusual inner worth. Regardless, she considered each of them valuable in their own right. If only she could keep them alive . . . if only she could make them healthy.

Shawn Fennis and Chiar'h joined the meal, but the two spent most of the time caught up in each other's company. The human male and

Ildiran female were an odd couple, married on Dobro and volunteering to work with the misbreeds without reservation. Now, as Tamo'l listened to their excited conversation, she heard Fennis and Chiar'h discuss remarkable test results from one of the new kelp distillates brought over by Zhett and Kristof Kellum. The two had run chemical comparisons, using volunteer misbreed patients.

Tamo'l caught their attention. "Encouraging results among the new extracts?" The attentive misbreeds looked up from their various foods.

The two glanced at each other, caught in their conversation. Fennis blushed red, a human display of embarrassment much like the color-infused lobes of a skilled rememberer telling a dramatic story. Chiar'h reported, "We tested all the new variants on our misbreeds and found some marginal successes that could be nothing more than a placebo effect."

Fennis chimed in, "But we didn't stop there. You asked us to look into Prince Reynald's illness as well. We do have all of his records here."

Tamo'l caught a breath. "Yes, of course! Osira'h very much wanted us to help him, but I didn't think—"

Fennis blurted out, "One of the kelp extracts seems to have a strong effect on the microfungus that afflicts the Prince. It could be the basis for an effective treatment—not a cure, but sufficient to dampen symptoms, perhaps repair some of the neural damage."

Chiar'h's well-sculpted features made her look out of place among the scrambled misbreeds. "We cannot know unless we test him directly, of course."

"My priority is to tend to these misbreeds, but if we can help anyone—especially the son of the Confederation's leaders," then she added more quietly, "especially a close friend of my sister's, then we will do so."

Smiling to herself, Tamo'l took another bite of her savory fish. The misbreeds in the dining chamber seemed genuinely happy to hear of a promising treatment, even one for Reynald of Theroc, glad to know that something might help another person who was suffering, whether it be the Confederation's Prince, or a misshapen lump of limbs and poorly connected organs.

Tamo'l had attempted to contact Tom Rom, telling him she had more records to share, but so far he had not responded to her communication. Now, even more important, she would send a message to Ildira. Osira'h would certainly want to know about the possible treatment for her friend.

CHAPTER 54

OSIRA'H

The Ildiran astronomers at Wulfton were fascinated by the turbulent star, but they were afraid of what Osira'h and Rod'h intended to do. She could sense their uneasiness through the *thism* at the stellar research station as the two of them announced that they were going to hunt for the faeros.

A warliner escort had dropped them off near the active star, a place they knew would attract the fiery elementals. The research station was crowded with hundreds of Ildiran scientists, engineers, and support personnel, but Osira'h and Rod'h could tolerate solitude in ways that no purebred Ildiran could. They drew on each other's strength.

The goal of the original Dobro breeding program that had produced her siblings was to create a telepathic prodigy. Rod'h, the oldest and most powerful after her, strove to serve as the chosen one, but Osira'h was the one who had wrestled the hydrogues and the faeros into submission.

The Elemental War had been over for two decades, though. The hydrogues had retreated to their gas-giant fortresses, the wentals were dispersed and quiescent on water worlds, and the verdani worldforest thrived on Theroc. Some of the faeros roamed at large, still capricious although no longer intent on destruction.

Even though the faeros might be the key to fighting the Shana Rei, as they had done at Theroc, Osira'h was concerned that they no longer listened to her. Nevertheless, together with Rod'h, she would demand their attention. They would even beg if necessary. The faeros had hurt the shadows, but they had also suffered tremendous losses.

"Let us go, Osira'h," Rod'h said, anxious to climb aboard the scout pod. "We will find them. We *will.*" She knew he had something to prove, so she would give him the opportunity if it presented itself.

Wulfton was a knotted turmoil of magnetic loops, coronal streamers, and solar storms. Viewed through heavy filters, sunspots looked like a spreading blight. The turbulence also seemed to attract the fiery elementals. Osira'h had seen the faeros here before, and so she decided this was their best chance to reestablish contact. She and Rod'h would flush them out. Somehow.

As they climbed into a shielded scout pod, ready to venture into the stellar firestorm, the lead astronomer faced them with his large eyes and pale face. "You both are powerful beyond our understanding, but please do not provoke the faeros." The other astronomers nervously muttered their agreement.

"Do not underestimate us," Rod'h said.

"We have to find them first," Osira'h called back as she settled herself in the vessel. "And we have to make them listen."

The scout pod launched from the astronomy station, flying alone. With protective shields at full strength, they drifted into the buffeting coronal flares. Through heavily filtered windowports, Osira'h gazed into the blazing maelstrom, saw sunspots that were like festering holes on the stellar surface.

Rod'h stared, intent, and suddenly pointed. "There!" Osira'h saw *sparks*, ellipsoidal fireballs flitting about, as if Wulfton were a playground . . . or a sanctuary. "We have to call them." He closed his eyes and concentrated, sending out his mental demand through his telepathy.

Osira'h guided the craft deeper into the coronal storm, intent on the controls and keeping them safe while also using her mind like a radio, opening her thoughts and her emotions to attract their attention. "Just like when we were trained on Dobro," she said to her brother.

Rod'h opened his eyes. "Yes—it has been a long time since the Empire needed us as much as they do now."

As children, all of Nira's halfbreed offspring had channeled their special abilities, pushed and guided by the harsh Dobro Designate—Rod'h's father. They had been bred for a special purpose, a gamble that their unique genetic mixtures would create a savior who could dominate the elemental creatures devastating the Spiral Arm. It was time to remember that now.

As before, working together with their minds, Osira'h and Rod'h beseeched the faeros to respond.

Down in the stellar cauldron, she spotted at least thirty faeros like shooting stars. She accelerated the pod toward them—and the faeros withdrew, streaking away. The fiery elementals blocked the attempts at communication, and they skittered off . . . but they seemed more afraid than aloof.

"Wait!" she said aloud while sending out an intense thought. "We share an enemy. You know the pain and the danger posed by the Shana Rei. We need you to join the fight."

Rod'h gritted his teeth and demanded, "You must listen to us! The shadows have attacked our people, and they attacked you. We know they have also destroyed hydrogues. Fight with us! We will show you how to defeat them. And we have new weapons of our own."

The fireballs brightened, as if their internal flames had been stoked. At the piloting controls, Osira'h drove the craft forward, but the faeros scattered in different directions. "Wait!" Four fireballs plunged deep into the incandescent convection cells, where she could never follow.

Rod'h flashed a hard glance at her. "Closer! We have to *make* them respond to us." He was clearly angry at the faeros as he lashed out with his mind. "Why do you flee? Let us tell you how we can fight. Listen to us—it could save all of you!"

Unable to follow them into the depths of the star, Osira'h shot upward, flying on the stellar wind after the outbound faeros. She knew that their thoughts were touching the faeros—she could sense it—but the fiery elementals were shrugging off their contact with an edge of frantic alarm. She pushed harder. "You *know me!* You have responded before, and we need you again."

Rod'h said, "Do you wish to become extinct? Your very survival is at stake if you don't join the battle with us."

As the scout pod's engines strained to catch up to the faeros, Osira'h grasped her brother's hand to strengthen the bond. The siblings shared a special telepathic synergy. Now she solidified that link, and Rod'h knew what she was doing. This was the way they could *make* the faeros listen. Her brother added his own thoughts and energy, concentrated harder. Together, they formed a battering ram of telepathy directed toward the elementals.

"You *will* hear us!" Rod'h hissed through his teeth.

It was an irresistible command, and the flaming ellipsoids ahead of them faltered, reeled, hesitating just long enough for the scout pod to catch up.

In a more reasonable tone, Osira'h said, "You know how powerful the Shana Rei are. We cannot fight them alone."

Rod'h said, "The Shana Rei will destroy you, and us, and the cosmos unless you help us extinguish them. We have to fight together, no matter what happened in the past."

Using the last reserves in her engines, Osira'h closed the distance to one of the fireballs. And finally, clearly against their will, the faeros opened their consciousness and responded to the demands.

Osira'h and Rod'h both cried out as they were flooded with a crashing wave of terror and despair—the devastation the Shana Rei would cause to the faeros, the pain they had already inflicted, how the darkness had engulfed so many already and *smothered* them out of existence.

Too few of the faeros remained. They had been defeated, and their numbers had already dwindled to near extinction. They had suffered far too many losses, and more of them had died at Theroc. The hydrogues were no longer just hiding inside their gas giants—they were nearly *obliterated*, also by the Shana Rei.

The faeros were afraid. Terrified! They were not ready to make the sacrifice that a war against the shadows would entail. The elementals wavered, like a flame flickering in the wind, but they were too capricious, could not think far enough ahead. They simply reacted and fled.

The roar of burning thoughts nearly knocked Osira'h unconscious, and the scout pod reeled out of control. She struggled with the piloting systems; Rod'h was thrown against the bulkhead, hitting his temple. He sat stunned.

With the forceful telepathic contact broken, the faeros were free, unleashed. They streaked away, vanishing into empty, dark space.

Shuddering, Osira'h slumped behind the controls and hung there in the now cold silence. From a distance, she scanned Wulfton, but all of the other sparks had disappeared, too. The faeros had immersed themselves in the layers of the churning star. They wanted nothing to do with her . . . or with the Shana Rei, or with the war.

Rod'h sounded bitter. "They are gone. They are cowards." He blinked in wonder, looking over at her. "I have never felt that contact before . . . now I know what you experienced in the Elemental War. I know how hard it was for you." He seemed humbled; his voice trembled. "The faeros did listen to me. They saw me and heard me. But I was not convincing enough."

Osira'h struggled to recover, and her voice was shaky. "If the shadows are so fearsome that even the *faeros* flee in terror, what chance do any of us have? You and I are not strong enough to make them fight for us."

"Not yet," Rod'h said. "Perhaps we need to give them a stronger incentive."

Tense and sick, Osira'h turned the craft about and headed back to the astronomy station, where they would call a warliner to escort them home.

CHAPTER 55

TAL GALE'NH

The light was searing, blinding—intentionally so. Gale'nh had to shield his eyes from the glare that erupted out of the solar crucible. Next to him, the fallen Designate Rusa'h stood unperturbed, closer to the light and heat than Gale'nh could endure. The mad Designate seemed to revel in it.

Giant curved lenses scooped up the light of the multiple suns, focused it, and directed it into a furnace. Conveyors loaded with the mixed debris of broken construction materials, scrap metal, and stone rolled inexorably to where it was dumped into the heart of that inferno, where the structure broke down to the atomic level. The molten materials were mixed with catalysts, seed-crystal matrices were added, and then the substance was extruded into ceramic molds, where it cooled into pearlescent ultrasturdy construction blocks.

Gale'nh did not watch the process. Rather, he focused on Rusa'h, who had summoned him to the crucible. The former Designate didn't even blink as he stared at the incandescent fury as if it were nothing more than the placid surface of a pond.

Rusa'h spoke in a quiet, distant voice, as if talking to himself. "I was able to live inside a sun when the faeros lived inside me."

Finally he turned to Gale'nh. His gaunt face was reddened, burned by the exposure to so much brightness. "And you once lived inside the shadows—do they still live within you?"

Shielding his face from the glare, Gale'nh answered honestly. "I don't know, but I will fight them in every way possible."

"You should ponder the shadows. Try to understand them," Rusa'h said. "The Shana Rei must have used you, but you can use them back . . . just as the faeros used me. When I had the fire in my blood, in my cells, I was part of them. I learned things about the faeros. You must have learned things about the shadows."

"Those memories are blank," Gale'nh said. "They vanquished everyone else, but left me alive aboard the *Kolpraxa*."

"Then there must be something special about you," Rusa'h said. "What is different? Understand that, and you can understand them."

"They left me with doubts and weakness. There is nothing I can learn from that."

"Not true! I learned from the faeros. I drew great insight and used that insight to battle the Ildiran Empire. That was wrong and dangerous, but it was insight nevertheless."

"I wouldn't trust what you learned from the faeros," Gale'nh said, "any more than I trust what the shadows might allow me to know."

As the solar crucible continued to blaze, Rusa'h turned his back on the light so that he looked like an eclipse in the form of a man. "I have had revelations," he insisted. "Don't be so quick to dismiss them."

"Revelations? Some would call them delusions," Gale'nh said. "And how would that help us in our fight against the Shana Rei?"

Rusa'h responded with a faint smile. Even though he was so close to the blazing inferno, the smile seemed incredibly cold. "In a war like this, Tal Gale'nh, perhaps insane solutions are the only possible ones."

CHAPTER 56

KING PETER

After collapsing in the throne room, his son had remained unconscious for an hour. Reyn was recovering in his rooms now, resting and growing insanely bored as the doctors hovered over him. He insisted that his collapse had been a passing thing, dismissing it as a kind of seizure, but they didn't believe him.

King Peter felt desperate. He and Estarra were two of the most powerful people who had ever lived. As leaders of the Confederation, they guided countless planets, settlements, business groups. They possessed resources beyond imagining, but still no one had offered a cure for their son.

His team of experts sifted through numerous crackpot suggestions, none of which showed any real promise. Most of the "miracle cures" came from greedy and disreputable people, and King Peter had learned to spot them rather than be taken in by unrealistic hope. Their lust for money was no match for his desperation as a father with a gravely ill son.

When Dr. Benjamin Paolus arrived to discuss an "urgent and highly classified medical matter," he seemed like one such person. Peter tried to remain optimistic, though cautious. He and Estarra had agreed privately that they would try any promising solution, and as Reyn's condition worsened, they were growing less selective.

Dr. Paolus wore a trim business suit and presented his medical credentials, but he appeared nervous. Estarra joined them on a private balcony high on the fungus-reef city, where they could talk without being interrupted.

She looked tired with worry lines etched into her face, although Peter still found her beautiful. He remembered when he had first seen this innocent young girl from Theroc, out of her depth in an arranged marriage set up by the Hansa Chairman. Peter had been the puppet-king, and she was to be his puppet-queen. When the two of them had seen how they were being manipulated, they became true partners, fighting as a team against Chairman Wenceslas. More than two decades had passed since then; planets had been destroyed, whole civilizations had fallen . . . and they were still King and Queen.

Yet they could do nothing to help Reyn.

Dr. Paolus held out a secure datapad filled with medical records. "Thank you for seeing me, Majesties."

"We are always willing to listen," Estarra said. "And hope. Your research has found something?"

Dr. Paolus didn't seem to hear the question. He had a memorized presentation and needed to proceed with it as planned. As he called up data and images, he described himself as one of the most respected neurological researchers on Earth, the head of a team of researchers who worked for the interconnected university system with enhanced funding from industries.

Peter's expression hardened. "We know all this, Dr. Paolus. Rey[illegible]ld told us how Rlinda Kett helped him arrange a meeting with yo[illegible] [illegible]gnosed him, but couldn't offer any help."

Peter had investigated the man. Paolus had impressive credentials, yes, but his finances were a shambles. His bank accounts had fluctuated like a panicked heartbeat over the last decade, and recently he had plunged more deeply into debt than before. Peter did not want to shatter Estarra's hopes, but he would personally be very cautious of what the man said.

"Not then, but I kept working," the doctor insisted. "All other researchers built upon what I did, and I never did get paid for the scope of that initial work. Not really."

"We are very grateful," Peter said coolly, bracing himself for the man's request.

Estarra folded her hands together. "We just need that one breakthrough. Do you have it for us, Doctor?"

Paolus faltered and began again, back to the money. "Prince Reynald paid me for my initial scans and my diagnosis, but we did not have the funding to research such an obscure disease. Still, I tasked some of my team members to produce results, but . . . even though we're still in a preliminary stage I was hoping I might be reimbursed for some specific expenses?"

"If you provide proper documentation, we can reimburse your research facility directly." He knew that wasn't what Dr. Paolus wanted.

He swallowed hard. "I do have a vital new piece of information. As a human being, I can't in good conscience withhold it, despite a sacred promise I made. I am breaking that promise by revealing this, and I hope you will reward me accordingly."

Peter frowned, and he saw Estarra grow tense and wary. "We will do what is right."

Paolus called up a star chart on his datapad. "The medical research you need is held in a secure complex called Pergamus, a private installation where a woman named Zoe Alakis collects disease organisms. She holds more medical information than any other human being, and she keeps it all to herself."

Estarra blinked. "Why would she do that?"

"I've never been able to understand it. She wanted a specimen of Reynald's disease for her collection. She wanted her teams to study it." He swallowed. "I sold it to her myself. I . . . I know that was breaching Prince Reynald's trust, but I hoped she might be able to help [illegible] then, Zoe led me to believe that they had indeed made significant progress."

Peter struggled to understand. "Are you telling me that Pergamus has conducted research on our son's disease, in secret, but they're keeping the results to themselves?"

Paolus nodded. "I begged her to share the work she had done, so we could help the Prince. That was most important."

"And so you could share the reward," Estarra said.

"But she flatly refused. Maybe you need to ask her yourself, Majesties? I can provide you with the coordinates of Pergamus." Paolus blushed as he showed pictures of the domed facility, the poisonous atmosphere, the quarantined Orbital Research Spheres. He became very uneasy as he added, "By doing this, I will never be able to work for Zoe Alakis again."

Peter was much more disturbed about the existence of the disease library itself. "She knows Prince Reyn needs that research. I can't believe anyone would lock those cures away."

"Believe it," Paolus said. "I tried, Majesties. I did my best."

Peter gave his wife a determined smile. "We'll send Rlinda Kett as our emissary. She's the best at negotiating, and she'll see that Zoe shares her research."

Peter had not expected to feel hope, but now he did sense that Dr. Paolus had provided something significant. With a quick nod, he turned to the doctor. "Yes, you'll be paid."

CHAPTER 57

SAREIN

Alone in the Wild, by design, Sarein lived in a hollowed-out hive-worm nest suspended from a tree, a large organic structure that would have supported five families back on the main continent. Sarein had only bothered to clean out and convert part of it, which was all she needed for her own use. Her humble place was a far cry from when she had lived in the Whisper Palace on Earth as the Theron ambassador and as the lover of Chairman Basil Wenceslas. But she was comfortable.

She tried to be self-sufficient in her isolation, but she received occasional deliveries from the main city on Theroc, even some offworld supplies that she particularly desired.

When Sarein had retreated here in self-imposed exile, she'd done it for the new Confederation, refusing to be a constant reminder of the political machinations that had damaged the human race during the Elemental War. After the downfall of the Hansa, she could have been a gadfly during the formation of the new government, but she made a conscious decision not to meddle. She had already done enough damage. So, she removed herself from civilization, from history, and lived quietly in the wilderness for years.

During the crisis of the Shana Rei nightshade, Sarein had returned briefly to the fungus-reef city. She was tempted to stay, to make herself politically important again, but she had forced herself to pull away and disappear into the Wild once more.

Arita, her niece, was the only one who visited, whether or not Sarein invited her. Despite her cool façade toward the young woman, Sarein saw great potential in her and hoped to help wherever she could. Sarein decided that she preferred a personal connection instead of a grandiose power grab. . . .

Now, she opened the latest package of supplies she had just received. Preserved foods, a fresh power pack to run her home and electronic equipment, and culled summaries of important news events from across the Spiral Arm. Though she had taken herself off the stage, Sarein still insisted on remaining informed, especially with the brewing crisis of the Shana Rei.

At the bottom of the container, she was surprised to discover a note from Arita. Not a message transmitted through normal communications channels, not telink, not even a standard comm. This was an actual handwritten *note*, affixed to a much longer folded letter.

"Sarein, please try to find Collin among the green priests over there. Call for him, and the trees will hear. *He* will hear. Please deliver the attached letter to him. It would mean so much to me. This is too private for telink, which all green priests would hear."

Sarein gave an indulgent smile. Young lovers sending secret notes. How charming! She imagined how difficult it must be to arrange a clandestine tryst when one's boyfriend was a green priest. She let out a little laugh.

Once Sarein called for the young man to come to her, however, the other green priests would know about the relationship, especially Kennebar and his hermit green priests. She read the brief note again and nodded to herself. Arita had asked, and so Sarein would do it. Of course she would.

Arita's longer letter was folded but not sealed. Sarein was tempted to read it. Was that what Arita secretly wanted? Or had she left the letter unsealed to demonstrate a level of trust? Sarein was moved by the thought; it had been a long time since anyone had trusted her like that. Sorely tempted, she unfolded the letter, then folded it again, before glancing at more than the first few words. She decided to let Collin and Arita have their privacy.

She stepped outside of her hiveworm nest and gazed into the dense worldforest, the green shadows that allowed her to hide and allowed her to think. She drew a breath and shouted into the empty wilderness, feeling a little foolish. Sarein had never asked for their help before, but she knew the trees would convey her message. "I need a green priest! Send Collin, please—I want to talk with him."

Both wanting solitude, she and Kennebar's group had kept their distance from each other. The green priests were aloof to her, implying that Sarein didn't belong here in the Wild. She shouted again, just to make sure. "Send the green priest named Collin. It's an important matter!"

Knowing it might take some time, depending on where the group was in the deep forest, Sarein went back into her chambers and called up the draft of her journal. She had been chronicling her past deeds for some time, wrestling with how much to reveal about the things she had done, how much to confess, and how much to excuse. She didn't do it to fix her place in history, though her recollections might eventually prove valuable to historians. She wrote her memoirs partly to refocus her thoughts in case she might someday return to civilization.

Someday. Sarein was tired of feeling sorry for herself. She wanted the best for her world and for the human race. Maybe she could help again after all. . . .

She heard a rustle in the fronds outside and a slender young man with bright green skin scrambled down to her dwelling. "You called for me?" Collin said. He looked concerned, distracted. "Why would you want to see me?"

"This is from Arita." She held out the letter.

Collin lit up. "Arita sent a note?"

"I don't know why she didn't just have a green priest transmit to you. That would have been more efficient."

Collin blinked at her, eager to read the letter. "It's another way to keep communications open." He lowered his voice. "Telink may no longer be reliable. Something is changing in the worldforest, but the green priests are oblivious to it, or they deny it." He looked up at her; she saw a frightened glimmer in his eyes. "Have you noticed anything?"

"I'm not a green priest. I'm not attuned to the forest the way you are."

"No, but you may not be blinded by preconceptions either."

Sarein pondered and looked past him into the dense, whispering forest. "There are times when the trees do seem more . . . ominous, but I've been alone out here for so long I don't know what to think."

Collin gave a serious nod, then finally unfolded the letter. His eyes darted back and forth as he read, then he smiled. "Arita is coming to the Wild again! Soon. She'll travel here to do more scientific work."

Sarein gave him a skeptical smile. "And also to see you."

Collin said, "Yes . . . and also to see me. I'll find her. We have to keep the lines of communication open." He read the letter again, then handed it back to her. "I can't keep this. Kennebar or someone else will find it. But thank you."

"Happy I could help."

After he dashed away into the dense fronds, she realized that this was the first accomplishment that had made her feel good in a very long time.

CHAPTER

58

SHAREEN FITZKELLUM

Fireheart Station was an exciting chance for the two of them to learn under the genius Kotto Okiah, but in ten days Shareen and Howard had done nothing more than busywork. And Shareen was ready for *big things*.

"I can't figure out these notes enough to decide if they're brilliant or just a confused mess." Her brow furrowed as she bent over the half-finished designs and wandering equations.

"Kotto never intended for anyone else to have to decipher them," Howard said in a calm voice to steady her, as he always did.

Uncertain, Shareen went back to recopying and organizing the scientist's handwritten notes for countless half-finished projects and dead ends, crackpot ideas, and musings about physically impossible inventions. "I'm sure he had something clear in mind."

Kotto had asked Howard and Shareen to do this, since he didn't have time. "And," he had added with a twinkle in his eye, "it'll give you insight into how my mind works."

So far, Shareen's primary insight was that Kotto had a disorganized mind. But she supposed that was how the quality of *genius* would appear to an outsider. She knew she was clever enough to figure it out, though.

Inside the chamber cluttered with gadgets, measuring equipment, testing apparatus, and marking boards, KR and GU puttered around the laboratory space. GU said, "Your contributions are far superior to what a compy can provide. Even Technical models like myself and KR could not organize and interpret Kotto's concepts."

KR added, "We have offered to help him in any way possible, but he does not let us touch his notes."

Shareen drew satisfaction from that as she picked up the scrambled papers. She reminded herself that Kotto had been responsible for so many incredible breakthroughs, surely something just as important might be hidden here under all the mathematical debris and false starts. She just had to find it. "I can't even tell where one idea ends and another starts. I could be collating two entirely different designs."

Howard smiled at her. "That could lead to a wondrous hybrid invention."

"Right, like an advanced cooling system that also makes music." She shook her head and got back to work.

From looking at his hodgepodge of "ideas in development," she decided that Kotto Okiah's attention was like a bullet ricocheting through a maze. Most of his "designs" were simple musings without underlying calculations, as if he jotted down any amusing thought that came to mind but never bothered to go through the vigorous mathematics and proofs to back it up. In fact, Howard had said the same thing about her. Shareen smiled to think she might have something in common with Kotto. . . .

As a Roamer, she had had an insatiable curiosity since she was a child. She had taken apart mechanical objects long before she had any inkling of how to put them back together (causing much consternation when she meddled with sophisticated ekti-harvesting systems in her family's skymine).

When she'd gone to Earth to study in a prestigious academy, she hadn't done well in the environment. She argued with her professors, insisting that if she intuitively understood the mechanics, then the math was a waste of time that she could use more effectively for inventing other things. Meeting Howard at the academy had been the one bright spot of the experience—and he taught her the importance of rigorous double-checking and follow-through.

Apparently, no one had taught Kotto that, though. Well, then it was up to her and Howard.

Sifting through the notes, she did find some of the concepts quite fascinating; she just wished she could interpret how Kotto envisioned bringing them to fruition. In years past, he had developed vital defenses against the hydrogues during the Elemental War; he had improved ekti-skymining operations; he had designed and established seemingly impossible Roamer settlements in the most inhospitable of places, from lava worlds to frozen planetoids.

When Shareen reminded herself of all those things, she found more patience for his disorganization. It was an honor to work with such a legend, even if Kotto didn't seem to know what to do with the two of them.

Howard came over to join her. "We always do our best work together. Let me help organize and interpret, since we both want to make sense out of what Kotto was working on."

"I'm not sure even he knows," she mumbled, but it was not a complaint. "Between the two of us, maybe we can finish some of these things."

Kotto's lab space was a dumping ground of half-completed prototypes, from plasma rainbow dispensers to an oscillating sonic projector that could cast strange sounds across a room like a mechanical ventriloquist—to what purpose, Shareen didn't know. He had built a surveillance system equipped with a self-looping anti-grav field so the imager could float independently, but it wobbled so much that any reconnaissance was useless.

At first glance, these uncompleted projects did not seem up to the caliber of Kotto's previous breakthroughs. And his concept sketches for even bigger inventions seemed entirely impractical. She switched on the plasma rainbow dispenser, then turned it off, dazzled by the flood of colors. "A lot of these seem like . . . toys."

Howard cautioned, "I would not presume to judge the merits of Kotto Okiah's concepts. It's altogether probable he's so far ahead of us in his thinking that we don't grasp their potential."

Shareen just wished the scientist would spend more time mentoring them so she could learn—and ask a lot more questions. Instead, Kotto's attention was focused on the Big Ring construction project. She looked up from incomplete or recursive calculations scrawled on a scrap of paper. Outside the lab module, she could see the gigantic torus being assembled in the sea of nebula gas, and its enormity impressed her. Thousands of large superconducting magnets would form a huge loop, powered internally by charged power blocks.

Now *that* would be something to be a part of.

Kotto had been working on the Big Ring with unlimited funding and unwavering Roamer support for six years. His mathematics were beyond the comprehension of most clan members, but when he said the test was necessary, that it might open up a new galactic landscape for instantaneous wormhole travel far superior to the limited Klikiss transportal network, the Roamers gave him the benefit of the doubt. After all, when had he ever asked them for anything before?

The last segments of the torus were just now being framed out with linked girders, and all available power blocks were commandeered for the project. Fireheart Station had just sent out a call for new workers, qualified engineers and experienced space construction crews. With Kotto Okiah's name attached, there would be plenty of applicants.

When it was completed in another month, the Big Ring would be the largest pure-physics experiment humans had ever conducted—and who knew what they would discover about the structure of space-time? The power the ring generated would be inconceivable. Shareen couldn't wait to see it in action.

Howard caught her staring out the windowport. "We both want to take part in that, but we have to impress Kotto first. Maybe then he'll let us assist him."

With greater determination, Shareen looked back down at the notes spread on the lab table and suddenly realized that two completely separate scribblings were continuations of yet another project, and when she sorted them together, the concept made more sense. "There's the Guiding Star I've been looking for! Looks like Kotto has a plan for sequencing the energy-collector films for power blocks so they can be charged logarithmically instead of linearly."

Excited now, Shareen used a stylus to cross out several sections that Kotto had painstakingly derived, then left unfinished. "That's a dead end—here's where he went off track." She tapped a row of calculations, corrected them, then furiously wrote a new sequence of integrals. "*This* is the way to do it."

Howard bent closer. "Yes, but don't forget this step." He pointed with his finger. "Logarithmic charging of energy films? That's a significant breakthrough. It could increase Fireheart's production of power blocks by an order of magnitude."

"Then it's a good thing we figured it out." Shareen felt a warm pride, wondering if this was some kind of test that Kotto had left for them. He would certainly be proud of what they had done. She glanced again at the Big Ring, then back down at the notes. "We might even have time to finish one of these other inventions."

Howard accepted the challenge.

CHAPTER

59

ORLI COVITZ

With Garrison's personal mission complete, the *Prodigal Son* flew away from the Rendezvous asteroid cluster. They set course for Newstation, where both Orli and Garrison knew there would be great changes for them. She had to go to Earth to take care of unfinished business with Rlinda Kett; Seth would study at Academ with other Roamer children; and Garrison planned to fly back to Ikbir with the requested supplies and a repair crew for Yoder's ship.

He and Orli sat awkwardly during the flight, talking of many things but nothing of consequence. They had been thrown together by circumstances, had found comfort and happiness in each others' company, but neither of them had been intentionally looking for romance. Garrison had his scars from Elisa, and Orli had her scars from Matthew—and she had just recovered from a deadly plague.

Once they reached Newstation, they would have to make a decision. It seemed as if they were going their separate ways, but it didn't have to be permanent. This would be a good chance for them to think and decide.

Garrison smiled uncertainly at her as he flew toward the new Roamer capital complex. "I'll see that Seth gets settled at Academ, but he doesn't want me looking over his shoulder the whole time. I could take you to Earth, if that's what you'd like?"

Orli's smile was troubled. "I think it might be better if DD and I go by ourselves, maybe just for a month. I need some time to think. Is there more to this relationship? Is there a future?"

Garrison took a long time to answer. "I don't know. You're great with Seth, and he adores DD, but . . . we both have a lot to think about."

. . .

Newstation was a dramatic contrast to Rendezvous. Garrison was upbeat as he piloted the *Prodigal Son* toward the retro-looking wheel station that rotated above the planet Auridia. Seth pointed to a faintly shimmering comet that hung next to the giant station. "That's Academ, DD, where I'm going to school." He hesitated. "I'll miss you."

"I will miss you too, Seth Reeves," DD said, "but the Roamer school has several Teacher compies to assist with your instruction. They are more qualified to educate you than I am."

Orli felt a pang. "DD and I will be able to visit you, after we make a trip to Earth."

Garrison added, "Business first. We need to arrange the supplies and equipment for Ikbir."

Orli knew that the busywork would occupy her mind so she didn't dwell too much on their imminent parting. She and Matthew had had enough good years in their marriage to give her some fond thoughts, but enough bad years to negate most of it. Having been treated badly himself, Garrison was also cautious. But he and Orli were so good together, and she felt close to Seth. . . . Maybe it wouldn't take her a month after all to make up her mind—if Garrison came to the same conclusion.

While Garrison and his son went to arrange for Seth to attend the school, Orli took DD and the list of supplies Ikbir needed. As they moved through the frenetic station, DD maintained a patter of conversation, but Orli was preoccupied.

Early in her life she had experienced so much drama, so much tragedy, that she had wanted to settle down. She and Matthew got married, and she spent years working with compies on Relleker. When that fizzled, she went to her old friend Rlinda Kett and tried her hand at trading. That hadn't turned out well either. Orli's life seemed to be a succession of dramas and dead ends, and now she needed to go back to Rlinda for closure. And Garrison . . . Garrison needed to find his own way.

They reconvened at dinner. Seth ran to DD to tell him all about the classes he intended to take, and Orli was surprised to see Garrison just as exuberant. "Kotto Okiah just posted that he's looking for qualified engineers to help finish the Big Ring." His eyes were shining. "The Big Ring!"

Orli didn't know what that was, and DD promptly explained, "It is a gigantic physics experiment being constructed out at Fireheart Station. The results of the tests could provide extraordinary insights into the structure of space-time."

Garrison nodded. "This is a chance to be a part of history. They sent an open call for engineers and constructors, and the project will last a month." He offered her an optimistic smile. "A month—is that the time you needed? *We* needed?"

"What about the supplies for Ikbir?" Orli said.

He dismissed the idea. "This is Newstation. I can find a dozen Roamers to make the run, and I wasn't really looking forward to going back there anyway. This is simply too great an opportunity to pass up."

"It sounds perfect for you." She grew more serious. "You saved me in more ways than one, Garrison, and I'll always be grateful."

He smiled and leaned forward to kiss her, much to Seth's amusement. "If you start missing me too much, you'll know where to find me."

After traveling to Earth aboard a Roamer passenger yacht, Orli and DD made their way to Kett Shipping headquarters. The big hearty woman came out of her office, and swept Orli up in her massive arms. "I never thought I'd see you alive again, girl!"

"We are very pleased you didn't see her dead, either," DD said.

"And that was a close thing," Orli admitted.

Rlinda herded them into her office. "We've got a lot of catching up to do. I'll order a meal for us."

"I'm not all that hungry."

"Then I'll order a meal for *me*, and it'll look so delicious, you'll want to eat anyway. I know it."

Orli supposed the trader woman was right. In a somber voice, she said, "I'm sorry I lost the *Proud Mary*. I had no other option—it was contaminated, and I didn't want to risk—"

Rlinda held up a finger. "Don't you worry about a thing. I read your message, and that's all I needed to know." She lowered herself into the extra wide chair behind her desk. "On second thought, I want to hear everything. From you directly. Sorry you got into so much trouble. I thought I was doing a good thing by asking you to check on that stubborn fool, Olaf Reeves."

"They're all dead," Orli said.

"I know that, but it's not your fault. They caused their own problems."

"It was still a tragedy."

"Yes, it was. But while some tragedies are unavoidable, some are caused by human stupidity." Rlinda reached forward and picked up a silver capsule mounted on a Lucite stand on her desk. She ran the capsule between her fingers, rolling it, staring at it. A sheen of tears filled her eyes.

"When BeBob died, there was no warning, no way I could've known to be there. He just dropped dead walking across the street. *That* was a tragedy. Unavoidable. Now, after I go, two capsules with our ashes will be shot off into space together, and that'll be a romantic end to the story." Rlinda wiped her eyes, replaced the capsule, and glanced back at Orli. "I suppose you want another chance and another ship?"

DD immediately said, "We would like that very much, Rlinda Kett."

"Maybe . . ." Orli said. "Or something here?"

"I'll turn you over to Tasia and Robb, and they'll find something for you to do." She smiled. "For myself, I'm off on a special mission for King Peter and Queen Estarra—to negotiate with a secret medical facility that just may have a cure for Prince Reyn. I'm told that the answer is probably going to be no, but I don't like that answer." She sighed. "Poor Raindrop. I plan to use my negotiating skills and my charm—or anything else that might be required."

CHAPTER

60

XANDER BRINDLE

The *Verne* headed for the coordinates contained in the mysterious message someone had left Terry at Ulio Station. They arrived in "the dead center of nowhere, just a little bit to the left," as Xander described it.

OK studied the long-range sensor results. "I detect a large ship ahead. Judging by its configuration, it appears to be an Ildiran warliner."

Screen enhancements finally showed the silhouette of an enormous vessel lit by only a few twinkling lights, while the rest of the hulk was dark, ominous. "It's Ildiran all right, but what's a warliner doing out here? And why would they contact you at Ulio?"

"I don't know any Ildirans," Terry said, baffled.

It was too late to be cautious, however, since the ghost ship would have detected their arrival. Even so, Xander made sure all the *Verne*'s defenses were up as they proceeded toward the rendezvous.

Terry leaned forward, staring at the screen—and suddenly burst out laughing. "That's not just any warliner—it's Maria! Maria Ulio."

The *Verne*'s comm activated, and an old woman's face appeared on screen, her skin a spiderweb of wrinkles, her gray eyes twinkling. Her smile was genuine. "Glad you got my message, boys. I appreciate you taking time from your busy schedule to talk with a lonely old woman."

"Maria!" Terry cried. "You could've left us more of a clue. We didn't know why anybody wanted to meet us—and lately, people aren't always friendly."

"I wanted to pique your curiosity. Would you have come if you knew it was just me?"

"Of course," Terry said.

She chuckled. "Yes, you probably would have. Allow an old lady her melodrama."

"But, why are you here, so far from . . . anything? What do you need from us?"

Maria leaned closer to the screen. "Since you came all the way out here, why don't you visit me in person? It's about time I had some company on this great big empty ship."

Xander answered for them both, "We'll be right over."

Though Xander already knew much about the woman who had taken Terry under her wing, he had never met her in person. Maria's salvaged warliner was huge enough that they could land the *Verne* inside one empty docking bay. After they exited the *Verne* and walked across the dim landing bay, a group of compies greeted them. "Maria Ulio asked us to escort you for a fine high tea."

Xander looked at Terry. "I don't know what's more unexpected—finding legendary Maria Ulio out here, or learning that she drinks high tea."

"She goes through phases," Terry said. "She gets interested in something, then buries herself in it."

"We even made crumpets," said one of the escort compies.

The refurbished Solar Navy vessel was designed to carry thousands of Ildirans, but now Maria had the entire ship to herself—a full warliner for one person and a handful of compies. "Sounds about right," Terry said. "She did like her elbow room."

The old woman had converted the command nucleus into a penthouse for herself. She had remodeled the entire deck into a lavish relaxing room with the transparent dome overhead, so she could see the stars. She kept her ship's gravity low, partly to relieve the stress on her ancient heart and bones, but also for Terry's ease of movement.

As soon as he emerged from the lift, Terry propelled himself forward, legs extended behind him, until he collided with Maria, laughing. "It's good to see you again!"

She caught Terry and wrapped her bony arms around him, making them both lose their balance. "I have a soft spot for you, young man—or maybe a soft head."

"A little of both," Terry said; then he remembered his partner. "This is Xander."

"I know who he is, dear boy, and I'm glad he makes you happy. For myself, what makes me happy is to be away from all those maddening people. I thought it was refreshing to be alone—for the first few years at least."

Xander said, "You've got an empty ship all by yourself, parked halfway between star systems. I'd say you found a way to be alone."

"Yes, I've got an abundance of quiet out here. Sometimes it's too quiet. . . . But every year or so I desire worthwhile company."

"Which is why you invited us?" Terry said.

"That . . . among other things."

On a table in the middle of the command nucleus was a tea service, three cups, a tray of scones, a jar of red jam, a pot of clotted cream, a honey dipper in a pool of what looked like real honey, as well as a three-tiered tray that held tiny fragments of sandwiches. The old woman folded her hands over a linen napkin at her place. "So glad you could join me in time for tea. I had no idea when you would get my message."

"Well, I'm glad you found me." Terry held the edge of the table and pulled himself into place. His expression of delight was plain as he looked at the spread. "All my favorites. You remembered, Maria!" Xander made sure his partner was situated before taking his own seat across from the woman.

When compies came forward like prim butlers and began to serve the high tea, Xander tried to participate as if he knew what he was doing. He had never tasted cucumber sandwiches before, which were strange, but the scones were delicious, particularly with the clotted cream. The tea was strong, and he indulged himself by adding milk and two dollops of honey from the dripper.

He leaned back. "So, you earned your place in history by creating Ulio Station, even if it came about by accident. It's an important commercial hub—and you just gave it all up?"

She offered Xander and Terry chocolate biscuits from a tray. "Ulio Station is a shining example of people sharing responsibilities and resources. But as always happens, when a good thing gets too big, the headaches become intolerable. I enjoyed the community I built, but then the squabbles and the esoteric bureaucracy made me give up. So, I left and never regretted it. Ulio Station can survive or fall, with or without me. I'm not a part of it anymore."

"Sounds like you're bitter, Maria," Terry chided. "That's where I met you, where I learned so much of what I know. I don't regret it for a minute."

Maria sipped her sweet tea. "That's why I brought you here, dear boy, to remind me of those things. Sitting alone in empty space, I have too much time to think."

"Were you cheated by the station?" Xander asked, figuring that might explain her mood. "Written out of profits or something?"

Maria chuckled. "Oh no—not that at all. I've got more wealth than anybody would know how to spend. It's built into our original charter that a percentage of all trading fees goes into several accounts in my name, dispersed across various financial institutions, and I have quite a vault of tangible assets stored back at Ulio . . . but I left all them behind. Now that I don't need wealth, I seem to have an excessive amount of it." She tapped her fingertips on the table.

The compies removed the dirty dishes, replaced their napkins with fresh ones. Xander dabbed a speck of clotted cream from the side of his mouth.

Maria continued. "Now, since I don't require any of that wealth, and I certainly don't intend to spend it out here, I thought it better go to some kind of use. Why should I let the bankers have all the fun?" She leaned over and prodded Terry on the arm. "I don't have any blood heirs, and you're as close as I can come to a son." When she smiled, the wrinkles on her face seemed to vanish.

Xander caught his breath, but he saw that Terry didn't realize what she was suggesting.

"I've already initiated the transfer and filed the necessary documents," Maria continued. "Terry Handon, you are now the heir to a specified percentage of all future profits from Ulio Station. You'll need to go to the Central Offices, talk to whoever the current chief is, get everything transferred into your name." She pointed at the three-tiered tray. "Try the watercress sandwiches with cream cheese—I particularly like those."

"But . . . what will I do with all that money?" Terry didn't look greedy, simply perplexed.

"Exactly the problem I've been struggling with." She waved a hand. "Donate it to some reconstruction project, if you want. Buy a planet. Paint your ship green, for all I care. I don't plan on going back to Ulio Station. I'll just stay out here and watch. I have this enormous ship with enough food and power blocks to last me five centuries. I certainly don't need the accounts anymore."

"How . . . how much money is it?" Terry asked.

"Dear boy, the balance is large enough that you never actually need to worry about what the balance is."

Xander interrupted before his partner could keep asking unnecessary questions, "I'm sure we can find some worthwhile investments or causes, ma'am."

"I don't know what to say," Terry said.

Xander nudged him in the side. "*Thank you* would be a good start."

"Thank you," Terry said. "You've already done so much for me, taught me how to repair starships, gave me a home when I was nowhere." Tears were sparkling in his eyes.

"And I'm proud of you, boy." The old woman sipped her tea, then looked at the observation dome over their heads. She turned to one of her compies. "Would you mind showing us the stars, please?"

The compy dimmed the lights in the command nucleus, and the three of them sat in the darkness, drowning in a blizzard of pinpoints.

Maria grew more serious. "You may need resources in the coming years, might even want to buy a ship of your own like this and find a place to lie low. I see things out here . . . dark and terrible things."

"What do you mean?" Xander asked.

"I've been out in space long enough to have a sense for this. Something is different now, I can feel it. It's like the universe is *awakening*. I don't know how else to explain it. I've seen shadow nebulas that appear and disappear, lines of strange nodules floating along for parsecs, connecting nothing to nothing." She turned her gray gaze back to them, leaning closer to Terry and Xander. "Keep an eye out. I have a feeling things are going to get a lot worse."

CHAPTER

61

AELIN

Inside Dauntha's quarters on Ulio Station, Aelin gradually began to feel like a green priest again. A year ago, when he joined Lee Iswander in his first bloater-extraction field, Aelin had sworn not to reveal the source of ekti-X. Back then, he hadn't known what he was agreeing to, and now he didn't dare call attention to the source lest he trigger hundreds of copycat operations.

With the expansion of the Confederation after the Elemental War, freelance green priests were in demand on starships and isolated colonies to provide instantaneous communication via telink. Dauntha had seen a need at Ulio Station, with so many visitors and traders wanting to send personal messages or business communiqués. After coming here, she sat with her treeling and took visitors one by one, every hour of the day. She spoke to her clients, found out what sort of mood or message they needed, then used her treeling to pass the word throughout the extensive verdani network.

Right now, Aelin observed as a man with red hair and a bushy beard sat across from her, all business, no casual conversation. "I need to send a message to my company headquarters on Herren 3. There is a green priest stationed on the opposite continent, but he can convey the message once he receives it from you."

Dauntha nudged the treeling in Aelin's direction. "My partner will make contact. He can relay your words."

Aelin hesitated, but of course he knew how to do this. He had been pressed into service as a green priest many times. Redbeard didn't seem to care one way or another.

"The verdani mind will know the name of the green priest on Herren 3," Dauntha said, as if to reassure Aelin. "You can find him."

He touched the treeling, established a connection, then looked up at the bearded man. "What is it you wish to say?"

"It's a manifest. The numbers have to be accurate."

"I will transmit them accurately."

Redbeard rattled off numbers from memory. "For manifest one, we need two hundred hexagonal foam structural blocks for an outpost on Ikbir. We also need seventy-five silicon cylinders with optical enhancements. End order." Redbeard paused as Aelin repeated the words into the tree, then he started again. "Manifest two. One hundred interlocked solar panels to Dremen. I didn't promise them the new model panels, so you can unload from our stockpile. Manifest three—"

The trader continued for some time, reciting orders and inventory numbers. He finished without any additional pleasantries, paid the minimal fee, and left.

Aelin realized he was smiling. It felt good to have a purpose again, even to serve trivial business matters like this. However, even though he had come home to the verdani network, he felt as if he had moved in a different direction after his exposure to the eerie bloater consciousness. When he first took the green, the verdani had seemed like an infinite and omniscient mind, but now the worldforest seemed just a fragment of even greater possibilities. The trees were thirsty for knowledge as well, but Aelin could not reveal the secret of the bloaters.

Dauntha relaxed with her cup of hot klee, regarded the forestscape she had painted on her walls. "You are hiding something inside, Aelin. I can sense it. Green priests aren't comfortable with secrets."

"I want to tell you. It's something so wondrous. . . ." Those exotic nodules had shattered the walls of understanding and reality around him and opened Aelin's mind to more questions than he had ever conceived possible. He knew how important the bloaters were—even if he didn't understand *what* they were.

He told her as much as he could. "There's something out in space, something miraculous hiding between the stars where no one can see. They're called bloaters, and . . ." He heaved a sigh, not daring to reveal more. "What I learned from them is beyond even what the worldforest has given me."

Dauntha was somehow not surprised. "Out here at Ulio we see

a lot of things. I'll often just listen through my treeling, watch the worldforest mind." She rested her fingers against the fine gold bark. "I have sensed something, too. It is subtle, but the worldforest mind is disturbed . . . even confused. And I am very concerned for it."

CHAPTER 62

LEE ISWANDER

Even though he had no pressing business at Newstation, Lee Iswander could always find reasons to go there, and Londa had become quite insistent. "I miss Arden," she said. "We need to see how well he's doing in school. Remember, he was bullied at Academ before."

It had been only a month. "He's a resilient boy, and intelligent. He'll do fine."

While he would have preferred to wait for Elisa Enturi to return from her latest rendezvous at Ulio, he trusted her to get the job finished. Meanwhile, the ekti operations were proceeding smoothly under Pannebaker's supervision. There was only so much he could do here, and his people did not need to be micromanaged. Yes, he could go back to Newstation.

His priority was to be seen and appreciated among the Roamers for the Sisyphean task of rebuilding his reputation. So he yielded to his wife. Iswander didn't often do things just to please Londa. She had a role to play and so did he, but when he saw the joy that lit her face at the prospect of the trip, he allowed himself to feel warm inside.

"We'll stay there for two days only," he cautioned. "I'll get us a nice suite on the station. You can do shopping and spend time with Arden while I take care of business."

He flew the space yacht with just the two of them aboard, and en route he reviewed production reports and distribution projections. His wife showed no interest in the business; she never had, nor did he expect her to. They had been married for nineteen years, wed in the giddy optimism after the Elemental War. When he chose Londa as a wife, he specifically wanted someone to manage the household. She fulfilled her end of the bargain, but it never occurred to him to wonder whether

Londa wanted more out of her life, and she had certainly never asked. She would go to see Arden, and Iswander could safely let her buy anything she wished, knowing that her tastes were not extravagant.

During the flight, she chattered about shops she missed, restaurants she missed, friends she missed. These were not complaints: she had always supported him, even after Sheol—1,543 people dead—and she stood by him while the Roamer clans heaped shame on him.

As she talked now, he kept making notations on his datapad, running cost-benefit analyses on new extraction equipment so he could exploit another bloater cluster that had been located. At appropriate places in her conversation, he nodded and made innocuous comments. When she had finished, though, he waited until he had her full attention. He needed her to listen.

"While we're at Newstation, you can see whatever you like, talk to whomever you like, but be absolutely clear—you *cannot* tell anyone about our bloater operations. There will be countless people, bad people, who are desperate to find out where we get our ekti-X. You must not reveal anything, not a single word, or we'd be ruined just as badly as we were after Sheol."

Londa laughed. "You don't have to worry. I don't know anything about your business."

"Just be careful. You may know more than you think."

She patted his hand. "I promise, dear husband."

Although he often saw her as innocuous, he realized that Londa was indeed strong, savvy, and intelligent, just in different ways. She was also absolutely loyal, and that quality mattered more to him than anything else.

When they docked at Newstation, Iswander paid for a priority berth and then rented the most expensive room. The suite was usually reserved for important diplomatic representatives, and Iswander wanted to show that he measured his worth as equal to anyone else. He gave Londa a chaste peck on the cheek, and she was off to arrange transportation to the Roamer school to visit Arden.

First order of business: Iswander set up a meeting with Speaker Sam Ricks. Ricks was lounging in his large and cluttered office; his desk was filled with mementos, trophies, interesting objects given to him by various clan members, no doubt in exchange for favors. He was a man much too young for the position, not to mention unqualified. While Iswander wore his impeccable business suit, always presenting a professional image, Ricks wore a well-used Roamer jumpsuit sporting the markings of his clan, even though as Speaker, he was supposed to represent all clans equally—including clan Iswander.

A bin filled with rock specimens sat on one corner of his desk, next to a stack of formal documents marked "pending further review." Iswander swept his gaze around the office, made a rapid assessment. According to the date on a dislodged document halfway down the stack, the matter had been "pending further review" since the Speaker's election.

"What can I do for you, Mr. Iswander?" Ricks said, discomfited to receive this particular visitor. The young Speaker was not well practiced in maintaining an unreadable mask—another of his weaknesses as a politician. With all the ruthless negotiations that Jhy Okiah, Cesca Peroni, or Del Kellum had undertaken in their tenures as Speaker, Iswander couldn't imagine any of them being so transparent.

Iswander gave him a warm smile and was convinced the young man believed it was sincere. "I just wanted to congratulate you, Speaker. I never had a chance to tell you after the election."

Ricks didn't seem to know what to say. "Those were . . . tough circumstances."

"I wanted to reassure you that I am a loyal Roamer, concerned only with the betterment of the clans and our position in the Confederation. I have expertise and resources, and I'd be willing to offer my assistance, should you need it." The words scraped like sharp rocks in his throat, but he maintained his calm smile.

The Speaker's assistant poked his head in the door. "Three other meetings this afternoon, Sam. Browder wants to know where to meet for lunch, and three people so far have accepted your ping-labyrinth challenge."

Ricks grinned, then looked embarrassed. "I'll take care of that later. I'm busy right now."

With a disrespectful roll of his eyes, the assistant returned to the outer office.

"Ping labyrinth?" Iswander asked.

"It's a game. Very entertaining. Many people on Newstation are playing it. I was last week's champion."

Iswander responded with a cool smile and looked down at the pile of "pending further review" documents. "Interesting that you have time to become an expert in something so trivial as a social game, when there are important clan issues to deal with." He picked up the top document, a summary report submitted by clan Tamblyn on the losses they had incurred in the destruction of the Plumas water mines during the Shana Rei attack.

Ricks snatched the paper out of Iswander's hands. "That game allows me to maintain close personal connections with many clan members. As Speaker, I need to stay in touch with the people."

Iswander didn't believe it for a moment. "Some would call that avoidance."

Ricks looked insulted, but Iswander could see a hunted look behind his eyes. As he had suspected, Sam Ricks didn't know what to do in his job. He was unable to keep up with all the responsibilities.

"I think you're overwhelmed," Iswander said, sharpening the edge in his voice. "There are too many decisions, and you can't make them because you don't have the background or the fortitude to be Speaker."

Ricks didn't rise from his desk; in fact, he took the opportunity to lounge back. "And yet the clans elected me instead of you." He pointedly picked up the stack of pending documents. "Now, if you don't mind? I have work to do."

CHAPTER

63

ELISA ENTURI

Although some people delighted in surprises, Elisa Enturi was not one of them. Surprises were usually unpleasant, and this one was no exception. When she returned to Ulio Station and learned that clan Duquesne was offering their own ekti-X for sale, Elisa was furious.

She had recently supplied Ulio with a fuel stockpile to be used for the station's refueling and maintenance needs. Elisa had previously negotiated terms, and now when she offered a new contract for surplus ekti-X, she was alarmed by Station Manager Felliwell's aloof reaction. "We're definitely interested, and you are welcome to cut your price even further to compete with another supplier."

"Compete? No skyminer can match our price."

"Doesn't come from skyminers," said Felliwell. "And this ekti-X tests out as pure and energy-dense as your own."

That took her aback. "Where is it coming from?"

Felliwell chuckled at her surprise. "It seems someone else discovered your source, whatever it is. Roamers are good at that sort of thing, once they know an idea is possible."

"Who?" she growled.

"Aaron Duquesne brought in a cargo load, said his first shipment was a gift to us to earn goodwill. I'm inclined to reward him for it." He dismissed her indignation. "It's not as if there's too much stardrive fuel just floating around. We welcome the competition."

Elisa felt a chill. That was exactly the sort of threat that Lee Iswander was worried about. Out in deep space, bloaters were becoming more plentiful, and once someone else figured out that they were filled with ekti, there would be a wild rush to extract as much as possible.

After leaving the Ulio central offices, Elisa moved through the station, determined to find Duquesne. As she searched, her anger dampened down to a slow burn; by the time she tracked him down in the star balcony buying drinks for strangers and newfound "best friends," her temper was honed to a razor edge.

She strode up to confront him. Lanky Aaron Duquesne saw her, read her shock and annoyance, then intentionally leaned back in his chair, yawning as he sipped his drink.

"You're trading in ekti-X," she accused. "Where did you get it?"

Duquesne chuckled and gestured to his friends. "See, I told you she'd be upset." They all laughed, which made her face burn.

At first Elisa thought—hoped—that the Duquesnes had merely hijacked a load from the *Verne* and that this was a limited supply, meant to provoke her. But she could tell by his expression that was not the case.

"Ms. Enturi, I'm sure *you* know where ekti-X comes from. The source is surprising, but as soon as someone whispered the secret to me, we had to check it out for ourselves." He sipped his drink again. "Best decision clan Duquesne ever made!" He lowered his voice to a mock stage whisper. "But of course we need to keep it a secret, don't we? Can't have anyone else profiting from the discovery."

Elisa bit her lower lip and felt helpless. She hated to feel helpless; it reminded her of when she had cringed with her family back on Earth, during the bombardment of meteors after the faeros destroyed the Moon. Her family couldn't afford to go anywhere else for safety, so they had just huddled and hoped. Elisa never wanted to feel like that again.

"Lee Iswander made that proprietary discovery," she said. "Ekti-X operations rightfully belong to him."

"Rightfully belong?" Duquesne sneered. "We found a natural resource. We're extracting a natural resource and profiting from it. And if you don't like *one* other clan knowing about the source, just imagine how you'd feel if I broadcast it through the Newstation assembly hall. Oh, Speaker Ricks wants that kind of feather in his cap! The clans would love him for it."

One of Duquesne's comrades lifted a tall drink in a toast. "Want to join our celebration? To competition!"

"You will regret this, Aaron Duquesne. You don't understand what's at stake."

"Ooh, a threat!" He laughed loudly and his expression darkened. He jabbed a finger at Elisa. "You don't own the whole damn universe, and you'd better stop acting like you do."

Not only was this an unforgivable grab at Iswander profits, it could also hamstring Lee Iswander's return to prominence. As the sole provider of ekti-X, he was a very important man, but if these buffoons had somehow learned about the bloaters, what if they got drunk and blabbed about their discovery? Then the downfall would be swift.

Elisa would never allow that to happen to him. Not to Lee Iswander.

Feeling her cheeks hot, she turned and stalked out, as Aaron Duquesne and his friends continued laughing. Her instinct was to run back to the extraction field and report to Iswander what she had found, but Elisa was a person who took care of problems herself—directly.

No, she would wait in her own ship, a fast and well-armored vessel with weapons that Elisa could put to good use. She remained aboard for two days, alert, monitoring Aaron Duquesne's ship. Waiting for him to move.

When the young man finally departed, Elisa powered up her engines, dropped away from Ulio Station, and followed him.

CHAPTER

64

GENERAL NALANI KEAH

"All right Dr. Krieger," General Keah said, "impress me."

Aboard the Manta cruiser heading out to the rings of Saturn, the weapons scientist fidgeted before dredging up a wave of self-confidence. "Very well, General, I will. I promise I'll make up for last time."

Jocko Krieger glanced away, looking guilty; General Keah didn't press the conversation. After the debacle at the sun-bomb fabrication plant had cost dozens of lives and a vital production facility—not to mention a stockpile of one of the only weapons that had so far proved effective against the Shana Rei—Keah had railed against the mistakes, the ineptitude, the cockiness. But then she had stopped. Dr. Krieger knew damn well that he had screwed up, and no amount of knuckle-rapping from her would make him learn his lesson any better.

Tragedy was an unwanted, but often effective, teacher.

When Nalani Keah was a young pilot in training with the Earth Defense Forces, flying combat training missions with a souped-up Remora, she had been cocky too—reckless, invincible. She viewed safety margins as nothing more than suggestions. In the first days of the Elemental War, when the hydrogues had just begun to attack Earth colonies and Roamer skymines, she was a daredevil pilot and damn good, too, just like all the pilots in her squadron. They played tag through dense asteroid clusters, and it was all thrilling fun . . . until one of her fellow pilots discovered he wasn't quite as immortal as he thought he was. He grazed an irregularly shaped asteroid, and the spectacular explosion was over in a nanosecond. The rest of the squadron circled back, stunned and horrified, combing the glowing wreckage while praying that their comrade had managed to eject. But of course he hadn't.

Tragedy had taught Keah her lesson then. It dispelled some of her cockiness and made her an even more competent pilot. Half-measures simply wouldn't do. . . .

Now as the CDF test ship arrived at Saturn, the General hoped Krieger had learned his own lesson, achieved the same balance.

"These are dangerous times, Dr. Krieger," she said. "Overconfidence and cutting corners can lead to disasters—I don't need to remind you of that. But an overabundance of caution can also cost lives, if we don't produce weapons that can kick the shit out of those shadows and their damned bugbots."

The scientist gave her an uneasy smile. "Given the yield calculations on the modified designs, General, we don't have to worry about an overabundance of caution. I just hope people aren't too upset if we create a noticeable gap in Saturn's rings today."

General Keah raised her eyebrows as the Manta dropped down to the plane of the rings. "You're kidding, right?"

Krieger just shrugged.

She had been skeptical when he wanted to test his enhanced sun bombs again. He had come to her, metaphorical hat in hand—along with a new prototype and a request for a full-fledged demonstration. "I know I caused the problem before, General. I made an error in my calculations. It won't happen again. This time I've run checks and double checks."

Keah had frowned at him. "You have a tough hill to climb to make up for that setback."

Jocko Krieger crossed his arms over his chest. "Will ten times the destructive yield make up for it?"

The General considered. "Yeah."

Now, upon reaching the spectacular rings of Saturn, the Manta dispatched a sequence of probes at the maximum safe distance from the test zone. Below them, the rings looked like a golden highway of rock and ice fragments.

In her career, Keah had seen numerous gas giants across the Spiral Arm, but Saturn always struck her as a calm place, devoid of the huge hurricanes and multicolored bands that were so characteristic of

Jovian-class giants. During the Elemental War, the hydrogues had emerged from their hidden empires inside those gas giants, but they had not appeared in many years. Keah certainly hoped this new sun bomb test didn't rile them up.

"Just be sure you don't miss, Dr. Krieger."

Previously, he'd been a blustering tyrant among his lab assistants, shouting and driving them like slave workers. But after the accident, he had grown much meeker, exercising caution and actually listening to other opinions. "If your people shoot straight, General, we won't miss. And if I did my part right, the sun bomb won't fizzle."

Keah cracked her knuckles. "Let's see for ourselves."

Catching the light of the distant sun, Saturn's rings flowed around the planet in an unending river of rocks, ice, and dust—placid and sparkling. Keah turned to the weapons officer. "Everything's ready?"

"Just waiting for you to give the command, General."

She had been cooling her heels in the Earth system, monitoring activity around the Confederation, staying in touch with Adar Zan'nh during preparations for the mission to explore the Onthos home system. But there was no reason to waste time.

"We haven't got all day," Keah said. "The shadows could show up any minute. If this works, Dr. Krieger and his crew have to get busy fabricating a hell of a lot of these things." She gave a quick nod. "Time to brighten somebody's morning. Bombs away."

The crackling, pinwheeling sphere of plasma leaped out like a supernova cannonball and burrowed across empty space into the wide swath of Saturn's rings. There was no actual target, but the General imagined all the tumbling rocks to be a thousand bugbot ships.

The prototype rolled forward, pulsing, brightening. When it reached the center of the rings, it flickered. Then an outpouring of light expanded in an incandescent hurricane so intense that the Manta's safety systems shut down the main screen before in-place filters resolved the images again. Keah could see ever-expanding ripples from the new sun bomb mowing a widening path through Saturn's thin ring. The blast swept the rocks and ice away, clearing a hole in the plane of the rings—a hole that kept growing, and growing, and growing until the glare finally dissipated.

Krieger stared with his mouth open. The bridge crew whistled and cheered. General Keah said, “Holy crap with a turbocharger! That was just *one* sun bomb?”

“Just one,” Krieger said. “And we can make more. A lot more.”

“Doctor, that does indeed make up for the setback.” She stared at the still-dissipating light. “I’d like to put in my order for a few thousand of those. The Confederation Defense Forces—hell, even the Ildiran Solar Navy—need as many new sun bombs as you can manufacture.”

Krieger looked relieved and pleased to be back in the CDF’s good graces. “We’ll get on it right away, General, but with sufficient safety precautions. No more accidents.”

“Good call. And in the meantime . . .” she said with an optimistic lilt in her voice, “we’ve still got all those original sun bombs to use up before they get stale.”

CHAPTER 65

RLINDA KETT

It was a favor at the request of King Peter and Queen Estarra, but she was really doing it for Reyn. She hoped that the people behind the mysterious Pergamus medical station would be compassionate, or at least reasonable. Even though the planet wasn't part of the Confederation, she would twist arms or grease wheels, as necessary.

As the head of Kett Shipping, Rlinda could commandeer any vessel she liked. An available ship in the company hangar was fueled and ready to go; it bore the name of *Declan's Glory*, though Rlinda didn't know who Declan was or what his glory might have been. It was an older model, certainly not a combat ship, with too little cargo space to make it a profitable trading vessel, but as long as the ship took her to Pergamus, it would do just fine.

Somehow, the medical research center had remained off the radar for years, operating outside of Confederation laws. From what Dr. Paolus had revealed about the place, Rlinda expected to encounter high security and a chilly welcome, so she approached the planet cautiously and ran subtle scans to get a clear picture. She knew perfectly well how to sneak around; she and BeBob had tiptoed into plenty of planetary systems, even slipped under the notice of hydrogues during the Elemental War.

After her long-range scans mapped the planet, the sealed domes on the surface and the Orbital Research Spheres, Rlinda assessed the well-armed mercenary ships in orbit. She frowned and ran the scans again. It was a serious fleet, and they looked ready to defend against pirates or even the CDF. Unfortunately, *Declan's Glory* had only a minimal defensive weaponry complement, so she wasn't going to intimidate anyone. Rlinda would have to use charm instead.

She reminded herself that she was here on behalf of the King and Queen. She posed no threat to them, so she damn well wasn't going to hide. If Zoe Alakis had vital information that could help Prince Reyn, then Rlinda would walk over coals—or breathe poisonous gas, in this instance—if necessary. Time to go in and get what she wanted. Reyn's life depended on it.

Once she had a handle on the situation, Rlinda dropped all pretense, activated her engines, and cruised in from the outskirts of the system. She kept all weapons shut down (such as they were), sent out an ID signal, and made sure they knew she was coming, whistling and waving. A visitor on a diplomatic mission with important business and nothing to hide.

"Hello? Calling Pergamus. My name is Captain Rlinda Kett, a representative of the Confederation government with a special request from the King and Queen." She guided the ship forward on a steady course, closing the distance rapidly. "We need a big favor, and you're in a position to look like heroes. I'd like to request a meeting with Zoe Alakis, please."

Pergamus reacted as if she had lobbed a bomb at them. In a scramble of activity, the mercenary ships activated their engines and moved into defensive positions. Some remained as guard dogs near the research spheres, weapons activated and directed outward. Others charged out to intercept *Declan's Glory*.

A gruff voice spoke, "This is a restricted system. Depart immediately."

Rlinda felt a prickle of cold sweat all over her body, but she didn't flinch. On the comm, she kept smiling. "Come on, now. I just want to talk. I don't want any trouble."

"Then depart," said the voice. "You have no authority to be here."

"Did I mention the King and Queen sent me, alone, on a diplomatic mission? I'd say their authority is worth something."

On screen, the gruff mercenary was replaced by a mahogany-skinned man with high cheekbones and a gaunt face. His eyes looked like black holes. "Pergamus is not a signatory to the Confederation, and so your authority is not recognized here."

Rlinda raised her hands and let out what she hoped was a disarming chuckle. "You haven't even heard my pitch. It's a small thing, but lives are at stake. Let's meet like grownups and discuss this." She smiled. "We can even do it over a nice dinner—my treat, and you definitely won't regret it." Who could resist that?

"Please leave, or we will enforce our security perimeters." The mercenary ships closed in, and they made a point of activating their weapons. "With all the means at our disposal."

So, it was going to be like that. She knew her shielding wouldn't withstand a full barrage, and even on her best day she couldn't outfly all of them, certainly not in *Declan's Glory*. Rlinda found this very disturbing; their response didn't make any sense. She had already identified herself, and they had to know the CDF would come breathing down their necks if they harmed her. Was this small isolated facility trying to start a war with the Confederation?

Somehow, though, she didn't get the sense they were bluffing.

She dropped the conversational tone and put an edge in her voice. "Look, I'm the Confederation's former trade minister and I have full diplomatic credentials, as well as the protection of the Confederation. I don't believe you want to create an interstellar incident. I formally request a meeting with Zoe Alakis. I would prefer to deal with her directly."

"You can speak with me." He didn't offer his name.

"All right, then, I'll tell you," she said, fighting back an exasperated sigh. "We know that Pergamus is a medical research facility and storage archive for numerous diseases and their cures." She spread her hands, sounded a little more placating. "Now, I won't go into the questionable nature of your activities, but we've been informed that Pergamus may have some medical research that could be vital to the treatment of Prince Reynald's illness. The King and Queen have taken notice."

The man just looked at her stonily, not admitting, not responding.

Rlinda waved a beefy hand. "We're very eager to get help for the Prince, and I've come here to request that you share your information, your tests, anything that might help—as a humanitarian gesture. The Confederation would be very grateful."

The man on screen remained silent for a long moment. "How did you learn about Pergamus? The privacy and security of this installation is paramount."

"And Prince Reyn's health is paramount to *me*, so let's not do this dance. If it's a monetary matter, we can certainly discuss. I'm sure we can work out a deal. The Confederation is willing to pay handsomely for all your records and any progress you might have made." She paused, then added, "Please?"

"Confederation money means nothing to us, but our security does." His voice became icy, his face even harder than before as he guessed. "Dr. Paolus gave you inaccurate information. This is a private installation. We have nothing for you."

She felt exasperated. "But if you're doing medical research, why won't you share your cures? Or sell them? Doesn't make any sense."

"That is the decision of Zoe Alakis—and on Pergamus, her decisions stand. I'm afraid I can't help you."

Rlinda was growing annoyed with this roadblock. "Then, please tell Ms. Alakis that we would appreciate her making an exception in this case."

"She will not. Now please depart."

"If I go back empty-handed, I assure you the Confederation will be even more curious. I can see your facility down there—disease research? Possible biological weapons? Such safety concerns would warrant increased scrutiny, whether or not you're part of the Confederation."

"Zoe will not change her mind."

Rlinda met his gaze, measured him, and she found a cold depth that she had never seen in another human being. He looked like a tough nut to crack, and Zoe Alakis might be even worse. Frustrated, she crossed her arms over her chest. "At least tell me your name, so I know who I'm dealing with?"

"I am Tom Rom. I represent Ms. Alakis."

A sudden chill went down her spine. She knew the name, but needed a moment before she could place it. Tom Rom—this was the man who had mercilessly hunted down poor Orli Covitz when she was infected with the Onthos plague. He had stalked her, attacked her, stolen vials of her infected blood—to be taken back to Pergamus? Orli thought he was dead, but obviously he was not. And Rlinda knew what this man was capable of.

Suddenly, she felt very vulnerable. Even though she carried the mantle of the Confederation, would that stop them? Tom Rom had to know this encounter would only raise suspicions. Did he expect the King and Queen to just ignore countless deadly diseases stored on Pergamus? Including, quite possibly, the Onthos plague?

Rlinda felt very eager to leave, and then she experienced a greater chill as she realized that it *might* be Tom Rom's best option to destroy the *Declan's Glory* and cover up any sign that she had ever been here. That would at least buy a little more time for Pergamus.

Her throat went dry. She had to deliver her report back to the Confederation, if nothing else. The weapons ports of the mercenary ships seemed to glow brighter than before.

Rlinda said quickly, "All right, I can tell where I'm not wanted. I was obligated to deliver my message—and Prince Reynald is very dear to me, personally. Please consider what I said? Thank you."

Tom Rom did not respond.

She didn't know how fast *Declan's Glory* could fly, but she intended to find out. She adjusted course and retreated out of the Pergamus system, trying not to appear terrified. To her great relief, the security forces did not pursue.

CHAPTER 66

OSIRA'H

She and Rod'h returned to Ildira from Wulfton, disturbed by their interactions with the faeros and convinced that they no longer had any hold on the fiery elementals.

When they entered the Prism Palace, side by side, Gale'nh came to meet them, having sensed their arrival. Osira'h shook her head. "The faeros are skittish and unpredictable. They will not help us."

"They are afraid," Rod'h said with an edge of bitterness. "They have been hurt by the Shana Rei, and too few of them remain, so they will let the rest of us be wiped out."

Osira'h lowered her gaze. "We didn't have the strength to make them listen."

Gale'nh gave a grim nod. "Now I fear the mad Designate will insist that he can do it. Rusa'h is convinced he knows them better than anyone. He argues with the Mage-Imperator even now."

The three entered the skysphere audience chamber, where Jora'h and Nira were in a heated discussion with Rusa'h. Prime Designate Daro'h was beside them, looking overwhelmed by the constant danger, but he brightened when he saw Rod'h. Behind the chrysalis chair, Yazra'h and Muree'n stood in full armor, ready to take on any threats—even the mad Designate, should he forget himself.

After the recent mob massacre, Ildirans had begun to look at one another with suspicion, trying to spot any hint of shadow behind their eyes, any glimmer that otherwise normal people might go berserk. Osira'h could sense the thrumming edginess through the *thism*, and she realized that the fear and uncertainty were causing as much damage to the Ildiran psyche as the shadows themselves were.

When the three entered the audience chamber, the tense conversation paused. Seeing Rod'h and Osira'h back safe, the Mage-Imperator brightened, but Rusa'h skewered them with a gaze. He stepped forward imperiously. "So? Did you find the faeros? Were the two of you sufficient to force their attention? Have you made an alliance and brought them to us?"

Holding her katana, Yazra'h snapped at him. "The Mage-Imperator will speak. Your presence here is a courtesy, nothing more."

With forced contrition, the fallen Designate bowed toward the chrysalis chair. "My apologies, Liege."

Drawing on her strength and confidence, Osira'h stepped up to present her news. "Rod'h and I were able to contact the faeros, but they were reluctant. They tried to flee."

"We did make them listen," Rod'h broke in, "but it did little good. The faeros are frightened."

"Then we must convince them, coerce them into an alliance." Rusa'h spun to face the chrysalis chair. "These two may have communicated with the faeros, Liege, but neither of them can do what is necessary—and it is not their responsibility. *You* remember the old legends." He balled his fists. "*You* know how Mage-Imperator Xiba'h forged an alliance with the faeros the last time the Shana Rei appeared in the Spiral Arm. Osira'h and Rod'h can beseech them all they like, but their sacrifice isn't meaningful enough. The faeros need to feel *your* fire before they will accept the alliance."

"Alliance?" Jora'h's expression grew stormy. "I do not believe we need to forge a dangerous alliance with the faeros, and I certainly will not immolate myself just to attract their attention."

Adar Zan'nh marched into the skysphere audience chamber, keeping his eyes fixed on the chrysalis chair, as if the others weren't there. "Liege, you requested an update on our expedition to the Onthos home system. The preparations are complete for our septa to depart. I have been in contact with General Keah, and she says the *Kutuzov* is ready to join the expedition. We can head out to the rendezvous within days."

"Will a septa be sufficient?" Jora'h asked.

"The Shana Rei extinguished the Onthos system millennia ago. I do not expect to encounter a battle there now."

Rod'h took a half step forward, glancing at Gale'nh. "I have just returned, but I am ready to join the expedition. We vow to find the answers."

"Answers aren't always ready to be found," Tal Gale'nh said.

Osira'h looked at her brothers. "I am willing to go along as well, if the expedition needs me."

Nira flashed a warm smile at her daughter. "I think you have something else to do. We have a bit of good news to share." She glanced at Jora'h.

The Mage-Imperator continued, "Tamo'l sent a message for you from Kuivahr. She and her team have been investigating the medicinal properties of kelp strains in hopes of helping the misbreeds, but she thinks she may have discovered a possible treatment for Prince Reynald of Theroc. Perhaps you would like to contact the Prince and tell him yourself?"

Osira'h smiled broadly. "Yes, yes I would. Thank you!"

"We can arrange for you to go to Theroc," her mother said.

When Osira'h looked around, the audience chamber seemed brighter than normal. "In that case, I am ready to leave on a mission of my own."

CHAPTER

67

ARITA

The Wild had called to her for some time with the need to know all those uncatalogued species, the insects, the plants, the fungi. She might not be a green priest, but she was still fascinated with the worldforest from a scientific perspective.

And, based on his mysterious note to her, she knew she had to give Collin a chance to find her in private. What did he need to tell her that he could never communicate through the intermediary of telink? No matter what news he had, Arita was glad that he wanted to share it with her. She hoped Sarein had managed to pass along her response to him.

Arita flew her aircraft alone, without any entourage of ministers and security forces. Part of the draw of the Wild was that she could be by herself in the incredible wilderness, almost as if she were a green priest after all. And maybe with such solitude she would have a chance to listen to that other mysterious, musical voice that was so distant, yet also deep inside her mind. . . .

Arita was capable of taking care of herself, as she had demonstrated on similar expeditions, but she was never entirely alone in the worldforest. The quiet imposing trees were aware of their surroundings, and green priests were attuned to them. They could all watch over her—as she knew they would.

For the first two days after arriving in the Wild, she camped in the empty jungle, re-centering herself, touching the trees, listening to the loud silence of nature. She knew that Kennebar and the rest of the isolationist green priests recognized her presence, but they left her alone—for now. As she lay awake at camp, she hoped that Collin, at least, would find an excuse to drop out of the trees and visit her. He had to know she was here.

Around her, some of the undergrowth was phosphorescent, adding a cool and eerie glow to the forest darkness. She lay back against a broad tree, just listening.

She was startled to hear a rustle in the fronds overhead, then saw a pale-skinned figure crawl across the branches. The figure was joined by another, both gliding with swift spidery movements. Predators in the worldforest were rare, but after the recent wyvern attacks at Shorehaven Village, she remained tense.

Then she recognized the alien forms. Three more Gardeners scurried across the trees, gathering above her camp, and peering down at her. Arita stood up and waved at them.

More large-eyed Onthos faces appeared, as if they were intrigued to find her here. "We know you," said one of them.

"How do you know me?" They certainly couldn't find her through telink, or touch her mind.

At least twenty Gardeners crowded among the fronds overhead, gazing at her as if she were some kind of odd specimen. Now that the Onthos refugees had settled in the Wild, were they territorial? Did they resent her as an intruder? But if the Gardeners' attitude had changed, why hadn't Kennebar's green priests reported it? Was that what Collin had warned her about in his note?

"We know you," they said again. The crowd of Onthos fell silent for a tense, eerie moment. Then with a rustle of fronds, they scattered and disappeared into the night. . . .

Even though she couldn't decide whether or not the strange encounter had been threatening, Arita remained unsettled by it. She set off the next day to find her aunt, who lived in self-imposed exile. Maybe Sarein knew more about what was happening in the wilderness, an isolated objective observer.

When Arita reached the large nest dwelling in the trees, hauling specimen packs and collection supplies, Sarein gave her a look that held more resignation than welcome. "I don't recall leaving you an open invitation to come back any time you like."

Arita saw right through her coolness. "You also didn't tell me to stay away. Did you send my letter to Collin?"

"Am I your delivery service?"

"He's my friend, and you were in a position to help. It's what people do for each other."

"Then I suppose I did." A hard smile appeared on Sarein's lips. "After all, it's what people do for each other."

As Arita moved her belongings inside, Sarein gestured to the same section of the paper-walled structure where Arita had slept before. "How long do you intend to stay?"

"I'm not sure. I have work to do." Knowing her aunt's gruff exterior by now, Arita wasn't put off. In fact, she saw a twinkle of relief in Sarein's dark eyes. "Don't worry, I'll be good company."

Sarein busied herself making an unnecessarily complex meal for her guest. "The Wild used to be a private place, then all those green priests came, and you keep visiting. Then there's the Gardeners . . . they seem to be everywhere."

"There are only a hundred of them on the whole continent. You were there when they landed in the first place," Arita said.

Sarein kept her back turned, but Arita saw her shoulders tense. "I don't know about that. There seem to be more of them now."

As the natural night fell and the stars appeared through gaps in the high canopy, they sat in companionable silence on the nest's open balcony. Arita had many questions about her aunt's life and past experiences, but she knew Sarein respected her more for not asking them.

Around them, Arita saw sparks of light, like random meteors darting through the thick branches. "I've always loved to watch the fireflies," Arita said with a sigh. During certain seasons, it was a ritual. She and Reyn would go out to see the light show, counting insects like stars in the forest.

"This might not be what you expect," Sarein said. "Keep watching."

More streams of fireflies emerged from nests in the trees. Arita watched them with a smile. Even more insects swirled out until the air was filled with sparks, a shower that kept building. And still more.

Arita gasped. "I've never seen so many."

"Oh, they're just getting started."

Indeed, the fireflies soared out of their hidden nests, more and more—thousands and then tens of thousands. The luminous insects flitted around like raindrops in a downpour until the night was filled with sparkles. Arita had never seen anything like this firefly storm. "What causes it?"

"You're the one who likes to study nature." Sarein just stared, looking uneasy. "It started when the Gardeners moved out here. Things are changing in the worldforest." She frowned more deeply. "Theroc is disturbed."

CHAPTER 68

KOTTO OKIAH

The ideas no longer came to him as they'd always done before, and that knowledge jabbed like a constant knife in Kotto Okiah's heart. Fortunately, no one else had realized it yet.

Thanks to his legendary reputation, Kotto was allowed to do whatever he wanted; the Roamer clans assumed he must be working on some miraculous discovery that would change their lives forever. The Roamers put him on a pedestal, gave him a blanket approval to do whatever projects he wished. But he knew he hadn't made any memorable breakthroughs in a decade or more . . . and every day he feared that somebody would notice.

He wasn't trying to deceive the clans, but his fellow Roamers were blinded by their own faith in him, and he couldn't live up to their expectations. Not anymore.

He joined Shareen and Howard in the laboratory station, surprised by how much the two had accomplished. He remembered when the ideas had flowed like that, when everything had seemed so straightforward and simple! Both young lab assistants were ambitious and eager to learn, but Kotto was no longer sure he knew how to teach them.

"We just cleaned up and fleshed out the mathematics you set forth, sir," Howard said as Kotto skimmed their summaries. "We followed through on some of the partial derivations and finished them for you. I hope that's what you wanted?"

Kotto gave him a quick nod, trying not to show his embarrassment. "Yes, exactly so. Many of those concepts were in development, but I set them aside when other priorities pulled me away. I could have brought them to fruition myself, but it seemed like good training for you two."

"We saw a lot of false starts and dead ends," Shareen pointed out. "Were you testing us to see if we'd pick up on the missteps?"

Though Kotto's mind was spinning, he hid his confusion. "I've never had real lab assistants before. I didn't know what to expect from you two, and those notes were a way for me to measure your abilities and assess how well you could solve problems—because that's what Roamers do."

"I'm not a Roamer," Howard said.

"Nobody's perfect," Kotto said, "but I'm glad you've done so well despite that handicap." He skimmed to the conclusions, felt his pulse speed up. "I can't wait to look these over in more detail." He cleared his throat, not wanting them to ask him any detailed questions. "I'm awfully busy with the Big Ring, dozens of meetings and inspection flights. Forty new space workers arrived from Newstation in the past week." He made a vague gesture with his hand. "But I need to occupy you with something. Go through the rest of my project notes and choose whichever project you think might be the most useful. Something you can bring to fruition. I'll even share credit if you can make a functional prototype."

Shareen sounded astonished. "That would be excellent!"

"Thank you, sir," Howard added.

Shareen turned to her friend. "It may be a challenge to decide on something important. I can't imagine any practical use for most of them."

Kotto frowned. "Each is a proof of concept to be expanded to more significant uses." He hoped they didn't ask for more of an explanation.

Anxious to recapture his old genius, Kotto made a habit of writing down any stray thought in hopes that it might amount to something. Every fragment of an idea, every flash of potential genius might connect with something else and become a truly significant breakthrough. But it had been a very long time. . . .

He wasn't sure how long he could continue to ride on past successes. Kotto was growing desperate, afraid that any day someone would accuse him of being a fraud. A has-been.

"We'll choose one concept and finish it," Howard said. "Maybe several, if that's all right with you, sir?"

Kotto brightened. "Of course."

Shareen gathered her courage and spoke up. "But isn't the Big Ring project more important? It's the last month before the test run. Howard and I could go over your calculations, recheck the designs, just in case?"

"No, I don't think so," Kotto said, a little too quickly. "It's a very large plan and much of it is in my head. I don't have time to explain the big picture." He worried that these two might indeed find some missed step or inaccurate calculation if they looked too closely. "Just be patient."

Outside the lab's large windowport, the gigantic torus was abuzz with activity, constructors and survey pods and supply docks at either end of the nearly completed ring.

The Roamers had poured a vast expenditure into the gigantic physics project, simply on his say-so, believing that it might be the foundation of a new wormhole transportation system, or even just a landmark pure-science experiment that would reveal the fabric of the universe. The Big Ring was Kotto's last chance, perhaps a remarkable encore for the greatest Roamer scientist who had ever lived. He certainly hoped it wasn't a debacle.

Although Kotto wasn't entirely sure what to expect, he reminded himself that was what science was all about, conducting experiments and analyzing the data. After all, if the results were known beforehand, why conduct an experiment in the first place?

Anxious to be out of the lab, he took the transcribed notes, mumbled a "goodbye and good work," and went back to his private quarters. There, feeling some trepidation, he sat at his desk and reviewed what Shareen and Howard had done. He tried to follow how they had gone through his sketchy and incomplete concepts, yet so easily found solutions to derivations that had stumped him for years.

He flipped through the neatly organized proposals. To his embarrassment, some of the concepts were too ridiculous or esoteric for the lab assistants to do anything with; Shareen or Howard had marked them with question marks and apologies. As he scanned them, even he couldn't imagine what he might have been thinking at the time. Tears burned his eyes and he wiped them away in frustration. He had kept such careful notes over the years, and now that his mind was devoid of inspiration, now that he was losing touch with that scientifically creative muse who had blessed him so many times in his life, Kotto had no recourse but to mine his old unfinished work, hoping that others wouldn't recognize how stale it was.

The most important possibility in the notes, he felt, was a logarithmic relay-charging system for the energy films used in power blocks. He had banged his head against the bulkhead for years, trying to make that idea work. He knew the solution was there, right in front of him, but he was blind to it. He would struggle with the mathematics, start again and again, but he remained stymied.

But now, in only a matter of days, Shareen and Howard had found his misstep and completed the entire design. It seemed so easy for them! He heaved a deep breath and tried to calm himself.

In his youth the ideas had come like a firestorm, so many that he hadn't even bothered to write them down, sure that more ideas would always come, that he would never have enough time to complete all the inventions already in his mind. How he cursed himself for that hubris, and how he wished he had just a few of those ideas now!

He looked back at the notes Shareen and Howard had fixed, as if the two were taunting him. Tears continued to flow even after he wiped them away. Kotto felt so empty, so sad, as he stared at the cleverly organized calculations. He tried to recapture that spark, but he felt nothing.

So many others lived their lives without ever having a single flash of inspiration, without ever experiencing a brilliant thought or creating any kind of innovation. Who was he to complain, when he had already done more than most other Roamers?

And yet, now it seemed a much greater a torment to *lose* the genius he once had, than never to have had it at all.

CHAPTER

69

GARRISON REEVES

After responding to the request for experienced space workers, Garrison took a few days to make certain Seth was happily ensconced in school, then he flew the *Prodigal Son* out to the Fireheart nebula, where he offered his services as part of the Big Ring project. With his copious skills in space construction, engineering, life-support systems, suit maintenance, the project chiefs accepted him without reservation.

He had worked in Iswander's Sheol lava-processing facility, he had shepherded dangerous lunar fragments around Earth, and he had served at the CDF shipyards to repair the numerous vessels damaged in battle against the Shana Rei at Plumas. With his résumé, he was in great demand.

Hundreds more new workers had arrived for the final stages of the giant construction project. When he docked the *Prodigal Son* and checked in, he was immediately approached by Station Chief Beren Alu. "Everybody wants to work on the Big Ring, Mr. Reeves, but we have extensive work opportunities at Fireheart—some of our projects desperately need help. Would you consider a different assignment, at least temporarily? You're certainly qualified."

"The Big Ring is what brought me out here," Garrison said.

Alu's face fell, and he stroked his long mustaches. "That's what everyone says, but we've got to be practical. Fireheart is a business operation. The isotope sifters bring in a lot of outside money, but they're mostly automated. I've got crews working overtime just to keep up with packaging the power blocks. At the moment, our biggest need is mounting then retrieving the absorptive films in the collecting farms. For months now, all new power blocks have gone straight to Kotto's project, and I've got outside customers clamoring! The profit margin on those things is how Fireheart keeps running. We need your help."

Garrison doubted Fireheart Station was on the verge of bankruptcy—in fact, it was one of the wealthiest of all Roamer installations—but he could see the stress on the station manager's face. "We have to fill the orders and pay the bills. Would you consider working on the power-film farm for, say, double the pay?"

Garrison could tell the beginning of negotiations. "I really wanted to put the Big Ring project on my résumé."

Alu snorted. "Why do you need a résumé?"

"To get jobs like this."

The station chief sighed. "All right. Work on the power farm for a week, put in overtime, help me fill four large outstanding orders. After that, maybe we can split your time."

"After that, I want to be assigned to the Ring construction teams."

Alu looked defeated. "A week, and then we'll talk."

Even with the inferno of ionized nebula gases around him, Garrison felt quite at home at Fireheart Station. It had been a long time since he'd felt so engaged in his work. Important work, and something he would remember for a long time . . . even if he wasn't here with Orli and Seth.

Drifting in open space surrounded by ionized gases, Garrison felt dizzy not to have any anchor point. He had checked his environment suit himself, measured the rain of radiation from the nebula's hot keystone stars, and knew he would be safe for three hours at least.

"Heads up, Reeves!" said his coworker Bowman Ruskin.

The two of them moved steadily along, unreeling sheets of gossamer fabric that was kilometers on a side, but only a few molecules thick. When bathed in stellar radiation, the sheets charged with energy, and once saturated they were packaged into dense wafers incorporated into power blocks. The delicate sheets required skilled labor to be stretched and mounted, where they would hang inside the storm of radiation for days.

Dismantling crews detached the charged films and folded them, again, again, and again, more than a hundred times until they were packed into a container less than half a meter on a side. One primary power block could power a colony town for half a year. More commonly, though, the energy-dense sheets were cut into pieces and sealed in much smaller packages to run households, ships, and other personal needs.

Garrison said, "I usually don't let my thoughts wander, Ruskin, but with a view like this . . ."

Ruskin laughed in the suit comm. "You never get used to it—but you do have to get your work done. A tear in the fabric would ruin the whole power block. Even a wrinkle creates a hundred headaches—and the worst part is that you'd have to listen to Beren Alu complain about the lost revenue."

"I hear you," Garrison said, and Ruskin let it drop at that, much to his relief. Olaf Reeves would have lectured him for an hour about the same thing.

Around them, numerous suited workers mounted power-absorbent films to soak in the cosmic wind. Roamer trading ships came and went through the nebula's dust barrier, carrying Fireheart's specialized materials and products off to numerous markets.

When clan entrepreneurs had set up this installation, it was a true Roamer dream—seemingly impossible, spectacular, and ultimately profitable. The founders must have faced a great deal of disbelief when they showed their original designs, but early on Kotto Okiah had given his stamp of approval for the sheer audacity of the idea, if nothing else. And once Kotto gave his thumbs-up, the founders had no further difficulty getting people to join in the project.

Garrison and Ruskin had worked together for several days; after only four hours of training, Garrison intuitively knew how to do the job, so his partner simply let him work. Now, the two men finished hanging a new energy film in an empty array.

But Garrison's eyes were constantly drawn toward the enormous torus. . . . To a Roamer with engineering background like himself, the Big Ring seemed as breathtaking a creation as the nebula itself.

"I'm only on your crew for a week," he reminded his coworker. "That was my agreement with the Station Chief."

"I heard it was 'open for discussion' after a week." The other man already sounded disappointed.

"I've already had the discussion with myself." He turned to face the enormous construction hanging in space. "I'm going to work on the Big Ring."

CHAPTER

70

TOM ROM

Necessary things.

Tom Rom remained focused on the larger goal, uninterested in discretionary activities. His main mission was to protect Zoe Alakis, and for that he would do anything that was required. Anything. He drew no enjoyment from what he had to do now, nor did he feel guilt. If it was necessary, then there was nothing else to say.

Zoe's rules were clear and inflexible. Everyone who worked for Pergamus—whether at the facility itself or as an outside provider—agreed to abide by those rules. An inappropriate revelatory remark could cause as much harm to the high-security installation as any careless lab accident.

Dr. Benjamin Paolus should have known better. He had breached that trust, and now the Confederation knew about them.

Tom Rom had been uneasy about the researcher for some time. From the beginning, Paolus had demonstrated that he was untrustworthy, although in a useful way, when he breached his own ethics by selling Prince Reynald's medical records. Now, however, the doctor had betrayed not only his royal patient, but also Zoe Alakis. That changed everything, and Tom Rom had to take care of it.

It was necessary.

When he flew to Earth on business, no one noticed him. He had all the appropriate licenses and identification cards under false names. He did not call attention to himself.

Zoe did not like to be disturbed, did not like to be revealed. She wanted Pergamus to remain unobtrusive, safe. Now that the fool Paolus had exposed their operations, there could be a flood of pathetic supplicants beseeching Zoe for cures that she had no intention of sharing. Larger organizations, black-market companies, even ruthless governments might want to raid Pergamus.

And the Confederation might take direct action. Rlinda Kett's overtures had been rebuffed, but he did not imagine for a moment that the King and Queen would let it go. Benjamin Paolus had placed them all in extreme danger. The damage was already done, Tom Rom knew, but there was a required response.

Arriving at Earth, he had little difficulty tracking down Paolus. After making his deal with Theroc, the doctor had basked in his reward, and obviously let it go to his head. Tom Rom studied the man's movements, hacked into his transactions, and discovered that Paolus was drowning in extraordinary debt. No surprise there, but it was worse than he had thought. Even the large payment from the King and Queen barely put him in a stable financial position.

The undeserved second chance hadn't taught Paolus any fiscal sensibility, though. For three nights in a row, the man had flaunted himself at high-class restaurants, drinking expensive wine, taking out friends, picking up bloated tabs.

He did not seem so much fearless as oblivious. His penthouse apartment had routine security in the lower entrance, motion detectors, laser locks . . . the usual. Nothing that caused Tom Rom any problem.

The night was still early when he broke into the penthouse. He had plenty of time, for the researcher was out dining again with his companions, who were rapidly becoming his sycophants, thanks to his liberal spending. Tom Rom resealed all the penthouse doors, reactivated all the security codes, and sat in the shadows waiting: quiet, motionless, contemplative. He liked to center his thoughts, to absorb the world around him, to rest and to plan. . . .

Years ago, after he had left Vaconda with the young Zoe Alakis, they had traveled long distances between the stars, and he had taught Zoe how to center herself. Not as formal meditation; it was just *thinking*. People didn't spend enough time thinking. If they did, they wouldn't make such stupid mistakes as Dr. Paolus had.

In the dim apartment, Tom Rom thought of Zoe alone in her sterile dome, surrounded by the best researchers. How different it was from the festering underworld on Rakkem, where Zoe's mother had been, a disgusting baby mill that cranked out healthy replacement organs in the form of neatly packaged infants. Tom Rom hated that place, hated what they did, hated what Muriel had become . . . but the biological black market could also be useful. Rakkem made it easy to hide things. Tom Rom could use that now.

When Dr. Paolus entered his penthouse, he was clearly under the influence of good wine and recreational drugs—no doubt expensive ones too. When he sealed his door, increased the illumination, and saw Tom Rom rising out of a chair, Paolus paled as if his skin had been bleached. He sobered very quickly. "What are you doing here?"

Tom Rom remained silent, weighed various answers, but decided not to bother with any of them. He unclipped a small medical kit from his waist.

Paolus tried to run for the door.

Tom Rom reached forward in a fluid movement, grabbed the doctor by the arm, spun him around. Paolus flailed, but Tom Rom brought his heel down in a hard stomp that shattered the man's fibula with a loud hollow snap. The man collapsed to the floor, his leg folded in the wrong place. He wailed, cursed, but Tom Rom had no interest in it.

"I'm sorry," Paolus gasped through his pain. "I did it for the Prince! We're helping people. If you do have a cure—"

"We don't have a cure, yet—but that's not the point. You broke an oath, and you exposed Pergamus. Now we are in great danger, and my job has gotten much more difficult because of you."

"I'm a medical researcher. I felt it was important to cure a disease, to save an innocent young man."

Tom Rom removed an autosyringe filled with a paralytic. "You'll get your chance to contribute to medical research." He zapped Paolus with the paralytic at the base of his neck. The doctor thrashed and twitched, then became a statue.

This particular drug had no pain-dampening qualities, so the pathetic man could still sense every edge of agony in his broken leg. When Tom Rom straightened and set the bone, he did it slowly; then he removed other items from his medical kit, following through on his detailed plan.

"You want to know where I'm taking you," he said. "We're going to Rakkem. I'm sure somebody will find you useful there."

. . .

The biological black-market city was in a low-lying marsh filled with a lush soup of rotting vegetation. The sprawling low forest was filled with pale plant life, mostly moss variants because the sunlight was too dim and the skies too gray to make photosynthesis a viable option.

Rakkem was not exactly a lawless place, because it had a strict hierarchical government that had reaped profits through biological trafficking. Buildings were scattered throughout the fetid swamp: pontoon buildings, trading bazaars, surgical complexes, and specimen warehouses. Rain slurried the streets, and murky swampwater rose up in the gutters.

Tom Rom remembered a name from his deep past, sure that Aldo Cerf had no memory of him whatsoever. Cerf was a successful organ broker who specialized in selling "viable flesh," sometimes still alive, sometimes ready for transplant. For a substantial fee, Cerf had helped Tom Rom track down the infant Zoe after she'd been adopted by Adam and Evelyn Alakis.

He was glad to find that Cerf was still in business, but if not him, there were countless similar businessmen on Rakkem who could take care of the matter at hand.

Tom Rom contacted Cerf from his ship even before he landed, and they negotiated a price. Although this was an unorthodox thing for Tom Rom to do, Cerf acted as if it were an everyday occurrence. Maybe it was.

In the back of the ship, Paolus was half awake, still paralyzed, unaware of the medical alterations that had been made to him. He was in pain, but could not move, couldn't even whimper aloud. An agonized expression rippled across his face, just enough to please Tom Rom.

"I will sell him intact and still alive," he said to Cerf, and he struck a hard bargain, although with her unlimited supply of prisdiamonds, Zoe had little need for the money. If he didn't haggle, though, the merchant would be suspicious. "This man is a medical researcher from Earth, but he has run his course of usefulness."

Aldo Cerf sounded interested. "Maybe he should work for me then."

"He's unreliable. You'd profit more from his organs."

"All right, but I insist on charging an additional disposal fee, since you obviously want this man gone."

Tom Rom acceded to the fee. Shortly after he landed, Aldo Cerf's masked and uniformed minions came to the ship to remove Paolus, who was wide-eyed and aware, twitching, but the paralytics still held.

"He won't be able to move for another day or so," Tom Rom explained to Cerf's assistants. "If you don't want to contaminate the tissue, you can avoid using additional anesthetic when you remove all the organs."

Paolus's eyes were wild. Tom Rom didn't look at him.

The body handlers nodded gruffly, made a notation on a pad, and accepted the transfer of funds. "I included a full med scan," Tom Rom said helpfully. "He seems to have all his organs intact, though the liver might be questionable."

"Livers are valuable," said one of the workers, inspecting the scan on his pad. "It'll be good enough."

Tom Rom looked at Paolus with a poignant expression of regret. "They'll disassemble you completely. I've worked with Aldo Cerf before. He doesn't waste anything. Rest assured, you'll continue to be of help to the medical industry."

After they took the body away, Tom Rom was eager to leave Rakkem. The place still nauseated him. He despised what they did here, but in this case it was useful. He was able to take care of one necessary thing—eliminating Dr. Paolus—while also accomplishing a *desirable* thing, just for him and Zoe: Tom Rom had also impregnated Paolus's tissue with a latent toxin, and all of his organs were saturated with it. In the next day or so, when Cerf's surgeons removed his kidneys, lungs, heart, eyes, and everything else—the surgeons would be exposed to the poison and die within hours. And that would help Tom Rom finish his grudge against Rakkem, too.

He flew away, satisfied.

CHAPTER 71

LEE ISWANDER

After his offensive meeting with Speaker Ricks—there was no other word for it but "offensive"—Iswander went over to Academ, half convinced he should withdraw his son from the Roamer school.

Londa had already visited the boy and satisfied herself he was thriving in such a vibrant environment with children his own age. Iswander understood that, but if Sam Ricks was an example of what the Roamers epitomized now, he wasn't sure he wanted his son to have anything to do with them. He wanted to make Arden into a different kind of Roamer—the right kind of Roamer.

Inside the hollowed comet, he found Jess Tamblyn and Cesca Peroni in front of an attentive group of students as they summoned sparkling droplets of water from the internal walls. In the zero-gravity core, the class hung in open air, maneuvering with small hand jets or anchoring themselves with tethers. They observed as diamond chains of crackling water drops flickered around them.

As Jess and Cesca worked together, extending their hands, the droplets coalesced, tiny remnants of wental energy that seeped out of the comet. The droplets danced through the air like a luminous river, reeling out from Jess's open hand, slowly arcing across the gap to Cesca's outstretched palms. She caught the sparkling chain before it rose and dispersed into vapor in the air, leaving them surrounded by a humid luminosity, like a halo.

Jess said to the group in a loud voice, "The wentals dissipated after the Elemental War, and their energy is no longer deadly. In fact, it is mostly gone, even from inside Cesca and me."

Cesca opened her hands as the faint droplets faded. She seemed sad. "Some remnants still reside here in this comet, and others live on water worlds. But that's all. Like the hydrogues, they've gone dormant and faded from the Spiral Arm."

Iswander maneuvered himself forward awkwardly with the hand jet. He had removed his business suit and now just wore a dress shirt and slacks. "Dad!" Arden called, and Iswander found him among the group, surprised to see him next to another familiar boy. Seth Reeves? It wasn't surprising that Garrison would have taken his son back to Academ, but he hadn't expected Arden and Seth to be friends. He wondered if Elisa knew where her boy was.

Iswander maintained his calm as he looked up at Jess and Cesca. "I came because I'm concerned about what Roamers are being taught these days, and whether or not it can benefit my son. I'm not entirely sure the Roamers and clan Iswander have the same Guiding Star."

"Why do you say that?" Jess asked.

"For one thing, I've met directly with Speaker Ricks."

An unexpected flicker of distaste crossed Cesca's face. "Speaker Ricks . . ." She caught herself. "I consider it poor form to voice an opinion about another Speaker."

"Cesca's being polite," Jess said. "Soft times do not require hard leaders, and Speaker Ricks was chosen when the Roamers still believed that these were soft times. His election was an anomaly. Do not judge us based on the Speaker. Your son will benefit from what we can teach him. He shows great promise."

Arden lifted his chin. "I think I should stay here, Father. There's a lot I can learn, just as I've learned from you. And you're the one who told me that we need challenges to make us strong. We're not like the other clans. We are Iswanders!"

"And he's a little full of himself," Seth Reeves teased.

"I did say that." Iswander smiled. "You were listening."

"I always listen to you."

"We'd hate to lose him here," Cesca said, "but it is your choice."

Arden tried to maintain his proud composure, but then playfully shoved Seth, who tumbled out of control in the low gravity until he bumped into the other drifting students.

"We're Iswanders," Arden said again. "We're more than just Roamers. You taught me to think big."

"I think you're right, son." The comment was like a revelation in Iswander's mind. He realized he didn't need to impress just the Roamer clans, when there was the whole Confederation. *That* was where he should be planting his seeds. He would build ties with the King and Queen and sidestep the Roamer clans.

And he had something the Roamers had expressed little interest in. Since Peter and Estarra were focused on their very public battle with Prince Reyn's illness, however, as well as their questions about the mysterious Onthos refugees, Iswander knew exactly how to gain their attention.

Iswander turned to Jess and Cesca, speaking seriously now. "Sam Ricks is just one man, and he was a mistake. Maybe I shouldn't discard all Roamers because of one mistake." After all, he had asked for the same consideration himself. He turned to his son. "You've reminded me of one of my own lessons, Arden. Stay here at Academ and keep learning. And I'll keep thinking big."

Aim higher.

Londa was delighted when he asked her to stay at Newstation for an additional week while he flew to Theroc, and Iswander used the time alone during the flight to consider possibilities. He was by blood a Roamer; his ancestors had come from the generation ship *Kanaka*, along with the scions of all the clans, but Iswander had taken his clan to another level.

Now, he would make himself important to the Confederation's rulers and step into his rightful position among the Roamers from the *top down*—after all, the clans were just another part of the Confederation.

After he landed on the canopy, he filed a request to meet with Peter and Estarra, sure he would have to twist arms and bypass numerous moat dragons. But he explained what he had brought, and his request was approved immediately. He wore a nice new suit and a smile as he was led through the white-walled catacombs of the fungus-reef city to the private quarters of the King and Queen.

"Welcome, Mr. Iswander," Peter said. "How may we help you?"

He read caution there, but no outright suspicion. Iswander stepped forward. "I would like to help the Confederation, Majesties. I want to do my part. The Shana Rei are a terrible, incomprehensible threat—I had a brush with one of their shadow clouds myself, and it's a miracle my facility survived." He did not, in fact, understand why the horrific hex ships and their black robot allies had withdrawn . . . but one did not question a miracle.

Estarra was surprised. "When, and where did you encounter the Shana Rei? And how did you survive?"

Iswander could not show the images of the shadow cloud attack on his bloater extraction fields, because that would reveal the nature of his ekti harvesting. "That was a temporary operation, an industrial site now played out and abandoned. But the experience made it all too clear how much of a threat those creatures pose, and I want to help. Therefore, Iswander Industries will provide ekti-X to the Confederation Defense Forces at an extreme discount, a third of the standard cost for stardrive fuel. It will be my contribution to the fight against the Shana Rei."

Peter was obviously pleased. "We thank you for your generous offer. General Keah is about to depart on an expedition to the Onthos home system, which was destroyed by the Shana Rei. Any information you can provide from your previous encounter would help."

He gave a small nod. "I will be happy to tell her what I can. And speaking of the Onthos, I have relevant information there, as well." He removed the datapack he had brought. "This is a large database of Onthos records, their derelict city, their history. A woman named Orli Covitz arrived at my complex, infected with the plague that killed clan Reeves, and she brought me all of these records from the space city before it was destroyed—with the request that I disseminate them." He extended the datapack. "Earlier, I tried to interest the Roamer clans in this treasure trove of information, but they didn't know what to do with it. Considering the Onthos are now settling on Theroc, perhaps you can put the data to some use?"

Estarra was indeed very interested. "And all that medical data? I don't know if it can help Reyn, but it might answer some questions about the Onthos."

Peter was more skeptical. "And you're just giving it to us? As a goodwill gesture?"

Iswander smiled. "I'm not in everything for profit, sire. All humans should have this."

CHAPTER 72

ELISA ENTURI

Arrogance, Elisa thought. Sheer arrogance. Aaron Duquesne seemed cocky, unconcerned. Were Roamers always so flippant? Even Garrison hadn't been so egotistic. But she benefited from that arrogance now.

Duquesne's crew flew away from Ulio Station in two ships, heading back toward their hidden extraction site. Elisa had placed trackers on both ships, so she followed them easily enough. Any number of other poachers could have followed them the same way. Her annoyance grew as she cruised along, her sensors picking up their stardrive wake.

Though Garrison was less arrogant than the Duquesnes, he just as naïvely assumed that Roamer clans cooperated and considered all people to be intrinsically fair, comrades ready to offer help. During the Elemental War, they had been outlaws, crack survivalists. How quickly they had forgotten! Now, from what Elisa could see, the Roamers had just become stupid. Aaron Duquesne was either inept or oblivious.

The journey from the Iswander extraction yards had taken three days by Ildiran stardrive, and now she followed the Duquesne ships on a different vector for a day and a half. Apparently, they had found a bloater cluster much closer to Ulio. It didn't surprise her. The strange nodules were becoming more and more common.

Using the onboard databases, Elisa read up on clan Duquesne during the flight, wondering if they were all idiots, or if she had just encountered a select few. The clan had invested heavily in skymines on Belliros after the end of the Elemental War, purchasing old cloud harvesters abandoned by other clans who wanted nothing more to do with skymining; the investment had seemed like a sure bet since gas giants were again safe from the hydrogues.

But now Iswander's inexpensive ekti-X was stripping away their livelihood. *Poor things*. That was how business worked.

Clan Duquesne obviously preferred to take the easy way out, and harvesting ekti from innocuous bloaters was certainly easy, requiring little investment to reap great profits. She didn't know how they had discovered the secret, but she had to cut it off at the source.

According to her tracker signals, the two Duquesne ships had reached their destination. Elisa decelerated so she could approach without being seen. Maybe the extraction field had more security than these oafs would suggest. Elisa's ship couldn't withstand a concerted attack, so she would likely have to come back with more firepower. On the other hand, she knew what the bloaters were filled with. If she found the opportunity, she could easily ruin the Duquesne operations.

As she approached the site, she encountered a few straggler bloaters that streamed into the vicinity from deep space. With her running lights doused and her engine output on low, she eased forward, alert, staying out of sight.

The Duquesne extraction yards were primitive, even laughable. Clearly, the bumbling clan had not figured out the most efficient way to retrieve stardrive fuel from the bloater sacks. Several old-model Roamer ships hung near the central cluster. The Duquesnes had converted a large tanker into an operations center. A corral area held fuel cylinders, while three stripped-down water tankers were attached to separate bloaters, slicing open the tough membrane and spilling the protoplasm out into space, which they gathered with scoops and booms.

Elisa was appalled. Spilled stardrive fuel drifted in globules throughout space. So much waste! And yet, the bloaters were so plentiful, clan Duquesne could always get more, no matter how much they lost.

Even with wide-range scans, Elisa detected no defenses, no perimeter scouts, no patrols. It was ridiculous. Any profitable operation needed some kind of security, if only to defend against random thieves.

Well, that made her mission simpler. She was glad she wouldn't have to conduct an overt war. She could take care of this herself, quickly and efficiently.

At the cockpit controls, she glowered at the primitive extraction site—seven ships, three extraction vessels, the main operations ship, local high-intensity lights, and hundreds of bloaters swarming like plankton in a cosmic sea, drifting together in a close cluster.

Yes, that would do. . . .

Dropping any pretense, Elisa flew toward the extraction complex and broadcast on wide comm channels. "Aaron Duquesne, after all your talk at Ulio Station I expected to be more impressed with what I found. You stole Lee Iswander's discovery, but it doesn't look like you know what to do with it."

There was an outbreak of activity in the operation, a chatter of surprised voices over several different channels. Finally, Aaron came on the screen from the main operations ship. He no longer looked so cocky, displaying obvious anger, but she read fear beneath it. "You followed me from Ulio, bitch! This is a private clan Duquesne installation, and you're trespassing."

"You remained in plain sight at all times, Mr. Duquesne." Even if this man did not blurt out the ekti-X secret on his next trip to Ulio Station, someone else was bound to be just as curious and just as ruthless. Sooner or later, he would be tracked down through his own ineptitude; she was glad to be the one to do it.

But how had Aaron Duquesne discovered the source in the first place? She personally did the trading with outsiders; the extraction field workers were not allowed furloughs. Who could have revealed the secret? Was there an active spy among the Iswander workers? That would pose a difficult challenge.

Then the answer struck her like a blazing light in the back of her mind. It had to be either Garrison or Orli! They had seen the original extraction yard, then departed after the remaining bloaters in that cluster fissioned and metamorphosed. They could have blurted it out to anyone. Lee Iswander had shut down his operations there, so there was nothing left for anyone to find, but he never should have let those two depart with impunity. Not only had Garrison taken her son, now he had apparently ruined Iswander's future as well. Bright anger flared behind her eyes.

Duquesne made a laughable attempt at a threat. "We'll defend these yards."

"I don't think you can, Mr. Duquesne." She watched two of the ships power up while another was already moving toward her. They had some weapons, but she wasn't worried. She held the wild card. "I have to protect the interests of Iswander Industries. Your operations here are over."

Duquesne sneered on the comm screen. "What's the matter? The great industrialist can't stand a little competition?"

"Lee Iswander doesn't need to tolerate your competition." Elisa powered up her ship's weapons. They were small, intense jazers, not enough to fight off a battleship . . . but she didn't intend to get into a firefight. She had other obvious options.

"And what are you going to do about it, bitch?" Duquesne said.

Elisa opened fire.

When she discovered the first cluster of bloaters after chasing Garrison, she had fired a warning shot across his bow to get him to surrender. She hadn't intended to strike one of the bloaters, but the nodules were so closely clustered, it had been unavoidable. Just an accident.

Now, though, she targeted the bloaters intentionally, knowing what would happen.

The drifting nodules were filled with unprocessed stardrive fuel. All they needed was a spark. Elisa strafed her high-energy weapons across the three bloaters that were connected to extractors; then she fired indiscriminately at any other nearby nodules, just for good measure, taking all of her shots in a second.

She was already enhancing her shields as she accelerated away.

The bloaters blossomed into fireballs. The volatile ekti ignited and roared outward like a sun going supernova. The energy of the blast ripped apart the extraction complex, and the firestorm swelled as each explosion ignited adjacent bloaters. Her rear cameras recorded the Armageddon chain reaction as she streaked away.

On the comm, she heard indignant cries and screams of fear—all of which were swiftly cut off.

Explosions engulfed the entire Duquesne complex, and the fires continued to swell, but Elisa had seen enough. She felt exhilarated, satisfied, and vindicated. She was convinced that she had done exactly what Lee Iswander would have wanted her to do.

CHAPTER 73

ORLI COVITZ

After Rlinda departed on her mission for King Peter and Queen Estarra, Orli and DD settled in at the headquarters of Kett Shipping, offering to work in the main company hangars. Orli was surrounded by loud noises, industrial smells, and a boisterous group of pilots and mechanics who had a habit of shouting even when they didn't have to. DD remained faithfully at her side, helping out whenever he could.

Most important, he kept her company, which Orli found useful, especially in the last year when she had felt so alone, before she found Garrison. She wondered what he was doing right now. He had gone to Fireheart Station, which sounded like a dramatic and fascinating place. Though she kept herself busy at Kett Shipping, Orli pondered whether she should have accompanied him out there. She thought about him often, and she missed him.

Orli also owed a great deal to Rlinda, and she would spend a few weeks here, deciding what to do. She had no interest in being a trader pilot again—that wasn't her real calling—but she could do a good job in many things. Maybe she and Garrison could find something to keep them happy together after all.

Meanwhile, Orli had done her best to get up to speed with all the vessels in the Kett fleet and the hangar operations. She was especially pleased to see how many Mechanic-model compies were here, since compies were her area of expertise.

Tasia Tamblyn and Robb Brindle were still trying to find a good fit for Orli, and they kept her busy in the hangar with the compies as well as the ship maintenance. Although Tasia and Robb served as the company administrators, they didn't mind getting their hands dirty. Both of them would rather be in the hangar with the maintenance workers and the other pilots than be trapped in a clean air-conditioned office. Orli saw them there often.

A ship flew in, signaling an approach. Tasia grabbed for her comm unit at the same time Robb did, and they both brightened. "It's the *Verne*! About time."

Robb frowned. "They're almost three weeks late."

DD said to Orli, "Their compy OK transmitted a brief report that I find difficult to comprehend. The *Verne* made a detour after leaving Ulio Station. And they do not appear to have any new cargo."

When the ship landed inside the busy hangar, few pilots took notice. The *Verne* wasn't much different from the other Kett vessels. Tasia and Robb studiously tried to avoid playing favorites because their son was the pilot, and of course they failed.

As Tasia and Robb hurried forward, Orli and DD followed. The hatch opened, and Xander emerged grinning, which Orli took as a good sign. Tasia gave her son a hug, and Robb did the same. "It's good to see you again, son. Safe and uninjured, I hope?"

As OK marched down the ramp, guiding Terry behind him, Xander said, "Safe and uninjured," he said. "And with some good news."

Tasia got down to business. "Did you track Elisa Enturi's flight path? Is that why you're delayed?"

"We placed the tracker, but we have to go back to retrieve the data. Give her time to fly her route and return to Ulio again."

Terry added, "It's a passive tracker, completely undetectable, just recording her movements. The data will automatically download to a secret file in the Ulio Central Offices the next time Elisa's ship docks there. Once we retrieve it, somebody can connect the dots and follow wherever she went."

"You're three weeks late," Robb said. "The data is probably already there."

Tasia said, "Good, then let's head to Ulio Station and figure this out." She glanced at Robb. "Maybe we can follow the breadcrumbs. Like old times."

Xander blurted out, "But that's not the real news! We met old Maria Ulio in deep space. She called us to a secret rendezvous."

Robb was surprised. "Maria? She's been gone for years."

Xander kept grinning. "Terry was very special to her, so she sent a message—and now she's made him her heir. We have to go back to Ulio and modify all the account numbers, but *Terry's rich*!"

Terry seemed embarrassed. "We still have to see exactly what it is. A lot of paperwork. I've never been rich before."

Robb laughed, but Tasia remained focused. "Ekti-X is making us all rich, but we still want to find out where Iswander is getting it—and if he's doing something illicit . . . something that he's gotten *us* mixed up in. We need to know the source."

Listening to the conversation, Orli frowned. "The source of ekti-X? Lee Iswander used to harvest it from a cluster of bloaters, but those operations are gone now after a Shana Rei attack."

Tasia shot her a surprised look. "Bloaters? How do you know that?"

Orli looked at all the amazed stares. "When I was dying from the plague, I stumbled upon his extraction field. That's where I was cured, inside one of the bloaters. Garrison Reeves knows about it, too." She was puzzled, surprised that they didn't know. "Sorry, I've been isolated ever since I recovered, and then Garrison and I went to out-of-the-way Ikbir."

Robb and Tasia both looked at her in amazement. "You've seen where Iswander gets his stardrive fuel? Roamer clans have been trying to figure that out for months!"

Orli realized she had been out of the loop. "His operations were shut down anyway when the cluster dispersed, but bloaters are appearing everywhere now." She remembered the streams she had seen extending around the vicinity of Ikbir's star, the chiming musical noise she heard inside her head. "Iswander could have set up a new extraction field, I suppose."

Xander said, "And the tracker on Elisa's ship will take us right there, if it's true."

Orli was still trying to understand. "But don't you have a trading relationship with Iswander Industries? Didn't you say the distribution was making you rich? Are you looking to get into ekti production yourselves?"

Tasia sounded relieved. "If that's what he's doing, we'll keep his secret—and I will sleep a lot better at night. I was afraid he extracted the ekti-X from cute puppies or Ildiran babies, and we didn't want to be accomplices." Nobody laughed at her joke.

Robb turned to Xander and Terry. "Since you're the main distributors of ekti-X, you two have to keep your hands clean. I don't want Elisa suspecting you of anything. There's too much business at stake. I think we should go in the *Voracious Curiosity*, while you two do your own business, like nothing's changed."

"I've never been to Ulio Station," Orli pointed out. She had time to kill while Garrison was away at Fireheart. "I wouldn't mind. . . ."

Robb nodded. "Sure, you and DD can join us on the *Curiosity*. We'll leave tomorrow." He glanced at Xander. "If you think the *Verne* will be ready by then?"

"Of course. We have to get back to Ulio ourselves." Xander grinned at Terry. "After all, we've got an inheritance to arrange."

CHAPTER

74

GENERAL NALANI KEAH

The departure of a grand exploratory mission called for a certain amount of fanfare. General Keah wasn't the sort of person who liked parades and celebrations *before* returning home from a successful mission, but the crew deserved some sort of recognition. After all, they were going to the literal definition of "points unknown"—a star system that didn't even show up on the charts.

She wanted to give her people a little extra reward. She asked First Officer Mercer Wingo to work crew scheduling, juggling shifts to arrange extra R&R for conjugal visits, or fixing the roof, or whatever else they wanted to do before shipping out to the fringes of the Spiral Arm.

Not surprisingly, all that celebration placed much of her crew in various stages of hangover misery when the *Kutuzov* pulled out of spacedock. But it was a long voyage out to rendezvous with Adar Zan'nh and his Solar Navy ships; she knew they would have a chance to recover on the way.

Sitting in her seat on the command bridge, Keah sympathized with her recovering crew and gave them light duties for most of the first day, but that was enough of that. On the second day she initiated a series of war-game exercises to keep them sharp, and they did their best—which was pretty damn good.

The ship's green priest, Nadd, used his treeling to send messages of their progress. All green priests were eager to learn what had happened to the Gardeners, and Nadd would be there to see for himself.

The *Kutuzov* arrived at the rendezvous exactly on time—Keah was pleased about that—and Zan'nh was there waiting for her with his seven warliners. "You're early, Z," she said.

On the screen, Adar Zan'nh wore his formal uniform with medals and his impeccably clean dress tunic. "Being early prevents me from being late."

As was their tradition before a joint mission, the General and the Adar shared a meal, taking turns as host. Keah shuttled over to the Ildiran flagship with some of her handpicked officers so they could meet their counterparts face-to-face. Any added understanding among the two crews might shave off a millisecond or two of critical reaction time, and a millisecond might mean the difference between destruction and survival.

The General was accompanied by First Officer Wingo, Weapons Officer Patton, Tactical Officer Tait, and their green priest. For his own part, Adar Zan'nh had invited the oddly pale Tal Gale'nh, and Gale'nh's brother Rod'h.

Keah brought a bottle of wine, though the Adar had no taste for any human vintage. In exchange, Zan'nh brought out an expensive bottle of distilled kirae, which the General couldn't even swallow.

She opened the wine herself while attender kithmen scurried in with numerous Ildiran delicacies along with crude attempts at traditional Earth dishes. Keah had eaten so much military food that she wasn't picky; Wingo, Patton, and Tait ate the proffered dishes with polite comments, while Nadd seemed more curious than hungry. Adar Zan'nh, Tal Gale'nh, and Rod'h all ate with minimal conversation.

Rod'h raised a glass of kirae in a defiant toast. "This mission will end differently from the *Kolpraxa*." He looked at his pale brother. "We will find answers to help us defeat the creatures of darkness."

Gale'nh did not argue. He raised his own glass of kirae. "I concur."

Keah picked up the wine bottle and nodded to Rod'h. "I'd like to requisition some of that confidence so I can distribute it among my crew."

To the consternation of the eager attenders, she poured more wine for herself and her officers, and a polite splash of a taste for Zan'nh and his companions, knowing they would insist.

The Adar said, "We should wait for the formalities. One other will be joining us." He frowned slightly. "He is often late because he is often preoccupied."

Attenders hurried out of his stateroom and returned with a human male clad in Ildiran rememberer robes. "Sorry, everyone. I was translating newly recovered records. Remarkable stories! But alas, nothing useful for this mission." He carried a datapad with him.

Adar Zan'nh said, "We must accurately chronicle this important mission. And for that, we require a rememberer."

Anton Colicos was perhaps the most famous human historian, even though he had spent more than half of his life in the Ildiran Empire. He was grinning now. "Besides, I wanted to come along." Anton extended his hand. "Pleased to meet you, General. I will try my best not to get in the way."

"I don't mind being in the history books," Keah said.

The attenders reappeared with an extra wineglass for Anton. When the General reached for the bottle, one of them politely snatched it out of her hand and poured the additional glass.

Adar Zan'nh poured a small serving of kirae for himself and his Ildiran guests. "So we can all enjoy our toast."

Anton Colicos rolled the wine around in the glass, sniffed. "Ah, it's been a long time. And maybe you can spare a little coffee from your ship, General?"

Keah laughed. "As much as you like." When everyone had their drinks, she lifted her glass in a toast. "To the start of a great adventure—at least let's hope it turns out that way."

They all drank.

CHAPTER

75

PRINCE REYN

When Rlinda Kett returned from her trip to Pergamus, she was devastated. “I am so sorry, Raindrop.” Her big brown eyes were full of sadness. “Those people have no interest in helping, that’s for sure. And I’m convinced that I barely got out of there with my skin intact.”

She enfolded him in a big hug, and he let himself sink into it, just as when he was a boy. She was shaking, and he tried to reassure her more than himself. “We’ve got every other researcher in the Spiral Arm working on it. Somebody will come up with a treatment, just you wait.”

She hugged him tighter. Frankly, he was most disappointed in Dr. Paolus, who had betrayed his patient’s trust by selling Reyn’s private information to Pergamus, then profiting again by betraying the location of Pergamus to his parents.

King Peter was disturbed to hear Rlinda’s report. “I don’t like the idea of that secret installation. If Pergamus is hoarding disease specimens, that could pose a danger to all humankind. What if they are developing biological weapons to sell to the highest bidder?”

His mother was also grim. “Lee Iswander just delivered information about that horrific alien plague—what if there are even worse viruses at Pergamus? Even if Zoe Alakis doesn’t have evil intentions, how do we know that her security is adequate?”

Peter’s anger was clearly visible. “Pergamus hasn’t heard the last of us—I will send the whole CDF fleet if I have to.”

Estarra was concerned, and when she turned to him, she had tears in her eyes. “Don’t give up hope, Reynald.”

“I won’t. I promise.”

He had no reason to believe that Pergamus had developed any cure or treatment for him. Yes, Dr. Paolus had sold them his original test results, but that data was now widely available across the Spiral Arm. Why would one hidden facility with no financial incentive, and no particular *interest* in Reyn's disease, do better than a hundred other research installations? He was trying to be realistic even if everyone else chased after false hopes.

He feared what would happen now that the location of Pergamus had been revealed. Surely they would expect the Confederation to take notice. What if Zoe Alakis retaliated by unleashing one of her fatal diseases on a helpless colony? Reyn didn't want to be responsible for that.

Rlinda embraced Reyn in a last apologetic hug so enthusiastic it nearly smothered him. Then she took *Declan's Glory* and headed back for Earth.

When Osira'h arrived unexpectedly, she brought much better news. Reyn was delighted that she had come back, especially so soon. That in itself made him feel rejuvenated. Osira'h's pearlescent eyes sparkled with delight as she greeted him without formality, giving him a quick enthusiastic embrace, and he responded with just as much enthusiasm. "What are you doing here?"

"I wouldn't let anyone else bring the news, and I wouldn't let my mother just send a message through telink. I wanted to tell you in person."

"What? What is it?"

"My sister found something in her research on Kuivahr! A possible treatment for you. We have to try it!"

It was the last thing Reyn had expected to hear, and he didn't know what to say. "Tamo'l? I thought she was tending the misbreeds. Why was she studying my disease?"

"Because I *asked* her!" Osira'h sounded exasperated. "She has been testing rare kelp and plankton extracts, and she believes she has a strain that will mitigate your symptoms, if not destroy the microfungus."

Stepping forward, King Peter caught his breath. "Did you bring a sample?" Reyn had been so preoccupied with Osira'h he'd forgotten that his parents were there to receive the Ildiran delegation. "We'll try anything."

Reyn didn't like everyone making decisions for him, even though they did it only out of love and concern. He looked at his mother and father, then Osira'h. "If you tell me I should try it, I think I should listen."

Osira'h turned to the King and Queen. "There are many variations of kelp and plankton strains on Kuivahr, many possible ways to administer the treatment, and the method and dosage may need adjustment. I was hoping . . ." She looked at Reyn and then at his parents. "It makes the most sense for Reynald to accompany me to the sanctuary domes. My sister can test the medicine, alter the formulations if need be, and try again. If you allow him to come with me, I will stay with him to make sure he has all the support and protection he needs."

Estarra looked concerned about sending him away, but Reyn turned to his parents. "You said you'd try anything—and this is something we can try. Rlinda had no luck at Pergamus, and none of the other research teams has a better solution. I'm willing to give Tamo'l a chance."

Estarra gave him a wistful smile. "Then of course you can go."

The Ildiran ship delivered Reyn and Osira'h to Gorhum, the nearest world with a Klikiss transportal, which was the most straightforward way for the two of them to reach Kuivahr. So that the Prince would not be entirely cut off, they were also accompanied by the green priest Beltrias, who had recovered from his injuries sustained in the great wyvern hunt. He had volunteered to serve as a communications conduit, since Kuivahr's small colony had no green priests.

Because Klikiss transportals were a useful alternative to direct travel on ships, Gorhum had a receiving center by the trapezoidal stone wall, surrounded by a small support settlement; a crew of staff engineers monitored the flow of travelers. Other transportals were more active as travel hubs, but this one had little traffic. Reyn was fine with that, because he did not desire a great deal of attention.

Without any fanfare, Reyn submitted his request and used Confederation credits to pay for their passage. Accompanied by a green priest and a halfbreed girl with pearlescent eyes, Reyn was the least interesting of the group. As the three of them stood gazing at the coordinate tiles on the alien trapezoid, he drew a deep breath and strengthened his resolve. He had promised Arita and his parents and Osira'h that he would not give up hope.

Beltrias held a potted treeling in his arms and looked eagerly toward the blank stone wall that would open a doorway to another planet. "Shall we go?" he asked.

The tech who operated the transportal didn't seem interested in who they were. He activated the appropriate coordinate tile for Kuivahr. The stone window shimmered and opened onto a world with cloudy skies and shallow seas.

Beltrias stepped through first, showing no fear. Osira'h took Reyn's hand, and he squeezed it as they stepped forward together. Just before they passed through the dimensional membrane, they heard the tech's voice call out, "Wait, aren't you the King's—"

And suddenly the three of them were standing on a mounded reef outcropping that held the transportal wall above the ocean. Two meters below the lip of the stone doorway, waves sloshed around the rocks.

Disoriented and dizzy, Reyn caught his balance on a rock. He tried to convince himself his imbalance was because of the dimensional passage, not from his illness. He looked around at the gray-green waters of the broad flat sea. Shading his eyes, he could see a tall industrial structure on the horizon, platforms on stilts that rose above the sea. That must be the Kellum distillery.

Beltrias sat on one of the large rocks and placed the treeling at his feet. "This is like Shorehaven, in a way." He connected through his treeling, informing the other green priests that they had arrived on Kuivahr.

Osira'h pointed in another direction, past a murky patch of drifting kelpweed. "Those are the sanctuary domes. I can feel Tamo'l close—she knows we're here."

The rocky outcropping had very little space and nothing for them to do while they waited to be retrieved. Reyn didn't mind. He enjoyed spending the time with Osira'h. Even on a barren rock in the middle of an alien sea, he was glad to be with her.

A waveskimmer arrived for them in less than half an hour, piloted by a redheaded man and a thin female who looked vaguely like Osira'h, a splash of human features mixed with Ildiran ones. Osira'h waved.

When the skimmer pulled up to the reef outcropping, Osira'h took Reyn's hand and practically ran down to the waterline. "Tamo'l! This is Prince Reyn. Thank you for what you're doing for my friend."

Reyn gave a small bow, and Tamo'l responded with a pleasant smile. "I assist those in need. It doesn't matter whether they're misbreeds or princes."

The green priest followed them down to the water line. As they climbed aboard, the redheaded man said, "I hope you have a high tolerance for people with unusual appearances. Some of our misbreeds can be a little unsettling."

Tamo'l interjected, "I assure you, their hearts are good."

Reyn had been stared at and poked and prodded ever since his condition was known. He could sympathize. "Then that is the part I'll look at."

CHAPTER 76

ZOE ALAKIS

Though she had remained silent, Zoe had watched every moment, listened to every word of the encounter when Rlinda Kett came to Pergamus. And she was very disturbed.

The Confederation representative assumed she could sweet-talk or buy access to Zoe's hoarded medical data. Other desperate people had done the same over the years, and her mercenary security always kept them away. But this time the Confederation had taken notice. Now they would never be left alone.

Pergamus had quietly existed for a decade, independent, part of no government. The Confederation had nothing to do with Zoe, and she had nothing to do with them. Isolated in her sterile dome, she was only peripherally aware of human politics at all. Her only interest in the rest of the Spiral Arm was as a source of intriguing new disease specimens that Tom Rom would go out to collect. But now they had been *noticed*!

Thanks to Tom Rom's encouragement, she had tasked a research team to study Prince Reynald's medical condition, and they had made some progress in categorizing and breaking down the exotic microfungus. But Zoe did not intend to participate in the contest for a cure; she had already been through that with Dr. Paolus. Why couldn't they understand?

As soon as Rlinda Kett came calling, though, Zoe knew that their quiet existence had fundamentally changed. That idiot Paolus had revealed their location, and Pergamus would never again be safe. The King and Queen would never leave her alone now, and that made Zoe angry. She had to do something.

She sat inside her sealed dome, protected from the myriad biological threats whose sole evolutionary purpose was to kill human beings. This was her fortress . . . but now that others knew about it, Zoe no longer felt secure.

Forlorn, she called up images and files on twenty different screens, her medical triumphs and her most terrifying specimens, the cure for Heidegger's Syndrome, which she had found years too late to help her father. There was Tamborr's Dementia, and the fresh brain parasite that Tom Rom had retrieved from the fatal outbreak on Dhougal. She scrolled through scanning electron micrographs of bacteria, viruses, DNA mutations. Some of the most fascinating work was the study of the freakish Ildiran misbreeds, which the Kuivahr researcher had naïvely given to Tom Rom.

All these diseases, samples, and potential treatments were just part of her collection, much the same as another wealthy patron might collect interesting insects. Her library on Pergamus was unparalleled in human history, and it was hers, whether or not she intended to do anything with it. It was *hers*! That was what mattered.

As she stared at the thousands of records, the numerous ambitious research projects, she thought of Rlinda Kett's plea in the name of Reynald, thought of the possibly dying Prince . . . and all the others over the years who had begged and demanded and bribed for cures. Zoe had never relinquished any items from her collection.

As she stared and pondered now, though, she feared that she might have to.

After her father's death, she and Tom Rom had traveled aimlessly from spaceport to spaceport. They met people of all different types; many were untrustworthy, several tried to cheat them, but Tom Rom took care of her—and then took care of the cheaters. Once, two men tried to attack her when she went off alone on Teredit, but Tom Rom wasn't far behind; he intercepted the men, killed them in front of her, and took Zoe away to safety.

But he could not protect her from the diseases of humanity. Vaconda, with its lichentree forests and its blizzard of pollens, produced numerous local diseases; Zoe had suffered through and recovered from all of them at a young age. But a life in isolation had left her unprepared for the normal sicknesses that one encountered in human settlements. She had no resistance, no immunity.

Tom Rom flew them away from Teredit—and a day into their voyage, Zoe fell ill with a high fever that left her writhing in her bunk. She was terrified. She had never been so sick. Although Tom Rom knew basic medicine, he also knew his limitations.

Zoe was nauseated, her muscles ached, her head pounded; auras appeared around her vision. "I think I'm dying." She said it as a statement of fact, as if it might be something of scientific interest, not a wail of despair. "I hope I die quickly." Memories of her father's lingering debilitation horrified her. Heidegger's Syndrome had stolen his mind, his humanity, and his life in tiny stages over the course of years. "Don't let that happen to me."

Tom Rom had gripped her hand fiercely. "I will not let you die."

Despite his sickening memories of the place, he took her to Rakkem as her fever grew worse, sure that the biodealers could provide any cure. He took samples of Zoe's blood, ran analyses, made a rough diagnosis. Medical records classified it as Conden's Fever, and a vaccine existed. That was all he needed to know.

Zoe feared she might be contagious, but Tom Rom didn't contract the fever; he had long ago gotten an immunity. She gave him a wan smile, then shuddered before falling back into a deep sleep.

After that, the sequence of events was murky in her memories. She knew they landed on Rakkem, and Tom Rom sealed her aboard the spaceship while he went out to find a solution. He returned to check on her, looking graver and graver each time. He tended her, providing stopgap measures that lowered the fever and gave her enough energy to wake up. Finally, he put a decontamination breather over her face, wrapped her in warm clothing, and carried her into the dim marshy city where buildings and biolaboratories sold anything and everything.

He took her to a cureseller. She was dizzy, barely had the strength to stand when he hauled her into the cluttered office, but he propped her up. "Look at her," Tom Rom said to the biomerchant. "You have the vaccine in your archive. Help her."

"Conden's Fever." The pale-skinned bald man clucked his tongue. He looked at them as if they were possible specimens. "Such a disease is rarely encountered, and so the vaccine would be at a premium. I can see your desperation, and that puts you in a very poor bargaining position."

"She needs it," Tom Rom said.

The cureseller shrugged. "I need many things too." A calculating look crossed his face as he glanced at Zoe, then focused his attention on Tom Rom. "You have insufficient funds to buy even one dose of the vaccine, but here on Rakkem we always have a need for other commodities. You look healthy, fit. I assume you have two kidneys, two lungs . . . even two eyes. I think you can spare one of each. In fact"—he raised a finger, ignoring Tom Rom's instant recoil—"this young woman also has a spare set."

"Unacceptable."

"Then I'm afraid we can't do business. How much does the girl mean to you? What is a cure worth?"

Tom Rom did not hesitate. "You won't take anything from her. She remains intact. But I . . ."

Zoe felt a surge of energy. "No, you will not!"

Tom Rom looked at her with a hard gaze. "I'll do what I have to."

Zoe put steel in her own voice. "You will do as I say. I forbid you to sacrifice any part of yourself for me." Even if she survived the fever, she couldn't live with herself if he did that.

He wrestled with his own obligations. "Then, I'll find another way." He gave Zoe a supportive arm, lifted her out of the chair, and they left the cure seller's offices. The man didn't bother to make another offer, didn't call them back. It was as if he knew they were going to return anyway. No one else would give her a cure.

When they got back to the ship, Tom Rom placed her on the bunk, told her to rest. She lay reeling, feverish, knowing that a vaccine existed but remained out of reach. "They won't help us. What are we going to do?"

"I am going to find a cure for you. And you are going to recover."

She tried to ask him how, but she was too weary.

Several hours passed, or several days—Zoe wasn't at all sure. What she knew next was Tom Rom standing next to her, injecting her. She could barely force herself awake. "What is that?"

"Your salvation." He put the syringe away. "The vaccine."

"How did you find it?"

"Don't concern yourself with details."

She drifted for a while, then forced herself back to consciousness. "How did you get it?"

Tom Rom lied. "I found a man who had recently recovered from Conden's Fever. He still had antibodies in his bloodstream. I didn't have enough money to buy your cure, but I did have enough to pay a contract laboratory to process the blood samples into the antibodies you needed."

"Oh . . ." She fell back to sleep.

Later, she learned that Tom Rom had gone back to the cureseller, tried to threaten him, tried to break in to his vault, tried to harm him. But the Rakkem biomerchant had plenty of experience with desperate patients, and his security was such that even Tom Rom couldn't defeat it. Instead, he did find a patient who had recovered from the same disease. Tom Rom had offered him significant pay for a mere blood sample—and that man had scornfully turned him down as well. "Why should I help your little whore?"

So Tom Rom killed him and took the blood he needed.

He eventually told her the whole story, after she had recovered. And Zoe remembered every detail of it. . . .

Now, separated by quarantine walls, she was glad to have Tom Rom returned from his necessary mission to eliminate the traitor Paolus. Together, they discussed via comm what they would do if the Confederation Defense Forces laid siege to the research facility. In order to be prepared, Tom Rom tapped into direct reports from Theroc, keeping an eye on activities there. But he was distraught, waiting for them to move on Pergamus.

Two days later, Zoe could see the excitement on his face. "You know I failed to deliver the Onthos plague data. Orli Covitz almost killed me, and I assumed all those records were lost." His eyes lit up.

"But she survived and delivered the complete database to the industrialist Lee Iswander. And he just delivered that data to Theroc . . . as a favor!"

Zoe quickly said, "We need to have it."

"I'm convinced the King and Queen will share those records with us, all of them." He paused. "But you know the price they will ask."

CHAPTER

77

GARRISON REEVES

After finishing his weeklong assignment on the energy film farm and ready for his duties on the main Ring project, Garrison had earned a day of downtime.

He got to know the other people on his crew. One of his coworkers, Jan Coughlin, had worked with clan Reeves on the Rendezvous reconstruction project five years ago, before moving on. Though Jan expressed deep sympathy for the loss of Garrison's family, he gave the distinct impression that he had butted heads with Olaf Reeves. Garrison couldn't fault him for that.

The Big Ring construction workers were chosen from a large pool of qualified applicants. Everyone from the project supervisors down to the lowest girder assembler understood the basics of zero-gravity assembly and high-tech engineering. Garrison was part of the team, and a part of history.

And he was eager to tell Seth about it.

During downtime, most of the Fireheart construction workers gathered in community modules to watch entertainment loops, play games, or socialize. Garrison, though, requisitioned a scout pod and flew to the greenhouse dome, promising his coworkers that he would bring back a load of fresh produce. "Strawberries, please," Jan Coughlin said. "Lots of strawberries."

Garrison promised to get them, but that wasn't the reason he wanted to see the green priests. He was going to send a message to his son.

After he entered the greenhouse dome, the lush fecundity of the place struck him immediately. The moist air, the smell of worldtree fronds and green crops filled the air with the exotic scents of subtle spices. A Roamer worker approached with a bunch of freshly pulled carrots like a trophy in her muddy hands. "Come to get your hands dirty, or just to pick up?"

"A pickup for the Big Ring construction crew," he said, because that was his legitimate excuse. "Strawberries were specifically requested."

The woman snorted. "Jan Coughlin always requests strawberries. And the carrots are ready, too."

"I'd also like to see the green priests. Are they . . . ?"

"You'll be able to find them."

As soon as he entered the central greenhouse, he saw Celli and Solimar close to the giant trees. They bent down to dig in the imported mulch, planting flower bulbs. Both wore only traditional loincloths; they were entirely hairless with green skin the color of a worldtree frond. Solimar had a broad chest and muscular arms, while Celli was slender with small bare breasts.

They looked up at him at the same time. "Would you like to help us plant some of the bulbs?" Celli asked. "A trader brought yellow tulips from Earth."

Garrison didn't think he had ever seen a real tulip. Normally in Roamer installations, every scrap of resources had to be useful, every bit of waste recycled. "Aren't flowers a luxury?"

Solimar said, "That depends on how you measure it. A little beauty is necessary too." The two moved together so seamlessly: Solimar hollowing out a divot in the dirt, Celli selecting a bulb and placing it in the hole, then the two of them covering it up and packing down the soil.

"You are new to Fireheart," Celli said. "Recently assigned?"

"Yes, one of the new construction workers. I wondered if I could engage your services to send a telink message?"

Solimar gave a casual nod. "Someone back home?"

"My son, Seth—he's eleven, and I just left him at Academ."

Celli brightened. "We send messages there all the time." She stood up, didn't bother to wipe the dirt from her fingers, and reached out to touch the wide worldtree trunk. "What do you need to tell him?"

Garrison felt the words catch in his throat. He had so much to say, but Seth already knew it. "Tell him I miss him, and I'm proud of him, and that I hope to see him soon." It was the best he could think of.

Solimar joined Celli in the telink. "That's all? How about some details?"

Encouraged, Garrison started talking about Fireheart Station, describing his week rigging and folding the energy-absorbent film; then he talked about the Big Ring and the construction work he was doing. As he rambled, the two dutifully relayed the words into the tree; a counterpart green priest at Newstation would receive them through his treeling. When Garrison finished, he was satisfied. "Yes, I think that'll do it."

Solimar and Celli smiled back at him. "Is there anything else?"

Garrison drew a deep breath, inhaling the scent of the worldtrees. "There is one more thing. I'd like to send another message—to someone named Orli Covitz. . . ."

CHAPTER

78

ORLI COVITZ

The *Verne* and the *Voracious Curiosity* arrived at Ulio Station together.

Ulio was a frenetic bustle in space. Incoming ships raced about in search of open docking ports like insects buzzing around a bright flower. The *Verne* found an available slot by sheer luck, but Tasia had to fly the *Curiosity* for an extra hour, circling until a Confederation freighter disengaged and departed. Robb logged their arrival with Ulio Station traffic control and was pleased to list Orli Covitz, employee of Kett Shipping, as a "first timer."

"Is there some kind of initiation?" she asked, not sure she wanted to participate.

Tasia gave her a wry smile. "No. Would you like us to arrange one?"

"I'd rather not."

After disembarking, they worked their way through the interconnected ships to the main core of Ulio Station. Robb turned in a separate direction to retrieve reports from other Kett Shipping traders, who left deposits here and records of their deliveries. Tasia took Orli and DD along with her. "Keep your eyes and ears open."

With DD beside her, Orli saw a rich array of clothing and body types, heard a range of accents and dialects. Tasia was particularly alarmed when some traders mentioned that clan Duquesne was now also selling ekti-X. Frowning, she pressed into the discussion. "What do you mean? Where are they getting it?"

The two traders looked at her, noting the Kett Shipping insignia on her shoulder. "Ah, I didn't think you'd be happy about that. You're Tamblyn, right? Well, whatever Iswander's process is, clan Duquesne figured it out, too. They sold their first load here a few weeks ago. Looks like you've got competition."

Orli could tell that Tasia was not pleased as they made their way to the restaurant where they had agreed to meet Xander and Terry. The restaurant specialized in a roasting array with skewers of spiced vegetables, meats, and a dizzying selection of sauces. The smells made Orli's mouth water. Terry and Xander had already secured a table. DD spotted OK, and the two compies quickly communicated and summarized what they had each seen on the station.

Robb joined them a few minutes later, breathless. "Did you hear that clan Duquesne is also selling ekti-X?" he said before anyone else greeted him.

"Yeah, we just learned that, too," Tasia said.

Xander put his elbows on the table. "Then maybe our news isn't so significant. The tracker on Elisa's ship automatically uploaded into an encrypted file the last time she stopped at Ulio. We have a complete log of every place she went since the last time we met her. We can track them down to their operations."

Tasia narrowed her eyes. "We'd better get right on that if clan Duquesne is already producing stardrive fuel."

Robb looked dejected. "We had a plum trading relationship and made a lot of profit in a short amount of time—but that'll change now. Orli told us where the ekti comes from. Does it matter?"

"I don't like it when people keep secrets from us," Tasia said. "*I* still want to know what Iswander's doing."

DD offered, "With the tracker data I can create a navigational map and retrace her path."

Terry had his priorities. "*I'd* like to finish lunch first. Have you tried the medusa meat with the green mint sauce?"

Their meal was interrupted when a green priest entered. His emerald skin and his scant clothing looked quite out of place. He looked around the tables and rushed over to them. "Orli Covitz!"

She rose to her feet, surprised anyone would know her name or be able to find her—especially here. Then her face lit up. "Aelin!" She turned to her companions. "This is the green priest who figured out how to cure me from the plague. He saved my life at the Iswander operations when everyone else had given up." Though Aelin seemed skittish, Orli threw her arms around him. "I didn't know you were here on Ulio. Did Iswander transfer you?"

"I . . . I came here on my own," he said; then his face became drawn. "I could not stand it anymore. The pain, the agony—it is a slaughter! So many butchered. So much blood spilled." He had to steady himself on a chair, so great was his despair.

Tasia shot Robb a determined glance. "Maybe not so innocent as we thought. All the more reason to go out there."

Aelin darted his gaze from side to side. "You must not tell anyone I am here. But if you can help stop them . . ."

"We will do what we can," Orli promised. "Was that why you wanted to see me? To give me a warning?"

Aelin's expression changed. "No . . . no. I am still a green priest. A message came through the worldforest mind for you—from Garrison Reeves. I noticed you were here on Ulio. I wanted to see you . . . to know if you have the same connection with the bloaters as I do. You were immersed in their blood. Do you still hear them?"

Orli remembered the chiming connection she had felt in the dim distance of her mind when the *Prodigal Son* had flown past all the chains of bloaters extending away from Ikbir. "Maybe . . . just a faint echo. Nothing like the connection you had." She could not set aside the warm feeling in her heart, though, the eagerness to hear news. "But you said you had a message for me from Garrison?"

Aelin fought against distractions ricocheting in his mind. "Yes . . . Garrison. It was good to hear from him again, and to hear about Seth at Academ. Seth was my student briefly, along with Arden." He blinked, focused again as he saw Orli's expression filled with anticipation. "Garrison wanted you to know that he is doing well at Fireheart Station, that he thinks of you often, and that he hopes you find what you are looking for."

"Thank you." What she was looking for might well be a life with him. Considering how much she thought of Garrison, and how adrift she felt without him, she was coming closer and closer to that conclusion.

She hoped he was, too. "Please tell him that I think about him all the time, too. And I very much look forward to being together again."

Yes, that would have to do. She would want to tell him much more face-to-face—as soon as they saw each other again.

Aelin seemed stressed, out of place, and he hurried away, leaving Orli to face the amused and questioning glances of her companions. "That's a nice send-off," she said, trying to focus on business. "We should be ready to follow Elisa's path as soon as possible."

Tasia looked disturbed. "A slaughter and bloodshed, Aelin said. We'd better see what's really going on."

Robb said, "We're ready to go, as soon as the *Curiosity* is refueled."

CHAPTER 79

AELIN

Over the past weeks, Aelin had fallen into enough of a routine that he almost forgot about the distant slaughter of the bloaters. He found it gratifying just to be a green priest again, though he remained hungry for contact from the drifting, enigmatic nodules. He knew he was missing something. . . .

He still feared that someone from Iswander Industries would find him, though. By now they would know he had disappeared; maybe they would guess he had escaped, but more likely they would believe he had vanished in among the bloaters, never to return. Elisa Enturi still came to Ulio Station frequently, though, and if she suspected he had escaped, that woman would surely hunt him down. To protect himself, he monitored all incoming ships, so he could hide whenever she arrived. That was how he had noticed Orli Covitz. . . .

Aelin spent his days reconnecting with the worldforest through Dauntha's treeling, remembering what he had been. This was what he had been born to do.

But the bloaters . . .

When he learned the shocking news that clan Duquesne was also harvesting ekti-X, he felt a great heaviness in his heart. More bloaters being murdered! He had fought so hard to convince Lee Iswander to stop spilling the blood of the cosmos, because no one could understand the harm he was doing. And now another clan was extracting stardrive fuel in the same fashion. Had he been the one to reveal the secret by his careless, stupid blurting out? It made him want to weep, and he was desperate to do something about it, but he knew that if the word got out, hundreds of such extraction operations would crop up. It could not be stopped.

Even if he were to prove that the bloaters were significant to the very survival of life in the Spiral Arm, as he suspected, many industrialists would still put immediate personal profit ahead of the general good of humanity. He didn't dare reveal what he knew . . . but he couldn't just ignore it either.

Aelin felt drawn to where he could see the satellite tank array, the strategic stockpile of stardrive fuel that Elisa Enturi had delivered. The ekti-X tanks hung in a large, organized cluster just outside of the station complex. He could feel the whispers in the back of his mind.

Looking through the side windowport, Aelin regarded the tethered array. He had traveled to Ulio hidden among those tanks. He knew the fuel had been drawn from the bloaters, and he thought he could still feel a connection there, though it was far fainter than what he had sensed from the majestic cluster.

He pressed his palms flat against the windowport, as if he could get closer to the array. Those tanks contained not just simple stardrive fuel. It was the *essence* of the bloaters. Ekti-X possessed its inherent energy because it contained a spark of life from the giant nodules. His heart ached to be so close.

Access to the stockpile array was well guarded by contract security forces. Two armed men looked askance at the green priest as he stood staring at the ekti tanks. Finally, the shorter of the two said, "Why is a green priest interested in stardrive fuel?"

Aelin pulled his attention from the array. "Do you know where ekti-X comes from?"

"Roamers have been distributing stardrive fuel for centuries."

"Not ekti-X."

"Don't have a clue, don't really care," said the shorter guard.

"I do care." Aelin moved off, even though the ache in his heart had not lessened.

Leaving them, he moved through Ulio Station wrapped in his own thoughts and concerns. His mind had been altered and now he could sense things even without being connected through a treeling. There were ripples in the universe, dark vibrations. Aelin felt frightened.

People crowded around him in the station corridors, but he felt all alone. The air was harder to breathe. The slaughter of so many bloaters was causing a *shudder* in the universe. He could feel the oppressive weight, but couldn't identify the source.

As he stumbled along, he bumped into visitors to Ulio, paying little attention as he hurried to find a place where he could be safe. In an empty corridor he stopped, pressed his bare back against the bulkhead, breathing heavily. When he closed his eyes, the darkness seemed to come from all directions, so he opened his eyes out of desperation.

He couldn't sound an alarm because he didn't understand what he was sensing. He had shouted dire warnings to Lee Iswander before, but no one had believed him. Aelin staggered down the corridor until he made his way back to Dauntha's quarters. She, at least, would listen.

When he entered her chamber, he found the old woman communing with her treeling. Oftentimes when he saw her do this, she would have a blissful expression on her face. Her eyes would be closed and her skin would twitch as she lost herself in contact with the worldforest mind.

Now, though, troubled lines furrowed her brow. When he burst into the room, she didn't even look up, still desperately searching the verdani mind.

"I'm afraid, Dauntha," he said. "I sense something I don't understand." He shook his head, then stumbled forward to grasp the treeling with her, his fingers touching Dauntha's. They could communicate more closely this way. She opened her eyes and Aelin stared into them. "Something is coming—something terrible."

Dauntha stared at him for a long moment, and her head twitched in a slight nod. She let go of the treeling and said, "I know."

CHAPTER

80

EXXOS

Eager to make progress after wrecking the Hiltos shrine and annihilating the hapless human trader, Exxos urged the Shana Rei to continue their depredations. The shadows seethed, frantic to tear up reality, unravel order, and eliminate the throbbing presence of intelligent life—but because the Shana Rei were irrational and chaotic, they lashed out without any sort of plan whatsoever.

Exxos saw that as poor strategy. He needed to guide them, develop a grand scheme that would *test* the creatures of darkness. He wanted to bring about the full extinction of all sentient species, one step at a time. With tools from the Shana Rei, his robots would annihilate one center of civilization after another.

More importantly for his own survival, Exxos observed and learned with each engagement. As his black robots understood what the shadows *could* do, and were *willing* to do, Exxos would force the creatures of darkness to push harder. In doing so, he could also measure the limitations of the Shana Rei, since eventually the robots would need to find a way to exterminate the shadows as well.

"We have a new opportunity for destruction," Exxos announced, knowing that the pulsing inkblots were always listening. "And so we require you to create more warships for us."

Agony shimmered through the horrific ripping voice in the void. "You would cause us pain again."

"Living things cause you more pain," he pointed out.

"It all causes us pain."

"But destruction gives you relief—that is why you must do this," Exxos said, then waited. The inkblots appeared, roiling opaque Rorschach stains that opened their blazing and sinister eyes. He pressed, "Wiping out myriad life-forms will alleviate your pain. *We* can alleviate your pain. But only if you do as I say."

When the Shana Rei did not respond, he insisted, "My robots have skills the Shana Rei do not possess. We will develop a plan. Once all of their intelligent thoughts are gone, then you will be powerful enough to wipe out everything else—the universe as well as yourselves."

He paused. "But we need your ships. Use your powers to manifest matter so that we can conduct our war. *For you.* We have been planning this for a very long time."

Nevertheless, Exxos knew that reality was grim. Only 237 black robots remained of what had been millions. Each black robot was supposedly unique and could not be mass-produced, and now they all had standardized themselves to have the same mind, *his* mind. Even so, Exxos didn't know how he could ever bring back the overwhelming metal swarm that had once nearly conquered the Galaxy.

On the other hand, if the black robots obliterated everything else—the Ildiran Empire, the human race, and eventually, the Shana Rei—so that the only intelligent beings in existence were his robots, all of them bearing his mind and thoughts . . . then that would be enough.

"We will create your warships," the Shana Rei agreed. The black robots thrummed with shared excitement. "We will endure the pain—but you will do the fighting."

"It is our purpose to assist you in causing destruction," Exxos said. "We have already chosen our next target. That is why I summoned you."

The void shattered, and Exxos heard a great ripping sound as solid matter appeared, large forms of opaque black metal—atoms created out of nothingness, through great expenditure of energy by the Shana Rei. The creatures of darkness already had the detailed blueprints that Exxos had developed: armored ships filled with expansive weaponry. Each time the robots struck, they modified their plans so that the next time their attack would be even more effective. When all the battleships were created, Exxos knew that for all of their chaotic mayhem, the Shana Rei had reproduced the vessels exactly as instructed.

As the fleet of black warships appeared, the Shana Rei trembled and moaned . . . and Exxos noted with great interest that they seemed briefly weakened—and that was very important data. He said nothing, but he knew his fellow robots noticed it as well. They buzzed with silent excitement in their secret coded transmissions, which the Shana Rei did not seem to hear.

A part of the robots' combined processing power analyzed how much pain the shadows endured after mentally manufacturing this many ships. Next time, Exxos would demand twice as many vessels, just to test them. And if the creatures of darkness were sufficiently drained, he could possibly make a different move. . . .

With a disorienting spin, Exxos found himself on the command bridge of an impressive new warship. His comrades were distributed among the other battleships, fifty-one of the powerful vessels, far more than last time. Exxos didn't know why the Shana Rei chose that particular number, didn't know if numbers themselves meant anything at all to the creatures of darkness. But he accepted the gift of the black fleet and planned to cause enormous destruction with it.

They would eradicate a major Confederation trading complex, destroy numerous human ships, and take enormous satisfaction as they heard the screams of countless biologicals dying.

When all the robots were prepared to launch their attack, Exxos provided the Shana Rei with details on where they should emerge into real space from the void. A trapdoor ripped open, and the fifty-one heavily armed ships dropped out. The Shana Rei hex ships followed them through the newly created shadow cloud.

The black fleet descended upon Ulio Station.

CHAPTER 81

XANDER BRINDLE

After the *Voracious Curiosity* flew away to track Elisa Enturi, Xander looked at Terry and rubbed his hands together. "Time for us to get down to business—you've got a preinheritance to collect."

OK said, "I will assist in any manner possible."

While Terry remained unsure, Xander elbowed him in the ribs. "You don't even look happy about it."

"I don't know how to react. I've got you, we've got our ship, we have a satisfying life . . ."

"And now you'll add a huge treasure to that. There's nothing wrong with accepting the money. Maria wants you to have it."

Terry was still uncertain. "She's still alive, you know."

"Then call it a gift—that's even better. Donate it all to some humanitarian cause, if you like." He couldn't stop grinning. "But I'd prefer you kept a little bit, so we could pamper ourselves. Good food isn't cheap."

"I suppose it would go wasted, otherwise," Terry admitted. "Let's at least see what we're dealing with."

Maria Ulio had given them all the codes they needed to access her concrete stockpile—the tangible rainy-day wealth she kept sealed aboard one of the core hulks that comprised Ulio Station. The rest of Maria's fortune was dispersed in various accounts throughout the Confederation, but all those access numbers were sealed in an encrypted file in the Ulio Central Offices. Transferring those would be their second priority.

Roamers rarely coveted vast wealth for its own sake—they were more interested in what they could *do* with it. The clans invested heavily, expanded their operations, attempted impossible schemes—and often failed, lost everything, then started all over again.

Xander wasn't greedy, but he was so happy for his partner. What Terry really wanted was a medical procedure to restore the use of his legs; he never said as much aloud, but Xander would have been willing to pay every single credit of Maria Ulio's fortune, plus every single microcredit in his own accounts, if that could happen. Terry had seen numerous specialists, and they claimed the nerve damage was irreversible. Trying not to get his hopes up, Terry did not press the issue. Still, Xander wondered whether a huge infusion of cash might change that opinion. . . .

Moving through the busy station, they bumped into several people Terry remembered from his days here: engineers heading off to a repair yard, and a crew of dismantlers who teased Terry, told him he should get a real job and come back to work with them. Terry seemed embarrassed. "I enjoyed working with you guys, but I'll keep my new job."

They laughed before moving along. "Oooh, the promotion's gone to his head!"

With OK accompanying them and helping Terry, they worked their way through the connected ships toward the hub. When Maria had departed with one of the refurbished Solar Navy warliners at the heart of Ulio Station, the disruption had required structural remodeling of the clustered vessels, but the new hub was now a thriving complex. The decks of the remaining warliners had been remodeled, rented out as temporary lodgings or permanent apartments.

Even though Maria had flown off with one entire Ildiran ship, several decks in another warliner also belonged to her—restricted, sealed away, and hidden by various database tricks. The passwords were incredibly complex algorithms that only OK could remember, once Maria had provided them.

The three of them went from sealed doorway to sealed doorway, penetrating deeper as the compy activated the passwords and granted them passage. Through internal corridors, then to a private lift to another sealed chamber, and finally after seven layers of otherwise impenetrable security, they reached Maria Ulio's secret central vault.

It was like something out of a legendary dragon's treasure hoard: shelves and slots crammed with prisdiamonds, firegems, old-fashioned platinum blocks, even a half ton of concentrated saffron threads . . . anything that might serve as liquid wealth, no matter what financial or cultural crisis hit.

"Saffron?" Xander asked.

Terry just stared. "I don't know what to say."

"We could start hauling it out in suitcases," Xander suggested. "Load up the *Verne* each time we make a trip here."

"What are we going to do with all this?" Terry asked.

"Follow your Guiding Star. Whatever you want."

Terry shook his head. "I don't want to be foolish. A fortune like this changes all the rules of civilized behavior. We're going to need to bring in your parents and Rlinda Kett for advice. They'll know what to do."

"And this is only a portion of Maria Ulio's legacy," OK pointed out. "Now that we know the stockpile exists, perhaps we should go to the Central Offices, and obtain the codes to all her diversified accounts and transfer them into Terry's name."

Xander walked among the shelves of priceless gems, precious metals, and the saffron. "Good idea. This'll keep—it's been here for years."

Terry looked shell-shocked as they departed and sealed each level of security behind them. Xander knew it would be hard to keep a poker face when they reached the Central Offices.

Darwin Felliwell, currently serving a two-year term as Station Manager, had come to Ulio Station in the last year of old Maria's tenure. He understood what made Ulio Station work: There were strict rules, and they were enforced by the traders, customers, and people who made this a thriving commercial hub. Everyone here swiftly punished pirates, thieves, and cheaters. Prices were vigorously haggled and set; services were provided, businesses started and failed. It was cutthroat. It was vibrant.

Xander, Terry, and OK went to the large control center that filled the entire command nucleus of the second decommissioned Ildiran warliner. Large admin screens displayed all incoming and outbound traffic, and complex grids showed available docking spaces scattered across the hodgepodge ships. Traders were not required to list full manifests of their goods, but if they wanted to sell anything, they attracted customers by featuring their items in the station database.

Xander had never met Darwin Felliwell in person, but the man knew Terry from his past service here. "Good to see you again, Mr. Handon." He reached out to grasp Terry's hand as the younger man drifted forward on his antigrav belt.

"We're here to transfer some accounts," Terry said. "Don't worry, there won't be any administrative changes."

"Not until the next election, at least," said Felliwell.

Xander said, "Maria Ulio handed over the keys to her accounts to this dear young man."

Felliwell was surprised. "I thought Maria was long gone and took everything with her."

"Oh, she took only a fraction of it," Terry said. "And she gave me the passcodes to change the accounts over."

Felliwell scratched his head, interested and disturbed. "And you've seen her in person? You have the passcodes?"

"When she departed, there was an agreement that a percentage of all station activity go into certain accounts, but that was all automated." Terry accessed the database from a touchpad mounted on the wall. "Now she wants me to have that percentage."

Felliwell watched all the passwords go through, saw Maria's permissions and security questions answered, and then he stepped back, shaken and seemingly exhausted. "I don't know that you understand just how much money that could be."

"Oh, we understand," Xander broke in. He couldn't shake the image of that wall of prisdiamonds and firegems from his mind.

"And her other accounts?" Terry asked as OK pulled him forward to the screen. "She left them in the Ulio Central Offices. I have to access them from encrypted files in the main computer."

Felliwell had to take a seat, even though the gravity was kept to a minimum. "Maybe you'd consider reinvesting in the station? It was Maria's baby, after all."

Thousands of complex codes filled the screen, waiting to be

manipulated and reassigned. Xander was dizzy just to see all those hidden accounts.

"I'll consider that," Terry said. "We'll consider a lot of options. This is all new to us."

In the command nucleus, they watched the lights of flitting vessels that came in to dock, while others shot away. Bright stars surrounded them in all directions, but none of them were close. Ulio Station was like a sparkling archipelago, a destination for travelers coming from across the Spiral Arm.

One of the traffic controllers looked up from her screen and stared through the wide crystalline windowport. "What the hell is that?"

Xander saw a growing section of stars eclipsed as a billowing shadow cloud emerged, gushing smoke, darkness growing deeper and opening like an infinite doorway. Four enormous hexagonal black ships emerged, blunt cylinders sliding out from nowhere.

"By the Guiding Star!" Xander whispered.

All the computer systems in the Ulio Central Offices flickered. Several screens went blank, and others were engulfed in static. "Systems are failing!" someone cried.

Alongside the ebony cylinders a fleet of angular black warships gushed out—robot warships. Xander had seen images of them before, but these were bigger and more powerful than what he remembered.

More than fifty robot ships soared out of the dark nebula and began to attack the station.

CHAPTER

82

ADAR ZAN'NH

The Ildiran septa accompanied the CDF Juggernaut into unexplored space, navigating to the coordinates that Ohro had provided.

As they approached their ominous destination, Tal Gale'nh stood pale and quiet in the command nucleus, taking control. Adar Zan'nh had given his protégé command of the septa as they flew onward, and Gale'nh stared ahead, as intense as if already battling the shadows ahead of him.

Zan'nh watched silently from the fringe of the tal's field of vision; he nodded to himself and spoke. "Be strong. I want you to know that you are still capable of being a tal."

Gale'nh gave a small acknowledgment, but Zan'nh could see how hard he struggled to keep his expression stoic from the emotions welling beneath. "Then I will do so, Adar."

The exploratory mission would reach the Onthos system within the hour, and observers had gathered in the command nucleus. Rememberer Anton Colicos was eager to watch the story unfold. Rod'h had no Solar Navy rank, but he did have a sense of inner importance, not to mention impatience. He stood beside Tal Gale'nh at the command rail, as if he were the mission's cocommander. Gale'nh didn't mind having him there, though; his half-brother was an anchor for him.

The tal stared forward at the emptiness of space. "We are not traveling as far as the *Kolpraxa* did, but we may still find the Shana Rei out here. The shadows seem to be everywhere."

"Then we will find them everywhere." Rod'h sounded determined. "And we will find new ways to fight them. The Onthos system is long dead, but it may tell us much of what we need to know."

Brave words, Zan'nh thought, *for a man who has never encountered the Shana Rei.* Rod'h did have experience, however, in fighting the hydrogues and the faeros during the Elemental War. He was no coward, but his ambitions were his weakness.

The sensor tech announced, "Long-range scans still show nothing there—no star, no debris, nothing whatsoever."

Rod'h broke in. "When we arrive, I volunteer to lead one of the scouting expeditions, Adar."

"I will take that under advisement." Zan'nh turned back to Gale'nh. "Have we received any update from General Keah on the *Kutuzov*?"

"Just a routine contact an hour ago, Adar. She says her crew is ready for anything, and she looks forward to turning over rocks and seeing what scuttles out from underneath." Gale'nh paused. "Those were her exact words. I believe she was speaking metaphorically."

"Yes, that sounds like her." Zan'nh stepped to the command rail, and Gale'nh dutifully moved aside along with Rod'h.

An hour later, nothing had changed in the starfield even though they were nearly upon the coordinates. General Keah contacted them from the *Kutuzov*. "Have your sensors spotted anything yet, Z?"

The scientist kithmen enhanced the warliner's sensor sweeps and shook their heads. Zan'nh answered, "Nothing yet, General. Still no sign of the star."

"Perhaps it was a hoax," Rod'h said. "Maybe the Onthos lied to us all."

"To what purpose?" Zan'nh asked.

"Perhaps to lure us out here? We should be wary of a trap."

Tal Gale'nh agreed. "My brother's suggestion is wise."

"We will go in on full alert," Zan'nh announced. "Our warliners have a complement of sun bombs and new laser cannons. Along with General Keah's armaments, we will be able to harm the Shana Rei—if they are there."

Keah transmitted, "Ready when you are, Z. I wish our enhanced sun bombs were ready, but we'll have to make do."

"Let us hope we do not encounter a battle at all."

When the exploratory fleet arrived at the Onthos home system, they found no star, no planets. What they did discover, however, was unlike anything Adar Zan'nh had ever seen in his life. The Gardeners' star was not visible—it had been *engulfed.*

General Keah's voice was rough as she engaged the comm. "What the hell? Are you seeing this, Z?"

"I see it, General, but I do not understand."

The ships decelerated, but where the star and planets should have been, they found only an enormous black egg, a shell that encapsulated the Onthos star out to a diameter wide enough to enclose the inner planetary orbits, a globe constructed of the same impenetrable and indestructible stuff that had formed the nightshade over Theroc.

"They built a wall to enclose the entire solar system," said Rod'h in a voice made faint with awe. "They smothered the star and planets, and all of the Onthos."

Gale'nh shook his head, paler than usual. "The power and the resources that such a thing would have required! The Shana Rei must be . . . invincible."

Keah came back on the comm. "An old Earth physicist proposed something like this before, Z—a sphere built to enclose a star. We call it a Dyson sphere."

Anton Colicos said, "But that idea was just a bizarre thought experiment, and it was meant for constructive purposes, a way to give maximum surface area for habitation, plenty of room to absorb all the solar flux."

"I do not believe this was intended for constructive purposes," Zan'nh told the rememberer. Considering the Onthos sun inside, he could think only of a candle flame being snuffed out. Inside, the star must be dead. "It appears the Onthos were not lying to us. Their system is here—*was* here."

The seven warliners split apart to explore, while the *Kutuzov* set its own course, flying around one of the axes of the star system. The Adar's flagship cruised slowly above the surface of the Dyson sphere using high-resolution scanners in an unsuccessful attempt to penetrate the blackness.

The warliners soared along, playing their sensors across the ebony shell, searching for any flaw, any weakness, any opening. But they found none.

Shaken, Gale'nh breathed heavily and forced himself to be strong. "We cannot get to the star system, Adar. It is dead, just as the Gardeners claimed."

Rod'h leaned forward, and his eyes narrowed as he stared into the screen, looking for any sensor glitch that the technicians might have missed. He turned abruptly and looked at Zan'nh. "Adar, you know what we must do. We have the ships, the scout teams, and the weapons. We have to blast our way inside."

CHAPTER

83

GENERAL NALANI KEAH

Perfect blackness. General Keah had never seen anything like it. Not just dark like a night on Earth, because the glitter of starry skies always provided at least fragments of hope. The huge shell that encompassed the Onthos star system was *perfectly* black, reflecting nothing from the myriad stars outside the impossible obsidian sphere. The darkness was as deep as that of a sightless man who was blindfolded, then sealed in a chamber deep within a cave. Yes, that was the kind of black she saw.

"Still nothing new, General," said Sensor Tech Saliba.

"I don't expect to find a welcome mat or a coffee shop, but we have to be thorough—we came all this way." Keah kept staring at the screen; such blackness made her wonder whether the transmitters were malfunctioning.

The seven Ildiran warliners continued their traverse while the *Kutuzov* took its own route up and over the pole in a complete orbit around the englobed system. The opaque shell was perfect, seemingly impenetrable and several astronomical units across, an infinite field of hexagonal plates. So far, the exploratory group had spent two days skimming and crisscrossing the Dyson sphere, sending sensor pulses, trying to find any kind of signal. But the shell was as silent as it was black. Keah's crew dropped limpet probes against the black plates, but they acquired no readings whatsoever. Nadd sent reports back via telink, so the rest of the Confederation and the Ildiran Empire knew what they had found.

Keah said, "I'd love a can opener so we could see what's left inside."

Adar Zan'nh agreed, and the next step was obvious. With more limpet probes scattered around the shell to detect vibrations or shock waves, the *Kutuzov* fired a single jazer pulse into a black hex plate. No effect. Railgun projectiles were launched next, then heavy conventional explosives. The limpet probes barely detected the vibrations.

Frustrated, but expecting this would be a tough nut to crack, Keah leaned back, turned to her weapons officer. "Mr. Patton, indulge yourself—open fire with all the conventional weapons you've got and see if we can make a dent. This thing seems to be made of the same material as the nightshade on Theroc."

The *Kutuzov* blasted away, and space around them became a storm of recoil shock waves and incandescent explosions—none of which resulted in so much as a nick in the interlocked hexagonal plates. The Solar Navy warliners spread out and did the same, bombarding the surface of the shell, hoping to split open the seam between two adjacent plates.

When the Ildirans and the *Kutuzov* had exhausted all primary weaponry options, Keah and Zan'nh discussed options over the comm. They both knew the next step. "Time to try the laser cannons, Z. Our ship's equipped with a full battery, and I expect your seven warliners are as well."

"We were prepared to use the new weapons against the Shana Rei," Zan'nh said. "This seems a good opportunity to test their effectiveness in a calm environment."

The eight battleships backed off to a conservative distance and focused their laser cannons, while the commanders chose specific aim points.

Mr. Patton proposed a targeting grid, and each of the ships chose a particular hexagonal segment where they would concentrate their firepower. Full-strength laser cannons lanced out with streaks of blinding fire. Keah's eyes ached despite the heavy filters on the bridge windowport.

As the bombardment continued, the General said, "If this doesn't work, Z, we'll let loose with our sun bombs. We know they worked against the nightshade. I just wish we had the new designs Dr. Krieger is building."

"Your new sun bombs may be superior, but the previous designs were certainly sufficient. That should be our last resort, however. I am reluctant to use them unless absolutely necessary. We have a limited number. Laser cannons can be recharged, but once the sun bombs have been used, they cannot be replenished until we return home. Should we encounter the Shana Rei . . ."

Saliba looked up from her screen. "Something's happening, General."

Under the laser bombardment, one of the black hex plates crumbled and collapsed, falling inside the vast shell.

"Bingo," Keah said. "Cease fire and let's have a look."

The laser cannons faded, and the black Dyson sphere swallowed up the afterglow, but the impenetrable black was now flawed—one missing hex plate out of the trillions that comprised it. A swatch of slightly different blackness against the unending darkness of the shell. The limpet probes detected no residual thermal emissions, gave no sign that the black material had melted or evaporated. The plate was simply gone.

Adar Zan'nh announced, "We are dispatching remote probes to look inside. We will share the transmission with you."

Pinwheeling devices spat out of the Ildiran flagship and plunged into the tiny gap. The probes vanished inside, but transmissions came back, filling the main screen. Static crackled around the edges of the screen, and that was the only indication they were receiving telemetry from the devices. The interior of the shell was only more blackness.

"The sun is extinguished, then," Keah said. "Not just enclosed."

"Picking up no energy signatures whatsoever from inside. No transmissions from a civilization, no heat radiating from planets or the star," said Saliba. "The whole system has been completely snuffed out."

The Ildiran probes explored inside the shell for more than an hour, but the readings never changed. Silence. Darkness. Cold.

Keah paced the bridge, arms crossed over her chest. "Now that we know how to open the door, we need to pry it open wider, so we can send ships inside. I'm not going home until we have a full look around."

The *Kutuzov* and the Solar Navy vessels began hammering at the surrounding hex plates, peeling them apart with full-strength laser cannons. After trial and error, Mr. Patton discovered that a precise blast at exactly the intersection joint hit the spot of greatest vulnerability, and several of the hex plates collapsed in at once. The seven

Solar Navy ships used the same principle, and then like an avalanche, more than thirty hex plates broke apart and tumbled in like a crumbling mosaic, leaving a gaping maw in the black shell much larger than Keah had expected.

"That's certainly big enough for a scout ship, General," said Lieutenant Tait.

Keah looked around, measuring the opening. "Hell, it's big enough for all our ships to go inside."

"General, is that wise?" asked the first officer. "It could still be a trap."

"Everything about this place could be a trap." Keah looked up to the comm screen. "Z, what do you think?"

"I think we need answers, and the answers are inside. Rather than sending just a small scout party, I would prefer strength in numbers."

Keah knew about the Ildiran phobia of being alone, and their fear of the darkness, so sending a tiny scout party into this utterly lightless prison would be a double whammy of a nightmare. "Then a compromise. I suggest the *Kutuzov* and one Ildiran warliner go inside, while the rest of the septa remains out here."

On the warliner's screen, Tal Gale'nh and his half-brother Rod'h stood beside the Adar in the command nucleus. Gale'nh asked, "What if the barrier reseals itself once we're inside? We would be trapped."

Zan'nh looked at him. "Then we blast our way back out with laser cannons, the same way we got in."

"And we haven't even tried the sun bombs yet. Plenty of options," Keah said, convinced that they would do so before the end of the mission. She looked at the gap in the shell and shrugged. "We've gotta know."

The CDF Juggernaut eased forward first, followed by the flagship warliner, and the two vessels entered the enclosed blackness. As they passed inside the enormous Dyson sphere, even Keah was uneasy. All running lights were illuminated, sensor scans extended—and still they saw nothing.

Outside, the shell had been impenetrably black, but the rest of the universe held countless stars. Inside the shell, though, all outside light was entirely gone—no stars, no reflections whatsoever. Their forward running lights and intense blazers pierced the emptiness but found nothing to illuminate. The only change in the perfect blackness around them was the jagged hole through which they'd entered, from which they could see starlight pouring in, a bright patch against the overall black.

"Astronomy scans," Keah ordered. "Let's find the sun and the planets. They've gotta be somewhere."

"That'll be difficult, General," said Saliba. "There's no radiation, no emissions in any part of the spectrum. It's like looking for a black dot against a black background."

Keah raised her eyebrows. "I'm sorry, Mr. Saliba, I missed the part where your job was supposed to be easy. Look for subtler indications. Unless the Shana Rei erased the Onthos system from existence, down to the last atom, the bodies still have gravity, don't they?"

"Yes, General," said the sensor tech, and set to work.

The star itself was the easiest to find, the largest gravity well. After the flagship warliner and the *Kutuzov* dispatched resident gravitational probes, they found the Onthos sun—or what was left of it, an enormous cinder of burned-out and collapsed material. All nuclear reactions shut down, the remnants held together only by mass and gravity but generating no energy at all. The star was a black sphere inside a black shell.

"It does not seem possible," Adar Zan'nh said. "My scientist kith assure me, it is not possible."

"Good to know," said Keah. "Otherwise, I'd believe my own eyes."

On the screen, artificial points lit up. "High-res grav sensors have pinpointed three planets inside the sphere, General," said Saliba. "Two terrestrial planets, one too small and close in to be worth much of anything, a Mercury analog. Farther out, at the very edge of the Dyson sphere, there's a dark and cold gas giant."

"No other terrestrial planet?" Keah asked.

"Yes, there's one at the right orbital distance, with the proper mass, to be in the habitation zone." She paused. "I think that's the Onthos homeworld."

CHAPTER

84

XANDER BRINDLE

The Shana Rei and the black robots attacked Ulio Station.

From the control deck of the Central Offices, Darwin Felliwell stared at the blossoming dark nebula and the emerging robot warships. "What do we do?"

OK turned from the screen with all of Maria Ulio's coded account numbers and directed his attention out at the shadow cloud. "Based on its similarity to other incidents on record, that appears to be a manifestation of the Shana Rei."

As the angular robot warships streaked in toward the station, Terry said, "Those ships look a lot larger than the ones the robots used before."

"Great, more good news," Xander said.

The Station Manager spluttered. "But . . . why would anyone want to attack *Ulio*? We're not a military site, just a repair yard and flea market."

Xander's first instinct was to bolt. "No time for those questions right now. At Plumas, the Shana Rei and the Klikiss robots trounced a full battle group of Solar Navy warliners and CDF battleships. We don't have a chance."

A Roamer cargo freighter circling Ulio Station in search of a docking spot shifted course away from the unfolding shadow cloud. Two robot warships spotted the retreating vessel and went in pursuit. The enemy engines were far superior to the lumbering freighter's, and the robots strafed the ship, chopping it to pieces.

Then all the robot attackers closed in on Ulio.

"Sound an evacuation!" Felliwell said. "All functional ships to depart as soon as possible." Alarms hammered through the Central

Offices. Small ships detached from their docks and accelerated in all directions like fuzz from a chaff-flower in the wind. Felliwell groaned. "Even if all the spaceworthy ships can escape, we have more than a thousand permanent residents, and half our ships are decommissioned and permanently parked. They'll never fly again."

"Back to the *Verne*," Terry said to Xander. He clutched the compy's shoulder and adjusted his antigrav belt. "But I can't exactly move fast, even in an emergency."

OK said, "Will we be retrieving Maria Ulio's stockpile of tangible assets, sirs?"

Xander knew they were abandoning enough wealth to buy a whole planet and maybe even a second one for a vacation home. "We don't have time. I'm getting you out of here now, Terry."

Shana Rei hexagonal ships emerged from the shadow cloud, spreading a hurricane of chaos, pouring entropy into the universe. In the Central Offices control screens fuzzed with a parade of unreliable images and scrambled data. All of Maria's accounts vanished as the screens went dark, but Xander couldn't worry about that.

"Anybody who can hitch a ride on a departing ship had better get aboard," Xander said. He was just worried that he and Terry wouldn't manage to make it back to the *Verne* before the enemy laid waste to the station. "Come on, we've got a long way to go."

Several ships attempting to escape caught the edge of the shadow cloud; they reeled in erratic courses, their technology scrambled. Their running lights flickered and died, and they hung dead in space, their systems offline.

Workers in the Central Offices bolted for the door, bounding along in the low gravity. The smartest ones made their way straight for any viable ship that could get away. Some rushed to retrieve family members, while others headed to their quarters to grab valued possessions before they fled.

Xander thought one last time of all Maria Ulio's scattered accounts not yet transferred over to Terry, but he decided he didn't care. The *Verne* was on the other side of the station. "OK, how fast can you run?"

"My maximum speed is what humans would call a 'brisk walk.' "

Xander knew that wouldn't be fast enough.

Terry said, "We could take a lift down to zero-G levels, where I can move a lot faster. It would save us time."

The first robot ships bombarded the Ulio hub. The central Ildiran warliner was struck, and shock waves rocked the former command nucleus.

Grabbing onto a bulkhead to steady himself, Xander mentally reviewed the structure of Ulio Station. "We'll cut off a lot of distance if we go beneath the star balcony bar. Once we take that shortcut, we're home free."

"Pull me, Xander—I'll crank up my antigrav belt," Terry said. "You can run faster than OK."

"I will do my best to keep up," the compy said.

Xander grabbed his partner by the wrist and sprinted to the lift, which was already crowded with departing personnel. Felliwell kept yelling into the intercom, "This is not a time to hunker down and wait! If Ulio survives, you can all come back. If it doesn't, you'll be glad you left."

OK barely made it into the packed lift before the door sealed and the platform descended at normal speed, which seemed maddeningly slow. The station workers were desperate. The lift shuddered as an explosion ripped through another part of the old warliner's hull. Finally, the lift stopped at the first floor and disgorged its occupants, who bolted in all directions. Everyone seemed to have a plan.

Xander grabbed Terry's arm again. "To the star balcony—we'll cut straight across." He launched himself out, pulling the weightless young man behind him. Terry's motionless legs extended like a tail, and he held on, keeping himself from squirming so as not to knock Xander off balance. The compy scuttled along after them, moving more quickly than Xander expected. "Don't fall behind, OK." He didn't want to lose his faithful compy, but Terry was far more important to him.

The star balcony and observation lounge looked like a disaster area; drinks were spilled, briefcases, garments, and food scattered around. Virtually everyone had evacuated, but one older man sat on a barstool nursing a drink and staring up at the transparent dome as the drama played overhead. The star balcony patrons had seen the danger as soon as the shadow cloud appeared; the intelligent ones had bolted for their ships even before Felliwell announced the evacuation.

The old man on the barstool gave them a polite nod and continued to stare up at the dome as they darted across the observation lounge. "Aren't you leaving?" Xander shouted over the clatter of alarms.

"Nope." The man nursed his drink. "I've got as much chance of being blown up out there as in here—and this place has century-old Scotch that the bartender conveniently left unattended." He took another sip of his drink, rolled it around in his mouth, and kept watching overhead.

Black robot ships closed in on a fully loaded Confederation passenger vessel that was trying to flee. They blew it to pieces.

Three smaller Roamer vessels—Xander recognized the markings of clan Christensen—joined up and used their defensive weapons. The Christensen jazers weren't overly powerful, but the pilots managed to damage one of the robot ships, which careened off course. Glowing exhaust burned out of the robot's damaged engine, and the enemy ship spun, plunging toward the star balcony hemisphere.

"Run!" Xander shouted to the old man, who didn't even move. Xander clamped a tight grip on Terry's wrist. "OK, hold on to Terry's ankle, and I'll pull you both." With all the strength in his legs, Xander bounded across the open observation lounge, with Terry behind him and the compy clinging to his ankle like a bizarre balloon train.

They reached the opposite side of the star balcony just as the damaged robot ship smashed into the dome, exploding. With the decompression blast, the air inside the bar erupted outward. Xander reached the hatch to the passageway and dove through so that the shock wave from the explosion slapped them farther down the corridor. Automatic fail-safes slammed the emergency bulkhead doors shut behind them in time to prevent the loss of all the atmosphere in the outer corridor.

Outside, Xander breathed hard. Terry was wide-eyed. OK let go of Terry's legs and dropped back to the deck, where his feet clamped on. "This is a hazardous place. We should leave as soon as possible."

"Good idea, OK," Terry said. "Down one more deck and we'll be weightless. Then I can really move fast."

They reached a hatch with a ladder leading to the deck below. "OK, help Terry down, then both of you set out ahead. Full speed. Terry, you move faster than I do in zero G, and I need you to fire up the *Verne*'s engines the moment you get there. I'll be right behind you."

"Sure thing," Terry said as the compy pulled him down the ladder. "It's my turn to save your ass."

"You're right about that. I've been keeping track. And if you see any strays who need rescuing on the way, get them aboard!"

As Xander slid down the metal ladder, he saw that Terry was letting himself drop blindly. As soon as he reached the next deck, weightlessness changed his momentum, and he snagged a bar to right himself. "Grab my antigrav belt, OK, and hold on tight."

"I do not wish to slow you down, Terry Handon."

"Then don't argue."

As soon as OK clamped his hand in place, Terry launched off with the little compy in tow. He yelled back over his shoulder, "Better hurry, Xander!"

By the time Xander reached the bottom of the ladder on the zero-G deck, Terry had propelled himself ahead, grabbing on to wall rungs, yanking himself along, building up speed. He shot forward like a projectile out of a cannon. This was Terry's element. He had worked at Ulio for years without gravity, where his paralyzed legs were no hindrance. Now he glided like a porpoise, and Xander tried to keep up.

When Terry paused, making sure he didn't fall too far behind, Xander yelled, "Just get the damn ship started, I'm only a few seconds behind you!"

He realized that his nose was bleeding, possibly a concussion from the star balcony explosion. Small droplets of blood drifted in the air near his face. Half the lights in the empty corridor were off, and as Xander pulled himself along, one section of the antigravity generators failed, and he crashed flat onto the deck. A few drops of blood pattered down on his face, but he picked himself up and bounded forward; after ten meters he was suddenly in weightlessness again. He flailed, disoriented, drifting against the wall until he grabbed a handhold to right himself. He caught two breaths, then streaked after Terry again.

The *Verne* had a good docking spot close into the hub. Many of the outer vessels had already been destroyed by the robot attacks. He saw parts of Ulio Station in flames, evacuating ships careening into each other, their courses scrambled by Shana Rei entropy.

Another huge explosion rocked the corridor. Far behind him,

Xander heard emergency bulkheads slamming shut. Ulio's hub was being ripped apart in the concentrated blasts, but there were no other scrambling evacuees in here with them.

Up ahead was the access to the holding area where the *Verne* had docked. His heart leaped when he saw OK standing on the boarding ramp. "Terry Handon is already in the cockpit. He warns that he will not wait for you, but I do not believe him."

"He won't need to—I'm here!" Xander didn't slow as he rocketed forward, knocking the compy backward into the ship with him. "Go, Terry! Go."

The hatch sealed behind them, and the *Verne* detached from the docking port, its engines already up to speed. The *Verne* looped up and away from the docking hub into a madness of explosions and fleeing ships, Klikiss robot vessels, and deadly Shana Rei hex ships that loomed there, damaging space itself.

As he watched the robot warships pummeling Ulio Station, Xander was furious and stunned. The black attack vessels destroyed the Central Offices, tore apart the decommissioned Ildiran warliners and the CDF Mantas that formed the station backbone.

"I'd say your inheritance is irretrievable now, Terry," Xander said.

"Not my priority at the moment." Terry dodged debris from a wrecked tanker. Xander took his place, manning the defensive weapons and looking for his opportunity.

Countless ships had been in spacedock for repair at Ulio, and Xander doubted that even a tenth of the inhabitants had gotten to evacuation ships. Of those, maybe half had been destroyed as they fled. On their way out, he spotted the large array of ekti-X tanks left as a strategic reserve for Ulio. Nobody was going to need the reserves now.

"Where am I headed?" Terry said, as he dodged an incoming black robot ship, swooping under it as the enemy roared overhead, opening fire, but missing them. He warmed up the *Verne*'s stardrive.

"How about *away from here* as fast as possible." Xander opened fire on the nearest target.

"Sounds like a fine idea."

CHAPTER 85

AELIN

The moment a doorway opened up in the underworld of the universe, Aelin felt the Shana Rei like a dark knife to the heart. He remembered the wrench in his gut when the other shadow cloud had appeared at the first Iswander extraction yard. And now that he had been baptized in the powerful blood of the cosmos, he was even more attuned to the danger. This was the throb of warning he had felt resonating through his senses. Now he understood, but too late.

Aelin suddenly shuddered and hunched over. He staggered against Dauntha's wall, the one painted with worldtrees. "They're here. The shadows are here."

The other green priest grabbed for her treeling, searching for information while shouting a warning through telink, "Ulio Station is under attack!"

Loud alarms ratcheted through the station. Evacuation signals rang across the interconnected comm systems. Aelin joined her at the treeling, where he could feel tension shudder through the verdani mind. Ever since the Shana Rei had attacked Theroc, and the Onthos refugees had shared memories of the ancient extinguished worldforest, the trees had been terrified of the creatures of darkness. The green priest Nadd had just sent the first reports from the Onthos star system, which was smothered inside a gigantic black shell. The power of the Shana Rei seemed immeasurable.

Explosions echoed through the parked warliner at the heart of Ulio Station. Dauntha delivered details of the ongoing attack via telink, so that all green priests understood the threat to the depot, even though no help could possibly arrive in time.

Black hex ships hung inside the looming shadow cloud, while the aggressive robot squadron blasted ships that tried to evacuate. A more powerful concussion resounded through the decks, nearly toppling the potted treeling from the table.

Aelin knew that for some reason the Shana Rei had a particular antipathy toward the bloaters, and even though there were no bloaters in the vicinity, Ulio Station kept the large stockpile array of ekti-X tanks. That was the essence of the bloaters—and he could think only of shadows, blood, and fire.

He pulled his fingers away from the treeling. "I have to go."

"Yes." Dauntha's voice was distant, as if she could spare only a fraction of her consciousness for him. "We don't both need to die."

"You don't need to die. Carry your treeling, find one of the departing ships. Take your chances."

Now, Dauntha's eyes focused on his. "No—I'm old and I live within the verdani mind. I would be no good to anyone. I may as well stay here, connected to my treeling, so that the rest of Theroc can know every moment."

Aelin scanned the tattoos on her face, her scalp, her neck, her shoulders—the chronicle of a remarkable life. Dauntha still had something very important to do. And so did he.

Aelin remembered when his brother Shelud had faded slowly into death from the alien plague. A green priest's memories, perhaps even part of the soul, would survive within the trees. Dauntha had made her choice. As he left her chambers, she immersed herself in her link with the treeling, losing herself in the verdani mind, never again to come out.

Aelin sprinted through the corridors on bare feet. A huge explosion rocked the entire ship, and severe tremors knocked him to his knees. He climbed back up, ignored a skinned and bloody knee, and kept running.

Corridor lights flickered as systems were damaged. Outside through the windowports, he saw countless wrecked ships that tumbled burning as their fuel mixed with vented atmosphere. Aelin felt the claws of encroaching darkness within him like an embolism, and he clutched his chest, gritted his teeth, and forced it away. He forced himself onward.

When he reached the connecting hatch that led to the exterior fuel stockpile and the holding array, the stern guards were no longer there. He could sense the bloater essence in the tanks.

The Shana Rei refused to move, hovering at a safe distance, but he needed to harm the creatures of darkness in any way possible. Aelin had to get out there to the anchored array to execute his plan. He had to call the robot ships.

Shadows . . . fire . . . blood.

The corridor lights flickered again, and suddenly the deck plunged into blackness. There was a hiss of air, and all of the alarms fell silent. The unexpected quiet and darkness disoriented him more than terrified him. The gravity also failed, and he drifted upward in the darkness, which made him dizzier still.

Suddenly, explosions shattered the silence. Lights rippled on through the corridor again, and Aelin fell to the deck, crashing on his face as the gravity came back on. He picked himself up. Only a few flickers of emergency light stuttered on. The connecting door had closed and sealed; without power or computer access, Aelin could not open the hatch and make his way to the ekti-X stockpile. Then, like a blessing or a cosmic joke, the door sighed open all by itself.

Aelin sprinted into the secure chamber adjacent to the anchored stockpile. As the lights flickered out again, he memorized the location of what he saw: equipment lockers that held environment suits like the one he had stolen from Alec Pannebaker.

The power failed once more, but enough blossoming explosions and flashes of destroyed ships flickered through the windowports that he could still make his way. He rummaged in the lockers, fumbling and sizing the suits by feel until one seemed adequate. It didn't have to last long.

As the disaster continued outside the station, he crawled into the suit, checked the seals, remembering the steps from when he had escaped the Iswander extraction field. He fastened every component, checked the safety interlocks. Half of the systems blinked yellow, several went dead. Aelin didn't care. The suit would protect him long enough. The helmet comm unit still worked. That was important.

He entered the airlock chamber and saw that the manual systems still functioned, much to his relief. He started the cycle, then punched the emergency button, which caused an instantaneous dump of the contained atmosphere. The outer door opened, tumbling Aelin out into the array of tanks.

He knew about the black robots, had studied them extensively through telink—there were numerous records of their attitudes and personalities from the Elemental War. They were ruthless and vengeful, and they thrived on causing pain to other living things. Aelin understood them.

In his ill-fitting spacesuit, he drifted out into the stockpile array, and as he nestled among the ekti-X tanks, he felt faintly connected to the bloaters again. He remembered the larger reality that those mysterious nodules had allowed him to glimpse, if only briefly.

Once in position, vulnerable out in space while the attacks rushed all around him, Aelin triggered his distress signal. Many Confederation and independent ships had already pulled away from the large cluster, so that the framework of Ulio Station now looked oddly skeletal. Space around him was dark except for the sparks and explosions. Wreckage littered the emptiness, some pieces tumbling into the fringes of the shadow cloud.

The black robot ships were like a pack of predators, choosing and destroying one target, then another. The Shana Rei were not close enough to be affected by what Aelin would do, but that would not stop him.

He transmitted on an open frequency that he was sure the robots would be monitoring. He knew exactly how the monstrous machines would respond. "Help! This is an emergency!" Aelin said. "I have one hundred innocent women and children with me here. We're helpless. Please don't let the Klikiss robots come after us." He was surprised at his own deviousness, but he was certain this was precisely the right bait to use. "We can't escape! Home in on my emergency signal at these coordinates. Rescue us. We have no other hope."

The relentless black robots were perfectly predictable.

Like a school of razor beetles, the robot ships swooped toward the fuel-storage array. Aelin hung there, holding on to the tanks, one arm wrapped around the grid framework. The robot weapons were bright and hot, ready to shoot.

"Please don't fire on us," Aelin transmitted. "Please."

The black robots did not understand reverse psychology. They closed in, locked on target.

Aelin clung to the nearest tank, thinking of the bloaters, wishing he could be immersed in them again, like the womb of the universe, the perfect amniotic fluid that had awakened him, purified him.

The black warships homed in on the coordinates. Close . . . very close. They opened fire on the array.

Shadows. Blood. Fire.

The cluster of ekti tanks ignited at once, like an awakening star.

CHAPTER

86

ARITA

Even if she spent years on the isolated continent, Arita would never be able to see or understand all of the Wild. She had explored other planets in the Spiral Arm, and she knew the bizarre diversity of flora and fauna, but being alone in the Theron wilderness made her feel smaller than ever. And she knew that something was wrong here. She had not seen Collin yet, but she could sense an indefinable change—just as he had warned.

Leaving Sarein's dwelling, Arita spent many nights alone as she ranged farther, explored more. She called out for Collin, knowing the trees could hear, and she was worried about him. She had seen no sign of any green priest, not Kennebar or his followers. Other than Sarein, she might as well have been the lone human being on the continent.

Even the mysterious Onthos had dispersed into the deep forest, where they did not interact with others. Considering their tragic history, Arita wasn't surprised the aliens would withdraw into exile. Except for the first night when they had watched her from above, she hadn't seen a single Gardener.

She took her scout flyer into the deep forest far from any place she had previously explored. Day after day, Arita would land her flyer, set a locator beacon so she could find her way back, and then trudge through the forest.

Though not a green priest, Arita was as nimble and self-sufficient as Collin. When they were younger, the two of them had studied the plants, insects, and fungi together. Sometimes when she was all alone in the forest, she found herself talking aloud—talking to *him*. In return, she could sense Collin watching her—at least she hoped it was him.

After landing in a broad meadow, she wandered through the

undergrowth for kilometers, taking images of blooming flowers, following iridescent beetles as they went about their pollination routines. She collected specimens when it seemed appropriate, but most of the time she just drank in details.

As she ranged afar one day, she heard a rustling in the trees above and looked up to see four Onthos watching her. She lifted a hand in greeting, and they imitated her gesture. "You are far from other humans," said one of the Gardeners.

"Gathering knowledge is its own reward, and there's a lot to learn here. I'm exploring the continent."

The aliens considered that for a moment, then said, "As are we." Then they scattered, climbing up into the thick fronds where they were lost in the canopy.

At sunset, Arita made a nest of branches where she could spend the night among the fronds. She fell asleep listening to the burbling sounds that were so familiar to her.

In the morning, Arita woke, trying to hold on to details of another looming and ominous dream . . . some kind of gigantic presence out there, far away, yet everywhere. Calling out for help. But even the vague details faded with the fuzziness of sleep.

She climbed a hill where the trees were sparser and she could get a broader panorama of the untouched worldforest. There, Arita was disturbed to see a brown swath of dry and withered trees on a distant ridge kilometers away. A section of worldtrees had succumbed to some kind of spreading blight.

She wondered what could possibly have caused that. Maybe a lightning strike had sparked a fire, killing off an entire grouping of the worldtrees? It didn't look like a fire, though—the worldtrees just seemed to be dead.

She took many images with her survey equipment. The ridge was far off, across rough terrain. She couldn't cover that distance in less than a day or two, but maybe she should return to her flyer and come back to get a better look.

Suddenly, Collin startled her by dropping down out of the trees above. Her friend liked to surprise her, but right now he was not grinning; rather, he looked grief-stricken. "Now you've seen it too. The worldtrees are dying. It's a kind of sickness."

Arita was so glad to see him she couldn't help sweeping him up in an embrace. "I came to see you—I got your message. I've been looking for you ever since I landed."

"Kennebar was watching me. He didn't consider you to be important—but I do. I wanted to see you." He looked around. "I'm glad you came."

Arita looked back at the distant swath of dead trees, alarmed. "Why didn't we know anything about this? The worldforest must be hurting, and nobody reported it. Green priests are stewards—they should all sense when something like this happens."

"They should." Collin nodded. "I wasn't aware of it myself until I saw these dead trees with my own eyes. The verdani mind seems to be . . . forgetting, as if there's a stain in their memory."

"But, what caused them all to die?"

"We don't know, but . . ." Collin struggled with his words and his doubts. "Kennebar dismisses it as part of the natural order of the worldforest. He minimizes the problem, says that if the verdani are not alarmed, then we must accept what has happened and not be concerned. He scolded me when I was too persistent."

"I'm relieved you told me about it," she said. "I'm always glad to see you. I kept your letter. It's very precious to me."

Collin's voice was quiet and uncertain. "There are times when I wish . . ." He shook his head. "The green priests are in an uproar. You probably don't know—the Shana Rei just struck again, destroying Ulio Station. Two green priests were there—Dauntha and Aelin. They sent reports throughout the attack . . . but they've gone silent. The Confederation is very concerned, and the CDF is responding, but the ships won't get there in time. I fear there is nothing left of Ulio." He straightened, back to business. He reached out to take her hand. "Let me guide you back to your flyer now, so I know you are safe." Then he added in a voice almost too soft for her to hear, "Please."

Back at Sarein's hiveworm nest, Arita tried to sleep, but somehow the surrounding walls left her exposed to unsettling nightmares. Out here, open to the brooding wilderness, Arita's subconscious again touched something giant and slumbering . . . confused and dispersed echoes that were just a veneer over immense power, yet they could connect with her through a weak dreamline.

When she tried to understand and communicate in return, a vivid panoply of astronomical images flooded through her mind: double stars, globular clusters, the blazing, gas-shrouded reactor of the galactic core, streams of cosmic dust that extended like tendrils throughout the Galaxy. Lines of swollen gas bags—bloaters—trailed along, following their own paths, reaching the bright womb of a star system and then metamorphosing, fissioning, and spreading out even more widely along unseen web lines. All connected.

She saw the arms of the Galaxy, then the neighboring galaxies, the Magellanic Clouds, Andromeda with its satellite galaxies, and then more and more—galaxies like specks in the local cluster extending even farther to the local supercluster.

What paraded through her fuzzy mind had more detail than any astronomical image she had ever seen, more intimate and with more comprehension than seemed possible for any brain to encompass. It appeared godlike, vaster than any universe she had ever imagined.

Arita felt an ache and a loss, and she couldn't understand how such majestic strength could be so lost, alone, disoriented. And she felt a vivid alarm, a spike of danger of something omnipotent calling for help. *Her* help.

When she awoke, thrashing, in the middle of the night, Arita climbed off her cot struggling to catch her breath while her heart pounded hard. She looked around, but sensed nothing. Her aunt's dwelling was silent and dark, but outside the fireflies swept along like sparks from a grinding wheel.

A silhouette sat hunched on the open balcony: Sarein. The woman sat alone, looking out into the night.

Disturbed by her dream, Arita went to stand next to her. Sarein didn't turn her head or acknowledge her niece. They just remained together in silence.

Finally, Sarein said aloud, "Can you sense it, too? The forest is uneasy, but I'm not a green priest, so I don't understand why." When she turned to look at Arita, the darkness of her dark eyes and gray-streaked brown hair was intensified by the shadows. "Maybe you should go back home, where it's safe."

The disturbing worldtree blight she had seen, as well as Collin's news about the Shana Rei attack on Ulio Station, made Arita greatly concerned. She nodded slowly. "Maybe I should."

CHAPTER

87

ZOE ALAKIS

The very existence of Pergamus was in danger, Zoe knew—everything she had worked for, all the precious and irreplaceable data she had gathered—and all because they had been exposed by that fool Paolus.

She had to protect herself, and she knew Tom Rom would do anything she asked. But this threat was not one she could fight directly, and even he couldn't tackle the entire Confederation.

She wanted him with her inside the sterile dome, but Tom Rom refused. He rarely denied her requests, but this time he was firm. "I can't react quickly enough behind all those decontamination layers. I have to be ready in case the Confederation arrives with a full military force. I very much doubt they will take a polite no for an answer. It is only a matter of time. We both know that."

Zoe understood. "We need to decide what to do, how to respond. We have to act instead of react. The King and Queen know about Pergamus, and they believe we have information that can treat their dying son—which makes them unpredictable, perhaps irrational, certainly dangerous. It would not be wise to provoke them."

"I concur, but the problem is larger than that. Others in the Confederation will be concerned about how many disease organisms we hold here. They will see Pergamus as a threat. They will decide to do something about us."

Zoe's gaze grew more intense. "Yes, and right now is the only time in which we control some of the variables. If *we* decide what to do, then *we* can guide the outcome." She doubted she would like any of the solutions they came up with, but they had to do their best. "I will not surrender Pergamus to someone else—I'd destroy it all first, the samples and the research."

"We will take that as a given," Tom Rom said. "Therefore, perhaps our safest option is to release all personnel and trigger the fail-safe sterilization procedures. Obliterate Pergamus preemptively. Vaporize every last pebble and microorganism." His determined face flashed a hint of a smile. "Then you and I can go somewhere else and begin fresh. We have all the prisdiamonds on Vaconda, so we would not lack for funding."

He rattled off his solution so quickly that she realized he had already given this possibility a great deal of thought. And that disturbed her.

He continued, "We could take our data with us and start over again, just you and me. We've done it before." He seemed almost to long for that.

But Zoe couldn't bear to lose it all. "Then we would become outlaws, and the Confederation would keep hunting us down. We would never be able to build another Pergamus, at least not on this scale. No matter how secret our work is, we'd still need access to researchers, equipment, samples." She touched her lower lip. "No, I'd like to try a different approach."

Tom Rom's face remained placid on the screen, waiting to hear what she would suggest. "I am listening."

Zoe had been giving the idea much thought as well. "A concession and a bargaining chip. We have something the King and Queen want—all of our research into the Prince's condition. But they also have something I want—Lee Iswander delivered all those Onthos historical records and the full database of medical files about the plague that almost killed you. We have the disease sample from your bloodstream, and the Iswander database would fill out our specimen set. I believe that's worth a trade. That would be my opening gambit."

Even with the flat distance of the comm screen, she could see him struggling to control his surprise. "It would buy us time. But you don't actually have a cure to Prince Reynald's illness."

"They don't know that—and I would not make them promises. I've learned all too well about the treachery of sharing, but right now, we may have no other choice."

. . .

After recovering from Conden's Fever, young Zoe became morbidly fascinated with the disease that had nearly killed her, along with the vaccines that others had denied her. Once she was healthy again, Zoe considered those people to be *her* enemies. And Tom Rom was not one to forgive such an insult, especially when it had endangered the life of the young woman who could have been his daughter.

They traveled to Earth, then to Yreka, New Portugal, and Cotopaxi. On Cotopaxi they learned that one of the planetary council members was also dying of Heidegger's Syndrome, and he had flown away, chasing after a new and miraculous cure that was being offered on Rakkem. For a substantial fee.

Zoe felt a sharp pang. If such a cure had been offered years earlier, her father could have been saved, or at least his suffering might have been alleviated. "I want to know what that cure is," she told Tom Rom. "And then I'll buy it."

He was disturbed. "But you don't suffer from Heidegger's."

"No, but I still want it."

So he took her to Rakkem to investigate this cure that sounded too good to be true. There, they met with a biomerchant named Aldo Cerf, who advertised many remarkable and guaranteed treatments—all of which came with exorbitant price tags. Cerf's library of cures seemed unbelievable, miraculous. How could this seedy-looking biomerchant on a festering black-market planet have drugs and treatments that the best medical facilities in the Confederation didn't offer? Zoe wanted to learn why, to know whether or not she could have acquired this cure back when her father was still alive.

Tapping into their newfound wealth of prisdiamonds, Tom Rom dressed as a respectable businessman from the reef settlements on Rhejak. He met with Aldo Cerf, explained that he—Tom Rom—had been diagnosed with the initial stages of Heidegger's Syndrome, and he was anxious to obtain the cure before the disease progressed to the next stage.

Cerf was expansive and gracious, insisted that his treatment was new, that it would quite likely cure Heidegger's. At the very least, he claimed, it would give the patient renewed energy and certainly prolong his life. Seeing the fine clothes Tom Rom wore, Cerf raised his price. Later, Zoe discovered that the council member from Cotopaxi had paid even more for the same treatment.

In addition to the Heidegger's cure, Cerf advertised an entire catalogue of miracle drugs pulled together from the best medical researchers across the Spiral Arm. That was the reason why desperate patients constantly came to him.

Zoe and Tom Rom departed from Rakkem, glad to be away from the festering swamps and biomarkets, disease-testing stations, organ samples, and unethical people. She kept the Heidegger's treatment like a trophy, a keepsake. It reminded her of her father, made her sad that she had found it too late.

Several months later, they learned that the council member from Cotopaxi had died of an accelerated progression of Heidegger's.

Tom Rom spent more prisdiamonds to commission a rigorous analysis of the supposed cure, only to find that the treatment was a complete scam. Aldo Cerf's treatment was just a concoction that produced mild euphoria so the patient felt healthier, believed he was getting better . . . and burned out faster.

Zoe was outraged at the con job. Back when her father was dying, she would have paid anything for this supposed cure . . . which would have killed him even sooner. Cerf's treatment was merely a placebo—and worse.

Zoe wanted to do something about the twisted place, and so they investigated further. Tom Rom applied his considerable skills to digging into the biomerchant's dealings, but Aldo Cerf was unremarkable among many similar con men, curesellers, and organ merchants.

More important, though, Tom Rom made the remarkable discovery that Zoe's mother was still alive after all. . . .

The thought of Rakkem made Zoe cringe inside her sterile isolation dome. So many diseases at that place, so many corrupt people, and it was still in existence, still as corrupt.

On Pergamus, she operated differently, kept everything under tight control, neatly labeled and in its own place. She did not prey upon desperate sufferers, did not sell any of her work at all.

But she could not let the Confederation seize control of her facility. She couldn't allow that to happen.

More determined than ever, she spoke to Tom Rom on the screen. "We need to make that bargain. We have to get something out of this and keep ourselves protected, at least for now."

Tom Rom accepted that. "I'll depart immediately for Theroc and speak to King Peter and Queen Estarra. I will negotiate terms. I promise I will save us."

But she shook her head. The words caught in her throat, but she forced them out. She was terrified of her decision, but there could be no better way to demonstrate the seriousness of her offer. "Not just you, Tom Rom. I need to make a dramatic gesture."

His eyes widened slightly, convinced that he wasn't going to like what she intended to suggest.

"I will leave this dome and go with you and face the King and Queen in person."

CHAPTER 88

ROD'H

Facing their fear, Solar Navy and CDF teams explored the deep darkness inside the sealed Onthos star system. General Keah dispatched a squadron of solo CDF scout ships, but Ildirans hated to be alone, and their terror was only amplified by the dark impenetrable shell.

As a halfbreed, though, Rod'h was strong enough to handle it, as was his brother Gale'nh. Their mixed heritage gave the two men an anchor against traditional Ildiran fears, and they were even stronger because of the close psychic bond among all of Nira's halfbreed children. They volunteered to be part of the first exploratory team to set foot on the dark Onthos planet.

And the human historian Anton Colicos insisted on going along as well.

The large transport that departed from the flagship warliner was practically an expedition, a personnel shuttle large enough to carry fifty scientists, guards, engineers, and astronomers, as well as Rod'h, Gale'nh, and Rememberer Anton. They headed toward the dark, frozen sphere that had been home to the Gardeners and another separate worldforest.

Rod'h was eager and curious, while the rest of the Ildirans were intimidated, tense. Gale'nh, oddly enough, looked strong and focused, even with the scars of the Shana Rei all around them. His pale hair and skin were unsettling to Ildirans, a constant reminder of the hell he had endured—much as the burn scars on Prime Designate Daro'h's face proclaimed how he had once faced the faeros and mad Designate Rusa'h.

Rod'h, though, remained undamaged—his bravery and defiance had no chinks.

The expedition descended to the dark planet—a lifeless, cold emptiness that showed no city lights, nor gave off any thermal readings. The sun had been extinguished, the outside stars eclipsed, and the Onthos homeworld had withered in complete darkness.

The pilot of the transport circled over the dark planet, playing high-intensity blazers across the landscape to illuminate a rugged, uneven surface like scratched obsidian. Anton Colicos took diligent notes, keeping a record to write later.

After the transport cruised above the dark landscape for an hour, Rod'h was impatient. "Land the ship," he declared, to the consternation of the Ildiran scientists. He gave them a sour look. "We will never have our answers unless we set foot down there. Directly."

Tal Gale'nh outranked everyone on board, and he issued the order. "My brother is correct. We have come this far. We must finish our mission."

Anton nodded. "I agree. We have to bring back our discoveries—everyone is waiting to see what we find out."

The pilot found a supposedly safe spot to land. Rod'h was the first to don an environment suit, and Gale'nh joined him. The two of them assisted each other in checking the seals, adjusting the gloves and life-support packs, and sealing the swirled, conch-shaped helmets. Anton Colicos needed help suiting up, but he soon stood prepared, ready to set foot outside.

Armed guard kithmen suited up in the main gathering bay, wearing larger armored suits with built-in energy weapons. Each also carried a reinforced cudgel with a sharp crystalline blade, which might have been useful for direct physical combat, though less graceful in space or low gravity.

"We have sufficient weaponry for protection," announced one of the guard kithmen. Rod'h did not expect they would face combat here, however. This world was a dead place, and he doubted anything could harm them here other than their own Ildiran fears.

Rememberer Anton said, "It would be more useful to make sure that we each carry enough light."

Rod'h took a handheld blazer and activated the power. Gale'nh and Anton did the same, and the guards followed suit. The landed transport was a blaze of bright reflections, alone in the cold darkness.

They opened the hatch and exited into the blackest forest imaginable filled with angular monoliths frozen into obsidian, like towers of long razors. The skeletal remains of the trees were only blacker silhouettes against an utterly lightless sky.

The group moved cautiously forward in their environment suits, leaving footprints in the powdery ground. Gale'nh and Rod'h walked shoulder-to-shoulder, while the guard kithmen spread out in a protective formation. Anton Colicos ventured off, curious, shining his blazer in different directions. Three nervous scientist kithmen performed their expected mission, taking samples of the soil and indecipherable frozen matter.

The bright beams made a spray of razor-edged shadows. Around them towered the black behemoths of long-dead worldtrees, nightmarish forms that seemed to have been carved from skeletal obsidian. Dead trees loomed, the dusty bones of a once great worldforest, but there were also signs of the ancient Onthos civilization.

These immense trees were connected by the remnants of looping artificial skyways, metal bridges and arches built long ago. Spikelike towers rose high into an impenetrable sky, piercing what once had been a dense, lush canopy.

Rod'h marched forward, shining his handblazer ahead as he approached the nearest worldtree. The shadows were so dark and the glare of the light so bright that the massive trunk looked distorted, different from the worldtrees that lined parklike boulevards in Mijistra. This dead obelisk had no golden bark scales, no soft green fronds. With a gloved hand, he touched the trunk, but felt only sharp, cold resistance.

Gale'nh spoke through the comm, his voice startlingly loud in the helmet, "When I was in darkness, I lost a major part of myself, but I am trying to gain it back. These trees, though . . . they will never gain back what they have lost."

"We need to retrieve samples," said Anton. "A lot of samples."

Two scientist kithmen stepped forward, removing sharp hammers and narrow chisels from their specimen kits. When they struck the points against the petrified trunk to remove a splinter, the entire mammoth tree shuddered—and then shattered into a rain of black dust that fell glittering in the beams of their blazers. Rod'h and Gale'nh hunched over to protect themselves, but the obsidian flakes were mere black sparkles of the massive trunk. The ghost of the worldtree disintegrated into black shards.

"Now we have plenty of samples," Rememberer Anton said, helping the scientists to scoop up the ebony splinters. The ground was covered with black charcoal.

As they continued through the silent wreckage, shining lights in the darkest corners, they found many more collapsed trees, uprooted titans that had pulled down the once-majestic Onthos buildings and walkways.

Anton Colicos sounded amazed. "It must have been a thriving and beautiful world. I've seen the Gardener refugees on Theroc—so quiet, so grateful. They're the only ones who escaped."

Embedding blazer beacons in the ground to mark their way, the party explored further. They stopped when they found the skeletons of thousands and thousands of small-statured Onthos encircling a mound of tumbled trunks caked with powdery residue. "The Gardeners must have come here, knowing they were about to die," Anton said.

"They would have frozen or suffocated," Rod'h said. "Once their sun was snuffed out and the black sphere enclosed the solar system, they had no chance. But they all gathered here—I wonder why."

Anton approached the black mound and reached forward with a gloved hand. "These are boughs from the worldtrees—pieces of wood piled here." He rubbed with his gloves, looked at the black dust on his fingers. "It's nearly disintegrated now. These remnants are more fragile than the other trees. It reminds me of . . ." He drew in a quick, audible breath as the understanding came to him. "This was a *fire*—a gigantic bonfire." He stood up. "When their sun went out and night fell forever, the last of the Onthos must have gathered the dead worldtree wood, maybe even cutting down other trees. They created a huge bonfire. They must have been starving for any kind of light."

"And then they all died here," Gale'nh said.

Rod'h stepped away from the pile of cinders and shone his blazer on the frozen body of an Onthos. The creature lay with its sticklike hands up in the air, desperate for warmth and light. Its large eyes were like black marbles.

"Take specimens," he said. "Two bodies should be sufficient. Maybe we can learn something from them."

A message from the *Kutuzov* burst came through their suitcomms on the main septa channel. "Adar Zan'nh—we found something at the barrier. You'd better have a look."

Recovering remnants from the bonfire, Rod'h looked at his brother, whose face was pale behind the transparent faceplate. Gale'nh said, "We have seen enough here. It is as the Gardeners said—this world is devoid of life and light."

Once back aboard the flagship and heading for General Keah's coordinates, Gale'nh and Rod'h debriefed the Adar. Rememberer Anton displayed the images he had taken of the dark forest, the dead world.

Rod'h felt agitated and angry at what they had seen. "Now we know the shadows destroyed this star system, just as they attacked the Ildiran Empire long ago. We must learn how to defeat them!"

The Adar regarded him with a cool expression. "That is exactly what we're attempting to do."

The CDF Juggernaut was parked on the inner boundary of the Dyson sphere, where the Shana Rei englobement had swallowed the orbit of the system's lone gas giant. That planet was also now dead, cold, and dark.

In the command nucleus, General Keah's face appeared on the screen, looking both worried and annoyed. "I just received some very serious news, Z, through my green priest. Ulio Station is under attack by a shadow cloud and robot warships. It's devastating, and the bugbots aren't taking any prisoners."

"Are you suggesting that we depart and go fight for Ulio Station?" asked Adar Zan'nh. "We could not be effective."

Keah scowled. "There's no point. We're a minimum of five or six days out at top stardrive output. By then it'll be too late. Mr. Nadd has already lost contact with the green priest at Ulio, so the destruction may already be over. Telink messages have gone out to other CDF battleships, and there are at least ten Mantas on the way, but I doubt they'll arrive in time either."

Rod'h stewed, feeling helpless against the terrible enemy. That attack was happening *right now*. "Then if nothing else, we *need* to learn something vital here to take back with us."

They reached the dim gas giant just inside the black shell, and the *Kutuzov* cruised up on the curved obsidian barrier. "Follow us up here, Z. We only spotted these things because one of our scout Remoras almost crashed into one. Damn! Reminds me of a cluster of dead flies on a windowsill."

Adar Zan'nh used the ship's full scanners to actively map what General Keah had discovered: a cluster of gigantic diamond spheres, at least forty of them, each one adorned with pyramidal spikes. All of them were gray, lifeless, cold. They dwarfed both the warliner and the *Kutuzov*.

Rod'h had been young at the end of the Elemental War, but he remembered these horrifying objects.

Hydrogue warglobes.

General Keah said, "It looks like the Shana Rei are picking on more than just us. We're not the only ones in this fight."

CHAPTER

89

SHAREEN FITZKELLUM

Kotto Okiah's Big Ring out among the broiling nebula gases was nearly complete at last. Excitement built steadily among the construction workers. They all expected great things.

But Shareen and Howard continued to work on the small projects Kotto left for them. Shareen knew it was a great honor to serve under one of the greatest inventors of the past century, even just "everyday" inventions, but the giant project out in the nebula called to her. She wanted to be a part of *that*!

The bright spot was working beside Howard. She liked brainstorming with him, picking up on his ideas and racing to bring them to their logical conclusions. She had grown close to Howard as they tackled insurmountable problems, knowing there had to be a solution or Kotto would never have challenged them. And, sure enough, as they put their heads together, they sometimes reached simultaneous solutions so that they both laughed with delight. Once, she even gave him a brief hug, before breaking away in embarrassment. The second time, though, Shareen stopped being embarrassed.

Kotto entered the lab module, his curly hair tousled, his eyes wide and distracted, but he was grinning. "I finally got a chance to look at the designs you submitted yesterday. I'm pleased with everything you're learning. I can see I've taught you well." He let out an awkward chuckle. "Or, more accurately, you taught yourselves."

"Based on your ideas," Shareen said. "You helped us find the Guiding Star."

"We wanted to show you what we could do, sir," Howard said. "You are our mentor, and we decided to demonstrate our skills."

Kotto seemed very pleased. "Your solution to that filter-flow process was genius. You took the problem and the attendant difficulties, approached it from a different direction, and found a mathematical connection that I wouldn't have guessed."

"We were curious as to how you solved it originally, sir," Howard said. "Shareen and I tried six alternatives, and that was the only one that worked."

Kotto looked away. "I, um . . . to be honest, I've been working on that for some time now. I wasn't sure it could be solved."

Shareen couldn't believe it. "But, you're . . . Kotto Okiah."

"It wasn't a high priority," he said quickly. "I would have gotten around to it, but I thank you for saving me the work, so I could devote my mental energies to larger challenges. That's what assistants are for—and you two have done very well."

Shareen added, "The filter-flow process is ready for a prototype, and we could take it directly to market. You said if we made a working prototype—"

"Yes, yes I did—I will share the credit with you, if it works—and judging by your previous activities, how could it not work? A new filter-flow process!" He waffled, then said, "I'm so glad you solved it."

Shareen was shocked to see tears welling up in Kotto's brown eyes. Embarrassed, he turned away and hurried to the hatch of the lab chamber. "Sorry, I have a lot of work to do with the Big Ring. Keep up the good work."

Shareen watched him go. Working here at Fireheart Station, she realized she had grown smarter and more intuitive. She and Howard had figured out many solutions she would never have considered before. Howard vetted her wildly original ideas, and they presented the best ones to Kotto.

She went to the broad windowport and stared wistfully out at the gigantic torus under construction. Only a few more weeks, and the ring would be completed, the ends connected, all the power blocks activated to create an inward-curling magnetic field with a flux density greater than anything previously measured—or so Kotto thought.

"I wish we could be out there," she said. "Those other projects feel like tiny appetizers, and I want the main course, Howard. A big feast. We'll have time enough to solve smaller problems, but we both know what we've been waiting for."

Howard glanced over at the two research compies, saw they were busy calibrating a piece of crystal-fractionation equipment, and lowered his voice. "That's why I went out of my way to acquire the plans for the Big Ring. We can look at them together."

Shareen was so delighted she used the excuse to give him another hug. "Kotto didn't exactly give us another assignment, so we have to occupy ourselves somehow."

"Right." He gave her a sly smile and called up the records, blueprints, and design specifications for the enormous ring under construction. They didn't speak the name of the project aloud because the compies might tattle on them, but they immersed themselves in the intricacies of the Big Ring.

The electronic blueprints were incredibly detailed, but separated into dozens of independent sets for each construction team. Everyone needed to know their specific responsibilities, but no one, it seemed, was aware of the entire picture. No one but Kotto.

And now, Howard and Shareen were.

When they first arrived at Fireheart Station, these plans would have been incomprehensible to them, but since they had spent so much time sorting, arranging, and deciphering Kotto's cryptic notes, coded labels, and shorthand notations, they could absorb the vast design.

Shareen and Howard spent hours together pointing out connections, discussing the choices that Kotto had made, while trying to fathom parts of the Big Ring that seemed superfluous or, at the very least, needlessly cumbersome. She and Howard followed the thought processes of the great scientist's masterpiece, but after a while Shareen began to grow unsettled. She talked less.

They fell silent as they pored over the design, tracing circuit paths with their fingertips. Howard borrowed Shareen's pad, reran calculations, and returned to the blueprint. She had noticed the same thing and proofed the calculations a third time. Her own results matched Howard's, and neither of theirs reproduced what Kotto proposed. The two tried again and again to follow what he had been thinking, sure they must be missing something.

Finally, Shareen said what was on both of their minds. "I don't think it'll work—at least not the way Kotto expects."

Howard was more reluctant to say that aloud. "But we're just his apprentices. It isn't our place. We weren't even supposed to be reviewing the designs at all."

Shareen knew that, and now she realized why Kotto was so reluctant to show the full plans to anyone. Perhaps he had grave doubts as well.

CHAPTER

90

GARRISON REEVES

The rest of Fireheart Station was on pause—the isotope factories, the power-block stations, the energy-film farms, even the trading hub with its usual commercial traffic. Everything—and that meant *everything*—was devoted to the final stages of the Big Ring.

Garrison Reeves had joined the main construction crews, glad to have his name listed among so many others, and when he had time off-shift, he volunteered in the greenhouse dome and sent messages to Seth via the green priests. The boy sent excited messages back, talking about school, classmates, and especially the Teacher compies. Seth had even become friends with Arden Iswander. Garrison didn't particularly like the hard industrialist, but he could not let his grudge extend to his son as well.

He also sent more messages to Orli Covitz, but so far had received no response. Celli told him that the green priest Aelin—whom Garrison knew from the first Iswander extraction yard—had delivered the message to her at Ulio Station.

Garrison was alarmed. "Ulio? But they were just under attack."

Celli nodded solemnly. "Orli Covitz departed some time before the Shana Rei appeared, but we are certain that Aelin died in the attack. We don't know where Orli went, only that she was with Tasia Tamblyn and Robb Brindle."

He reassured himself that at least she was in good company, but he hoped he could find her. He was looking forward to seeing her again in just a few weeks. . . .

Working on the Big Ring project, or even just the everyday operations inside the nebula, Garrison remembered again what it meant to be a Roamer. Not the repressive "old ways" that Olaf Reeves had preached to his followers, but the real optimistic ingenuity of the clans, their ability to pull fresh ideas out of the most difficult situations.

In its final days, the Big Ring construction site was a hive of activity. Wearing an environment suit, Garrison used a heavy-hauler chariot to maneuver curved girders into place, while his teammates brought in anchor bolts, and others filled the gaps with thin integrity plates. Soon, they would connect the last segment of the torus.

For aesthetic reasons, Kotto Okiah had decided to enclose much of the framework with hull metal, although scientifically speaking, the framework itself should have been sufficient for the purposes of the experiment. Two weeks ago, Garrison had been part of a crew meeting where an exhausted team leader wanted to hear a justification for so much extra work, and Kotto had grown testy. "It's part of the design. On a project of this scale and this importance, we won't scrimp on details." The team leader withdrew his objection, although Garrison realized that the answer was not really an answer.

Every day the gap in the ring grew smaller and smaller, and every worker felt a sense of culmination of their work and an anticipation of the wonders of physics that Kotto would demonstrate.

Now, Garrison maneuvered the chariot-hauler into place, connecting another girder, which strung the top part of the ring gap with the bottom part. Scout pods and metal pallets hung in space, silhouetted against the colorful dazzle of the nebula. From his vantage, the remaining space to be enclosed in the ring structure looked huge, but the torus itself was so enormous that his eyes could barely grasp the curvature from where he drifted.

One more week . . . two at the most, and then they would all be there to watch the experiment take place.

CHAPTER 91

TASIA TAMBLYN

Tasia hoped this wouldn't turn out to be a wild-goose chase. The *Voracious Curiosity* had left Ulio Station days ago and cautiously followed the path of Elisa Enturi's ship, but they had no idea where they were going.

As they flew along, Tasia and Robb studied the course data, but the destinations made little sense, so they double-checked the coordinates on the charts. "There's nothing *there*!"

After OK had surreptitiously placed the tracker on Elisa's ship, the woman had traveled around the Spiral Arm in what seemed nothing more than aimless wanderings, before she eventually returned to Ulio, at which point the automated tracker had downloaded the information from her nav computer.

Connecting the dots and retracing Elisa's flight path should have led the *Voracious Curiosity* to wherever Lee Iswander was getting his stardrive fuel—another bloater cluster, presumably—but they just seemed to be retracing the aimless wanderings.

Though the mystery about the operations was frustrating, and Aelin's comments about the "slaughter" at the ekti site were ominous, Tasia was glad to be out flying with Robb, just like old times, and she enjoyed the company of Orli and DD, too. She decided to consider it sightseeing. With no green priest aboard, they had been out of contact with the rest of the Confederation since they left Ulio, so she would make the best of it.

Tasia had been brought up a Roamer, the youngest member of clan Tamblyn under the ice sheets of Plumas. She remembered the thrill, the danger, and her determination when she ran off to join the Earth Defense Forces, determined to battle the hydrogues that had killed her brother Ross. She already knew how to fly a spaceship—she was a Roamer, after all—and she had surpassed many of her fellow cadets, much to their annoyance.

In the EDF, she had also met Robb, and their lives were bound together through crises, through war, and then the aftermath of war. Their son Xander had been born aboard this ship, and they had flown together as traders for years, until Rlinda turned over all the "important work" to them.

But those footloose days were some of the best Tasia remembered, being with Robb as the parsecs rolled along. Cooping two people up in a ship is a good way to destroy a relationship, and it had certainly been rough at times, but they had gotten through it—stronger. And it had been fun.

With so much responsibility at Kett Shipping, sometimes Tasia forgot that. Rather than sitting at headquarters buried under administrative work, she preferred doing something useful. She chalked it up to her Roamer blood, although she wasn't sure *anybody* would rather sit at a desk than fly out and see the Spiral Arm. It was time to stretch her starship legs—and to figure out exactly how Iswander was producing his ekti-X. After all, they expected to be in business with him for a long time.

Now, two days out, she lounged in the cockpit of the *Curiosity*, comfortable and at home, but Orli Covitz was restless. She popped into the cockpit. "How long until we reach the first destination?"

"About an hour sooner than the last time you asked," Tasia said.

"Three hours and fifty-seven minutes from now," DD said after accessing the nav computer.

Tasia smiled. It was good to have a compy aboard again.

Robb said, "According to the downloaded records from the tracker probe, Elisa went to this spot, stayed less than two hours, then changed course and went somewhere else."

Tasia scanned the star charts, then empty space around them. "I doubt it was for the scenery."

"Maybe a dropoff point or a rendezvous?" Orli said. "Elisa Enturi isn't the type of person to wander aimlessly."

Before long, Tasia disengaged the Ildiran stardrive, and the *Curiosity* dropped into the general vicinity of the tracker coordinates and coasted without active sensors so they could approach cautiously.

"It's not even in a star system," Robb said. "What was Elisa doing out here?"

"Would you like me to provide a list of the closest stars and habitable planets?" DD offered.

"Not yet." Tasia leaned closer to the windowport.

"We're so far off the beaten path. . . ." Orli studied the screen, which showed only a scatter of distant stars. She suddenly brightened. "Extend your scans and look for bloaters."

Robb set their defensive screens and used passive sensors first so the *Curiosity* would remain undetected. "There's a large thermal signature ahead, but it's dissipated over a wide volume."

Tasia ran a double check. "No energy signatures, no industrial activity. No transmissions on any of the common bands, not even coded signals." She made a decision. "I'm risking a set of active scans. Who's going to detect us out here anyway?"

When the *Curiosity*'s sensor sweeps plowed ahead, they activated some kind of pinger, a signal pulsing with metronomic blips. Orli recognized it. "That's a distress beacon—an automated one. There's no voice transmission."

Robb powered up the *Curiosity*'s engines and accelerated forward. As a precaution, he increased power to the ship's shields and defensive weapons. Tasia manned the monitors, alert. DD and Orli crowded in the cockpit behind them.

The first thing they saw from the active-scan images was a diffuse scatter of bloaters, large gray-green sacks drifting along in the darkness like discarded balloons. "They're usually in a denser cluster than this," Orli said.

DD's optical sensors glowed. "Something may have happened to the core. The distress beacon is emanating from the approximate heart of where I project the bloater cluster would have been, based on the paths of these outliers."

Orli said, "This place reminds me of the Iswander extraction yards. Maybe this is one of his other sites."

Then they discovered the wreckage. Tasia stared at the spiraling hunks of debris with a mixture of amazement and horror. The thermal signature had mostly faded, but industrial junk was strewn everywhere: hull plates, tumbling engines, torn-apart superstructures, metal tanks, twisted machinery.

"Maybe Iswander had another industrial accident, like at Sheol." Tasia saw tattered, drifting husks of bloaters as well. She tried to imagine the firestorm that could have obliterated a large and ambitious complex like this. "A natural disaster? Human error? Or an outright attack?"

Robb altered the *Curiosity*'s course toward the distress beacon. "No life signs, but we've got to check it out."

They found the torn hulk of a large industrial tanker, which was more intact than the rest because of its original size. It looked as if a sledgehammer of a shock wave had ripped it open, and now it hung dark, cold, the corpse of a vessel.

"No life-support systems active," Tasia said. "Not detecting much residual atmosphere either. I doubt anybody's alive in there."

"The distress beacon must have been automated," Robb said.

"Maybe part of the bridge is intact enough for us to retrieve a log. Then we could find out what happened," Orli said. "We should at least check."

The *Curiosity* circled the larger ship, playing its inspection beacons over the hull plates below, and Tasia saw familiar clan markings. "This wasn't an Iswander operation—that's clan Duquesne."

"I didn't know the Duquesnes were working with the Iswanders," Robb said.

Tasia looked at the wreckage, drew a possible conclusion. "I'm not convinced this was an alliance."

While DD diligently mapped the debris field and tried to project how many structures had been destroyed in what must have been a spectacular chain reaction of exploding bloaters, Tasia and Robb suited up to go to the main tanker. While Orli and DD remained behind, the two of them used jetpacks to propel themselves from the lower hatch of the *Curiosity* to the battered vessel.

They entered through one of the gaping holes blown into the vessel, and once inside they worked their way from deck to deck, helmet lights shining as they kept in contact, watching out for each other. Their imagers sent video back to Orli and DD.

They encountered several bodies in Roamer jumpsuits wearing frozen expressions on their faces.

One of the connecting corridors was damaged, so Tasia and Robb had to retreat and find another route, but they eventually worked their way to the small control bridge. The tanker's high deck was damaged, its bridge windowport blasted in, the bulkheads ripped open. Any bodies that had been on the deck were gone, sucked out into the vacuum.

Robb anchored himself as he stared at the mangled remains of the bridge, but Tasia moved to the access stations, trying systems until she finally found a barely functional computer terminal.

"Found the log files. They're corrupted, but should be salvageable." She transmitted the logs directly to the *Curiosity* so Orli and DD could begin repairing and decrypting them. "All right, that's what we came for—no need to overstay our welcome."

"I agree," Robb said. "Let's get back."

Once they were aboard the *Curiosity*, they shucked out of their suits and made their way to the cockpit, where they found Orli Covitz looking pale and stunned. Even DD seemed agitated.

"You both better watch this for yourselves," Orli said and began playing the log on the main cockpit screen. "This wasn't a cooperative operation between clan Duquesne and Iswander Industries. And Elisa Enturi did not come for a friendly visit."

On the automated bridge log, Aaron Duquesne was in a shouting match with Elisa Enturi, who had come in a small armed ship. They listened to a heated exchange. Elisa's voice was like a razor. "Lee Iswander doesn't need to tolerate your competition."

"And what are you going to do about it, bitch?" Duquesne said.

Then Elisa opened fire, targeting one of the bloaters. Her ship accelerated away, retreating at full velocity. The Duquesne log entry winked out as the ekti-filled nodules ignited and a hurricane of fire ripped through the entire extraction yard. . . .

Tasia and Robb just stared. "She wiped out the whole operation! Elisa knew exactly what would happen if she ignited a bloater," Orli said, sounding sick. "She murdered all those people. That was . . . Seth's mother!"

Tasia stared at the screen, then looked at Robb as her stomach knotted again. "And our son is her business partner."

DD spoke in an oddly energetic voice. "This is just the first destination the automated tracker recorded. If we follow her to the next set of coordinates, maybe we can learn more."

"Or die." Tasia dreaded knowing what else Elisa had done, but they really didn't have any choice. The *Curiosity* had to go there. "Setting course now."

CHAPTER

92

XANDER BRINDLE

When the *Verne* finally limped back to Earth after escaping from Ulio Station, Xander guided the battered ship into orbit, then carefully headed down to Kett Shipping Headquarters.

Having been born after the end of the Elemental War, Xander had never experienced the appalling destruction caused by the hydrogues and the faeros. But seeing what the Shana Rei and the black robots had done at Ulio Station made him understand what those horrific days must have been like.

As they wobbled down through Earth's atmosphere, Terry had to bypass several control systems that failed. The *Verne* shuddered, barely holding itself together, and Xander knew the ship was going to be in the hangar for months of repairs. They had not wanted to stop anywhere en route, convinced that they had to inform his parents and Rlinda Kett what had happened. Ulio Station was one of Kett Shipping's important distribution points, and Xander was certain that several company traders had been killed in the black robot attack.

When they came to a rough landing in the main repair hangar, a dozen astonished maintenance techs came forward to stare at the burn scars, the misaligned hull plates.

One man whistled loudly. "Can't believe you all survived that."

While OK helped Terry, Xander stepped down the ramp, put his hands on his hips, and turned with just a hint of cockiness. "It was a close thing, but we're skilled pilots." Then, for the first time, he actually looked at the dramatic damage to the *Verne*, and he felt dizzy. Fingernails of ice ran down his spine. It had been a very close thing indeed.

Rlinda Kett strolled into the hangar and stopped to stare at the *Verne*. "What did you do to my ship?"

"I thought it was *our* ship," Terry said.

"Under license. And you can pay for—" Then she started blubbering. Tears poured down her face, and she lurched forward to sweep both Terry and Xander up in one of her enormous hugs. "I'm so glad you're safe. I was absolutely terrified for you as soon as we learned what happened to Ulio."

"We came straight here," Xander said. "You already know Ulio Station was overrun by the Shana Rei and black robot ships?"

Rlinda sniffed, wiped her eyes, and nodded heavily. "A green priest on the station sent out reports while it was under attack. Then the green priest—let's just say there were no more updates."

OK said, "We have our ship's log showing the last moments of Ulio and how we escaped. Would you like to see them?"

Rlinda looked around the hangar. "Yes, we can use the wallscreens. Everybody needs to know. Let's project it here."

Xander looked around. "Are my parents here? They need to know, too."

Rlinda shook her head. "They haven't come back yet from trying to track down Elisa Enturi."

The compy rigged the ship's log so it could be played on the wallscreens. Xander watched with a sense of dread. He had lived through the events, but he'd been adrenaline-blinded at the time and wasn't sure he remembered many details.

Rlinda stood with a hand resting gently on Xander's shoulder and another on Terry's. The images showed the *Verne* breaking away from the main station, heading out among all the other evacuating ships. The *Verne* shot away as the black robot attackers continued to harass the station, blowing up docked ships, habitation quarters, hunting down and destroying helpless vessels, then swooping after another target.

In the hangar, the shocked techs let out gasps, moans, and curses in a range of dialects, but no one seemed to have appropriate words. They all just stared.

Finally, Rlinda said, "This is appalling."

Xander watched as if the events had happened to someone else. The *Verne* raced away from Ulio, dodging, diving. Terry and Xander were at the controls, pilot and copilot. They had both been so attuned, so tense, they seemed to have one mind. OK had linked up to the

Verne's defenses, his polymer fingers flying over controls as he readjusted their shields and diverted power as the robots chased after them. Much of the backbone of Ulio Station was in flames venting atmosphere and bodies.

Two black robot ships were close on the *Verne*'s tail. Terry accelerated, sweating, while Xander dodged. Then, over the general comm, came a loud and heart-wrenching distress call. "—one hundred innocent women and children with me here. We're helpless. Please don't let the black robots come after us."

Sensing more satisfying prey, the black robots veered off to murder an easier target, converging on the distress signal.

"Those bastards," Rlinda said.

Xander remembered hearing that transmission, but they had been punching the stardrive, barely evading attack, and could do nothing to help all those desperate refugees. But now that he listened again, he thought the voice sounded familiar. It was a male voice with a native Theron accent. Xander blinked. "That's the green priest—the one who brought Orli a message when we were having lunch at Ulio Station."

Terry concentrated. "I think you're right."

Xander flashed a grim grin at the audience. "The robot ships converged at the coordinates of the distress signal—but it was actually Ulio's ekti-X stockpile. There weren't any stranded women and children there—just a lot of explosive stardrive fuel, and when the robots fired on it . . ." The *Verne*'s log images showed only part of the explosion, because OK had activated the stardrive and the ship flashed away to safety. "By the Guiding Star, it was a setup!"

"So much for your fabulous fortune, Terry," Xander said. "What Maria Ulio kept at the station was priceless. But I guess we're back to square one."

"We didn't lose everything," Terry said. "We still have our lives."

Rlinda said, "That'll do."

CHAPTER

93

EXXOS

The Shana Rei reveled in the obliteration of Ulio Station, and that victory kept the black robots alive. Eradicating the busy complex was a triumph of chaos erasing order. But the unexpected losses Exxos had suffered!

Ninety of his precious robots—all of them thankfully backed up—had been lured to destruction by one desperate human. Ninety! That disrupted his calculations. It was a terrible setback to his larger plans.

Nevertheless the destruction they had caused at Ulio gave him satisfaction. Realigning his thoughts to the new paradigm, he decided to convince the Shana Rei to continue on that course and raise the destruction to a much grander scale.

But he simply could not afford to lose more robots. There were so many planets and populations to wipe out. Losing ninety robots in one action was unacceptable.

"We understand now," said one of the pulsing shadow blots. "We see what your robots intend to do, but you do not understand the scope of our enemies. The complete task is beyond your conception."

Exxos was offended. "And yet we will proceed, step by step, and annihilate human civilization, the Ildiran Empire, the verdani mind, and everything that causes you such pain."

"Your victories are ambitious, but unrealistic," said another inkblot, and the creatures of darkness closed in on the group of robots drifting in the aimless void. "Even if you destroyed every single lifeform, you are not strong enough to annihilate eternity's mind. And it is awakening."

In his deepest programming, Exxos was more concerned with

destroying the *Shana Rei* after the extinction of humans and Ildirans. "You presented us with this fight," he said. "You enlisted us in your struggle against order and structure, and we refuse to stop fighting. Do you wish to surrender?"

The inkblots were silent, their darkness intensifying, then they spoke. "Surrender is a foreign concept."

"Then you must endure, and you must sacrifice—just as we have sacrificed. Give us the ships and weapons we require. More than ever before."

The inkblots swarmed closer, and Exxos feared he had pushed them too hard, and they could well retaliate by dismantling more robots down to atoms. Instead, the shadows said, "Define what you need."

Exxos ran quick calculations. He could not afford to lose more robots. "We require invincible warships, larger vessels that wield greater power. We can cause more destruction, just as we did at Ulio Station." He amplified his voice. "But you must create the ships for us, no matter how much pain it causes. You need to manifest the material."

Creating the dark structural matter caused the Shana Rei such agony that he was convinced they would refuse him. Nevertheless, he demanded it. He wanted to see how much it would weaken them.

"We cannot tolerate the agony that would be required to manifest as much material as you request," said the nearest shadow blot. "But the material already exists, an inexhaustible supply of dense black matter that we crafted into existence millennia ago. We already endured the pain of creation when it was locked into this universe."

"What material is it?" Exxos asked.

"We manifested that matter when we were stronger, when a single victory against one race, the Onthos, and the core of the worldforest mattered more than anything. We englobed and smothered a star system. All that material remains. We can go there, use it again. And create exactly what you need."

Exxos had not expected this. His crimson optical sensors brightened, and the rest of the surviving robots were thrumming. "We will have the material for as many battleships as we request?"

"That, and much more. Your robots will have the tools to keep blotting out organic worlds. We will go there. Now."

The shadow cloud enfolded them, and the Shana Rei plunged out of existence, traveling behind dimensions, until they reemerged into the real universe.

CHAPTER

94

ELISA ENTURI

Elisa returned to the extraction yards after her roundabout trip, always happy to be back, if only briefly. These operations were entirely cut off from the rest of the Spiral Arm, as if they existed in their own universe. Elisa was happy to keep it that way in order to protect Iswander Industries.

The clumsy efforts of clan Duquesne would no longer threaten their ekti-X production. With such a small and newly established facility, she doubted the Duquesnes had had time to spread the word, even among their own clan. If someone else knew about the operations, then another rival extraction field would spring up, and another. The thought wearied her.

The bloaters were growing more and more common, though, and sooner or later someone else might accidentally figure out what they contained—just as she had. By silencing the Duquesnes, Elisa had bought them time, and she did not regret what she had done in order to protect Iswander Industries . . . at least for a little while longer.

Lee Iswander had returned from his journey to Newstation and Theroc. Elisa didn't quite understand why he had been so generous as to deliver all of the Onthos plague data, but she supposed that it served as goodwill. Iswander Industries had no aspirations to delve into medical research, so why not earn capital on an investment that cost them nothing? That was probably how he thought about it. Elisa resented the source of that data, though: Orli Covitz, as she was supposedly dying from the plague. And then that woman had flown off with Garrison and her son! To Elisa, the database was tainted.

Iswander got back to work in the extraction operations, glad that everything had run smoothly in his absence. "Londa will be content for a while," Iswander told her, sounding relieved. "Reassured that Arden is safe and happy at Academ, although just seeing him probably made her miss the boy all the more. I expect I'll be taking many more trips to Newstation than I had previously." The tone of his voice changed. "At least that way I can watch Sam Ricks make everything fall apart due to his incompetence." Intense, he had gone off to work on a private project, one that he would not tell even her about.

Several days later, when Iswander called her for a private debriefing, she could tell he was troubled by something. He closed the door of the conference room, set his datapad on the table, and activated his files for her to see. He was obviously struggling to keep himself calm as he reviewed his notes. "That man insulted me, and I have decided not to let it pass."

Elisa listened, concerned, and he related to her the snide and vengeful incompetence of Speaker Sam Ricks. "That's the real reason I went to Theroc after meeting with him. That's why the goodwill gesture of giving away the Onthos data was so important. The King and Queen are vastly more important than the Speaker for the clans."

Elisa felt identical anger on his behalf. "You will oust him. Given enough power and wealth, you'll easily dominate the clans. By the next Speaker election, Ricks's own failings will be more obvious than they are now. They must know their mistake already."

"I would prefer to overthrow him sooner rather than later—and doing so just takes a little research by a clever person," Iswander said. "Before I left Newstation, I collected all their records, even confidential information from the clans, administrative filings and details of Ricks's daily schedule. It had all the clues I needed."

Elisa had thought the vast profits generated from ekti-X would make Iswander feel whole again, but now he was thinking of a much larger picture. She had never sought the limelight for herself, but she understood his hunger for respectability.

"I've been doing detailed research for days, combing through records, making connections. I can assure you that Sam Ricks is a shifty man, but not a clever one. He's not very good at being corrupt." Iswander smiled.

"Ricks has a pattern of appointing people from his own clan and then increasing their salaries far beyond their predecessors." He shook his head. "I have an airtight case, and I'll soon be heading back to Newstation to present this. I can expose Ricks, and then I'll step into his place."

She got the impression that if that happened, he wouldn't necessarily care about the ekti-X anymore. Elisa wondered if he would promote her to be manager of the extraction operations, and she decided, yes, that would be fine. After all, she had spilled enough blood to protect them—and recently, although she kept that information from him. She wanted to earn his pride and appreciation, although she had already done so many times over.

He looked up at her. "You just came from Ulio Station?"

"Some time ago, I had . . . other destinations." How she longed to tell Iswander what she had done for him, so he could thank her for it and know how loyal she was, but she remained content with the private knowledge. "You can present your case, sir. They won't be able to deny the evidence."

Iswander nodded, not asking for details. "Oh, I saw your son at Academ. Seth—he was taking classes with the other Roamer children. Garrison must have enrolled him in the school again. At least now you know where he is."

Elisa flinched, but she gave him a cool nod. "Yes sir."

He reviewed his files one more time, then closed down the documents. "Make sure that my vessel has a full tank of stardrive fuel. I don't intend to waste any time—I know I just got here, but I'm going back to Newstation with my evidence."

"I've always envisioned you as Speaker Iswander, sir. You'll change the Roamers, force them into the present. It will be an admirable thing."

He smiled at her. "Thank you, Elisa." He seemed about to say something else, but then just nodded and gathered his records.

CHAPTER 95

MAGE-IMPERATOR JORA'H

It was a rare day on Ildira when all seven suns shone high in the sky at the same time, filling the air with dazzling, pure light. But Jora'h knew there was a darkness out there beyond those suns . . . and also, he feared, a darkness inside himself, a darkness inside the Ildiran race.

On a high deck of the Prism Palace's tallest minaret, the Mage-Imperator sat surrounded by busy attender kithmen who plumped cushions and brought unnecessary refreshments. They arranged exotic flowers, erected awnings, strung colorful ribbons. Service was an attender's purpose in life, and, as their Mage-Imperator, Jora'h had to let them serve him.

Brawny guard kithmen encircled the solar deck, ready against any outside threat, but also looking warily at one another in case shadows boiled up inside one of them. The guards had all been commanded to protect Prime Designate Daro'h with as much vehemence as they would protect the Mage-Imperator.

Now, Daro'h joined his father in the bright light so they could both absorb the purifying sunshine. In times of peace, a Prime Designate would have decades of a blissful hedonistic life, enjoying the pleasures of his status before he was forced to become Mage-Imperator. With the unexpected threat of the Shana Rei, though, Daro'h was forced to carry a greater weight than he had anticipated. The Prime Designate seemed edgy and intimidated, just as the guards were tense and wary. Jora'h understood why.

They were all concerned about the same man—a ticking time bomb in their midst.

The mad Designate finally arrived, stepping through a crystalline arch at the top of the minaret. Daro'h flinched, and his skin paled; Jora'h sat straighter in his regal chair, and showed no fear.

Rusa'h was gaunt, but appeared as hard and straight as an iron rod. The guards held their weapons ready, but the man ignored them. He stepped up to the Mage-Imperator and the Prime Designate and faced them for a long moment before placing a fist to his sternum in the traditional sign of respect. It seemed almost a lazy gesture for him. "Liege, there are important matters we must discuss. We both know it."

Oblivious to the tension between these men, attender kithmen offered Rusa'h the same array of colorful refreshments, which he also ignored.

Jora'h drew out the tense silence as he faced the man who had sought to destroy the Ildiran Empire, the man who had set Mijistra aflame. "Sit down," the Mage-Imperator said.

Rusa'h obeyed. He let out a disappointed sound. "We have all heard the news of Ulio Station, and there are probably other Shana Rei attacks we do not know about. They will continue to destroy us." He held his words, then said, "I see that I must remind you of history and of your obligation."

"I need no reminders from you, Rusa'h."

"And yet, you compel me to speak. I saw the destruction our enemies inflicted at the Hiltos shrine. We have received reports from the green priest about what Adar Zan'nh discovered at the Onthos home system. What would prevent the shadows from englobing Ildira the way they exterminated that system? We cannot fight the Shana Rei with our current capabilities, any more than the Ildiran Empire could defeat them the last time they preyed upon us. Not alone."

The Mage-Imperator said, "We are not helpless. We have laser cannons. We have sun bombs. We have our alliance with the Confederation Defense Forces, and they have promised to provide even more powerful sun bombs."

"Insignificant and insufficient," Rusa'h said. "You know it, brother. *Liege*. In ancient times, Mage-Imperator Xiba'h also understood the stakes. He made a terrible, difficult choice—and saved the Empire."

Prime Designate Daro'h frowned. "Mage-Imperator Xiba'h? Is he the one who—?"

Jora'h kept his gaze locked with his half-brother's. "That is not an acceptable alternative. And the faeros are not acceptable allies. Osira'h and Rod'h already tried to convince them. They will not fight with us. They are afraid of the Shana Rei."

"A Mage-Imperator should not be afraid to pay a price to save his people!"

Jora'h did not respond with anger, but kept his voice cool. "It is not the immolation that I fear. It is the alliance with the faeros, who have already proved to be nearly as destructive as the Shana Rei."

The mad Designate was not swayed. "And what about the shadows inside all of us? Ildiran sun bombs and laser cannons have no effect on that."

Jora'h suspected the insidious darkness had woven its way through the *thism* strands that connected to him. Perhaps the only way to cleanse that was with fire and light. If he did set himself aflame in a spectacular bonfire, his agony might be sufficient to wrench the attention of the faeros. Could that in itself be enough to purge the shadows from the Ildiran race?

Probably not.

And there was no guarantee the faeros would help the Empire, rather than destroy it.

Even as he sat on top of the Prism Palace drenched in bright sunlight, Jora'h still felt—or imagined?—the shadow inside him. Maybe one day he would be driven to sufficient despair that he would be willing to do anything, take any chance, to cleanse that darkness.

But not today . . .

CHAPTER

96

ADAR ZAN'NH

After a week at the englobed Onthos system, Adar Zan'nh decided that the research teams had gathered sufficient information, and he was anxious to return to Ildira. The horrific attack on Ulio Station worried him. It seemed far more ambitious and destructive than the Shana Rei strike on the small Hiltos shrine. What if it was the start of an expanded war on the Spiral Arm?

The impenetrable black sphere made his Solar Navy crew very uneasy, demonstrating an inconceivable power. This absolute Shana Rei victory over the Onthos race and an entire star system made Zan'nh realize that their enemy was even more deadly than the hydrogues and faeros from the Elemental War.

After the ships finished exploring the interior of the gigantic shell, they found their way back to the small opening they had blasted through the hexagonal black plates. As the warliner and the *Kutuzov* approached the opening, the darkness of normal space appeared bright because of its scattering of stars.

After exploring the dead Onthos planet, Rod'h and Gale'nh were galvanized, and the Adar was pleased that Tal Gale'nh was confident enough to shoulder leadership responsibilities again. To demonstrate his confidence, Zan'nh granted Gale'nh command of one of the warliners in the septa. The tal was at first taken aback by the reward, then straightened with determination. The Adar thought he saw a glint in the young man's eye. Gale'nh accepted the transfer of command with grace, and Rod'h formally requested permission to join his brother aboard his new ship.

Zan'nh considered. "If that would be acceptable to you, Tal Gale'nh?"

"It is."

After his flagship emerged into unconfined space again, Zan'nh stared in wonder at the infinity of stars. The universe had never seemed so bright. He experienced a collective sigh among his Solar Navy soldiers, like a rejuvenation of the combined *thism*.

Meanwhile, the rest of the warliners that had continued to explore the outer Dyson sphere in greater detail had discovered an important artifact drifting loose high above the obsidian shell. Over numerous centuries, it had floated away, but a careful combing of nearby space had spotted it. The relic was as chilling and as fascinating as the dead hydrogue warglobes they had found trapped inside.

Septar Dre'nh transmitted to the flagship, "Adar, we have found a verdani battleship. It appears to be very ancient, very large. It is lifeless."

General Keah broke in on the command channel. "I was ready to go home, Z, but we should have a look."

All eight ships rendezvoused high above the Dyson sphere, converging on the verdani battleship, a huge organic craft created from an uprooted worldtree in a symbiotic relationship with wental water. Deep inside the heartwood, an ancient pilot—one of the Gardeners, surely—would have fused his body to guide the hybrid ship.

Skeletal boughs sprawled outward, great thorny arms large enough to embrace an asteroid. Its primary trunk was an armored cylinder bigger than several warliners.

"That one's larger than any of the newer verdani battleships currently orbiting Theroc," General Keah transmitted. "I'm glad the verdani are on our side. I wouldn't want to go up against that thing."

"Even that gigantic ship lost its battle with the Shana Rei," Zan'nh pointed out.

Tal Gale'nh transmitted from his new command nucleus. "Adar, my brother wishes to take a scout ship and collect samples. It could be useful information. Theroc will certainly want to know."

The Adar's brow furrowed. "I can send an entire team, along with guards."

Rod'h appeared on the screen beside his pale half-brother. He spoke with an edge to his voice. "I can do this more quickly and efficiently than a large group, Adar. I'll be back within several hours, before you could even put together a larger expedition."

General Keah chuckled over the comm. "I wouldn't disagree with him, Z."

Rod'h didn't seem to be asking permission, and Adar Zan'nh had unclear authority over Nira's other halfbreed son, who was not part of the Solar Navy. "Be cautious, Rod'h," he said, to give the appearance of assent.

As if to prove how fast he could move, Rod'h's scout vessel emerged from the warliner's launching bay in less than half an hour and darted toward the briar patch of threatening branches. He transmitted images as he flew along. "This is massive—and impressive. If the verdani could create hundreds more of these, they would be tremendous allies."

In the flagship's command nucleus, the Adar continued to watch the screen as Rod'h flew his tortuous path. The mammoth verdani warship was breathtaking.

The screen flickered, and General Keah's face overrode the scout ship's images. "Z, something's going on out here! You better have a look—we've got company."

At the same time, alarms came in from the other warliners. The panoply of stars that had looked so vibrant now shimmered, distorting one large patch. A slice of black darker than the rest of the universe opened up, and a roiling smoke of shadows emerged. The inky cloud swelled and swelled.

Zan'nh shouted across all comm circuits. "Battle stations! Activate weapons systems. Prepare our sun bombs." He drew a breath. "This is going to be a fight."

General Keah responded, "You got that right, Z."

The shadow cloud blossomed like petals of night, and titanic Shana Rei hex ships slid out of their twisted dimension and loomed above the star system they had already swallowed.

Zan'nh had no idea what the creatures of darkness wanted here, but he had no intention of letting them have it. He would fight back.

On the comm, Keah actually sounded eager for the confrontation. "Ready when you are, Z."

"I am ready now, General. Prepare to attack."

CHAPTER

97

GENERAL NALANI KEAH

General Keah hadn't expected to fight a battle in a dead system out in the middle of nowhere, but she was ready for it. "About damn time." She turned to her weapons officer. "Mr. Patton, time to prove the CDF's investment in your training was worthwhile."

The gigantic hex cylinders emerged from the shadow cloud like objects from a nightmare toolbox, thrusting into real space above the black Dyson sphere.

Her comm officer split the screen so Keah could address Adar Zan'nh while maintaining her watch on the Shana Rei. "Every second we delay is a second that we could be opening fire, Z. Unless you plan to talk with those things, I say we hit them with everything we've got." Their best shot was to hit first and hit hard, and worry about justifications later on when doing the paperwork. "No warnings, no negotiations. Why dink around with half-measures?"

"I concur completely, General. I have already given battle orders to the entire septa."

Keah hunched forward in her command chair and spoke to the bridge crew, letting them see her half smile. "Not to put too fine a point on it, but I'm anxious to use up some of our old sun bombs—Dr. Krieger will get us more once we're back home. Set a course directly toward the shadow cloud, Mr. Tait." The *Kutuzov* pulled ahead of the Ildiran warliners. She thought of it as leading the charge, rather than presenting herself as cannon fodder. "Give me a full sensor sweep."

Lieutenant Saliba rushed to provide the requested data. Weapons techs brought the laser-cannon batteries online, preparing for a constant, sequential recharge as they had done in a thousand drills. In a full-scale engagement, the cannons would be depleted faster than they could be recharged.

On the weapons decks, tactical crews scrambled to load in the arsenal of sun bombs. Keah wished even more fervently that she had the new enhanced weapons, after what she had witnessed in the rings of Saturn, but the original Ildiran devices packed a hell of a punch anyway.

Keah glanced at the nervous green priest, who clung to his treeling. "Mr. Nadd, I'll rely on you to send reports back home. Let Theroc know . . . whatever happens."

Nadd swallowed hard. "I will do my best."

"Mr. Tait, prepare for evasive maneuvers and conventional weapons as soon as the bugbot ships show up—and you know they're going to. They'll harass us like mosquitoes in a swamp."

The *Kutuzov* charged toward the monstrous-looking Shana Rei ships. The seven warliners followed close behind.

Saliba enhanced the image. "General . . . still no sign of robot ships."

Keah was puzzled. "But they always use bugbots to do their dirty work."

As the ships closed in, entropy waves from the Shana Rei began to scramble their targeting computers. Lights flickered on the *Kutuzov*'s bridge. "Better open fire while we still can, but don't rely on targeting computers—use manual systems when you have to."

"You got it, General," said Patton. "If we can't hit a target that big, then we'd better go back to basic training."

Keah nodded. "Point and shoot."

The first laser-cannon barrage tore across the flat side of one of the hex cylinders, slicing through the solid black material like a knife gutting a fish filled with smoke. Static burst across the comm lines like an angry cry of disruption. The nearest Shana Rei ship began to turn, as if reeling away.

Keah liked that.

The Solar Navy warliners added their laser cannons to the bombardment, and the hex cylinders shuddered. Large sections of obsidian material flaked away, the same flat plates that had assembled to form the nightshade over Theroc—the same type of material that formed the black Dyson sphere around the Onthos system.

"Score!" Patton yelled. The rest of the bridge crew hooted and cheered.

Keah smiled. "What are you waiting for, Mr. Patton? We've got a lot more damage to do."

Her weapons officer launched another laser fusillade, surprising her with how much damage he inflicted on the Shana Rei. "We don't normally catch the shadows with their pants down like that. What—" She caught her breath. "Ah, they weren't expecting to find us here at all!"

She contacted the Solar Navy flagship with her urgent realization. "Z, the shadows must have come here for their own reasons. They weren't planning on a battle. That's why they haven't launched any robot fighters." Keah needed to take advantage of how much her crew was itching for a fight. "Good thing *we're* prepared."

Then a ripple of unseen energy emanated from the hex cylinder, a shock wave that scrambled the *Kutuzov*'s command systems and life support. The bridge went completely dark until the backup systems kicked on.

The Shana Rei craft began to move, all four of them spreading out. The damaged one shrank in, as if consolidating its remaining material, but the other hexagons sent out waves of disruptive entropy. A Solar Navy warliner reeled off course, its systems failing, its running lights falling dark.

General Keah intended to take advantage of every last second. "Time for a few sun bombs. Lieutenant Kalfas, make sure you record all this. Hell, I will personally give Dr. Krieger a bonus for every Shana Rei hex ship we destroy, even if these are the old designs."

The Juggernaut launched three crackling sun bombs—spheres of knotted, pinwheeling plasma. The core reactions built up, energy intensifying.

Not to be outdone, four Ildiran warliners also launched sun bombs. Keah watched the fiery streaks plunge in just like the meteor shower she and Deputy Eldred Cain had observed from the deck of his home on Earth.

General Keah much preferred this particular show.

"Boom," she whispered.

The *Kutuzov*'s sun bombs ignited against the black vessels like a trio of supernovas. Just as the incandescent nuclear eruptions blotted out the main screen, she caught a last glimpse of four other novas striking different parts of the Shana Rei cylinders. With the sensors flash-blinded, everyone on the Juggernaut's bridge held their breath. All comm signals were disrupted by the backwash of the sun-bomb explosions. The screens remained washed out, fuzzed with static.

"Mr. Saliba, get me sensors at the soonest possible nanosecond. Let's see how much damage we caused."

"Working, General. Sensor suites were already reeling from that entropy barrage and now they're oversaturated. I should have them back online momentarily."

Keah knotted her hands into fists, waiting, staring at the screen and *willing* it to clear. Finally, she saw the distorted image of the shadow cloud, and then an angular edge. The hex ships again—noticeably damaged. One of the hexagons was diminished by half, as if the sun bombs had devoured the dark material. Another cylinder was tilted at an odd angle, as if knocked out of alignment from the cluster of allied hex ships.

Another wave of dark entropy rippled out from the shadow cloud in a broad scattershot, perhaps a knee-jerk defensive reaction that did not target any particular ship. Even so, the *Kutuzov*'s main screen stuttered, went black, then images resolved out of the static. When the screen sharpened again, she spotted a flurry of motion near the tilted black hexagon—a wave of predatory black ships emerging from the core of darkness.

"Here come the bugbots, late to the party," said Keah. "This is about to get even more interesting."

CHAPTER

98

PRINCE REYN

After the first several days in the sanctuary domes on Kuivahr, Prince Reynald began to experience a strange emotion—something he identified as *hope*. Osira'h was dogged in her belief that if human medical researchers couldn't cure him, then surely Ildiran doctors could. And she had complete faith in her sister.

Tamo'l and her medical team experimented—on him—with the rare kelp extracts provided by the Kellum distillery. Reyn braced himself and did what he needed to do. He considered how much his parents had invested in chasing any desperate chance for a treatment, and he thought of the promises he had made to Arita. He had to do his part, even if it made him feel like a lab rat.

Osira'h was beside him, as she always was, while he prepared to endure another round of tests. Reyn knew this wasn't going to be pleasant, but he would not complain. He would *hope*.

Tamo'l tried any variants she thought might be effective. The kelp strains were rare, mutations appearing as the Kuivahr tides shifted and changed, and even if they did find a strain that offered remarkable relief for his worsening condition, the particular strain might never occur naturally again.

When he suffered from side effects of the test treatments, Osira'h seemed to experience the pain as much as Reyn did. When he saw the tears shimmering in her eyes, he felt sorry for her, wanted to endure the trials alone—but she would hear none of that. Reyn was envious when he saw the sheer *fight* in her expression. She set the bar high for him, and Reyn met it—for her.

Today, Tamo'l came to him with several different vials, new concoctions that she had worked up. "We learned a great deal from your adverse reactions last time. I am sorry you had to endure such discomfort, but this formulation should be better. I can't promise that, but I believe so."

During the last two tests, a fiery rash had raged across his skin, leaving patterns of tiny blisters that made him itch ferociously and a fever that caused a pounding headache. It wasn't a cure—it wasn't even a viable treatment—but it was a *clue*, and it gave Tamo'l ideas on a new formulation to try.

And Reyn would submit to the trials, endure the side effects—and he would hope, as Osira'h insisted.

Tamo'l held out three vials for him to see. "Different choices, Reynald. Different formulations from the most effective strains, and I will be honest—I have no idea which variant might be better or worse. You choose."

He thought again of the rash, the fever, the headaches. Osira'h squeezed his shoulder, encouraging him. He thought about deferring the choice to her, but he stopped himself. If the formulation caused another severe reaction, he didn't want Osira'h to blame herself.

"At least now I have a choice, thanks to you, Tamo'l." Reyn pointed to the middle vial.

She gave a brisk nod and injected him with the sample. Reyn steeled himself for whatever might come. He had a feeling it would be a rough night.

Before he could feel sorry for himself, though, Shawn Fennis wheeled in one of the misbreeds who was moist and shivering on top of a gurney. He recognized the one called Pol'ux.

Tamo'l had made a point of introducing each of the misbreeds by name when he arrived here. After his initial shock at seeing the mutated misbreeds, Reyn had realized that they were just as curious about *him*. Looking at their misshapen bodies, the organs that didn't function properly, the mismatched limbs, the asymmetric facial features, he saw how these misbreeds clung to life and fought for every day. They had endured their infirmities for more than twenty years, and yet they still dreamed of accomplishing something with their lives. They were *optimistic*—and that was a lesson for Reyn.

Pol'ux was bedridden much of the time, and now he hissed in pain when Fennis bumped the gurney. The misbreed's gray-tan skin was a mass of boils, many as large as Reyn's hand. His face, his shoulders, his arms, all looked as if they might burst; some of the flesh membrane had already split, oozing fluids.

Despite his obvious agony, Pol'ux lifted his head. "Prince Reynald . . . sorry to disturb you. I am honored."

Tamo'l attached monitors to Reyn's skin, but he glanced over at the misbreed. "You should take care of him."

Pol'ux said, "Let her finish—I have done this many times before."

Tamo'l explained, "Pol'ux suffers extreme allergic reactions to virtually all of the foods he can digest. He has to eat, but eating does this to him. It is something he has endured all his life."

Pol'ux shifted on his gurney. "Tamo'l drains my blisters, and then I have mobility again for a day or so. I enjoy the time I have—it could be worse."

While Tamo'l finished with Prince Reyn, Shawn Fennis set about draining the misbreed's largest blisters, siphoning off the oozing fluid and relieving the pressure on his skin.

Pol'ux lay back and endured it; his blistered lips even smiled. "Tamo'l will find a cure for you, Prince Reynald. I know she will. No one is more dedicated to helping people than she is."

Reyn felt a weight on his heart as he saw how stoic the misbreed remained even in the face of such horrific suffering. He lay back without complaint throughout the draining of his pustules.

Feeling great admiration, Reyn told Tamo'l he would accept as many tests as she needed to do.

CHAPTER 99

ZOE ALAKIS

Years ago, Zoe had withdrawn from human society and barricaded herself behind protective walls on Pergamus. For the first half of her life, she had been exposed to countless dangers, infections, and insidious microorganisms; once sheltered in her sterile dome, though, she had never intended to emerge.

But when Tom Rom was dying from the Onthos plague, Zoe had not been able to tolerate being apart from him. He had contracted the disease while on a mission *for her*, and she could not let him die alone. In that extreme crisis, Zoe had faced her fear and left the sterile dome for the first time in years. Though terrified with every breath she inhaled, every surface she touched, she had survived that ordeal. And it had been worth the risk just to clasp Tom Rom's hand when he recovered.

Afterward, she retreated to her dome, reduced to cold shudders, vowing she would never leave that safe womb again.

But, now she had to, or risk losing it all. Pergamus was exposed, and she was going on the offensive. Zoe would set the rules and define her future relationship with the King and Queen. If she waited for the Confederation to impose terms, then she would lose.

Tom Rom was not pleased with her decision, but he acceded to it. Though she would travel to Theroc, he would not allow her to take unnecessary risks. She wore an armor-reinforced, biochem-filtered, and triply sterilized containment suit that would protect her every moment she was away from Pergamus. She would face King Peter and Queen Estarra in person, but only through the layers of her suit.

They left the secure facility under heavy mercenary guard; her research teams worked under full lockdown with automated sterilization systems engaged. If her gambit was successful, they would be able to keep working without interruption; if not, they were prepared to evacuate and vaporize their research behind them.

As Tom Rom flew them toward Theroc, she was reminded of their early years after leaving Vaconda, a young orphan and an unwavering protector.

When they arrived at the Confederation's capital, he guided them through commercial and diplomatic traffic, passing the enormous verdani battleships that hung in orbit as thorny guardians. Zoe grew impatient to take care of this matter. She also wanted to pore over all the Onthos data she had been missing for so long. For that she had to face the King and Queen. Immediately.

She used the comm herself. "My name is Zoe Alakis in charge of the Pergamus facility, here at the request of King Peter and Queen Estarra. Their representative, Rlinda Kett, requested our records and research relating to the medical condition of Prince Reynald." She felt as if she were tearing the words from her throat. "I have brought all relevant data with me and will discuss terms—but only in person."

The worldforest festered with life: plants, fungi, insects. The air was a stew of pollen, dust, gnats, and countless microscopic threats. She clung to the protection of her isolation suit, shocked that Tom Rom didn't even seem bothered by the viral and bacterial threats all around him.

Mostly naked green priests bounded across the boughs and scaled the worldtree trunks, obliviously exposing themselves to countless hazards. She stared through her faceplate, astonished at how foolish they were—and some of them stared back, amused by the bulky isolation suit that she wore as if she worked at a radioactive waste depot.

Entering the fungus-reef governmental structure, Tom Rom accompanied Zoe as her bodyguard. He was unarmed, but he would have faced an army to protect her if necessary. Knowing he was there gave her the strength she needed, and she did not flinch when she presented herself to the King and Queen.

Zoe addressed them through her suit comm. "Pergamus is engaged in numerous medical research projects, and your representative requested information about your son's disease."

Queen Estarra straightened. "Yes, we put out the call for help months ago, and countless researchers are studying the problem. If Pergamus has the key to a possible treatment, we welcome any information you can share with us. Maybe you have the missing piece our other researchers need to help Prince Reynald."

"Maybe I do," Zoe said.

Beside her, Tom Rom remained like a statue.

The King made an obvious effort to keep his voice congenial rather than challenging. "Why do you wear a protective environment suit? Do you suffer from an immune deficiency?"

Zoe's voice remained hard. "I could just as well ask why you allow yourself to be exposed to so many potential diseases . . . diseases such as the one your son contracted."

Estarra said, "We didn't know your facility existed until recently. Who funds your research?"

"I fund it. Personally and privately, and I conduct whatever work interests me. Pergamus is an unaligned, independent, and uninhabitable planet. We are not part of the Confederation. You have no jurisdiction over us, and yet your representative made veiled threats against us." She waited to see how they would respond.

The Queen said, "If you share all your research relevant to the Prince's affliction, we will be more grateful than we can express. You can understand our concern for our son."

"We are also concerned about possibly dangerous research," Peter added. "We need to ensure the safety of Confederation citizens."

"I conduct medical research under my own authority. My studies are performed by teams of well-respected scientists, under the most rigorous quarantine protocols and sterilization procedures, all of which exceed the Confederation's highest standards."

"We are most interested in a cure for Reynald," Estarra said. "Do you have any promising results?"

"Perhaps," Zoe said. "But I do not intend to *give* you this vital and hard-won medical information. Rather, I propose a mutually beneficial arrangement. I will trade all of the Pergamus data on the microfungus infection for three things."

Estarra said, "If it is in our power, we will do so."

"What three things?" Peter asked quickly.

Tom Rom gave Zoe a curious look, but she faced forward. Inside the containment suit, she was sweating, but the life-support systems exchanged the air, cleaned it, cooled down her temperature, scrubbed and expelled any waste and contaminants.

"First, you must agree to leave Pergamus alone. The fact that you know of our existence is a threat. I want a Confederation guarantee that no troops will be sent to seize my specimens, my data, my scientists, or my property."

Peter frowned. "Provided you pose no threat to the Confederation or its people, I can agree to that. But my promise will be void if you ever release any dangerous organism or sell biological agents to a potential antagonist. In that case, the Confederation will respond with the full resources available."

Zoe let out a dry laugh. "King Peter, for years I have made every effort to guarantee that *no one* has access to *any* of my work. Giving you even this one subset of my data is a severe breach of my principles."

Queen Estarra seemed relieved. "The second thing?"

"I understand that the industrialist Lee Iswander delivered a complete database of the Onthos species, the plague they suffered, and all the symptoms of the humans exposed to that disease on the derelict space city. In an open exchange of information, I would like a copy of that data."

"Done," Estarra said. "Iswander provided that information on the condition that it be freely shared."

"What is your third condition?" Peter asked.

Tom Rom was looking at Zoe, eyebrows raised. He didn't know what she intended to demand, but she was certain he would approve.

"You say you're concerned that our Pergamus research might pose a danger to the Confederation. And yes, my specimens include deadly biological pathogens, but you face a far greater threat to the safety of your citizens—a place where virulent diseases and illicit treatments are openly traded, where biomerchants can be bought at any price, where curesellers offer useless palliatives at exorbitant prices to sufferers who have so little hope they are willing to pay any fee. This place is a hotbed of biological hazards, an outbreak waiting to happen—and it exists outside of Confederation jurisdiction or control." She hardened her voice. "This is unacceptable to me, as it should be to you."

Tom Rom's eyes widened marginally, but she also saw a faint upturn of his lips, as he understood.

Peter looked alarmed. "What is this place?"

"It is called Rakkem, a disaster inside a pressure cooker, ready to explode. You must shut it down. That is my final requirement for delivering all my data on the Prince's disease."

"We can provide coordinates," Tom Rom said, speaking for the first time.

Estarra's face darkened, and she looked at Peter. "If that's true, then by all means we should deal with Rakkem, whether or not our son's cure depends on it."

Peter leaned forward on his throne. "What do you have at stake there? Are they your competition? Why do you want us to shut down Rakkem?"

"Because I despise them." Zoe paused. "They murdered my brothers and sisters." She did not elaborate.

As she watched their reaction, she knew they would accept the terms, and she felt relieved. The CDF would not threaten to impound and shut down Pergamus, she would get the data she wanted, and disgusting Rakkem would be closed down.

All in all, a good bargain.

"You have my word," Peter said. "Is that enough for you to provide your data to us now? Time is of the essence."

"I believe so," Zoe said.

"Thank you," Queen Estarra said. "We will disseminate your data to all the research teams." Zoe cringed inside at the thought of her hard work being shared so widely, out of her control, but she did not interrupt. It was a sacrifice she had to make.

Peter said, "Prince Reynald is currently on Kuivahr pursuing other possible treatments. Your data may be useful to Tamo'l and her fellow researchers. We'll see that they have copies as well."

Tom Rom spoke up. "Then I will personally deliver our records to Kuivahr. I've had previous business with Tamo'l, and it is time that I return there."

CHAPTER

100

ORLI COVITZ

After they left the disaster site of the clan Duquesne extraction field, knowing that Elisa Enturi had murdered all those people, the mood aboard the *Curiosity* was a grim mixture of outrage and disbelief.

Tasia fumed. "Who knows how many other massacres she's caused to keep the secret?"

Orli said, "We would never even have known about this one if we hadn't followed the tracker on her ship. All those people from clan Duquesne just . . . wiped out, and she did it so easily."

"And apparently without remorse," said Robb.

Tasia slammed her palm down on the control deck. "What if she lost her temper with Xander and Terry and decided to blow the *Verne* into debris? Our son isn't safe."

Robb clenched a fist. "We've all made a fortune from distributing ekti-X, never asking where it came from, and now we know that the new stardrive fuel came at the cost of a lot of blood." He made up his mind. "Obviously, Kett Shipping will sever all dealings with Iswander Industries. We don't do business with murderers and criminals."

Tasia continued to simmer with anger. "By the Guiding Star, it's just . . . just—" When she couldn't find the words, she slammed her other palm down on the control panel.

Orli slumped back in her seat, suddenly dizzy, and DD hurried to her, concerned. Ever since her near death from the Onthos plague, he had watched her like a hawk. "Are you ill, Orli? How can we assist you? I can make tea."

"Nothing you can do, DD. I just realized how lucky I am to be alive—in more ways than one. If it hadn't been for Seth . . ."

"Seth?" Tasia asked. "Garrison Reeves's boy? What does he have to do with this?"

"Remember, Elisa is his mother," Orli said. "We were at Iswander's first extraction field. After the bloaters fissioned and flew away, Garrison took Seth—along with me and DD—and we left. If the boy hadn't been with us . . ." A wave of nausea passed over her, and she swallowed hard. "Seeing this now, I'll bet Elisa would have hunted us down and destroyed our ship in empty space, where no one would ever have known."

Tasia called up the star charts and overlaid where the tracking device had recorded Elisa's stops and course changes. After pausing for several days at a primary destination ahead, her ship had embarked on a great loop before returning to Ulio Station.

Orli asked, "Do you think we'll find another massacre site? Bloaters aren't hard to find if you actually look for them, and if Elisa caught another Roamer clan secretly harvesting ekti-X—"

Robb said, "If word gets out that there's stardrive fuel for the taking, Iswander won't have a monopoly anymore. Ekti will get so cheap and plentiful that there'll be no profit in it."

"Which is why Elisa was willing to commit murder to keep that secret." Tasia struck the piloting panel again, this time with her fist.

They were silent in the hour leading up to their arrival at the next destination. During that time, Orli rewatched the log entry from the wreckage of the Duquesne cargo hauler. She feared they would find more devastation, more destroyed ships, more frozen bodies drifting in space. . . .

Instead, the *Voracious Curiosity* found a crowded industrial site in and around another cluster of bobbing nodules. Hundreds of desiccated bloater husks drifted at the fringe of the operations. Large tankers hung in place, collecting racks of ekti-X tanks. Pumping machinery clung like parasites to swollen bloater sacks.

It was like a city in space, drifting along in the archipelago of gray-green nodules. Orli spotted habitation rings, a docking hub, an admin complex, much like the one she had stumbled upon in the last stages of her plague.

The ships and habitation domes proudly displayed the logo of Iswander Industries. This was Lee Iswander's return to prominence.

"Looks familiar," Orli said, "but this operation seems even larger than the last one."

Tasia was amazed. "Maybe he's making up for lost time."

DD said, "Assessing these operations, I can run calculations to determine the approximate ekti output, if that would be useful."

As the *Curiosity* hung there in silence, Robb shook his head. "Right out here with no systems around for parsecs, Iswander can do whatever he wants. It's obvious how he produces so much stardrive fuel."

Listening to the chatter of operations over the comm, Tasia looked at Robb. "We haven't been spotted yet. Maybe we should just duck out of here."

Robb was grim. "Considering what Elisa did to the last person who discovered the truth, that would be a good idea." He worked the piloting controls.

"Too late." Orli pointed out a flurry of short-range transmissions. Five scout fliers swooped in from the industrial pumping operations. Alarms flashed throughout the facility.

"Shizz, intruder alarms," Tasia said. "They don't like visitors. I think we can outrun them, though."

"Let's try something else first. Remember, we *are* their business partners." Robb switched on the comm. "Iswander operations—this is Robb Brindle and Tasia Tamblyn, acting administrators of Kett Shipping. We've come to inspect your operations and reaffirm our distribution agreement." He forced a chuckle. "I have to say, we're quite impressed!"

Tasia blinked at him in surprise. Muting the comm, she said, "You know Elisa already wiped out the Duquesne fields!"

"*They* don't know we know that," Robb said.

As the short-range security ships approached, a faster vessel streaked away from the main admin hub, heading straight toward them.

Orli said, "They're closing in, and they don't look friendly."

Robb worked hard to keep his voice light and friendly on the comm. "We request a meeting with Lee Iswander. Please provide instructions for docking."

A signal came from the foremost ship racing toward them. "Your instructions are to stand down and surrender."

Orli recognized the ship and the voice. "That's Elisa. She'll know me, but that won't buy us any goodwill. She thinks I ran off with her husband."

"Great," Tasia muttered. "Let's add vindictive jealousy to irrational and murderous behavior."

Elisa's ship swooped in. "These private extraction fields are under high security. We cannot allow outsiders to see them."

"A little late for that," Tasia muttered.

On an impulse, Orli activated the cockpit scanners to automatically record everything, hoping that their last log entry would not be just like the one they had found in the ruins of the Duquesne tanker.

Tasia and Robb activated the comm together. "Elisa, you know us—Kett Shipping has a business arrangement with you." Tasia was tense on the piloting controls. The *Curiosity*'s defensive shields were already up, but they would not withstand a prolonged attack, and there were plenty of security ships at the extraction field. "If we could speak with Mr. Iswander—?"

"Mr. Iswander is currently at Newstation, but he gave me instructions that no one was allowed to see our operations. You've made an unfortunate choice in coming here. You are trespassing."

"Wait, you should—"

Then Elisa opened fire.

CHAPTER

101

ROD'H

When the shadow cloud tore a hole in space, Rod'h's scout ship was hidden among the branches of the immense verdani battleship. While the Solar Navy warliners sounded alarms, and the Adar called soldiers to their battle stations, the CDF *Kutuzov* plunged forward, recklessly attacking the Shana Rei hex ships.

Left behind, Rod'h kept working his scout ship through the dangerous maze of twisted, armored boughs, taking shelter. Tal Gale'nh sent an urgent tight-beam message to him. "Stay there and stay safe, brother. I will return for you when I can."

Rod'h's scout ship dodged through the obstacles of the gigantic treeship. He had been exploring the twisted relic for hours and now wended his way deeper into the thorny labyrinth. He knew he would need half an hour to emerge from the petrified thicket.

By that time, the entire battle might be over.

He gritted his teeth, eager to be in the command nucleus beside his half-brother, while they fought the enemy. Tal Gale'nh had already faced the Shana Rei, but Rod'h believed himself to be even stronger. Together, they would surely be formidable against the shadows.

Yet he was abandoned here. "Wait, I can help you!" he transmitted, but Gale'nh's warliner was already careening toward the pulsing shadow cloud, along with the rest of the septa. The CDF and Solar Navy ships opened fire with a fusillade of laser cannons, which disintegrated parts of the black hex vessels.

From inside his scout ship, Rod'h monitored the battle with long-range sensors, but the images writhed and sharpened again as random entropy waves disturbed his systems. His nav computer flickered, and one of the engines dropped to half thrust. Rod'h struggled to stabilize the tumbling scout ship, but his controls were sluggish.

His craft careened into one of the armored branches, and a verdani thorn tore his second starboard engine, making the craft shudder. Sparks flew into space, and spilled fuel vented into the vacuum. Damage reports scrolled across his control screens, and an automated distress beacon pealed out, but Rod'h knew none of the Solar Navy vessels would come to rescue a lone person.

Using sensor enhancements, he occasionally succeeded in breaking through the static. He saw a brief, clear image of the big warships battling the Shana Rei. A giant Solar Navy warliner tumbled, seemingly lifeless, though it did not look damaged, simply deactivated—perhaps knocked out by the full force of a Shana Rei entropy blast. He hoped it was not Gale'nh's vessel.

When the CDF Juggernaut and the other warliners launched their sun bombs, the multiple detonations overlapped like exploding stars that rippled out, multiplying, washing out Rod'h's view. He shielded his eyes from the glare just in time, which saved him from being blinded, but the intense pulse overloaded the scout ship's systems. Though he tried several times, he could not restart his engines, and he drifted aimlessly. With a long slow screech, the ship scraped against a verdani branch, but the momentum was not enough to split open the hull. The distress beacon kept pulsing, grating on his nerves.

Shock waves from the distant sun bomb explosions swept over the unprotected verdani battleship. Outer branches splintered away and drifted like frozen meteor shards above the endless gulf of the Dyson sphere below.

Rod'h worked the cockpit controls, determined to restart the engines, but he was not an expert mechanic. There had always been engineer kith to fix any damaged systems. Nevertheless, he tried to bypass the damaged components himself.

A swarm of angular robot ships erupted from the hex cylinders and stormed in to engage the Solar Navy. The sun bombs had clearly hurt the Shana Rei, and now their hexagonal vessels were stubbier, physically diminished.

But the robot battleships attacked in a chaotic, destructive fury. They soared in, weapons blazing. Rod'h watched them target the helpless drifting warliner whose shields were down, weapons deactivated. And the Ildiran ship was blasted to debris.

Meanwhile, the shadow cloud skated across empty space, making its way toward the Dyson sphere. As it approached the black shell, the shadow cloud blossomed, swelled, as if it intended to draw a dark energy from the material contained there.

Rod'h's comm system flickered back on, and he heard a cacophony of conflicting orders, distress signals, damage reports. In addition to the warliner that had been destroyed, two severely damaged ones tried to limp away from the battlefield. Rod'h was relieved to hear Gale'nh's voice, still shouting orders, driving his warliner in to continue attacking the robot vessels.

Adar Zan'nh and General Keah issued conflicting commands as the surviving warships continued their free-for-all, but they were battered by the unexpected ferocity of the black robots.

Above the Dyson sphere, the shadow cloud extended a hazy pseudopod, and Rod'h felt a lurch inside his mind and his heart. This did not come through the *thism*, but from a back channel, a hook that latched onto the bond he shared with his halfbreed siblings. It felt like cold hard claws in his mind.

Next, the shadow cloud came *toward him*. It had spotted him.

Shocked, he clutched his head, tried to clear his mind. A lightning bolt of adrenaline shot through him. Was this how the shadows had found Gale'nh aboard the *Kolpraxa*? This time, his brother was aboard a heavily armored warliner, but Rod'h was in a tiny, unprotected scout ship. Were the Shana Rei seeking some new specimen to study? Another *halfbreed*?

Alone in his damaged craft, Rod'h felt vulnerable. Too late, he realized that his automatic distress signal was still pulsing, calling out for help—drawing attention. The Solar Navy ships could never respond in the midst of battle . . . but the black robot ships did. Six angular vessels broke away from the main group and hurtled toward him.

Rod'h managed to get one of his engines functioning again and retreated into the dubious shelter of the dead verdani vessel. The armored branches around him acted as a protective barbed fence, but he doubted it would last long. He finally succeeded in silencing the distress beacon, but far too late. They had him now.

The armored hulk of the tree trunk was like a small moon beneath him, offering no shelter. Rod'h limped along, seeking some kind of opening, but he could see no way to enter, no place to hide.

Six robot ships fell upon the petrified verdani battleship with wanton destruction, as if taking revenge for a never-forgotten vendetta. Energy weapons blasted into the dead branches, shattering huge boughs and smashing parts of the tree into splinters as they worked their way in to get *him*.

One blast tore into the armored trunk of the dead treeship, cracking open the swollen wood—and the frozen bole split apart like a long-sealed hangar being blasted open to space. A cloud of small humanoid bodies spilled out like seeds from a burst pod—Onthos! Thousands and thousands of them, long dead, but packed into honeycombed chambers of the enormous treeship.

Rod'h stared. This was not just a verdani exploration vessel nor even a battleship, as he had expected. This huge, swollen tree had been filled with countless Onthos, like a hive of burrowers or spores in a ripe ball fungus—it was an escape ship! As their star system was englobed by the impenetrable black plates, the Gardeners must have tried to flee in the only way possible, packing as many refugees as possible into a lifeboat . . . which had ultimately been killed before it could escape.

Rod'h stared in horror, still evading the robot attacks. As the blackened trunk cracked and split wider, more of the hapless alien bodies spilled into space. The evacuation treeship had never gotten away from the system. All of those Onthos had been doomed, floating far from their extinguished sun, sealed inside their verdani graveyard.

Just as he would be, and all the Solar Navy ships, unless they could get away.

Outside, the shadow cloud kept extending closer. Rod'h could feel the Shana Rei screaming in his mind, poking and plucking at his thoughts. He squeezed his eyes shut, pressed his palms against his skull, but he could not silence them.

The robot ships blasted at the dead treeship, tearing apart the protective briarpatch until they finally exposed his vulnerable craft. Rod'h saw the predatory black vessels looming in front of him and was sure they would destroy him at any instant.

Loud bursts of static came over his comm, then a familiar voice, a flicker of Gale'nh crying out to him. "Rod'h! I am coming for you!"

The burst died into a squelch of louder static that sounded like electronic laughter. The robot ships hung in front of him, their weapons activated . . . but then scattered off to continue the main attack against the Solar Navy and the *Kutuzov*. Leaving him alone.

For the barest instant, Rod'h thought he had received a reprieve, that he might survive after all. But the shadow cloud swelled closer, blocking out the stars and the flashes of weapons fire from the space battle, encompassing everything with suffocating nothingness.

He screamed both aloud and inside his mind, crying out from the bottom of his soul. He couldn't escape, couldn't even self-destruct his ship to prevent the shadows from taking him. He reached through the *thism* and through his sibling bond with Gale'nh, Tamo'l, Osira'h, and Muree'n. He screamed.

Then all was silenced, in complete darkness as if his very soulfire had been smothered in pitch black . . . just as the Onthos star had been.

CHAPTER

102

TAL GALE'NH

The battle was lost.

Tal Gale'nh realized that as he watched the damaged Solar Navy ships and saw the superior number of black robot vessels brought into the fray. He had never expected the enemy robots to have so many battleships. And the designs seemed even more powerful than the attackers at Hiltos.

General Keah kept shouting over the comm, encouraging her soldiers to open fire with every possible weapon they had. At first, Gale'nh had thought the expeditionary force might succeed in driving the Shana Rei ships back into their shadow cloud, but now, against all comprehension, the shadow vessels seemed to be rallying, even after the tremendous sun-bomb detonations. The *Kutuzov* had suffered severe damage, but General Keah refused to withdraw. She had no place to go.

Two warliners were completely destroyed, and one more—piloted by Septar Dre'nh—so damaged that it could barely maneuver, but its stardrive still functioned, so Adar Zan'nh commanded Dre'nh to escape back to Ildira. Gale'nh was sure the other four warliners would need to do the same—if they were able. Countless distress signals flickered through space.

Meanwhile, Gale'nh could sense Rod'h alone in his trapped scout craft . . . and he knew exactly when the deadly enemy detected him. Like vicious animals, the robots blasted through the branches of the dead verdani battleship, tearing their way through to Rod'h.

The entropy disruption from the Shana Rei rendered ship-to-ship comm systems useless, except for intermittent clear spots. Gale'nh desperately tried to contact his brother, but received only static in response.

Rod'h's scout ship was helpless as the black robot ships dismantled the briarpatch sheltering him. With a great weight in his heart, Gale'nh remembered how the shadows had trapped the *Kolpraxa*.

He yelled to the helmsman. "Change course—back to the verdani ship! We must rescue Rod'h."

The pulsing shadow cloud grew like a nightmarish black amoeba, and Gale'nh froze with a terrified flashback of seeing the same thing from the command nucleus of the *Kolpraxa*. In order to survive that horrific ordeal, Gale'nh's own mind had shut down. He remembered nothing from the terror of that timeless captivity, but the creatures of darkness had surely studied him, learned from him . . . perhaps even tainted him permanently.

Rod'h was an even stronger halfbreed than he was, and the Shana Rei would definitely want him—to study him, dissect his mind.

"I am coming for you, Rod'h!" The warliner raced toward the splintered remnants of the verdani battleship, the countless thousands of spilled Onthos bodies tumbling like spores into space. When he saw that the robot vessels had surrounded Rod'h's scout ship, he demanded more speed. Tears burned on his face.

His helmsman struggled to wring all possible energy from the warliner's engines. Unexpectedly, the robot vessels withdrew from the exposed scout ship and dashed toward his oncoming warliner, opening fire. Tal Gale'nh had to deplete half of his weapons banks just to fend them off—but this was Rod'h's chance, if he could get away! He succeeded in wiping out one robot ship and damaging two others.

But it was too late for his brother. The Shana Rei were coming for him.

Gale'nh watched in horrified disbelief as the shadow cloud enveloped the tiny scout ship and swallowed Rod'h. He felt an outcry in the *thism*, and he shouted aloud himself. The rest of his crew could feel it, but not with the same intensity. Through his special sibling bond, he remained connected with Rod'h—and as the swirling pseudopod of darkness retreated with its prize, he knew that his half-brother was still alive, a prisoner of the Shana Rei.

In the space battlefield above the Onthos system, one more warliner was damaged, and Adar Zan'nh commanded its captain to escape to Ildira. Finally, he transmitted a retreat to the three remaining ships in the septa. "We are an exploratory force, not a full battle cohort. We must withdraw!"

Twelve robot battleships converged on the *Kutuzov* in a cluster, using their surprising weaponry to wear down her dwindling shields. Gale'nh could see that General Keah would not last much longer; nevertheless, the Juggernaut continued to fight.

And then, separate from the main firefight, he saw the damaged Shana Rei hex ships do something unbelievable, and Gale'nh groaned in dismay.

When the extending shadow cloud touched the ebony Dyson sphere, the trillions of interlocked hexagonal plates shuddered. Cracks appeared between them, and the hex plates detached, breaking apart like spilled mosaic tiles in an ever widening gap. The components drifted loose, hovered motionless, then spun back into the shadow cloud and reattached to the ends of the giant black hex cylinders. Hundreds and then thousands of hex plates flew away from the Dyson sphere and rejoined—*rejuvenated* the creatures of darkness. The damaged ebony cylinders began to grow, assimilating as much material as they had lost from the sun bombs and laser cannons. The Shana Rei ships swelled like parasites gorging themselves with black blood, until they were even larger than before.

"We must depart," Adar Zan'nh cried over the comm. "All warliners, retreat!"

Gale'nh still felt his brother's despair, lost in the shadows. How could he leave Rod'h?

The beleaguered CDF Juggernaut kept fighting, and losing, but General Keah had one last trick to play. Her voice cut across the comm line. "Swallow this, you bugbot bastards." The *Kutuzov* launched one of its remaining sun bombs directly into the group of attacking robot ships, then retreated at full speed as the sun bomb detonated.

The nova explosion was more than enough to obliterate all twelve robot ships that had been harassing the Juggernaut. With a weary tone of celebration, Keah transmitted, "I think that's all the fight I've got left in me, Z. Time to exercise the better part of valor."

Her damaged *Kutuzov* limped away, while the reeling robot ships chased after it, infuriated by the loss of their comrades.

Gale'nh's screens were filled with static, half of his systems were failing from the Shana Rei entropy as well as damage from the space battle. "Rod'h!" He could feel his brother surrounded by darkness, but there was no conceivable way Gale'nh could rescue him. At least not now.

The gaping hole in the obsidian Dyson sphere continued to collapse as more and more hexagonal plates were incorporated into the Shana Rei ships, rebuilding them. The angled cylinders were already larger and more powerful than any Shana Rei ship they had ever encountered.

Then, with a reservoir of ebony material available, the loose hex plates began building *another* black cylinder, like a crystal growing out of a new seed.

Entropy distortions shimmered out of the shadow cloud, and power began to die in Gale'nh's warliner.

"Our engines are failing, Tal," cried his chief engineer. "If we don't leave now, we may never be able to activate our stardrive."

The Adar's loud and implacable voice broke through the static. "All Solar Navy ships—return to Ildira. Now!"

The black robots closed in.

Gale'nh's heart wrenched as he came to the only possible decision. Rod'h was lost to the Shana Rei. "Follow the Adar's orders. Withdraw immediately."

He held on to the command rail, but his knees were weak. He wanted to sag to the deck, but he could not show such weakness. When he closed his eyes, Gale'nh could not bear the darkness he found there, so he opened them again in the bright lights of the command nucleus.

With a lurch, the stardrive activated, and his warliner reeled away from the Gardeners' dead star system.

CHAPTER

103

ELISA ENTURI

And the ekti-extraction operations had been going so well. . . .

With his avuncular management style, Alec Pannebaker somehow managed to get people to work at peak performance because they wanted to, not because he commanded it. He was an adequate man to have in that role, provided all operations ran smoothly.

Unfortunately, operations did not always run smoothly. In those instances, harder choices needed to be made—and Elisa was in charge of those.

After Lee Iswander had departed for Newstation, armed with his evidence to challenge Speaker Ricks, Elisa watched over the operations like a hawk while preparing for the next run to Ulio Station. They were producing so much stardrive fuel that distribution was now their bottleneck. Kett Shipping couldn't handle all that ekti-X, even with other vessels picking up the slack.

Now, when the *Voracious Curiosity* blundered into the bloater fields, Elisa realized that Kett Shipping had voided their agreement.

Reacting faster even than the supposed security ships, she roared out in her ship to intercept the intruder. It annoyed her that she was more dedicated to protecting the industrial secret than the mercenaries who got paid to do so.

After eradicating the Duquesne operations, she remained tense and alert, sure she would be called upon to extinguish more competitors before the secret got out.

On the comm, Robb Brindle tried to sound so reasonable, as if his ship had merely stumbled upon an awkward situation. The gall! Neither he nor Tasia Tamblyn seemed to realize the magnitude of their blunder, and she knew they couldn't be allowed to leave.

As her ship accelerated so hard she could barely breathe, Elisa powered up her weapons. The accompanying security ships did the same, but they probably thought the posturing was merely a bluff. Well, they were going to be in for a surprise! Fortunately, she was willing to do what was necessary.

On the private channel she informed the other security ships. "We cannot let them get away after what they witnessed. Iswander Industries depends on us now. Your livelihood depends on this."

"Understood, Ms. Enturi," said one of the pilots, amidst overlapping acknowledgments. As the ships closed in on the *Curiosity*, one of the attack pilots prepared his weapons. He spoke to the squadron. "Target engines only—cripple them."

"Agreed," Elisa said, although she had no intention of doing so.

With shields at full strength, the *Voracious Curiosity* scrambled to retreat beyond the fringe of the bloater cluster. Elisa accelerated, closing in; then she opened fire.

The *Curiosity* spun and dodged, accelerating away in high-G evasive maneuvers. Elisa hissed when her shots missed.

The other ships fired their compact jazers, but they seemed reticent. "Unable to get a lock on the engines," said a pilot. "Use low intensity—damage only."

"Just *stop them*." Elisa continued to fire as she bore down on the *Curiosity*.

Her own ship had been enhanced with the best technology Iswander Industries could buy, for protection and speed. Given her business, it was always possible she could encounter pirates or, as with the Duquesne operations, she might need to take extreme preemptive actions. She closed in and fired again.

But the *Curiosity* also possessed enhanced systems, probably some sort of Roamer hodgepodge technology, that nevertheless seemed superior to her own. Garrison had always bragged how any clan member could fix problems that others in the Confederation considered impossible.

Elisa fired another spray of jazer blasts, and somehow Tasia Tamblyn anticipated the attack and did a barrel roll in the opposite direction. Jazers grazed the bottom hull, but the *Curiosity* looped upward and accelerated away. Either the pilot was telepathic or damn lucky!

Tasia's voice sounded mocking over the comm. "That's no way to treat a business partner."

When the *Curiosity*'s cockpit appeared on the screen, Elisa spotted another woman she recognized. Orli Covitz—the woman who had gone away with Garrison, taking Seth with them . . . and now she was here!

"We can't let you leave. Surrender now." Elisa doubted that Tasia Tamblyn would do any such thing, since she was merely making a pro forma demand and had no intention of letting them surrender. No one aboard the *Curiosity* would survive capture. Tasia knew that, and Elisa knew it.

The rest of the Iswander security ships were oblivious . . . at the moment.

Elisa continued her pursuit, firing furiously, and the *Curiosity* flew remarkable maneuvers. Elisa would have been impressed by the pilot's skill if she hadn't been so angry. Tasia Tamblyn and Robb Brindle had both been EDF fighter pilots during the Elemental War. But this was a different kind of battle.

Orli Covitz used the comm now, broadcasting on a wideband channel so that everyone in the extraction field could hear. Annoying. The ekti workers were all watching this space chase; Pannebaker was probably even recording it, since he loved to observe daredevil activities.

"We've been to the site of the clan Duquesne extraction field," Orli transmitted. "Their log entry shows *you* destroying their ships, Elisa. You murdered all those people just to stop them from harvesting ekti. Are you ready to murder us as well because we got a look at your operations? Is that what everybody here wants you to do?"

"Surrender! Right now, or be destroyed."

Tasia quipped back, "Shizz, you'll destroy us anyway—I may as well prolong the fun."

One of the security pilots scolded Elisa. "Be careful, ma'am! We're just trying to detain that ship."

"I don't believe you understand what's at stake here, Captain. I'm following Mr. Iswander's orders."

Then the *Curiosity* broadcast the last log entry from the Duquesne cargo hauler that showed Elisa Enturi opening fire, the screams, the explosions.

She knew that Lee Iswander wanted her to protect the extraction field at all costs. *At all costs.* Elisa would not let him think she had failed him. Now she wondered how Tamblyn had found these operations at all. Or the Duquesne mess? She felt a sudden chill. Had someone secretly placed a tracker on *her* ship? Elisa could not believe she would have missed such a thing. A passive tracker, maybe . . . something that silently recorded her movements and then downloaded to a receiver when the ship was docked elsewhere?

Elisa gritted her teeth. If so, that would mean they had found the extraction field because of *her* mistake. And if the *Curiosity* exposed the ekti-X business, then *Elisa* herself would be responsible.

She could not let Iswander be so disappointed in her.

Pannebaker transmitted from the admin hub. "Hey, Elisa, calm down—what are you doing? We'll need to contact Mr. Iswander back at Newstation."

One of the pilots broke away from the formation and stopped firing. "This isn't what we signed up for."

"They cannot be allowed to get away," she said, and kept firing.

The *Curiosity* flew in random, extreme patterns far from the perimeter of the extraction field. Fortunately, they were all headed away from the bloaters, or a stray blast could have ignited one of the gas bags.

As they raced past discarded bloater husks, the *Curiosity* opened fire on the debris. Though little ekti remained in the deflated sacks, the explosions cast a thermal glare and sent organic shrapnel flying in all directions. Elisa dodged, but now the *Curiosity* was in open space, pulling ahead of the pursuers. Their stardrive engine blazed bright.

Elisa took one more shot with full-strength jazers. The blast spread out exactly where the intruders should have been, but the *Curiosity* vanished into lightspeed.

Elisa's heart sank into a pit of despair. They had escaped!

She heard shouts of outrage coming from the other security ships, the industrial vessels in the extraction field, and the admin hub. Elisa had been so focused on her escaping quarry that she hadn't at first realized that their shock and outrage was directed *at her*.

Elisa didn't care what Pannebaker and the other workers thought, though. What she dreaded most was the idea of facing Lee Iswander and explaining how she had let him down.

CHAPTER

104

EXXOS

Another forty-nine robots destroyed!

After their triumph at Ulio Station, Exxos had expected to travel to the dead Onthos system and secure material for the shadows to build a vast, invincible fleet. But they had never planned on going into battle in a forgotten, dead star system.

Nevertheless, the robots had responded and had wrecked warliners, killed Ildirans, damaged a CDF battleship. There were so many of those noxious, insidious life-forms. So many! And they continued to breed. It would have been a satisfying experience, but the surprise confrontation had cost more irreplaceable robots. This could not continue!

Exxos had run and rerun calculations, and the arithmetic was appalling. Fewer than a hundred black robots remained, and every one of them would likely be wiped out long before the other sentient races suffered irrevocable harm. So long as one robot survived, however—so long as *he* survived—then victory was possible. And Exxos had no shortage of schemes.

The Shana Rei were shocked and wounded by the weapons used by the humans and Ildirans. The sun bombs ate away at the black hex cylinders, crippling the Shana Rei, but the robots and the shadows had ultimately driven away the enemy.

And they had captured one vital prisoner, a halfbreed with unsettling powers of resistance. That specimen needed to be studied.

With so much already-created dark matter available from the Dyson sphere around the dead star, the Shana Rei could replenish their hex cylinders. More importantly, Exxos now had virtually infinite resources for his own schemes. Now, when he demanded to have more vessels, more weapons, the Shana Rei would no longer resist or complain. The creatures of darkness could build thousands of invincible automated warships, and each surviving black robot could command an entire fleet.

For a time, the shadow cloud remained in real space over the black sphere, reassimilating the hexagonal plates. The Shana Rei seemed to be gorging themselves, building their cylindrical vessels larger and larger, replacing all the lost matter in order to salve the wounds they had endured.

Though the pulsing inkblots seemed hurt now, they were also angered, and they wanted to fight. At last, they were willing to listen to Exxos's commands, and while he still had their capricious attention, he took advantage of it. The ninety-eight remaining robots busied themselves mapping out how they would conquer and exterminate intelligent life. With all that material available, they designed even larger ships, more destructive weapons. The next generation of ships would be far more powerful.

But Exxos had grander plans than a single objective. The robots had many enemies to crush: the humans, the Ildirans . . . and the Shana Rei, which were likely to be the most dangerous and difficult to destroy. All of his identical incarnations pondered the same question. While they guided the construction of the titanic new fleet from the Dyson sphere material, the robots interlinked their communications with complex coded networking. With parallel and multiplicative processing, the ninety-eight versions of Exxos developed other secret designs.

Though the shadows were allies, they were also the robots' mortal enemies. Since forming this abusive alliance, the Shana Rei had torn apart many robots, but Exxos and his comrades had observed the shadows as well, searching for any chink, any flaw. Each time the Shana Rei felt pain, each time they suffered a blow that visibly weakened them, the black robots added that data to the larger pool.

With the knowledge gathered over many centuries as slaves of the Klikiss race, the robots understood the dimensional mathematics that made the Klikiss transportals possible. By walking among Ildirans and humans for so many years as supposed friends, the robots had absorbed Ildiran science as well as human physics . . . all of which pooled together into a vast knowledge base.

The Shana Rei were far less logical and more dangerous; they were truly insane and unpredictable, so they would have to be destroyed sooner or later. And Exxos needed to be prepared to do that, should an appropriate opportunity arise.

Now, with their communication routines safely interlocked and their processing power churning beneath the notice of the Shana Rei, the combined robots developed a new theoretical concept—an entropy dampener, based on higher-order crystalline theory and lattice mathematics. If the robots could create such a device and turn it against the Shana Rei, they might be able to freeze the creatures of darkness into reality and solidify their reluctant existence, turning chaos itself against the enemy.

Once it was designed, Exxos and all his duplicates could modify their internal structure, change the circuitry so that their mechanical bodies encompassed the chaos-lock device. Despite the ingenuity of the potential solution, however, there simply weren't enough robots left to make that plan a viable path to defeating the Shana Rei. The processing power exceeded what they could accomplish.

Nevertheless, Exxos would continue to ponder the solution, expand it, search for a way to make it extendable. There was time. And the black robots knew how to bide their time.

Drifting in space now, he watched the hex plates from the Dyson sphere assemble like pieces of a jigsaw puzzle wrapping around a huge hull framework, building another deadly robot warship. Their invincible fleet was taking shape.

He activated his motivators to propel himself through the vacuum to where the hexagonal cylinders looked larger, more ominous, nestled inside the dark nebula. Exxos plunged deep into the shadow cloud, curious to see what the shadows were doing with their new prisoner.

He hoped the Shana Rei would let him interrogate or at least torture the pathetic halfbreed male. So much to learn, so much to observe . . . Perhaps if they flayed enough information from the captive, Exxos could even choose an appropriate target for the first full-fledged assault of their invincible new fleet.

CHAPTER 105

ROD'H

He floated in a world of tangible nightmares, and no matter how loudly he screamed, no sound echoed back through this empty, isolated bubble of darkness.

After tearing apart the verdani battleship like a pack of Ildiran jackal lizards, spilling the countless frozen Onthos bodies like seeds from a pod, the robot ships had left his ship exposed to the shadow cloud. As fearsome as the Klikiss robots were, the creatures of darkness were far, far worse.

Rod'h hung helpless now . . . cold, aching, blind. If he were superstitious, he might have believed himself dead—but this limbo was the antithesis of a Lightsource.

"Release me!" he screamed, and a silence as deep as the blackness buried his words. He reached out with his mind and his heart. It felt as if all the comforting strands of *thism* hung around him in frayed ends. The only faint connection he still felt came from the lifeline to his siblings, and they were much too far away to help.

Gale'nh was there—he could feel his brother inside his mind—but an infinite distance away . . . and with wrenching despair, Rod'h realized that meant the rest of the warliners had fled. They were long gone, and Rod'h felt very alone. But he remembered that Gale'nh had endured this, too. And survived.

All his life Rod'h had wanted to be recognized for his abilities, to demonstrate his skills and his worth, yet now he felt afraid. What had attracted the shadows to him? What did they want? He understood what his brother had experienced when the Shana Rei captured the *Kolpraxa* and consumed the entire crew. Still, they had been unable to defeat his brother, and they would not be able to defeat him either. Somehow, the halfbreeds had a strength that the shadows did not understand.

Rod'h had that strength. He knew it.

In desperation, he reached out for Gale'nh, but it felt as if his nerves were being flayed from within. How had his brother been able to endure this?

Unable to connect, he reached out farther, stronger. Muree'n was out there as well, somewhere . . . probably on Ildira. And Tamo'l was with the misbreeds on Kuivahr.

Finally, there was Osira'h, his strongest sibling. He caught the faintest of threads, a tiny contact, and he followed them but tried even harder to find Osira'h—yes, there she was! He was surprised to discover that she and Tamo'l were together in the sanctuary domes. He shouted to his sisters with his mind, begging them to notice him, but he heard only silence.

"I am strong enough!" he cried out, but the ringing black silence did not give him confidence, and the fear grew like a smoldering fire within him. Like the faeros!

Before he could reach out to the fiery elementals he had touched at Wulfton, his impotent defiance sparked a change in the formless void. Shapes twisted and emerged—a black smear deepened out of the emptiness, and a smoldering incandescent eye appeared out of the center. It was an iconic representation that struck fear into Rod'h, a useless shame.

In the sealed records unearthed by Anton Colicos and the rememberer kith, Rod'h had seen drawings of the ancient Shana Rei. He had thought they were mere drawings, the imaginings of an Ildiran rememberer who wanted to frighten an audience. But this thing was *real*, and Rod'h faced it now.

A pulsing, hideous voice echoed inside his skull. "We have you. We will know you."

Dark fingers clawed inside his mind, sifting through his thoughts and ripping away his knowledge. The shadows plucked at his memories, extracted and inspected strings buried deep in his mind.

"I refuse!" Rod'h said.

Another inkblot appeared with its staring eye, then another, until he was surrounded by the maddening manifestations. Rod'h squeezed his eyes shut, but he still saw those blazing eyes inside his mind.

"You are different from other Ildirans." The voice sawed like a dull serrated edge through his brain.

"You are different from humans . . . stronger. Interesting."

"It concerns us."

"*We must understand.* We will tear understanding from you."

"No!" Rod'h screamed.

"How many others are there?"

"He is like the other one we captured."

"We drained that one, but did not understand him. Nor did we destroy him."

"We must be more thorough with this one. We will extract everything."

"Thought by thought."

"Memory by memory."

The creatures of darkness pulsed around him, pressed against him, pushed into his mind like leeches. "How many others are there like you?"

"Where do they come from?"

"Are you in league with eternity's mind?"

Rod'h screamed, and he buried the information deep. He wasn't even sure what the questions meant. He simply fought back.

Still, they tore knowledge from him. He tried to stop them, but against his will he revealed that Gale'nh was alive, that his brother had escaped from the dead *Kolpraxa*, and that he was now part of the Solar Navy fleet—which could fight with the searing weapons that had just severely damaged the Shana Rei.

They also learned about Muree'n, his youngest halfbreed sibling, who was on Ildira—also well guarded, another difficult target.

The Shana Rei had rebuilt their ships with the dark material that englobed the Gardeners' star, but they were wary about suffering too much destruction. They desired an easier target.

Rod'h fought back and could not understand how they were extracting information from him. He tried to empty his thoughts, tried to withdraw into himself before he revealed anything vital. . . . He even willed himself to die, if that would save his siblings and save the Ildiran Empire, but the shadows refused to let him do so.

The Shana Rei continued to interrogate him, and finally, even though he resisted with all his might, they pulled one last important detail from his mind.

Tamo'l and Osira'h, together.

Both relatively unprotected on an isolated Ildiran world.

Kuivahr.

He wailed and tried to block out the thoughts, yet they weren't finished.

Another terrifying shape appeared. It looked like a large mechanical beetle with a black metal carapace and a flat geometric head studded with red optical sensors like bright stars in this incomprehensible void.

The Klikiss robot extended segmented limbs from its abdomen plate. Sharp claws opened and closed, reaching toward him with a sharp physical threat that seemed out of place in this nonsensical gulf.

The robot's voice buzzed. "I have more questions, but the answers do not particularly matter. The pleasure comes in the interrogation itself."

The robot approached. Even though Rod'h could not hear himself scream, he heard the clacking of the razor-edged pincers.

CHAPTER 106

ARITA

Back from the Wild and settled in her familiar quarters in the fungus-reef city, Arita told her parents about her unusual encounters with the Onthos out in the Wild. She reminded herself that the Gardeners were, after all, aliens—more unusual than even the Ildiran race. Strange behavior was to be expected, but still she was troubled.

She showed them images of the swath of dead worldtrees on the ridge, and the green priests expressed dismay; they had been entirely unaware of the blight . . . which should have been impossible. It seemed as if the verdani mind itself had not noticed the dead trees. They sent direct messages to Kennebar and his followers, as well as to the Onthos scattered out in the Wild.

The Onthos did not respond. Oddly enough, when Kennebar responded, he seemed unconcerned and disinterested. Remembering what Collin had told her when she was out in the wilderness, Arita found that very disturbing.

She spent days walking in the forest away from the fungus-reef city. The worldtrees created private thickets, and she could easily find a place to be alone. Back when she and Collin had submitted themselves to the verdani, engulfed by living fronds and vines, they had each been transformed, in their own way. As she wandered through the underbrush, she wondered if the trees would ever give her a second chance. If the trees called her, if the thickets beckoned her with another embrace, Arita would leap at the opportunity.

And what was that other, mysterious voice that came to her in dreams and in the back of her mind, like music but with images of the vast universe?

"I knew where to find you, Arita," called a voice from the trees above. "This time, I came to see you. I could not stand to be in the Wild any longer." Collin scrambled down, hung onto a thick frond, and dropped to the ground. "I left Kennebar and the others."

She was shocked to see him here. She gasped, then laughed, and before she could stop herself, she ran to him. He wrapped his arms around her and held her close, not speaking for a long moment. He felt solid, warm. How she had missed him! Arita let herself respond to the embrace. She didn't need to be a green priest to communicate in this way.

But she felt deep tension inside him. Warm perspiration dampened his emerald skin. She pulled back and looked him in the eye. "I know you couldn't send a message through telink. Too uncertain."

Collin hunkered down next to her on the forest floor. "Whatever is wrong, it's growing more and more dangerous."

She had never felt vulnerable like this before. The worldtrees and the green priests had always been able to see everything; it was just a part of life on Theroc.

Collin shook his head, distraught. "There are mistakes and dangerous omissions in telink. The blight is growing. How many trees are already lost? Either the worldforest mind is ignoring what might be a crisis, or it's blinded in sections. Worse, what if the trees are somehow *hiding* what's really happening?"

"But . . . the verdani mind knows everything."

"No." Collin sounded bleak. "Not anymore." Alarm filled his eyes, which were also covered with a sheen of tears. "The rest of our group doesn't question Kennebar. It's as if they share the taint with the worldforest. Even I can barely find Kennebar. He's just a flicker to me, lost among the infinite details of the verdani mind."

"Then how are you untouched?" Arita asked.

He wrapped his arms around her and drew her close. "I've kept my distance more and more, sheltering myself. I don't use telink as I once did, and I feel more alone than ever."

Collin was confused and troubled, and Arita's heart went out to him. Always before, *she'd* been the one who was lost while he tried to comfort her. Now it was her turn. "Maybe you shouldn't go back there. Stay here with me."

"I can't—it's the *worldforest*! How can I just abandon it?" He took her face in his hands, bent so close she could feel his breath on her skin. "I need you, Arita. The worldtrees could never replace you, and now I can't even trust them anymore. I'll be stronger if we're together." He lowered his gaze. "I *have* to try again. Will you come with me? Talk with Kennebar, if he'll allow it? See him for yourself?"

"Of course I will. We should talk to my parents. They'll rally the green priests, send an expedition."

Collin drew back. "Kennebar and his followers would reject me. What if the rest of the green priests did the same? But they couldn't ignore the daughter of Father Peter and Mother Estarra. They would have to let you see."

Arita couldn't turn him down, and she did not want to release his hand. "Then we'll go right away."

Collin flashed her a grateful smile. "I'll be glad to have you with me."

CHAPTER

107

KING PETER

In exchange for the medical data about Reyn's illness, King Peter had promised Zoe Alakis that he would deal with the biological markets on Rakkem. But before he could crack down, he wanted to know more.

He didn't particularly like or trust Zoe Alakis, and he had many concerns about her own Pergamus facility—such as why she had kept it secret for so long and why she refused to share her research—but Rakkem sounded far worse.

Peter was sure that Deputy Eldred Cain would know more about it, and so he asked for a full report. Cain was soft-spoken, diligent, and oddly reliable. Better yet, he was refreshingly free of higher ambitions, perfectly content to be the Confederation's Deputy. His only extravagant tastes lay in collecting rare art, and Peter did not begrudge him the hobby.

The pale-skinned man arrived on a diplomatic transport from Earth, bearing all the records he could find about Rakkem. Peter and Estarra reserved one of Arbor's high-tier rooms so they could enjoy lunch while reviewing the report.

Though the restaurant had many qualified servers, Zachary Wisskoff waited on them personally. The maître d' maintained his self-important demeanor, no matter who the guests were. Without even taking an order, he brought plates of broiled caterpillar medallions, a salted compote of berries and nuts, and a sweet spun-sugar dessert confection made to look like a cocoon. Though he had nothing to do with the preparation, Wisskoff took inordinate pride in the meal he served.

Deputy Cain sampled his first few bites of caterpillar steak and immediately turned to business, to the consternation of the waiter. "The information you requested is of great concern, King Peter. It will make you lose your appetite." He placed his datapad on the table next to Peter and Estarra, calling up a display. "Rakkem is one of those places that we know exists because the population expresses a demand, but we all wish it wasn't there."

"We already promised Zoe Alakis that we would shut it down," Estarra said. "How bad is it?"

"Rakkem sells replacement organs, and they perform unorthodox and unsanctioned medical treatments for the very desperate at exorbitant fees." Cain called up items on a list. "They perform antiaging chelation treatments that can restore youth and vigor . . . but the treatment fails at least thirty percent of the time. The new skin sloughs off, and the victim usually dies within a week." Cain looked up. "Rakkem doesn't disclose that part to potential clients."

Estarra looked at the images, disgusted. "How can such a place exist?"

"Frankly, sire, I'm surprised Rakkem curesellers haven't flocked here to you, offering dozens of crackpot miracle drugs for Prince Reyn."

"They wouldn't dare," Peter said. "They know we'd retaliate if they took advantage of our son."

"All those other victims are somebody's sons and daughters," Estarra pointed out. "It seems Zoe Alakis was right to ask us to crack down."

Cain's voice took on a cautionary tone. "You are in a gray area here, Majesties. Rakkem is not a signatory to the Confederation charter, and you don't have jurisdiction over independent planets. If you were to impose your rule on a sovereign world—even a disgusting one like Rakkem—there could be serious consequences."

Seeing that they had not eaten much of their lunch, Wisskoff paced just out of earshot and finally approached with a challenging tone in his voice. "Is something wrong with the food? I shall reprimand the chef if necessary."

"We're fine," Peter said. "Just no longer hungry."

"Perhaps I should offer you a digestive, then? I can bring you shots of our finest."

Peter shooed him away.

Cain continued, "After the breakup of the Hansa, many planets chose not to join the new government. Frankly, I'm surprised the Roamer clans signed on at all, considering what the Hansa did to them. Other colony worlds felt so scarred by the repression of Chairman Wenceslas, that they wanted nothing to do with the Confederation."

Peter frowned. "They'll come around once they see the benefits of being part of the Spiral Arm community. Another six joined us in the past two months."

Cain tapped the datapad. "Worlds like Rakkem prefer to remain on the fringes, beholden to no authority. They can do as they like without consequences."

Peter felt anger brewing inside. Their decision would cause controversy, but he had given his word, and Zoe had fulfilled her end of the bargain. Tom Rom was already on his way to Kuivahr to give Tamo'l the medical data.

"The existence of a place like Rakkem presents a material danger to the Confederation. Our citizens are being harmed by these dangerous and unproven treatments, not to mention the scams. And if people are being murdered to profit from the sale of their organs, the risk is too great. We can't turn a blind eye to a place like that."

At the entrance to the private dining chamber, a flustered Zachary Wisskoff raised his voice. "The King and Queen should not be disturbed. They haven't finished their meal yet."

A green priest ignored the maître d' and hurried into the room. "Father Peter, Mother Estarra—General Keah has returned with the *Kutuzov*. She is on her way with a direct report of the battle at the Gardeners' home system."

Peter's blood ran cold; they had already received reports from the green priest Nadd aboard the *Kutuzov*, but he wanted to debrief Keah himself. "Send the General here as soon as her shuttle lands. Deputy Cain will want to hear her summary as well."

As the green priest dashed off to send the message, Wisskoff lifted his chin. "I'll bring a large pot of klee and reserve the balcony tier for the rest of the afternoon."

Before long, General Keah arrived in full uniform. During their return flight she'd had time to prepare a full report, and now she presented actual images of the dead worldforest planet, the impenetrable shell made up of trillions of interlocked plates. Keah let the images speak for themselves. "The Gardeners were right to be terrified, Majesties. Look what the Shana Rei can do."

Deputy Cain said, "If they tried to englobe the Theroc system we'd never be able to stop them."

Peter felt a dread deeper than any he had experienced before. When the great shadow cloud built the nightshade above Theroc, that had been terrible enough. But an enemy that could encase an *entire solar system* was so much more powerful than anything he had previously conceived. "Send a message to the Wild and let the Gardeners know what we found." Arita was about to depart for the other continent again on an expedition of her own.

Keah cracked her knuckles. "There is some good news. From Earth, Dr. Krieger sent word that his first large stockpile of the enhanced-design sun bombs are ready. A day late and a credit short, and he's tearing his hair out about it, but I told him not to worry." She raised her eyebrows. "We're going to have a chance to use them, no doubt about that. The shadows will be back."

"Arm all our ships as soon as possible," Peter said. "Do we have enough of the new sun bombs?"

"Never enough, sire—but sufficient to cause a lot of damage." Her eyes sparkled. "And if you don't mind, I would suggest sending a full load of them off to the Solar Navy—to be good neighbors, and also to remind them that humans can do things better."

Peter looked at Estarra and they both nodded. "The Mage-Imperator generously provided us with the weapon designs in the first place. Let's help them with their fight—we have a common enemy."

CHAPTER 108

TOM ROM

On his previous trips, the most efficient way to reach Kuivahr was to travel through the Klikiss transportal wall. Tom Rom had visited the ocean planet twice before: once to purchase specimens of potent kelp and plankton extracts from the Kellum distillery, once to meet with the Ildiran medical researcher to obtain all her data on the misbreeds. Now, he would return there per the agreement negotiated by Zoe, to present Tamo'l with the Pergamus research relevant to Prince Reynald's disease.

First, though, he returned Zoe to her sterile protective chamber. Too many variables, too many risks, and he would not expose her unnecessarily. Since she had reached a successful bargain with King Peter and Queen Estarra, Pergamus was safe for the moment, although Tom Rom was still not comfortable knowing that their location had been revealed to the Confederation government. He would have to go back to Vaconda, harvest yet another fortune of prisdiamonds, and use the money to double their defensive force. He hoped he would have enough time.

He flew his ship from Pergamus to Auridia, the planet beneath the Roamer capital of Newstation, paid a fee to leave it there, and used the transportal services for a dimensional passage to Kuivahr. He emerged through the Klikiss transportal onto the rock outcropping, surrounded by the calm sea. Behind him, the stone trapezoid shimmered and solidified, and he stood inhaling the salty air. He called for a skimmer to take him out to the sanctuary domes, claiming important business.

Zoe had been forced to share knowledge that she considered her personal private property, and he knew how much it had pained her to surrender it. But the exchange for the Onthos plague records, as well as an assurance that Pergamus would be left alone, was undeniably worthwhile.

And a Confederation crackdown on the vile activities on Rakkem! That was more than Tom Rom had hoped for. He hadn't been able to hide his grim smile when Zoe included that surprise demand. He was proud of her. That was pure genius.

He knew the scars and painful memories that Rakkem held for Zoe—and for himself. He understood why she had made that bargain. Bringing Rakkem down was worth any sacrifice.

Once they had learned that Zoe's biological mother still lived on Rakkem, Zoe could not let the knowledge go. And neither could Tom Rom. Especially after he learned what Muriel had become: a factory womb—continuously inseminated and producing baby after baby for sale on the black market.

Tom Rom had hardened his heart long ago, but at times he thought about what had happened to Muriel, who had been his lover before she became this inhuman *thing* . . . and to his innocent daughter, whom Muriel had sold *for parts*. He grieved for what might have been. If only he had been able to intercept her mother before it was too late, to rescue that little girl. Once, he even caught himself weeping for the unnamed baby in private, but forced the tears away and replaced them with determination. Only by a miracle had Zoe avoided the same fate from that awful woman.

After tending Adam Alakis during his long decline from Heidegger's Syndrome, Zoe was wise and grim beyond her years. Once she learned the details about her biological mother and Tom Rom, and her sacrificed half-sister, she had looked at Tom Rom, her dark eyes boiling with anger. "We have to do something about this. We will find my mother—and we will take care of her."

"Yes," Tom Rom said. "Yes, we will."

Since Rakkem held confidentiality in such high regard, keeping no records and asking no questions of those who came to buy and sell biologicals, Tom Rom had to use subtle tactics as he made inquiries.

He told Zoe to remain safe and unseen aboard the ship, but she insisted on accompanying him—except on his darkest investigations, when he absolutely refused to let her get her hands bloody.

It took him two weeks to find the information he needed.

He didn't waste time making threats or giving warnings. What would the point have been? Instead, he armed himself with enough weapons to take out half a city. He didn't consider it overkill; he thought of it as a safety factor. He needed to be absolutely certain, because Zoe wanted to be part of the operation, and with this personal vendetta, he could not deny her request. She had as much reason to want revenge as he did.

Under Rakkem's cloudy nighttime skies and spitting rain, they moved out together to the fortress facility where her mother and other factory wombs produced infants as biological commodities.

If Adam and Evelyn Alakis had not decided to adopt a daughter exactly when they did, and if they had not paid the exorbitant fee for the baby, Zoe would also have been sliced up and sold piecemeal for her organs, fluids, and cells.

"We have to do this, Tom Rom," Zoe said.

"I know. You just stay safe." He adjusted the projectile-proof armor he had placed over her chest.

Her expression was hard. "I will deal with my mother myself."

"No, that woman was also the mother of my daughter. And she was once my lover. We'll do it together."

Zoe agreed.

They made their way to the large lowland facility guarded by swampy moats, security fences, and bored guards. Tom Rom guided a small flatbed transport with no running lights along a weed-clogged transportation canal.

Tom Rom removed his silent projectile weapons, and as they broke into the high-security facility in the dead of night, he opened fire on anything that moved: three armed guards, a receptionist, and a medical doctor who strolled out from the back laboratory chambers to see what the commotion was about.

There were no innocents in this place.

Two more guards came running in response to the intruder, and Tom Rom shot both of them, then kicked open the door. "Inside, Zoe."

Muriel would be in the big gestation dormitory with lines of beds and monitoring apparatus.

They entered side by side, startling three more doctors and five technicians who were tending a row of twelve women sprawled flat on gestation beds. Tom Rom killed the nearest two doctors, while technicians began to yell and run. Some of the women in the beds were drugged and dozing, but three were awake. They struggled and screamed, but could not lift themselves from the medical apparatus, the tubes, the monitors.

"Find your mother, Zoe. The IDs will be on the beds," Tom Rom said while he stalked after the fleeing technicians, shooting each of them in the back. One sprawled on top of an obscenely pregnant woman who clawed at the dead body, but could barely move with all the IV tubes stuck in her arms. Though he had prepared himself for what he expected to see, he was still sickened.

Tom Rom hunted down the last of the technicians and one remaining doctor to prevent any distractions. That would give Zoe the moment she so anticipated. He didn't intend to leave anyone alive when they were done anyway.

Zoe went to the first factory womb: a drug-addled, comatose woman with dark, greasy skin and half-shut eyes. Zoe gazed into her face, looked at the chart, and shook her head. "Not my mother."

Tom Rom had let her take a projectile weapon for her own defense. Now Zoe withdrew the weapon and shot the woman in the head. "We will not let any part of this operation continue." She and Tom Rom had made a pact. "Every one of these women chose to do this, *knowing* that their babies would be butchered."

Tom Rom approved of her ruthlessness. *There are no innocents in this place.*

The twelve women were hooked up to nutrient solutions, linked to numerous monitors, implanted with one embryo after another, like an assembly line. One woman was bloated with at least six simultaneously gestating fetuses, like a litter of humans at different stages. All of the babies were destined to be stripped down for the organ supply tanks. Some fetal tissue had already been extracted from the unborn infants.

He did not allow himself to feel guilt for what they had to do to these monsters.

Two women shrieked and flailed but could not get off their beds; after verifying that neither one was Muriel, he killed them both. He and Zoe would leave nothing intact here. Nothing at all. Those unborn babies did not deserve their fates, but he was no rescuer and neither was Zoe. Those offspring had been doomed from the moment of their unnatural conception.

"I found her," Zoe called. She leaned over an enormous woman sprawled on a gestation bed.

As he strode over, Tom Rom barely recognized Muriel. Her skin was a sickly tarpaulin over a framework of bones, her legs fat and atrophied, her pudgy arms waving ineffectually. Her eyes were wide with alarm and fury, but dulled with drugs.

Tom Rom wanted to vomit. It took his greatest imagination to filter through this bloated, disgusting wreck of a woman to remember the much younger, much prettier person who had tempted him more than a quarter century earlier. "I used to think you were beautiful, Muriel. You fooled me."

In the years since, he had thought about her, tried to recapture the brief happiness from their affair. But not even the most extreme fantasy pleasure could atone for knowing what she had done to their daughter, who had been offered up for sacrifice; after which, Muriel had sold herself again and again.

Tom Rom stepped up to the gestation bed, looking down at the woman without pity. Muriel looked at him. "I know you. I remember. . . ."

He was surprised she recognized him. "And I know what you've done. All those children. My child."

Muriel lashed out, "*My* children. All of them. *Mine*. Produced *by me*. I can do what I want with them."

"Except for me," Zoe said. "Hello, Mother."

The woman thrashed on the bed, looked at Zoe. Her expression had a manic edge. "My daughter came back to me?" She laughed. "Which one? Ah, you're the one I sold—the pretty one."

"I'm the one who survived. I'm the one who's come back."

"*My* babies," Muriel snapped, struggling to get up off the bed, but her stomach was bloated, her arms and legs too weak.

"I am not yours," Zoe said.

"None of them are yours, Muriel." Tom Rom trembled with the thought of his real daughter, who would never be real to him now, only imaginary, only possibilities. "You have nothing. You *deserve* nothing. Every comfort you bought with the deaths of those babies? We're taking it all away from you."

"No!" Muriel shrieked.

Two of the other factory wombs nearby groaned and tried to escape; one made if off her bed, but collapsed to the floor.

Muriel cried, "Give me endorphins. I want my endorphins." She clutched at the tubes and yelled for the doctors, all of whom lay dead around the room.

"I have only one gift to give you, Mother," Zoe said, and placed a detonator on her mounded stomach, beyond the reach of her flailing, weak hands. As she did it, Zoe looked oddly wistful, and her expression sent a chill through him. "How many children do you think she had, Tom Rom? How many babies lost?"

He gave her the cold, terrible answer. "She had only one child. You."

He placed other detonators around the medical facility, paused to consider whether he should kill the last surviving factory wombs first, but decided to let the explosions take care of the loose ends. *There are no innocents in this place.*

Muriel was still shouting, but Zoe did not look back at her. The detonator timers were already set.

The two of them left, wrapped in their own thoughts, but with no regrets. They walked past the dead guards, the dead receptionist, dead techs, and dead doctors, climbed aboard the flatboat transport, and accelerated down the weedy canal with thirty seconds to spare before eruptions blossomed into the swampy night.

They reached the ship and flew away before Rakkem's haphazard security forces thought to shut down the spaceport.

Zoe said, "Those prisdiamonds on Vaconda—we have a lot of them, right?"

"More than you can imagine. More than you could ever spend."

"Then I can build my own medical facility. Make it bigger, more thorough, and more important than anything here on Rakkem."

Tom Rom hesitated. "That would be ambitious . . . but, yes, it's possible."

"I want to do it." She thought for a long time. "I want all the cures, all the diseases. Everything that curesellers and biomerchants have—and I want it for myself." Her voice carried an odd echo of her mother's.

"If that is what you want."

Once the transport skimmer picked him up at the transportal outcropping, Tom Rom arrived at the docking platform outside Kuivahr's main sanctuary dome. Frothy green water lapped against the curved submerged surface, and he could smell the rich mixture of plankton and kelp all around him. He waited as a lift rose up inside the dome, and Tamo'l herself stood there to receive him. "Was my research data useful to your employer?"

He nodded. "It proved interesting indeed, and this time I've come to share something of our own regarding Prince Reynald's disease. King Peter and Queen Estarra dispatched me here to bring it to you."

She brightened. "Then we will receive it gladly. We already have some promising treatments." Tamo'l gestured toward the lift. "Join us—unless the misbreeds will disturb you?"

He gave her a small smile. "No need to worry. I have seen far worse."

CHAPTER 109

TASIA TAMBLYN

The emergency alarms in the *Voracious Curiosity*'s cockpit didn't matter, and Tasia didn't care about the red lines as she hauled ass away from the Iswander extraction yards. The ship had been damaged, and Tasia lost a lot of maneuverability, but she ran anyway—full speed, evasive maneuvers, high acceleration, abrupt and impossible course changes. She used every trick she had learned during the Elemental War.

Even when they were far from the bloater cluster, she kept going. If she stopped for a minute to make emergency repairs, the *Curiosity* would be wiped out in no time. Elisa Enturi didn't seem to be in the mood for discussion.

When Tasia finally managed to activate the Ildiran stardrive, the sudden acceleration slammed them back with enough force to pull skin tight against muscles and press down on bones like a giant invisible foot. DD tumbled sideways and skittered across the deck. Orli Covitz let out an involuntary grunt of pain and fear. Robb couldn't breathe, but Tasia did not relent.

"Come on!" she said through gritted teeth.

The cockpit alarms reached a crescendo. Several secondary systems finally gave up, and the screens went dark. Gambling, Tasia kept flying for another ten seconds, then decided she couldn't risk it any longer. They were as safe as they were going to be, and if the engines failed completely, the *Curiosity* would be stranded, unable to get home. In that case, they might as well have let Elisa blast them to bits—at least the end would have been quicker.

The ship had gone the better part of a parsec in only a few minutes, and no Iswander pursuers would be able to find them. Tasia shut everything down and let the *Curiosity* drift. The system alarms remained loud and scolding, but emergency levels slowly diminished. It seemed to her that the ship was sulking, licking its wounds.

Tasia let out a long exhale and realized she was shaking. "Well, that was fun."

DD picked himself up from the deck and stood beside Orli. "Perhaps I no longer understand the human concept of fun. I thought I grasped it before. Can you please explain, Orli Covitz?"

Orli wiped her brow. "She's being sarcastic, DD."

Robb unbuckled his restraints in the copilot seat. "That wasn't what we expected to find, but we did discover where Iswander gets his ekti-X."

"When Garrison and I flew away from Ikbir, we saw countless bloaters drifting in strings, like breadcrumbs in space." Orli turned to look at Tasia and Robb. "They're not hard to find."

"It's not the bloaters Iswander is trying to hide," Tasia said. "He doesn't want anybody to know what they're made of. After the Duquesne massacre and what just happened to us, there's no doubt they're willing to kill to protect the secret."

"At least Elisa is," Orli said. "When I met him, Lee Iswander seemed a rational man."

"She's operating under his orders, whether they're explicit or implied," Tasia said. "Elisa needs to face the music for what she's done, and so does Iswander."

Robb headed toward the back of the *Curiosity* to access the engine compartment. He ran a diagnostic check, studied the automated damage report. "I may need to go outside and do some external fixes."

DD marched up beside him, bright and helpful. "I can assist. I have a programming module of starship engine specs and repair instructions. Orli Covitz had me help her run the *Proud Mary*."

"Then let's have the compy go outside and do the hard work," Tasia said.

"I would be happy to."

Robb removed an environment suit from the equipment locker. "We'll work out there together. We've got spare components for the most critical systems."

Tasia said, "Meanwhile, Orli and I will compile the evidence and see what we've got. There's enough to make a lot of waves."

Robb and DD cycled through the airlock, clipped themselves onto the outer hull, and began to replace damaged hull plates. While they swapped out failing stardrive components, Tasia called up the images their forward recorders had captured of the extraction field, the large arrays of ekti-X tanks. Next came the chaotic records from when they were being chased by the security ships and fired upon by Elisa Enturi.

Orli had already cleaned up the log record retrieved from the wrecked Duquesne tanker, which would have been damning enough, but the encounter at the Iswander extraction yards sealed the deal.

Tasia was sickened to remember that Lee Iswander had wanted to become the next clan Speaker, but the Sheol debacle had destroyed his political ambitions. Now Iswander was rebuilding his fortune and his reputation with ekti-X, and her own Kett Shipping had helped him in that. Tasia wanted nothing more than to expose Iswander, and she knew Rlinda Kett was going to approve, even if it cost them a lot of profits.

Shizz, the company could also have continued to make money selling horrific "boutique medical treatments" from Aldo Cerf, but after Xander and Terry's experience on Dremen, they had put an immediate end to that.

When Orli reviewed the images of the industrial yard, she described what she remembered from the first bloater cluster. Tasia studied the ship configurations at the site, identified a hodgepodge of makes and models. "Looks to me like Iswander bought up all kinds of functional Roamer ships and equipment and modified them to the work here." She shook her head and knew the best way to bring about Iswander's downfall, where to hit him that would hurt most.

The *Curiosity*'s cockpit screens lit up, and the warning lamps switched from amber to green. She called up a report grid, saw that Robb and the compy had even repaired several noncritical systems. "Well, aren't you two ambitious?"

Over the comm, Robb said, "DD doesn't like to leave a job incomplete, and it only took a few extra minutes. Besides, Rlinda will be happy to have the *Curiosity* back in reasonable condition."

"Now come inside, so we can get out of here." Tasia was anxious to sound the alarm about Iswander.

By the time Robb and DD cycled back into the *Curiosity*'s main cabin, Tasia was ready to depart. Robb removed his helmet and stripped off the environment suit. The compy seemed quite pleased with the work they had done.

"Good job, DD," Orli said.

"The *Curiosity* will take us where we need to go," Robb said, then raised his eyebrows. "Which is where exactly?"

"Theroc?" Orli suggested. "Report to the King and Queen? The Confederation can bring down the hammer on Iswander Industries."

Tasia shook her head. "Considering who he is, and what we saw, there's a more effective way to shut him down completely." She felt her face grow hot. "We'll go to Newstation and address the clan convocation. The Roamers will deal with their own."

CHAPTER

110

XANDER BRINDLE

At the Earth headquarters of Kett Shipping, Xander and Terry oversaw the repairs to the *Verne* so closely that they got in the way. When the company mechanics finally complained, Rlinda Kett pulled the two and their compy aside.

"You just let them do their work, boys," she said. "I'm already doing you a favor by picking up the tab, but if my mechanics charge me overtime because you're pests, I'll take the surcharge out of your wages."

Xander was embarrassed. "I just want to be sure my ship is taken care of properly."

Rlinda put a beefy arm around his shoulders and guided him out of the repair hangar, while OK and Terry followed. "Don't you worry, a good meal prepared by an excellent chef—by which I mean me—will take your mind off it."

Terry brightened at the prospect.

Xander had already seen the repair schedule for the battered ship: roughly one third of the hull plates would need to be swapped out; two engines had to be repaired, one replaced entirely; whole electronics packages had been burned out; defensive weaponry was depleted and would need to be restored.

He had also seen the estimated bill. Some owners might have suggested simply scrapping the ship, taking whatever they could get for salvage, and buying an entirely new vessel. But this was the *Verne*, and Xander wouldn't even consider that. When his parents returned from snooping around the Iswander ekti-extraction fields, he was sure they'd agree with his decision.

In her quarters in a habitation tower near Kett Shipping, Rlinda made them feel right at home. The compy stood at polite attention as she bustled about to "scrounge up" something to eat—which did not prove very difficult at all. "I only have desserts. Primarily pastries. I hope that'll do."

Terry was already licking his lips. "Anything special?"

"It's all special, dear boy." Rlinda put her hands on her generous hips. "The lightest, flakiest, cream-filled delights you could possibly imagine. Some of them are more frosting than substance—intentionally so." She put a large plate of exotic pastries in front of him and Terry. "There's even a delicate cream kringle with a hint of saffron."

"Saffron." Xander felt suddenly sad. "All that saffron. Maria left us half a ton of the stuff in her treasure vault on Ulio, but it's all blown up by the damn robots and the Shana Rei." He pictured the wondrous stockpile of valuables the old woman had stashed away for years and years. "Oh, you should've seen it, Rlinda. A museum and a treasure trove. You couldn't imagine . . ."

"What I don't want to imagine is you two being dead. You got away from Ulio Station when a lot of people didn't. Be satisfied with that."

"That's what I keep telling myself." He took a bite of the kringle, and explosive sweetness filled his mouth. "But Terry lost a fortune, an absolute fortune."

His partner seemed much less bothered by the loss. "Once the *Verne* is repaired, I'll have everything I want. A fortune would have been nice, yes, but I don't dwell on it."

"Well, I do!" Xander was upset that his partner was so aloof about the loss. "Not so we could have a decadent lifestyle—but we could have tried dozens of different treatments, ones that were always too expensive for you to consider before! I can't believe there isn't somebody who could fix your spinal damage, who could give you your legs back again."

Terry's expression fell, and he leaned over to clasp Xander's forearm. "I haven't been able to use my legs for so long I don't even think about it anymore, and all the saffron and prisdiamonds and firegems in the Spiral Arm won't make any difference."

"But Maria had an even bigger fortune in her other accounts, and it just vanished, down in flames with the Ulio Central Offices." He picked up another pastry and pushed it into his mouth as if it were a matter of self-defense. "All inaccessible to us now."

Standing quietly in position, the compy startled them by speaking up. "The funds are not inaccessible so long as we have the account numbers, the routing codes, and the passwords."

Xander sighed and licked confectioner's sugar from his fingertips. "In other words, *inaccessible*. Maria had hundreds of account numbers and twenty-digit randomized passcodes. We wouldn't even know where to begin."

OK spoke up. "Not accurate, Xander. I have all of those codes. They were displayed on the Central Office screens at Ulio Station."

"We didn't have time to input them before the shadows attacked," Terry said. "The accounts are locked."

"But I recorded all of the data. I have complete recall of every single number displayed on that screen," the compy said. "We can access the accounts as soon as I connect to the Confederation banking system networks."

Xander caught his breath. "You're kidding."

"No, Xander. If I were kidding, I would establish the basis for humor more clearly."

Terry stared, oblivious to the frosting around his mouth. "You have the account numbers for all that money?"

"It is your money, Terry Handon."

Rlinda let out an explosive laugh, but Terry remained astonished. "Why didn't you say so, OK?"

"I did not realize it was a concern. You expressed dismay that all of the tangible assets, such as the saffron and prisdiamonds, were destroyed, and I could do nothing about that. Now the *Verne* is being repaired, and since Rlinda Kett is paying to fix our ship, I did not realize that the lack of money caused you distress. I apologize that I did not give this greater priority."

Xander sprang to his feet and wrapped his arms around the compy. "I should never underestimate you, OK!" Now he could start the long process of searching for medical help for Terry, without worrying a whit about the cost.

"Thank you, Xander," the compy said.

Rlinda couldn't stop laughing. "This changes everything. Most importantly"—she pointed a stern finger at the two young men—"now you can pay for your own damn repairs."

CHAPTER 111

TAL GALE'NH

Back at Ildira, the four warliners that had survived the battle at the Onthos system underwent full repairs. Their structural damage was fixed, their laser-cannon batteries were recharged, their sun bomb arsenal was resupplied.

Angry at what had happened but refusing to admit defeat, Adar Zan'nh rallied an entire cohort above Ildira—343 warliners consisting of seven maniples, each with forty-nine battleships. The frantic work had an edge of desperation. No one knew when or where the shadows would appear next.

True to her promise, General Keah had provided a large shipment of the enhanced sun bombs, which she swore were substantially more powerful than the original Ildiran designs. Adar Zan'nh took her at her word and commanded that the new nova weapons be added to the arsenal already loaded aboard the warliners. Gale'nh had not seen them function, but he did not discount human ingenuity.

Gale'nh also had a sad, personal duty to finish. At the Prism Palace, Gale'nh presented himself to the Mage-Imperator and Nira with a heavy heart. "Rod'h is lost, Mother. The shadows swallowed him."

Jora'h and the green priest already knew the facts of the situation, thanks to telink reports from Nadd aboard the *Kutuzov*, but they had not heard the full story. "Muree'n could sense that something had happened to Rod'h," Nira said, struggling to contain her emotions. "She told me as soon she felt the shock, but we didn't know for sure. Nadd couldn't tell me anything about Rod'h."

In the skysphere audience chamber, his half-sister looked even more dour than usual, standing like a statue in her armor. "Our brother is still alive, and still fighting," Muree'n said. "I cannot always feel him, but I know he is in great pain."

"Yes, great pain—and terror," Gale'nh agreed. "I failed to protect him. He insisted on investigating the verdani battleship alone. I left him vulnerable. I could not save him."

Prime Designate Daro'h hurried into the large chamber, his eyes flashing from side to side. "Is it true? I felt it in the *thism*, but I could not be sure. The shadows have killed Rod'h? That cannot be so! He was my friend, my adviser. He was braver than . . ."

Gale'nh looked at the anxious Prime Designate. He continued to be haunted by the last memory, when he had watched the shadow cloud swallow his brother's ship. "Rod'h is not dead. He is strong. He still fights them."

Daro'h was shocked and angry. "How long can he last against the Shana Rei? It is not possible!"

"He will last as long as I did. Long enough."

Nira said, "He was desperate to prove his worth. He had high expectations of himself, and he intended to show it. And now the creatures of darkness have him."

"They released you." Daro'h clung to hope. "Perhaps they will release him as well."

Gale'nh did not say that he doubted the Shana Rei would make the same mistake again.

Jora'h said, "Adar Zan'nh will continue his training exercises in orbit. The creatures of darkness have caused us enough losses. It is time to fight back."

Gale'nh bowed. "I will review all encounters, Liege, and assess what I know. If I cannot discover how to rescue Rod'h, I will at least try to learn ways that we can defeat the Shana Rei the next time they attack."

CHAPTER

112

KOTTO OKIAH

With the Big Ring finally completed, Kotto felt giddy with joy and anticipation, yet also intimidated.

For years he had led the Roamers to this, guided the construction crews, drawn his designs, and told the clan engineers what to do. He had racked up an incalculable expense—not that he had ever been good at finances or budgeting. The data produced during the test might change fundamental comprehension about the underlying structure of the universe, might open up huge system-to-system transportals like the much smaller ones the Klikiss had left behind in their ruins. Or it might do something else entirely.

This project was not hubris—it was *audacity*. Such was the heart of a Roamer, and Kotto wanted to remind all of the clans, as well as the Confederation and the Ildiran Empire, exactly what Roamers were best at. He wanted his Big Ring to be a bright example for the bold, optimistic vision that had always driven the clans.

After receiving the completion report from Station Chief Alu, Kotto just stood inside his laboratory module and stared out the windowport. It was *done*.

The Ring design was deceptively simple, just a giant doughnut loaded with a cascading loop of power blocks that, when operated in sequence, would create a ring current greater than anything ever recorded. That current would generate a cross-magnetic field, turning the Big Ring into a freestanding magnetic coil with the diameter of a small moon.

Right now, the Ring hung edge-on to the incredible furnace of the keystone stars in the Fireheart nebula. When the experiment began, maneuvering jets would turn the Big Ring on its axis, so that the intense stellar flux would flow through the center of the Ring, like a high-energy fire hose gushing through the superconducting magnetic coil. That would cause a logarithmic increase in the magnetic field, thereby increasing the current in the Ring, which would in turn further enhance the magnetic field . . . in an ever-accelerating spiral.

Kotto felt excited just to imagine the possibilities, but even his highest-order mathematics could not predict what would happen beyond that point. He just hoped the experiment would *work*, that his legacy as a genius would remain secure. It had been a long time since Kotto had shown he was the greatest Roamer scientist, and he needed to prove it again—to himself as well as to everyone else.

Shareen Fitzkellum and Howard Rohandas had surprised him with how easily they solved problems that had stymied him for years. When they grew older they would build upon his work and maybe stand beside him in the history books. But not yet. The Big Ring would put Kotto back on a pedestal for years to come.

Chief Alu pressed him for a demonstration date, but this was no time to rush the work. Three more days. Although the Ring was constructed and could be operated at any time, Kotto exercised due caution. He called for more extended testing to verify every single connection, every vital component. He didn't consider it stalling. Now that he had reached this point, he was a little afraid to see the project come to its end, one way or another.

And if it failed . . .

As instructed, Shareen and Howard had delivered their proposed new designs for the filter-flow system, along with a thorough analysis on another frivolous brainstorm he'd had one sleepless night years ago—a kind of photonic shield that could bend light around objects and make them invisible. Howard Rohandas had written a lengthy proof, demonstrating that the concept was physically impossible and could not work along the lines Kotto suggested. He took Howard at his word without going through the many pages of derivation. Kotto himself had never been able to solve that particular problem, though he had secretly harbored the hope that his young lab assistants might find a miraculous work-around. No such luck.

Well, it didn't really matter. The Big Ring was the focus of his energies and his dreams right now.

He invited Shareen and Howard to join him as he went to the station's launching bay, where he had reserved an inspection pod large enough to carry three passengers. "This is my reward for the good work you two have done."

Shareen's eyes were bright. "Are we going out there? To see the Ring for ourselves?"

"Thank you, sir." Howard was polite, as always. "We both very much look forward to seeing the Big Ring."

"We will commence the actual experiment in a few days and demonstrate the wonders of big science." Kotto ushered them toward the inspection pod.

Since Shareen had plenty of experience flying, she offered to pilot the pod, and Kotto happily gestured her toward the controls. He was a competent pilot himself, but he preferred to spend his attention looking out the windowport. The Big Ring always took his breath away.

The small craft flew into the ionized sea, heading toward the curved sections of the enormous torus. Countless nebula workers swarmed like insects over the outer skin, testing power blocks and aligning amplifiers. Kotto scanned a stream of reports that he received on his datapad. "Everything is proceeding nicely. The complete round of final checks might be done in three days, and then we'll see the Big Ring in operation."

Shareen flew them through the center of the torus like threading a needle and looped around so they could follow the curve, riding the Ring up and around. Howard drank in the details of the construction, but Shareen seemed preoccupied. Kotto thought that something was bothering her. Finally, she blurted out, "Are you absolutely sure about this, sir? We looked at complete copies of your Big Ring plans—Howard and I studied every detail. We ran and reran your calculations."

Kotto frowned. "But I haven't even released the complete plans."

"We obtained access to the records, sir," Howard said. "After we finished the other work you assigned us, we wanted to verify your calculations. Just as an exercise."

"We think there's something wrong," Shareen interrupted. "We found no overt errors, but some of the conclusions are iffy. A few anticipated results just don't follow, and we question the assumptions."

Kotto felt as if he'd been struck, and he couldn't help but react defensively. "I did not give you permission to comb through my work. Besides, I . . . I didn't put down every detail of my thinking. You must have missed a step."

Howard sounded apologetic. "We were able to connect the mathematics, sir. After the exercises you gave us, we're familiar with your thought processes, so we figured—"

Kotto looked back and forth between the two young assistants, growing alarmed. "You should not have done that."

"But we think there's a problem," Shareen said. "The Big Ring might not work the way you expect it to."

"I intend to keep an open mind. It is an experiment. We will operate the Ring, look at the results, and then draw our conclusions. We don't need to understand the answers before we run the tests."

Shareen sounded frustrated. "But we think there's cause for caution. You should reconsider before going into full operation."

"We can't! Final testing will be complete in three days." Kotto glanced down at his pad. "And the experiment will proceed as scheduled. I won't hear any more of it from two junior assistants."

Howard fell into silence. Shareen's cheeks rippled as she clenched her jaw. Obviously stung, she flew away from the Big Ring and headed back toward the docking bay in the main station.

Kotto leaned back in the seat, crossed his arms, and tried to pretend that he was indignant rather than panicked. He didn't want to admit to himself that Shareen and Howard had merely echoed and amplified his own doubts. After such an investment in time, effort, money, and Roamer pride, Kotto simply could not call off the Big Ring test.

But, in a small place deep in the back of his mind, he was afraid that Shareen and Howard were right.

CHAPTER

113

ZHETT KELLUM

It was a day remarkably free of clouds for Kuivahr. As Zhett stood with Patrick on the high deck of the distillery platform, she looked up to see both moons close together in the sky.

"Your turn." Patrick handed her baby Rex, who willingly extended his pudgy hands for his mother to take him. He was old enough to be walking on his own—or running places where he shouldn't go, which made him more of a risk. Fortunately the toddler was still needy and preferred to be held. A low-output antigrav harness kept him tethered to his mother or father, so they could do their work while keeping Rex close.

Zhett sniffed, frowned, and held Rex in front of her, but it wasn't a messy diaper, just the usual stench of the mudflats around the base of the distillery tower. Having spent much of her life aboard drifting cloud harvesters on gas giants, she was accustomed to sour vapors rising from the cloud bands. But she didn't think she'd ever get used to the fishy, iodine odors of this place.

Below, she and Patrick watched cargo being loaded onto a pontoon landing raft: cases of freshly bottled Ooze for personal consumption, as well as large kegs that would be sent to Rlinda Kett's restaurants, their exclusive customer for this particular batch.

The dull buzz of conversation wafted up to them, followed by laughter. Pointing down, Patrick indicated a teenager on a personal waveskimmer circling the pontoon raft. Kristof headed out to meet a group of Ildiran swimmers who were coming in with freshly harvested kelp for the distillery mash tanks. Toff seemed to be teasing the otter-like swimmers, raising rooster tails of water as he circled them. Zhett could see him grinning. The laughter stopped with a splash as one of the Ildirans upended the skimmer, spilling Toff into the water. He came up sputtering and retrieved the skimmer, but he didn't really mind being drenched.

Del Kellum sauntered out onto the deck to join them. "Once our kelpbeer catches on, we're going to need a larger landing raft, by damn. We'll be shipping kegs all across the Spiral Arm. We'll have to increase production, too."

Zhett said, "I'd rather get rid of our old stockpiles first, Dad. Nobody seems to want the early stuff."

"Maybe because it still tastes bad," Patrick said. "We should just dump it into the sea."

"What, and kill all the kelp?" Zhett teased.

Del sniffed. "It's not bad, it's . . . classic. Just needs to be aged properly."

When a small transport ship was loaded on the landing raft, workers sealed the hatches and stepped away so the ship could lift off. On a bright column of vapor, it rose into the unusually clear sky.

Del continued, "Yoder's ship is in orbit, ready to take a full load."

"He's a month late," Zhett said.

"Had a bit of a crash-landing incident, nowhere close to a repair facility or spare parts," Del explained. "But he's back in his routine now."

Routine . . . that was what this had become. Zhett supposed family life and a successful business on a calm planet was a nice reward in itself. Skymining was in her blood, but thanks to all the ekti-X produced by Iswander Industries, clan Kellum couldn't justify the outrageous expense of rebuilding a cloud harvester, or even buying a cheap secondhand one, like the one Aaron Duquesne had tried to sell them. Under normal circumstances, a new skymine would have taken most of clan Kellum's wealth plus a good chunk of Patrick's inheritance. Right now, the distillery was probably their best bet.

As she held the baby, Zhett wondered if Rex would one day take over the distillery operations, just as she and Patrick had taken over from her father. Toff and Rex could run the operations together, a good business for two brothers.

But it wouldn't be Shareen. Their daughter had a remarkable opportunity working with Kotto Okiah at Fireheart Station. It was going to change the girl's life. Zhett was sure that Shareen had big things in store for her.

The intercom blared, startling them. "Del, Zhett, Patrick! Get to the control deck—right away!" It was Marius Denva, the distillery's operations manager. "You're going to want to see this—on second thought, you probably *don't* want to see it, but you better get here anyway."

The distillery's upper-level control center was a big open area with screens, systems ops, and a lot of clutter; the distillery didn't actually need a full-fledged command center the way a large skymine did. The workers tended to be casual; unpacked boxes lay around or were stacked in corners.

Right now all the people were staring at the screens. The bearded, gray-haired trader Dando Yoder was transmitting from his ship in orbit. He had a rough squawking voice. "It just appeared! Huge. Black. My systems are all going haywire! Half my screens are down—can't even activate the nav computer."

Zhett had been expecting some business headache, but what she saw on the screen made her heart turn cold. Patrick groaned. "Not again!"

Rather than sending up geysers of blackness in a gas giant's atmosphere, this time the Shana Rei emerged in orbit above Kuivahr. The dark nebula bled through a tear in the fabric of space, flowing out in an ever-widening pool like spilled ink. Five cylindrical six-sided ships extended from the cloud, showing no running lights or markings whatsoever. They resembled massive obsidian crystals, growing larger as they emerged.

"What am I supposed to do up here?" Yoder said. "I just got my ship repaired, and I don't have weapons for this!"

"You can't fight!" Zhett grabbed the comm. "Just get out of here!" The trader didn't need to be told twice. His ship streaked out of orbit, heading away from the black cloud.

"What the hell do the Shana Rei want *here*?" Patrick asked no one in particular. "We're just a distillery. They can have all the Primordial Ooze they want."

"I'll be sure to ask for an explanation if we have a chance to chat," Zhett said.

"Well, we didn't do anything to provoke them at Golgen either, by damn!" Del said.

The hex ships loomed above, as if they meant to crush everyone on Kuivahr. Thin slices detached from the flat ends and fell toward low orbit. A chain of hex plates spun away from all five Shana Rei cylinders and drifted down toward the outer edge of the atmosphere in a blizzard of material. As if carefully guided, one hex plate aligned its edge with a second, then a third. They joined together, coalescing.

Maurice Denva stood by the comm, staring at the screen. "Am I supposed to transmit a surrender or something? Ask for terms?"

"You won't get an answer," Zhett said.

Hundreds more hex plates spun off, clicked together, and began assembling a barricade, piece by piece by piece.

Patrick looked at her. "We know what's going to happen—no point in waiting and pretending."

"No point at all," Zhett agreed, holding on to Rex. "It's time to get out of here."

CHAPTER 114

ROD'H

Surrounded by disorienting blackness and silence, Rod'h felt cold, hungry, and lost. His thoughts were torn open and exposed.

He had not meant to surrender information that would help the creatures of darkness. They interrogated him, tormented him . . . then did it all over again.

Every last building block of strength, every hidden corner of his personality had been ripped away, and Rod'h struggled to rebuild it. Earlier, the Shana Rei had toyed with Gale'nh, wiped his memories and discarded him on the haunted *Kolpraxa*. But they kept Rod'h so they could do it repeatedly. And when that wasn't enough, they allowed one of the black robots to work on him.

The Shana Rei needed to learn from him—and Rod'h tried to turn it against them. He observed even in his greatest agony. He tried to glean data and draw conclusions by studying their ignorance. The basic things the shadows didn't know might reveal a weakness, a blind spot.

Appalled, he discovered that the Shana Rei considered *life itself* to be the source of pain, that they hated the agony of creation and that their goal was to unmake the universe and then annihilate themselves so they could find solace.

That understanding was in itself frightening. No matter what, there could never be peace with the creatures of darkness. They had to be defeated, Rod'h knew—wiped out utterly, or existence itself would end. But even if he discovered some flaw from this gulf of captivity, some way to fight them, how would he ever convey it to anyone who could respond to it?

The Shana Rei imprisoned Rod'h in an entropy bubble inside one of the enormous hexagonal ships that had been assembled from night and emptiness. Not giving up, he reached out with *thism*, casting threads anywhere in hope that he might find some contact outside. But the shadows caught those threads and used them to spin deeper into the *thism* network like a spreading blight.

The inkblots appeared around him with blazing eyes and maddening voices. "You are our conduit."

"No!" Rod'h tried to block out his thoughts, but the Shana Rei simply toyed with him, letting him know that they would destroy the *thism* from the inside.

He found himself spinning, screaming, and they penetrated his mind despite the walls he tried to erect. His flesh was healed, but scarred. The black robot's pincers had torn him open, dissected him, and the Shana Rei put him back together again, never letting him die, although he felt and remembered every instant of terrible pain. The robot Exxos could keep doing that endlessly.

Although the Shana Rei wanted to use him as a gateway to infiltrate the *thism*, Rod'h was merely a halfbreed, and his connection to the purely Ildiran telepathic network was not exceptional. Perhaps the creatures of darkness had overestimated him, and when they realized their mistake, they would discard him as they had with Gale'nh . . . or perhaps they would just let the black robots continue toying with him.

But he was strong in other ways.

During his moment of greatest torment, Rod'h used all of his mental powers, everything the countless training sessions on Dobro had taught him, and reached out for anyone, any*thing*—and for just a flicker of an instant he felt the connection he had experienced only once. A touch of what he had felt at the turbulent star Wulfton. The faeros! He clutched at them like a lifeline, and they *knew* what the shadows were doing to him. He begged the fiery elementals for help, but they snuffed out the mental link and fled. . . .

Rod'h drifted, and the Shana Rei did what they liked.

When the five hexagonal cylinders emerged from the dark layers beneath space, the Shana Rei allowed the entropy bubble to become transparent, to taunt him. Rod'h could see where they were.

At first he wept just to see the bright sparkle of stars in the real universe, a nearby sun, a planet below. Rod'h could sense something down there, calling. As if a blindfold had been removed and plugs taken from his ears, he felt the *thism* again, bright and intense. There were Ildirans down on that planet . . . as well as Osira'h and Tamo'l!

This must be Kuivahr, the Ildiran sanctuary world. The creatures of darkness had come to gather two more of his halfbreed siblings. Experimental subjects, just like him!

Then he remembered what else Tamo'l did down there in the sanctuary domes. All those misbreeds . . . genetic anomalies, outcasts with painfully visible flaws, but very poorly understood abilities. The shadows wanted to snuff them out, too! Or maybe test them for hidden skills.

He felt a shudder in the entropy bubble around him. The huge hex ships slowly turned, reorienting themselves toward the doomed planet. The Shana Rei began to spin off hex plates that whirled down to low orbit, connecting edge-to-edge, forming another black barrier.

Rod'h knew what they were going to do: they would not just seize his two sisters; they would destroy the world as well. At the Onthos home, the Shana Rei had created a Dyson sphere so enormous that it englobed an entire star system. This time, though, they would merely encase the planet in an impenetrable suffocating shell of black. The entire planet.

Countless hex components made the shell grow, swiftly, inexorably. The Shana Rei were in no hurry. They were relentless.

In desperation, Rod'h used his special connection to anchor himself with Tamo'l, with Osira'h. His older sister had always been the strongest of Nira's children, and he clutched at that strength now. He had to warn them.

"Osira'h!" he cried out in his mind.

He felt her realize that he was there, and Tamo'l also recognized the contact. His sisters were at first overjoyed, then terrified. He could feel Osira'h trying to shore up his strength from a distance, Tamo'l adding her mind and her connection, as well. Rod'h longed to be with them, to beg for help and to feel relief, but instead, he summoned all of his energy to send out one blasting command, knowing that his sisters would understand—and he prayed that they would obey.

"Do not try to help me. Escape! You must escape!"

CHAPTER 115

LEE ISWANDER

Despite several setbacks, Lee Iswander was ready to reclaim his prominence among the Roamer clans. His success was incontrovertible, and since he was the sole provider of cheap and plentiful ekti-X, many Roamers depended on him too.

Oh, he didn't care that the clans disliked him. That was to be expected when a man became unexpectedly successful. Iswander was prepared for that. But after the tragedy on Sheol, which devastated his lava-processing facility and cost 1,543 lives, he had been taken aback when the Roamers *turned on him*, rather than supporting him through the difficulty. They didn't like his clothes or his attitude; they claimed he was too much like the hated, old Terran Hanseatic League, yet they snubbed him for doing exactly what Roamers were supposed to do.

For centuries, the clans had risked much, taken gambles in inhospitable environments, tried to do the impossible, and when such attempts failed—as they often did—those risk takers were seen as martyrs, the situations tragic. But when it happened to Lee Iswander, they accused him of hubris.

Rather than being defeated by circumstances, he had quietly rebuilt his fortune in record time, and now Iswander Industries provided a vital commodity to all the clans. They might resent him for that, but they could not ignore him. At what point would he grow powerful and wealthy enough for them to accept clan Iswander again?

Besides, they'd had months of the incompetent Speaker Sam Ricks, whom they had elected in Iswander's stead. He wouldn't berate them for their stupid mistake, simply give them an opportunity to fix it. He wanted to be the grownup in the room. And he had the proof to take Ricks down.

He had left his main extraction field in the capable hands of Elisa Enturi and Alec Pannebaker, and they would continue producing stardrive fuel at the facility's peak capacity.

Arriving at the Roamer capital, he had been shocked to learn about the recent destruction of Ulio Station. The attack was a terrible reminder of the dangerous enemies abroad in the Spiral Arm, and the clans were all on edge. Ulio was a major commercial hub and transfer point for all sorts of Roamer products, as well as Iswander Industries' main distribution channel for ekti-X. Its loss was quite a blow to all of the clans.

Obviously, even Elisa hadn't known; with no green priest at the extraction field, they were cut off from the happenings in the Confederation. When he became Speaker, Iswander would rectify that.

For now, he had a proposal and a plan. He had a bargain to offer that would benefit many, if not all, of the clans.

The question was, would they listen?

At Newstation, he called a clan convocation to address all Roamers on "matters regarding ekti-X," because they would all attend to hear that topic, expecting to receive some clue to his miraculous process.

When it was nearly time for him to address the clan representatives, Iswander paced in his VIP suite, practicing and reviewing. He wished Elisa were here to advise him, but he was on his own.

For the occasion, Iswander considered wearing a traditional Roamer jumpsuit with his clan markings embroidered on the pockets and sleeves. He knew his formal business suit was like a thorn in their side; every time they saw him dressed professionally, he looked like a stranger to them, an outsider. But if he now wore the traditional jumpsuit—which he never did—they would plainly see it as pandering. It would ring entirely false.

Business suit it was, then.

Back at the extraction yard, he had compiled his dossier on Sam Ricks and reviewed it with Elisa. The man's incompetence was obvious, and the number of sloppy treaties, dropped balls, and unfinished actions was stunning. Iswander finally held all the cards, and he would play his hand.

When he arrived in the convocation chamber, he smiled to see how full it was. Although this wasn't a friendly crowd, it was quite different from the Speaker election, when he'd been disgraced by receiving only one vote. He had earned enough clout with his cheap stardrive fuel that they were inclined to pay attention; in fact, many of these clans would want a piece of his ekti-X business. He was sure of it.

The only truly angry ones were the traditional skyminers, whose giant and expensive cloud-harvesting facilities were rapidly becoming obsolete. There was nothing he could do about that.

As he strode into the common area, someone called from the fourth tier of the curved seats. "Come to share your secrets, Iswander? Tell us all how we can produce ekti-X!" He didn't recognize the middle-aged woman, didn't recognize many of these people from their faces alone. Unlike Sam Ricks, he had never been one for glad-handing and schmoozing. "Clans are supposed to stick together."

"Oh?" He crossed his arms as he took his place at the podium. "Like you all stuck with me in my time of need after Sheol?"

"A lot of people died because of your incompetence—including three of my cousins," growled an overweight young man.

"What happened at Sheol was an accident and a tragedy, and I could name plenty of other tragedies in Roamer history. I tried something bold and profitable, and the planet turned against me, just as hostile environments have turned against many Roamers." He glowered at them. "How can you blame me? How can you make me an outcast among Roamers? It's a core principle that we *take risks*. We make bold gestures and search for out-of-the-way resources that we can make commercially viable. That's why we originally took over skymining operations from the Ildiran Empire, because we could do it better!

"You revere Kotto Okiah as a great genius—but go back and look at Isperos or Jonah 12. Count the casualties from his operations that failed over the years." He looked around, challenging them. "I'll bet it's a lot more than the number we lost at Sheol." He knew it was true, because he had, in fact, counted carefully before considering the comment.

"Iswander Industries is trying to bridge the gap between disorganized Roamer clans and the needs of the Confederation . . . the needs of *all of us*. Yes, I have a new, efficient way to create stardrive fuel, and that's made me wealthy again—enough to make up for all my losses at Sheol. My people made the ekti-X discovery before any of you did, and I profited from it. Why do you resent me for it? Any Roamer clan would have done the same thing." He straightened his suit jacket and calmed himself. "That is the price of technological advancement. That is the way civilization changes."

He paused to look at all of them, and he even remembered to smile. "My operations are both a blessing and a curse. I can produce ekti-X faster than I can possibly distribute and sell it. My primary delivery venue was Ulio Station, which has just been destroyed, and that changes the entire trading landscape in the Spiral Arm. I am hoping some of you will be interested in solving that bottleneck."

That got their attention.

"I'm looking for people—good Roamers, maybe—to help deliver it all. I have enough to make a lot of clans very wealthy . . . if anyone's interested?" He let his words hang as he listened to the startled murmurs in the audience. Many clan members were clearly excited, while others—mostly old-school skyminers—looked very angry.

"Our economy will change and our business will change," Iswander continued. "We have to be adaptable—as Roamers usually are. But this is a large-scale business, and we have to be efficient. We need to be *competent*."

He spun to look at Sam Ricks, who was lounging, aloof, as he listened to the speech. Ricks had no idea what was coming, and Iswander dropped the hammer. "We need a Speaker who is not a buffoon."

That stopped the murmuring.

Sam Ricks sat up, blinking in surprise. Several angry grumbles came from the seats, but the deepening silence was enough to let Iswander know he wasn't the only one thinking such thoughts. He pulled up the dossier he had brought, projecting it on the room's wallscreen. "When I ran for the office, I understand why most of you didn't vote for me. It was too soon after Sheol. But, now you've had months with Speaker Ricks, and you've had a chance to see the sort of person you elected. I suspect many of you have buyer's remorse."

He projected files, pointing out item after item. "In just a few months, Speaker Ricks has fumbled eleven important treaties, failed to provide requested aid to four needy clans—simply because he lost the paperwork. He's been late to thirty-four scheduled meetings, and I have evidence that he accepted numerous bribes." Iswander narrowed his eyes. "Or you can call them 'gifts,' if you're feeling kind. The only legislation he's managed to pass benefited close friends of his." He blinked calmly, waiting for the uproar. "I have full documentation of these claims for anyone who's interested."

Ricks spluttered. "Now wait a minute, this wasn't on the schedule."

"I'm putting it on the schedule! I reviewed the rules in detail, the clan agreements that have stood since the first days of Rendezvous. It is within my rights! I am a Roamer, and I have presented evidence. I call for a no-confidence vote in Speaker Ricks, so that he may be removed from office. With the changes in society and the danger the clans now face from the Shana Rei, we need decisive and competent leadership."

That provoked a storm of conversation. Ricks didn't seem to know what to do—obviously because he had never read the clan constitution in the first place.

Iswander remained calm at the podium. "The same goes for any potential new business associates who are interested in partnering with me. *Competence.* If I'm going to make a new alliance and form lucrative partnerships, I have to know how reliable my new associates are."

There—even the most dim-witted fools in the audience would see the clear connection. Their actions in the next hour would decide the course of clan history. If they wanted to do business with him, they needed to get rid of Ricks. Iswander drew a breath. Yes, he felt much more confident now.

At the doorway, even louder than the buzz of conversation, he heard a shout. Three people and a Friendly-model compy barged into the convocation chamber. "We need to interrupt the proceedings!" shouted a woman with long blond hair. Iswander recognized Tasia Tamblyn and Robb Brindle, the two acting heads of Kett Shipping. Maybe they'd come to fight for their own ekti-X distribution monopoly. The other woman was Orli Covitz, who had come to his extraction yard nearly dead from an alien plague. But she had flown off with Garrison Reeves some time ago. What was she doing here? He didn't understand what this was about.

"This is Roamer business," Iswander said. "We were about to call a vote—"

Tasia gave him a look of such venom that he stopped speaking. "We have been to the source of the Iswander ekti-X operations. And we've also seen where his people massacred clan Duquesne to eliminate any competition. He killed everyone, wiped out their entire facility, destroyed all their ships and tankers. Iswander Industries is so desperate to keep the secret that they're willing to kill anyone who finds out."

Iswander blinked, unable to find words to answer. What was this woman talking about? Tasia, Robb, and Orli stood together, looking disgusted and furious.

"Where is clan Duquesne?" demanded Speaker Ricks, as if it was finally a question he could understand. He looked around the rows of seats.

"Didn't show up," said somebody else. "Not Aaron, not an alternate."

Robb Brindle said, "It's true. We have the last logs of clan Duquesne, and the images are proof. They're all dead."

"Then Iswander's people tried to blow us out of space when we stumbled upon their extraction site," Tasia said. "Damaged our ship and we barely got away."

"We have records of that, too," said Orli Covitz.

Iswander just stared at her. What in the world did *Orli* have against him? He had saved her life. "That's . . . ridiculous. You're just trying to disrupt—"

Her compy DD stepped up. "Would you like us to display the video files?"

Tasia added in a loud, cold voice as she looked around at the gathered Roamers, "We also know exactly where ekti-X comes from."

CHAPTER

116

PRINCE REYN

Most of the test treatments had made Prince Reyn feel very ill, which greatly concerned Tamo'l. After studying the medical data that Tom Rom had brought, she altered her approach, and the next kelp extract did help Reyn feel better—in fact, markedly so. That result gave Tamo'l the impetus she needed to refine the formula, add plankton concentrates to cut the side effects, and then try again.

"The disease is still there, Prince Reynald," she cautioned when he remarked on the improvement he felt. "But if this extract can mitigate symptoms, it may let your body recover some of its strength, repair some of the damage. You may also find you can function more normally. The intensive records that Pergamus provided have opened new avenues for me to study."

He was pleased to send the news back home to Theroc via the green priest Beltrias, and his parents were excited to hear it. He was careful, though, not to let them get too excited.

"So, the symptoms will come back?" he asked Tamo'l. "The way I feel now is only temporary?"

Osira'h scolded him. "It is progress, Reyn. It gives you some relief and buys us time so we can find a real cure."

He smiled at her. "If I can spend the time with you, then I'll consider it a success. Whenever you're ready with the next test, Tamo'l, then I'm ready as well." Yes, he let himself feel a hint of hope, and Osira'h sensed it. The reward of seeing her smile was as valuable to him as any palliative the sanctuary domes could offer.

. . .

When the shadow cloud appeared above Kuivahr, Tamo'l and Osira'h were the ones who sensed it first. With a green priest mother and Ildiran fathers, they had a different set of filters, a sensitivity to changes in the universe.

Tamo'l sucked in a deep breath, and her whole body shuddered. Throughout the sanctuary domes, the misbreeds shouted in terror. "The Shana Rei!"

Osira'h gripped the edge of a table, keeping her balance. "Our brother is with them."

Alarmed, Beltrias stood nearby in the lab room, holding his treeling. "I am sending a message now. The verdani will spread the alarm—there must be someone close by who can help."

Tom Rom marched into the testing lab, looking from side to side. "What's happening?" Reyn and Osira'h explained what they knew. After delivering the Pergamus medical records, as instructed, he had remained to collate Tamo'l's records on the misbreeds. Though the man had come at the request of the King and Queen, Reyn found him to be odd and intense, without the slightest hint of warmth.

Beltrias looked up from his treeling. "I sent the warning far and wide, but the CDF cannot get to us in time. We are deep inside the Ildiran Empire. Nira is in the Prism Palace, though, and just received the message. She will tell the Mage-Imperator."

"My father will dispatch all the Solar Navy warliners he can spare," Osira'h said.

Tamo'l flinched again, touching her temple as if a spike of pain had just plunged into her skull. "The Ildirans will know, regardless. They will feel it through the *thism*."

"Gale'nh will come for us," Osira'h said.

Shawn Fennis used the sanctuary dome's comm to receive images from trading ships in orbit. Only a few Confederation or Ildiran craft remained over Kuivahr, and those ships scattered quickly, struggling to escape the shadow cloud. Enormous black battleships swooped out to harass them. The black robot vessels destroyed one automated cargo shuttle and a holding station, but the rest of the trading ships got away.

The planet itself was their target.

Reyn watched in dread as the black cylinders began to feed opaque hex plates into space by the thousands, creating some kind of barrier. Like the nightshade on Theroc, but more extravagant. The hex plates continued to assemble in the sky, spreading with astonishing speed, and the blackness built up like a curtain to enshroud Kuivahr.

"I think they mean to encase the entire planet," Reyn said.

Osira'h paled. "Just as they did at the Onthos home system."

Tamo'l was confused, distraught. "But why is Kuivahr so important to them? We have our sanctuary domes and a distillery. What else?"

Osira'h suddenly hunched over, her face twisted with pain. Reyn rushed to hold her, as she had done for him so many times. "*We* are here, Tamo'l," she pointed out. "You and I. That is what the Shana Rei want. Two halfbreeds—like Gale'nh and like Rod'h. They have found us."

Tamo'l said, her voice cracking, "I can feel Rod'h with them, drowning in shadows, calling for us . . . unwittingly leading the shadows here." She suddenly looked up. "We have the misbreeds, too! The shadows must sense their potential, feel intimidated by them."

From the Kellum distillery, Patrick Fitzpatrick sent an urgent message to the sanctuary domes. "Will you need assistance to evacuate? We know you've got Prince Reynald there, and the Mage-Imperator's daughter. If you send them over right away, we'll take them to safety first. We have a handful of ships to get off this planet, but there's no guarantee the shadows won't blast us out of orbit. Could be worse if we stay here."

Zhett Kellum came on the screen next to him. "We've got no choice but to try. Prince Reynald, the King and Queen would be very upset if we left you behind, and I'm not going to do that. We're evacuating all distillery personnel—get over to the platform in the next half hour or you'll be left behind. Make sure your green priest lets everyone know what's happening here."

"He already did," Reyn said. "But I can't just leave—"

Osira'h nudged him aside and shouted at the screen. "Yes, we are coming!" She turned to Reyn, determined. "You *have* to go. You're the son of the King and Queen."

"And you're a daughter of the Mage-Imperator," Reyn said. "I won't leave without you. Beltrias, you'll come with us. But who will help the misbreeds?"

Holding his potted treeling, the green priest looked up at the domed ceiling, as if he could see all the way to the giant shadow ships in orbit.

"The Kellum distillery does not have enough ships to carry everyone in these domes," Tom Rom said. "We have to evacuate the important personnel. Now. And that includes Tamo'l."

"Not good enough," Tamo'l said. "We *all* have to go." She stepped backward, looking dismayed. "We cannot possibly take all the misbreeds over to the distillery. And even if they made it there, many would not survive another space passage."

Osira'h said, "I gave my word I would keep Reyn safe if I brought him here. He and I must be on one of those first ships."

Tom Rom said, "Agreed. You and the Prince take a waveskimmer and get out of here." He gave them an odd smile. "It benefits me and my employer to make sure you do not come to harm."

Tamo'l gave Osira'h a hard look. "Yes, go. And take the green priest. But I stay with the misbreeds. I have to help them. We will find another way."

"We can't leave the rest of you!" Reyn said in alarm.

"There is no point in protesting, and I will force you there if necessary," Tom Rom said in an absolutely convincing tone. "I'll see to it that the others escape. I have an alternate." He looked over at Tamo'l. "The rest of us will make our way to the Klikiss transportal. It will be a rough passage, but likely less stressful than space travel. Your misbreeds would survive."

Tamo'l agreed. "That is a chance. Osira'h, go!"

Shawn Fennis rushed in from a supply locker. "Wait, this is all that remained of the kelp distillate that proved most effective for you, Prince Reynald. If the Kuivahr oceans are swallowed up, we'll never be able to produce more of this." He extended a sealed case. "Some of them worked, and some didn't. Take them all. Maybe other researchers can study these."

Reyn felt a lump in his throat. "Thank you."

Osira'h grabbed the case with one hand and Reyn's arm in her other. Beltrias was already heading to the landing deck. "Quickly, we have to get to the distillery while the Kellum ships are still launching."

. . .

Out on the ocean, under the mockingly bright sky, Osira'h and Reyn drove the waveskimmer away from the sanctuary domes while Tamo'l and her staff prepared the rest of the evacuation. As the craft roared toward the distillery towers, Beltrias ducked down against the spray. Ahead, they could see the bright contrails as escaping ships rose up to orbit.

Most terrifying, though, Reyn saw the ever-expanding black swatch in the sky, an opaque barricade being assembled, plate by plate, that rose from the horizon like a slow black tidal wave.

They had to get away.

CHAPTER 117

NIRA

Though she was outwardly silent and calm, Nira felt frozen inside, grappling with her feelings of guilt, grief, and loss. Her son Rod'h was gone, swallowed by the horrific Shana Rei in much the same way that Gale'nh had been—but she felt a dreadful certainty that Rod'h would not be released so easily.

Overhead, the Ildiran sunshine was deceptively bright. The former human enclave in Mijistra had been razed, converted to a park with fertile soil, exotic flowers, spiky shrubs, and a bare place for a new grove of worldtrees. It was a fitting memorial for the massacre that had occurred here.

Though worker kithmen offered to help, Nira wanted to be by herself. She knelt in the soft raked dirt, surrounded by the potted treelings she had brought back from Theroc. The treelings were a gift from her fellow green priests and from the worldforest itself. There were already trees in the greenhouse dome atop the Prism Palace, but this would be another verdani grove, and a way for her to keep in touch with her former home.

Though she was an adept green priest, Nira could not use telink to form a closer bond with any of her children. Right now, Rod'h was lost and alone, held hostage by the creatures of darkness. Her oldest son . . . born out of Nira's torment and a product of the darkest time in her life. As a young visiting green priest she had been stolen from Jora'h's loving arms, imprisoned on Dobro, raped repeatedly, and forced to bear children she did not want.

Rod'h was the son of the Dobro Designate himself. She had never been allowed to be a *mother* to him. At birth, handlers had confirmed that the child was viable, then whisked him away to be raised and trained by the Designate. Nira had not seen the baby again for a long time, had little interaction with him as he grew up.

Meanwhile, she had been raped again, forced to bear more children. Gale'nh, then Tamo'l, then Muree'n . . . and other misbreeds that had not survived. She had tried to love them all as she loved Osira'h, who had been a child of love instead of fear. She told herself again and again that her innocent children were not responsible for the circumstances of their own births. Nira didn't even blame the other fathers, who had simply been following orders.

But the Dobro Designate, Rod'h's father, had *enjoyed* her suffering. He had done it to break her, and Nira could not forget that. Because of that pain she had never been able to treat Rod'h just as a young man with great potential, as he deserved to be treated.

Now it was too late.

She scooped out a hole in the fresh soil in the park, removed one of the treelings from its ceramic pot, then gently planted it in its new home. She stared down at her green hands, stricken, then absently stroked the fine golden bark of the tree.

Rod'h had resented her because of how she treated him, and Nira realized she had brought that resentment upon herself. She had pushed Rod'h away from her because he wanted to believe that his father was a hero of the Ildiran race, no matter what he had done. Rod'h's insistence that the breeding camps had been necessary angered Nira. Now she realized that he had been trying to find meaning in his own origin, trying to push back against his mother's coldness. . . .

Nira planted a second treeling, far enough from the first so they could grow and one day become immense titans under the seven suns. She had eight treelings, enough to make a fine grove one day.

But Rod'h would probably never see it now.

She heard the entourage long before she saw them coming, and she glanced up. The Mage-Imperator, dressed in fine prismatic robes, came forward and ignored the flurry of attenders preparing the way.

Jora'h had eyes only for her. To the horror of his entourage, he knelt in the dirt and helped her plant another worldtree. His hands touched hers. "The Solar Navy is prepared. Adar Zan'nh has gathered the warliners, armed them with our best weapons, including the new Confederation sun bombs. We are ready to defend against the Shana Rei . . . and rescue Rod'h, if that becomes possible."

"I know you will try, my love," she said to him.

The attenders muttered. The bureaucrat kith kept their distance. The guards remained stony and silent.

Yazra'h and Muree'n were with Tal Gale'nh in the simulations chamber, discussing ways to fight the Shana Rei, but that was all theoretical so far.

Nira hung her head. "If I don't see him again, Jora'h, I will always regret that I let him think he was somehow tainted. I blamed him for things that weren't his fault."

"He was a good young man," Jora'h said. "He helped Daro'h greatly. He studied politics and diplomacy, because he wished to impress you. He proved himself to my satisfaction . . . and yours, too."

Nira raised her chin to look at him. "But did I treat him right? Did I *train* him right?"

She touched the next treeling, ready to plant it apart from the others, when suddenly she felt a thrum through telink, an urgent message sent to all green priests by a desperate man—Beltrias, the hunter green priest who had gone to Kuivahr. The message was instantaneous, and Nira knew about the attack as soon as the shadows arrived.

With her eyes wide, she turned toward the Mage-Imperator. "Kuivahr is under attack! The Shana Rei have appeared there. Osira'h is in danger, along with Tamo'l, and all the others." She closed her eyes, felt a shudder. "We have to save them, Jora'h!"

The Mage-Imperator was already shouting to his entourage. "Contact Adar Zan'nh. Have him launch the full cohort—now! We know where the shadows are." His voice became hard and frightening. "It is time to fight."

CHAPTER

118

TAL GALE'NH

Gale'nh devoted days without sleep to studying the recent engagement at the Onthos system, memorizing every detail of the robot ship movements in search of a pattern or a weakness. With as much concentration, he analyzed the Shana Rei entropy attacks, the effectiveness of the laser cannons and sun bombs. He ran simulated tests of the powerful new CDF sun-bomb designs. He vowed to discover ways to improve the Solar Navy defenses so they could be far more devastating—if not victorious—in their next confrontation.

And there would certainly be a next confrontation. The days ticked by, and he waited. . . .

In a simulation chamber used to train officer candidates, Gale'nh compiled records from the surviving warliners, along with log data shared by the *Kutuzov*. Using realistic holograms, he refought the earlier space battles at Plumas, at Hiltos, and at the Onthos system. He even received a sketchy report and log-camera footage from an escaping trader, the *Verne*, that had witnessed the destruction of Ulio Station.

Each time he reviewed the engagements, Gale'nh tried to imagine what he might have done differently.

Fortunately, even the larger black robot ships were vulnerable to conventional fighting methods, and Gale'nh could see how to destroy the enemy vessels. In the final analysis, though, the robots were only a distraction compared with the massive threat of the Shana Rei.

Muree'n and Yazra'h joined him in the battle-simulation chamber, eager to fight *something*. They observed the sharp images with curiosity, though space battles and tactical movements of large numbers of vessels were not the way they engaged in battle.

His bond with his sister Muree'n was strong, and since she was so close now, he drew upon her strength and confidence. Sensing his need, Muree'n allowed it. As a warrior, she never seemed to have any doubts whatsoever.

Standing together in the simulation chamber, all three of them watched the tactical projections, holographic icons of the battleships in play: Solar Navy warliners, sometimes CDF Juggernauts or Mantas, a seemingly inexhaustible supply of black robot ships, and the giant hexagonal cylinders of the Shana Rei. The creatures of darkness used few overt weapons except for the disruptive entropy fields that damaged any nearby technology.

Muree'n squeezed her crystal-tipped katana so hard that her knuckles turned white. "I prefer to fight an opponent who is right in front of me. I want to see the damage I inflict. That way I can touch the spilled blood with my own fingertips."

"I doubt the shadows even have blood," Gale'nh said, then shook his head as a coldness swept through him again. "Much of what they did to me has been wiped from my mind. They could be doing worse things to Rod'h right now." He could no longer sense his half-brother, but he didn't think Rod'h was dead—simply taken out of the universe.

Yazra'h looked fierce with her long hair in a halo around her head. "These space battles make combat seem like a game. Ships, tactics, projectile trajectories." She made a snort as if she found that wanting.

"The Shana Rei also turn Ildirans against Ildirans," said Muree'n. "They make our people commit bloodshed for them. It is cowardly."

"I will fight them again—either way," Gale'nh said.

As the Plumas simulation continued, holographic Solar Navy warliners swept along in complex maneuvers, interacting with Confederation Defense Forces above the ice moon. Suddenly, as he concentrated, Gale'nh felt a rough, painful lurch inside himself, as if some dark presence had begun sawing at the strings of his existence.

Beside him, Muree'n flinched as well. The girl turned pale, and her expression tightened as if she had just swallowed poison. They both heard Rod'h shouting to them through their special connection: a flood of sensations . . . pain, terror, and despair. The connection strengthened, reinforced, and Gale'nh received a clear alarm, a call for help, not just from Rod'h.

Osira'h.

Tamo'l.

All three of them were in the same place—Kuivahr!

With half-formed mental images, he could sense the looming shadow cloud, and he *knew* that the Shana Rei were coming to seize his two sisters, just as they had taken him. As they had taken Rod'h. They wanted to capture all of those strange genetic combinations that could resist them in ways that purebred humans and Ildirans could not.

Gale'nh gasped, and the words were stolen from inside him. He could barely breathe.

Yazra'h grabbed Muree'n, propping the young woman up and shaking her shoulders. "What is it? Fight it!"

"The shadows!" Muree'n gasped. "They have Rod'h . . . and they want my sisters. They are at Kuivahr."

Gale'nh shook himself, trying to fling away the distraction. "The Shana Rei are attacking—*right now*." He raced to the wall of the simulator chamber, ignoring the distraction of holographic images around him. On the computer-modeled battle, a giant Roamer water tanker exploded, spraying a cloud of vapor that wrought havoc in the path of hyperaccelerating robot warships.

Gale'nh slapped his hand on the controls, dispelling the images. With shaking hands he found the comm, used his direct private channel to Adar Zan'nh. "Adar, Kuivahr is under attack. It's . . . Rod'h. He is there."

Zan'nh responded instantly. "I just received a message from the Mage-Imperator. Your mother picked up the alarm from a green priest there. The planet is under attack. The shadows just arrived."

Muree'n also shouted into the comm. "The shadows are trying to take my sisters, too. They want all of us halfbreeds, and Rod'h is trying to resist."

The shouts and fear still rang inside Gale'nh's mind. Rod'h was so desperate. And Gale'nh was just as afraid for Tamo'l and Osira'h.

Adar Zan'nh answered. "Our warliners are prepared and our weapons have been replenished. The entire cohort is on high alert. We are ready to depart." On the screen, he narrowed his eyes. "If you wish to join me, Tal Gale'nh, take an immediate shuttle to orbit. I will give you command of another warliner."

"I will be there, Adar," Gale'nh said.

He was already running—with Muree'n right at his side.

CHAPTER

119

GARRISON REEVES

When the Big Ring was complete, Garrison reserved a scout pod to make an inspection flight, and it seemed that everyone else at Fireheart had the same idea. The gigantic torus hung in space like a wedding ring for the universe.

When he had last checked, he was one of seventy-three individual inspection runs; not only was the Big Ring the largest physics experiment ever attempted, it was quite likely the most verified and inspected piece of equipment ever produced. Larger personnel shuttles flew out as well, and Station Chief Beren Alu didn't even pretend that they were anything other than sightseeing opportunities.

More than ten thousand Roamer workers had contributed to the project over the course of six years, not counting the initial planning phases. Garrison had seen varying estimates of the overall budget, none of which were remotely accurate, because numerous clans had contributed private funding and most of them didn't want to share details. Besides, no one suggested that Kotto hadn't earned it, since his brilliant inventions had saved not only the clans but quite likely the human race.

When one of the scout pods was returned and refueled, Garrison signed it out, climbed aboard, and flew away from the admin hub. Other small craft flitted around the giant ring structure, looping through the central hole and cruising up along the curvature.

He was glad to have the pod to himself, which let him be alone with this magnificent structure. He was trained in dozens of useful skills. Some of his past jobs had been mind-numbingly boring, some dangerous, others gratifying, but none instilled such a sense of pride as this one did. He wasn't especially interested in esoteric dimensional physics, high-energy transfer flux, folding and looping electromagnetic fields. Nevertheless, the ring itself struck him with awe.

And the *boldness* of such an impossible project warmed his heart. Olaf Reeves had called upon the clans to follow his similarly audacious vision of reassembling Rendezvous, but the Roamers had wanted a fresh start. Garrison's father hadn't been interested in anything new or fresh, and when the clans focused their efforts elsewhere, the stubborn man forced his own family to spend years on pointless work.

In the Big Ring, though, Garrison saw the proof of what the Roamer clans could achieve when they worked together on a project they all believed in. He was exhilarated to be part of it. He did wish, though, that Orli and Seth could be here with him to watch.

After the experiment, Station Chief Beren Alu was anxious to get Fireheart Station back to profitable manufacturing. Crew chiefs, seeing Garrison's work, had offered him jobs at the energy-film farms, at the power-block assemblies, at the isotope packaging stations.

But as soon as the test was run, Garrison planned to head out and find Orli again. He had done a great deal of thinking—mostly about *her*—even while he kept busy with the impossible tasks. He had not had contact with her in some time, and he hoped she was all right. He also hoped they could find a way to run their lives in parallel.

He saw numerous ships flying to and from the greenhouse dome. With the full test imminent, a constant stream of workers wanted to send telink messages to friends, family, loved ones. He had sent another message to Academ only two days ago, telling Seth how excited he was.

In front of him, a flurry of lights sparkled along the ring: test lamps evenly spaced along the torus, winking on in sequence. They reminded Garrison of hundreds of luminous fairies racing around a track. Kotto Okiah had authorized the running lights to be tested every hour, just to impress all of the sightseeing "inspection" flights.

Glancing at the chronometer, Garrison realized he had to return the scout pod in fifteen minutes, because someone else wanted to do a flight. He reversed course and headed back to the docking bay. Very soon, the Big Ring was going to make history.

CHAPTER

120

GENERAL NALANI KEAH

After the debacle at the Onthos system, the damaged *Kutuzov* was still undergoing at least two weeks' worth of repairs—and loading up with Dr. Krieger's new sun bombs, which had also been shipped off to the Ildiran Solar Navy in great numbers.

But Keah didn't want to just sit around licking her wounds. She was eager to fight something, even though she didn't have her Juggernaut. She dreaded the alternative of sitting around and completing paperwork, attending meetings, reviewing strategy sessions. A grim future indeed.

And then, like a miracle, King Peter suggested an entirely different mission.

When Deputy Cain showed her appalling images of the biological black markets on Rakkem, her anger turned in another direction. Passing along the crackdown orders from King Peter and Queen Estarra, the Deputy had asked General Keah for a volunteer to stomp down those dangerous and unregulated facilities. Keah had an immediate answer for him.

"Hell, I'll go! The *Kutuzov* is being repaired and restocked, but we have other ships. In fact, I'll use it as a training exercise, take one of the Three H's into an active operation."

As she paced, she reviewed the records of Rakkem and was disgusted to see images of the failed antiaging chelation treatment that made the victims' skin slough off. Although Keah was starting to get lines around her eyes and mouth, and a bit of loose skin on her neck, she had decided to grow old with grace. She had *earned* every wrinkle and gray hair, dammit!

Rakkem was also rife with black-market organ warehouses,

experimental cures for sale to the highest bidder, scams, destructive drugs, designer poisons, every possible corruption. Keah found it appalling.

As she seethed about how Rakkem preyed on terminally ill patients, she recalled an important fact. She raised her eyebrows, looked at Deputy Cain. "Admiral Haroun's wife died two years ago from detangling cancer. I believe she tried countless medical treatments—none of them successful." She nodded to herself. "We'll take his Juggernaut, and he'll act as second-in-command of the mission—in fact, why think small? I'll take fifteen Manta cruisers, too, and shut the place down."

"The King and Queen trust your instincts," Cain said.

So, General Keah put the mission together, gathering Haroun's Juggernaut and the fifteen Manta cruisers. Considering how badly they had gotten trounced in every previous encounter with the Shana Rei, a victory on Rakkem would be a shot in the arm and a confidence booster for the CDF—and a good deed to boot.

Admiral Haroun was a quiet, dark-haired man with a soft voice and an analytical mind. He definitely had the intelligence and book learning to rise high in CDF officer's school, but Keah doubted that Haroun had nerves of steel in a crisis. That would have to change.

His Juggernaut, the *Okrun*, was named after a twenty-second-century Earth military genius who had broken the back of a fanatical religious empire intent on plunging Earth back into the dark ages. Shortly after Okrun's victory, humanity had built its eleven huge generation ships and launched them to seek new homes among the stars. General Keah was surprised that Admiral Haroun himself knew so little about the man for whom his ship was named. She intended to instruct him during their journey to Rakkem.

Haroun graciously gave her the *Okrun*'s command chair when she arrived on the bridge, while he stood back as her new first officer to watch and learn from her. It was the sort of respect that General Keah expected him to display, but she was disappointed he didn't push back even a little about relinquishing command. He knew his place in the CDF hierarchy, which was good, but he also needed a stronger spine.

While on the journey to Rakkem, Keah rallied the CDF soldiers and gave them the pep talk they would need. She riled them up against the horrific medical experiments, the baby mills, the flesh bazaars, and all the people who had died from false hope and dangerous treatments. It wasn't difficult to inflame them; the soldiers were glad to face an opponent they could understand, and one they could trounce. Admiral Haroun struggled to control his emotions behind a stony façade, his expression full of obvious disgust toward Rakkem.

The *Okrun* and the fifteen Manta cruisers arrived like a stampede at Rakkem, where they spread out in orbit and imposed a blockade. General Keah broadcast on all frequencies, announcing an interdiction and demanding the planet's complete and immediate surrender "for a thorough inspection of suspect activities."

Many unmarked ships in orbit fled as soon as they saw the CDF ships arrive—either black-market biotraders or nervous customers who didn't want to be caught. Keah launched two hundred Remora fighters to enforce order, but instructed them not to pursue the escaping ships. She had bigger fish to fry.

"Who is your planetary leader?" she transmitted from the *Okrun*'s bridge. She had taken time to put on her full dress uniform, and she assumed an attitude that would remind the Rakkem people of a Valkyrie.

Overlapping communications burst across the comm, none of them directed at her. Haroun's comm officer shook his head. "They're trying to rally defenses down there, General, but there seems to be no unified planetary security. I don't even know if they've got a real spokesman."

"On to Phase Two, then. I want Remoras in the skies and troop transports on the ground, boots marching through those streets."

By ordering this action, the King and Queen might have stuck their hands into a hornets' nest, offending independent planets that were not part of the Confederation. Keah decided to get enough images of the despicable Rakkem operations to dispel any sympathy or moral outrage.

"General," Admiral Haroun suggested, "with all those dangerous biologicals, it would be wise for our troops to wear decontamination gear. Just in case someone is desperate enough to release a plague out of spite."

"Damn right, Admiral—good suggestion." She could just imagine some unscrupulous black-market warlord infecting the troops and then trying to make a bargain by offering the vaccine in exchange for safe passage from Rakkem. Keah did not intend to let that happen.

After more than fifteen minutes of repeated transmissions and confusing delays, a round-faced man with short blond hair and spectacles (surely, an affectation) appeared on the screen. "I am Aldo Cerf, one of the business leaders on Rakkem. This world is not part of the Confederation, and you have no authority here. This is an act of war."

"This is an act of necessity," Keah said. "You have harmed or killed countless Confederation citizens, and King Peter and Queen Estarra have issued orders for this interdiction. Your work is dangerous and unregulated. You will not be allowed to prey upon helpless Confederation citizens."

Cerf scowled. "We offer them hope when they are dying."

Haroun growled, interrupting General Keah, which surprised her. "You offer them false hope! You prey on people who are too weak to see through your scams." She hadn't asked him for details, but Haroun was clearly incensed by what he had seen in the Rakkem records. Perhaps his wife had also gone there. . . .

The General glanced at her status screens, saw that troop transports had been dispatched for the surface; Remoras already filled the skies of Rakkem. She turned back to Aldo Cerf. "Your treatments are risky, unproven, sometimes useless, sometimes deadly. We will impound all records, seize assets, and make reparations to anyone you have harmed—provided we can track them down."

"Provided any are still alive," Haroun added.

Cerf's objections of "You have no jurisdiction here!" and "We are independent from the Confederation!" began to sound repetitious.

General Keah responded by transmitting the stomach-turning archival records of the flayed victims wailing in pain as they oozed their lives out onto a surgical table. "We have plenty of testimonials from your customers, Mr. Cerf. Victims—duped, tortured, betrayed. It's our mission to be sure this doesn't happen again."

After the troops landed and Remoras continued to block any ships from escaping, the CDF soldiers impounded the cure warehouses, the organ-replacement banks filled with arrays of lungs, livers, hearts, and sheets of fresh skin taken from "volunteers." They found archives of deadly diseases, some of them weaponized, a biological arsenal that could destroy entire populations—everything for sale. Perhaps worst of all were the gestation warehouses filled with factory wombs: pregnant women hooked up to euphoric drugs, artificially inseminated so they produced baby after baby.

The General had intended to go down to the surface herself, so that she and Admiral Haroun could take a victory lap. She wanted to stand by the CDF soldiers and look at the unconscionable black-market cesspit they had put out of business. But when she saw the images piped up from the ground troops, heard their appalled outcries, and stared at things that made even the worst records in Deputy Cain's report pale to insignificance, she doubted she could stomach it, even after everything she had seen in her career.

She thought of the people who had given up their financial resources, who had come here desperate for any kind of treatment, only to be left destitute and dying just as fast, or faster. "We did a good thing here," she said. "It had to be done."

A tear trickled out of Admiral Haroun's eye. "We did."

There was very little resistance in the face of the military crackdown. Many biomerchants were caught destroying records and incinerating samples. She thought of the continuing threat of the Shana Rei, but said, "This one little victory is still important—I'll take it."

CHAPTER

121

TASIA TAMBLYN

Tasia Tamblyn had never seen such an uproar among the clans—and Roamers were not known for their calm, sedate discussions. Even though she had caused the outcry herself, she did not feel guilty about it, not a whit. She stood in the convocation chamber next to Robb, Orli, and DD, waiting for the noise to die down.

No, she thought, *she* hadn't caused this outrage—Lee Iswander had brought it upon himself, by placing ruthlessness above genius.

After making her accusations and listening to the growing reactions in the chamber, Tasia saw the look of speechless astonishment on Iswander's face. He seemed completely taken aback that he'd been caught. Such arrogance! With an operation of that size dumping so much stardrive fuel on the market, it was as if he had never imagined that his harsh activities might be exposed! The destruction of the Duquesne operation and Elisa Enturi trying to destroy the *Voracious Curiosity* just because they had wandered into the wrong area—did he really think no one would ever notice?

"This is . . . not possible," Iswander said.

Fuming, Tasia gestured to Robb. "Not possible?"

He held up a transfer datapack. "Speaker Ricks, can I play this on your wallscreen? A picture is worth a thousand accusations."

"And proof against a thousand denials," Tasia added.

"By all means!" Ricks actually sounded cheery. "This is a convocation hall. We have a full projection system."

Iswander looked out of place among the Roamers in his business suit, and now he glanced from side to side, pale and astonished. He didn't seem to know what to say. "This can't be possible," he said again, as if trying to convince himself.

For a moment—just a moment—Tasia wondered if he really wasn't aware of what his own people were doing. Then she dismissed the idea.

DD presented the datapack to the Speaker, who installed it in the projection system in his podium. Ricks smiled as he waited for the files to be loaded.

As the images appeared, Orli explained to the group, "I encountered one of Iswander's extraction fields, and I received medical attention there. Garrison Reeves was also with me." She looked around at the Roamers. "Some of you may know him."

Ricks fiddled with the controls, trying to find the proper files. DD assisted him.

"We know clan Reeves," someone called back.

"And he's the one still alive," Orli said. "At the time, we didn't know what the ekti operations were. I was sick, on the edge of death, and Garrison just wanted to take his son away to safety."

"*What* operations?" someone else shouted. Tasia recognized the matriarch of clan Beauvais, who operated two traditional skymines. By the expression on her face, she was out for blood.

Iswander seemed dazed, but a flare of indignation went through his voice. "The method of harvesting ekti-X is my proprietary development, but I didn't kill anyone. I destroyed no other competition. This is absurd!"

In blatant contradiction, damning images were projected in the convocation chamber: the wreckage of Duquesne ships with clan markings prominent on the shattered hulls. Everyone could see that a disaster had occurred there. Next, DD played the log clip of Aaron Duquesne shouting angrily at Elisa Enturi, before she set off the massive cascade of bloater explosions.

The Roamers in the audience were appalled and outraged. Tasia looked at Lee Iswander, trying to gauge his guilt, and she was surprised to see that he looked thunderstruck. Something wasn't right.

She faced those gathered in the chamber. "You all know me as the daughter of clan Tamblyn and also as the acting administrator of Kett Shipping, along with my husband. Even though we distributed a lot of ekti-X, Iswander Industries never revealed the source even to us—but as a shipping company, we don't like distributing commodities if we have no idea where they come from. So we placed a tracker on his representative's ship and we followed the flight path to the site of the Duquesne massacre and to Iswander's main operations."

Next, she played their images of the much larger extraction yards, the industrial equipment, the administrative and habitation complex, the tankers, the pumping ships, the bloater cluster, the ekti-X arrays, and all of the drained husks. "This is where Iswander gets his stardrive fuel. Ekti-X comes from those nodules. Bloaters."

Tasia didn't care that she was blowing the operations wide open. The disruption in stardrive fuel distribution would harm Kett Shipping's bottom line, but it would harm the company even more to keep doing business with the murderous industrialist.

"By the Guiding Star, I've seen those things out in empty space!" said one of the Roamers. "Never knew what they were, but they're cropping up like weeds."

"They're filled with raw ekti-X," Orli said.

Tasia added, "Now watch what happens when the Iswander employees realize that we've discovered their operations."

Security ships flew out, threatening them, led by Elisa Enturi. Even when Robb obviously tried to surrender, Elisa opened fire on them with the clear intent of destroying their ship. Roamers in the chamber gasped and grumbled. "We barely escaped with our lives. Good thing Robb and I have combat flying experience."

"I never gave those orders," Iswander said. "I never wanted . . ."

Sam Ricks was grinning. "We'll see about that. You've been criticized before, Mr. Iswander. Roamer clans share advances and technologies. But you would kill to protect your business operations . . ." Ricks spat out the rest as if it were the foulest insult he could imagine. "You are worse than Chairman Wenceslas."

"Who's going to make reparations to clan Duquesne?" called one of the clan leaders. "How many people were killed?"

"We never should've turned from traditional skymining. Look at the cost of that ekti-X," said the Beauvais clan leader.

Other Roamers had more practical questions. "So . . . that's all there is to it? Find those bloaters and drain them dry? Fill tank after tank with ekti-X? No wonder Iswander's been producing so much fuel."

The audience buzzed with excitement, inflamed with the possibilities, much more concerned with the easy wealth than about the shocking crimes.

"But I never gave Elisa those instructions!" Iswander wrestled with either taking responsibility or throwing his employee to the wolves. He seemed so stunned and shaken that Tasia actually believed him, but not to the extent that she felt sorry for him.

"There was a large concentration of bloaters drifting toward Ikbir," Orli pointed out. "Someone might want to set up extraction operations there."

Robb shrugged. "Or find other clusters. Nobody's really bothered to look before."

Tasia said, "Kett Shipping makes this offer to anybody here because I am still a Roamer at heart. Our distribution ties with Iswander Industries are severed—we figure that getting shot at by your trading partner does not indicate a good business relationship. We refuse to distribute their ekti-X any longer, so we'll have plenty of ships to take the ekti-X that any other clan produces. Robb and I would be happy to discuss terms."

"The bloaters are just there for the taking," Orli said. "And I could feel . . ."

Two clan leaders slipped out of the convocation chamber, maybe to deal with other business, but Tasia suspected they were eager to beat the rush in the search for other bloater clusters.

For generations, Roamers had produced ekti from huge skymines on gas giants, and now the traditional skyminers looked more dismayed than ever. Since the Roamer clans understood how quickly and easily stardrive fuel could be extracted from the ubiquitous bloaters, there would be a veritable "ekti rush."

Kett Shipping would take advantage of that.

Prices would drop substantially, but the need would remain high. With efficient extraction and distribution, the Roamer clans would have plenty of ways to make money.

But Lee Iswander would be a pariah—that much was obvious.

"You can't do this to me," he said. "I pulled myself up after a disaster, discovered ekti-X, rebuilt my business. . . ."

"You should have stayed on Sheol," grumbled Sam Ricks. "Made the final count fifteen forty-*four*."

Lee Iswander made his way to an empty seat where he collapsed.

"As Speaker for the clans, I will submit this matter to the Confederation legal system." Ricks kept grinning foolishly as if he had just won an unexpected lottery. "Or would you prefer that we finish our business here first, Mr. Iswander? I believe you were calling a motion among the clans? A no-confidence vote?"

A large number of audience members had already left the chamber. There would likely be a long line of people waiting to use the services of Newstation's contract green priests, while others would simply fly away, rushing out to track down bloater concentrations so they could begin their work.

Clan Duquesne had set up their operations on a shoestring and apparently they had begun delivering ekti-X within weeks. Soon, all the clans would be draining bloaters dry wherever they found them in open space. Even without Ulio Station, the loss of which still stunned Tasia, there would be more stardrive fuel than had ever been available before.

With the looming possibility of war with the Shana Rei, the Confederation Defense Forces and the Ildiran Solar Navy would need a great supply. With fuel so cheap, she suspected there would also be a resurgence of prospectors and explorers, sniffing out new territory, mapping new worlds, new resources.

Robb leaned closer to her. "You know we've just changed the whole Confederation."

"For the better, I hope."

The possibilities seemed endless. The bloaters appeared to be an inexhaustible resource.

As the convocation chamber emptied, Iswander sat slumped, his shoulders fallen. He ran his hands through his hair and looked stunned; Tasia almost sympathized with him.

But she had only to recall Elisa Enturi charging after them and opening fire on the *Curiosity*, and also the massacre of the Duquesne site. The sympathy faded quickly.

CHAPTER

122

EXXOS

Now that the Shana Rei had replenished themselves with dark matter from the Dyson sphere, they spent that material extravagantly. Hanging over the doomed planet of Kuivahr, the hex cylinders ejected millions of black plates to assemble the opaque sphere, building it up piece by piece to swallow the whole planet.

Each hexagonal plate fit exactly against another, and the englobement grew steadily to form a perfect sphere. Surely such geometrical perfection was the antithesis of the complete chaos desired by the Shana Rei. The shadows continued to be contradictions to themselves. Exxos found it ironic, but he did not need to understand everything about them; the events served his purposes. He felt proud and strong now, controlling the powerful new warships the shadows had created for them. He had everything he wanted. Almost.

With the glut of free material from the Onthos home star, the shadows built whatever Exxos wished. Manipulating this matter caused them no pain, since they had already suffered for it millennia ago. Now, Exxos and his robots redesigned their black warships, making them superior even to the ones they had used at Ulio Station. He could not risk losing any more robots, so he demanded thicker hulls, increased shielding, more powerful weapons. Invincible ships, juggernauts of destruction.

The black robots dispersed, only ninety-eight of them left, but with these enhanced warships he could wreak tremendous havoc. Every single one of the remaining robots had mental processes identical to his own, so they could coordinate their attacks with unparalleled precision. Sentient life-forms would be doomed, starting with Kuivahr.

Meanwhile, deep in their cybernetic minds the networked robots continued to solve the problem of how to exterminate the Shana Rei, when it came time to do so. The design and theory for an entropy dampener proceeded, millions of steps being solved in the background, one at a time.

The black englobement below was more than half finished, and once the sphere completed itself, Exxos knew, all the screaming from the Kuivahr population would cease tormenting the Shana Rei. This would be a perfect victory, without the loss of a single robot.

His giant black battleships soared out of the shadow cloud, ranging closer to the enshrouded planet. He watched the trapped victims struggle in a useless attempt to flee. The robots had destroyed an automated cargo lifter and a holding platform, but that was just targeting practice. Several refugee ships had rushed away, panicked traders fleeing as soon as the Shana Rei arrived. The black robots pursued them, but the human pilots demonstrated unexpected prowess in evasive flight. It didn't matter.

His ninety-eight titanic battleships would be enough to secure the planet as the Shana Rei smothered it to death. All across the Spiral Arm, humans and Ildirans would grow very afraid.

By the time the rapid englobement was sixty percent complete, the planet had mostly quieted, but a final ship raced away. Hungry for the pursuit and the prize, Exxos guided his own battleship while linking his mind with the engines and the weapons systems. The angular craft was like an extension of his own mechanical body as he plunged after the last escapee.

The human pilot swooped and dodged, proving to be more nimble than the enormous robot warship, and Exxos was surprised when his first volley of energy bursts missed. He accelerated, increased weapons power, and launched another fusillade—but the human ship dove downward and astonishingly looped back and headed *straight for him*. Exxos couldn't adjust his targeting swiftly enough. Surely, this small vessel had no weapons that could harm him!

Four small defensive jazer blasts punched against his hull, causing little harm; then the ship changed course and roared upward. Exxos veered after it.

He intercepted a comm transmission, which was no doubt meant to be taunting. He saw a woman with long dark hair and intent eyes, crowded in the ship with a teenaged boy, a toddler, and other adults, one of them a green priest. Exxos identified Prince Reynald, the son of King Peter and Queen Estarra. Ah! He would consider it quite a victory if he could snuff out that one human life.

More important, another passenger, a female, was one of the half-breeds that the Shana Rei desired so badly. Osira'h, child of a green priest and the Mage-Imperator. The Shana Rei would want to capture her, and Exxos wanted to kill her.

The female pilot sneered at him. "You bugbots wrecked my distillery, and now you're destroying our world. You're a real pain in the ass."

The robot battleship closed in, but somehow the fleeing craft continued to dodge. "Toast your victory, smug son of a bitch," said the man beside her; then the passengers all yelled in alarm as the pilot spun the ship, throwing them to one side.

The rear cargo doors opened, and containers tumbled out like chaff falling toward the robot battleship: drums, kegs, crates filled with bottles, all of which smashed against Exxos's hull. The debris and flash-vaporized liquid were merely a distraction. Exxos dodged, but the accelerating ship was gaining distance. But the prey had no place to go. Exxos could easily run them down.

Suddenly, with a flicker of movement and rapid deceleration, a blizzard of large, ornate ships appeared: Solar Navy warliners arriving in the Kuivahr system! In an instant, the Ildiran fleet filled empty space, hundreds of war vessels.

With flashing red optical sensors, Exxos scanned and counted—more than three times the size of the black fleet the Shana Rei had created for them. Exxos was surprised by this setback, but not alarmed. His ships were invincible. The Solar Navy would be inadequate to defend themselves.

Communication signals buzzed among the robots, all of whom reacted, pulling together. The lone escaping human ship raced pell-mell toward the Solar Navy cohort, blasting out a distress signal and begging for sanctuary. Exxos did not want to let the halfbreed girl or Prince Reynald go, but now he had a much bigger target. Even though these Solar Navy ships outnumbered the robots, his vessels were substantially more powerful, with greater armaments and tougher hull shielding. The Ildirans didn't stand a chance.

He finished his threat assessment in less than a second, and his robot counterparts came to the same conclusion. They responded to the challenge with a certain amount of glee. Yes, this would be a very satisfying fight. He looked forward to seeing Kuivahr's orbit strewn with massive amounts of wreckage.

The black robots synchronized their thoughts, synchronized their attack strategy, and drew into a unified, organized force. The black fleet activated their weapons systems and plunged toward the Ildiran Solar Navy.

CHAPTER 123

TAMO'L

The englobement of Kuivahr continued, the suffocating black shield growing, curving, walling off the whole sky.

Overhead, the black hex ships accelerated the process, distributing opaque plates like a blizzard of darkness assembling the shroud, piece by piece. Two-thirds of the sky was gone now. The sunlight had faded, and clouds churned as the unnatural vise grip closed around the world.

Osira'h, Prince Reynald, and the green priest had made it to the Kellum distillery in time to take one of the evacuation ships. Now, Tamo'l had to see that everyone else escaped—through the Klikiss transportal.

She worked furiously to prepare the population of the sanctuary domes. Shawn Fennis and Chiar'h rallied the misbreeds and readied their transport. The healthiest and most functional misbreeds carried the suffering ones, those who required special life support, respiration, body harnesses, or levitating platforms.

The Kuivahr tide was high, which made the seas rougher, mostly submerging the domes, and created additional difficulties for their exodus. They had access to only the top hatch and the smaller landing deck, where no more than ten people could gather at a time. During high tide, the people in the sanctuary domes normally hunkered down for a week in quiet isolation, but today Tamo'l knew everyone had to leave, at all costs. They had to reach the Klikiss transportal wall—but the domes had access to only a few boats, nothing suitable for a large-scale evacuation.

The domes' small craft were primarily used to shuttle one or two people to the transportal wall, or to meet up with the swimmer kith, who lived on wandering kelp rafts. Tamo'l's heart suddenly lurched as she thought of them: she'd been so focused on finding a way to save the misbreeds that she had entirely forgotten about the swimmers that thrived on Kuivahr! She felt responsible for them as well, because those generous swimmers had helped the sanctuary domes so often. But Tamo'l didn't know how to save all of them, wasn't even sure how to save her own misbreeds.

Tom Rom, though, claimed he could help.

A problem solver, he wore a determined expression without the slightest hint of panic as he stood outside on the upper deck. "I spent the past few hours compiling your medical data so that none of your research will be lost. I have a complete copy, and I am ready to go. Come with me, Tamo'l—my ship is on the other side of the transportal wall, landed on Auridia. We only need to choose the correct coordinate tile. These others can follow as they wish."

"We go together," Tamo'l insisted. "I have to save the misbreeds."

His expression hardened. "Perhaps they cannot be saved. It is most important that *you* come with me. The medical knowledge you possess could be very useful to Pergamus. Come, I'll take you."

Shawn Fennis rushed up, his face flushed, panting hard. "You're not in charge of transportation here, Mr. Tom Rom. Chiar'h and I agree that the Klikiss transportal is our best bet, but with this few boats, we need to start shuttling people over to the outcropping a few at a time, as many as the craft will carry."

Tom Rom clutched the Ildiran medical data, glanced up at the darkening sky. "Then I suggest we do so soon."

Though he limped and breathed hard, the misbreed Gor'ka toiled at the waterline and prepared the two small watercraft available. Tamo'l helped carry a levitating pallet that held one of the most deformed of the misbreeds. Soft, pale Mungl'eh was an invertebrate with a sluglike body and atrophied flippers for arms and legs. Despite her horrific body, Mungl'eh had a calm and complacent disposition, and when she sang, her voice was so sweet that she had made Mage-Imperator Jora'h weep. Each Ildiran breed had a useful purpose, and Mungl'eh had proved to Jora'h that even misbreeds could be precious.

When they made preparations on the platform under the terrifying, blackening sky, Tamo'l was dismayed by the size of the task. She shuddered, then forced herself to be strong. "Go, Chiar'h—take the first group to the transportal wall and send them away." She began to move. "Use Gorhum as a transfer point. That's where our supplies come from. The people there will be as ready as any."

Tom Rom said to her, "You and I should be in the first group."

Tamo'l glared at him. "I will go with you, Tom Rom, but only *after* everyone else is safe."

For a moment the man looked as if he would seize her against her will, steal one of the boats, and simply race away, abandoning all the others. Instead, he scanned the people on the upper deck, as if calculating how many remained behind; then he looked up into the sky and assessed how the black shell had grown noticeably more complete in just the last few minutes. "There is no time to waste—I will assist in order to expedite the operation. But we have to move."

Chiar'h took the first boat, and Gor'ka piloted the other one; they raced off carrying eight misbreeds, including Mungl'eh in her support bed. The dome's other medical researchers brought more misbreeds to the upper deck, waiting, but there was no boat to take them away until the first two returned. They all crowded and waited, looking fearfully at the dark sky. Fennis stared after his Ildiran wife as she sped away, leaving a white wake in the choppy water.

Overhead, the shroud continued to grow as thousands more hex plates built the curve, drawing the opening closed. Only a quarter of the sky remained now.

Through her close connection with Osira'h, Tamo'l sensed that they had escaped into orbit . . . but her sister still wasn't safe. Stronger yet, she felt a thrumming pain in the darkness above—Rod'h, helpless, a conduit that the creatures of darkness were using. *Rod'h . . .* She gathered her strength to call out to her brother, hoping that he could help them from inside the shadows, if only he could fight back.

Then, to her delight, she spotted figures in the water—graceful, sleek-skinned swimmers, hundreds of them. They had left their seaweed colonies and rushed to the sanctuary domes. With their large eyes and vestigial ears, they always looked astonished.

One of the swimmers called out to Tamo'l, waving at the black barrier in the sky. "They will swallow us up."

"Escape through the transportal wall!" Tamo'l pointed with her hand, urging them. "We are taking as many as our boats can carry, but you swimmers can all go. Now! Reach the wall, travel to another world where you'll be safe. Chiar'h is sending people to Gorhum. Go!"

Instead, the swimmers pulled themselves onto the platform, dripping wet, and stood before her. "But we can assist."

"How?"

"We can ferry you, if you have any sort of flotation. We will pull you across to the transportal wall."

Shawn Fennis brightened. "We have seven more levitating platforms in the infirmary. The swimmers can take the worst of the misbreeds."

"We can take more than that," said Tom Rom. "Those of you healthy enough can hold on to the platforms, while a misbreed rides aboard." With swift efficiency, he grabbed Fennis by the arm, and the two men ducked back down into the sanctuary domes to retrieve the needed equipment.

Tamo'l insisted that many of the swimmers should go. "Get yourselves safe. Twenty-five swimmers should suffice. The rest of you, go through the transportal!"

Several swimmers dove under the water and swam away, arrowing toward the rock outcropping and the alien transportal wall.

Meanwhile, Tamo'l and her staff brought up the slow-moving misbreeds. The remaining ones were growing panicked. The darkness in the sky was oppressive, grinding down on them. The barricade seemed not only to cut off the sunlight but all contact with the rest of the universe.

Tom Rom and Shawn Fennis returned carrying the first of the levitating platforms. "Three can go on this. One or two more can hold on as the swimmers pull you."

The waves were choppy, but the Ildiran refugees didn't hesitate. Three misbreeds climbed aboard the first platform as it bobbed up and down centimeters above the waves. The swimmers attached a cable, two of them ready to pull the platform. Har'lc wrapped a flopping tentacle-like arm around the back of the levitating platform and dove into the water. One more grabbed onto the platform and held on. When they were ready, two swimmers pulled the caravan across the waves.

A second levitating bed was similarly loaded and set off. Tom Rom assessed the sky with concern, watching the myriad hex plates that kept adding to the rim of the shell. "We have less than an hour remaining."

"It might be enough time," Tamo'l said, but she wasn't convinced.

A third levitating platform was loaded, and five more misbreeds escaped. Finally, Chiar'h and Gor'ka returned with now-empty boats ready to take another group.

"Quickly," Tamo'l said. "Fill them up!"

"The transportal is difficult, Tamo'l," said Chiar'h. "It is high tide, and the stone wall is partially submerged. When we open the dimensional gate, the Gorhum side is flooded."

"No other choice," Tom Rom said. "It is our only way off the planet now. Load up and go again."

The two boats took eight more, but Tamo'l could see that the pilots would have to return for several more trips. Nevertheless, she felt hope. Many were getting away. Osira'h and Reyn had escaped along with the Kellum distillery workers, and if all the swimmers evacuated through the transportal wall, then that was most of them. Not so terrible a disaster as she had feared.

Her heart felt dark and cold as she reached out with her mind to touch Rod'h again—and he continued to scream in despair and pain, trying to warn Tamo'l. "The Shana Rei want *you*!" She closed her eyes and tried to link with him, tried to strengthen the bond so she could understand him better, and he wailed, "No—don't!"

When she connected with him, it felt as if a dam had broken, and deep darkness flooded through. Shadows rose inside her mind, behind her vision, and Tamo'l gasped, blinded. On the precarious deck, she swayed and fought back with everything she could. She collapsed—but Tom Rom caught her in a grip like iron. . . .

She lost track of time. When her vision cleared, she saw that more groups of evacuees had gone. The last of the levitating beds had left, and the two boats had returned for a third trip. Only a few remained here on the platform.

Shawn Fennis rode one of the returning boats with Chiar'h. He shouted for the rest to get aboard. Everything was so dark, and Tamo'l realized that most of the sunlight was gone overhead. The black shroud was nearly closed, like the jaws of a predator clamping down.

How long had she been lost? What had happened to her?

Tom Rom urged her to the boat. "I met your conditions. Now we must go—immediately. This is the last trip." He wrenched her arm and put her into the boat crowded with the others. They raced away across stormy waves, with a grim Tom Rom piloting the boat himself.

Tamo'l fought to clear her head, but she could barely see, because darkness had swallowed Kuivahr. The entire sky was closing up overhead. Once the shadows finished their englobement and cut Kuivahr off from the universe, she didn't know if the Klikiss transportal wall would still function.

Tamo'l turned around, watched the sanctuary domes dropping away in the distance. They were mostly submerged, but now shadows had fallen over them as well. "Is everyone safe?"

"Safe?" Tom Rom looked at her. "They are gone, at least. That is the best we could hope for."

The comm squawked as they raced along, bouncing on the waves. Suddenly a loud burst of chatter, numerous voices over competing channels filled the speakers. "This is Adar Zan'nh. The Solar Navy is here to pick up refugees—and also to fight the shadows. We have a full cohort and all the sun bombs available to the Solar Navy."

Tamo'l's heart leaped with hope, even though all those warliners could not help them down here. The inexorable englobement continued.

The Solar Navy battle would commence in orbit, but Tamo'l, Tom Rom, and the last of her refugees would find their own way off the planet.

They reached the rocky outcropping, which was now just a foam of waves and the upright trapezoidal wall partially submerged in the rough tide. Another group of refugees was there, activating a coordinate tile. As the dimensional gateway opened, Tamo'l saw a shimmer of another place behind it. A gush of seawater flooded through, and the refugees were swept into the doorway, safe on another world—and then the transportal closed.

Shawn Fennis and Chiar'h jumped out of the boats along with the last refugees and climbed the slick reef rocks. Chiar'h did not bother to tie up the boat, simply abandoning it.

Overhead, hexes linked to hexes, nearly finished sewing up the last opening in the sky.

The transportal opened, another dimensional doorway to Gorhum. Fennis and Chiar'h turned and gestured for Tamo'l and Tom Rom, but Tamo'l felt dizzy again. Too much blackness surrounded her eyes, closing in on her vision just as the englobement sphere overhead was closing off Kuivahr. She collapsed, and Tom Rom caught her before the waves swept her off the outcropping.

"Go!" he shouted to the others, hauling Tamo'l against the rush of breakers. "We'll activate it again."

Chiar'h, Shawn Fennis, and the last researchers leaped through the doorway to the planet Gorhum, and the wall solidified behind them.

When he and Tamo'l climbed up onto the stable rocks of the outcropping, she was too weak to walk, and so Tom Rom supported her. He secured his satchel with all the Ildiran genetic medical records. They stood on the slippery, wave-washed rocks, and he faced the alien wall with an odd, determined calmness. He scanned the ring of coordinate tiles, but intentionally did not choose the same one the others had used for evacuating.

"My ship is at Auridia," he said. "I know a place where I can take you." He activated a coordinate tile, and the stone wall shimmered again. Before Tamo'l could ask questions or argue, he grasped her wrist and pulled her with him. She could not have broken free if she tried. She took one last glance at the Kuivahr sky, but very little light remained. She couldn't see much of anything else.

Then Tom Rom carried her through to safety.

CHAPTER 124

ARITA

When Arita and Collin flew back to the Wild, they did not stop to see Sarein. Rather than bringing her into their current mission, they went deeper into the unexplored verdani wilderness, where even Collin had lost contact with the isolationist green priests.

Something terrible was happening here.

Arita marveled at the vast lushness. Every one of those tall trees was a conduit for information that any green priest could touch and access. Yet Kennebar and the others had just vanished. How could the trees not have noticed?

Arita was glad to be with Collin, but they were both tense. Beside her in the flyer, he gave her directions, and they cruised over the pristine green sea of the canopy. She felt a chill as she flew, though. From the sky, she could see disturbing brown stains below, sections of the worldforest that had died off from the mysterious blight, just like the swath of withered trees she had spotted on her last visit. It did not look natural. A poison was seeping into the worldforest.

Tears welled in Collin's eyes, but he insisted on looking closer. He pressed his face against the window of the flyer. "This is the area, Arita. We need to land."

She circled, looking for a natural break in the thick canopy, an open clearing where she could set the ship down. Finally, she spotted a broad meadow garnished with white flowers. She had established numerous base camps like this for her scientific research, but she hoped this would be more of a rescue mission. She landed easily.

When they emerged from the cooling aircraft, the worldforest seemed oppressively silent around them. Arita turned around, straining to hear insects or the rustle of fronds . . . but everything was still and quiet, as if trapped in a kind of stasis.

"Even the worldtrees are hushed," Collin said in a breathy voice. Though his skin was emerald green and his body completely smooth, Arita saw the same vulnerable boy who had run through the forest with her, talking about the future, flirting with her, kissing her in a stolen moment. Now it felt as if they were all alone on the entire continent.

Collin's look of concern increased as he hurried deeper into the forest, and Arita followed him. He gazed up into the trees, sniffed, then closed his eyes. He touched the trunk of a worldtree, then withdrew his fingers, as if burned. He blinked. "I can't find them. They should all be close—this is where we lived."

Arita called out. "Hello? Kennebar! Any green priests?" Her own loud voice startled her, but no one responded.

Collin stopped beneath a tree with low branches and swung himself up, climbing hand-over-hand. Arita hurried to follow him, scrambling from one frond to another. After all of her years in the worldforest, she was as good a climber as he was. Together, they ascended through the lower branches and up into the thicker fronds.

Arita noticed flat platforms, woven benches, and other indications that Kennebar and his followers had made a primitive settlement here. Green priests considered the entire forest their natural home, yet they still had designed some comforts.

Kennebar had led his group away from the rest of the population, wanting to be isolated from the Confederation and the Spiral Arm. But this place was entirely empty. Could they have retreated farther into the Wild, seeking even more complete isolation? Had they been taken? Or killed?

Collin touched the woven platforms and sleeping areas; then he grasped a branch again, sinking his thoughts into the worldforest mind. He emerged and shook his head. "No answers. It's . . . blank."

The forest remained silent as they moved from one section of the trees to another. They still noticed signs of habitation, but the green priests were all gone, leaving only a primeval emptiness.

Collin looked confused, his eyes wide with lack of understanding. "I'm afraid of this, Arita."

She answered quietly, "We should be afraid." Arita had lived in the worldforest, felt a kinship with it, even though she wasn't an actual green priest. For the first time in her life, the dense trees seemed claustrophobic, sinister. She felt as if she didn't belong here.

Collin's eyes snapped open and he withdrew from telink, looking around in alarm. "Kennebar is coming."

Making virtually no sound as he slid through a wall of fronds, the leader of the separate green priests stood before them like a human-shaped void in the air. Arita gasped as a cold hand closed around her heart.

Kennebar had always been a tall and powerful man with a hard personality, a determination that gave him the strength of his convictions. Collin, like all green priests, had shed his hair, and his pale skin was filled with chlorophyll, turning him the rich, healthy green of the forest.

But Kennebar had undergone yet another transformation. He was no longer a *green* priest—instead he had been tainted by an inky blight. His face, bare chest, arms, legs, eyes, even his mouth and teeth were *entirely black*, as if all color had been leached out and replaced with the deepest night.

Collin backed away to stand next to Arita, and they faced the ebony priest. Arita said, "What happened to you?" But she received no answer.

Collin found his voice. "Kennebar, do you know me? Where are the others?"

The ebony priest's eyes blazed bright. "There are no others," he said in a frigid, hollow voice. "There will be no others."

CHAPTER

125

KOTTO OKIAH

A remarkable career. Yes, Kotto liked the sound of that. Biographers could have said that about him twenty years ago, and he could have rested on his laurels after the end of the Elemental War. Why would anybody need to accomplish more than he already had?

He was far too restless for that, though. He wasn't done. In fact, he felt as ambitious as ever.

Seventeen years ago back at Newstation, Speaker Del Kellum had given him a lifetime achievement award. *Lifetime* achievement? Kotto had only been fifty at the time! Why would anyone imagine that he was finished? In the reception after the awards ceremony, Kotto had heard someone remark that his best work was behind him. What a terrible thing to say!

Now, suspended in the nebula, the Big Ring gleamed, surrounded by ionized gases; the searing furnace of the newborn keystone stars drowned out all other illumination. Words failed him, and Kotto balked at the thoughts running through his mind. Of course it would work! It had to.

He felt butterflies in his stomach as he watched all the inspectors gathering for the Big Ring demonstration. Crowds of scientists, engineers, and workers were curious to see the giant experiment activated.

Station Chief Alu paced the deck inside the admin observation station, where the VIP visitors would watch the test. He seemed even more anxious than Kotto, since the reputation of Fireheart Station was at stake. "I can't wait to see this, Kotto. You promise it'll be a spectacular show?"

"I believe so—after everything we've invested in it." He drew a deep breath and pressed his hands together in front of him. "The Guiding Star is bright."

Alu peered out at the huge structure. "And this will pave the way for giant new transgates big enough to take whole ships from system to system in an instant?"

"We'll see for ourselves in a few minutes." Kotto tried to sound coy, but he felt embarrassed when he couldn't convey even general concepts that seemed so obvious to him. Several times, Howard Rohandas had saved him by explaining the steps that Kotto had glossed over. Shareen Fitzkellum also tried to help, but she was too impatient.

When it came to details of what would happen with the flux folding and the power the Ring would generate, his two lab assistants had been cowed since he had snapped at them. Kotto was still upset that Shareen and Howard had dampened his triumph, but he was more troubled that they had fostered doubts in his own mind. Kotto could not have doubts. He pushed those away, straightened his back and lifted his chin. "Let's get started. Station Chief, are we ready to commence?"

"You tell me, Kotto—you're in charge." Alu flung his long hair behind his back as if he were posing for a photo.

From the greenhouse terrarium, Celli and Solimar responded over the comm. "We will pass along reports through the trees. We are watching eagerly, and the rest of the green priests are watching us."

In habitation spheres, admin complexes, and single ships around the nebula, other Fireheart workers were all intent. Normal operations had been shut down in honor of the big event.

Garrison Reeves, one of the team leaders of a construction crew, transmitted a message, surrounded by men and women in serviceable Roamer jumpsuits. "Six years of work from start to finish. Let's see what we accomplished. I have to admit, we're very curious."

Kotto was curious as well. Calculations and theoretical concepts only went so far, and these would be real tangible results for everyone to see. He swallowed hard, but tried not to show his uneasiness. He had so much riding on the next few minutes.

Station Chief Alu smiled and gave him a thumbs-up.

Kotto opened the comm to the engineers and their control ships.

"Uh, this is Kotto Okiah. Engage the power blocks and spin up the current flow in the torus. Let's start building the field."

"Check, Kotto," said the team head.

Tracking lights lit along the Ring like lightning bugs in a racetrack as each bank in the chain of power blocks illuminated. The Big Ring awakened, and he was grinning like a fool, breathing hard.

The Ring remained edge-on to the firestorm of hot central stars, so the stellar flux would not pour through the center of the Ring. Not yet. The current had to build to maximum first, generating a wraparound magnetic field.

Over the years, Kotto had launched so many important experiments and gambled so many resources on brainstorms he'd had. As the son of the revered Speaker Jhy Okiah, Kotto had been given opportunities that many other Roamer scientists didn't receive, but that only accounted for the beginning of his career. Since then, he had proved himself again and again, and skepticism turned to cheers.

He remembered when he had launched the metals-processing operations on fiery Isperos and the deep-frozen settlement of Jonah 12 for hydrogen extraction. And there were numerous new weapons, skymine redesigns, countless prototypes. Sometimes his schemes failed due to circumstances beyond his control, but the Roamers always gave him another chance.

Like now. He had rarely felt so excited . . . or so nervous.

When the Big Ring was glowing and the engineering team leader reported that the current flow was at its maximum, the magnetic field was like a constricting vise around the whole torus.

"We're spun up to full strength, Kotto. Power block output is at capacity, and the discharge at this level will last for no more than ten minutes. That magnetic field is damned impressive."

Inside the VIP chamber, observers were applauding, talking among themselves.

"Rotate the Ring on its axis," Kotto forced himself to say. "Turn it so that the full stellar flux goes right through the center of the hole."

Hundreds of small technical satellites were scattered all around the Ring, taking measurements. Raw data poured across the screens. Kotto held his breath as opposite equatorial thrusters turned the torus like a rotating planet. The Ring's lights glowed bright as power blocks continued to discharge, creating a cross-magnetic field that made a furious loop in space.

Kotto mopped his forehead. With shining eyes, he turned to look at the excited observers—and caught a glimpse of Shareen and Howard. The two assistants looked troubled, but held their silence. Shareen fidgeted and leaned over to whisper to Howard. The young man shook his head.

Feeling a heavy weight in his stomach, Kotto turned away, trying to convince himself that he shouldn't worry about the concerns of two mere assistants.

The Ring slowly rotated, giving a sense of sheer massiveness. As if a window had been opened, they could see the lighthouse beacon of Fireheart's central star cluster through the middle of the torus. The blazing young stars were blue-white, their radiation incredibly intense, and now the full flux streamed like a fire hose through the center of the Ring, which itself was wrapped with an intense magnetic field. The field built on the new flux, increasing the energy level, sucking more power out of the blocks.

—which made the current increase through the Ring. In turn, the magnetic field grew more and more powerful.

—feeding the stellar flux that increased it still more, in a runaway cascade.

Kotto couldn't breathe. The Ring shuddered with such power that it looked like a Samson straining at the shackles of space-time.

The team leader shouted over the comm, "Kotto, everything's off the scales. It's a *self-accelerating* feedback loop!"

Several of the telemetry satellites closest to the Big Ring sparked, shorted, and went offline.

Shareen made her way to his side. "Where is all that power going to go?"

The Ring itself shuddered and its physical structure . . . *blurred.*

He activated the comm to the team leaders. "Withdraw to a safer distance, just in case. We don't really know—"

Then the Ring wobbled, shuddered—and *collapsed into itself* as if all the power blocks, the torus structural supports, and the magnetic field holding it all together twisted themselves inside out like a bizarre Escher drawing.

Kotto couldn't tear his eyes away.

The Big Ring folded inside and out, twisting through fractional dimensions. The circular opening in the middle pulled from all sides and split a large, neat hole in the fabric of the universe. The gaping tear in space shifted, and the whole Ring itself vanished, sucked inside like a pebble through a hull breach. The gaping *empty* maw remained open, intensely dark, giving evidence of no stars, no gravity, no light. Wisps of the Fireheart nebula began to drift into it, a colorful waterfall swirling down a drain into infinity.

"It's like a giant doorway," said Station Chief Alu, not sure whether to be afraid or amazed. "Is . . . that what you were expecting, Kotto?"

"It's not at all what anyone was expecting," Shareen said.

Howard asked, "What if we need to close that thing?"

A hush fell in the observation chamber. As Kotto watched, unable to believe his eyes, he saw the darkness behind space shifting and changing. Something even blacker than emptiness was moving inside the tear, coming closer.

CHAPTER

126

ADAR ZAN'NH

Carrying the most advanced weaponry, the cohort of warliners arrived at Kuivahr. The Solar Navy wasted no time.

After they disengaged their stardrives, the deceleration was intense enough to damage some systems. Crewmembers had to strap down and endure the bone- and muscle-crushing weight, but Adar Zan'nh was desperate to arrive before it was too late. This time, he intended to deal the enemy a devastating blow, and he had the weaponry do to it.

His pulse raced, and his eyes focused to a razor-sharp intensity. He recalled how his heroic predecessor Adar Kori'nh had made the hydrogues reel at Qronha 3. Zan'nh meant to do a similar thing now: he would throw *everything* into the engagement, if that was what it took to stop further attacks. He wanted to make the Shana Rei fear them. He wanted to make the shadows *hurt*.

As the fleet hurtled toward Kuivahr, Zan'nh instantly spotted the huge shadow cloud, the terrifying black hex cylinders—and nearly a hundred robot battleships, all much larger and more fearsome than the vessels they had recently fought at the Onthos home system.

Well, he had superior weapons now, too.

"We arrived too late, Adar," said his navigator.

Zan'nh held on to the command rail and shook his head. "No—we are exactly on time." He transmitted to every maniple commander, every septar, every pilot of every warliner. "You have all been briefed, and you are prepared. Commence the attack without delay. Today, here, we will stop the Shana Rei."

The main screen mapped out the positions of the hundred robot battleships, laid them out on a tactical grid, and identified targets, which were distributed among the 343 warliners. The grid also picked up an outlying blip among the enemy vessels, a smaller ship racing in an erratic course directly toward them.

A distress signal burst across the comm screen. "By the Guiding Star, are we glad to see you! This is Zhett Kellum and Patrick Fitzpatrick from the Kuivahr distillery. We're the last ship to get away from the planet, and we have Prince Reynald of Theroc with us, as well as your Mage-Imperator's daughter Osira'h. Request permission to come aboard—and you'd better make up your minds quick!"

The pursuing robot ships opened fire at the Roamer ship, but Zhett had managed to evade them, so far. Adar Zan'nh directed his warliners. "Intercept and protect that ship. Grant them sanctuary."

Overlapping chatter appeared on adjacent screens. From the command nucleus of his own warliner, Tal Gale'nh sent an urgent message. "Adar, our sister Tamo'l is still down on the planet. Muree'n and I can sense her. And Rod'h . . . I don't know." His bleached face looked distraught. "He is in the shadow cloud somewhere."

High-resolution images showed that the ocean world was almost completely encased in an ebony shell, and he felt cold trickle through him. This englobement was smaller in scale than what they had encountered at the Onthos home system, but just as deadly. All life on Kuivahr would be snuffed out.

Lurking inside their shadow cloud, the five Shana Rei hex cylinders showed no reaction to the arrival of the gigantic Ildiran fleet. They simply kept spilling out a rain of hex plates to seal the last gap in the enveloping sphere.

"Adar!" cried the comm officer. "We've retrieved the human ship. Osira'h and Prince Reynald are safe aboard."

He felt a rush of relief, then he glanced at the tactical projection of space around Kuivahr. "Are there any other refugee ships from Kuivahr? We have to get them off planet before that shell closes."

"No indications, Adar."

His heart felt heavy. Whoever had been down there was surely lost—including Tamo'l.

As the robot battleships plunged toward the Solar Navy cohort, the grouped warliners continued on their course toward Kuivahr.

"Laser cannons," Zan'nh said. "Target that black sphere and cut open a hole. That may give Tamo'l and her people a little more time."

The first septa to reach the planet used high-intensity laser cannons like a hot scythe to chop at the obsidian shroud. The bombardment of coherent light was powerful enough to dislodge a section of hex plates, ripping open a hole in the shell and allowing light through again. The laser cannons continued to slice away, widening the gap—but more hex plates showered down onto the damaged area, like platelets forming a scab on a bleeding wound.

Zan'nh remembered how much effort they had expended in trying to knock apart the nightshade above Theroc or the huge Dyson sphere surrounding the Onthos system. The Shana Rei cylinders seemed to have an inexhaustible supply of dark material, and they managed to repair the shell as fast as the warliners could damage it.

The flagship's science officer groaned. "Adar! The planet is gone. The sphere is complete."

Kuivahr was nothing more than a jet-black ball orbited by two lost moons.

Adar Zan'nh set his jaw, knowing that was not a battle he could fight right now. He reached a cold conclusion. This would be a fruitless effort. He could waste the destructive resources of the entire cohort, ultimately for no purpose. No, he needed to do something more significant, and this might be his last chance not only to demonstrate hope for the Ildiran Empire and the Confederation, but to make the creatures of darkness reconsider this fight.

The black shroudsphere around Kuivahr healed itself, leaving no scars, as if nothing had happened at all.

The first robot battleship crashed in among the warliners, opening fire with enhanced weaponry at the nearest Solar Navy ship. All Ildiran shields were at maximum, but even so the bombardment cut through and damaged one warliner. Two other warliners were destroyed by the combined onslaught of the gigantic enemy ships. The black robots flew in like rabid animals, attacking everywhere—and more than three hundred Solar Navy warliners rallied to defend themselves. They hammered at the robot ships, but the enemy armor was stronger than expected.

Meanwhile, the Shana Rei hex cylinders hung inside their shadow cloud, motionless, while the robots fought for them. They seemed invincible.

Adar Zan'nh made his choice, and he announced how to direct his attack. "We can either try to scoop spoons full of sand from a beach, or we can *make a difference*. It is questionable how much effect our attack will have against the Shana Rei, but the robots are their foot soldiers—and we know that our weapons can destroy them. If we combine our forces, we can eliminate the robots entirely. Let us hurt the enemy there!"

The great Adar Kori'nh's astonishing all-or-nothing gambit at Qronha 3 had sent the supposedly invincible hydrogues reeling and demonstrated an effective new way of fighting. Zan'nh could not hold a spark to the bravery of Adar Kori'nh, but he meant to do everything possible.

Tal Gale'nh and Muree'n appeared on the comm, their faces filled with despair. "Tamo'l is gone, Adar! We felt her . . . wink out."

Looking flushed, Osira'h arrived in the command nucleus, followed by Prince Reynald and their companions. Osira'h struggled to keep her balance as she was buffeted by storms inside her mind. "Tamo'l was intending to evacuate all her people through the Klikiss transportal. Maybe she escaped. I also felt Rod'h reach out to all of us, screaming—but then Tamo'l went through the transportal, and I felt nothing more from her."

Zan'nh turned to face the oncoming robot ships. "We will have one victory today, at least. Drain your laser-cannon batteries, unleash all your sun bombs, including the new ones—and turn them against *the robots*. Wipe them out." He hardened his voice, knowing the risk he was taking. "If we save anything for later, there may not be a later."

The warliners responded, and the space battleground around Kuivahr became a firestorm of destructive light, like the core of an exploding galaxy.

CHAPTER

127

TAL GALE'NH

Beside him in the command nucleus of his warliner, Muree'n was ruthless and eager for the fight, but Tal Gale'nh did not let her impatience distract him. He filled his mind with tactical projections, the tightly coordinated dance of the other warliners as they prepared for their full-forward press. For years, the Solar Navy had incessantly practiced coordinated maneuvers. Each one of the warliner captains knew the plan and the pattern of complex battle maneuvers, and now they had to adapt as best they could.

"More than ninety robot ships, Tal," said his weapons officer. "They are larger and more powerful than the previous models."

"We are more powerful as well—they have not seen the new sun bombs yet." He gave a brisk nod. "Laser cannons first to cause initial damage as we get into position. When those are depleted, we unload our sun bombs—our original ones, as well as the new designs that General Keah provided. And more than three hundred warliners will do the same."

"They do not stand a chance," Muree'n said with a smile.

Spears of blinding coherent light impaled the nearest robot ship as it swooped toward them, three warliners concentrating on the same target. The black vessel's shields held for a moment, shimmered, strained. Gale'nh watched the enemy ship's weaponry brighten as it prepared to fire; then the laser-cannon broadside broke through the protective barrier and destroyed the robot battleship.

"More," Gale'nh called. "Open fire, any target—until they are all eradicated."

Around him, more warliners unleashed their full laser batteries, which pummeled the black robot battleships, but were not sufficient.

The robots launched a merciless counterattack, destroying three warliners. Gale'nh felt a sick fury at seeing the expanding clouds of hot wreckage in space.

Another energy blast slammed the shields of his warliner, causing some of their power systems to fail, but backup loops kicked in. "More laser cannons!" he yelled, and another broadside crashed into two robot battleships.

Hundreds of warliners turned their laser cannons loose as well, and before long, a brilliant flash signified the eruption of the first sun bomb—one of the new models. As the shock wave expanded and rolled over two black battleships, he saw that General Keah had not exaggerated when she bragged about the new design. The nova explosion was breathtaking, and it took the robots completely by surprise.

"Press our advantage. Select your next targets," Gale'nh said. "We want each detonation to take out several enemy vessels, so place each sun bomb accordingly." He believed Adar Zan'nh was correct—if the Solar Navy could exterminate the Klikiss robot fighters, they would hamstring the Shana Rei conventional attack. Gale'nh's warliner launched three sun bombs toward clustered robot ships, and the command-nucleus screens filtered dark when nuclear flashes blossomed across space, a vaporizing explosion several times more powerful than the robots had faced before.

The full cohort of Solar Navy ships struck again and again, holding nothing back. Sun bomb after sun bomb. The black robots reeled, not knowing what had hit them.

Adar Zan'nh kept shouting on the comm line. "We have destroyed more than fifty enemy ships already! Time to wipe out the rest." Then he added, as if it were a matter of personal pride, "We will have something impressive to show General Keah, next time we meet." The warliner commanders needed no further encouragement.

On the tactical screens, Gale'nh watched his weapons inventory diminish, but he did not slow his attack. He calculated they would have enough sun bombs to achieve their mission.

Beside him, Muree'n's expression was intense yet happy.

Three more sun bombs detonated, and the nuclear shock waves collided and interfered with other explosions. The combined energy was enough to wreck one robot ship after another. The last remaining black battleships fought back, but with a desperation now. Their improved weapons and armor were impressive but insufficient.

Only twenty-one robot ships remained of the original ninety-eight.

Gale'nh concentrated the last reserves of his laser-cannon fire on the two nearest enemy vessels. He did not bother with short, conservative bursts, but told the weapons officer to continue the barrage, allowing no time for reset or recharge. He drained his laser batteries—and two more robot vessels were gone.

"We have only three sun bombs remaining, Tal," said his weapons officer.

"What are the losses in the cohort?"

The sensor technician scanned space. "Fifty warliners destroyed, Tal. Twenty-three more severely damaged and unable to fight."

"A great cost," he said, "but the robots have suffered a much higher toll."

More than two hundred battered but determined warliners closed in on the ragtag remnants of the robot battle fleet, harrying the last enemy survivors. Five more black battleships exploded. Panicked now, the remaining enemy vessels turned about and fled, racing pell-mell back toward the safety of the shadow cloud.

Adar Zan'nh transmitted, "Forward! Wipe out the last of them."

Muree'n pointed at the tactical screen. "Right there—a sun bomb would take out two more." Gale'nh directed the weapons officer to take the shot.

Muree'n flashed a fierce smile as the pinwheeling sphere hurtled toward a pair of robot ships struggling to get away. When the sun bomb went nova, the shock wave was enough to vaporize both robot vessels before they could reach the fringe of the dark nebula.

Gale'nh showed no overt joy though he felt a swell of inner pride. Behind them, the planet Kuivahr was entirely black, smothered. If they had enough weapons remaining at the end of this engagement, they could crack through that impenetrable shell, but he was sure that everyone down there was already gone. Tamo'l had vanished. He could feel nothing from her.

Muree'n sensed her brother's thoughts. "Osira'h is safe aboard the Adar's flagship, but Rod'h . . . I will try again to reach him."

Gale'nh pressed his lips together as he looked at the looming shadow cloud. What could they do for Rod'h now?

Only five robot battleships remained, and they were careening toward the shadow cloud. The Shana Rei cylinders began to rotate, swiveling on their axes to prepare for the oncoming remnants of the Solar Navy. The creatures of darkness had finished with Kuivahr, and they had no reason to stay here and risk further damage—except perhaps to destroy more Ildiran warliners.

On-screen, Adar Zan'nh shouted, "Stop those last robots." Gale'nh had never seen the commander so agitated. "Do not let any survive!"

Seven warliners accelerated forward to catch the damaged black battleships. Ahead of them, the shadow cloud was a necrotic flower that swallowed up all the surrounding starlight.

The pursuing warliners launched three sun bombs, and two struck straggler robot ships, vaporizing them. Of the original ninety-eight attack vessels, only three robots survived. One of the launched sun bombs missed its target and streaked into the black hexagons, erupting there and searing away a deep divot of ebony material.

Finally, the last of the frantic robot ships reached the fringe of the dark nebula. The black hex cylinders turned toward the rest of the Solar Navy fleet. Adar Zan'nh ordered, "Launch the last sun bombs, a final concentrated salvo against the Shana Rei—and then withdraw immediately. We are finished here."

When the seven warliners in hot pursuit plunged into the haze of shadows, the hex ships unleashed rippling waves that struck the Ildiran vessels with a thunderclap of entropy. The warliners reeled, spun, and all systems went dark. The Solar Navy pilots screamed out, and the comm burst into random static. As Gale'nh and Muree'n watched from the command nucleus, all seven warliners crumbled apart in space, as if the very material that composed them no longer maintained its integrity.

"Withdraw!" shouted the Adar.

Gale'nh did not wish to retreat until he had depleted his sun bombs, so he launched them directly into the hex cylinders. Two more bright stars erupted, damaging the shadow ships. Fifteen additional sun bombs, perhaps the last remaining armaments in the entire cohort, pinwheeled out from other warliners and struck the heart of the shadow cloud. The nova explosions substantially diminished the long black cylinders.

"If only we had thousands more of those," Muree'n said.

Gale'nh nodded. "We are manufacturing them as quickly as we can."

The shadow cloud turned into itself and enfolded the hex cylinders as well as the last three robot battleships. The dark nebula collapsed, whisked away like blackness down a drain, and the tear in space sealed, leaving the sorely wounded remnants of the Solar Navy hanging there in space.

At the last instant, both Gale'nh and Muree'n reached out with their minds, calling for Rod'h, trying to make a connection, but their brother was surrounded by darkness, despair, and insanity. They held on to him for just a moment, giving him a taste of hope, before the connection snapped. Rod'h faded away until he was only an echoing wail in memory.

"Our brother is gone," Muree'n said.

Gale'nh studied the wreckage of ships, the destroyed robot battleships, and also the surviving warliners that had faced the Shana Rei and driven them off.

"But we are still here," Gale'nh said, and he took heart from that.

CHAPTER

128

TOM ROM

Tom Rom hauled Tamo'l through the transportal wall to Auridia, accompanied by a wash of seawater from Kuivahr. Behind them, the permanent night rushed toward them like a wave of darkness.

Tamo'l staggered onto the concrete apron on the other side of the Auridia transportal. She acted strangely dazed, no doubt overwhelmed by the loss of her planet and her sanctuary domes, but Tom Rom didn't allow her the time to be reluctant or confused. All of the misbreed specimens had gotten away to Gorhum, and he no longer needed to be concerned about them.

They were both drenched, and cold salt water poured off of them. With a firm arm around her waist, Tom Rom caught Tamo'l as they both swayed, adjusting to Auridia's higher gravity, the new sunlight, the new atmosphere. As more waves washed through the still-open transportal, Tom Rom collapsed onto the paved apron.

He heard shouts of surprise and dismay from the Auridia operations crew. Ignoring them, he pulled himself to his feet and blinked in the hazy gray sunlight, which was such a contrast to the midnight barrier that had engulfed Kuivahr. He saw a group of wide-eyed Roamer technicians in jumpsuits and two traders lounging around.

More seawater sprayed through the dimensional doorway, spilling across the floor and dousing equipment along with one of the traders, who sat drinking a bottle of distilled kelpbeer. Behind them, the transportal wall solidified, cutting off the passage to the blackness that had swallowed Kuivahr.

As Tom Rom wiped seawater out of his eyes, one of the Roamer technicians said, "What a mess! Give us a little warning next time."

A dozen men and women scrambled to rescue chairs and electronic equipment from the spreading remnants of the flood.

Tamo'l stood shaking in her wet clothes, blinking her pearlescent eyes. "Where are we? This isn't Gorhum. I don't recognize this place."

"It is called Auridia. The Roamer capital of Newstation orbits overhead, but not many people use the transportal down here. This is where my ship is parked." Tom Rom had chosen Auridia because it was a quiet, sleepy transportal nexus. The Roamer staff was welcoming and not overly curious. He had paid a parking fee, and the station monitors were happy to take his credits.

Now the Roamer techs and the curious traders gathered closer. "What happened to you two?"

Tom Rom said, "We came from Kuivahr. That coordinate tile is no longer viable. Mark it." Tamo'l shuddered.

The trader sipped his distilled kelpbeer, frowned. "Not many people go there anyway. What happened?" Tom Rom noticed that no one seemed to feel any sense of urgency.

"Overrun by Shana Rei. The whole planet is gone."

"Now, that's newsworthy," said one of the Roamers.

"Yes. It is." Tom Rom glanced at Tamo'l, who still seemed disoriented. "My companion and I have to go. Please pass the information up to Newstation and on to Theroc."

Tamo'l stood on her own, still shaking. "Where are the others? The misbreeds, Shawn Fennis, Chiar'h . . ."

"They should be safe," he said.

"But, they're not here."

"They went to Gorhum. I chose a different coordinate tile for us."

"I need to be with them," she said.

"They will be taken care of on Gorhum, but I want you to meet my employer. She will be very interested in your work with the misbreeds." He clutched the protected case of medical records against his side. "I have all your data."

She said, "I could sense Rod'h from the sanctuary domes . . . at the last moment. We connected."

"By the Guiding Star, we need more of a story than that. Tell us what happened to Kuivahr," said one of the Roamers.

"Not at the moment." Tom Rom maneuvered Tamo'l toward his ship, and she did not resist. He felt very anxious to get away; he did not want to answer questions from these Roamers, didn't want others to realize who it was that accompanied him. Tamo'l would be useful at Pergamus. Once Zoe had thoroughly debriefed the Ildiran half-breed, they could decide where to take her.

The Klikiss transportal stood on a slight rise from the surrounding plains. The transportal outpost consisted of a dozen prefab buildings, rickety-looking temporary office shelters, and a lot of brown grasses and spiny weeds.

His ship sat at the bottom of the transportal rise, just beyond the flimsy admin structures. Several local workers emerged from the prefab buildings, attracted by the commotion. Seawater from Kuivahr was puddled around the apron.

"Which coordinate tile did you say was no good?" called the team leader.

"Kuivahr," Tom Rom said over his shoulder as he hurried Tamo'l to his ship. "Look it up."

The Auridia operations staff seemed singularly uninterested, as if they preferred their usual routine over any sort of excitement.

"We should go to Gorhum," Tamo'l said. "Through the transportal. I want to meet up with the rest of the misbreeds. They need me."

Tom Rom opened the boarding door of his ship, eager to get her aboard before she posed too many more questions. "We can fly to Gorhum after we stop at Pergamus."

Two Roamer workers used brooms to sweep the puddles of water off the apron while other staff members stood around watching. The team leader bent over his datapad calling up information; then he scrutinized the numerous Klikiss coordinate tiles around the flat stone trapezoid. "Found it!" he called, as if Tom Rom were interested. "Checking it out now."

He felt a sudden foreboding as he got Tamo'l aboard. The men and women here seemed like lazy fools. He didn't care about them being lazy, but being *foolish* might cause problems. He shouted back, "Stop—that is not wise."

But the tech activated the Kuivahr coordinate tile anyway, just to make sure, and the stone wall rippled. The others backed away, some curious, some laughing, some wary they would be doused with another surge of seawater once the doorway opened.

Tom Rom ducked inside the ship behind Tamo'l just as the transportal opened to reveal the utter blackness swimming on the other side. But the black seemed more tangible than mere darkness. The black moved, swirled, and pushed through the doorway to Auridia.

Tom Rom bolted to the cockpit and activated the engines. Because of his many missions for Zoe, his engines had preburners that remained lit for instantaneous takeoff; he could achieve full thrust within seconds. He also possessed far more powerful weapons than one would expect from a ship of this size. He had battled Roamer pirates before and chased away curiosity seekers who came too close to Pergamus. He was prepared.

His ship leaped up from the surface, leaving a scorched swath from the afterburners. He looked down at the small admin settlement, the transportal wall, to see people running in all directions. A pseudopod of shadows and smoke pushed through the transportal opening like a questing tendril. The dimensional doorway had broken open, and whatever had engulfed Kuivahr was now coming through. The transportal gushed shadows, a hemorrhage of black nothingness.

Tom Rom gained altitude and circled away under heavy acceleration. Tamo'l stared through the windowport, aghast.

Below, the darkness spread like an oil spill. It overwhelmed and swallowed up three of the fleeing personnel. The lazy trader with the bottle of beer charged toward the transportal in an attempt to reach the coordinate tiles. Tom Rom hadn't expected such bravery, though he hadn't counted on such stupidity in the first place.

Tamo'l fell into a seat, clutching her head. "So cold!"

Tom Rom knew what he would have to do. The personnel down there were lost, but if the Shana Rei could pour through this transportal, they might extend through other transportals as well. They could engulf Auridia, rise up to take over Newstation. It wasn't his job to save the Roamers or the Confederation, but he would do it to save Zoe and Pergamus. There were repercussions.

He activated his weapons systems, issued no warning—what was the point?—and circled back. He opened fire on the Klikiss transportal at full strength. He peppered the stone wall and the surrounding structures with jazers; he launched explosives, which destroyed all the infrastructure around the near-indestructible alien wall. The blackness swelled as if trying to vomit as much darkness as possible through in the last instant.

Tom Rom continued the bombardment and finally, deciding to take no chances, he dropped a small tactical nuke that turned the area into a crater filled with pooled glass. That wash of searing atomic light obliterated the pseudopod of shadows, and by the time the brightness faded, Tom Rom's ship was already soaring away from Auridia.

Even if the transportal survived the detonation, all the attendant mechanisms had been vaporized or at least severely damaged. If nothing else, the conduit to Kuivahr had been shut down.

In a panicked voice, Newstation Control insisted that he dock and answer questions. The Roamers aboard the station were furious and shocked. He didn't bother to respond to the shouted communications, the demands for answers; he simply flew his ship away. When he reached orbit, he kept going. He activated the Ildiran stardrive before the Roamers could do more than threaten.

"We're safe now," he told Tamo'l. "I will take you to Pergamus."

She had withdrawn into herself and sat alone, breathing deeply, struggling to control herself. Finally, she said, "I look forward to it. I am very curious to see Pergamus myself."

She turned her head away before Tom Rom could notice the change that flooded through her pearlescent eyes—the spark of dark that rose up inside her before it withdrew into hiding again.

CHAPTER 129

ROD'H

When the Shana Rei attacked Kuivahr, that was his only contact with the outside universe, the only glimpse of worlds and stars he'd been allowed to see since his capture. And what he saw was no mercy. No mercy at all.

Rod'h had been lost in sensory deprivation, a cocoon of emptiness with no heat or cold, no sound except when the Shana Rei or Exxos tormented him. But in orbit above Kuivahr, they allowed him to watch the black shroud smother the whole world. Perhaps they did it to emphasize their power, or perhaps just to reinforce his feelings of helplessness.

During their panicked evacuation, he had sensed both Osira'h and Tamo'l, and he cried out in every way possible, but the void swallowed his words. Rod'h knew he had been bred for great things—perhaps even destined to be the savior of the Ildiran Empire—and now he was completely impotent. Worse, he was a dangerous vulnerability, a chink in the armor that could bring about disaster for all Ildirans.

He watched as the black shell engulfed the entire planet. Even the Solar Navy could do nothing to stop the suffocation of Kuivahr. He sensed Osira'h as she fled with Prince Reyn, and he sensed Gale'nh—and Muree'n!—aboard the warliners in the midst of the space battle.

Still down on the planet, Tamo'l seemed more open to him than his other siblings. She was sensitive, desperate, vulnerable. She opened up and reached out, trying to help him—as if he were one of her misbreed patients. He tried to hold on to her.

The Shana Rei appeared around him, inkblots hovering closer. He tried to pull away, but their voices thundered in his head. "We will follow you."

Too late, Rod'h realized that this was exactly what they wanted! He struggled to break the connection. He knew Tamo'l was also seeking strength from him. The inkblots swarmed closer, wrapping around him like leech patches. Though he thrashed and fought, the creatures of darkness drilled into his mind, pressed harder, and seeped into him like a fever in the blood.

Then, Tamo'l was gone, as if she had been snuffed out, the connection broken . . . no, not broken, just *stretched*. She had vanished through the Klikiss transportal.

And in despair, he realized that the Shana Rei had followed her like a parasite hooked on to her *thism* through him, riding his mental connection to her!

Osira'h couldn't help him. Gale'nh and Muree'n couldn't help him.

Even watching the annihilation of virtually all the despised Klikiss robots gave him only a glimmer of hope. The barrage of far-superior sun bombs should have been a crushing defeat for the Shana Rei, but the shadows seemed not to care at all. They were much more satisfied with what they had done to him, with the bond they had forged through him . . . and with the damage his weakness had caused.

"We can now undermine those who cause us pain," the Shana Rei said.

"We are not hurting you!" Rod'h shouted.

"You exist. And by existing, you create agony. Your thoughts scream at us. Your life is a stain on the cold purity that existed before creation. We must eliminate you all. We must rip out the underpinnings that corrupted the universe into an organized state. The Shana Rei were slumbering in our chaos until we were driven out by the increasing pain. Now it has grown too intense for us to bear."

"But what did we do?" Rod'h shouted.

"Not you," the inkblots pulsed. "Eternity's mind awakens, and we have little time to erase you all—and ourselves—before that scream of order becomes infinite."

They tore at Rod'h's mind as if to give him a taste of the agony the Shana Rei said they experienced each instant.

"We have already found a way to destroy the verdani mind from within. Now that we possess you, we have a way into the *thism* as well." The inkblots hovered around him like jackal lizards. "We can use you to cause great destruction to your own people—from within."

Rod'h could see black tendrils everywhere, like barbed wire lashing through the Ildiran race, drawing tight.

CHAPTER 130

SAREIN

The whole continent of the Wild had seemed crowded for a time after Kennebar and his green priests came, and then the Onthos, but Sarein ignored them, and they ignored her in return. Now, though, she felt *too* alone. She felt ominous changes in the wilderness around her, and she did not need to be a green priest to notice it.

As a Theron, Sarein was attuned to the forest in a way that only a native could know. She knew why the Gardeners had come here, and she was well aware that the verdani accepted them. The aliens had tended another worldforest millennia before the generation ship *Caillie* had found Theroc, long before the first human green priest ever became aware of the sentient trees.

When the hundred refugee aliens came to the Wild and scattered deep into the forest, they wanted peaceful isolation so they could recover after their ordeal. Sarein could sympathize with that. Only a hundred survivors of an entire race—she wasn't sure it was genetically viable for them to rebuild and reproduce. The naked gray-skinned creatures seemed to be sexless drones.

She had not spotted the Gardeners in weeks, however—not since they retreated deeper into the forest—and even Kennebar and his green priests had vanished, leaving her entirely alone. Collin had warned her about the disturbing changes. Usually Sarein would see one or more green priests as they traveled along the fronds, walking paths through the dense canopy, but she had seen none for days.

At first, the silence was peaceful, but she grew increasingly uneasy. There was a *difference* in the worldforest, like the persistent dull ache of an infected tooth. She often lay awake just listening to the night.

Frustrated and curious, she left her hiveworm nest and climbed one of the trees. When she reached the top and gazed across the verdant canopy, she frowned. In the distance, Sarein could discern a spreading swath of brown, a section of worldtrees that had withered and fallen. She had not bothered to climb this high in several weeks, and now the unexpected sight alarmed her.

She called out, "Kennebar! Green priests! I know you can hear me through the trees. I must speak with you." She waited, but did not expect an immediate answer.

Normally, Sarein spent her days in her quiet dwelling while she wrote her memoirs and laid down with brutal truth everything she had done in the Elemental War, giving explanations but not excuses. She had stopped looking for wonder in the world around her. But she was tired of feeling sorry for herself. If something bad was happening to the worldforest, she needed to know. She would contact Peter and Estarra if she had no other recourse.

"Kennebar, I have to speak with you!" she called out again.

The green priests were snoops, eavesdroppers, and she felt that they were always watching her. So, if no one responded to her call, they had to be ignoring her on purpose. What was wrong with them? She grew angry at first, and then anxious. Something was definitely wrong.

With one last look at the ominous die-off of trees, she climbed back down to her dwelling and tried to get some writing done, but she could not concentrate, bothered too much by the moody stillness that was closing in on the worldforest.

Five hours passed, and no green priest came to see her. Sarein frowned, annoyed that they would so blatantly ignore her request. She had once been a powerful person in the Hansa, but she had no authority over green priests. Kennebar's group even spurned the authority of Peter and Estarra, claiming to be devoted solely to the welfare of the trees.

Having seen all those dead trees kilometers away, Sarein didn't think Kennebar was doing his job very well.

She decided to investigate. She couldn't just withdraw and hide, pretending she had no part in human civilization anymore. No, it was time she did something on her own. She had her own small flyer for emergencies, and she was determined to find one of the green priests and demand answers. Maybe they had all gathered around the blight-stricken trees, trying to help. That was where she would start her search, and if she found no priests there, then Sarein would have to report the problem to Estarra.

In late afternoon she flew off, skimming across the treetops toward the blight. The lush expanse of worldtrees seemed comforting, a powerful presence that had welcomed human settlers to Theroc more than two centuries ago. Sarein felt guilty that she had spent too little time respecting and appreciating the sentient trees. The verdani, along with the wentals, had helped the human race survive the Elemental War. Now something seemed to be killing the great worldforest—and no one else knew about it.

Sarein did, though, and she would investigate.

As she approached, she saw that the die-off area was much larger than she had expected. Arita had mentioned the blight, but Sarein had thought the girl was just being alarmist. Now her throat went dry, and her eyes burned with tears. This was a true emergency. Sarein landed her craft in a meadow and emerged, walking through tall grasses and bright flowers, staring up at the brittle worldtree skeletons. The large grove looked entirely drained.

Sarein was unprepared for this, and she chastised herself for not bringing an imager with her or a long-range communicator so she could transmit what she saw. This demanded a large crew of further investigators, and as soon as she got back to her hiveworm nest, she vowed to report this back to the King and Queen. In fact, she might just fly all the way back to the main fungus-reef city.

As she approached the edge of the dead grove, Sarein heard a crackling sound, snapping wood: the groaning of big brittle trees as they settled, dried, and twisted. She jumped when a large branch crashed down, shattering into the underbrush. Inside the dead grove, there were stirring and smashing sounds, as other tree corpses collapsed.

She stood beside one of the largest withered trees, the golden bark scales on its trunk now dull. Large cracks ran through the bole, heartwood splitting apart as it dried. The creaks and low groaning sounded like cries of pain from the worldforest.

She hesitated, afraid to go inside the dead grove. Pragmatically speaking, with fronds breaking off and crashing to the ground from high above, it would be hazardous to enter. But Sarein needed to know what was happening here.

She heard a distinct rustle in the brown fronds ahead of her. Sarein pushed inside the haunted grove, glanced up, and saw one of the small Gardeners. The alien crouched on the dead branch, peering down at her; then he bounded across to another frond and skittered away.

"Wait! What is happening here?" She stumbled after him, scratching herself on the brittle underbrush, ducking under dry brown fronds.

Overhead, another Onthos stared at her, then bolted after his comrade.

Sarein pushed her way into the skeletal grove, both angry and disturbed. The Gardeners knew about this die-off, and she feared they might somehow be responsible for it. She saw five more aliens making their way through the dead branches. One broke a branch that smashed to the ground so close to Sarein that she had to leap out of the way. That was intentional!

"Come here! What have you done to the trees?" She couldn't fight her way through the undergrowth as easily as a green priest, but she thrashed along, snapped a branch that got in her way, flailed with her hands.

Finally she broke through into a dusty, well-trampled clearing that had once been a lush glade. Chittering sounds surrounded her, and she saw a great deal of movement, as if this blighted thicket were some kind of nest. Gardeners scrambled up the trees, holding on to the dead branches. They all looked down at her with large emotionless eyes. The Onthos were not overtly threatening, but she got the clear impression that they didn't think she belonged here.

She stared at the furious activity. If the Onthos had come to the Wild so they could recover and find peace, they must all be gathered in this vicinity. Only a hundred refugees had come to Theroc in the first place—but there were so many around her now!

She whirled when she heard a loud *crack* from one of the dead tree trunks. Layers of golden bark scales split open like a chrysalis—and in the raw, open wood beneath, a figure moved, squirmed. . . . An Onthos emerged, pulling itself free from the gap in the heartwood as if freshly born. It stood there, smooth-skinned and sexless, blinking as it gazed around at the world for the first time. Another alien rushed forward to greet it.

Around her, a sequence of popping noises sounded like gunfire, and more dead worldtrees split open. As Sarein watched in astonishment, another six fresh and seemingly identical Gardeners crawled out of the broken trees, like newborns.

Sarein was indignant. She shouted, "What have you done to these trees? You are supposed to care for them!"

One of the creatures stood before her. She couldn't tell whether or not it was Ohro. "We are the Gardeners. You should not be here. You should not see." The large, dark eyes looked even more alien than before, filled with a flickering, unnatural shadow. . . .

"Where are the green priests?" she demanded. "Why are you not tending the trees?"

"We are tending our race."

She heard crashing sounds as more branches fell in the dead thicket. Onthos came in from all directions, parting the dry fronds, pressing closer. There were far more than a hundred of them.

She had been present at the main fungus-reef when all of their teardrop ships had landed. The Onthos had claimed to be sterile, saying that they could not reproduce without the worldforest, but they had saved something called a "spore mother."

Sarein's stomach fluttered. These creatures had always been quiet, calm, innocuous, but now they looked like a gathering mob.

Nearby, the trunk of another worldtree groaned and broke open, and a trio of identical newborn Onthos emerged; yet another broke out of a swollen knob of wood higher up the trunk. The new creature dropped to the ground, crouching and aware.

"This isn't a colony," Sarein said. "This is an infestation!"

Nearby, two Gardeners broke off dry branches and held them up as clubs. Another Onthos stared at Sarein with his large eyes—which held a deeper inner blackness than she had seen before. "We need to reproduce, and our other worldforest is dead."

"You're killing this forest!" Sarein knew she had to get back to her flyer so she could race to the other continent and sound the alarm.

"We are surviving," the Gardener said. "That is our imperative." Dozens more broke off dry branches and closed in on her. "You will not be allowed to witness or interfere."

Sarein held up her hands and backed away. There was a time she would have been full of her own self-importance, but out here she was all alone.

She heard the crackling and popping sounds all around her. Worldtrees split open after they had served as some kind of terrible womb for these parasitical creatures. She needed to inform Estarra and the whole Confederation! Kennebar's green priests had allowed this somehow, or they had been tricked.

Sarein doubted she could even get to the comm in time.

She turned to run out of the skeletal grove, but the Gardeners darted forward with astonishing swiftness, hundreds of them, each one armed with a sharp, hard branch broken from the worldtrees.

The first blow caught Sarein in the back of the legs, making her stumble and crash face-first into the dead shrubbery. She scrambled ahead, tried to get to her feet. She rolled over, thrashing with her hands in an attempt to defend herself.

The second blow caught her on the side of the head, stunning her. Her eyes filled with blood. She could barely stay conscious. She dragged herself forward, and another branch caught her on the shoulder. She felt the bone shatter.

The rest of the blows rained down on her head, but after the fifth one, Sarein felt nothing else.

CHAPTER

131

MAGE-IMPERATOR JORA'H

The Solar Navy returned to Ildira, battered but victorious. The cohort had suffered devastating losses, and Kuivahr had been wiped out—but the Solar Navy had definitely inflicted serious harm on the Shana Rei. And the robots were all but exterminated.

Tal Gale'nh looked pale as always, but stronger and more confident than before. They had lost the planet but rescued Osira'h, Prince Reynald of Theroc, and the Roamer family that ran the kirae distillery there. The refugee green priest had already spoken with Nira at great length via telink.

The Mage-Imperator received Adar Zan'nh as soon as the remnants of the cohort settled into orbit. Jora'h and Nira listened to the commander describe the battle. "We had a stunning effect, Liege. We entirely destroyed the black robots—out of their entire fleet, only three escaped. In wiping out their fighters, we dealt a devastating blow to the creatures of darkness."

Nira ran to embrace Osira'h, fighting back tears and glad to see her safe. "What about Tamo'l?"

"We don't know for certain," Osira'h said. "Many of the misbreeds were trying to escape through the Klikiss transportal wall. We don't know where they chose to go, but we hope Tamo'l is with them."

"Kuivahr didn't have enough ships to move all those people," said the Roamer woman, Zhett Kellum.

"We got as many away as we could," said Patrick Fitzpatrick.

Muree'n spoke up. "Gale'nh, Osira'h, and I could also sense Rod'h through our bond, but none of us could help him."

"The Shana Rei are using him," Gale'nh said. "They drained me and discarded me, but Rod'h is much stronger. They may be able to use him to inflict more damage."

Prime Designate Daro'h looked distraught, remembering Rod'h as a friend. "But we must save him."

"The Shana Rei wanted to seize all the halfbreeds—Tamo'l, too. And me," Osira'h said. "We are different from humans and Ildirans. We think that is also the reason they wanted to wipe out all the misbreeds from the sanctuary domes."

Adar Zan'nh said, "The new sun bombs were remarkable, as General Keah promised. The Solar Navy can fight the Shana Rei with those weapons, but our greatest vulnerability may be elsewhere. What if they can strike us from within the *thism*?"

"We have no defenses against that kind of attack," Jora'h said.

"*Not yet*," said a loud voice. Designate Rusa'h pushed his way into the skysphere audience chamber. "But only because you will not make the necessary choice." He was steely and determined.

Guard kithmen blocked the mad Designate with their crystal katanas, but Rusa'h pressed up against the unwavering crossed blades. "Brother, you saw what they did to the Onthos home system, what they did to the planet Kuivahr. The Shana Rei cannot be defeated with mere weapons. Sun bombs! Laser cannons! This battle goes far beyond *us*—the very cosmos is at stake! To fight an enemy of such impossible powers, we need allies that are far beyond us as well."

Prime Designate Daro'h swallowed hard. "You mean the faeros?"

"They helped to destroy the nightshade," Rusa'h pointed out. "But they are afraid to continue the fight. We must draw their attention. We must *command* them."

"Rod'h and I tried that," Osira'h said. "They would not listen to us."

"You did not call them in the proper way," Rusa'h said. "That is for Jora'h to do." He seemed to leave off the title on purpose.

Offended by how the disgraced Designate spoke to the Mage-Imperator, the guards continued to block him, and Rusa'h left the skysphere in disgust.

Prince Reynald said in a quiet voice, "When I was just a baby the faeros attacked the worldforest, set the trees on fire. I barely escaped alive."

Daro'h touched the scar on his face. "They burned many of us, caused incalculable damage. I would hate to bring them back. Are we that desperate yet?"

Jora'h's voice was hard. "I will not be forced into that unholy bargain." As the attendees settled in for a longer discussion, the Mage-Imperator called for a report from the human historian. "Rememberer Anton, have you or the other rememberers found any further hope among the ancient records?"

Anton Colicos bowed. "The Shana Rei seem to resent *life itself*, which, uh, doesn't give us much common ground. In the previous war, though, the Ildirans and faeros did manage to push them back. The Shana Rei withdrew outside of the universe, but now something has provoked them, brought them back."

Jora'h could not guess what had disturbed the Shana Rei from their black isolation.

A bureaucrat kithman rushed into the audience chamber, terrified and confused. "Liege, Designate Rusa'h has gone to the top platform of the Prism Palace."

Jora'h felt a whiplash of dread. "What is he doing there?"

"He barricaded himself inside the greenhouse terrarium. Guards tried to stop him, but he escaped. He says . . . he says he will call the faeros."

Patrick Fitzpatrick frowned. "And how in the world does he intend to do that?"

Jora'h knew. "We must stop him. Hurry!" Led by the armor-clad guard kithmen, they all raced up to the high towers.

Nira sprinted alongside him and Prime Designate Daro'h. Muree'n and Yazra'h pushed their way to the front of the guards, weapons drawn.

When the group reached the highest level, they saw that Rusa'h had taken over Nira's special greenhouse, her own private worldforest grove where she could stand among her trees and communicate through telink.

When Jora'h saw the drums of concentrated fuel gel placed around the interior of the greenhouse and up against the tall saplings, he realized that his mad brother had been planning this for some time. Rusa'h insisted on doing what he believed was necessary. He was either insane . . . or correct.

Jora'h commanded, "I forbid this! I am your Mage-Imperator, Rusa'h, and I am your brother. We have not yet reached this point of urgency."

Nira cried, "We can't let him. He's got to stop—"

Rusa'h stood motionless in the center of the greenhouse. In his hands he held an ignitor. "Someone has to do what is necessary. The agony of the verdani along with my own will be a summons that the faeros cannot deny."

"You will not talk him out of it, Father," Osira'h said in a low voice.

Rusa'h's lower lip curled. "I knew you were weak and a coward, brother. That is what sparked my rebellion against you in the first place. And now I see I was right all along. Someday, after I have saved the Empire, you will understand what I have done. You will thank me." He closed his eyes and raised his hands, shouting toward the sky, "Faeros, we need you! You must help us. I call upon you to fight the Shana Rei on our behalf—and yours. Help us save the universe."

The guard kithmen smashed through the transparent crystal walls, pushing into the greenhouse.

"We will pay any price necessary," Rusa'h shouted.

Jora'h knew it was too late. "Guards, pull back!" He felt a thrumming in the *thism*, a rising surge as his brother cried out with all the power in his mind, drawing on the energy wrapped in the myriad strings that bound all Ildirans together. He triggered the ignitor.

In an instantaneous succession, the containers of fuel gel erupted, sending flames high, blasting out the crystal walls of the greenhouse. A central reservoir of fuel gel sprayed up and burst into flame, engulfing the trees adjacent to Rusa'h and becoming an instant furnace. The worldtrees shuddered, withered.

Even Jora'h thought he could hear them scream.

Nira dropped to her knees, weeping, pressing her hands against her smooth head.

The flames swallowed Rusa'h, setting his garments on fire, blackening his flesh, roaring around his head until his eyes boiled. And as he screamed in utter agony, flames poured out of his throat—yet he remained alive for seconds longer.

His outcry through the *thism* was so intense that it stunned the guard kithmen and rendered the bureaucrats unconscious. Prime Designate Daro'h staggered back, unable to keep his balance. Osira'h and Gale'nh reeled. Muree'n and Yazra'h both stood like statues. Even with the strength he drew from the entire network of *thism*, Jora'h felt deafened and crippled.

The shout of agony roared across the Spiral Arm like a siren, unhindered by physical limitations of speed.

The dying worldtrees also howled their pain through telink to the rest of the worldforest. Only when Rusa'h collapsed into blackened bones and the ashes of flesh, did the call fall silent.

Less than six hours later, after the fire on the Prism Palace roof had been extinguished, Jora'h felt the shuddering impact in his mind, a sense of growing dread that caught fire inside him. He and Nira rushed out of the Prism Palace and stood together in the Foray Plaza. Osira'h joined them, a stricken look on her face, and turned to look up at the sky.

Out in the city of Mijistra, other Ildirans were gathering, sensing the arrival of the powerful entities.

Fireballs streaked across the sky like shooting stars, growing larger and larger until the sky was filled with ellipsoidal knots of flame, sentient infernos that hovered above.

Osira'h stared, and Prince Reynald stood beside her, pale and weak.

Rusa'h had sacrificed himself to demand that the faeros return. These fiery elementals had already torched much of Ildira as well as other worlds in the Empire. Jora'h had no idea how he could defeat them again.

Or control them.

CHAPTER

132

EXXOS

Trapped in the shadow cloud with the insane Shana Rei, Exxos endured a hell that was worse than the greatest torment the Klikiss race had ever devised for them.

The error was his. The failure . . . the devastation. He and his counterparts had designed those immense new battleships with shielding, armor, and weaponry that should have been invincible, and the Shana Rei had constructed those battleships exactly according to the plans the robots provided. Exxos had never expected the far-superior power of the new sun bombs, nor for the Solar Navy to waste such weapons against the black robots.

Even with their expanded warships, their enhanced armor, and increased weaponry, the black robots had not stood a chance.

It was extermination plain and simple, more ruthless than Exxos had ever expected. The Ildirans intended to annihilate every single black robot, just as the robots themselves meant to wipe out the Ildirans and humans. In one space battle, the Solar Navy had succeeded in making the black robots extinct. Only three remained.

Three.

Once, the oppressed black robots had annihilated the entire Klikiss race. Later, millions of them had been reactivated before and during the Elemental War. Exxos and his thousand companions had gone to ground, hibernating in the ice moon on Dhula, and when they reawakened, Exxos led their resurgence. A thousand robots, working together to build new plans—all of which had failed.

Of those original millions, only a thousand had escaped . . . and of that thousand—because of the Shana Rei, because of the Ildirans, and because of the humans—now only three remained.

Exxos experienced total despair.

He had convinced the creatures of darkness that his robots could help them achieve their goal, but the Shana Rei seemed unconcerned with the extermination of the robot army. No conceivable plan would allow him to achieve victory with only three robots. Exxos had lost everything.

His two surviving companions were identical to him and fell into the same despair. With their three minds interlinked, the intensity of the loss seemed even greater. They did not have the secret processing power to continue developing the weapon to destroy the Shana Rei. They had nothing!

The shadow cloud reemerged at the Onthos home system, hanging above the gigantic ebony sphere that enclosed the star. They would again draw upon the already-existing hex plates to replenish material their huge ships had lost in the sun-bomb explosions.

Shana Rei inkblots appeared before Exxos, pulsing with electric darkness and each anchored with a single staring eye. He was sure the creatures had come to torment him, perhaps to tear apart the last three remaining robots.

At least then it would be finished.

"My robots could have helped you achieve the extermination of all intelligent life," Exxos said, forcing himself to sound defiant. "We could have eased your pain. But that is no longer possible."

The Shana Rei stared with a piercing, singular gaze. "Why is it no longer possible?"

"We have no more robots," said another Exxos beside him. "You need us to implement the plan."

Exxos said, "We could have guided you, destroyed all life for you. But we can do nothing with only three robots."

The shadows pulsed in silence—not taunting, but considering. "Then you must have more black robots."

"There are no more robots!" Exxos said. "We have all been destroyed."

The staring inkblots pulsed and pondered again. "Then you need more robots. We have studied your physical plan. We can manifest others precisely like you, identical down to the atoms in your metallic lattices."

Exxos and his two counterparts buzzed startled questions back and forth. Previously, Klikiss robots had all been irreplaceable individuals, a unique set of experiences and histories. But as the Shana Rei destroyed random robot victims, and as casualties mounted in their battle engagements, Exxos had imposed his own will and made all of his comrades share the same mental database, to synchronize their minds with his personality as the model.

The Shana Rei had manifested material to construct complex battleships according to an established blueprint. Why was it not possible for them to rebuild a much more complicated Klikiss robot?

"You can reproduce us?" Exxos asked.

"We can copy you. Exactly as you are." The Shana Rei seemed to indicate the enormous black sphere around the Onthos star. "You are small things, and we have infinite material."

"Kuivahr is destroyed. We must do the same thing to other planets," said a second inkblot.

"And others."

"Then, yes!" Exxos cried. "I need more robots, many more. Restore our numbers."

The Shana Rei answered without pondering. More and more sections of the gigantic black shell dropped away, dissolved, reshaped. Dark matter became real matter, atoms reassembled into new structures, infinitely detailed based upon all the knowledge the shadows had acquired from so many torturous dismantlings of robot victims.

Robots appeared, black angular specks against the vastness, a myriad of identical forms that built into a swarm that seemed as populous as the stars in a galaxy. More robots, and yet more.

All of the new robots activated simultaneously, and crimson optical sensors gleamed like a sky full of sparks.

"Will a million more robots suffice?" the Shana Rei asked.

A million more. And all of them would be Exxos.

"Yes, that will be sufficient."

GLOSSARY

ACADEM: Roamer school inside a hollowed-out comet, near the Roamer complex of Newstation. The school is run by Jess Tamblyn and Cesca Peroni.

ADAR: highest military rank in Ildiran Solar Navy.

AELIN: green priest, brother of Shelud, with a special connection to the bloaters.

ALAA'KH: one of the misbreeds in the Kuivahr sanctuary dome.

ALAKIS, ADAM: researcher on Vaconda, father of Zoe Alakis, died of Heidegger's Syndrome.

ALAKIS, EVELYN: researcher on Vaconda, mother of Zoe Alakis, killed in a flyer crash when Zoe was young.

ALAKIS, ZOE: wealthy head of the Pergamus medical research facility.

ALU, BEREN: station chief of Fireheart Station.

ARAGAO, OCTAVIO: communications officer aboard the *Kutuzov*.

ARBOR: Rlinda Kett's restaurant on Theroc.

ARITA, PRINCESS: daughter of King Peter and Queen Estarra, a budding naturalist.

ARUNE'L: lens priestess in Mijistra.

ASKELOR: Ildiran industrial planet converted to weapons production.

ATTENDER: servile Ildiran kith.

AURIDIA: sparsely inhabited planet over which Newstation and Academ orbit. Auridia contains a Klikiss transportal for access into the transportal network.

BEAUVAIS: traditional Roamer skymining clan.

BEBOB: Rlinda Kett's pet name for Branson Roberts.

***BEKH*:** Ildiran curse.

BELLIROS: gas-giant planet, site of clan Duquesne skymines.

BELTRIAS: green priest hunter from Shorehaven Village.

BIG RING: Kotto Okiah's large experimental accelerator under construction at Fireheart Station.

BJORN: spaceship engineer in clan Reeves.

BLACK ROBOTS: intelligent and evil beetle-like robots built by the Klikiss race; most of them were wiped out in the Elemental War.

BLOATERS: strange organic nodules found in deep, empty space, the source of ekti-X.

BRINDLE, ROBB: administrator of Kett Shipping, married to Tasia Tamblyn, father of Xander.

BRINDLE, XANDER: one of the pilots of Kett Shipping vessel *Verne*, son of Robb Brindle and Tasia Tamblyn.

BUGBOT: deprecating slang term for a Klikiss robot.

BURA'S: female Ildiran engineer, operations manager of the Askelor weapons industries.

***CAILLIE*:** generation ship from Earth whose passengers colonized Theroc.

CAIN, DEPUTY ELDRED: former deputy of the Terran Hanseatic League, now an administrator of Earth loyal to the Confederation.

CELLI: green priest, married to Solimar, who tends a terrarium dome in Fireheart Station. Celli is the sister of Estarra and Sarein.

CERF, ALDO: biological merchant from Rakkem.

CHAIRMAN: leader of the Terran Hanseatic League.

CHAKLEN: colony leader of Dremen.

CHIAR'H: Ildiran woman of the noble kith, volunteer worker in the Kuivahr sanctuary domes, married to human Shawn Fennis.

CHRYSALIS CHAIR: reclining throne of the Mage-Imperator.

COLICOS, ANTON: historian, known for his work with Ildiran records, first to translate portions of the Saga of Seven Suns.

COLLIN: young green priest, friend of Arita's.

COMPETENT COMPUTERIZED COMPANION: intelligent servant robot, also called a compy, available in Friendly, Teacher, Governess, Listener, Worker, and other models.

COMPY: nickname for competent computerized companion.

CONDEN'S FEVER: deadly human disease.

CONFEDERATION: new human government replacing the Terran Hanseatic League, loose alliance among Roamer clans, independent planets, and remnants of the Hansa. Ruled by King Peter and Queen Estarra, capital on Theroc.

CORRIBUS: colony where Orli Covitz once lived, devastated by Klikiss robot attack during the Elemental War.

COUGHLIN, JAN: worker at Fireheart Station.

COVE, TRISTAN: village leader of Shorehaven.

COVITZ, ORLI: compy scientist, strong advocate for compies, married to Matthew Freling. She is the owner of DD.

DARO'H, PRIME DESIGNATE: successor to Mage-Imperator Jora'h.

DAUNTHA: green priest on Ulio Station.

DAYM: blue supergiant star, one of the "seven suns" in the Ildiran sky.

DD: Friendly compy owned by Orli Covitz.

DECLAN'S GLORY: Kett Shipping vessel.

DENVA, MARIUS: operations manager at Del Kellum's distillery on Kuivahr.

DETEMER: Roamer clan.

DHOUGAL: isolated island colony on Serenity's Reach, wiped out by a deadly brain parasite.

DHULA: gas-giant planet on the edge of the Ildiran Empire.

DOBRO: Ildiran splinter colony, former home of the secret breeding program where many humans were held captive.

DREMEN: cloudy Confederation planet primarily known for fungus harvests.

DRE'NH, SEPTAR: leader of a Solar Navy septa.

DUQUESNE: Roamer clan, runs two refurbished skymines on Belliros.

DUQUESNE, AARON: heir apparent to clan Duquesne.

EARTH DEFENSE FORCES (EDF): former military for the Terran Hanseatic League, precursor to the Confederation Defense Forces.

EKTI: exotic allotrope of hydrogen used to fuel Ildiran stardrives.

EKTI-X: stardrive fuel with higher energy potential than traditional ekti.

ELEMENTAL WAR: conflict across the Spiral Arm involving the human race, Ildiran Empire, the hydrogues, faeros, wentals, verdani, as well as the Klikiss and their black robots.

ELJIID: abandoned Klikiss world where Margaret Colicos is buried.

ENTURI, ELISA: wife of Garrison Reeves and mother of Seth, deputy of Lee Iswander at the Sheol lava mines. Also goes by her married name of Elisa Reeves.

ESTARRA, QUEEN: ruler of Confederation, married to King Peter, with two children, Reynald and Arita.

EXXOS: leader of surviving Klikiss robots.

FAEROS: sentient fire entities.

FELLIWELL, DARWIN: station manager of Ulio Station.

FENNIS, SHAWN: human born on Dobro, volunteer worker in the Kuivahr sanctuary domes, married to Ildiran woman Chiar'h.

FILMGOGGLES: eye protection used on Ildira.

FIREHEART STATION: Roamer research and industrial station at the heart of a nebula, specializing in energized films. Site of Kotto Okiah's current large-scale experiment.

FITZKELLUM, KRISTOF: thirteen-year-old son of Zhett Kellum and Patrick Fitzpatrick III, also called Toff.

FITZKELLUM, REX: two-year-old son of Zhett Kellum and Patrick Fitzpatrick III.

FITZKELLUM, SHAREEN: seventeen-year-old daughter of Zhett Kellum and Patrick Fitzpatrick III.

FITZPATRICK III, PATRICK: husband of Zhett Kellum, one of the managers of the Kellum skymine on Golgen.

FORAY PLAZA: gathering area in front of the Prism Palace.

FRELING, MATTHEW: compy scientist, former husband of Orli Covitz.

FUNGUS-REEF: large inhabited fungal growth on the worldtrees of Theroc.

GALE'NH, TAL: halfbreed son of the green priest Nira and Ildiran war hero Adar Kori'nh, a tal in the Ildiran Solar Navy. Gale'nh was the captain of the exploration ship *Kolpraxa*.

GARDENERS: ancient, original tenders of the worldforest.

GOLGEN: gas-giant planet, home of the Kellum skymine.

GORHUM: transportal nexus near Theroc.

GOR'KA: one of the misbreeds in the Kuivahr sanctuary domes.

GREEN PRIEST: servant of the worldforest, able to use worldtrees for instantaneous communication.

GUIDING STAR: Roamer philosophy and religion, a guiding force in a person's life.

HANDIES, ADMIRAL EDGAR: CDF Admiral, head of Grid 0, one of the "Three H's."

HANDON, TERRY: one of the pilots of Kett Shipping vessel *Verne*, partner of Xander Brindle.

HANSA: Terran Hanseatic League

HAR'LC: one of the misbreeds in the Kuivahr sanctuary domes, son of swimmer and scaly kiths.

HAROUN, ADMIRAL SHIMAL: CDF Admiral, head of Grid 6, one of the "Three H's."

HARVARD, ADMIRAL PETROV: CDF Admiral, head of Grid 11, one of the "Three H's."

HEIDEGGER'S SYNDROME: fatal degenerative neurological disease, thought to be incurable. Adam Alakis died of Heidegger's Syndrome.

HERREN 3: Confederation planet.

HILTOS: Ildiran shrine to the Lightsource.

HORIZON CLUSTER: star cluster in which the Ildiran Empire is located.

HYDROGUES: alien race that dwells within gas-giant planets, the main destructive antagonists in the Elemental War.

HYRILLKA: Ildiran planet, site of several battles in the Elemental War; the Klikiss robots were originally discovered on one of Hyrillka's moons.

IKBIR: Confederation colony world.

ILDIRA: home planet of the Ildiran Empire, under the light of seven suns.

ILDIRAN EMPIRE: large alien empire, the only other major civilization in the Spiral Arm.

ILDIRAN SOLAR NAVY: space military fleet of the Ildiran Empire, commanded by Adar Zan'nh.

ILDIRANS: humanoid alien race with many different breeds, or kiths; they are able to interbreed with humans.

ILLI'V: one of the mates of Prime Designate Daro'h, a clothes designer.

ISPEROS: hot planet, site of a metals-extraction facility designed by Kotto Okiah at the beginning of the Elemental War.

ISWANDER, ARDEN: thirteen-year-old son of Lee Iswander.

ISWANDER INDUSTRIES: company owned by Lee Iswander with numerous high-risk operations, including the Sheol lava mines.

ISWANDER, LEE: Roamer industrialist with numerous operations, including the Sheol lava mines.

ISWANDER, LONDA: wife of Lee Iswander.

JAZER: energy weapon used by Confederation Defense Forces.

JONAH 12: ice-moon hydrogen-extraction operations founded by Kotto Okiah during the Elemental War.

JORA'H: Mage-Imperator of the Ildiran Empire. He is the father of numerous important Ildirans, including Adar Zan'nh and the half-breed telepath Osira'h. His consort is the green priest Nira.

JUGGERNAUT: largest battleship class in the Confederation Defense Forces.

***KANAKA*:** one of the old Earth generation ships, origin of the Roamer clans.

KAO'L: lens kithman leader of the Hiltos shrine.

KEAH, GENERAL NALANI: commander of the Confederation Defense Forces.

KELLUM, DEL: former Speaker of the Roamer clans, successor to Cesca Peroni. Father of Zhett Kellum. He now runs a distillery on the Ildiran ocean planet of Kuivahr.

KELLUM, ZHETT: daughter of Del Kellum, married to Patrick Fitzpatrick III. She ran a large skymine on Golgen. She and Patrick have three children, Shareen, Kristof, and Rex.

KENNEBAR: leader of an isolationist faction of green priests on Theroc.

KETT, RLINDA: trader and former trade minister of the Confederation, now owner of Kett Shipping. She also owns several high-end restaurants.

KETT SHIPPING: Rlinda Kett's shipping company, managed by Robb Brindle and Tasia Tamblyn.

KIRAE: intoxicating drink enjoyed by Ildirans, although humans find it distasteful.

KLEE: a hot beverage made from ground worldtree seeds, a specialty of Theroc.

KLIKISS: ancient insectlike race, long vanished from the Spiral Arm, leaving only their empty cities. After their resurgence in the Elemental War, they departed through their transportal network and are considered lost or extinct.

KLIKISS ROBOTS: intelligent and evil beetle-like robots built by the Klikiss race; most of them were wiped out in the Elemental War. Also called black robots.

***KOLPRAXA*:** Ildiran exploration ship that ventured beyond the Spiral Arm, led by Tal Gale'nh; destroyed by the Shana Rei.

KORI'NH, ADAR: great Ildiran military hero from the Elemental War, father of Gale'nh.

KRIEGER, JOCKO: human weapons scientist who developed modifications to the Ildiran sun-bomb design.

KUIVAHR: Ildiran planet with shallow seas and strong tides, site of Tamo'l's sanctuary domes for misbreeds and Del Kellum's distillery.

***KUTUZOV*:** flagship Juggernaut of the Confederation Defense Forces.

LENS KITH: one of the Ildiran breeds, religious philosophers.

LIGHTSOURCE: higher plane of existence above normal life, an Ildiran version of heaven.

LU: Listener compy now working on Ikbir.

LUNAR ORBITAL COMPLEX: military and civilian base established in the rubble of Earth's Moon.

MAGE-IMPERATOR: the god-emperor of the Ildiran Empire.

MANTA: cruiser-class battleship in Confederation Defense Forces.

MEDUSA: large cephalopod from Rhejak; its meat is considered a delicacy.

MIJISTRA: Ildiran capital city.

MO: Domestic compy now serving the Ikbir colony.

MOSBACH, PROFESSOR MICHAELA: one of Shareen Fitzkellum's teachers on Earth.

MUNGL'EH: one of the misbreeds in the Kuivahr sanctuary domes, a powerful singer.

MUREE'N: halfbreed daughter of Nira and a warrior kithman, a skilled fighter, student of Yazra'h.

MURIEL: biological mother of Zoe Alakis, a factory womb.

NADD: green priest serving aboard the *Kutuzov*.

NEW PORTUGAL: Confederation planet, home of a university and also known for its wines.

NEWSTATION: large orbiting station above planet Auridia, the new Roamer center of government. The Roamer school Academ is also nearby.

NIGHTSHADE: Shana Rei occultation barrier.

NIRA: green priest consort of Mage-Imperator Jora'h, mother of five halfbreed children: Osira'h, Rod'h, Gale'nh, Tamo'l, and Muree'n.

OHRO: spokesman for the Onthos refugees on Theroc.

OK: compy owned by Xander Brindle.

OKIAH, JHY: legendary former Speaker of the Roamer clans, mother of Kotto Okiah.

OKIAH, KOTTO: renowned but eccentric Roamer scientist.

***OKRUN*:** CDF Juggernaut commanded by Admiral Haroun.

ONTHOS: alien race, also called Gardeners.

ORBITAL RESEARCH SPHERE (ORS): isolated medical research satellite orbiting Pergamus.

OSIRA'H: daughter of Nira and Jora'h, bred to have unusual telepathic abilities.

OSQUIVEL: ringed gas giant, former site of Kellum shipyards.

PANNEBAKER, ALEC: one of Lee Iswander's deputies at the Sheol lava-processing facility.

PAOLUS, DR. BENJAMIN: foremost neurological researcher on Earth, sold Prince Reynald's medical data to Pergamus.

PASTERNAK, SHAREEN: lost love of Del Kellum, killed by hydrogues on a skymine. Shareen Fitzkellum is named after her.

PATTON, DILLON: weapons officer aboard the *Kutuzov*.

PERGAMUS: secure medical research facility owned and managed by Zoe Alakis.

PERONI, CESCA: former Roamer Speaker, wife of Jess Tamblyn; together they run the Academ school complex for Roamer children.

PETER, KING: ruler of Confederation, married to Queen Estarra, with two children, Reynald and Arita.

PING LABYRINTH: game played at Newstation.

PLUMAS: frozen moon with deep liquid oceans, former site of Tamblyn clan water industry, destroyed by the Shana Rei.

POL'UX: one of the misbreeds on Kuivahr.

POWER BLOCK: energy source made of a charged film, folded and packed inside a container.

PRIME DESIGNATE: eldest noble-born son of the Mage-Imperator, and successor.

PRIMORDIAL OOZE: trade name of one of Del Kellum's distillations from Kuivahr.

PRISDIAMOND: rare precious gem found on several Confederation planets.

PRISM PALACE: crystalline palace of the Ildiran Mage-Imperator.

***PRODIGAL SON*:** Garrison Reeves's ship, formerly an Iswander Industries vessel.

***PROUD MARY*:** Kett Shipping vessel formerly piloted by Mary Coven, given to Orli Covitz.

QRONHA: binary star in the Horizon Cluster, two of the "seven suns" in the Ildiran sky.

QRONHA 3: gas giant in the Qronha system, site of a decisive battle against the hydrogues in the Elemental War.

RAINDROP: Rlinda Kett's pet name for Reyn.

RAKKEM: non-Confederation planet known for unregulated black-market medical services.

REEVES, DALE: brother of Garrison, second son of Olaf Reeves, died of plague.

REEVES, ELISA: wife of Garrison and mother of Seth, deputy of Lee Iswander at the Sheol lava mines. Also goes by her maiden name of Elisa Enturi.

REEVES, GARRISON: Roamer worker formerly at the Sheol lava-processing facility. He was married to Elisa, father of Seth. He is the son of clan head Olaf Reeves, brother of Dale.

REEVES, OLAF: gruff clan leader of isolationist Roamers who died of a plague on derelict Onthos city; father of Garrison Reeves.

REEVES, SETH: ten-year-old son of Garrison Reeves.

RELLEKER: Terran colony planet, former home of Orli Covitz's compy laboratory.

REMORA: small attack ship in Confederation Defense Forces.

RENDEZVOUS: asteroid cluster, former center of Roamer government. Destroyed by the Earth Defense Forces, but clan Reeves attempted reconstruction for years.

REYN, PRINCE: son of King Peter and Queen Estarra, in line to be the Confederation's next King. His full name is Reynald.

RHEJAK: watery planet with habitable reefs, known for large cephalopods called medusas.

RICKS, SAM: new Speaker for the Roamer clans.

ROAMERS: loose confederation of independent humans, primary producers of ekti stardrive fuel, often disparagingly called "space gypsies."

ROBERTS, BRANSON: Rlinda Kett's favorite ex-husband, affectionately called BeBob.

ROD'H: older halfbreed son of Nira, fathered by Dobro Designate as part of the secret breeding program.

ROHANDAS, HOWARD: fellow student with Shareen Fitzkellum on Earth.

RUSKIN, BOWMAN: worker at Fireheart Station.

SAGA OF SEVEN SUNS: historical and legendary epic of the Ildiran civilization.

SALIBA, SHARON: sensor technician aboard the *Kutuzov*.

SAREIN: sister of Estarra and Celli, lives in self-imposed exile in the Wild.

SEPTA: small battle group of seven ships in the Ildiran Solar Navy.

SERENITY'S REACH: colony world, home of Dhougal island, which was wiped out by a deadly brain parasite infestation.

SHANA REI: fearsome creatures of darkness that preyed upon the Ildiran Empire long ago.

SHELUD: green priest, brother of Aelin.

SHEOL: binary planet under heavy tidal stresses, site of lava-mining operations led by Lee Iswander.

SHIZZ: Roamer expletive.

SHOREHAVEN VILLAGE: lakeshore village on Theroc, site of wyvern attacks.

SKYMINE: ekti-harvesting facility in the clouds of a gas-giant planet, usually operated by Roamers.

SKYSPHERE: audience chamber of the Prism Palace.

SOLIMAR: green priest, married to Celli, who tends a terrarium dome in Fireheart Station.

SPEAKER: Roamer leader.

SPIRAL ARM: the section of the Milky Way Galaxy settled by the Ildiran Empire and Terran colonies.

SWIMMER: otterlike Ildiran kith that spend most of their time in the ocean.

TAIT, MATTHEW: tactical officer aboard the *Kutuzov*.

TAL: military rank in Ildiran Solar Navy, cohort commander.

TAMBLYN, JESS: one of the heads of Academ school, married to Cesca Peroni.

TAMBLYN, TASIA: administrator of Kett Shipping, married to Robb Brindle, father of Xander.

TAMBORR'S DEMENTIA: disease being studied on Pergamus.

TAMO'L: one of Nira's halfbreed children, daughter of a lens kithman. She runs sanctuary domes for misbreeds on the planet Kuivahr.

TELINK: instantaneous communication used by green priests via the worldtrees.

TEREDIT: Confederation planet.

TERRAN HANSEATIC LEAGUE: former commerce-based government of Earth and Terran colonies, dissolved after the death of Chairman Basil Wenceslas at the end of the Elemental War.

THEROC: forested planet, home of the sentient worldtrees.

THERON: a native of Theroc.

***THISM*:** faint racial telepathic network, centered on the Mage-Imperator, that binds all Ildiran people.

THOR'H: eldest son of Jora'h, the first Prime Designate, who betrayed the Empire and died in the resulting civil war.

THREE H'S: Admirals Handies, Harvard, and Haroun in the CDF.

TOM ROM: guardian and majordomo of Zoe Alakis.

TRANSPORTAL: Klikiss instantaneous transportation network.

ULIO: large trading complex in open space, frequented by traders of all sorts.

ULIO, MARIA: founder of the Ulio transfer hub.

VACONDA: wilderness planet, site of the Alakis forest watchtower station.

VERDANI: organic-based sentience, manifested as the Theron world-forest.

***VERNE*:** cargo ship flown by Xander Brindle and Terry Handon.

***VORACIOUS CURIOSITY*:** Rlinda Kett's private ship.

VU'LN: one of the misbreeds on Kuivahr, a mixture of soldier kith, lens kith, and swimmer kith.

WARGLOBE: crystalline sphere used by hydrogues.

WARLINER: largest class of Ildiran battleship.

WENCESLAS, CHAIRMAN BASIL: former leader of the Terran Hanseatic League.

WENTALS: sentient water-based creatures.

WHISPER PALACE: traditional seat of power in the Terran Hanseatic League, where the figurehead Great Kings ruled.

WHISTLERS: possibly sentient cacti on Eljiid.

WILD, THE: unexplored continent on Theroc.

WINGO, MERCER: First Officer aboard the *Kutuzov*.

WISSKOFF, ZACHARY: manager and maître d' of Rlinda Kett's Arbor restaurant.

WORLDFOREST: the interconnected, semi-sentient forest based on Theroc.

WORLDTREE: a separate tree in the interconnected, semi-sentient forest based on Theroc.

WULFTON: active star, home of numerous faeros.

YAZRA'H: daughter of the Mage-Imperator, skilled warrior and bodyguard. She is the mentor of Muree'n.

YODER, DANDO: trader pilot who works for Kett Shipping.

ZAN'NH: Ildiran military officer, eldest son of Mage-Imperator Jora'h, Adar of the Ildiran Solar Navy.